Hidden Kingdom

ALSO BY AMANDA HOCKING

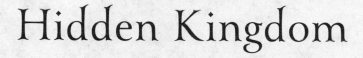

Hidden Kingdom

THE KANIN CHRONICLES

The Complete Trilogy

Amanda Hocking

Wednesday Books
New York

HIDDEN KINGDOM: FROSTFIRE. Copyright © 2014 by Amanda Hocking. ICE KISSED. Copyright © 2015 by Amanda Hocking. CRYSTAL KINGDOM. Copyright © 2015 by Amanda Hocking. All rights reserved. Printed in the United States of America. For information, address St. Martin's Press, 175 Fifth Avenue, New York, N.Y. 10010.

www.stmartins.com

The Library of Congress Cataloging-in-Publication Data is available upon request.

ISBN 978-1-250-14861-2 (trade paperback)

Our books may be purchased in bulk for promotional, educational, or business use. Please contact your local bookseller or the Macmillan Corporate and Premium Sales Department at 1-800-221-7945, extension 5442, or by email at MacmillanSpecialMarkets@macmillan.com.

First Edition: November 2017

10 9 8 7 6 5 4 3 2 1

frostfire

PROLOGUE

four years ago

As dawn began to approach, the celebration finally wound to a close. Even though I had been working for over twelve hours, I felt wide awake and even a little buzzed, like I'd gotten a contact high from the energy around me, not to mention the thrill of completing my first real assignment as a tracker.

Since my graduation was still several months away, I hadn't been given any major detail or heady responsibility. My duties for the night involved standing at attention during the formalities, and surveying the rooms for signs of trouble the rest of the night, which mostly meant directing the increasingly inebriated party guests to the bathroom.

But still, I had been here, working alongside other trackers and even the more elite Högdragen—the guards charged with protecting the Kanin kingdom. That's why at the end of the night, despite the growing ache in my bare feet, I was a little saddened to be relieved of my duties.

King Evert and Queen Mina had opened the doors to all the Kanin in our capital of Doldastam, and there were over ten thousand of us living here. With that many people streaming in through the doors for an impromptu party, the royal couple needed all the hands they could get, including trackers-in-training.

We'd just gotten word a few days before that another tribe, the Trylle, had defeated our shared enemy, the Vittra. For the past few months, our King and Queen had been quietly preparing the Kanin. If the Vittra had taken out the Trylle, we would have been the next logical target, since we were wealthier and more powerful than the Trylle. We were too strong and plentiful for the Vittra to go after first, but once they conquered the Trylle and turned their army to Vittra, they would be strong enough to go after us.

But when the Trylle did away with the Vittra King and his entire army, they did away with our impending war as well. So naturally our good King Evert found reason to celebrate, which was how I'd ended up working a party until the early hours of the morning.

By now the King and Queen had retired to their chambers for the evening, and nearly all of the guests had gone home. A handful of trackers and Högdragen stayed on to oversee the party until everyone had departed, while the cleaning crew had begun the unenviable task of taking care of the mess.

Since so few people were left, I was relieved of my duty and sent home for the night. I felt a bit like Cinderella then, her lovely coach turning back into a pumpkin, as I walked slowly into the front hall. Though I had been wearing the trackers' formal uniform—a tailored, frosty white suit, all crisp and new since this was the first time I'd worn it—instead of a gown given to me by a fairy godmother, at the end of the night my uniform would be put away, and I wouldn't perform any more duties until after I graduated.

Once I did graduate, I'd be given a silver sash to hold my sword, but until then they didn't quite trust me with a weapon, not that I'd really needed one for a celebration like this anyway.

As I made my way toward the front door, unbuttoning my jacket and letting it fall loose, I let out a heavy sigh. Many of the kerosene lamps had gone out, leaving the large entrance glowing dimly. The white banners that decorated the high stone walls of the palace had begun to sag, and silver confetti carpeted the cool floor.

The creak of a heavy door closing gave me pause, because it sounded like the door to my father's office. I glanced down the narrow corridor off the main hall, and sure enough, I saw my dad emerging from his office. His black hair—which he normally kept smoothed back—had become slightly disheveled, and his tie was loosened, with the top buttons of his shirt undone.

"What are you doing?" I asked in surprise. "I thought you went home hours ago."

"I had some paperwork I needed to finish up." He gestured to the office behind him as he walked slowly toward me, suppressing a yawn as he did.

My dad worked as a Chancellor for the kingdom. I knew

that Dad took his job very seriously, and he often worked late nights, but I'd never known him to work quite this late before.

"Paperwork?" I raised an eyebrow. "While a party was going on?"

"We needed to send a letter to the Trylle." Dad gave a half shrug, which did little to convince me that that was really why he was still working. "They're poised to oversee two kingdoms now, and it's in our best interest to align with them."

"And you needed to do that right now?" I pressed.

"It could've waited until the morning," Dad admitted, and his mouth turned to a sheepish smile as he shoved his hands in his pockets. "I wanted to see how your night went. It is your first big night on the job."

"It went well," I said, then paused when a wave of doubt hit me. I tried to replay the night in my head, searching for any mistakes I might've made. "I think."

"I'm sure you did wonderful," Dad assured me, and his grin broadened, stretching into one of pride and affection. "Every time I looked over, I saw you standing at attention. You looked so grown up and so . . . official."

"Thank you."

"My little girl is all grown up," he said wistfully and reached to tousle my blond waves.

"*Dad.*" I ducked away from his hand, but I couldn't help but smile at him. "Can you at least wait until we're out of the palace to get all mushy?"

He opened his mouth, probably to point out that we were alone, but then we both heard the sound of footsteps coming down the corridor. Instinctively, I stood up straighter and put my shoulders back. I was about to start buttoning my jacket back up, but then I saw Konstantin Black walking right toward my dad and me, and for a second I forgot to breathe.

We allowed movies and music from the human world, but the true rock stars of our society were the Högdragen. They had been ordinary Kanin who worked their way up to powerful positions of respect and authority, and none had done it quite so quickly or with as much flare as Konstantin Black. Still in his twenties, he was already the Queen's personal guard—the youngest in recorded history to have such a position.

His black velvet uniform, embellished with silver thread and jewels, was the most luxurious of all the Högdragen uniforms, and even though it was standard for Kanin in his position, his somehow seemed even more divine. His silver sash caught the dim light from the lanterns and managed to glint a little. Even the diamond-encrusted bell handle of his sword sparkled.

He strode confidently over to us, and I tried to remain as blank and composed as I could, as I had been taught. But it was impossible to keep my stomach from doing flips inside me. For years I had been admiring him from afar—for his abilities, his strength, his composure, and, if I'm being honest, in more recent years for how handsome he was—and this was already the most personal encounter I'd had with him.

We'd been in the same room before, but always separated by a sea of people, since his duties kept him close to the Queen, and mine kept me far from her or the King. He'd brushed past me in halls. I'd seen him from the crowd as he'd demonstrated his skill in fencing games during the summer. But I'd never seen him really look at me before, or notice my attentive gaze among all the other adoring faces.

Now here he was, smiling as he stopped in front of us, and it had the same overwhelming effect as looking down from a great height.

I'd gotten so used to gazing at him from a distance, it was hard not to stare. The way his lips curved up slightly more on the left side as he smiled, or the shadow of stubble that had grown darker on the smooth line of his chin as the night progressed, or the way his black hair was slick and straight until it began to curl at the nape of his neck, where it stopped just above his collar.

"Chancellor, I wasn't expecting to see you here at this hour," Konstantin said to my dad.

"I was seeing my daughter home." Dad motioned in my direction, and Konstantin looked down at me. He wasn't much taller than I was, but he seemed to tower over me, with his gray eyes like smoke resting warmly on my face.

"It was your first night working something like this, wasn't it?" Konstantin asked.

I nodded. "Yes," I said, relieved that my voice stayed even and normal.

"You did very well." He smiled at me, causing my heart to flutter. "I'll put in a good word to your Rektor."

"Thank you very much, but that's not necessary," I told him firmly.

Konstantin laughed, the sound filling up the front hall and echoing through it. "Modesty is a noble thing, but it won't get you a coveted spot on the Högdragen. Take help whenever it's offered if you want to make it in this world."

I'd always insisted that I only looked up to him as a guard, as someone I wanted to emulate. But now, with the mere sound of his laughter sending pleasurable shivers through me, I couldn't deny that I'd been harboring a crush on him for so long it had begun to turn into something that felt dangerously like love.

"That's very sound advice, Konstantin," my dad said, pulling me from my thoughts, and pulling Konstantin's gaze from me.

"You sound surprised that I have good ideas, Chancellor," Konstantin said with a wry smirk.

Dad returned the smirk in kind and adjusted his loosened tie. "I think it's just the night wearing on me."

"Sorry, I should be letting you get on your way," Konstantin said apologetically, and my heart sank when I realized this brief exchange would soon end, leaving me feeling even more like Cinderella than ever before.

"Thank you." My dad nodded and stepped back toward the door, then Konstantin held out his hand.

"Actually, Chancellor, if I could keep you just a few minutes longer I might save you some trouble in the morning."

"What do you mean?" Dad asked.

"The Queen just went to her chambers, but before she did, she let me know that she wanted you to sign a document first thing in the morning to be sent out to the Trylle." Konstantin gestured to the grand windows above the door, which were starting to show the first hints of dawn. "And with morning so close, if you wanted to sign it now, you would have a few hours longer to sleep in."

"A document?" Dad shook his head. The bags under his eyes revealed how truly tired he was, and his dark eyes were confused. "I was drafting a letter for the Trylle. What was she working on?"

"I'm not entirely sure, sir. I believe she left it in her office, if you'd like to have a look at it," Konstantin said.

"I suppose I should." Dad nodded wearily, then turned to me. "You can go on, Bryn. I'll be home soon."

"No, it's all right," I replied quickly. "I can wait for you."

Dad shrugged in a way that said I could suit myself, and then he started down the corridor toward the Queen's office.

Konstantin went after him, but he turned back to me as he did. "Don't worry. We won't be too long, white rabbit," he promised me.

I turned away, hoping my cheeks wouldn't burn at Konstantin's use of a nickname. It was one I'd heard a few times in my life, but it never really stuck. *White* because of my fair complexion, and *rabbit* because that was the symbol of the Kanin.

As soon as they were out of sight, I put my hand on my stomach and let out a shaky breath. Having my first taste of official duty left me feeling intoxicated and light-headed, but that last exchange with Konstantin made me weak. I'd never been that interested in boys, preferring to focus on my training, but now I finally understood what my friends meant when they were going on about being in love.

But all too quickly the adrenaline from talking with Konstantin began to fade away, and for the first time all night I realized how tired I really was. I hadn't slept much the night before because I'd been so excited to work at the party, and corralling drunk Kanin townspeople was more work than it sounded.

Dad hadn't been gone with Konstantin for long, but my feet were beginning to throb and I needed to get home and get to bed. I knew where the Queen's office was, so I thought it would be best to go down and let Dad know that I was heading out. Plus it would give me a chance to say something more to Konstantin.

The office wasn't far from the front hall, and I'd almost made it there when I heard a surprised yell, a man crying out, "No!" I froze at first, trying to register it, then it was quickly followed by an agonized scream.

If my head wasn't swimming from the night, I would've noticed sooner. And a second too late—maybe even a split second too long—I realized that it was my father screaming.

I ran to the Queen's office and threw open the door.

When I've later tried to remember that moment, I can't see the rest of the room. It's all a haze and a blur, but the one thing that's focused—and it is in perfect, startling clarity—is Konstantin standing over my dad. His sword is drawn, and the blade is dark crimson with blood, as my dad lies bleeding on the floor.

Konstantin looked up at me. His handsome face, usually bright and confident, was chillingly blank. He almost appeared dead, except for his gray eyes—dark and frightfully alert.

"I'm sorry," Konstantin said simply. "I am bound to something much higher than this kingdom, and I must complete my mission."

"Bryn, get out of here!" Dad yelled as Konstantin raised his sword again.

Weaponless, I did the only thing I could do—I charged at Konstantin. As I ran at him, he pivoted, turning his sword on me. I felt the thin blade sliding sharply through my shoulder, but I barely registered the pain. The only thing that mattered was stopping Konstantin from killing my dad.

I knocked him to the floor, and I managed to punch once before he threw me off him. And then I heard other voices behind me. Other members of the Högdragen had been alerted by the yelling.

In a flash, Konstantin was on his feet and diving out the window behind the Queen's desk. Glass shattered, and the cold and snow billowed into the room. The other guards ran after Konstantin, but I went back to my dad, kneeling beside him.

His shirt was stained red, and I pressed my hand to the wound on his chest, trying to stop the bleeding. Dad put his hand over mine, and his dark eyes were filled with worry.

"I'm sorry I didn't get here sooner," I told him as I tried to blink back my tears.

"No, Bryn, you saved my life." He reached up, touching my cheek with a bloody hand. "You did amazing tonight."

I stayed with my dad, pressing my hand hard against his chest, doing everything in my power to hold the life in him, until the medical staff came and pulled me off. They whisked him away, promising that he would be just fine, and thankfully, they ended up being right.

But after they'd gone, I stayed behind, alone in the office. My crisp white uniform was now stained red with my dad's blood, mixing with my own from my shoulder wound. I stared out the broken window.

It was snowing so hard that it had already covered up Konstantin's tracks. Whatever I had been stupid enough to think I'd felt for Konstantin was gone. He had been my hero, but none of that mattered now. He'd tried to kill my dad, and now I would stop at nothing until he was brought to justice.

ONE

ambushed

April 8, 2014

Three years of tracker school—including extensive combat training, courses on social etiquette, and peer integration— and none of it ever changed the fact that I really hated human high school. Every time I started a new school to get close to a new charge, I found myself rethinking my career choice.

Back before I chose to go to tracker school, rather than finishing out Kanin high school to become a farmer or a teacher or maybe a horse trainer, I remember watching the trackers come and go from missions. They all seemed so worldly and powerful. They earned the respect and admiration of everybody in Doldastam.

I imagined the kinds of adventures they must be having, traveling the world. Most of them stayed in North America, but sometimes I'd hear stories of a tracker going off to England or Italy, and some even went as far as Japan.

The prospect of traveling and protecting my people sounded

exciting and noble. Then I had graduated, and I spent the next four years actually doing the job. If only I had known how much of my "missions" as a tracker involved wearing itchy school uniforms and trying to keep up on slang so I could fit in with spoiled rich kids, I might've reconsidered.

It was during lunch on my fifth day in Chicago, as I followed Linus off the high school campus, when I realized they were watching him, too. I wasn't exactly sure who "they" were, but I'd spotted the car—a black sedan with tinted windows— parked nearby several times since yesterday morning, and that was too much for coincidence.

As I trailed behind Linus and two of his friends, deliberately staying far enough behind so he wouldn't see me, I wondered if the mystery men in the sedan had noticed me yet. If they were staking out Linus, then they had to have seen me, since I'd been interacting with him. But that didn't mean they knew who I was. At least not yet.

Tracking was usually simple when done correctly. The first step was surveillance. I found the target—in this case Linus Berling—and for the first day or two I did nothing but watch him. The goal was to figure out who he was and what he liked, so it would be easier to earn his trust.

The second step was infiltrating his life, which was why I was wearing a ridiculous prep school uniform with a blue plaid skirt and a cardigan that felt too warm.

With a combination of bribery, charm, and a bit of Kanin skill, I'd gotten as many classes with Linus as I could, and started bumping into him "accidentally." We'd talk a little, I'd bring up his interests, laugh at his jokes, and ingratiate myself to him.

This would lead to step three. Once I had the target's trust, I'd drop the bombshell on them about who they really were, and hope like hell that they'd believe me. Usually they already had inclinations that they were different, and if I'd done my job right, everything would fall into place.

Then it was just a matter of getting them back home, preferably with trust fund in hand.

Now there was this issue with the black sedan, bogging things down right at the beginning of the second step, and I had to figure out what to do.

Linus and his friends from school had gone into a restaurant, but I didn't follow them. I stayed outside, watching through the front window as they sat down at a table. In his dark blue blazer, Linus's shoulders appeared broad, but he was actually tall and lean. After watching him fall half a dozen times during gym class, I knew he'd be no good in a fight.

The restaurant was crowded, and his friends were talking and laughing with him. Whoever was following him in the dark sedan, they were trying to be inconspicuous, which meant that they wouldn't want to create a scene in a place like this. For now, Linus was safe.

I walked away, going around the restaurant and cutting through the alley. When I came back to the street, the sedan was parked a few feet from me, but I stayed in the alley, peering around the corner. I did my best to blend in, and once again, I found myself wishing that I had more Kanin blood in me.

Even this close, the tint on the windows of the car was still too dark for me to see through. I needed more information, so I decided to call Ridley Dresden.

He was the Rektor, so he might have a better idea of what was going on. The Rektor was in charge of trackers, organizing placements, assigning changelings, and basically just keeping us all in order. Because of his position, Ridley was privy to more information than I was, and he might be able to shed some light on the sedan.

Before I called, I decided to use the video option on my phone. It seemed like a smarter choice, because then I could actually show Ridley the car instead of just describing it to him.

But when Ridley finally answered—shirtless, with his brown curls even more untamed than normal—I realized that maybe I should've sent him a text first, letting him know that I'd be video-chatting with him.

"Bryn?" he asked, and behind him I saw movement as someone got up, wrapping themselves in a dark comforter. "Is everything okay?"

"Yes. And no," I said, keeping my voice low so people walking by on the street wouldn't hear. "Sorry if I'm disturbing you."

"No, it's okay." He sat up straighter, and the rabbit amulet he wore on a leather strap around his neck slid across his bare chest. I heard a girl's voice in the background, but I couldn't understand her. "One second." He held his hand over the phone, covering both the camera and the mic, but I could still hear him promising to call her later. "Sorry. I'm back."

"Aren't you supposed to be working right now?" I asked, raising a disapproving eyebrow.

"I'm on a lunch break. It's called a nooner," Ridley said, meeting my gaze with a devilish gleam in his eye.

The year I graduated from the tracker program was the year Ridley became the Rektor. I hadn't really known him before that, but his reputation had preceded him. Everyone regarded him as one of the finest trackers, but though he was only twenty-four, he'd been forced to retire three years ago. He was still youthful looking, especially for a guy in his mid-twenties, but thanks in part to his persistent stubble, he couldn't pass for a teenager any longer.

But that was the only bit of his reputation that I'd heard about. He had a long history of being a serial dater, and this wasn't the first time I'd accidentally caught him in a compromising situation.

But over the years he'd proved himself to be an excellent Rektor and a loyal friend. So I tried not to fault him too much for his escapades.

"But anyway, what's going on with you?" Ridley asked. The glint in his dark eyes was quickly replaced by concern.

"Do you know anything about someone else following Linus Berling?" I asked.

His brow furrowed. "What do you mean?"

"Is there any reason for someone else to be tracking him?" I clarified. "Anyone else from Doldastam, or another Kanin tracker? Maybe even from another tribe?"

"Why would anyone else be following him?" Ridley shook

his head. "You're his tracker. You're the only one that should be on him. Did you see someone?"

"Not exactly." I chewed the inside of my cheek and looked up from the phone at the dark sedan, which hadn't moved. "I haven't seen any*one*, but this car has been following him." I turned the phone around to show it to Ridley.

"Which one?" Ridley asked, and I tilted the phone to show him more directly.

"The black one with the windows tinted. Do you recognize it?"

Ridley was quiet for a moment, considering. "No, I can't say that I do."

"I was afraid of that." I leaned back against the brick wall and turned the phone back around to me. Ridley had leaned forward, like he'd been inspecting the image of the car closely.

"You haven't seen anyone get in or out of it yet?" Ridley asked.

"No." I shook my head.

"It could just be a human thing," Ridley suggested, but he didn't sound like he believed it.

"I don't think so." I sighed. "I'm gonna go check it out."

"Okay." Ridley pressed his lips into a thin line and nodded once, reluctant to agree that I should put myself in a possibly dangerous situation. "Just don't do anything stupid, Bryn."

"I never do," I assured him with a smile, but that just caused him to roll his eyes.

"I mean it," he insisted. "Investigate, but do not interact with them until you figure out who we're dealing with. In the meantime, I'll see if I can run the plates or find out anything on that car. I'll check in with you later today, okay?"

"Okay. And I'll let you know if I find anything out."

"Stay safe, Bryn," Ridley said, and before he could say anything else, I ended the call.

According to the clock on the phone, I only had twenty minutes left of lunch and then afternoon class began. My options were limited, but I knew I didn't want to wait outside all day, hoping the passengers would make a move so I could see them. If somebody was after Linus, I needed to find out who it was before something bad happened.

So I walked out of the alley and straight to the car. Ridley might consider what I was doing stupid, but it was my best option. Out of the past twelve changelings I'd tracked, I'd brought twelve of them back home. I wasn't about to let Linus be the first one I lost.

I grabbed the handle of the back door, half expecting it to be locked, but it opened, so I got in. Two men were sitting in front, and they both turned around to look at me as I slid across the seat.

"What the hell?" the driver snarled.

When I saw who it was—his steel-gray eyes meeting mine— my heart clenched, and all the air went out of my lungs. For that moment everything felt frozen as he glared at me, then the rage and horror surged through me in a nauseating mixture.

I recovered as quickly as I could, holding back my anger, and smiled at him. Somehow in an even voice, I said his name. "Konstantin Black."

vengeance

His eyes narrowed, and his lip twitched ever so slightly. "Do I know you?"

"Not exactly," I admitted, not surprised that he didn't remember me.

The only time I'd spoken to him had been one of the most important and traumatic nights of my life, but that night he'd clearly had his mind on something else. Before that, I had only been one adoring fan out of thousands that he'd met in his tenure at Doldastam.

Konstantin had changed some in the four years since I'd last seen him—four long years since he'd attacked my father and disappeared into the night. His eyes seemed harder, and there were lines etched in the once smooth skin around them. He'd grown a beard, and his hair was a bit longer and wilder than I remembered him wearing it.

But he was still unmistakably him. I'd spent years nursing a schoolgirl crush on him, picturing that face in my daydreams, and then I'd spent years plotting my revenge against him, picturing that face in my nightmares.

Now here it was, his eyes mere inches from my own, and he had no idea who I was.

"You're a tracker," Konstantin realized, and the corner of his mouth curved up into a smirk. I remembered the way that smirk had once filled me with butterflies, but now it only made me want to punch it off his face.

"So you do know her? Or not?" his companion asked.

"No, I don't know her, Bent," Konstantin told him, and I glanced over at his partner in crime.

His friend—Bent, apparently—I didn't recognize, but by his features I guessed he was Omte. His skin was smooth, and he appeared to be tall, but he had the same lopsided square head and beady eyes of a hobgoblin. Not to mention he didn't seem that bright.

"You're a wanted man, Konstantin. What are you doing here?" I asked, instead of hitting him or spitting in his face. Despite my wish for vengeance, I needed to find out what he wanted with Linus Berling and what he was doing here.

"Same thing as you, I would guess," Konstantin admitted.

Pressing my hands on the black leather of the seat to keep from slapping him, I asked, "What do you want with Linus? You don't have a tribe to take him back to. What's the point of even tracking him?"

"We were just waiting for a chance to grab him, and then

we're—" Bent began, but then Konstantin shot him a glare and he fell silent.

"Kidnapping? Really?" I shook my head. "Are you planning to hold him for ransom?"

Konstantin pressed a button in the center console, and the doors clicked as they locked. "Things are far more complicated than they seem."

I licked my lips, and, going against my better instincts, I offered him an olive branch. "How about I make a deal with you? I won't kill you if you let Linus leave with me." Then I paused, recalling the last thing Konstantin had ever said to me: *I am bound to something much higher than this kingdom, and I must complete my mission.*

Konstantin tilted his head then, eyeing me as if he were seeing me for the first time. "Do I know *you*?"

Bent had apparently grown tired of me, and he turned around in the seat with a dopey, crooked smile plastered across his face. "Whatever. I'm taking care of her."

"Bent, maybe—" Konstantin began, but Bent was already in motion.

He leaned over the front seat, reaching for me. His hands were disproportionally large, like massive bear paws, but he was slow, and I easily ducked out of the way.

I grabbed a clump of his dark curly hair, and then I yanked his head to the side, slamming it into the back passenger window. I let go of him and leaned back quickly, then I kicked his head, crashing it into the window again. The glass was shatterproof, and it instantly turned into a crackled sheet as blood streamed down the side of Bent's head.

Konstantin reached over the seat for me—going after me for the first time—but I slid past him. Bent was now slumped unconscious on the backseat, and I climbed over him. Konstantin grabbed my leg as I pushed through the crumbled glass of the window, but thankfully I'd been wearing knee-high socks, so I wriggled out of his grasp. He was left with a sock and a shoe in his hand as I dove out.

I fell onto the sidewalk, scraping my knee on the cement, but I was up in a flash. Konstantin got out of the car, but I wanted to get to Linus before he went back to the school, so that I could take him far away from Konstantin.

He grabbed my arm, and I whirled on him and punched him hard in the stomach. It felt so good that I had to punch him again, harder this time. It wasn't quite the same as running him through with a sword, but it would do for now.

As he doubled over in pain, I said into his ear, "That was for my father. You should've taken the deal."

His grip tightened on my arm as realization dawned on him, and his eyes widened in surprise. "You're the Chancellor's daughter."

"Bryn Aven," I told him, still whispering in his ear. "Remember my name. Because I'm going to be the one that kills you." Then I kneed him in the crotch. He let go, and I stepped back.

"This man is a child molester!" I shouted, and pointed to Konstantin. "He tried to touch me, and he's staking out the school for more kids to molest!"

I was nineteen, but the uniform made me look younger. The sidewalks were crowded over lunch hour, and people had stopped to watch since I'd broken out of the car window. My knee was bleeding, and my clothes looked disheveled from fighting.

As people circled closer to Konstantin and several of them pulled out their cell phones to call the police, I slid back in the crowd. For a moment I stayed around, protected by a small sea of people, and I watched him.

He was looking right back at me, his eyes locked on mine. I'd expected to see anger or arrogance, but he wore neither of those. Instead, he almost seemed to look at me with remorse, and for a split second I felt my hatred of him softening, but I refused to let it.

In the investigation following Konstantin's attempt on my dad's life, nobody had ever been able to figure out his motive. By all accounts, Konstantin had been a good and loyal servant of the kingdom since he'd become a tracker over a decade ago. He'd never had any disagreements with my father, or the King or Queen.

But in the years following that, I'd decided that it didn't matter what his motive was. No reason would ever be good enough for what he had done, and even if he was filled with regret and someday begged me to forgive him, I never would.

The crowd was overtaking him, so I turned and ran down the block. People called after me, and I ran faster.

Since I was only wearing one shoe, it felt awkward, so when I reached the restaurant, I stopped and pulled it and my remaining sock off. The cold cement felt better on my feet than socks did anyway.

When I looked through the window, I saw that Linus was just finishing up, and I pushed down all of the emotions that seeing Konstantin Black had brought up. I had a mission at hand, and it required my full attention.

I didn't know how things would go with Linus. I'd only been talking with him for three days. In an ideal situation, I'd make a connection for two or three weeks, sometimes even a month, before I took a changeling back to Doldastam.

"Linus!" I shouted as I opened the door. A waitress tried to stop me, but I pushed past her and hurried over to his table.

"Bryn?" He stared up at me with confused brown eyes. "What are you doing here?"

"Do you trust me?" I asked, a little out of breath from running all the way here.

"What?" Linus looked over at his friend, who laughed nervously, and then back at me. "You're bleeding. Were you in an accident?"

"Okay, seriously. We don't have time for this." I glanced back at the door. Then I looked down at him. "Come with me if you want to live."

Both his friends burst out laughing at that, but Linus swallowed hard. The sleeves of his blazer had been pushed to his elbows, and I saw the subtle shift of his skin tone. It didn't completely change, but the olive color began to take on a bluish hue.

That was good. It meant Linus was scared, which meant he believed me.

"Miss, I'm gonna have to ask you to leave," a waitress was saying to me.

"Linus, we have to go. *Now.*"

He nodded. "Okay."

One of his friends asked incredulously, "Linus, are you seriously going with this crazy chick?"

He stood up, ignoring his friend, but he'd only taken a step away from the table when he tripped over his shoelace. I caught his arm before he fell, and he offered me an embarrassed grimace.

"You are so lucky I'm here," I muttered as I took his arm and led him out of the restaurant.

"What's going on?" Linus asked.

When we got outside, I looked back down the street. There was still a small crowd of people milling around where I'd escaped from Konstantin and Bent, but the black sedan was gone. They were on the move.

"I'll explain later. But right now we just have to get out of Chicago as fast as we can."

The car I'd rented was in the school parking lot, but there was a chance that Konstantin knew its make. And even if he didn't, he could still be waiting in the parking lot.

"Where are we going?" Linus asked as I hailed a cab.

"To get a car, and then home." I held the door to the orange cab open for him.

"But my home is here in Chicago." He looked puzzled as he slid into the car.

I smiled at him. "No, your *real* home."

THREE

changeling

"Doldastam," Linus repeated, the same way he'd been repeating it over the past day and a half. Every time he said it, he'd put the emphasis on a different syllable, trying so hard to match my pronunciation.

I'd rented a new car, and the drive from Chicago to the train station in Canada was over twenty hours, and we'd only stopped for gas and bathroom breaks.

Before we'd left Chicago, we'd swung by my hotel, and I'd changed into a much more comfortable pair of jeans and a T-shirt. But I hadn't had any clothes for him, and I didn't want to risk going back to his apartment. In Winnipeg, we'd stopped so I could pick up an appropriate winter jacket and hat for Linus, and I'd finally gotten him a change of clothes so he could get out of his uniform.

I didn't know if Konstantin and Bent were working alone or with others, and I wouldn't feel safe until we were back behind the walls of Doldastam. Really, it didn't matter if they were working with others. Seeing Konstantin Black was enough to unnerve me.

As confident as I'd tried to sound with him and as well as I'd fought him, I'd thrown up as soon as we got to my hotel. Coming face-to-face with the man from my nightmares had that effect on me.

But when I was around Linus, I did my best to keep my feelings in check and seem as normal as possible. I needed to be vigilant to keep him safe, which meant staying calm. So I sat rigidly next to him, staring out the window, and not letting my panic show on my face.

"Did I say it right?" Linus asked, and I could feel him looking at me, waiting for an answer.

"Yep. You said it great," I assured him with a forced smile.

"It's pretty out here." Linus motioned to the window, at the snow and tree-lined landscape of Manitoba as we sped through it.

"Yeah, it is," I agreed.

"This is where I was born?" Linus asked.

"Well, not out here, exactly. We're still a ways away from Doldastam, but yeah, you were born out here."

"I'm a changeling." No matter how many times he said this, Linus still managed to sound mystified every time. "I'm Kanin, and you're Kanin."

"Right," I said, because that was easier than correcting him. I was Kanin—sort of. He already had enough to digest without me breaking into my life story.

If he'd known more about what it meant to be Kanin, he'd be able to tell that I wasn't really one just by looking at me.

Linus had dark brown hair, cropped short and gelled smooth to tame the unruly curls, and eyes that matched. I, on the other hand, had easily managed blond waves that landed just below my shoulders, and my eyes were the color of the blue sky out the window. Even his skin was several shades darker than mine.

On his cheeks he had a subtle spotting of freckles. They weren't typical of the Kanin, but they seemed to suit him. Linus had an openness to his face, an innocent inability to hide any of his emotions, and his expression shifted from awe to pained confusion every few minutes.

He furrowed his brow. "I'm a troll."

The long drive up had given me plenty of time to explain all the big points to him, but he still couldn't completely process it. It usually took much longer, and that's why I often spent so long with the changelings before revealing the truth. It was much easier to understand when you had time to digest it instead of your whole sense of reality instantly being dashed away.

"I always knew I was different." He stared down at the floor, the crease in his brow deepening. "Even before my skin started changing color. But when that happened, I guess I just thought I was like an X-Men or something."

"Sorry, we're not superheroes. But being Kanin can still be awesome," I tried to reassure him.

He turned to look at me, relief relaxing some of his apprehension. "Yeah? How so?"

"Well, you're a Berling."

"I'm a what?"

"Sorry. Berling. That's your last name."

"No, my name is—"

"No, that's your host family's last name," I said, cutting him off. The sooner he started severing mental and emotional ties with his host family, the easier it would be for him to accept who he was. "Your parents are Dylan and Eva Berling. You are a Berling."

"Oh. Right." He nodded, like he should know better, and then looked down at his lap. "Will I ever see my host family again?"

"Maybe," I lied, then passed the buck so I wouldn't have to be the one to break it to him that he'd never again see the people he'd spent the past eighteen years believing were his mom and dad. "You'll talk about it with your real family."

"So what's so great about being a Berling?" Linus asked.

"Well, for starters, you're royalty."

"I'm royalty?" He grinned at that. Being royalty always sounded so much better than it actually was.

"Yeah." I nodded and returned his smile. "Your father is a Markis, and your mother is a Marksinna —which are basically Kanin words for Duke and Duchess."

"So am I a Markis?"

"Yep. You have a big house. Not quite as nice as the palace, but close. You'll have servants and horses and cars. Your dad is best friends with the King. You'll go to lavish parties, date the prettiest girls, and really, just live happily ever after."

"You're saying that I just woke up in a fairy tale?" Linus asked.

I laughed a little. "Kind of, yeah."

"Holy crap." He leaned his head back against the seat. "Are you a Marksinna?"

I shook my head. "No. I'm a tracker. Which is almost as far away from being a Marksinna as being human."

"So we're . . . ." He paused and licked his lips. "Not human?"

"No. It's like a lion and tiger," I said, using my go-to analogy to explain the difference to changelings. "They're both cats, and they have similar traits, but they're not the same. A lion isn't a tiger. A Kanin isn't a human."

"We're still, like, the same species, then?" Linus asked, sounding relieved.

"Yep. The fact that humans and trolls are so similar is how we're able to have changelings. We have to pass for human."

"Okay." He settled back in his seat, and that seemed to placate him for a few minutes, then he asked, "I get that I'm a changeling. But *why* am I a changeling?"

"What do you mean?"

"Why didn't my real parents just raise me themselves?" Linus asked.

I took a deep breath. So far, Linus hadn't asked that, and I'd been hoping he wouldn't until we got back to Doldastam. It always sounded much better coming from the parents than it did from a tracker, especially if the changelings had follow-up questions like, *Didn't you love me?* or *How could you abandon your baby like that?* Which were fair questions.

But since he'd asked, I figured I ought to tell him something.

"It started a long time ago, when humans had more advanced medical care and schools than we did," I explained. "Our infant mortality rate was terrible. Babies weren't surviving, and when they did, they weren't thriving. We needed to do something, but we didn't want to give up our ways completely and join the human race.

"We decided to use changelings," I went on. "We'd take a human baby, leave a Kanin baby in its place, and then we'd drop the human baby at an orphanage."

Other tribes brought that human baby back to the village, believing it gave them a bargaining chip with their host families if the changeling decided not to return. But that rarely happened, and we thought the insurance policy—raising a human child with intimate knowledge of our society—cost more than it was worth, so we left the human babies among other humans.

"Our babies would grow up healthy and strong, and when they were old enough, they'd come back home," I said.

"So you guys still have crappy hospitals and schools?" Linus asked.

"They're not the best," I admitted. "But that's not all of it."

"What's the rest?"

I sighed but didn't answer right away. The truth was, the main reason we still practiced changelings was money.

The Kanin lived in small compounds, as far removed from human civilization as we could manage. To maintain our lifestyle, to live closer to the land and avoid the scramble of the humans' lives with their daily commutes and their credit card debt, their pandering politicians and their wars, we refused to live among them.

We could be self-sustaining without living with the humans, but truth be told, we did love our luxuries. The only reason we ever came in contact with humans was because we wanted their trinkets. Kanin, like all trolls, have an almost insatiable lust for jewels.

Even Linus, who otherwise seemed to be an average teenage boy, had on a large class ring with a gaudy ruby, a silver thumb ring, a leather bracelet, and a chain bracelet. The only human man I'd ever seen adorn himself with as much jewelry and accessories as a troll was Johnny Depp, and based on his looks, I'd grown to suspect that he might actually be Trylle.

That's where changelings came in. We'd place the Kanin babies with some of the wealthiest families we could find. Not quite royalty or celebrity status, but enough to be sure they'd leave hefty trust funds for their children.

When they were old enough to be collected, trackers like myself would go retrieve them. We'd earn their trust, explain to them who they were, then get them to access and drain their bank accounts. They'd return to the Kanin community, infusing our society with a much-needed surge in funds.

So in the end, what it all came down to was tradition and greed, and when I looked over at the hopeful expression on Linus's face, I just didn't have it in me to tell him. Our world still had so much beauty and greatness, and I wanted Linus to see that before showing him its darkest flaw.

"Your parents will explain it to you when you get back," I said instead.

Linus fell silent after that, but I didn't even bother trying to sleep. When the train pulled into the station, I slipped my heavy winter boots back on. I hated wearing them, but it was better than losing my toes to frostbite. I bundled up in my jacket and hat, then instructed Linus to do the same.

I grabbed my oversized backpack and slung it over my shoulders. One good thing about being a tracker was that I'd been trained to pack concisely. On a trip I expected to last three or four weeks, I managed to get everything I needed into one bag.

As soon as we stepped off the train and the icy wind hit us, Linus gasped.

"How is it so cold here?" Linus pulled a scarf up over his face. "It's April. Shouldn't it be all spring and flowers?"

"Flowers don't come for another couple months," I told him as I led him away from the train platform to where I had left the silver Land Rover LR4 parked.

Fortunately, it hadn't snowed since I'd been gone. Sometimes when I came back, the SUV was buried underneath snow. I tossed my bag in the back, then hopped in the driver's seat. Linus got in quickly, shivering as I started the SUV.

"I don't know how much I'll enjoy living here," Linus said between chattering teeth.

"You get used to it." I pointed to the digital temperature monitor in the dash. "It's just below freezing today. That's actually pretty warm for this time of year."

Once the vehicle had warmed up enough, I put it in drive and pulled out on the road, heading south along the Hudson Bay. It was almost an hour to Doldastam from the train station, but Linus didn't say much. He was too focused on watching the scenery. Everything was still covered in snow, and most of it was unsullied, so it all appeared pure and white.

"Why are the trees like that?" Linus asked, pointing at the only vegetation that grew in the winter.

Tall evergreens dotted the landscape, and all of them were tilted slightly toward the east, with all their branches growing out on only one side. To people who hadn't seen it before, it did look a bit strange.

"It's called the Krummholz effect," I explained. "The strong wind comes from the northwest, making it hard for branches and trees to grow against it, so they all end up bending away from it."

As we got closer to Doldastam, the foliage grew thicker. The road narrowed, becoming a thin path that was barely wide enough for the Land Rover. If another car came toward us, we'd have to squeeze off the road between the trees.

The trees around the road seemed to be reaching for us, bent and hunched over, their long branches extending out toward the path. They had long viny branches, like weeping willows, but they were darker green and thicker than any willow I'd seen. These were actually hybrids, grown only by the Kanin people. They were made to help conceal the road to the kingdom, so humans would be less likely to stumble across us.

But no other car came. The empty road was normal. Other than trackers, no one really left the city.

The wall wasn't visible until we were almost upon Doldastam, thanks to all the trees hiding it. It was twenty feet tall, built out of stone by Kanin over two centuries ago, but it held up stunningly well.

The wrought-iron gate in front of the road was open, and I waved at the guard who manned the gate as we drove past. The guard recognized me, so he smiled and waved me on.

Linus leaned forward, staring up through the windshield. Small cottages lined the narrow roads as we weaved our way through town, hidden among bushes as much as they could be, but Linus wasn't paying attention to them.

It was the large palace looming over everything at the other end of town that had caught his attention. The gray stone made it look like a castle, though it lacked any towers. It was a massive rectangle, covered in glittering windows.

I drove through the center of town, and when I reached the south side of Doldastam, where the palace towered above us, I slowed down so Linus could get a better look. But then I kept going, stopping two houses away, in front of a slightly smaller but still majestic stone house. This one had a pitched roof, so it resembled a mansion much more than it did a castle.

"This is it?" Linus asked, but he didn't look any less impressed by his smaller home than he did by the castle.

"Yep. This is where you live."

"Wow." He shook his head, sounding completely awed. "This really is like a fairy tale."

FOUR

stable

I t was dark by the time I pulled the Land Rover into the garage, narrowly parking it between another SUV and a full-sized Hummer. I clicked the button, closing the garage door behind me.

Technically it was a garage, but in reality it was a massive brick fortress that housed dozens of vehicles and all kinds of tracker supplies. To the left of the garage were the classrooms and the gym where trackers trained, along with the Rektor's office.

I hadn't bothered to put on my jacket or boots after I had gotten Linus settled in at the Berlings' house, because I knew I was coming right here. The garage was heated, as were most things in Doldastam. Even the floor was heated, so when I stepped out of the SUV, the concrete felt warm on my bare feet.

I'd just gone around to the side of the car to get my bag out of the back when I heard the side door close. The Rektor's office connected to the garage, and I looked over to see Ridley Dresden walking in.

"Need a hand?" he asked.

"Nah, I think I got it. But thanks." I slung my bag over my shoulder and went over to the storage closets.

He wore a vest and a tie, with his sleeves rolled up above his elbow. But like me, he was barefoot. His dark hair was kept short, but it still curled a little. In that way, his hair fit him perfectly. Try as he might to be straitlaced, there was just a part of him that wouldn't completely be tamed.

I dropped my bag on the floor in front of the shelves and crouched down to rummage through it. I'd pulled out a couple fake passports—both for me and for Linus—when Ridley reached me.

"You don't look that bad," he said with his hands shoved in his pockets.

I looked up at him, smirking. "And here I didn't think you liked blondes."

As far as I knew, his last couple girlfriends had been brunettes, but that really wasn't saying much when it came to the Kanin. Like all trolls, the Kanin had certain physical characteristics. Dark curly hair; brown or gray eyes; olive skin; shorter in stature and petite; and often physically attractive. In that regard, the Kanin appeared similar to the Trylle, the Vittra, and, other than the attractive part, even the Omte.

It was only the Skojare who stood out, with fair skin, blond hair, and blue eyes. And it was the Skojare blood that betrayed my true nature. In Doldastam, over 99 percent of the population had brown hair. And I didn't.

"Come on. Everyone likes blondes," Ridley countered with a grin.

I laughed darkly. Outside of the walls surrounding Doldastam the world may have shared that opinion, as Ridley would know from his tracking days. But here, my appearance had never been anything but a detriment.

"I was referring to your run-in," Ridley said.

I stood up and gave him a sharp look. "I can handle myself in a fight."

"I know." He'd grown serious, and he looked down at me with a level of concern that was unusual for him. "But I know how hard dealing with Konstantin Black had to be."

I turned away from him, unwilling to let him see how badly it had shaken me up. "Thanks, but you know you don't have to worry about me."

"I can't help it," Ridley said, then waited a beat before adding, "It's my job."

I pulled open a cabinet drawer and flitted through the files, looking for the one with my name on it, and dropped the passports inside of it.

"It must've taken all your restraint not to kill him," Ridley went on when I didn't say anything.

"On the subject of your job, have you figured out why they were after Linus?" I bent over and dug through my bag, refusing to talk about it. I wouldn't even say Konstantin's name aloud.

"No. So far we've come up empty. I've scheduled a phone call with the Queen of Omte first thing in the morning, and I have a meeting at ten in the morning tomorrow with the King,

Queen, and the Chancellor." He paused. "I'd like you to be there too."

"I'm no good at meetings." That wasn't a lie, exactly, but it also wasn't the reason I didn't want to go to the meeting.

As the Chancellor, my dad would be at the meeting, and I didn't want to talk about letting his attempted murderer get away. I knew he would never hold it against me, but that didn't make me feel any less guilty.

I grabbed stacks of American and Canadian cash out of my bag. Ridley pulled his keys out of his pocket and unlocked the safe at the end of the cabinets. My own set of keys were buried somewhere in my bag, and it was a bit quicker to let him unlock it.

"You know more about this than we do," Ridley reasoned. "For the sake of Linus and the other changelings, we need you at this meeting."

"I'll be there," I said reluctantly. I crouched back down over my bag and dug out what was left of my tracker supplies—a knife, a cell phone, a mileage log, and a few other odds and ends— and began putting them in the cabinets.

"What are you doing out here, anyway?" I asked. "Aren't you off for the night?" His job was much more of a nine-to-five gig than mine.

"I saw you pull in." He leaned back against an SUV parked next to me and watched me. "I wanted to see that everything went okay."

"Other than the dustup, everything was fine." I shrugged. "I got Linus back, and he's getting settled in with his parents. I did a quicker intro than I normally do, but Linus seems to be taking this all really well, and I needed to get out and get some sleep."

His dark eyes lingered on me. "When was the last time you slept?"

"What day is it?"

He arched an eyebrow. "Wednesday."

"Then . . ." I paused, thinking. "Monday."

"Bryn." Ridley stepped over to me. "Let me do this. Go get some sleep."

"I'm almost done, and if I don't log it myself, then my jerk of a boss will have my head," I teased, and he sighed.

"Well, whatever. I'm helping you even if you don't want me to." He grabbed the logbook and started filling it out.

With his help, everything was put away and accounted for within a matter of minutes, leaving only my clothing and laptop in my bag. I started to pull on my heavy winter boots and jacket, and Ridley told me to wait there for a second. He came back wearing his charcoal-gray peacoat and slick black boots.

"I'll walk you home," he said.

"You sure?"

He nodded. "I'm done for the night, and you don't live that far anyhow."

That was an understatement. My place was a two-minute walk from the garage. Ridley lived farther than that, but honestly, most people in Doldastam did.

The night had grown even colder, and Ridley popped up the collar of his jacket and shoved his hands in his pockets as he walked. I was smart enough to wear a hat, so I didn't mind it so much. The snow crunched beneath our boots as we slowly walked down the cobblestone road toward my loft.

I turned to him and couldn't help but admire him in the moonlight—tall and strong with the beginnings of a light scruff. Ridley's looks could be a distraction if I allowed them to be. Fortunately, I was a master at reining in useless, dangerous feelings like attraction, and I looked away from him.

"I'm not gonna be in trouble, am I?" I asked.

Ridley looked over at me like I was insane. "Why would you be in trouble?"

"Because I'm not sure that the Berlings will be able to get Linus's money now. He's a few days shy of eighteen, and there's no telling what'll happen to his trust fund."

"You got him home safely. That's the most important thing," he said. "Everything after that is icing."

"So you think I did the right thing by taking him home early?"

"Absolutely." Ridley stopped walking, so I did too, and he looked down at me. Our path was lit by lanterns and the moonlight, and I could see the sincerity in his chestnut eyes. "You have great instincts, Bryn. If you thought that Linus was in real danger, then he was. And who knows what Konstantin Black would've done with him?"

"I know." I sighed. "I mean, I do. But what if his parents don't feel the same way?"

"The Berlings aren't like that, and if they are . . ." He shrugged. "Screw 'em. You protected their son, and that's all that should matter."

I smiled. "Thanks."

"No problem." He smiled back at me, then motioned to the barn just up the road. "Now go up and get some sleep, and don't forget about the meeting in the morning."

"See you tomorrow, Ridley."

"Good night."

I turned and jogged toward the barn, but he stayed where he was in the street, waiting until I'd made it inside safely. The lower level of the barn was a stable, but the stairway along the side of the building led up to a small loft apartment, and that was where I lived.

It was chilly inside, since I'd turned down the heat because I'd planned on being in Chicago for a month or more. Before I took my coat off, I threw a couple logs in the wood-burning stove and got it going. I had a furnace, of course, but the natural heat always seemed to feel better.

I could hear the Tralla horses downstairs, their large hooves stomping on the concrete of the barn, and their neighing and rustling as they settled in for the night. The Tralla horses were huge workhorses the Kanin had brought over from Scandinavia centuries ago, and they stood even larger than Clydesdales, with broad shoulders, long manes, and thick tufts of fur around their hooves.

The horses in the stable all belonged to the King and Queen, and, like most Tralla horses, they were only used for show, pulling a carriage through town if the Queen was making a visit or marching in a parade.

They could be ridden, and I did ride one horse—Bloom—as

often as I had the chance. Bloom was a younger steed with silvery gray fur. Even as tired as I was, I wanted to go down to say hello to him, maybe brush his fur while he nuzzled against me, searching my pockets for hidden carrots or apples.

But I knew I had to be up for the meeting, so I figured I'd better postpone my reunion with Bloom until the next day.

Instead, I settled in and put the rest of my things away. My apartment was small, taking up only a quarter of the loft space. A wall separated my place from the room where the hay bales and some horse equipment were stored.

But I didn't need that much space. I had my bed, a worn couch, a wardrobe, a couple shelves overflowing with books, and a chair and a desk where I put my laptop. Those were the only things I really needed.

While I waited for the loft to warm up, I changed into my pajamas. I'd decided that it was about as warm as it would get when I heard footsteps thudding up the steps. Based on the speed and intensity—like a herd of small but anxious elephants—I guessed that it either had to be a major emergency or it was Ember Holmes.

"Bryn!" Ember exclaimed as she threw the door open, and then she ran over and threw her arms around me, squeezing me painfully tight. "I'm so glad you're okay!"

"Thanks," I managed to squeak out as she hugged me.

Then as abruptly as she'd grabbed me, she let go. She'd barely even stepped back when she swatted me hard on the arm.

"Ow." I rubbed my arm and scowled at her. "What the hell?"

"Why didn't you call and tell me you were coming home?"

Ember demanded, staring up at me with piercing dark eyes and her hands on her hips. "I had to hear about it from Ridley that you'd been attacked and were leaving early."

"Thanks, Ridley," I muttered.

"Why didn't you tell me what was going on?" Ember asked.

"I didn't want word getting out." I sat back on my bed. "I thought it'd be best to keep mum until we figured out what's going on."

"Well . . ." She didn't know how to argue with that, so she brushed her bangs out from her eyes. "You can still tell me. I'm your best friend."

Ember was lithe and petite, standing at least four inches shorter than me, and I wasn't that tall to begin with. But she was a good fighter, quick on her feet and determined. I respected that about her, but that wasn't what bonded us together.

Like me, she didn't quite fit into Kanin society. In her case, it was because she was actually Trylle. Her father had worked for the Trylle Queen before they'd moved here to Doldastam four years ago. They hadn't exactly been welcomed with open arms. Outsiders never were, but Ember and her parents had made their place here.

She did have the added struggle of being a lesbian in a society that wasn't exactly thrilled about that kind of thing. But since she was a tracker, and not a royal with an important bloodline—or even Kanin—she'd gotten a bit of a break and tended to slip under people's radar. Not that Ember would ever let anybody keep her down anyway.

"I know. I'm sorry," I said. "Next time I'll be sure to tell you."

"So what happened?" She sat down on the bed next to me.

I shook my head. "There's not much to tell."

"Ridley mentioned . . ." Ember paused, her tone softening with concern. "He said that Konstantin Black was involved."

I lowered my eyes and took a deep breath, but I could feel her eyes on me, searching for any signs of trauma or despair. When Ember had moved here, it had only been days after Konstantin had left. She may not have been here for the attack, but she definitely witnessed the aftermath.

His attack on my dad had left my nerves raw and I was struggling to control my anger at both Konstantin and myself. Myself for not being able to protect my dad better, and for having had such strong feelings for Konstantin.

Ember, along with my friend Tilda Moller, had been instrumental in helping me deal with it. But that didn't mean I wanted Ember or anyone else to have to deal with it now.

"It was Konstantin," I said finally.

Ember didn't say anything for a minute, waiting to see if I'd continue, and when I didn't, she cautiously asked, "Did you kill him?"

"No." The word felt heavy and terrible in my mouth, and an ache grew in the pit of my stomach like a forgotten ulcer flaring up.

"Good," she said, and I looked up at her in surprise. "You don't need that on your conscience."

I scoffed. "His death I could handle. It's his life that I don't need weighing on me."

"I don't know what happened, because I wasn't there, but I

know that you did the right thing." Ember put her hand on my shoulder, warm and reassuring. "You always do. You got the Berling boy home safe and sound, and you're here and you're alive. So I know you did everything right."

I smiled wanly at her. "Thank you."

"You look exhausted. But I'm sure you had a very long trip back." Ember'd only been a tracker for a little over a year, but already she understood how taxing the journey could be, even without a run-in with my nemesis. "I'll let you get some rest."

"You have no idea," I admitted with a dry laugh.

Ember stood up. "I really am glad you're back. And your timing is perfect."

"What do you mean?" I asked.

"My birthday's on Friday, and the big anniversary party's on Saturday. You're back just in time for all the fun," Ember said with a broad grin.

I tried not to grimace. "Right. Fun."

The birthday party would be fun, but the anniversary party I'd been hoping to avoid. It would mean guard duty at the palace all night long, which sounded like it would be right up my alley. But every party or ball I'd guarded had always turned out to be nothing but trouble.

sovereign

The footman who answered the door to the palace helped me take off my coat, even though I assured him it wasn't necessary, and he nearly pulled off my blazer with it as I tried to wriggle away. I'd kicked off my boots, and before I could collect them he was already bending over and picking them up.

If I hadn't been in such a hurry, I would've insisted on doing things myself. Just because I was in the palace didn't mean I needed a servant doing everything for me. But as it was, I'd barely had time to shower, and I didn't have time to dry my hair, so it had frozen on the way over from my apartment.

I mumbled apologies to the footman and thanked him for his trouble. He offered to lead me down the hall to where the meeting was being held, but I didn't need it. I knew the building like the back of my hand.

The opulence of the palace was nearly lost on me by now. Like the exterior, most of the walls inside were stone or brick.

Two massive wooden doors opened into the majestic front hall, but despite the openness, it felt dark and cavernous, thanks to the gray tones of the stone.

The only natural light filtered through stained-glass windows featuring famous battles and royalty long since gone. At the right times of the day, when the light came through the window depicting the Kanin's voyage across the sea, the hall would glow blue, and when it shone through the window immortalizing the Kanin's role in the Long Winter War, the hall would shine blood-red.

The rest of the palace was designed much the same way. Since the palace had been built right after the Kanin settled Doldastam, the key to keeping the cold out seemed to be building as many brick walls with as few windows as possible. Not to mention an abundance of fireplaces, which was another reason the stone was so necessary. Less chance of the building going up in flames.

Not much had been changed in the palace since it was built. At least not in the wing where business was conducted. The private quarters where the King and Queen lived were updated when each new monarch began his reign, so they were much more personal, with wallpaper and wood floors.

Most of the palace did seem dark and cold, but there were elegant flourishes and royal touches. Masterworks of art and antique Baroque furniture were carefully arranged throughout. The kerosene lamps that still lit the corridors were made of silver and adorned with jewels. The ceilings were astonishingly high, and were often broken up by skylights that the poor servants had to constantly clear of snow so they wouldn't come crashing in under the weight.

As I jogged down the corridor, constantly pulling up my black slacks— my nicest pair, though they were too large—I barely even noticed any of the majestic trappings around me. When I reached the meeting hall, I paused outside the door to catch my breath and rake my fingers through my thawing hair.

Then I took a deep breath and opened the doors, and it was just as I had feared. Everyone was already here, waiting. Around a square table that sat ten, there were five of us.

King Evert Strinne sat at the end of the table, next to the crackling fireplace and a massive portrait of himself. He wore a handsomely tailored black suit, but he'd forgone a tie and left the top few buttons undone.

His wife, Queen Mina Strinne, wore her crown, though her husband did not. It was really more of a tiara anyway, silver and encrusted with diamonds. Her long brown hair was pulled back in a loose bun that rested on the nape of her neck, and she smiled warmly at me when I came in. This was a rather casual meeting, but she still wore an ornate gown of white and silver.

The table was wide enough that the Queen could sit next to her husband at the head of it, though her chair was much smaller than his. The dark wood of the high back rose a full two feet above the King's head, while Mina's only came up to the top of her tiara.

Directly to the King's right was Ridley. With a stack of papers in front of him, he smiled grimly at me, and I knew that my tardiness had not gone unnoticed.

Then, sitting to the left of the Queen, with the gravest expression of anyone in the room, was the Chancellor, Iver Aven. My father. His wavy black hair was smoothed back, unintentionally highlighting the silver at his temples, and he wore a suit and tie, the way he did nearly every day. The ire in his toffee eyes was unmistakable, but I met his irritation as evenly as I could and held my head high.

"Bryn Aven." King Evert eyed me with a severe gaze and his perpetual smirk. "How nice of you to join us."

"I'm sorry, my lord," I said with genuine contrition and bowed. "I overslept."

The last few days had worn much harder on me than I had thought they would, and I'd slept straight through my alarm, which led to a frantic scramble to get here on time. Although the fact that I'd only been a few minutes late was really a credit to my determination.

"She just got back from the mission late last night, and she didn't have time to sleep while she was transporting the Berling boy," Ridley said, coming to my aid. "She needed to remain vigilant after his attempted kidnapping."

"We appreciate your diligence, Bryn," the King said, but I couldn't tell if it was approval or condescension in his voice.

I smiled politely. "Thank you, Your Majesty."

"Why don't you have a seat, Bryn?" the Queen suggested, and motioned to the table, the rings on her fingers glinting in the light.

"Thank you."

I took a seat at the end of the table across from the King, and deliberately left empty chairs between myself and my dad, and myself and Ridley. While I loved my dad, and I thought the King approved of him as Chancellor, I always tried to put distance between us at occasions like this.

I didn't want anyone to think that I was relying on my dad and his position in the King's court to get where I was, or that Ridley showed me any favoritism because he was my friend as well as the Rektor. I earned everything on my own merit.

"So. Back to what we were saying." The smirk finally fell away from Evert's face and he looked to Ridley. "How are we even sure this was an attempted kidnapping?"

"Well, we're not," Ridley admitted.

"Are we sure that they were even going after the Berling boy?" Mina asked, her smoky gray eyes surveying the room.

"They all but confessed it to me," I said, and everyone turned to look at me.

"You spoke to him?" Dad asked, and worry hardened his expression. "How did that happen?"

"I got in the car, and I asked him what he was doing," I said simply.

"You got in his car?" Dad asked, nearly shouting. Then he clenched his fist and forced a pained smile, doing his best to keep control of himself in front of the King and Queen. When he spoke again, his voice was tight. "What were you thinking?"

"I was thinking that I needed to do my job, and my job was protecting Linus Berling." I sat up straighter in my chair, defending myself. "I did what I needed to."

"Chancellor, my trackers are trained to handle themselves in all situations." Ridley bristled a little, as if my dad were calling into question his abilities as a Rektor.

"Well, what did they say?" Queen Mina asked, bringing us back on topic.

"They said they were following Linus and waiting for their chance to grab him," I said.

The King sighed and shook his head. "Dammit."

"Did they say why?" Mina pressed.

"No. They refused to say why. Then they tried to prevent me from leaving, and things became . . . violent," I said, choosing my words carefully, and from the corner of my eye I saw my dad flinch, though he did his best to hide it. "One of the men— the one called Bent—was injured. But Konstantin Black evaded serious damage before I got away."

Dad couldn't help himself and whispered harshly, "You shouldn't have gotten in the car."

Ridley cast my dad a look from across the table. "Sir, Bryn can handle herself in a fight."

"It was definitely Konstantin Black, then?" the Queen asked. I nodded. "Yes."

"How can you be so sure?" King Evert looked at me skeptically. "Did you ever meet him?"

"Everybody in the kingdom knew who Konstantin Black was," Ridley interjected, attempting to spare me from explaining how I knew him so well.

"Only once," I said, speaking loudly but still clear and even. It was getting harder to keep a steady tone when the King was patronizing me about something I was certain of. "When

Konstantin stabbed my father. I'll remember his face until I die."

The King lowered his eyes, faltering only for a moment. "I'd forgotten you were there for his altercation with the Chancellor.

"What about this other man?" The King cleared his throat and continued, "The one called Bent. Do we know anything about him?"

"I've been doing some research and making a few calls." Ridley flipped through the papers in front of him and scanned his notes. "Bryn thought he might be Omte, and they can be reluctant to give any information. However, the Queen did confirm that a young man named Bent Stum was exiled from their community last year, but they wouldn't say why."

"So a wanted Kanin and an exiled criminal Omte joined forces to track down a changeling in Chicago? Why?" Dad shook his head. "And how did they find him?"

"I've been looking over all the paperwork on Berling's placement, and I can't see any sign of why it went wrong." Ridley shrugged helplessly. "The only people who should've known where he was were Linus's parents, and then Bryn."

"Did the Markis or Marksinna Berling tell anyone?" my dad asked.

"No." The King dismissed this instantly. "Dylan and Eva are too smart for that. They know better." Then he looked at me. "What about you, Bryn?"

"No, Your Majesty. I never tell anyone where I'm sent."

"You sure?" King Evert pressed. "You didn't mention it to any of your friends?"

"Bryn's one of our best, my lord," Ridley said. "If she says she didn't tell anybody, she didn't tell anybody."

"Well, somehow they found one of our highest-priority Markis changelings. If nobody told anyone, how the hell did they manage that?" King Evert snapped.

"I'm not sure, sire," Ridley admitted, but he met the King's annoyed glare.

"What about your files? You have it all written down, don't you?" the King asked.

"Yes, of course I do. But it's all locked away."

"Who has access to it?" King Evert asked.

"Myself and the Chancellor," Ridley said. "And, of course, you and the Queen would have access to anything you wanted."

My dad furrowed his brow as he considered this. "So, the people in this room."

"Obviously it was none of us, so it must be someone else," Queen Mina said.

The King looked over at Ridley. "What about you?"

Ridley shook his head. "I didn't tell anyone, Your Highness."

"Perhaps Konstantin Black was tracking the trackers," Queen Mina offered, and she turned to me. "Were you followed?"

"I don't believe so," I said. "Konstantin didn't know that Berling was being tracked at first, and I don't think he realized I was Kanin."

The King snorted. "Well . . ."

This time I didn't even try to keep the emotion from my voice, though it was a struggle not to yell. "I was born in Doldastam and raised here. I have pledged my fealty to this kingdom. I am as much a Kanin as any of you."

King Evert smirked, unmoved by my outburst. "I appreciate your service, Bryn, but you know that—"

"Evert, my King." Queen Mina reached over and touched his hand, and she looked up at him with deference. "If the girl has pledged her loyalty to you, then she is a Kanin, and by saving the young Markis Berling, she's proved it."

He looked at his wife, then shifted in his seat and nodded. "You're right, of course, my Queen. I apologize, Bryn."

"No apology is necessary, my lord," I said.

"Back to the matter at hand—what to do about Konstantin Black and Bent Stum?" my dad said. "Didn't the Trylle have a problem like this once? Their changelings were kidnapped by an enemy. What did they do?"

"They went to war," the King replied with a heavy sigh.

"We're not prepared for war," Queen Mina said quickly, as if anyone had actively proposed it. "The Trylle have a smaller population than us, but thanks to their heavier reliance on changelings they have many more trackers, and their army is at least twice that of ours."

"More than that, the Trylle knew who their enemy was," King Evert agreed. "They had that long-standing feud with the Vittra, so the Trylle knew exactly who to go after. Who would we even fight against?"

"Could the Omte be behind it?" Mina asked.

Ridley shook his head. "Doubtful. They're not smart enough

to have found the Berling changeling, and if the Omte Queen was aware of Bent Stum's activities, she would've denied his very existence."

"We don't even know if this is going to be a recurring problem," Dad pointed out. "The Berling boy may have been a one-time thing."

"He is the highest-ranking Markis in the entire Kanin now," Ridley said, thinking aloud. "Until the King and Queen have a child, Linus is actually next in line for the throne. We don't know what Black wanted with Linus, but it can't be good. He could have been planning an assassination."

"Or it could've been a plot for ransom. Both Konstantin and Bent have been exiled," Dad said. "Konstantin has been on the run for years. He has to be in desperate need of money."

The King nodded. "Until we learn otherwise, I think we should treat this as an isolated incident."

"But what if it's not?" I asked.

"It might not be," Evert agreed. "But what would you have us do? Bring all the changelings home right now? Send out all our trackers after Konstantin Black and Bent Stum, leaving Doldastam unguarded?"

"No, of course not, my King. But there should be a compromise," I argued. "Bring home our highest-ranking changelings, especially those over the age of twelve, and send a few trackers after Konstantin and Bent. I would gladly volunteer for that mission."

"Absolutely not," the King said, so swiftly that I was too

stunned to speak for a moment. He hadn't even considered what I'd suggested.

"But my lord—" I said when I found my words.

"We can't afford to bring in that many changelings, not this early," King Evert defended his veto.

"And can we afford to have our changelings kidnapped or slaughtered?" I shot back.

"Bryn," Dad said, trying to silence me.

"Tracker, I think you've forgotten your place," King Evert said, and I swallowed hard. "This is my kingdom, and my decision. Your invitation to this meeting was little more than a courtesy."

I lowered my eyes. "I'm sorry, my King. I'm only thinking of what's in the best interest of the kingdom."

"So are we, Bryn," Queen Mina said, much more gently than her husband had spoken to me. "Many of the highest-ranking Markis and Marksinna in the Kanin, not to mention the Kings and Queens from friendly tribes, will be descending on Doldastam this weekend. If there is a threat to our kingdom, then we will need all our guards here. And if this was targeted on Linus Berling in particular, then it's even more important that you, as his tracker, are here to keep him safe."

"The Queen is right, Bryn," Ridley said, but he sounded sympathetic to my position. "We don't know much right now, and our highest priority should be keeping the kingdom safe."

"Then it's settled," the Queen declared. "I will hear no more of this over the weekend. We have much to celebrate, and friends and dignitaries will be coming into town beginning to-morrow."

"You will stick with Linus Berling like he's your shadow," the King commanded me. "Help him acclimate and understand our community, the way you would with any other changeling, but you also need to be more vigilant, in case there is a price on his head."

I nodded. "Yes, my lord."

SIX

mistakes

The meeting appeared to be over, and the Queen was the first to make her exit. As soon as she rose from her place at the end of the table, the rest of us stood up. The backs of my legs smacked into my chair, and it creaked loudly against the floor.

"If you don't mind, I have much to attend to with guests arriving soon." She smiled at all of us as she gathered her dress, and she left the hall.

"I should be on my way, also," King Evert said. "Thank you for attending."

"My King," Dad said, stopping him before he left. "If I could have a word with you for a moment. It's about the new tax."

While the King and Queen were appointed to their roles by birth or marriage, the Chancellor was elected by the people so they could have a voice in the running of the government.

The King nodded. "Yes, of course, Chancellor. Let's walk

and talk." He and my dad left the room together, speaking in hushed tones.

"You always gotta make an entrance, don't you?" Ridley grinned at me as he gathered his papers together.

"I overslept, I swear. I didn't think I'd sleep for twelve hours straight." My pants had begun slipping down my waist again, and with the royalty gone, I was free to pull them back up without earning a scrutinizing look from the King.

"Well, you made it, so that's what counts."

I sighed and sat down, resting against the arm of the chair. "Maybe it would've been better if I hadn't come at all."

"You mean because the King got a little miffed there for a second?" Ridley asked as he walked over to me. "He'll get over it. And you weren't wrong."

"So you're saying I was right?" I asked with raised eyebrows.

"Not exactly." He leaned a hip against the table next to me, crossing his arms so his stack of papers was against his chest. "We need to protect here first, but once this anniversary party is over, then we should really implement your ideas. Even if Konstantin and Bent were only targeting Linus, we can't just let them get away with it."

"So you don't think this was a one-time thing?"

"Honestly?" He looked at me from behind his thick lashes and hesitated before saying, "No, I don't."

"Dammit. I was kinda hoping I was wrong." I ran a hand through my hair. "Anyway, thanks for having my back."

"I'll always have your back," Ridley said with a wry smile. "Or any part of your body."

I rolled my eyes and smiled despite myself. "Way to ruin a perfectly nice moment, Ridley."

"Sorry." He laughed. "I can't help myself sometimes."

"Mmm, I've noticed."

"Have you?"

He leaned back, appraising me, and there was something in his dark eyes, a kind of heat that made my heart beat out of time. It was something new, something I'd only begun to detect in the past few months. Most of the time when we were together it was the same as always, but more and more there was that look in his eyes, a smoldering that I had no idea how to react to.

I suddenly became aware of my very close proximity to him. My knee had brushed up against his leg, and if I wanted to, I could reach out and touch him, putting my hand on the warm skin of his arm, which was bare below where he'd pushed up his sleeves.

As soon as the thought popped into my head, I pushed it away.

The door to the hall swung open, and he lowered his eyes, breaking whatever moment we'd both been in.

"Good, Bryn, you're still here," Dad said as he came into the room.

Ridley looked up and gave me a crooked smile, then shook his head. "I don't even know what I'm talking about."

That's what he said, but it felt like a lie. Still, I'd become acutely aware that my dad was staring at us both, watching us look at each other, and the whole situation felt increasingly awkward.

Amanda Hocking

"Anyway, I should get back to the office." He straightened up and stepped away from the table. "It was nice seeing you again, Chancellor."

"You too." Dad nodded at him, then turned his attention to me. "I wanted to talk to you."

"What did you want to talk to me about?" I asked after Ridley made his escape. "A lecture on how I shouldn't put myself in danger? Or maybe how I should retire and become a teacher like Mom?"

"That would be nice, yes, but actually I wanted to invite you over for dinner tonight."

"I don't know, Dad." I hurried to think up some kind of excuse, *any* excuse. "I'm supposed to be spending time helping Linus get situated."

"Bryn, you just got back in town after being attacked."

"I wouldn't call it an 'attack' per se."

"Your mother wants to see you. *I* want to see you. It's been weeks since you've been over to our house." Dad used a tone so close to pleading that it made my heart twist up with guilt. "Mom will make a nice supper. Just come over. It'll be good."

"Okay," I relented. "What time?"

"Six? Does that work for you?"

"Yep. That'll be great," I said and tried to look happy about it.

"Great." A relieved grin spread across his face. "I know I said some stuff in the meeting that made you mad, but it's just because I love you and I want you to be safe."

"I know, Dad."

And I did know that. Dad was just trying to express concern. But I wished he'd do it in a way that didn't undermine me in front of my superiors.

"Good," he said. "Is it okay if I hug you now, or does that break your no-hugs-at-work policy?"

That was a policy I'd instated when I was fifteen and Dad had ruffled my hair and called me his "adorable little girl" in front of the Högdragen, making them chuckle. It was already hard enough for me to earn their respect without moments like that.

I nodded, and he wrapped his arms around me. When he let me go, I smiled and said, "Don't go making a habit of it."

We both left the meeting hall after that. Dad had work to be done, and so did I. I knew I should go down to help Linus Berling. Even without the King's order to guard him, as his tracker I was supposed to be the one helping him adjust to his new life here in Doldastam.

But right at that moment I didn't think it would be the best idea. The meeting had left me in a sour mood. Things had not gone well with the King, and I really needed to burn off steam.

I could spend an hour at the gym, then go down and help Linus. It'd be better for him if I got in my daily training anyway. If someone was coming after him, I needed to be strong and sharp enough to fight them off.

The gym in the tracker school had a locker room attached to it, where I changed into my workout clothes. As I pulled on my tank top, I was acutely aware of the jagged scar on my shoulder—the gift Konstantin had given me the first time we'd fought.

That only helped fuel my anger, and I pulled my hair up into a ponytail and strode into the gym.

The younger recruits in tracker school were running laps around the side. A couple of older kids were practicing fencing at the other end. Swordplay probably wouldn't be that useful in the outside world, but the Kanin liked to keep things old school. We were a culture steeped in tradition, sometimes to a maddening degree.

A few other full-fledged trackers were doing general workouts, including Ember Holmes and Tilda Moller. Tilda was lifting weights, and Ember hovered over her, spotting for her.

While Ember was a couple years younger than me, Tilda and I were the same age. We were actually the only two girls in our graduating tracker class, and that hadn't been an easy feat for either of us.

Tilda and I had become friends in kindergarten, when we'd both been deemed outsiders—me for blond hair and fair skin, and her for her height. As a child, she had been unnaturally tall, towering over everyone in our class, though as we'd gotten older her height had become an asset, and she'd filled out with curves and muscles that made her almost Amazonian.

Growing up, we were subjected to all kinds of bullying— mostly by the royals but even by our own "peers." I was quick to anger, and Tilda helped ground me, reminding me that my temper wouldn't help the situation. She bore the taunts with poise and stoicism.

Most of the time, anyway. In our first year at tracker school, a boy had made a derisive comment about us girls not being able to handle the physical training, and Tilda had punched him, laying him out flat on his back. That was the last time anybody said anything like that around her.

Hanging down over the weight-lifting bench, Tilda's long hair shimmered a luscious dark chestnut. But the only thing about her I'd ever been jealous of was her skin. As she lifted the barbell, straining against the weight, the tanned color of her skin shifted, turning dark blue to match the color of the mats propped against the wall behind her.

Unlike Ember and me, Tilda was full-blooded Kanin. Not everyone could do what she did either, the chameleonlike ability to blend into her surroundings. As time went on, it was becoming a rarer and rarer occurrence, and if the bloodlines were diluted by anyone other than a pure Kanin, the offspring would be unable to do it at all.

And that's why my skin had the same pallor no matter how angry or frightened I might get. I was only half Kanin, so I had none of their traits or abilities.

"Hey, Bryn," Ember said brightly, and I wrapped my hands with boxing tape as I approached them. "How'd your meeting go?"

As Tilda rested the barbell back in its holder and sat up, her skin slowly shifted back to its normal color, and she wiped the sweat from her brow with the back of her arm. By the grave look in her eyes, I knew that Ember had filled her in about everything that had happened with Konstantin.

She didn't ask about it, though. We'd been friends so long that she didn't really need to say anything. She just gave me a look—her charcoal-gray eyes warm and concerned as they rested heavily on me—and I returned her gaze evenly, trying to assure her with a pained smile that I was handling everything with Konstantin better than I actually was.

Of course, Tilda probably knew I was holding back, but she accepted what I was willing to give and offered me a supportive smile. She would never press or pry, trusting me to come to her if I needed to.

I shrugged. "I'm here to blow off steam, if that answers your question."

Ember asked with a smirk, "That bad, huh?"

"The King hates me." I sighed and adjusted the tape on my hands as I walked over to the punching bag.

"I'm sure he doesn't hate you," Ember said.

Tilda took a long drink from her water bottle, accidentally spilling a few droplets on her baggy tank top, and Ember walked over to help me. She stood on the other side of the punching bag, holding it in place, so that when I hit it, it wouldn't sway away. I started punching, throwing all my frustration into the bag.

"I have to learn to keep my mouth shut if I'll ever stand a chance of being on the Högdragen," I said, and my words came out in short bursts between punches. "It's already gonna be hard enough without me pissing off the King."

"How did you piss him off?" Tilda asked as she came over to us. She put one hand on her hip as she watched me, letting her other fall to the side.

"I was just arguing with him. I was right, but it doesn't matter," I said, punching the bag harder. "If the King says the sky is purple and it rains diamonds, then it does. The King's word is law."

I don't know what made me angrier. The fact the King was wrong and refused to see it, or that I'd once again botched my own attempts at being one of the Högdragen. That was all I'd ever wanted for as long as I could remember, and if I wanted to be in the guard, I'd have to learn to follow orders without talking back.

But I didn't know how I was supposed to keep my mouth shut if I thought the King was doing things that might endanger the kingdom.

I started alternating between punching and kicking the bag, taking out all my anger at the King and at myself. I finally hit it hard enough that the bag swung back, knocking Ember to the floor.

"Sorry," I said, and held my hand out to her.

"No harm, no foul." Ember grinned as I helped her to her feet.

"You make it sound like we live in an Orwellian dystopia, and I know you don't think that," Tilda said, but there was an arch to her eyebrows, like maybe she didn't completely disagree with the idea.

She'd never openly speak ill of the kingdom—or of anything, really—but that didn't mean she approved of everything that happened here. Neither did I, but Tilda always managed to handle things with more grace and tact than I could muster.

"No, I don't." I rubbed the back of my neck. "But I won't ever get ahead if I keep arguing with everyone."

"Maybe you will," Tilda said. "You've argued and fought your way to where you are now. Nobody wanted you to be a tracker, but you insisted that you could do it, and now you're one of the best."

"Thanks." I smiled at her. "Speaking of which, I'm supposed to be shadowing Linus, so I need to fly through today's workout. You wanna spar?"

"I think I'll sit this one out, since the last time you gave me a fat lip," Tilda reminded me, pointing to her full lips.

They had been briefly swollen and purplish last month when I accidentally punched her right in the mouth, temporarily marring her otherwise beautiful face. She'd never been vain or complained of the bumps and bruises we'd both get during our practicing fights before, but if she didn't want to fight today, I wasn't going to push her.

"Ember, you wanna go?" I asked.

"Sure. But you have to promise not to hit me in the face." She motioned a circle around her face. "I don't want any visible marks for my birthday party."

I nodded. "Deal. Let's go."

estate

I'd moved out when I turned sixteen three years ago, and it still felt kinda strange going back to the house I'd grown up in. It always looked the same and smelled the same, but there were subtle differences that reminded me it wasn't my home anymore.

My mom and dad lived in a cottage near the town square, and as far as cottages in Doldastam went, theirs was fairly spacious. It wasn't as nice as the house my dad had grown up in, but that had been passed to the Eckwells after my grandparents had died, since Dad had given up his Markis title.

Mom had probably grown up in a nicer house too, though she didn't talk about it that much. In fact, she rarely ever mentioned Storvatten except to talk about the lake.

As soon as I opened the door, the scent of seawater hit me. We lived over a half hour away from Hudson Bay, so I have no idea how Mom did it, but the house always smelled like the ocean. Now it was mixed with salmon and citrus, the supper she was cooking in the oven.

"Hello?" I called, since no one was there to greet me at the door, and I began unwinding my scarf.

"Bryn?" Dad came out from the study at the back of the house, with his reading glasses pushed up on his head. "You're here early."

"Only fifteen minutes," I said, glancing over at the grandfather clock in the living room to be sure I was right. "Linus was sitting down for supper with his parents, so I thought it would be a good time to duck out. If I'm interrupting something, I can entertain myself while you finish up."

"No, I was just doing some paperwork, but it can wait." He waved in the direction of his study. "Take off your coat. Stay awhile."

"Where's Mom?" I asked as I took off my jacket and hung it on the coatrack by the door.

"She's in the bath," Dad said.

I should've known. Mom was always in the bath. It was because she was Skojare. She needed the water.

Some of my fondest memories from being a small child were sitting in the bathroom with her. She'd be soaking in the clawfooted tub, and I'd sit on the floor. Sometimes she'd sing to me, other times I'd read her stories, or just play with my toys. A lot of time was spent in there.

Fortunately, Mom didn't have gills, the way some of the Skojare did. If she had, then I don't know how she would've survived here, with the rivers and bay frozen over so often. The

Skojare didn't actually live in the water, but they needed to spend a lot of time in it, or they'd get sick.

When Mom stayed away from water too long, she'd get headaches. Her skin would become ashen, and her golden hair would lose its usual luster. She'd say, "I'm drying out," and then she'd go take a long soak in the tub.

I don't think that was the ideal course of action for her symptoms, but Mom made do.

"Supper smells good," I said as I walked into the kitchen.

"Yeah. Your mom put it in before she got in the tub," Dad said. "It should be ready soon, I think."

Upstairs, I heard the bathroom door open, followed by my mom shouting, "Bryn? Is that you?"

"Yeah, Mom. I got here a little early," I called up to her.

"Oh, gosh. I'll be right down."

"You don't need to rush on my account," I said, but I knew she would anyway.

A few seconds later, Mom came running down the stairs wearing a white robe. A clip held up her long wet hair.

"Bryn!" Mom beamed at me, and she ran over and embraced me tightly. "I'm so happy to see you!"

"Glad to see you too, Mom."

"How are you?" She let go of me and brushed my hair back from my face, so she could look at me fully. "Are you okay? They didn't hurt you, right?"

"Nope. I'm totally fine."

"Good." Her lips pressed into a thin line, and her aqua eyes were pained. "I worry so much when you're away."

"I know, but I'm okay. Honest."

"I love you." She leaned down and kissed my forehead. "Now I'll go get dressed. I just wanted to see you first."

Mom dashed back upstairs to her bedroom, and I sat down at the kitchen table. Even without makeup, and rapidly approaching forty, my mom still had to be the most stunning woman in Doldastam. She had the kind of beauty that launched a thousand wars.

Fortunately, that hadn't happened. Although there had definitely been repercussions from her union with my dad, and they'd both sacrificed their titles and riches to be together.

Their relationship had been quite the scandal. My mom had been born in Storvatten—the Skojare capital—and she was a high-ranking Marksinna. My dad had been Markis from a prominent family in Doldastam. When Mom was only sixteen, she'd been invited to a ball here in Doldastam, and though my dad was a few years older than her, they'd instantly fallen in love.

Dad had become involved in politics, and he didn't want to leave Doldastam because he had a career. So Mom defected from Storvatten, since they both agreed that they had a better chance to make a life here.

The fact that Dad was Chancellor, and had been for the past ten years, was a very big deal. Especially since his family had basically disowned him. But I'd always thought that the fact that my mom was so beautiful helped his case. Everyone understood why he'd give up his title and his riches to be with her.

I'd like to say that life had been easy for my mom and me,

that the Kanin people had been as forgiving of us as they had been for Dad. But they hadn't.

Other tribes like the Trylle were more understanding about intertribal marriages, especially if the marriage wasn't among high-ranking royals. They thought it helped unite the tribes. But the Kanin definitely did not feel that way. Any romance outside your own tribe could dilute the precious bloodlines, and that was an act against the kingdom itself and nearly on par with treason.

Perhaps that's why they were slightly easier on my mom than they were on me. Her bloodline was still pure. It may have been Skojare, but it was untainted. Mine was a mixture, a travesty against both the Kanin and the Skojare.

"So how are things going with Linus?" Dad walked over to the counter and poured himself a glass of red wine, then held out an empty glass toward me. "You want something to drink?"

"Sure." I sat down at the kitchen table, and Dad poured me a glass of wine before joining me. "Linus is adjusting well, and he's curious and easygoing, which makes the transition easier. He's trying really hard to learn all of our words and phrases. He's even tried mimicking our dialect."

When trackers went out into the world, we were taught to use whatever dialect was common in that area, which was actually incredibly difficult to master. But in Doldastam, we returned to the usual Kanin accent—slightly Canadian but with a bit of a Swedish flare to it, especially on Kanin words. Linus's Chicago accent wasn't too far off, but he still tried to imitate ours perfectly.

Dad took a drink, then looked toward the stairs, as if searching for my mother, and when he spoke, his voice was barely above a whisper. "I didn't tell her about Konstantin. She knows you were attacked, but not by *whom*."

Dad swirled the wine in his glass, staring down at it so he wouldn't have to look at me, then he took another drink. This time I joined him, taking a long drink myself.

"Thank you," I said finally, and he shook his head.

My parents had a very open relationship, and I'd rarely known them to keep secrets from each other. So my dad not telling my mom about Konstantin was actually a very big deal, but I understood exactly why he withheld that information, and I appreciated it.

Mom would lose her mind if she found out. After Konstantin had stabbed Dad, she'd begged and pleaded for us all to leave, to go live among the humans, but both Dad and I had wanted to stay, so finally she had relented. It was my dad's argument that we were safer here, with other guards and trackers to protect us from one crazed vigilante.

But if Mom knew that Konstantin was involved again, that he'd attacked another member of her family, that would be the final straw for her.

After changing into an oversized sweater and yoga pants, Mom came down the stairs, tousling her damp hair with her hand.

"What are we talking about?" Mom touched my shoulder as she walked by on her way to the oven.

"Just that Linus Berling is getting along well with his parents," I told her.

She opened the oven and peeked in at whatever was simmering in a casserole dish, then she glanced back at me. "They don't always?"

"Changelings and their parents?" I laughed darkly. "No, no, they usually don't."

At times they even seemed to hate each other, not that that was totally outlandish. These were wealthy people, living in a childless home, when suddenly an eighteen- to twenty-year-old stranger going through a major bout of culture shock was thrust into their lives.

Maternal and paternal instincts did kick in more often than not, and an unseen bond would pull them together. Eventually, most changelings and their parents came to love and understand each other.

But that was over time. Initially, there was often friction, and lots of it. Changelings were hurt and confused, and wanted to rebel against a society they didn't understand. The parents, meanwhile, struggled to raise someone who was more adult than child and mold them into an acceptable member of the Kanin hierarchy.

"The whole practice has always seemed barbaric to me." Mom closed the oven, apparently deciding supper wasn't quite done yet, and sat down at the table next to my dad. "Taking a child and leaving it with total strangers. I don't know how anyone can part with their child like that. There's no way I would've allowed that to happen to you."

The Skojare didn't have changelings—not any of them. They earned their money through more honest means. The general population worked as fishermen, and they had for centuries, originally trading their fish for jewels and gold. Now it was mostly a cash business, and the royalty maintained their wealth through exorbitant taxes on the people.

That's part of the reason why the Skojare population had dwindled down so low compared to the other troll tribes. The lifestyle wasn't as lavish or as kind to those who weren't direct royalty.

"The Changeling practice isn't as bad as it sounds," Dad said.

Mom shook her head, dismissing him. "You were never a changeling. You don't know."

"No, but my brother was," he said, and as soon as Mom shot him a look, I knew he regretted it.

My uncle Edmund was five years older than my dad. I'd only met him a handful of times when I was very young, because Edmund was kind of insane. Nobody was exactly sure what happened to him, but by the time I was in school, Edmund had left Doldastam and now traveled the subarctic like a nomad.

"Exactly, Iver," Mom said. "And where is he now?"

Dad cleared his throat, then took a sip of his wine. "That was a bad example."

Mom turned back to me. "So with the Berling boy back, are you here for a while?"

I nodded. "It looks that way."

"Well, good." She smiled warmly at me. "With all this non-sense going on, you don't need to be out there."

"That is exactly why I do need to be out there," I said, even though I knew I should just keep my mouth shut. This was supposed to be a nice visit, and we didn't need to get into this again. It was an old argument we'd repeated too many times, but I couldn't seem to stop myself. "I should be out there protecting the changelings."

"We shouldn't even have changelings. You shouldn't be out there risking your life for some archaic practice!" Mom insisted.

"Would you like a glass of wine, Runa?" Dad asked in a futile attempt to keep the conversation civil, but both my mom and I ignored him.

"But we do have changelings." I leaned forward, resting my arms on the table. "And as long as we do, someone needs to bring them home and keep them safe."

Mom shook her head. "By being a tracker, you're buying right into this awful system. You're enabling it."

"I'm not . . ." I trailed off and changed the direction of my argument. "I'm not saying it's perfect or it's right—"

"Good." She cut me off and leaned back in her seat. "Because it isn't."

"Mom, what else do you want our people to do? This is the way things have been done for thousands of years."

She laughed, like she couldn't believe I was saying it. "That doesn't make it okay, Bryn! Just because something has been done for a long time doesn't make it right. Every time a changeling is left with a human family, they are risking their children's lives to steal from strangers. It's sick."

"Runa, maybe now isn't the time to have this discussion." Dad reached out, putting his hand on her arm. She let him, but her eyes stayed on me, darkened with anger.

"I'm not condoning the stealing," I told her.

"But you are," Mom persisted. "By working for them, by helping them the way you do, you are tacitly agreeing with all of it."

"The Kanin have a way of life here. I'm not talking about the Markis or the trackers or the changelings. I am talking about the average Kanin person, the majority of the ten thousand people that live in Doldastam," I said, trying to appeal to her sense of reason and fair play.

"They don't have changelings," I reminded her. "They work for their money. They're teachers and bakers and farmers and shop owners. They raise families and live quietly and more peacefully and closer to nature. They're allowed to leave, yet time and time again they choose to stay. And it's a good thing too. You don't know what the world is like outside the city walls anymore. You haven't been anywhere except Storvatten and Doldastam."

Mom rolled her eyes at that, but she didn't say anything, letting me finish my speech.

"The life for the humans, outside in the real cities, it's not like this," I said. "The drugs, the violence, the excessive commercialism. Everything is a product, even people themselves. I know that things here are not perfect. We have our problems too, but the way we live as a whole, I wouldn't trade it for anything.

"And the way that we support this lifestyle is with the changelings," I went on. "I wish there was a different way, a better way, but as of right now, there's not. And if the Markis and Marksinna didn't get their money from the changelings, they wouldn't have anything to pay the teachers and bakers and farmers and shop owners. This town would shrivel up and die. The things I do make this possible.

"I am part of what keeps this all together, and that's why I became a tracker. That's why I do what I do." I leaned back in my chair, satisfied with my argument.

Mom folded her arms over her chest, and there was a mixture of sympathy and disappointment in her eyes. "The ends don't justify the means, Bryn."

"Maybe they do, maybe they don't." I shrugged. "But I love this town. I think you do too."

A smile twisted across her face. "You are mistaken again."

"Fine." I sighed. "But haven't you ever loved a place?"

"No, I've loved *people*. I love you, and I love your dad." She reached out, taking Dad's hand in her own. "Wherever the two of you are, I'll be happy. But that doesn't mean I love Doldastam, and it certainly doesn't mean that I love you risking your life to protect it. I tolerate it because I have no choice. You're an adult and this is the life you chose."

"It is. And it would be great if every time I visited didn't turn into a fight about it."

"Is it so wrong that I want something better for you?" Mom asked, almost desperately.

"Yes, yes, it is," I replied flatly.

"How is that wrong?" She threw her hands in the air. "Every mother just wants the best for her child."

I leaned forward again and slapped my hand on the table. "This is the best. Don't you get that?"

"You're selling yourself short, Bryn. You can have so much better." Mom tried to reach out and hold my hand, but I pulled away from her.

"I can't do this anymore." I pushed back my chair and stood up. "I knew coming over was a mistake."

"Bryn, no." Her face fell, her disapproval giving way to remorse. "I'm sorry. I promise I won't talk about work anymore. Don't go."

I looked away from her so I wouldn't get suckered in by guilt again, and ran my hand through my hair. "No, I have stuff I need to do anyway. I shouldn't have even agreed to this."

"Bryn," Dad said.

"No, I need to go." I turned to walk toward the door, and Mom stood up.

"Honey. Please," Mom begged. "Don't go. I love you."

"I love you too," I told her without looking at her. "I just . . . I'll talk to you later."

I yanked on my boots and grabbed my coat from the rack. My mom said my name again as I opened the door and stepped outside, but I didn't look back. As I walked down the dirt road my parents lived on, I breathed in deeply. The cold hurt my lungs and stung my cheeks, but I didn't mind. In fact, I didn't even put on my coat, preferring the chill. I just held my jacket to my chest and let the fresh air clear my head.

"Bryn!" Dad called after me just as I made it around the corner past the house.

An errant chicken crossed my path, and when I brushed past,

it squawked in annoyance. But I didn't slow down, not until I heard my dad's footsteps behind me.

"Wait," he said, puffing because he was out of breath from chasing after me.

I finally stopped and turned back to him. He was still adjusting his jacket, and he slowed to a walk as he approached me.

"Dad, I'm not going back in there."

"Your mom is heartbroken. She didn't mean to upset you."

I looked away, staring down at the chicken pecking at pebbles in the road. "I know. I just . . . I can't deal with it. I can't handle her criticisms tonight That's all."

"She's not trying to criticize you," Dad said.

"I know. It's just . . . I work so hard." I finally looked up at him. "And it's like no matter what I do, it's never good enough."

"No, that's not true at all." Dad shook his head adamantly. "Your mom takes issue with some of the practices here. She gets on me about it too. But she knows how hard you work, and she's proud of you. We both are."

I swallowed hard. "Thank you. But I can't go back right now."

His shoulders slacked but he nodded. "I understand."

"Tell Mom I'll talk to her another day, okay?"

"I will," he said, and as I turned to walk away, he added, "Put your coat on."

history

Books were stacked from the floor all the way up to the ceiling thirty feet above us. Tall, precarious ladders enabled people to reach the books on the top shelves, but fortunately, I didn't need any books from up that high. Most of the ones people read were kept on the lower, more reachable shelves.

The height of the ceiling made it harder to heat the room, and since Linus and I were the first people here this morning, it had a definite chill to it. Disturbing dreams of Konstantin Black had filled my slumber last night, and I'd finally given up on sleep very early this morning, so I'd decided to get a jump start on acclimating Linus. He had quite a bit to learn before the anniversary party tomorrow night, where he'd be introduced to all sorts of royalty—both from the Kanin and from the other tribes.

I doubted anybody else would come to the library today, which would make it the perfect place for studying. The halls in the palace had been chaotic with the bustling of servants and guards as dignitaries from other tribes arrived.

Linus had very nearly gotten trampled by a maid carrying stacks of silken sheets, and I'd pulled him out of the way in the nick of time. The upcoming party had turned the normally sedate palace into bedlam.

The library was still a bastion of solitude, though. Even when everyone wasn't distracted by a hundred guests, it wasn't exactly a popular place to hang out. Several chairs and sofas filled the room, along with a couple tables, but I'd almost never seen anyone use them.

"It's okay that we're here, right?" Linus asked as I crouched in front of the fireplace and threw in another log.

"The library is open to the public," I told him and straightened up. "But as a Berling, you're allowed to move freely in the palace. The King is your dad's cousin and best friend. The door is always open for you."

"Cool." Linus shivered, and rubbed his arms through his thick sweater. "So is it winter here year-round?"

"No, it'll get warm soon. There's a real summer with flowers and birds."

"Good. I don't know if I could handle it being cold all the time."

I walked over to where he'd sat down at a table. "Does it really bother you that much?"

"What do you mean?"

"Most Kanin prefer the cold. Actually, most trolls in general do."

"So do all the tribes live up around here?"

"Not really." I went over to a shelf to start gathering books for him. "Almost all of us live in North America or Europe, but we like to keep distance between tribes. It's better that way."

"You guys don't get along?" Linus asked as I grabbed a couple of old texts from a shelf.

"I wouldn't say that, exactly, but we can get territorial. And most trolls are known for being grumpy, especially the Vittra and the Omte."

"What about the Kanin?"

"We're actually more peaceful than most of the other tribes."

After grabbing about a dozen books that seemed to weigh about half a ton, I carried them back to the table and plunked them down in front of Linus.

Apprehension flickered in his brown eyes when he looked up at me. "Do I really need to read all this?"

"The more you know about your heritage, the better," I said, and sat down in the chair across from him.

"Great." He picked up the first book off the stack and flipped through it absently. "I do like the cold."

"What?"

"The winters back in Chicago, they were always so much harder on my sisters. Er, host sisters," he corrected himself. "But the cold never really got to me."

"We withstand it much better."

Linus pushed the books to the side so it'd be easier for him to see me. "How come?"

"I don't know exactly." I shrugged. "We all came from Scandinavia, so that probably has something to do with it. We're genetically built for colder climates."

"You came from Scandinavia?" Linus leaned forward and rested his arms on the table.

"Well, not me personally. I was born here. But our people." I sifted through the books I'd brought over until I found a thin book bound in worn brown paper, then I handed it to him. "This kinda helps break it down."

"This?" He flipped through the first few pages, which showed illustrations of several different animals living in a forest, and he wrinkled his nose. "It's a story about rabbits and lions. It's like a fairy tale."

"It's a simplistic version of how we came to be," I said.

When he lifted his eyes to look at me, they were filled with bewilderment. "I don't get it."

"All the trolls were one tribe." I tapped the picture showing the rabbit sitting with the cougar, and the fox cuddling with a bird. "We all lived together in relative peace in Scandinavia. We bickered and backstabbed, but we didn't declare war on one another. Then the Crusades happened."

He turned the page, as if expecting to see a picture of a priest with a sword, but it was only more pictures of animals, so he looked back up at me. "Like the stuff with the Catholic Church in the Middle Ages?"

"Exactly. You've noticed that trolls have different abilities, like how you can change your skin."

"Yeah?"

"That's not the only thing we can do," I explained. "The

Trylle have psychokinesis, so they can move objects with their minds and see the future. The Skojare are very aquatic and are born with gills. The Vittra are supernaturally strong and give birth to hobgoblins. The Omte . . . well, the Omte don't have much of anything, except persuasion. And all trolls have that."

"Persuasion?"

"It's the ability to compel someone with your thoughts. Like, I'd think, *Dance,* and then you would dance," I tried to elaborate. "It's like mind control."

Linus's eyes widened and he leaned back in his chair, moving away from me. "Can you do that?"

"No. I actually can't do any of those things," I said with a heavy sigh, and he seemed to relax again. "But we're getting off track."

"Right. Trolls have magic powers," he said.

"And during the Crusades, those powers looked like witchcraft," I told him. "So humans started rounding us up, slaughtering us by the dozens, because they believed we'd made pacts with the devil."

It was actually the changelings that got hit the worst, but I didn't tell Linus that. I didn't want him to know the kind of risk our previous changelings had gone through, not yet anyway.

Babies that exhibited even the slightest hint of being nonhuman were murdered. They had all kinds of tests, like if a baby had an unruly lock of hair, or the mother experienced painful breast-feeding. Some were much worse, though, like throwing a baby in boiling water. If it wasn't cooked, it was a troll, they thought, but no matter—the baby was cooked and killed anyway.

Many innocent human babies were murdered during that time too. Babies with Down's syndrome or colic would be killed. If a child demonstrated any kind of abnormal behavior, it could be suspected of being a troll or evil, and it was killed.

It was a very dark time for humankind and trollkind alike.

"Had we made a deal with the devil?" Linus asked cautiously.

I shook my head. "No, of course not. We're no more satanic than rabbits or chameleons. Just because we're different than humans doesn't make us evil."

"So we were all one big happy family of trolls, until the Crusades happened. They drove us out of our homes, and I'm assuming that's what led us to migrate to North America," Linus filled in.

"Correct. Most of the troll population migrated here with early human settlers, mostly Vikings, and that's why so much of our culture is still based in our Scandinavian ancestry."

His brow scrunched up as he seemed to consider this for a moment, then he asked, "Okay, I get that, but if we're Scandinavian, how come so many of us have darker skin and brown hair? Not to sound racist here, but aren't people from Sweden blond and blue-eyed? You're the only one I've seen that looks like that."

"Our coloration has to do with how we lived," I explained. "Originally, we lived very close to nature. The Omte lived in trees, building their homes in trunks or high in the branches.

The Trylle, the Vittra, and the Kanin lived in the ground. The Kanin especially lived much the way rabbits do now, with burrows in the dirt and tunnels connecting them."

"What does that have to do with having brown hair?" he asked.

"It was about blending into our surroundings." I pointed to the picture again, pointing to where a rabbit was sitting in the long grass. "The Kanin lived in the dirt and grass, and those that matched the dirt and grass had a higher survival rate."

"What about you, then?"

"I'm half Skojare," I told him, and just like every other time I'd said it, the very words left a bitter taste in my mouth.

"Skojare? That's the aquatic one?"

I nodded. "They lived in the water or near it, and they are pale with blond hair and blue eyes."

"Make sense, I guess." He didn't sound completely convinced, but he continued anyway. "So what happened after we came to North America?"

"We'd already divided into groups. Those with certain skills and aptitudes tended to band together. But we hadn't officially broken off," I said. "Then when we came here, we all kind of spread out and started doing our own thing."

"That's when you became the Kanin and the Skojare, et cetera?"

"Sort of." I wagged my head. "We'd split off in different groups, but we hadn't officially named ourselves yet. Some tribes did better than others. The Trylle and the Kanin, in particular, flourished. I don't know if it was just that they were lucky in establishing their settlements or they worked smarter. But whatever the reason, they thrived, while others suffered. And that's really what the story is about."

"What?" Linus glanced down at the book, then back up at me. "I feel like you skipped a step there."

"Each animal in the story represents a different tribe." I tapped the picture of a cougar, his eyes red and fangs sharp. "The cougar is the Vittra, who were starving and suffering. So they began attacking and stealing from the other tribes, and soon the Omte, who are the birds, joined in. And it wasn't long until everyone was fighting everyone, and we'd completely broken off from each other."

"Which one are the Kanin?" Linus asked as he stared down at the page.

"We're the rabbits. That's literally what *kanin* translates into."

"Really?" Linus questioned in surprise. "Why rabbits? Shouldn't we be, like, chameleons or something?"

"Probably, but when the trolls named themselves, they didn't know what chameleons were. Not a lot of reptiles in northern Canada. So we went with rabbits because they burrowed deep, ran fast, and they did a good job of blending in with their surroundings."

Linus stared sadly at the books in front of him. "I don't think I'll ever be able to remember all this stuff, especially not with all the different tribes."

"Here." I grabbed a thick book from the bottom of the pile and flipped through its yellowing pages until I found the one I was looking for.

It had a symbol for each of the tribes, the actual emblems that we used on flags when we bothered to use flags—a white rabbit for the Kanin, a green flowering vine for the Trylle, a red cougar for the Vittra, a blue fish for the Skojare, and a brown-bearded vulture for the Omte.

Next to each emblem were a few short facts about each of the tribes. Not enough to make anyone an expert, but enough for now.

He grimaced and stared down at the page. "Great."

"It won't be that bad," I assured him.

As Linus studied the page in front of him, his brown hair fell across his forehead, and his lips moved as he silently read the pages. The freckles on his cheeks darkened the harder he concentrated—an unconscious reaction brought on by his Kanin abilities.

"Bryn Aven." A sharp voice pulled me from watching Linus, and I looked up to see Astrid Eckwell. "What on earth are you doing here?"

Her raven waves of hair cascaded down her back. The coral chiffon of her dress popped beautifully against the olive tone of her skin. In her arms she held a small rabbit. A smirk was already forming on her lips, and I knew that couldn't be a good sign.

"Working with Markis Linus Berling," I told her as I got to my feet. Linus glanced at both Astrid and myself, and then he got up. "You don't have to stand."

"What?" He looked uncertainly at me, like it was a trick. "But . . . you did."

"Of course she did," Astrid said as she walked over to us,

absently stroking the white rabbit. "She's the *help*, and I'm a Marksinna. She has to stand whenever anyone higher up than her enters the room, and that's everyone."

"As the Markis Berling, you only need to stand for the King and Queen," I said, but Linus still didn't seem to understand.

"Bryn, aren't you going to introduce us?" Astrid asked as she stared up at him with her wide dark eyes, but he kept looking past her, down at the rabbit in her arms.

"My apologies, Marksinna. Linus Berling, this is Astrid Eckwell." I motioned between the two of them.

"It's a pleasure to meet you," Linus said, and gave her a lopsided smile.

"Likewise. Are you going to the anniversary party tomorrow?" Astrid asked.

"Um, yeah, I think so." He turned to me for confirmation, and I nodded once.

"He will be there with his parents."

Astrid looked at me with contempt in her eyes. "I suppose that means you'll be there too."

"Most likely I will be assisting Markis Berling and the Högdragen," I said, and I didn't sound any more thrilled about it than she did.

"You better dig something nice out of your closet." She cast a disparaging look over my outfit. "You can't go to the party wearing your ratty old jeans. That might fly for the trashy Skojare, but you know that won't do for the Kanin."

I kept my hands folded neatly behind my back and didn't look down. As a tracker, I had to dress appropriately for many different occasions, and I knew there was nothing wrong with my outfit. I might be wearing dark denim, but they were nice.

"Thank you for the tip, Marksinna, but I'm certain that you won't be speaking derogatorily of the Skojare anymore, as their King, Queen, and Prince have already arrived in the palace for tomorrow's anniversary party," I replied icily. "You wouldn't want them to hear you speaking negatively of them, since they are King Evert and Queen Mina's guests."

"I know they're here," Astrid snapped, and her nostrils flared. "That's why I'm dressed properly today, unlike you. What would the King of the Skojare say if he saw you running around like that?"

"Since he's a gentleman, I'm sure he would say hello," I said.

Taking a deep breath through her nose, Astrid pressed her lips into a thin, acrid smile. "You are just as impossible as you were in school. I can't believe they let you be a tracker."

When she spoke like that, it wasn't hard to remember back when we'd been kids in grade school together. I couldn't have been more than six or seven years old the first time Astrid pushed me down in the mud and sneered at me as she called me a *half-breed*.

For the past century or so, the Kanin had been trying to re-duce their reliance on changelings. If there were multiple chil-dren in a family, only one would be left as a changeling. It wasn't uncommon for particularly wealthy families to go a whole gen-eration without leaving one.

And in Astrid's case, both her parents had been change-lings, so they were freshly infused with cash from their host families and didn't need their child to bring in more of an income.

So, unfortunately, that left me forced to deal with Astrid all through grade school. There were many times when I wanted nothing more than to punch her, but Tilda had always held me back, reminding me that violence against a Marksinna could damage my chance of being a tracker.

That hadn't stopped me from hurling a few insults at Astrid in my time, but that had been long ago, before I'd joined the tracker school. Now I was sworn to protect the Marksinna and Markis, which meant I wasn't even supposed to speak ill of them.

Astrid knew that, and it pleased her no end.

"Linus, if you ever need any real help, you can always ask me," she said, with her derisive gaze still fixed on me. "You mustn't be forced to rely on an inferior tutor like Bryn."

"Markis," Linus said.

Startled, she looked up at him. "What?"

"You called me Linus, but I'm your superior, right?" he asked as he stared back down at her. "That's why I didn't have to stand when you came in?"

"That's . . ." Her smile faltered. "That's correct."

"Then you should call me Markis," Linus told her evenly, and it was a struggle for me not to smile. "If I'm understanding correctly."

"You understand it right, Markis," I assured him.

"Yes, of course you are, Markis." Astrid gave him her best eat-shit grin. "Well, I should let you get back to your lessons.

I'm sure you have much to learn before tomorrow night's ball if you don't want to make a fool of yourself."

She turned on her heel, the length of her dress billowing out behind her. Once she was gone, I let out a deep breath, and Linus sat back down at the table.

"That chick seemed kinda like a jerk," he commented.

"She is," I agreed, and sat down across from him. "We went to grade school together, and she was always horrible."

"She wasn't a changeling?"

"No, she's been here every day for the past nineteen years."

"What was the deal with the rabbit?" Linus asked. He sounded so totally baffled by it that I had to laugh.

"Oh, it's kind of a tradition. They're Gotland rabbits, and legend has it we brought them over with us when we came from Sweden. Supposedly they helped us find where to build Doldastam and helped us survive the first cold winter."

"How did they help the Kanin survive?"

"Well, they ate them," I explained. "But not all of them, and now people raise them, and we'd never eat them because they're like a sacred mascot. Some of the Marksinna carry them around now, like rich American girls used to do with Chihuahuas. The Queen has a rabbit named Vita. You'll probably see it."

He laid his hands flat on the table and looked me in the eye. "Can I be totally candid with you?"

"Of course." I sat up straighter, preparing myself for any number of inflammatory statements he might make. "I'm your tracker. You can always speak freely with me."

"You guys are super-weird."

NINE

regret

"I can't do this," I announced as I threw the office door open. It swung back harder than I meant for it to, and when the doorknob banged into the brick wall, Ridley grimaced.

"If by 'this' you mean knocking, then yes, that's very apparent," he said dryly.

I flopped in the chair across from his large oak desk. A widescreen monitor for his computer was tilted toward the edge of the desk. Being trolls, we craved all things shiny and new.

Our love of such things extended to the latest gadgets and fastest technology, but once we had them, it seemed that we usually preferred the old ways of doing things. The Kanin royalty collected computers and tablets the way others did baseball cards—storing them in boxes and closets and out of sight.

That's why the Rektor's office contained a high-speed computer, a massive printer, and all sorts of devices that would make his work so much easier, but it was rarely used. Stacks of paper covered the desk, since, inevitably, most things were done by hand.

A bulletin board on one side of the room was overflowing with flyers. Reminders for meetings and trainings, sign-up sheets for less glamorous jobs like cleaning out the garage, and missing persons posters for the rare changeling who ran away.

Behind Ridley's desk were two massive paintings of King Evert and Queen Mina. The rest of the wall was covered in smaller eight-by-tens of the latest changelings who had come back, as a reminder of why we did the job.

Outside the office, classes were in session, so I could hear the muted sounds of kids talking.

"I can't stay here," I told Ridley.

"Like in this office?" He scribbled something down on a piece of paper in front of him, then he looked at me. "Or can you be more specific?"

"I can't stay in Doldastam," I said. His shoulders slacked, and he set the pen down. "Linus is safe. He's fine. There are tons of people here to watch him. I have no reason to stay."

"That's true," he said sarcastically, then he snapped his fingers like something had just occurred to him. "Oh, wait. There is that one reason. The King *ordered* you to stay and personally watch Linus."

I rubbed my forehead, hating that he was right. "I need a break."

"A break?" Ridley asked in confused shock, and for a few seconds he appeared speechless. "You're a workaholic. What nonsense are you going on about?"

"I'm not asking to do nothing," I clarified. "I need a break from here. I just got done breaking in the last changeling, and that went fine, but I was stuck here for weeks and weeks. And then I just got to go out after Linus, and I had to turn around and come back."

He ran a hand along the dark stubble of his cheek. "What's going on?" he asked, and his tone softened. "What happened?"

"Nothing."

"Bryn." From across the desk, he gave me a look—one that said he knew me too well to let me bullshit him.

Instead of replying, I turned away from him. I twisted the silver band around my thumb and looked over at the bulletin board, eyeing the wanted posters.

Any fugitive who was still at large had their picture up, even if they'd escaped years ago. The incident with Viktor Dålig had to have happened fifteen years ago, but his picture was still prominently displayed at the top of the wanted section. The bright red font for "wanted" had faded to more of a dull pink, but his picture was still clear and visible. The heavy dark black beard, his cold eyes, even the scar that ran across his face from just above his left eye down to his right cheek.

There were two new posters that popped out on crisp white paper with fresh ink. An updated one for Konstantin Black, and a brand-new one for Bent Stum. Even in his picture, Konstantin seemed to be smirking at me, like he knew he'd gotten away with what he'd done.

But his eyes caught me. Even in black-and-white, they appeared livelier than when I had seen them in real life. It was the look he'd had when I'd last seen him standing in the crowd in Chicago, and the same look he'd had when I saw him standing over my father. And it was his eyes that had haunted my dreams last night, but I struggled to push that back, refusing to replay it in my head again, the way I had been all morning.

"Bryn," Ridley repeated, since I hadn't answered him.

Reluctantly I turned back to look at him. "I just ran into Astrid Eckwell in the library at the palace."

Ridley shrugged, like he didn't know why that would bother me. "Astrid's an idiot."

"Yeah, I know."

"You never let her get to you."

I inhaled deeply. "I usually don't."

"What'd she say this time that got under your skin?"

"Nothing, really. It was just the same old crap." I started bouncing my leg up and down, needing to do something to relieve my agitation. "And usually I'm over it. But this time it was really hard for me to not punch her in the face."

"Well, I commend you on not doing that. Because that would've been very bad."

"I know. I think I've just been cooped up here too long." I shifted in my chair. "This winter is taking forever to end. And the King is being ridiculous. I should be out in the field, and you know it, Ridley."

"Shh." He glanced toward the open door. "Lower your voice. You don't want the new cadets to hear."

"I don't care who hears," I said, nearly shouting.

Ridley went over to the door and peeked out in the hall, then closed the door. Instead of going back to his chair, he came over to me. He leaned on the desk right in front of me, so he was almost at eye level.

He wore a button-down shirt and vest, but he'd skipped a tie today, so I could see his necklace. It was a thin leather strap with an iron rabbit amulet—his present upon becoming Rektor. The amulet lay against the bronzed skin of his toned chest, and I lowered my eyes.

"I know you're pissed off, but you don't need to get in a shit-load of trouble because an overzealous tracker-in-training tattles on you to the wrong person," he said, his voice low and serious.

Technically, speaking any ill of the King was a punishable offense. My saying that he was ridiculous wouldn't exactly get me executed, but I could end up stuck cleaning toilets in the palace, or demoted, even. The changelings were assigned to us based on our rank, and in terms of trackers, I was third from the top.

"You're right." I sighed. "I'm sorry."

"Don't apologize to me. Just don't act stupid because you're mad."

"I'm more valuable out in the field." I stared up into Ridley's dark eyes, imploring him to understand. "And I feel so useless here. I'm not doing anything to help anyone."

"That's not true. You're helping Linus. You know how lost and bumbling changelings are at first."

"He needs someone, yeah, but it doesn't have to be *me*," I countered. "I'm not actually needed here."

"I need you," Ridley said, with a sincerity in his tone that startled me. In the depths of his eyes I saw a flicker of that heat I'd seen before, but just as I'd registered it, he looked away and cleared his throat. "I mean, there's a lot going on right now. Royalty from all over are on their way right now. You're a big asset here. I wouldn't be able to handle everything without your help."

"Anyone can do what I'm doing," I said, deciding to ignore the heat I'd seen in his eyes. "I think that's why Astrid got to me. I already feel like I'm being useless, and she always does such a great job of reminding me how much better than me she is."

He shook his head. "You know that's not true."

I opened my mouth to argue that, but the door to the office opened and interrupted me. I looked back over my shoulder to see Simon Bohlin. Out of habit, I sat up straighter in my chair and tried to look as nonchalant as possible. I still wasn't completely sure how to act around him.

We'd broken up a few months ago after going out for nearly a year. I'd gone against my own rule about not dating other trackers because Simon was funny and cute and didn't seem all that intimidated by the fact that I could kick his ass.

But I don't know why it still felt so awkward. We hadn't even been that serious. Well, I thought we hadn't been serious. Then Simon dropped the *l*-word, and I realized that we wanted two vastly different things out of the relationship.

Simon had been walking into the office, whistling an old tracker work song under his breath, but he stopped short when he saw me.

"Sorry," Simon said. From underneath his black bangs, his

eyes shifted from me to Ridley. "Am I interrupting something?"

"No." Ridley stood up and stepped away from me. "Not at all."

"I just came in to get my orders for the new changeling," Simon said.

"Right. Of course." Ridley walked around to the other side of his desk, shifting around stacks of paper in search of the file for Simon.

"You're leaving?" I asked, flashing Simon the friendliest smile I could manage.

He nodded. "Yeah."

"When?"

"Um, I think later today," Simon said.

Ridley found the file and held it up. "That is the plan."

"So you're not staying for the party?" I asked.

Simon shook his head, looking disappointed. "Not unless it's in the next couple hours."

Then it hit me. Simon was a good tracker, but he'd always enjoyed the parties and balls here more than I had.

I stood up. "We could trade."

"Trade what?" Simon asked cautiously.

Ridley sighed. "Bryn. No."

"I'm supposed to stay here and shadow Linus Berling, but you were always so great with the changelings." I walked over to Simon, getting so excited by the idea that I forgot to feel strange around him. "You could get him all settled and act as his bodyguard, and I could go out into the field."

"I . . ." Simon hesitated. "I mean, I don't know if that's okay."

"But would you?" I asked before Ridley could object. "I mean, if it was okay."

"Why? What's going on?" Simon asked.

"Bryn's just going through a case of cabin fever, and it's making her act crazy," Ridley explained as he walked over to us.

"I'm not acting crazy," I insisted and stared hopefully up at Simon. "So, Simon, are you in?"

"Why don't you come back in, like, half an hour, and we'll have this all straightened out?" Ridley asked and started ushering Simon to the door.

Simon glanced back at me, then shrugged noncommittally as he left. Once he'd gone, Ridley closed the door. He turned around and leaned back on it, letting out a long sigh as he looked over at me.

"What I'm saying makes sense. It works," I insisted, already steeling myself for his protests.

"Sit down." He motioned to the chair.

He went over to the two chairs sitting in front of his desk and turned them so they faced each other. After he sat down, he gestured to the other one, so I went over and sat down across from him. He leaned forward, resting his elbows on his legs, and by the gravity in his eyes, I knew this conversation wasn't going the way I'd hoped it would.

"Do you want me to be completely honest with you?" he asked.

"Always."

"What the hell are you thinking?" Ridley asked with such force and incredulity that it surprised me.

"I . . ." I fumbled for words. "What?"

"Okay, truthfully, yes, I probably can pull some strings and make it happen. If you really wanted to get out of here, I could switch your assignment with Simon's."

I waited a beat, and he didn't add the *but*, so I figured I'd have to ask. "But you're not gonna do it?"

"No, I will," Ridley said. "If that's what you really want. And if you really want to blow your chance at ever becoming a Hogdragen."

I lowered my eyes, and when I tried to argue against it, my words came out weak. "It won't hurt my chances."

"This is the first time the King ever gave you a direct order, and it's a very simple one. And you can't follow it." Ridley sighed and leaned back in his chair. "You're already fighting an uphill battle to be a guard because you're half Skojare, not to mention there are only a handful of women in the Högdragen."

I gritted my teeth. "I know what I'm up against."

"I know you know that," Ridley said, sounding exasperated. "Do you even still want to be on the Högdragen?"

"Of course I do!"

He shook his head, like he wasn't sure he believed me anymore. "Then explain to me what the hell is going on with you right now."

"What do you mean?" I asked, but I refused to meet his gaze.

"You know this could ruin your shot at the one thing you

want most in the world, and yet you're still fighting against it. Why do you want to get out of here so badly?"

I clenched my jaw and found it hard to speak around the lump growing in my throat. "I let him go," I said, and my words came out barely above a whisper.

"Konstantin Black?" he asked like he already knew the answer.

I looked away, staring at the wall and struggling to keep my anger under control. Tentatively, Ridley reached out and placed a hand on my knee. It was meant to be comforting, and the warmth of his skin through the fabric of my jeans was just enough to distract me.

"You did the right thing," Ridley told me. "You did what you needed to do to protect Linus."

"Maybe I did." I finally turned to look at him, letting my cool gaze meet his. "Or maybe I could've snapped his neck right then, and we'd all be rid of him forever."

If he saw the ice and hatred in my eyes, he didn't let on. His expression was filled only with concern, and he didn't even flinch at my wishful thinking about murder.

"If you really believe that, then why didn't you kill him?" Ridley asked reasonably.

"The truth?" I asked, and suddenly I felt afraid to say it aloud. But with Ridley staring at me, waiting, I knew I had to finally admit it. "I don't think he wanted to kill my father."

"What? What are you talking about?"

"When I walked in on him, standing over my father with his sword bloodied, he apologized and said that he was bound to something higher than the kingdom," I tried to explain.

"So you think he . . . what?" His forehead scrunched, and he shook his head. "I don't understand."

"There was a look in his eyes. Regret." I thought back to Konstantin, and the pain I'd seen in his smoky eyes. "No, it was remorse."

"Remorse?" Ridley sat up a bit straighter. "You think you saw remorse in his eyes? So, what? You just forgave him?"

"No. *No,*" I said adamantly. "I'll never forgive him. But I think he regretted what he did, even before he did it. And it doesn't make sense. I need to know why he did it."

"He could just be insane, Bryn," Ridley said, going to the only reason that anybody had ever been able to come up with for Konstantin's behavior. "Your dad had never had a cross word with him, and then one night Konstantin just snapped."

"No. He's too smart, too calculated. And now with this attack on Linus . . ." I chewed the inside of my cheek as I thought. "It's all connected. He's plotting something."

"If he's still working toward some ultimate goal, then he doesn't regret it," Ridley pointed out. "If he felt genuine remorse, he should be looking for absolution, not trying to hurt more people."

"Not if someone else is pulling his strings," I countered. "And if someone is, I need to find out who it is."

"Konstantin might be an innocent pawn in all of this?" Ridley questioned doubtfully.

"No. I don't know what is motivating him, but he drew his sword against my father with his own hand. That fault lies entirely with him."

Konstantin may have come to regret what he'd done. He could even cry about it every night, but it didn't change the fact that he'd done it, and he knew exactly what he was doing. When I went into the Queen's office that night, he was preparing to finish the job as I watched.

Regardless of what guilt he might feel or what reason might drive him, Konstantin had still acted of his own accord.

"You want to leave here so you can find him and hold him responsible," Ridley said.

"Yes." I looked up at him, pleading with him to let me go, to let me finish what Konstantin had started. "He needs to be brought to justice, and so does anyone else he's working with."

"Justice? Does that mean you'll drag them all back here? Or are you gonna kill them all?"

"Whichever one I need to do. But I'm not letting Konstantin get away again," I told him, and I meant it with all my heart. I'd never killed anyone before, but I would do whatever I needed to do.

Ridley seemed to consider this for a moment, then he pulled his hand back from my leg—leaving it feeling cool and naked without his warm touch—and he rubbed the back of his neck. "You can't go after him alone, and you can't go right now."

"Ridley—" I began, but he cut me off.

"I don't care if you think Linus doesn't need you and the King is an idiot. You are needed here right now." Ridley held up his hand, silencing any more protests I might have before I could voice them. "At least for the time being. Once everyone is gone after the party, and Linus is settled in, if you still need to go on your personal vendetta, we can talk about it. We can make it happen."

"We?" I shook my head. "You don't have to be a part of this."

"But I am anyway." He lowered his head and exhaled deeply. When he looked up, his dark eyes met mine, and when he spoke, his voice was softer. "Stay."

"Is that an order?" I asked, but by the look in his eyes, I knew it wasn't.

"No. It's not," he admitted. "But stay anyway."

celebration

By the time I'd finished with Linus for the evening, it was nearly eight o'clock. After my meeting with Ridley, I'd wanted to spend as much time as I could prepping Linus. The next few days were going to be filled with overwhelming madness for the new changeling, and I needed to set my personal feelings aside to do my job.

I ran home just long enough to grab Ember's present, and then I made the trek to her place as quickly as I could. The cottage Ember lived in with her parents was over a mile away from the palace, nestled against the wall that surrounded Doldastam, separating us from the Hudson Bay.

The farther I went, the farther apart the houses were. Near the palace, the cottages and even some of the smaller Markis and Marksinna's mansions were practically stacked on top of each other. But at Ember's house, there was room enough for a small pasture with a couple angora goats, and I heard them bleating before I could even see them.

A rabbit hutch was attached to the front of a house, and a fluffy Gotland sat near the edge of the run, nibbling a pint-sized bale of hay. When it saw me, it hopped over, and I reached my fingers through the wire cage and stroked the soft white fur.

The sun was beginning to set, and Ember's party had been under way for an hour. I knew that I couldn't put it off any longer, so I said good-bye to the rabbit, and I knocked on the front door.

"Bryn!" Annali Holmes—Ember's mother—opened the door and greeted me with a broad smile as the warm air from inside wafted over me. "Glad you could make it."

"Sorry I'm late. I was stuck at work."

I peered around to see who was in attendance, and the small cottage was nearly overflowing. Imagine Dragons played out of the radio loud enough that they hadn't heard me yet, and I spotted Ember laughing in the center of the room. She always fared much better with attention than I did.

A toddler with dark brown hair sticking up like a troll doll came darting past, trying to escape out the door before Annali scooped him up.

"This is Liam," she said, and the little boy stared up at me with wide eyes, looking too adorable for his own good, and then in a bout of shyness he buried his face in the blue folds of his grandma's faded dress. "He's my son's youngest."

"So they made it in okay?" I asked.

Ember's older brother, Finn, worked as a guard at the Trylle palace. The King and Queen of the Trylle had come to town for the anniversary party, and Finn came with them as their guard. Since his parents lived in Doldastam, he'd brought his wife and two kids along for a visit.

"Yeah, they arrived early this morning. Why don't you go in and say hello?" Annali stepped back and motioned toward the living room.

All the gifts were stacked on the dining room table, which had been pushed up against a wall to make more room. I snuck behind the people, nearly sliding up against the wall to add my gift to the pile. Mine was wrapped in butcher's paper and tied up with twine, appearing rather plain compared to some of the brightly colored packages.

I'd meant to get Ember something nice in Chicago, but since I had to make an abrupt departure, I'd had to grab something quick in Winnipeg while Linus and I waited for the train. It ended up being a sweater that I hoped she didn't hate, and a ring with a fox on it that I thought she'd actually like.

There had to be over twenty people crammed into the small living room and dining room. Most of them were fellow trackers, but a few were people Ember just knew from town. She was much more sociable than I was.

Tilda was here, of course, along with her boyfriend, Kasper Abbott. He was a few years older than her, with black curly hair and a carefully manicured beard. Last year, he'd been appointed to the Högdragen, and though he was a very low-ranking member, I'd already begun hitting him up for advice.

In the center of the room, Ember laughed brightly, and Finn stood next to his sister. Though this was just a casual family gathering, he was dressed in a tailored vest and slacks, just like every other time I'd seen him. He held a little girl in a frilly dress on his hip, her dark wild curls pulled into two pigtails.

Next to him was his wife, Mia, who appeared to be pregnant again. Her hands were folded neatly, resting on top of her swollen belly hidden underneath her fitted emerald dress.

"Bryn!" Ember squealed in delight when she finally saw me. "You made it!"

She slid past her brother. When she reached me, she looped her arm through mine, knowing that I would hide in the corners of the room unless she made me actually join the party. "A girl only turns seventeen once, you know, and she needs her best friend at the party."

I hadn't noticed until she was up close, but her eye shadow had a bit of a sparkle to it. Her sweater dress even had a few strategically placed sequins, adding an extra shimmer as well. Several braids twisted through her hair, and then it was pulled back in an updo.

"You remember Finn, right?" Ember pointed to him.

"We've met a few times," I reminded her. He managed to get up here a couple times a year for a visit, bringing his family with him as often as he could. I knew that he was a retired Trylle tracker who now worked as a royal guard, and was Ember's inspiration for joining the Kanin's tracker program.

"How are you, Bryn?" Finn asked, smiling at me.

There was something almost strikingly handsome about

him, and I noticed it more when he smiled. But he emoted so rarely, and no matter what happened he seemed to stand at attention. I respected him for his training and obvious skill in working as a guard, but he was so closed off.

After I'd first met him, I'd asked Ember if he was secretly an android, and I'd only been half joking. The scary part was that Ember told me he'd actually loosened up a lot since he'd gotten married. I'd have hated to meet him before, if this was him relaxed.

"I'm doing well, thank you." I smiled politely at him. "How are you?"

"Can't complain."

"When are we eating cake?" the little girl asked.

"Not right now, Hanna," Finn told her, and that was about the only time I ever saw his expression soften. When he was interacting with his kids, he truly let his guard down.

"Here." Mia held out her arms for the little girl. "I'll take her and get her something. It's getting late for the kids." Hanna squealed in delight and practically jumped into her mother's outstretched arms.

"Sorry about that," Finn said, smoothing down his vest after Mia carried Hanna away to the kitchen. "She gets excited."

"Who can blame her? Everyone gets excited about birthday cake," Ember said. "My mom makes the *best* cake. She uses blueberries as the sweetener, and it's to die for."

Kanin, and really trolls in general, had an aversion to sugar, except for fruit. We didn't have much of a stomach for foods that weren't all natural, nor were we big into red meat. Most of our food was produced in Doldastam, thanks to special "green-houses."

We had a few gardeners that worked to keep fresh produce and wine year-round, and to cultivate flowers that could bloom in the snow. They used psychokinetic abilities to work against the harsh winters of the subarctic, and it took half a dozen of them to keep the garden up and running.

Kasper asked how to change a song, and Ember offered me an apologetic glance before dashing off to help. That left me standing awkwardly with her brother.

"So . . . are you going to be at the anniversary thing tomorrow?" Finn asked.

I nodded. "Yeah. I'm helping a new changeling adapt. But I would probably be there anyway, because of the added security. We should all be there tomorrow."

"That makes sense." He lifted his eyes, surveying the room of people chatting with one another. "Are they all Högdragen? That's what you call it, right?"

"No, most of them aren't." I turned and pointed to where Kasper stood next to Ember, going through her iPod. "Only Kasper is."

Tilda saw us pointing at her boyfriend, so she made her way over to where Finn and I were talking, and relief washed over me as Tilda came to rescue me from awkward party conversation as she had a hundred times before. I liked Finn well enough, but I doubted that the two of us could talk comfortably for very long.

"Did you say something about Kasper?" Tilda asked when

she reached us. It felt warm in the house—at least to me, after walking the mile here—but her dress left her well-toned arms bare, and she rubbed at them absently.

"I was just telling Finn that Kasper's on the Högdragen," I explained.

"That's true." Tilda smiled proudly as she looked back at her boyfriend.

"I've always been curious. How does the Högdragen work?" Finn asked "The Trylle don't have that."

I shook my head. "How do you protect the royalty?"

"Most trackers pull double duty as guards, and when they retire from tracking, many of them guard at the palace." He looked down at me. "It's like how you're working at the party tomorrow."

"I have basic training, but trackers aren't in combat that often. And we're not trained to work together, if there were an invading army," I countered. "The Högdragen have all kinds of specialized training."

"How often do you really have an invading army?" Finn asked. "When was the last time anyone's attacked you guys?"

"That's because they know how good we are. We're the only tribe that has a real army to speak of," Tilda added, bristling a bit. She held her head up higher, making her taller than Finn. "Nobody is equipped to go up against us."

"What about the business with someone going after the changelings?" Finn asked, undeterred.

I looked at him sharply. "What do you know about it?"

He pursed his lips and shook his head. "Not much. We've

heard rumblings back in Förening, and Ember mentioned a few things to me."

I glanced over at Tilda, wondering if I should say anything. Her gray eyes were hard, and her lips were pursed together in an irritated pout. If it were her choice, she wouldn't tell Finn anything. Not just because of his comments about the Högdragen—Tilda preferred to keep private business private. Ember was a bit of a gossip, which was why she'd become closer to me than she had with Tilda. I had a higher tolerance for that kind of thing.

"I'm not a gossip at the market," Finn said, sensing our unease. "I'm a guard, working with an allied tribe. Discretion is something I'm well versed in."

He had a point, so I relaxed a bit. Besides, he was Ember's brother, and she trusted him.

"As of right now, there is no business with any changelings," I told him matter-of-factly. "Two men went after one of our high-ranking Markis. That's all we know, and as far as the King and Queen are concerned, it was an isolated attack."

"And who stopped it?" He narrowed his eyes at me. "It was you, wasn't it?"

"I was—" I started to answer him, but I happened to glance past him and saw Ember go over to answer a knock at the door, barely audible over the music and chatter of the party.

When she opened the door, she let in a draft of cold air, along with Juni Sköld and Ridley. Juni came in first, and Ember helped her slip off her long black jacket. Once Ember took their coats to put them away, Ridley put his hand on the small of Juni's back, and as they walked toward the party, he leaned over and whispered something in her ear.

I had seen Ridley with plenty of girls over the past years, but that was because I'd barged into his office without knocking and caught him kissing someone, or I'd gone to his place after work and found a girl slinking out his door. This was the first time I'd seen him on an actual *date*.

"Bryn?" Tilda asked, leaning toward me. "You okay?"

"Yeah." I shook my head, clearing it, and then I looked back at Finn, forcing myself to keep my eyes on him and not wander to Ridley any longer. "As I was saying, I was tracking the changeling and prevented them from kidnapping him, yes."

"That's exactly my point." Finn folded his arms over his chest. "You're not a member of the Högdragen, and yet you were perfectly capable of fighting off two men without any of their training. Are they really necessary, then?"

"If anything, that's a testament to Bryn's work, not a condemnation of the guard," Ridley interjected. I looked over to see both him and Juni sidling up next to Tilda, joining our conversation.

"Ember really just invited everyone to this, didn't she?" I asked as pleasantly as I could and gave them a crooked smile.

He nodded and adjusted his narrow tie. "Apparently so."

"Ridley, this is Ember's brother, Finn," I said, making the introductions between the two of them. "Finn, this is the Rektor, Ridley. And this is . . ." I pointed to Juni, then feigned a memory lapse. "Sorry. I've forgotten your name," I lied, and Tilda gave me a peculiar look.

"Juni. Juni Sköld." She smiled, making a dimple on her smooth skin. "I went to tracker school years ago with Bryn and Tilda, but I flunked out, so it's no surprise that they've forgotten me."

"I'm sure Bryn didn't forget you," Ridley said, casting a look at me that I deftly avoided meeting. "She's just had a busy week."

"Well, it's nice to meet you both," Finn said, breaking the growing tension.

"Likewise," Ridley said. "So what were we talking about when I so rudely interrupted?"

"Finn doesn't understand the point of the Högdragen," Tilda said, filling him in with a hint of bitterness to her words. Her arms were crossed over her chest, and she turned to look at him as Ridley spoke, as if waiting for Ridley to tell him.

Ridley didn't seem that fazed by it, though. "The Trylle use trackers to guard the King and Queen, right?"

Finn nodded. "Correct."

"Wow, you guys don't have a guard?" Juni asked, sounding genuinely shocked. Her caramel eyes widened, and she put her hand to her chest, making her bracelets jingle. "That is so weird and kinda scary."

"How so?" Finn asked.

"The tracker program is hard, and I'm sure you understand that," Juni went on. "That's why I left. It's not for everyone. But the Högdragen is so much more than trackers are. They're the best of the best, trained to protect us from any number of dangers. I can't imagine feeling safe in Doldastam without them."

"You have the biggest tribe, though you are spread out quite a bit more than we are," Ridley said, elaborating on his date's position. "Förening is less than half the size of Doldastam. But you have the most money. You must have jewels and gems up the ass."

Finn scowled at Ridley's crassness. "I don't think I would use those exact words, but our wealth is well known."

"So why aren't you guarding it?" Ridley asked.

"We are," Finn persisted. "We just don't have a fancy name or a special program for it."

"I don't understand what your issue is with the Högdragen," Tilda said, unwilling to let his disdain for the guard go. She knew what the guard meant to both her boyfriend and me, and Tilda was fiercely protective when she felt people she cared about were being slighted. "Ember's talked about you. I know how important your sense of duty is to your people."

"It is," Finn agreed. "I'm not against the work you all do, but it seems to me that the Högdragen is just another form of elitism, just another class in the system that separates everyone."

Ridley's expression hardened. "We may not have fought wars recently, but we've prevented our share of violence. Viktor Dålig led an attack against the King fifteen years ago that resulted in four men dead." His words were solemn, the same way they were every time he mentioned Viktor Dålig's assault. "If it hadn't been for those men—the members of the classist system you don't understand—Viktor would've been successful, and he could've overthrown the entire kingdom."

Juni reached over, putting her hand on Ridley's arm and leaning into him. I bit my lip and looked away from them.

"You think trackers couldn't have stopped them just as well as members of the Högdragen?" Finn asked pointedly.

"I think that you have no idea what you're talking about," Ridley snapped, making Juni flinch next to him. "You've never served on the Högdragen, and you've never seen them in action. You grew up in a world where you were taught to honor and serve and never think for yourself, so you question anything that isn't exactly the same as you or the Trylle."

"That's not what– " Finn began, but Ridley cut him off.

"This conversation is taking a turn, and you seem like a very respectable gentleman. So, before I say something you'll regret, I'm going to go say hello to the birthday girl." He nodded curtly. "Excuse me." Then Ridley turned and walked away.

"It was very nice meeting you." Juni offered him a polite smile, then turned and went after Ridley, her long, dark brown locks bouncing as she hurried over to him.

"What did I say?" Finn asked, baffled by the hard edge in Ridley's voice. "I wasn't trying to be offensive or hurtful."

"Ridley's dad was on the Högdragen. He was one of the four men that Viktor Dålig killed," Tilda explained. "He died saving the kingdom."

unrequited

Finn apologized for saying anything that might've offended anyone, and I stayed and talked with him and Tilda a bit more, though both of them were careful not to bring up the guard anymore. Mostly Finn just talked about his home, since Tilda seemed strangely interested in what it was like raising a family while working as a tracker.

But how Finn managed to juggle taking care of two kids and his workload wasn't all that interesting to me, and I let my attention wander. Usually— and rather unfortunately—I kept finding my gaze landing on where Ridley and Juni seemed to be enjoying themselves.

No matter when I looked over, she always seemed to be laughing at something. She had to be one of the most cheerful people I'd ever met, which was part of the reason she hadn't been suited for the tracker program. It wasn't that she wasn't tough enough, exactly—she'd just been too friendly, too kind for a job that required a lack of emotion.

When Ridley wrapped his arm around her waist, she leaned into him, laughing warmly, her dark lashes lying in a fan on her bronze skin. Her hair fell down her back in long dark waves, and her dress hugged the full curves of her hips and chest beautifully.

She almost seemed to glow with happiness, a Kanin ability and one of the reasons why she'd had to leave the tracker program. Most of the Kanin who had the skin-changing ability would only blend in with their surroundings when they were distressed, but hers made her radiate when she was happy, and it simply darkened when she was upset. Despite her best efforts, she'd never been able to get it under control, and it had become a detriment.

So I understood exactly why Ridley had invited her here as his date. She may not have been suited to be a tracker, but in every other way, Juni was the perfect Kanin girl.

A painful twisting sensation spread through my chest, and I couldn't stand to watch them anymore. I wanted to make my escape, but on my way to the door Ember intercepted me, insisting that I stay for just a bit longer. But then Tilda—sensing my distress—provided a distraction for Ember and whisked her away so they could dance together to an Ellie Goulding remix.

It was Ember's birthday, so I could hardly go against her wishes, but I needed a break. I went upstairs, and at the end of the hall, heavy French doors led out to a small balcony. I'd left my coat downstairs, but that was just fine.

Pulling my sweater sleeves down over my hands, I leaned against the wrought-iron railing that ran around the balcony. I had no reason to be jealous of Juni. It didn't affect me at all that she was perfect. She was a wonderful, beautiful, nice person, and I had no reason to wish her ill.

In fact, I should be happy that she was apparently dating Ridley, since he'd always been good to me. He'd been nothing but kind, loyal, and supportive to me, and he deserved the same in return. Yes, he had done his fair share of philandering, but Juni was just the right girl to get him to settle down. And nothing about that should make me feel even slightly bad.

And yet . . . it did. It hurt so bad, I found it difficult to breathe.

Below me, goats were bleating in the moonlight, their pleas like those of a lovelorn suitor. I watched them nibbling at the blades of grass bravely poking through the snow, and I refused to acknowledge my feelings. They didn't make any sense, so I just pushed them away.

"Romeo, Romeo, wherefore art thou, Romeo?" I said to the goats, as if speaking to them would ease their loneliness.

"It is the east, and Juliet is the sun," Ridley said from behind me, startling me so much I nearly leapt off the balcony.

I'd left the French doors open, and I turned around to see Ridley standing in the doorway, the curtains billowing around him as the icy wind blew past.

"The balcony is actually facing the north," I told him once I'd found my voice.

"So it is. That would make you . . . Polaris?" Ridley surmised. He walked out on the balcony and closed the doors behind him.

"What are you doing up here?" I leaned on the railing again, so I wouldn't have to look at him.

"I came up here to shut the doors, because Ember's mom was complaining of a cold draft coming downstairs."

I grimaced. "Sorry. I meant to close the doors."

"But the real question is, what are you doing up here?" Ridley asked. He rolled down the sleeves of his shirt and folded his arms over his chest, trying to warm himself. "It's freezing out here."

"It's not that bad." I shrugged. "I just needed a breather."

"From what?"

I said nothing, preferring to stare out into the night rather than attempt to explain what I was feeling. He let it go, and we both stood in silence for a few minutes. Even the goats had fallen silent, and the only sound was the wind blowing through the trees and the faint music from the party below us.

"Did you know that I'm the oldest person here?" Ridley asked.

I thought about it, then shook my head. "Ember's parents are older than you."

"Now I feel much better." He gave a dry laugh. "I probably shouldn't have come here."

"Why not?" I looked at him from the corner of my eye.

He shook his head. "I'm older than the guy that has, like, a dozen kids," he said, referring to Finn.

"I think he only has two kids, and another on the way," I corrected Ridley.

"Still. That's a lot of kids for someone his age. He's, like, twenty-four, right?" He looked back down at the balcony and absently kicked a clump of snow stuck to the wood. "That's too young to have that many kids." Then Ridley looked up over at me. "I mean, isn't it?"

"Maybe." I shrugged, unsure of where the conversation was going, which only made me feel more flustered than I already did. "But I don't know what that has to do with you not coming to the party."

"I don't know. I'm just feeling old, I guess." He leaned his head back, staring up at the stars, and his breath came out in a plume of white fog. "I'm having a bit of an existential crisis lately."

"What do you mean?"

"Do you think you'll ever settle down?" Ridley asked, and I was grateful that he was still looking at the sky, so he couldn't see the startled—and probably terrified—expression on my face.

"You mean like get married and have kids?" I asked, buying myself some time until I figured out how I wanted to answer. "Or retire?"

"Both."

"No. Never," I said firmly, and at that moment it felt painfully true.

I would never retire, I knew that with every fiber of my being, but it wasn't until just now that I realized that love was off the table for me too. As my brief romance with Simon had proven, I didn't have the time or the inclination for a relationship. My career would always come first—as it should.

And hopefully that would put the final nail in the coffin of whatever I was feeling for Ridley. Because it didn't matter how I felt or whether he was with Juni or not. I would never be with Ridley. I had more important matters to tend to, and getting involved with my boss would only complicate and ruin everything.

"Never is pretty final," Ridley commented rather grimly.

"I know."

"I used to think that way," he admitted. He rested his arms on the railing beside me, leaning against it, and his elbow brushed up against mine. I could've pulled my arm away so I wouldn't be touching him, but I didn't.

"You are retired," I pointed out.

"No, I meant about getting married. I thought I'd never do it." He paused, letting the silence envelop us. "But now I'm reconsidering."

I swallowed hard and scrambled to think of something supportive to say. It took me far too long, but finally I managed, "Well, Juni seems nice."

"Yeah, she is." Then he said it again, as if convincing himself. "She's very nice."

"And beautiful," I added. "Stunning, even."

Ridley laughed softly at that. "Are you crushing on my date?"

"No. I'm just . . ." Just what? Trying to convince myself that I was happy for him? I didn't have anything, so I let it hang in the air.

"Did you really not remember her?" Ridley asked. "I mean, you guys are about the same age and went to school together, and there aren't *that* many people in town."

"No, of course I remembered her. Her name just slipped my mind," I lied.

"You have had a lot to worry about lately." His tone shifted from playful to thoughtful. "Is that what you were doing out here?"

"What?" I glanced over at him.

"Figuring out how you're going to exact your revenge on Konstantin?"

"Something like that," I muttered, feeling angry at myself that that wasn't actually what I'd been doing.

I *should* have been doing that, but instead I was stupidly and childishly trying not to think about how handsome Ridley looked tonight and the way his hair curled more at the end of the day, when the gel couldn't fight it any longer, and how the stubble darkened his jaw in a way that made me want to touch it, to feel it like sandpaper against my cheek if he leaned in for a kiss, and how badly I wished he were slipping his strong arm around my waist and whispering in my ear instead of Juni's.

"You should clue me in on your plans," Ridley said.

I looked at him sharply, terrified for a second that he'd been able to read my thoughts, but then I realized that he was talking about my plans for Konstantin. "Why? So you can talk me out of them?"

"No. I want to help." He turned to face me, putting his hand on the railing so his fingers brushed against mine. The metal felt icy cold, and his fingers felt like delicious fire against mine, radiating all through me. "I meant what I said earlier. I'm part of this too, and I don't mean just because I'm your boss. I know what this guy did to you and what he did to your family. I want to help you catch him."

It was too dark out for me to really see his eyes, but I could feel the heat from them, the new intensity I'd begun noticing when he looked at me sometimes, and it made my heart forget how to beat properly.

I looked away from him, unable to deal with the way he was looking at me, the way he made me feel, or even how close he was to me. His fingers on mine were cooling against the iron railing, but that didn't stop the heat from coursing through my veins.

And suddenly I couldn't stand it. I didn't want to be around him, making me feel a way that I refused to feel.

I stepped back from the railing, pulling my hand away from his. "Thank you. But right now my only plans are helping Linus get ready and surviving the anniversary party tomorrow night." I motioned to the door behind me. "Which means that I probably should be getting home to get some sleep."

"Good call. I should be heading out soon too."

I took a step backward, still facing him like I was afraid he would attack me if I turned away, and I reached behind me, fumbling for the door handle. Ridley moved closer. The balcony wasn't that big, so it only took a step and he was right in front of me, staring down at me. The light was coming through the glass doors, illuminating his face, and he appeared breathtakingly handsome.

The scent of his cologne blended perfectly with the winter air around us, making him smell tantalizingly clean and crisp, and I imagined that it came in a blue bottle with a name like Aspen or Evergreen. His chest nearly touched me, and for a second time I froze completely, terrified that he would kiss me and terrified that he wouldn't.

Then he reached around me, his arm pressing against my side in a way that made me involuntarily tremble.

"Let me get the door for you," Ridley said as he grabbed the door and opened it behind me. A subtle smile spread across his face, lightening it, but his eyes remained serious and fixed on me.

"Thank you," I mumbled, lowering my head so my hair would cover my face in case I was blushing. Then I slid under his arm and darted inside the house.

"If you wait a second, Juni and I could walk you home," he offered, and I couldn't imagine anything that sounded worse than walking home with him and his date after having a far too vivid fantasy about kissing him.

I had already turned away, hurrying down the hall before he could catch up to me. "Thanks, but I think I got it," I told him over my shoulder, and darted down the stairs.

As quickly as possible, I found Ember and, feigning a stomach bug, I made my excuses and escaped into the night. Just as I'd reached the door, struggling to pull on my jacket and thinking I'd made a clean escape, Juni found me.

"I'm sorry to hear you aren't feeling well." Juni looked genuinely sympathetic, which at that moment only succeeded in making me angrier. *Of course* she felt bad for me, when I was only leaving because my feelings for her date had just become all too apparent to me.

"I'll be fine," I insisted, and when she tried to say something more, I just turned and walked out the door. I think she was offering to walk me home when I shut the door in her face.

Instantly, I felt awful for being rude, and it wasn't like I'd wanted to be rude. I just needed space, a moment without Ridley clouding my thoughts and emotions, where I could breathe and focus on what really mattered.

By the time I reached my place, I was nearly jogging. Instead of going up to my loft apartment, I went to the barn below. Many of the Tralla horses neighed their greetings as I walked past them, but I was on a mission and I went down to the final stall, where "my" horse, Bloom, was waiting.

He wasn't really mine, because all of the horses belonged to the King and Queen. But Bloom and I had a special relationship. As soon as he saw me, he stretched his long neck out over the door and let out a delighted snort. He buried his snout in my hair, sniffing at me as I opened the stall door.

"I'm happy to see you too, buddy," I said, running my hands over him. His thick silver fur felt like satin under my fingers. I grabbed his bridle from the wall, and he happily let me slip it on over his head.

Usually I would brush him or pet him more, but I wanted to get out of here. I needed to feel the wind blowing through my hair. I led Bloom out of the stables, and he followed behind me, his massive hooves clomping loudly on the ground.

I didn't bother saddling him, but the reins were necessary. His long mane was far too soft and glossy to properly grip, and Bloom had a bad habit of stopping and starting quickly. That's why they rarely used him in the parades or to pull carriages, despite the fact that he was one of the most beautiful Tralla horses I'd ever seen. His body was an illustrious silver that shimmered in the light like platinum. Long bangs from his mane fell into his blue eyes, and his mane, tail, and the fur covering his hooves were a beautiful snowy white.

Bloom was a happy, friendly horse, but he loved speed. For an animal with his bulk and girth, one would think he'd be slow and clunky. But Bloom was light on his feet and astonishingly fast.

He headed over to the fence, walking in front of me, and he waited patiently until I came up beside him. I had to climb up on the wooden rails of the fence to climb onto Bloom, since he was so tall.

As soon as he felt me settled in, he lunged forward without waiting for a command from me. Fortunately, I knew that was how Bloom worked, so I already had the reins gripped tightly in my hands, and Bloom raced forward. The gate was open, so he ran out to the open road, running toward the wall.

That's where I usually rode him—along the wall that surrounded Doldastam. It gave him a long, clear path to run as fast as his thick legs would take us. And that was just what I needed. The wind stung my skin and made my hair whip back behind me, so I leaned forward, burying my face in Bloom's neck and urging him to go faster.

I closed my eyes, and it was just me and Bloom. Any thoughts about Ridley or Konstantin or anything else at all just fell away.

TWELVE

anniversary

The anniversary party was even worse than I'd feared.

An insane number of stuffy royals filled up the ball-room. The last time I'd seen this many people in the palace, it had been at the celebration after the Trylle had defeated the Vittra, and that hadn't exactly gone well.

At least that time it had been mostly regular Kanin folks, living it up and getting drunk. It actually had been a rather fun affair, until Konstantin Black ruined it. But this party was all Markis and Marksinna and Kings and Queens. Everyone dressed in their best, holding their heads up so they could look down on everyone else.

I was to spend the evening as Linus Berling's shadow, and that was both a curse and a blessing. He wasn't smug or pompous, so that was refreshing, but being stuck at his side meant that I had to spend far too much time listening to other royals issue backhanded compliments and mutter all sorts of derogatory remarks under their breath.

The dinner service began with King Evert and Queen Mina being seated at the main table in the center of the ballroom. All the guests waited in a procession to enter the ballroom, and as they did, the King's personal guard announced who they were and where they were from. Then they would greet the King and Queen and head to their own table.

As King Evert's cousins and closest friends, the Berlings were right at the front of the line—only entering behind King Loki and Queen Wendy of the Trylle; King Mikko, Queen Linnea, and King Mikko's brother Prince Kennet of the Skojare; and Queen Sara of the Vittra. The Omte Queen had declined to attend, but that was fairly standard for the Omte.

While Linus and his parents were seated beside the King, I had to stand behind Linus. I of course couldn't actually eat with them. I was only there to whisper in Linus's ear, telling him the names, titles, and tribes of the royals who were coming to greet us at the table.

Once all the guests were seated and dinner was served, I was allowed to duck away and sneak back to sit with other trackers. Ember, Tilda, Ridley, and Simon were all seated together at a round table in the corner, and Tilda had been nice enough to save a spot for me between her and Ridley. I didn't really want to sit next to him, at least not right now, but I didn't have a lot of options.

Tilda must've known that because she offered me an apologetic smile and a shrug of her shoulders.

For tonight, being a tracker was a much sweeter gig than being on the Högdragen. They all stood at attention in their black velvet uniforms around the edge of the room. Some were near the doors, some stood behind the royalty, and the rest just lined the walls.

We didn't even have to wear our uniforms tonight. I'd chosen a white and black lace dress with cap sleeves, not only because I thought it was beautiful, but because it allowed easy flexibility for kicking and punching. I actually found that short dresses were much less constraining in fights than jeans or tracker uniforms.

The Kanin trackers were only really here as backup, on the off chance one of the visiting tribes decided to start something tonight, while the Trylle and Vittra brought along trackers for the same reason. The Skojare didn't have trackers, but they had their own bodyguards, who were seated one table down from us.

"Is it weird for you?" Ember asked. She leaned on the table, but her eyes were looking over my head at the Skojare guards behind me.

A glass of red wine had been waiting at my place at the table, along with a plate of steamed vegetables, and I took a sip of the wine before answering her. "What do you mean?"

"Not being the only blonde here anymore," Ember said, and though I knew she didn't mean anything by it, I still bristled a little.

"She's not the only one. Her mom is blond too," Tilda reminded her.

"It's kind of nice, actually," I admitted and set my glass back on the table. "Just blending in with everyone else."

I glanced over at the Skojare. They ranged from nearly albino in complexion, with porcelain skin and platinum hair, to pale beige and golden, closer to my and my mother's appearance. But even looking around the room, it was a veritable rainbow of trollkind.

The Kanin actually had the darkest complexions of all the trolls, with the Trylle, the Vittra, and the Omte looking fairer in comparison. I'd never been able to even remotely blend in with the Kanin, but for the first time in a long while I didn't stand out like sore thumb.

"Really?" Ridley cocked his head and looked over at me, while I stared down at my plate of food and stabbed at a bit of broccoli. "I thought you always liked standing out in a crowd."

"Just because I always do doesn't mean that I like it," I told him flatly.

"I know you hate it, but I've always loved your hair." Ember reached across the table, gently touching a lock of hair that hung free from the updo I'd put it in. "It's beautiful, and it suits you."

"Are you petting her?" Tilda wrinkled her nose and pushed Ember's arm down. "She's not a cat, Ember."

As trackers, we were the lowest priority when it came to getting food, so when we had just gotten our second course—a squash stew that was meant to be served hot and thick but had grown cold and had been watered down to stretch it by the time it got to us—the Kings and Queens had already finished their meal.

King Evert stood up, clinking his glass to draw attention to himself. The chatter among the guests died down, replaced by the sound of chairs sliding against the wooden floor as everyone turned to look at him.

Most of the room was lit by candles on the tables and filling the massive iron chandeliers that hung from the ceiling, and while everyone could see, it was somewhat dim. But a bright electric bulb shone above the head table like a spotlight, and when the King stood up, the silver and diamonds on his tall crown glimmered like a disco ball. He wore the white suit he'd gotten married in, and it reminded me of what a Disney prince would wear, only with far more jewels and adornments, making it even more cartoonish than the actual cartoons.

"I want to thank you all for coming out tonight." Evert spoke loudly, so his voice would carry throughout the cavernous ballroom. I could hear it surprisingly well, even tucked away in the corner. "I know some of you have traveled great distances to be here with us, celebrating this special night with my wife and I, and we want to thank you all.

"I've never been much for public speaking, but I know my wife has a few words she'd like to say." He smiled and gestured to Queen Mina, who stood up next to him.

The bodice of her white gown was covered in so many diamonds I wasn't sure how she was able to move in it. Not to mention her jewelry. Her necklace was covered in such massive rocks, I wouldn't be surprised if it weighed ten pounds or more.

"As the King said, we both want to thank you all for joining us," Mina said. Her voice was softer, but she managed to project it well.

I'd heard her speak many times before, and I'd come to notice that when she talked in private, like in the meeting on Thursday, she had a normal Kanin accent. But when she spoke now, in front of larger crowds, she suddenly had a mild British accent, as if that would make her sound more proper somehow.

"Over the past five years, I have had the pleasure of being your Queen and Evert's bride." She smiled broadly when she spoke, and her hands were folded neatly over her abdomen. "And I can honestly say that these past five years have been far happier and far greater than I ever could've imagined.

"Growing up in Iskyla, I could only dream of a life like this," she went on. "For those of you that may be unfamiliar with Iskyla, it's a small Kanin village that's even farther north than Doldastam, so it's even colder and more isolated, if you can believe that."

This was met with a few chuckles, especially from other Kanins who knew of Iskyla. I'd never been there before, but most people hadn't. From what I'd heard about it, it didn't have any modern amenities like electricity or working phones. Plus, it was in the Arctic.

"My parents died when I was very young, but I still dreamed of getting out. I just knew that I was destined for something more," Queen Mina told us all emphatically. "Then, in the cold dead of winter five years ago, I was invited to a ball in this very room, as were so many of you, though I didn't expect much."

The ball Mina referred to had been actually very Cinderella-esque, as was much of her life, apparently. King Evert's predecessor, his cousin Elliot Strinne, had died rather suddenly with no wife or immediate heirs. This had led to a heated exchange among the royalty, with some lobbying for Elliot's young niece to take the throne, before the Chancellor finally decided that the then-twenty-three-year-old Evert would be more suited to rule the kingdom than a child.

After Evert had been King for ten years and still had no bride and no heirs, the leaders had begun to worry. They didn't want to put the kingdom in turmoil, the way it had been after Elliot's death. So they set up a ball where the eligible women were to come to meet the King, and that's how Mina met Evert.

"That night was like a fairy tale." Mina smiled and touched her husband's shoulder. "The instant I laid eyes on him, I was in love. Luckily for me, he felt the same way. Four short months later, we were wed. Every day since then has been the happiest day of my life, and I can only hope that the next five years of marriage will be just as magical as the first."

She beamed down at King Evert, giving him a look so sweet and adoring that it was almost uncomfortable to watch. And then, quietly, almost too quietly for us to hear, she said, "I am so grateful for you, my love."

Since that seemed to be the end of her speech, the crowd applauded warmly for her, and she offered us all a wide smile before sitting back down next to her husband.

"She's lying," Ridley said as he clapped halfheartedly for her. "She doesn't love him."

"Why do you say that?" Ember asked.

He shook his head and went back to spooning the now-freezing-cold stew. "Nobody loves anybody that much."

"And here you were going on and on about true love last night," I said, surprised by the bitter edge of my own words.

"Was I?" He lifted his head, resting his eye on me, and I quickly turned back toward my own stew. "I remember saying something about settling down, but nothing about true love."

"Same thing," I mumbled.

"I don't know. Some people love each other that much," Ember insisted. "I think the Trylle King and Queen are super into each other."

"I'm not saying that people don't fall in love. People fall madly in love with each other all the time. But that right there"—Ridley gestured behind him, toward where King Evert and Queen Mina were seated—"that was all an act."

"I think you're right," Tilda agreed, talking about the royalty in a way that was unusual for her. When I looked at her in surprise, she shrugged one shoulder simply and took a sip of her water. "Well, he is right. She was a small-town girl with big dreams, and marrying into money and royalty was her way to get what she wanted."

"That's all I'm saying." Ridley leaned back in his seat, a self-satisfied grin on his face. Since Tilda so rarely chimed in on matters like this, having her on his side seemed like a boon.

"Good for her, then," I replied glibly.

"Good for her?" Ember laughed. "You think it's good that she tricked the King?"

"She didn't trick him," I corrected her. "He needed a beautiful wife to bear him children, and that's what he got. Well, no kids yet, but she's still young. She wanted to make a better life for herself, and she found a way. Maybe not the way that you or I would've chosen, but it was one way to do it."

"Would you do that?" Ridley asked. "Would you marry someone you didn't love to advance your life or your career?"

"No, of course I wouldn't," I said.

"Would you even marry someone if you did love them?" he asked. I could feel his eyes on me, but I refused to look at him, preferring to finish my wine in big gulps.

Before I could answer, Evert announced that it was time for the dance, and waiters came out to start clearing the tables and moving them out of the way so there would be more room for people to dance.

Then I didn't have time to worry about Ridley's questions or the way his eyes seemed to look straight through me. I had to hurry and help the waiters take our plates away, and then I was on my feet with the other trackers, helping to stack chairs and push tables to the side of the room.

But that was just as well, because I had no idea how I would answer.

impropriety

At the end of the ballroom, a small orchestra played a mix of contemporary human music along with Kanin folk songs. A singer accompanied them, and she had a pristine voice with an operatic range. The songs would segue seamlessly from the Beatles to a Kanin love ballad, sung entirely in its original low Swedish, and then would switch to a beautiful rendition of Adele.

It was still early in the evening, so the dance floor was relatively full. Most couples swayed to the music, but some glided across the floor with the elegant, practiced steps that came from years of training. The royalty, especially those from Doldastam, lived pampered, sheltered lives with much free time on their hands, so many of them took up ballroom dancing to fill the time.

As the newest returning changeling and one of the highest-ranking Markis, Linus attracted a lot of attention, and his dance card was full. While he could be clumsy, and did trip over his own feet a few times, his dance partners didn't seem to mind.

I watched him from the sidelines, ready to swoop in if he needed me, but he seemed to be doing okay on his own. His dance moves might have been lacking, but he made up for it by being nice and rather charming, in an unassuming kind of way.

Tilda and Ember didn't have any charges to watch out for, so they were free to hang out with me, standing along the wall at the edge of the dance floor. Tilda wore a short flapper-esque dress that showed off her long legs, and as she swayed, the silver tassels would swing and bounce along with her. Even though we were supposed to be standing at attention at the side of the ballroom, Tilda couldn't help herself. She loved to dance far too much. With her eyes closed, her head tilted back slightly, letting her long brown hair flow behind her, she moved gracefully in time with the music.

"I wish I could dance," Ember lamented.

Tilda opened her eyes and glanced down at Ember. "Just dance. It's fun even if you're alone."

Ember stared forlornly out at the crowded dance floor. "When I was a kid, all I wanted to do was go to the palace and attend one of these balls. And now that I am, I'm stuck at the side, unable to join in or have fun."

"You've joined in. You got to have a nice meal, you got all dolled up, and you're listening to the music," I pointed out, trying cheer her up. "You're a part of it."

"Maybe," Ember said doubtfully, but then she shook her head. "No, you're right. I guess I just spent too much time daydreaming about dancing with Prince Charming. Or Princess Charming, as it were."

As the song ended, Linus politely extracted himself from the arms of a lovely but clingy Marksinna in her early teens, and he came over to where I was standing with Ember and Tilda. His cheeks were flushed, but he had a goofy, lopsided grin plastered on his face.

"How are you doing?" I asked Linus as he reached us.

"Good. I mean, I think I am." He ran a hand through his dark hair and his smile turned sheepish. "Did I seem to be making any mistakes?"

"No, you look like you're doing really good," I assured him. "Are you having a nice time?"

"Yeah. It's a little weird dancing with so many strangers, especially when I've never been that into dancing, but most of the people are nice." He glanced back toward where his parents were seated at a table. "And my parents seem really proud."

"They are," I said.

Linus turned back to me, his eyes twinkling. "Are you having fun? You look kinda left out here on the sidelines."

"I'm having fun." I smiled to prove it to him.

"Why don't you come dance with me?" Linus suggested. "Cut loose for a minute."

"Thank you for asking, but I don't think I should." I demurred as graciously as I could. "It wouldn't be proper."

"Not even for one song?" His eyebrows lifted as he stared down hopefully at me, making him appear more like an excited puppy than a teenage boy.

I shook my head ruefully. "I'm afraid not."

"I'll dance with you," Ember piped in and stepped closer to him.

"*Ember,*" I admonished her, but Linus had already extended his arm to her.

She waved me off as she looped her arm through his. "It's one song. It'll be fine."

"That's the spirit." Linus grinned and led her out to the dance floor.

I looked to Tilda for support, hoping she would back me up even though Ember had already disappeared into the crowd and it'd be too late to stop her. But Tilda just shrugged, still swaying her hips along to the music.

"Let them have their fun," she said, smiling as she watched them twirl clumsily away from us.

"Ember is such a rebel sometimes." I stood on my tiptoes, craning my neck in an attempt to keep my eyes on Linus and Ember as they weaved in between other couples.

"They're fine," Ridley said. I'd been so busy watching Linus and Ember that I hadn't noticed Ridley come up beside me. "I doubt anyone will even notice her dancing. Everyone's having fun, and most of the royals are getting drunk on wine."

"Linus actually asked Bryn to dance first, but she declined," Tilda told him, ratting on me even though I knew I'd done the right thing.

She had a mischievous glint in her eyes—parties like this always brought it out in her. While she hadn't had anything to drink tonight, Tilda seemed to get drunk on good music and good dancing. Her relaxed elegance made me feel so rigid in comparison.

"You probably should've said yes. He could actually use a lesson in dance moves." Ridley motioned to where Linus stumbled over Ember's foot, but she helped him keep his balance.

"In private I'll give him a few pointers," I said. "But it wouldn't be proper here. He's my charge. I shouldn't do anything that might blur the lines of professionalism."

"I love it when you talk clean to me, quoting training manuals like sonnets," Ridley teased, but I found his usual flirtation off-putting since I didn't know how to respond.

Seeing him with Juni last night forced me to realize that I had some type of feelings for him. That left me unsure of how to act around him, so I'd rather be around him as little as I possibly could. At least until the feelings went away. And they had to eventually, right?

"There's nothing wrong with being professional," I told him coolly with eyes straight ahead, staring at the dance floor.

"There's nothing wrong with dancing either." Ridley moved so he was standing in front of me, forcing me to look at him. "Come on. Why don't you dance with me?"

"We're working," I replied quickly, making him smirk.

"It's a party, and everyone's dancing. And as the Rektor, I am your boss." He held out his hand to me.

"So this is an order?" I asked, eyeing his outstretched hand and hating how tempted I was to take it.

"If I say no, will you still dance with me?" he asked.

Tilda elbowed me gently in the side. "Just go dance, Bryn."

Without thinking, I reached out and took his hand. His hand easily enveloped mine, and it sent flutters through my stomach, which I tried to suppress. His smile widened, and as he led me away, I glanced back over my shoulder at Tilda, who smiled reassuringly at me.

Once we'd lost ourselves in the sea of well-dressed trolls, Ridley stopped and I put my hand on his shoulder. I was careful to keep some distance between us, but when he put his hand on the small of my back, he pulled me closer to him.

"This isn't so bad, right? Nobody's gawking at us or chasing us with pitchforks," Ridley said, smiling down at me as we danced in time with a dramatic cover of "Love Is Blindness."

"Not yet, anyway," I admitted.

I glanced around just to be sure we weren't getting any dirty looks, but nobody really seemed to be paying us any mind. But I supposed that, based on the formal way both Ridley and I were dressed, and the fact that there were so many royals here from other kingdoms who didn't know each other, they didn't realize that we didn't belong here, dancing alongside them.

Ember spotted us through a break in the crowd, and her jaw dropped. Instinctively, I tried to pull away from Ridley, but his hand was unyielding and warm on my back, holding me to him.

"So what's going on with you?" Ridley asked, and when I looked up, his smile had fallen away and his dark eyes were strangely serious.

"Nothing's going on." I tried to brush him off with an uneasy smile.

"I feel like you're mad at me."

I hedged my answer and lowered my eyes. "Why would I be mad?"

"I don't know. But you've been giving me the cold shoulder all night." He paused. "You've barely even looked at me."

"It's not like I spend all my time staring at you," I said, finding it hard to look up at him even now.

"Bryn. You know what I mean," he insisted firmly, and I did.

I hadn't meant to put a wall between us, but I really didn't know how else to deal with things. He was apparently with Juni now, and even if he wasn't, he was still my boss, and a tracker getting romantically involved with a Rektor was definitely a bad move, one that could cost us both our jobs. It opened up too many possibilities for corruption, manipulation, and nepotism.

So there was no way Ridley and I could ever be together, even if he wanted to. Or even if *I* wanted to, and I didn't. Not really.

I finally willed myself to look at him, meeting his mahogany eyes, even though it made me flush with heat when I did. "I'm not mad at you. I promise."

"If I did something to upset you, you can tell me," he said in a low voice, distressed at the thought that he'd done something to hurt me. "That's, like, the foundation of our friendship. We're always honest with each other."

"I am," I lied as convincingly as I could.

"Good," Ridley said, not because he believed me, but because he didn't know how else to push me.

"Is this why you asked me to dance?" I asked, trying to lighten the mood. "So you could interrogate me?"

"No. I asked you to dance because I wanted to dance with you," he said simply. "You're a good dancer."

With that, he extended his arm and I stepped back away from him. Then he pulled me close, twirling me as he did, and I stopped with my back pressed against his chest. His arms were wrapped around me, and his breath felt warm on my neck.

We stayed that way for only a second, our hips swaying slightly, and my heart pounded so loudly I was terrified he could feel it, but I didn't want to pull away from him. I actually wanted to stay that way forever, with the orchestra swelling, and the singer reaching her crescendo as she warned about the blindness of love. Under the dim candlelight of a chandelier in a crowded ballroom, with Ridley's arms strong as they crossed over me, my body bound to his, I closed my eyes, wishing the moment would last forever.

But it was only a split second, and then he had my hand, and he spun me around again. This time, when he pulled me back into his arms, I extended my leg, the way the dance required. He dipped me down so low, my hair brushed against the floor, and my eyes stayed locked on his as he pulled me back up.

I stayed in his arms, my body pressed against his, feeling breathless and dizzy, and I knew it wasn't just from the dancing. I stared up at him, and I'd never wanted to kiss anybody as badly as I wanted to kiss him then.

But instead I found myself blurting out, "It's too bad Juni couldn't be here."

"Yeah." Ridley sounded out of breath himself, and he blinked, clearing his eyes of whatever had been darkening them. "Yeah, it is."

The song ended, so I pulled away from him and smoothed out my dress. I wanted to rush off the dance floor, retreating back in the shadows to stand with Tilda, but Ridley hadn't moved. He stood in front of me with a puzzled expression on his face.

"What?" I asked.

"Nothing." He tried to smile at me but it faltered. "Thanks for dancing with me."

Ridley turned and walked away, leaving me alone in the middle of the dance floor.

mission

E ven though I hadn't drunk much at the anniversary party, I awoke the next morning feeling hung over. I would've been happy to spend the entirety of the day snuggled deep within the recesses of my blankets. It was barely after daybreak when Ember came pounding up the stairs to my loft and threw open the door.

"Unless my building is on fire, go away," I told her as I buried my head underneath the pillow.

"Don't be such a grump. I have good news." Ember hopped on the bed with such force, it bounced me up. When I landed, I peered at her skeptically. "I'm leaving."

"Why are you leaving?" I lifted the pillow from my head and rolled onto my back so I could look up at her. "And why is that good news?"

"I got my next assignment." She beamed at me. "I'm heading out to get a new changeling."

"Congratulations," I said, but thanks to my sleepiness it came out a bit weaker than it should've.

Like me, Ember preferred being out on missions to being cooped up here in Doldastam. So even though it would be less enjoyable for me to be stuck here without her, I was genuinely happy for her.

"Thanks. I just came to say good-bye, and then I have to get going."

"You're leaving right *now?*" I pushed myself up so I was sitting, and glanced at the alarm clock on my nightstand. "It's not even seven in the morning. When did you get the assignment?"

"Like, twenty minutes ago. Ridley called me to the Rektor's office and gave it to me," Ember said. "He did not look excited to be up this early. I think he drank too much wine last night."

"Wait." I rubbed my forehead, trying to clear my head. "None of this makes sense."

Usually we got our assignments a few days to a week before we left. It gave us time to go over the changeling's file and get to "know" them before we met them, and we got our travel arrangements in order, like booking hotels and plane tickets, if needed.

On top of that, it had only been a few days ago that the King and Queen had ordered all the trackers to stay in Doldastam until after all the guests had cleared out. Some of the guests were leaving tonight, but the majority of them weren't heading out until tomorrow morning.

So, barring some kind of emergency, I didn't know why they

would send out a tracker before Monday afternoon. It didn't make sense.

"Ridley said that the King had called him early this morning saying that they got a tip, and they needed someone to get this changeling in right away," Ember explained.

"Which changeling?"

Ember pursed her lips and gave me a hard look. "You know I can't tell you that. Our missions are confidential until after we return."

As a matter of privacy and safety, we were never allowed to tell anyone where we were going or who the changelings were. It was to prevent things like what had happened with Linus, as well as the fact that the royals didn't always want it getting around how well-off (or how not-so-well-off) their offspring had been in the human world.

"I know, I know." I waved it off. "But what was the King's tip? What's so important that he roused Ridley in the middle of the night to start organizing your mission?"

Ember opened her mouth like she wanted to say something, but she couldn't seem to find the words. And that's when it hit me. It was so obvious, I couldn't believe I didn't figure it out instantly. I blamed my sleep-deprived brain for it.

"Konstantin Black," I said.

"They don't know for sure." Ember rushed to ease my anxiety.

"This is ridiculous." I threw the covers off me and leapt out of bed, barely noticing how cold the wood floor felt on my bare feet as I stomped over to my wardrobe.

"What are you doing?"

"I'm getting dressed." I threw open my wardrobe doors, hard enough that the wardrobe nearly tipped forward, but I caught it just in time. I grabbed a sweatshirt and pulled it on over the tank top I'd slept in. "I'm gonna go find Ridley and give him a piece of my mind."

"He's probably back in bed," Ember said.

"I don't care." I turned to face her. "I just can't believe he would do this. This should be my mission, not yours. If Konstantin is back, then I should be the one going after him."

Ember had been sitting on the bed, but she stood up now. Her hands were balled into fists at her sides, and she took a fortifying breath before speaking.

"Bryn. Stop." She spoke harshly enough to break through my frantic agitation, but by the tightness in her voice I could tell she was doing her best to keep calm and not yell at me. "First of all, what you're doing is incredibly patronizing. I am strong and smart and capable enough to handle this mission."

"No, I know that, Ember," I hurried to apologize. "You're an excellent tracker. I don't mean it like that."

"I know what your deal with Konstantin is, better than almost anyone," she went on. "So I get it. But I also know what a massive jerk he is and how much of a threat he is. I understand the danger, and I also understand how important it is to bring him back to stand trial for his crimes."

"I know," I said.

"But—and I mean no offense by this—I'm not clouded by my own personal feelings about him."

I wanted to argue with Ember on the last point, but I couldn't. Only a few days ago I'd confessed to Ridley that I wanted to kill Konstantin and that I wouldn't let him get away again. Since I'd seen him last week, I'd been replaying my fight with Konstantin again and again, thinking about how much worse I would hurt him if I saw him again.

My own need for revenge would make it impossible for me to think as rationally and impartially as Ember, so I fell silent and lowered my eyes.

"I understand the severity of the situation, and I've got it under control," Ember said at length. "That's why Ridley chose me and not you."

"I know that you're right and that he made the right choice. I just . . ." I trailed off.

"You still want to be the one going," she finished for me.

I looked up at her and nodded. "Yeah."

"I get it. But it's actually a pretty big *if* that it is even Konstantin. The reports were sketchy. They'd just heard rumors that he might be in the area of another prominent changeling."

"How do they know?"

"After the incident with Linus, they sent out Konstantin and Bent's pictures to all the tribes so their guards could keep a lookout. They're, like, Trolls' Most Wanted now," Ember explained. "A Trylle tracker was getting one of their changelings, and they thought they saw someone that looked like Konstantin, and that happened to be nearby where this changeling I'm going after lives."

"I know you can't tell me *who* or *where,* but can you tell me if you'll be close, at least?" I asked. "In case you need backup."

"I'll be less than a day's drive from Doldastam, if I need you."

"And you will call me if you need me? Or Ridley or Tilda or somebody, right?" I asked, and I was thinking more of Ember's safety than my own vendetta. Ember was a good fighter, but so was Konstantin, and he wasn't working alone.

"Of course I will," she promised me with a smile. "But I shouldn't. I'm sure everything will be fine. The Trylle tracker was probably mistaken, and I'll find a perfectly safe changeling and bring her home."

"How long do you think you'll be gone?" I asked.

"On the off chance that things get dodgy, Ridley wants me to try to make this a quick mission. I'm hoping a week will be good enough, but I also don't want to risk scaring the changeling off."

"Well, I was only in Chicago for five days, and Linus came back okay," I reminded her. "So I'm sure you'll be fine."

"I'm sure I will too."

"I should let you get going, anyway. If you need to get out of here right away."

Before she left, I hugged her tightly. Ember had gone out on missions before, but this was the first time I felt nervous for her. I was reluctant to let go of her, but eventually Ember pulled away. She smiled at me, promising that everything would be okay, before she turned and headed out my door. It took all my willpower to keep from chasing after her and following her.

FIFTEEN

repast

I'm not thrilled about this either," my mom said in a hushed voice, as if someone might overhear. Her gray jacket went down to her ankles, and she pulled it tighter around herself as we walked toward the palace. The large diamond studs in her ears glimmered when the sun poked through the clouds in the overcast sky.

"Then why are we doing it?" I asked, trudging along beside her.

"Because they're family, even if they aren't close," she explained with a hint of exasperation. "And because it's a nice gesture."

"But you don't even like them that much," I said, as if she needed me to remind her of that fact. "I don't even know them. *You* don't even really know them."

"I know. But they asked me." We'd reached the palace door, so she stopped and turned to me. The wind had left a rose on her cheeks, but that only made her look more beautiful. "And now I'm asking you."

"Your mother doesn't ask much of us, Bryn." Dad put his arm around her waist, showing his solidarity. "We can do this for her."

"Of course we can," I agreed, and smiled as genially as I could.

There was no point in arguing this or being sullen about the whole thing. It did help to know that my mom didn't enjoy it either, so the three of us were a united front, all pretending to be happy and polite for strangers.

Besides, I had to agree with my mom that it was a nice gesture. After my mom had eloped with my dad, she had been banned from visiting the Skojare, and at first that meant no contact at all. Slowly, their freeze-out had begun to thaw, and she had been allowed to return home for her mother's funeral ten years ago, which had opened the dialogue between her family and her again.

So this was a big step on their part. Queen Linnea Biâelse—the young bride of the Skojare King Mikko—was my second cousin, which made her my mom's first cousin once removed or some other ridiculous relation like that.

The King, Queen, and Prince of the Skojare had invited us for brunch since they were in town, and King Evert had been kind enough to allow us to use one of the meeting rooms in the palace to visit with them.

When we went into the palace, a footman greeted us and took our jackets and boots, and then he led us down to where the brunch was being held. My dad knew where everything was, and so did I, actually, but since we were here as guests of royalty, it was proper for the footman to show us in.

As my mom strode down the corridor, her long white dress flowed out behind her, and it made me happier that I'd chosen to wear a dress myself, although mine was much shorter than hers. My mom always looked beautiful, but she had taken the time to really dress for the occasion, looking more like she should appear on a red carpet than in the dark hallways of a frozen palace, so I knew this was important to her.

The footman opened the door for us, and King Mikko, Queen Linnea, and Prince Kennet were already seated at a long table decked out with fruit and pastries of all kinds. As soon as we entered the room, Linnea got to her feet, followed by Kennet, but the King seemed reluctant to stand.

"My apologies if we've kept you waiting," Mom said, curtsying slightly.

"No, of course not. We're early," Linnea assured her with a warm smile, and she gestured to the table. "Please, sit. Join us."

On the Queen's neck, just below her jawline, were two nearly translucent blue semicircles—her gills. They would've been virtually invisible, except they fluttered every time she took a deep breath.

Since her marriage to Mikko ten months ago, the royalty in all the kingdoms had dubbed her the "child bride." At only sixteen, Linnea had married a man twice her age, but that wasn't all that uncommon in societies like ours—where royal marriages were arranged to provide the best offspring and alignment of powerful families.

The Skojare possessed an odd elegance, as if they weren't human or trolls, but porcelain dolls come to life. While Linnea had that look—the pale, smooth features with undertones of blue, and the striking beauty—her face still had the cherubic cheeks of childhood, while her azure eyes had the youthful rebelliousness of a teenager.

Only her crown filled with sapphires, nestled in her platinum-blond corkscrew curls, gave the indication of her title. Her only makeup was bright red lipstick that stood out sharply against her alabaster skin.

Linnea took her seat between her husband and her brother-in-law, and my mom, my dad, and I sat down across from them, separated by the largest assortment of fruit I'd ever seen served at breakfast.

"I know that you're a relation of Linnea's, but I'm not sure that we've been properly introduced," Kennet said, grinning as he popped a grape into his mouth.

Kennet was a few years younger than the King, and they were unmistakably brothers. Both of them had darker complexions than Linnea, but not by much. Their hair was more of a golden blond, and they had blue eyes that were dazzling even by Skojare standards. Mikko had broader shoulders, and his jaw was a bit wider and stronger than Kennet's. Kennet may have been slighter and shorter than his brother, but he was just as handsome.

Like Linnea, both brothers had gills—nearly invisible until they breathed deeply. I had seen them before, but I still always found it hard not to stare.

"Runa is my cousin," Linnea explained brightly to the men, and motioned across the table to her. "This is her family, although I am embarrassed to admit I don't know them that well."

"No need to be embarrassed. We haven't spent much time together, but I am hopeful that we'll begin to know each other better." Mom smiled at her, then touched my dad's hand. "This is my husband, Iver. He is the Chancellor for the Kanin."

"And who is this?" Kennet was across from me, and he nodded toward me.

"Sorry, this is my daughter, Bryn." Mom squeezed my shoulder gently and leaned into me. "I didn't forget her, I swear."

"No, I didn't think you'd forgotten about her. I can't imagine how anyone could." He grinned at me and winked, and I wasn't sure how I was supposed to reply to that, so I started filling a plate up with berries.

Mom eyed Kennet for a moment, then began to fill her plate too. "So how are you enjoying Doldastam?"

"It's a very lovely town. So much bigger than Storvatten," Linnea enthused. "It is rather cold, though." She pulled her silvery fur stole around her shoulders then, as if she suddenly remembered the temperature. "And we're so far from the water. How do you handle that?"

"As soon as it begins to thaw, I swim out in the Hudson Bay, which isn't all that far from here," Mom explained. "The winters are much tougher, though."

Dad reached over, squeezing her hand. Both my parents had sacrificed so much to be together, but by leaving her family, her town, the very water she craved, my mom had arguably given up more.

"How do you get by?" Kennet asked. He folded his arms on the table and leaned forward. "How do you all occupy your time?"

"We all have our careers to keep us busy." Mom motioned between the three of us. "I teach elementary students, and that keeps me on my toes."

"What about you?" His eyes rested on me again as I picked at a strawberry. "Do you have a career?"

I nodded. "I do. I'm a tracker, and I plan to be on the Högdragen someday."

"Tracker?" Kennet raised a surprised eyebrow. "Isn't that a peasant job?"

"*Kennet!*" Linnea hissed, glaring at him.

"I meant no offense by that." He leaned back and held up his hands. "I was merely curious."

"Forgive my little brother." King Mikko looked at me for the first time since I'd entered the room. His voice was so deep, it was like quiet thunder when he spoke. "He has the awful habit of forgetting to think before he speaks."

"No forgiveness needed," I told him, and turned my gaze back to the Prince. "A tracker is a job mostly filled by nonroyalty, this is true. But as my mother and father both lost their titles as Marksinna and Markis when they were married, that makes me a nonroyal. A peasant."

"I am sorry." His shoulders had slacked, and there seemed to be genuine contrition in his aquamarine eyes. "I didn't mean to bring up class distinction. I was just caught off guard to hear that you had such a difficult job. I've gotten far too used to hearing people describe their jobs as simply being rich, or on the very rare occasion they may be a nanny or a tutor. It's exceptional to find someone who wants to work for something."

"It's very important to Bryn that she earns her place in this world, and she works very hard," Mom told him proudly.

"You seem like an intelligent, capable young woman." Kennet's eyes rested heavily on me. "I'm sure you're a wonderful tracker."

After that, conversation turned to general banalities. Linnea and my mom talked a bit about family members and old friends of my mom's. Kennet interjected some about the goings-on in Storvatten, but Mikko added very little.

Finally, when the banter seemed to run out, the room fell into an awkward silence.

"I very much enjoyed this brunch," Linnea said. "I do hope you can visit us soon. It can be so lonely in Storvatten. There are so few of us anymore."

This was an understatement. The Skojare were a dwindling kingdom. By best accounts, there were less than five thousand Skojare in the entire world—that was half of the Kanin population in Doldastam alone. That's why it wasn't quite so surprising that Linnea was related to us. All trolls were related, of course, but none so closely as the Skojare.

In fact, Mikko and Kennet were actually Linnea's second cousins, and if I understood correctly, my mom was related to them as well, though more distantly. But that's what happened in a community that small when you insisted on royals marrying royals, on purebloods with gills marrying other purebloods with gills to ensure the cleanest bloodline possible.

"Yes, we'll definitely visit as soon as we can," Mom said, and while I was sure it was convincing to them, I heard the tightness in her voice. She had no intention of visiting in Storvatten.

After we made our good-byes, the footman escorted us to the door. I waited until we were bundled back up in our jackets and walking away in the frigid morning air before I finally asked my mom why she'd lied.

"If you enjoyed the brunch, and you did seem to really enjoy talking about Storvatten, how come you don't want to go back there?" I asked.

"I never said I enjoyed the brunch," Mom corrected me, and she looped her arm through mine as we walked next to my dad. "I do like to reminisce sometimes, it's true. But there are few things I enjoy less than spending time with stuffy royals. I know you took that peasant comment in stride, but let me assure you, it's much better being raised a peasant than a royal."

"I'm very happy with the way you raised me," I told her. "I think you guys made the right decision giving up your titles."

"I know we did." She leaned over then, kissing me on the temple. "And besides all that, my life is here with you and your dad. There's no reason to revisit the past."

doldastam

While waiting in the entryway of the Berlings' mansion for Linus to get ready, I pulled my phone out of the pocket of my jeans, checking it for the hundredth time that morning. Ember had been gone for over twenty-four hours, and she hadn't texted me yet.

Ordinarily, she wouldn't check in with me when she was on missions. We would occasionally text or call just to chat and see how things were going, so logically it made sense that she wasn't briefing me and giving me updates on her trip.

But I would feel better if she did.

"So what's the game plan for today, teach?" Linus asked as he bounded up the curved stairway toward me.

"I'm not your teacher," I reminded him again, since he'd recently developed a penchant for calling me *teach*. "I'm your tracker. There's a difference."

"You teach me things. It sounds the same to me." He shrugged.

"Anyway." I decided to move on, since it was clearly a losing battle. "It's a nice day out, so I thought I'd give you a tour around town."

"That sounds great." He grinned. "I haven't really seen much outside of the walls of my house or the palace. It'll be good to get out."

While it wasn't exactly balmy outside, it'd warmed up just enough that the snow had begun to melt. When we stepped out of Linus's house, we were both treated to several huge droplets of water coming down from the roof.

It was the warmest day of the year thus far, and the gray skies had parted enough for the sun to shine through, so everyone seemed to have the same idea. On the south side of town, where Linus lived and the palace and all the royal mansions were, it was usually fairly quiet. But even the Markis and Marksinna were out, going for walks and enjoying the weather.

I showed Linus around his neighborhood, pointing out which mansions belonged to what royals. Astrid Eckwell was standing in front of her expansive house, letting her rabbit roam in the carefully manicured lawn, nibbling at newly exposed grass.

She smiled smugly at me as we passed, and while I told Linus that she lived there, I neglected to explain that her house should've belonged to my dad, if he hadn't married my mom and been disinherited. But he had, so everything that should've been his was passed down to the Eckwells.

As we got to the edge of the south side of town, the houses began getting smaller and sitting closer together. In the center of town, they were practically on top of each other.

What little yard the cottages did have usually had a small chicken coop or a couple goats tied up in it. It wasn't unheard-of to see chickens squawking about on the cobblestone roads or the occasional cow roaming free from its pen.

In the town square, I showed Linus all the major shops. The bakery, the general store, the seamstress, and a few other stores I thought he might find useful. He was surprised and some-what appalled to learn that we had a taxidermist, but many Markis liked to stuff their trophies when they went hunting.

"What's that?" Linus pointed to a brick building overgrown with green vines, untouched by the cold. A small orchard sat to the side of it, with apples and pears growing from the trees. A swing set, a slide, and a teeter-totter were practically hidden below the branches.

"That's the elementary school," I said.

"How are the vines still green?" He stopped to admire the building with its vines and white and blue blossoms. "Shouldn't they die in the winter?"

"Some Kanin have an affinity for plants," I explained. "It's a talent that's much more common in the Trylle, but we have a few special tricks in play, like keeping these alive and bright year-round."

The front doors were open, and he stepped forward to see that the greenery continued inside, with the plants twisting up over the walls and on the ceiling. Then he turned back to me. "Can we go inside?"

I shrugged. "If you want."

"This is the most unusual school I've ever seen," he said as he walked through the threshold, and I followed a step behind. "Why are the floors dirt?"

"It's supposed to take us back to our roots and keep our heritage alive. Some trolls even choose to have dirt floors in their homes."

He looked back at me. "You mean because we used to live with nature?"

"Exactly."

Drawings were posted up on the walls outside the classrooms. In child's handwriting, the pictures had "My Family" written across the top, and then stick figures of various moms and dads and brothers and sisters and even the family rabbit.

"All the kids go to the same place?" Linus asked, noticing that some pictures were simply signed *Ella* or *James,* while others had the title of Markis and Marksinna in front of their names. "The royals and the other town kids all go here?"

"Doldastam is really too small to support two elementary schools, especially when so many Markis and Marksinna are changelings," I said. "When we get older, we split up, with the royals going to high school, and the others going to specialized vocational training."

That was in large part why my childhood experiences hadn't been the greatest. Standing inside the school brought back all kinds of unpleasant memories, usually involving one Marksinna or another making fun of me for being different than the other kids. Astrid had been the worst, but she was far from the only one.

If it hadn't been for Tilda, I wasn't sure how I would've made it through. She was the only one I had by my side, through thick and thin.

But I found my thoughts drifting away from school to the King's Games as I looked down the long hall to the courtyard that lay beyond. Every summer we'd have the King's Games, which were sort of like a Kanin Olympic event, held out in the courtyard behind the school. Members of the Högdragen as well as elite trackers and occasionally well-trained townsfolk would compete in games of sport, like swordplay, jousting, and hand-to-hand, which was similar to kick boxing.

I remember once when I was ten or eleven, and I'd gone to see Konstantin in the games. Tilda had helped me climb up onto a fence so I could see, and we'd sat together, watching with equal fervor as Konstantin knocked his opponents to the ground. Konstantin held his sword to each young man's throat until he finally yielded, and the crowd erupted in applause.

"I almost thought that the other guy wouldn't surrender," Tilda had admitted breathlessly as Konstantin held his hands triumphantly above his head.

"Are you kidding me?" I asked her, with my eyes still locked on Konstantin. "Everyone always surrenders to him. He's unstoppable."

When I was a kid, that idea had filled me with wonder and admiration. Now it only filled me with dread.

"Hey, that lady looks an awful lot like you," Linus said, pulling me from my thoughts. I looked over to see my mom standing in the doorway to a classroom, ushering children out for a bathroom break.

"That's because she's my mom," I said, and lowered my head, as if that would make it harder for her to spot her adult blond daughter standing in the middle of the elementary school hallway.

"Really? Let's go say hi," Linus suggested brightly.

"No, we've got a lot to see," I said, and I turned and darted out of the school without waiting for him. I couldn't wait any longer if I didn't want to risk talking to her.

"Are you mad at your mom?" Linus asked, once he caught up with me outside of the school.

"What do you mean?" I asked, and continued our walk toward the north side of town.

"You just seemed to want to avoid her."

I shook my head. "No, it's not that. I just don't like mixing business with family."

"Why not?"

"She isn't supportive of my job, for one thing," I said, but that was only a half-truth.

"And what's the other thing?" Linus pressed.

I glanced over at him, with his earnest eyes and genuine concern, and I decided to tell the truth. "Most Markis and Marksinna don't exactly approve of her."

This seemed to totally baffle him, the way it would most people who saw past Mom's race to her kindness and strength and wit and beauty. But unfortunately, there were very few Kanin who could do that.

"Why not?" Linus asked in disbelief.

"Because she's Skojare, and I'm half Skojare." I stopped

walking and turned to him, since the conversation felt like it required more attention.

He shrugged. "So?"

"So . . . Kanin tend to look down on anybody that isn't Kanin, especially the royalty," I explained.

"That's dumb." He wrinkled his nose.

"Yes, it is," I agreed. "But it's the way things are."

"Why don't you change things?" Linus asked me directly, and for a second I had no idea what to answer.

"I . . . I can't," I stumbled. "But you can. You're part of an influential family. Someday you may even be King. But even if you aren't, you have the power to lead by example."

"You really think I can change things?" Linus asked with wide eyes.

"I do," I told him with a smile. "Now come on. Let's see the rest of town."

"So when you say people don't approve of you, what does that mean?" Linus asked, falling in step beside me. "Are they mean to you?"

I sighed. "I'd rather not get into it, if that's okay."

"All right," he relented, but only for a second. "But you can tell me stuff. We're friends now."

"Thanks, and I appreciate the sentiment, but . . . we can't be friends," I told him gently.

"What are you talking about? We *are* friends," Linus insisted, and this time I didn't have the heart to argue with him.

SEVENTEEN

confrontations

The fire crackled in my wood-burning stove, and I slipped out of my jeans—muddy and wet from the walk around town with Linus. Wearing only my panties, I pulled on an over-sized sweatshirt and went over to my bookshelf. After a long day, the only thing that sounded good to me was curling up in bed with a book.

I'd finally caved and texted Ember a few hours ago, but she hadn't replied. So I needed a good distraction. Most of the books I owned were old and worn, but I tried to pick up a few new ones every time I went out on a mission. I'd hoped to restock my shelves while I was in Chicago, but that trip had been cut too short.

Since I didn't have anything new, I decided to reread one of my favorites—a battered hardcover of *The Count of Monte Cristo* by Alexandre Dumas. It was wedged stubbornly between several other books, and I'd just finally managed to pull it free when I heard the creak of my front door opening.

I whirled around, brandishing the book with the intention of bludgeoning an intruder with it, but it was only Ridley, his black jacket hanging open and his hands held palm-up toward me.

"Easy, Bryn. It's just me."

"Why are you sneaking up on me?" I demanded, refusing to lower my book.

"I'm not *sneaking*. I just step lightly." He stayed in my doorway, letting a cold draft in around him. "Can I come in?"

I was acutely aware of the way I was dressed—no pants, with the hem of the sweatshirt hitting my midthigh, and the stretched-out neck left it hanging at an angle, revealing my left shoulder and bra strap, along with the jagged scar that ran below it. But I didn't want to seem aware of this, tried to act as if it didn't feel like a big deal to be standing half naked in my small apartment alone with Ridley.

So instead of rushing over to put on pants or hiding underneath a blanket, I shrugged and said, "I guess."

"Thanks." He came inside and closed the door behind him.

And then we stayed that way for a moment, neither of us saying anything. The only light in the loft came from the dim fire and my bedside lamp, casting most of the room in shadows. His eyes bounced around the room, never lingering on anything, and he licked his lips but didn't speak.

"Why are you here?" I asked finally, since it appeared he might never say anything. "You never come to my apartment."

"I've been here before," he corrected me. He shoved a hand in the back pocket of his jeans and shifted his weight.

I folded my arms over my chest. "You don't *usually* come here. Why are you here now?"

"Do you wanna sit down?" He motioned to the couch to the side of me, but I didn't move toward it.

"Why would I want to sit down? What's going on?" My blood pressure had been steadily rising since Ridley had opened the door, and my whole body began to tense up. "What happened?"

"It's nothing bad." He exhaled deeply and brushed his dark curls back from his forehead. "I mean, it's not as bad as it sounds."

"Just spit it out, Ridley."

"Ember ran into Konstantin Black on her mission."

For a moment I couldn't breathe, and I barely managed to get out the word, "What?"

"There was a small altercation, and she was hurt, but—"

That was all I heard, and all I needed to hear, and then I was scrambling to get out of there. I tossed my book down on the couch and ran over to my dirty jeans in the hamper.

"Bryn." Ridley walked over to me, but I ignored him.

"I need to get to her, Ridley," I said, nearly shouting by then, in a quavering voice.

"No, listen to me, Bryn." He put his hands on my arms, and I suppressed the urge to push him off and hit him. His grip felt solid and strangely comforting, so I looked up at him and tried to slow my ragged breaths.

"Ember is okay." Ridley spoke slowly, his words clear and calm. "She was injured, but it's nothing critical, and she managed to get out with the changeling. She's on her way home, and she'll be here tomorrow morning. You don't need to go after her."

I breathed deeply, letting his words sink in, and then I nodded. "She's okay?"

"Yes, I talked to her on the phone, and she sounded good." He smiled crookedly, trying to reassure me.

"What about Konstantin?"

Ridley didn't answer immediately, but he didn't look away, so I searched his eyes, looking for a glimmer of hope, but found none. His smile fell away, and I knew the answer

"He got away," I surmised.

"The important thing is that both Ember and the changeling are safe," Ridley reminded me.

"I know."

I pulled away from him, and at first he tried to hang on, but then he let his hands fall to his sides. I ran a hand through my hair and sat back on the bed behind me. My legs felt weak, and my shoulders ached. The sudden surge of anxiety and adrenaline, followed by the news of Ember's injury and Konstantin's escape, left me feeling sore and out of sorts.

"I should've been there," I said softly.

"No." Ridley shook his head and came over to sit down next to me.

My legs dangled over the edge of the bed as I stared emptily at the wall in front of me, but Ridley sat so he was facing me.

He rested one hand on the bed, supporting himself, and his fingers brushed against the bare skin of my thigh.

"Why did you send her and not me?" I turned to look at him, and he was so close, I could see my own reflection in his eyes.

"I knew she could handle it, and she did," Ridley said.

"But you didn't think I could."

"I didn't say that."

"Then why didn't you send me?" I asked thickly.

He swallowed, but his dark eyes never wavered from mine. "You know why."

"I could've gone with. I could've helped her. If I had been there, maybe she wouldn't have gotten hurt. Konstantin wouldn't have gotten away."

"Or maybe things could've gone much worse," Ridley countered. "You don't know what would've happened, and everything turned out okay."

"No, it didn't. He got away. *Again*."

"That's not your fault."

"It is my fault! Because I should've been there, and not here doing nothing." I looked away from him, staring down at my lap. "I should've killed him when I had the chance."

"Bryn." He reached out, putting his hand gently on my face and making me look at him. "It's not your fault. You did everything you were supposed to do. Konstantin Black isn't your fault."

"Then why does it feel like he is?" I asked in a voice barely above a whisper.

"I don't know." He brushed his thumb along my cheek, and I closed my eyes, leaning into his touch.

His other hand moved, so that his fingers were no longer brushing against my thigh, and he pressed it against the small of my back. I felt the bed shifting, and even though my eyes were closed, I knew he was leaning in toward me.

"You should go," I whispered, too afraid to open my eyes and see his face hovering next to mine.

"You sure?" Ridley asked, but he lowered his hand, and I felt the weight on the bed change as he moved away from me. I finally dared to open my eyes, and he was still sitting next to me, looking at me with an expression filled with concern.

"If Ember's coming back in the morning, I should get some sleep."

"But are you even gonna get any sleep tonight?" Ridley asked me honestly.

I gave a weak laugh. "I don't know."

"I could stay, keep you company until you fell asleep."

I didn't need him. Or at least I didn't want to need him. But I didn't want to push him away. Not tonight.

"Okay." I nodded, giving in to my feelings for him, at least in some small way.

"Good." He smiled, then slipped off his jacket. "When I came in, it looked like you were grabbing a book."

"Yeah, I was just gonna read before I went to bed."

"Perfect." He stood up. "You go ahead, crawl into bed and get comfy."

"Okay?" I was skeptical, but I did as he told me, sliding under the thick covers and lying back in my bed.

"Here's what I'll do," Ridley explained as he grabbed *The Count of Monte Cristo* from where I'd tossed it on the couch. "I'll read, you relax and fall asleep. Sound like a plan?"

I smiled up at him as he walked back toward me. "Sure."

He sat down on the bed beside me, over the covers with his legs stretched out next to mine, and he cracked open the book and began to read. Eventually his gentle baritone lulled me to sleep. I didn't actually remember falling asleep, but when I awoke with the early morning light spilling in through the windows, my head was on his chest and his arm was around me.

threats

I just can't believe she didn't call me," I muttered.

The Land Rover lurched to the side, and I jerked the wheel, correcting it just in time to keep us from slamming into one of the willow hybrids. Yesterday's early thaw had left puddles and melting snow everywhere that turned into ice today, making the road out of Doldastam more treacherous than normal.

Not that that slowed me down. Ember had texted me thirty minutes ago, letting me know that her train was almost to the station. I still wasn't sure how badly she'd been injured, and I didn't know if driving would be difficult or painful for her.

I'd been at Tilda's house—that had been my excuse to escape a rather awkward morning conversation with Ridley, saying that I'd promised to have breakfast with Tilda. I hadn't, but Tilda was who I ran to when I needed to gather my thoughts and get my wits about me. It'd worked out, because then Ember had texted me, and within minutes Tilda and I were racing to meet her at the train station.

"I'm sure she had her reasons." Tilda pressed her hands against the dashboard to keep from sliding all over as the Land Rover bounced down the road.

"She just lectured me about not calling her after my run-in with Konstantin, and then she turns around and does the same thing."

"Maybe Ember was afraid that you would freak out." Tilda let out a small groan when we hit a bump and she bounced into the air. "And I haven't the faintest idea why," she added drolly and shot me a look.

"I'm not freaking out," I protested, but I slowed down a bit. "She still should've called me."

"But she called Ridley, and she's safe, and that's what counts," Tilda reminded me.

We'd gotten far enough from Doldastam that trees were no longer crowding the path, and the road had widened and smoothed some, so she relaxed back in her seat.

"On the subject of Ridley," Tilda began, and I groaned inwardly. In my telling her about Ember's injury over oatmeal this morning, I'd let it slip that Ridley had spent the night, then Ember had texted me and we'd been on our way.

I tried to evade the question. "There is no subject of Ridley."

"But he did spend the night last night," she said carefully, making sure her words had no trace of accusation.

"He did, but nothing happened. It wasn't like that."

"Okay," Tilda relented, but I wasn't completely sure if she believed me. Hell, I wasn't sure if *I* believed me.

We lapsed into silence after that, so I turned up the music. Thanks to my earlier speeding, we managed to arrive at the station just as the train was pulling in. We'd made the trek in record time.

Ember hobbled off the platform, and her coat hung on her at a haphazard angle thanks to the sling around her arm, which appeared to be made from a couple different fashion scarves. A graze on her left cheek was red and puffy, but otherwise she didn't look that much worse for wear.

She stopped on the steps when she saw Tilda and me rushing toward her. "What are you doing here?"

"We came to give you a lift home and to make sure you're all right," I told her. "Are you okay?"

"I'll live." Ember smiled at us, then turned and gestured to a mousy girl standing just behind her, holding a massive Louis Vuitton suitcase. "This is Charlotte. She's my charge."

"Here, let me help you with that." Tilda ran up the steps to take the bag from Charlotte before it tipped her over.

"Thank you," Charlotte mumbled, but she seemed reluctant to let the bag go. Her eyes were wide and terrified, and her frizzy brown hair stuck out from underneath her knit cap.

"These are my friends Tilda and Bryn," Ember explained to her. "You can trust them. They're good guys."

"I'm sure you've both had a long couple of days. Why don't we get going?" I suggested.

I gingerly took Ember's good arm and led her down the

steps. Even with salt and gravel on the ground, the ice still made it slick in a few places, and it would be awful for Ember to take a tumble and hurt herself worse.

"What about my Land Rover?" Ember asked as we walked past the one she'd driven in to where I'd parked mine rather crookedly in my haste.

"We'll get it another day. Come on," I said. "Let's just get home."

On the ride back to Doldastam, it was hard not to ask Ember a million questions about her fight with Konstantin, but I didn't want to freak out Charlotte any more than she already appeared to be. Tilda sat with her in the backseat, speaking in soft comforting tones about the landscape and her family and how wonderful everything would be for her after she arrived.

Since Ember was injured, Tilda offered to take Charlotte to her parents and help her get settled in. Ember could return to her usual tracker duties once she was patched up, but for now, Tilda would work just fine.

"So what happened?" I asked Ember the instant Tilda and Charlotte had gotten out of the SUV.

"I was staking out Charlotte, like I'm supposed to, and then I had this sense of being watched," Ember said, recalling a scene that sounded familiar.

"I wasn't sure if it was just paranoia, but I decided that I'd better do something, just to be on the safe side," she went on, as I drove through town toward Ember's house. "I was on my way to Charlotte's house, trying to figure out what I'd say to her to get her to leave with me, but I was still scoping everything out, watching every car that went by and scanning for any signs of trouble.

"Then out of nowhere—and I mean like *nowhere*—Bent Stum jumped me."

"He jumped you?" I looked over at her, slumped down in the front seat, her eyes closed and her mouth turned down into an annoyed scowl.

"Yeah. That Bent is strong, but he's pretty dumb. He snapped my arm"—Ember grimaced and touched her broken arm gently—"but I managed to slide out of his grasp. He chased after me, but I managed to lose him when I cut through a backyard and down an alley."

"What happened? How'd you get Charlotte?"

"I got to her house, and Konstantin was already there." Ember paused to let out a pained sigh. "I don't know what his plan was, but when he saw me, he apparently decided that he needed to just go for it. He broke into her bedroom window and just snatched her."

"You mean he kidnapped her?" I asked, a little dumbfounded.

With Linus, back in Chicago, they had been staking him out, like they were planning a careful, quiet extraction. But with Charlotte, it sounded like a clumsy snatch-and-grab. Konstantin and Bent were getting more reckless, which meant that they were probably getting more desperate. That was a dangerous combination.

"Yeah, she was kicking and screaming at first, but he put his hand over her mouth to muffle it," Ember explained. "But it was enough to draw attention. Her parents weren't home, but one of her neighbors came outside and yelled that they were calling the cops."

"Wow." My jaw dropped. Discretion was the number one name of the game. I couldn't believe how risky Konstantin's behavior had gotten.

"Dragging Charlotte around really slowed Konstantin down, and I caught up to them easily and kicked out his legs. He got back up like he meant to fight me, but then we heard the sirens of the approaching cops. And he . . ." She glanced over at me for a moment, then shifted in her seat. "He took off."

"How'd you get Charlotte to come back with you?" I asked.

"She was in shock, so I used persuasion on her," Ember said, referring to her ability.

Persuasion was a psychokinetic ability with which she could make people do what she wanted by using her mind. Trackers were trained to use persuasion only when they had absolutely no other choice, since mind control eventually wore off and wouldn't make the changelings trust us more in the long run.

"I told her that she needed to trust me and come with me," Ember explained. "And she did, so I hurried to steal a car before the cops got there."

"You stole a car?" I asked, surprised, though not too much.

In our training to become trackers, we'd been taught how to steal cars, but I'd never actually done it in real life. Breaking human laws was discouraged, but we also knew that at times it was necessary. In order to get the changelings away from their family, we needed to avoid the police as much as possible, so we didn't end up in jail or have humans snooping around our business as trolls.

That's why we tried not to break laws, so we wouldn't attract unwanted attention from authorities. But sometimes, like in Ember's case, the only way to keep the changeling safe was to break the law.

"My options were pretty limited at that point," Ember said. "I had to get Charlotte out of there. I drove for, like, eight hours, then I stopped to get my arm in a sling and clean myself up, and then Charlotte insisted that we buy luggage and new clothes, which I obliged because I did whatever I could to get her here. Then we caught the train two towns over. I don't know if Konstantin followed us, but I doubt it."

"If he didn't go after you on the train, I'd say you got away safe. He has no reason to follow you here, because he knows where Doldastam is and that the Högdragen are waiting for him here," I said, thinking about what I would do to Konstantin if he set foot behind these walls again.

"I hope so." Ember sat in silence for a moment, then she turned to look at me. "I'm sorry I let Konstantin get away."

"No, there's no reason for you to be sorry." I smiled at her. "You got Charlotte out of there safe and sound, and you kept yourself alive. That's what really matters."

As I pulled up in front of Ember's cottage, she smiled wanly back at me. I got out of the Land Rover and then went around to help her. The goats were bleating loudly in the pasture next to the house, and I looked over to see Ember's mother, Annali, coming out of the pen. The bottom of her long dress was dark from melting snow and mud, and a few pieces of straw were stuck to her dark hair.

"Ember?" Annali asked, her words tight with panic, and she rushed over to us. "What happened? Has the medic seen you yet?" She touched her daughter's injured cheek, causing Ember to flinch a little.

The few medics in Doldastam weren't the same as you'd find in human society. They had medical training, so they could set bones, stitch up wounds, and even perform surgeries. But they'd been recruited from the Trylle tribe for a very specific reason—they were healers. Thanks to the Trylle's psychokinetic abilities, with a simple touch of their hands they could heal many minor biological ailments.

"I just got back. I haven't called yet," Ember said.

"Come in the house." Annali motioned frantically toward the house. "I'll call the medic."

She tried to help Ember into the house, but in her fear and frustration, she didn't seem to realize how rough she was being, so I told her to call the medic while I helped get Ember inside. As I got Ember settled on the worn sofa, her mother talked on the phone in the other room, speaking in irritated, clipped tones.

"You can head out if you want," Ember told me in a hushed voice after I draped a blanket over her.

"Nah, I can stay." I glanced over toward the kitchen, where Annali was continuing to swear at the poor person on the other end of the line. "I'd feel kinda bad leaving you alone with her."

"She means well, and she'll calm down." Ember moved the pillow behind her head. "I should probably get some rest anyway."

"I understand." I touched her leg. "Take care of yourself, and let me know if you need anything."

Ember nodded.

I went through the kitchen quietly, not wanting Annali to direct any of her anger at me, and I'd almost made it to the door when Ember stopped me. "Wait. Bryn."

"Yeah?" I turned to her, and she motioned for me to come closer. I went back to the couch, and sat down at the end, next to her feet.

"I was debating on telling you this, but . . ." Ember said so softly I could hardly hear her above her mother, "I think I should."

"What are you talking about?" I asked.

"When I was trying to get Charlotte, I knocked Konstantin to the ground. He got up slowly, and then we heard the sirens." Ember licked her lips. "He didn't leave right away, though. He said something to me, and then he took off."

"What did he say?"

She took a fortifying breath. "He said, 'Run along home, and tell that white rabbit to watch out.'"

"White rabbit?" I echoed. My blood was already pounding so hard in my ears I could barely hear my own voice, but I already knew exactly who Konstantin was talking about.

Ember's eyes were so dark and so solemn, they seemed to pull in all the light around them, like tiny black holes. "He means you, Bryn."

partnership

The number of people crammed into such a small space left it feeling stifling and humid, and everyone's voices blended together in one low, uncomfortable grumble. It was the same meeting room I had been in a couple days before, when I'd been having brunch with my distant Skojare relatives, but now all the tables had been pushed out and replaced with rows and rows of chairs.

I'd arrived ten minutes before the meeting was set to start, and it was already at standing room only. Somehow Tilda had managed to get a seat in the second row, and she offered me an apologetic smile when I came in, since she'd been unable to save me a seat.

Kasper Abbott stood at the side of the room, along with several members of the Högdragen. I wasn't sure if he'd gotten here too late to sit with his girlfriend, or if he'd just chosen to stand with the guards instead. But every tracker in Doldastam, including some of the senior class that hadn't graduated yet, was here, along with about a quarter of the Högdragen. Aside from Ember, who was still at home recuperating.

Ridley was already here, standing in the front of the room talking to a few trackers. He glanced up at me as I found a place in the back of the room, and I gave him a small smile, which he returned briefly before going back to his conversation. I hadn't talked to him since I'd kicked him out this morning, but we were both professionals, so I was determined to act normally around him. At least in situations like this.

I leaned against the wall while I waited for the meeting to get under way. It wasn't that much longer before my dad came in the side door. His head was down as he flipped through a huge stack of papers, so he bumped into a few people as he made his way to the front of the room.

"Ahem." Dad cleared his throat, still not looking up from his papers, and everybody kept on whispering and muttering, ignoring him. His normally clean-shaven chin was covered in salt-and-pepper stubble that he rubbed absently when he looked up at the room. "Excuse me."

With my arms folded over my chest, I glanced around the room, but not a single person had stopped talking. I tried to give my dad a look, encouraging him to speak louder, but he wasn't looking at me.

"If I could, uh, have your attention," Dad said, and I could barely even hear him at the back of the room.

"Hey!" Ridley shouted and clapped his hands together. He grabbed a chair, stealing it from a tracker in the front row, and then he climbed up on it. "Everyone. Shut up. The Chancellor needs to speak to you."

The room finally fell silent, and my dad gave him a smile. "Thank you."

Ridley hopped down off the chair, then offered the chair to my dad. "The floor is yours, sir."

"Thank you," Dad repeated, and with some trepidation, he climbed up onto the chair. "I want to thank you all for coming out for this. I know it was short notice." He smiled grimly. "We've got a lot of great trackers here, and even some of the Högdragen. So thank you.

"Let's get right into it, then." Dad held his papers at his waist and surveyed the room. "We have reason to believe that our changelings are under attack. Last week, Konstantin Black and an Omte associate of his, Bent Stum, went after Linus Berling."

Murmurs filled the room, and I could hear Konstantin's name in the air. Dad held up his hand to silence them, and reluctantly they complied.

"As most of you know, Konstantin Black is considered a traitor for crimes against the King and Queen, and, um, the Chancellor, specifically." He lowered his eyes for a moment, but quickly composed himself. "He's been on the run for the past four years, and we're not exactly sure what he wants with the changelings, but this no longer appears to be an isolated incident.

"Yesterday, Konstantin Black and Bent Stum attempted to take another one of our changelings," Dad went on. "He assaulted a tracker, but thankfully, both she and the changeling weren't seriously injured and made it back to Doldastam."

"You think he's going after other changelings?" someone in the audience shouted.

"Yes, that's exactly what we fear," Dad said. "There've been two incidents with Konstantin Black in the past seven days. We don't want a third. Which is why we've called you all here."

"Are we going after Konstantin?" Kasper asked, and I straightened up.

"We don't know where he is, or where he's going to strike next, so that doesn't seem prudent," Dad did his best to explain. "We're going after the changelings."

Everyone erupted in protests, saying how it wasn't possible or how it would ruin our economy. With over five hundred changelings between the ages of four months and twenty years old out in the field, we didn't have the manpower to bring back every changeling, and it would cripple our finances if we did. Not to mention that a lot of the changelings were still just kids, many under the age of ten. The American and Canadian police would have a field day if we kidnapped hundreds of children.

"Calm down!" Ridley shouted. "We have a plan, and before you guys get your panties in a bunch, you should at least listen to what it is, don't you think?"

"Konstantin's attacks haven't been random," Dad elaborated, once the room quieted down again. "The first changeling he went after was Linus Berling, who as you all know is next in line for the throne if the King doesn't produce an heir. The one he targeted yesterday was Charlotte Salin, who is right behind Linus in line for the throne.

"He's going after royalty," Dad concluded.

"But how is he getting this information?" Tilda asked, speaking for the first time since the meeting had started. "It's classified. Almost no one has access to it."

"We're not sure, but we're investigating," Dad assured her.

"As soon as we find the leak, we'll be able to find Konstantin and put a stop to this," Ridley added.

"But until then, we need to keep ourselves protected," Dad said. "That means more protection here in Doldastam, which is where the Högdragen come in. Linus Berling and Charlotte Salin need extra guards on them. The front gate needs to be locked at all times, and we need to instate a patrol to go around the wall. Doldastam must be impenetrable.

"As for the rest of the trackers, you'll be going out to get our more elite changelings that are coming of age. We think that's who Konstantin will target next, and we want you to get to them before he does." Dad pulled out his papers, looking down at them. "I've got all the placements right here. When I call your name, come up and get your file, and then you're to leave as soon as you're able.

"Tilda Moller and Simon Bohlin, you'll be paired together," Dad began.

"Paired together?" Tilda asked as she stood up.

"Oh, yes, after the incidents, we thought it would be best for the trackers to be paired up," Dad explained. "Both for your safety and for the changelings'."

"But what if we don't need to be paired up?" I protested, and Tilda gave me a look as she made her way to the front of the room.

"Everyone is paired up. No exceptions," Dad told me without looking up.

"But we're wasting resources," I insisted. "We only have so many trackers. If we pair up, then you're cutting our number in half. If we went on our own, we could get twice as many changelings."

"Or twice as many of you could end up dead." Dad pursed his lips and finally looked at me. "The King and Queen made the call, and the decision is final."

"I'm just saying—" I began.

"Bryn Aven, why don't you come up here and get your placement?" Dad asked. "That would probably make the rest of this meeting go much faster."

I groaned inwardly, but I went up to the front of the room, carefully maneuvering around trackers and guards. People had begun whispering and talking among themselves again, but they kept their voices low so they'd be able to hear my dad call their names.

"Where's my file?" I asked when I reached my dad.

"I already gave it to your partner." Dad motioned to Ridley, standing beside him, holding a manila file.

"You're retired," I protested.

"I came out of retirement for one last job," Ridley told me. "This is an important mission, and they needed the best."

"And that's me and you?" I asked.

Smiling down at me, he said, "I don't see anybody better here. Do you?"

TWENTY

enemies

The train ride to Calgary was long, and that should've been a good thing, since it gave me more time to go over the changeling's file. As soon as we'd been assigned, Ridley and I had gone to our respective homes, packed up our things, and within twenty minutes we were on the road out of town. I'd glanced over the file long enough to see where we were headed, noting that there would be a lot of downtime as we passed through the Canadian landscape.

That also meant there was plenty of time to have awkward conversations with Ridley. I hadn't spent this much time alone with him in . . . well, in *ever*, actually, since we'd be together for at least a few days on this mission.

This was coming right after we'd spent the night together—platonically, sort of. And right after I'd realized my feelings for him, feelings I was trying to will away or at the very least pretend didn't exist. Which was much harder to do when he was sitting right next to me, his arm brushing up against mine as I leafed through the file.

The cover page had all her basic information on it.

NAME: Emma Lisa Costar (*Jones*)
PARENTS: Markis Guy Costar and Marksinna Elsa
  Costar, née Berling
HOST FAMILY: Benjamin and Margaret Jones
BIRTH DATE: February 26, 1999
HAIR COLOR: Brown
EYE COLOR: Brown
LAST KNOWN ADDRESS: 1117 Royal Lane SW,
  Calgary, AB T2T 0L7

Paper-clipped to the top were two photos—a baby picture taken right after Emma was born, before she was switched at birth, and a composite photo of what Emma might look like now, based on her baby picture and her parents. I always thought the composite photos looked more than a bit creepy, but they had helped me find changelings in the past.

According to her birthday, Emma was just barely fifteen, but in the composite picture of her, she appeared younger. Her cheeks were still chubby, her eyes wide, her dark hair falling in ringlets around her face.

The packet of pages behind that had all kinds of information about her biological family, in hopes that it would shed some light on what she might be like, as well as information about her host family, to make it easier to find her.

I barely glanced through the packet, though, because I already knew a great deal about her family. Her mother—Elsa Costar—was Dylan Berling's sister, making her Linus's aunt and a cousin to the King. If something were to happen to Linus, when Emma returned from Calgary in a few years according to the original schedule, she would be next in line for the throne. Charlotte Salin—the changeling Ember had just rescued—was only next because she had come of age, and Emma Costar hadn't yet returned to Doldastam.

We kept very rough tabs on changelings while they were gone, since in general the Kanin liked to interact with humans as little as possible. That meant that, rarely, changelings would move or go missing, and we couldn't find them. On other tragic occasions, the changelings died while in the care of their host families, usually due to accident or illness.

The horrible truth was that we had no real way of knowing what was happening to changelings when they were with their host families. Most of the time it was nothing notable—their host parents generally loved and raised them like their own. But right now, when Konstantin Black was on the loose and going after changelings, it was a little scary not knowing where exactly Emma Costar was or if she was safe.

"Anything good there?" Ridley asked.

He sat low in the chair next to me, one of his legs crossed over the other, making his knee bump into mine every time he shifted. His head rested back against the seat, and his eyes were barely open, hooded in dark lashes so I wasn't sure if he even saw anything at all. In his hand he had a small lock of Emma's hair, taken from her when she was a baby and tied with a thin pink ribbon.

"Just the usual stuff," I said with a sigh and tried not to stare at Emma's hair as he twirled it between his fingers.

The Costars hadn't taken Emma's hair in a gesture of affection. It was a tool, an aid in helping trackers find her later. By touching something personal, most trackers had the ability to imprint on a changeling. Ridley couldn't read her mind, but he'd be able to feel if she was terrified or in pain—extreme emotions that meant that she was in trouble and needed our help.

This also turned the changeling into kind of a tracking beacon. If Ridley focused on her, we'd be able to find her. I wasn't sure exactly how it worked, but Ember had explained it as feeling a pull inside of you, like a tug from an invisible electrical current warming you from within and telling you which way to go, and the closer you got to the changeling, the stronger the feeling would get.

Ember had that ability, so did Ridley and Tilda and almost all the other trackers I worked with, as did their parents, and their parents before them. A Kanin's supernatural abilities were passed down through blood, and naturally the trackers were the ones who carried the tracking gift. Since my parents weren't trackers—my mother came from a tribe that didn't even have trackers of any kind—I was born without it.

That was one of the reasons it had been harder for me to become a tracker. I suffered a major handicap compared to everyone else, but I worked twice as hard to compensate for it.

Instinct, intuition, and sheer force of will seemed to make up for my lack of blood-borne talent.

"Are you getting a read on her?" I asked Ridley.

He shook his head. "Not yet, but we're still kinda far away."

"When we get to Calgary, we should go to her house straight off and scope it out." I closed the file and settled back in my seat. Ridley moved his arm so it rested against mine, but I let it. "We can check into the hotel after, but we should get a read on her, at least, make sure she's safe, and then we should come up with the best plan to interact with her.

"Obviously, since I'm younger than you and don't look like a thirty-year-old creeper, I should be the one to make contact," I continued, thinking aloud. "It's going to be a bit trickier, since she's younger than most changelings, but maybe that will work to our advantage. Younger kids tend to be more trusting."

"I have done this before." Ridley looked down at me, a wry smirk on his lips. "Believe it or not, I do know a few things about tracking."

"I know." I met his playful gaze with a knowing one. "I'm just coming up with a course of action." I moved my arm away from his. "I'm not used to working with someone."

"Neither am I, but I think we make a good team. We'll be fine." He reached out, putting his hand on my leg, but only for a second before taking it back.

"I don't know." I looked away, remembering the ominous warning Ember had given me this morning. "Konstantin seems out for blood."

"There's two of us, and we're both strong fighters. Hell, I'm an amazing fighter." Ridley tried to make a joke of it, but I wasn't having any of it, so his smile fell away. "If you could handle him by yourself, there's no reason to think that we can't handle him together."

"Except this time he's escalating," I reminded him. Ember had filled out a report and told Ridley in even greater detail about her fight with Konstantin and Bent, so he knew about Konstantin's blatant disregard for everything when he stole Charlotte from her bedroom.

"But we're prepared for it," Ridley countered.

"I still can't believe you're out in the field for this mission," I said, eager to change the subject from Konstantin and the sense of impending doom he filled me with. "Isn't it, like, illegal to un-retire?"

"No, we just don't often un-retire, as you so eloquently put it, because there's a reason we retired in the first place. For me, it was because my boyish good looks had given way to the ruggedly handsome features of a man, and for some reason teenagers find it creepy when grown men hang around high schools."

"Teenagers can be so unfair," I said with faux-disbelief. "Do you ever miss being in the field?"

He raised one shoulder in a half shrug. "Sometimes, yeah, I do. The one thing that does suck about being the Rektor is being stuck in the same place day in and day out. Don't get me wrong." He turned his head to face me, still resting it against the seat. "I love Doldastam, and I love my job. But it would be nice to see other places, like Hawaii in January."

"Did you ever go to Hawaii?" I asked.

"I didn't. I've tracked changelings to Florida and Texas, and once I went to Japan, which was definitely a trip. Mostly, though, I spent time in Canada," he said, sharing a familiar story. It seemed that only on rare occasions did changelings move someplace far away and exotic after we'd placed them. "What about you? What's the farthest your job has taken you?"

"Alaska. Or New York City." I tried to think. "I'm not sure which is farther away from Doldastam."

"You're young. You've got time. Who knows? Your next mission could be to Australia," Ridley said, attempting to cheer me up.

"Maybe," I said without much conviction. "Other than the lack of travel, you really like your job?"

"Yeah. The paperwork can be a bit much, but it's a good job. Why?" He stared down at me. "You sound skeptical."

"I don't know. Just . . ." I paused, trying to think of how to phrase my question before deciding to just dive right into it. "Why didn't you become a Högdragen?"

He lowered his eyes, staring down at his lap. The corners of his mouth twisted into a bitter smile, and it was several long moments before he finally answered. "You know why."

"No, I don't." I turned in my seat, folding my leg underneath me so I could face him fully. I could let it go, and part of me thought I should, but I didn't really understand why. So I pressed on.

"Because my dad was on the Högdragen, and he got killed for it," he replied wearily, still staring down at his lap.

"But . . ." I exhaled and shook my head. "I mean, I'm sorry for your loss."

Ridley waved it off. "It was fifteen years ago."

"Your dad died a hero," I said, as if that would offer some comfort. "He saved the kingdom. He died an honorable death."

"He did." Ridley lifted his head and nodded. "But he's still dead. My mom's still a widow. I still had to grow up without him. Gone is still gone."

"So what?" I asked. "You're afraid of dying?"

"No. Come on, Bryn." He turned to me, smiling in a way that made my skin flush for a moment. "You know me better than that. I'm no coward."

"No, I never said you were," I said, hurrying to take it back. "I didn't mean it like that."

"I know." He held up his hand, stopping my apologies. Then he let out a deep breath and looked away from me, staring out the window at the trees and lakes that the train raced past. "You know why my dad died?"

"Viktor Dålig killed him trying to overthrow the King," I said.

He laughed darkly. "No, my dad died because Elliot Strinne was a slut."

I shook my head, not understanding. "What are you talking about?"

"Elliot Strinne became King at a young age, and he thought he had all the time in the world to get married and have babies," Ridley explained. "So he decided to sleep with as many eligible young ladies as he could, and that meant when he suddenly fell ill and died of a rare fungal infection at the age of twenty-six, he had no direct heirs. The crown was up for grabs."

Ridley was telling me things I already knew, giving me a refresher of history lessons I'd learned in school. But he was doing it with a decidedly different twist, a bit of snark mixed with sorrow, so I let him.

"Viktor Dålig thought his young daughter should've been Queen, even though she couldn't have been more than ten at the time," he went on. "His wife was Elliot's sister, and she would've been Queen, if she hadn't died years before.

"All these freak accidents fell into place." He stopped for a second, staring off and letting his own words sink in with him. "There should've been a reasonable heir. But there wasn't.

"It was between the child Karmin Dålig, and Elliot's twenty-three-year-old cousin Evert, and the Chancellor had to make a call."

"It made sense," I said when Ridley fell silent for a minute. "It was a logical decision for an adult to be the monarch rather than a child."

"I'm not arguing about whether it was fair or just, because honestly, I don't care." Ridley shrugged. "All that mattered was that Viktor Dålig threw a fit because he felt like his daughter was being passed over."

"Then your dad, and other members of the Högdragen, stood up to him and his friends when they tried to throw a coup," I reminded Ridley.

"Viktor and his friends tried to assassinate a King arbitrarily placed there." Ridley gestured as he spoke, getting more animated the louder his voice got. "The Chancellor could've chosen Karmin Dålig just as easily as he had chosen Evert Strinne. But he didn't. And if Elliot had just gotten married and had a child, the way a King is supposed to, my father wouldn't be dead."

He shook his head, and when he spoke again, his voice was much lower and calmer. "You called his death honorable. He died in the hallway of the palace—a hall I have walked down a hundred times since that day. He died in a pool of his own blood, trying to protect a random stranger in a crown, because another man wanted that crown for his own daughter." He turned to me, his eyes hard and his words heavy. "He died for nothing."

"If you really believe that, how can you do any of the things you do?" I asked. "How can you stay in Doldastam, working for a King and for royals you despise?"

"I don't despise them, and I don't mind working for them. I *like* my job," he insisted. "I just refuse to lay down my life for something that doesn't matter."

"The crown may seem arbitrary to you, and to a point, it is. But for better or worse, our society works because it's a monarchy. Because of the King," I told him emphatically. "And you may think your father died for some jewels wrapped in metal, but he died protecting the kingdom, protecting you and me and everyone in it. And I'm sorry you don't see it that way."

"Yeah. I am too," he admitted.

"Maybe you shouldn't go on this mission," I said softly.

Ridley looked at me sharply. "Why?"

"There's a very good chance that Konstantin Black is going to try to kill Emma, or me, or you, or all of us." I tried to speak without accusation, because I wasn't mad at him and didn't think less of him. I'd just begun to fear that his heart wasn't in this, and that could result in somebody getting hurt. "I wouldn't want you to risk your life for something that you don't care about."

"Emma is an innocent girl. I won't let him hurt her, and there is no way I'd stand by and let you face Konstantin alone." Ridley reached over, taking my hand in his, and the intensity in his eyes made it hard for me to breathe. "I already told you that I'm in this with you."

distance

The house looked like it came straight from a fairy tale. It was a majestic Victorian mansion surrounded by a wrought-iron fence. Trees surrounded the property, all fresh and green thanks to the early warmth of spring, and a few of them had white and pink blossoms. Amid the bustle of a downtown metropolis, this was a slice of another world.

Since we planned on sneaking in, we wouldn't be going in through the front gate, which left us scoping it out near the back. Through the fence and the trees, I could barely see the end of the long, curved driveway, which seemed oddly crowded, with several cars parked in it. I leaned against the fence, trying to get a better look, but Ridley spoke, so I turned back to face him.

"She's not home," Ridley said matter-of-factly.

He stood a few feet behind me, the collar of his thin jacket popped to ward off the icy chill in the air. The wind came up, ruffling his hair. It was so rare to see his thick, wavy hair unstyled, and I realized that it was getting long.

After traveling all night to get here and sleeping on the train, neither of us had had a chance to shower yet, and Ridley hadn't shaved. We'd rented a car, parked it two blocks away from Emma Costar's house, then walked down to stake it out.

"Can you sense her?" I asked.

Ridley stared up at her house with one hand in his pocket, where he kept her lock of hair. His lips were parted just slightly, and his eyes darkened in concentration, then he shook his head once.

"No," he said finally, his voice nearly lost in the wind. "But it's ten in the morning. She should be at school."

"So you're still not getting anything on her?"

"Not yet." He glanced away from me, watching a car that sped by. "I'm probably not close enough. Or maybe it's just harder because I'm out of practice." He turned back to me, trying to give me a reassuring grin, but it faltered. "I haven't really done this in four years."

"Well, we should figure out which school she's in," I suggested.

"The file had listed two or three private schools in the area they thought she might be in," Ridley said. "Why don't we check into the hotel, then grab something to eat and start making a plan to get to her?"

"I need to get to a school, so I can get to know her."

"No offense, Bryn, but I don't think enrollment is gonna be

an option this time." Ridley smirked at me. "You can pass for seventeen, sure, but I sincerely doubt that anyone would take you for grade nine, and that's what grade Emma's in. We're gonna have to approach this a different way."

"Do you wanna break into her house?" I suggested. "Check out her room, see if we can find anything on her?"

He seemed to consider this, staring at her house with a furrow in his brow. "No. It just doesn't . . . feel right."

"What do you mean? Is this her house?" I asked.

"I don't know." He sighed. "Maybe. Let's just get out of here and regroup."

Ridley started to walk backward, away from me and away from the house. I stayed behind a few beats, glancing back at the house. He paused, waiting, so reluctantly I went after him. As we walked the few blocks down to our car, a police car sped by with its lights off, and Ridley regarded it warily.

We reached our hotel and checked in quickly, and Ridley spoke little. When I tried to press him about what was going on, he just said that he needed to get something to eat, and then hopefully he could think more clearly.

The diner we stopped at had an expansive organic vegan menu, which was nice and gave Ridley plenty of options to pig out if that would help him. I'd grabbed Emma's file, and I spread it open on the table beside me, leafing through it as I picked absently at a salad. When I glanced over at him, Ridley had his head bowed over his sandwich, his fingers in his thick hair.

"I still think it wouldn't be a bad idea to check out her school," I said.

He sighed. "We just need to find her and get out of here."

"What is going on with you?" I closed the file and rested my elbows on the table, so I could lean in closer to him. "You've been acting strange ever since we got here. Are you just freaking out 'cause you can't sense her? It's not a big deal, and we can still find—"

"It's not that I *can't* sense her," Ridley quietly interrupted me, staring emptily at his plate. "It's that it feels like there's nothing to sense." He looked at me then, the fear in his eyes conveying the gravity of the situation. "She just feels . . . cold."

"What does that mean?" I asked.

"I don't know," he admitted. "I've never felt anything like this before. But it can't be good."

"So . . ." I tried to take in what he was saying. "What do you want to do?"

"I think we should do an Internet search to make sure that's her house. I know her file says that's her last known address, but I'm not completely sure when that was updated," Ridley said. "And then we go to her house, and we wait there until she comes home—*if* she comes home—and as soon as she does, we basically grab her and get out of here."

I glanced around, making sure nobody was nearby, and when I whispered, my words were nearly drowned out by the Laura DiStasi song playing on the diner's stereo. "You want to kidnap her?"

"If we have to, yeah," he said without remorse. "Something bad's going on."

I leaned back in my chair, considering his idea, and then I nodded. "Okay. If it's what you think we should do, then let's do it."

He pulled out his smartphone and took the file from me, double-checking the spelling of the host family's name and the address. I dug into my pocket to pull out my wallet so we could pay for our lunch and then get out of here.

"Shit," Ridley said, and his whole body sagged. Under the dark stubble on his cheeks, his face had gone ashen.

"What?"

Instead of answering, he turned and held his phone out toward me, so I could see the ominous headline that had shown up during his search for Emma's address.

Emma Jones, Teenage Daughter of Software Mogul Benjamin Jones, Was Found Missing from Her Bedroom

I scanned the article below, and it went on to say that based on the ransacked state of her room, the authorities suspected foul play, and they were reaching out to the public to see if anyone knew anything about where Emma might be. Worse still, her family said Emma had only been gone since the early morning.

My heart dropped to my stomach. "We missed her by a few hours."

Amanda Hocking

"Then maybe we haven't missed her." Ridley shoved his phone back in his pocket and stood up in a flash.

I threw a couple bills on the table, then pulled on my jacket as I hurried after Ridley. An icy drizzle had begun outside, but Ridley hardly seemed to notice.

"We should split up," I suggested. "We can cover more ground that way."

"Good. That's smart. I'll go back to her house, see if I can get a better sense of where she might be. You should go back to the hotel."

"The hotel? Why?"

"You should get on your laptop, check out her Facebook, Tumblr, et cetera, see if her friends know anything and what people are saying online. You can also figure out what school she's at, and then you can go down and talk to them."

"All right," I agreed reluctantly.

"If I can't find anything at her house, I'll head down to the police station. I might get them to tell me something."

That wouldn't have sounded likely except that Ridley had mild persuasion. He only used it for tracking, and usually on people like host families or school officials. Or in this case he could get a police officer to tell us everything they knew about a missing girl.

I didn't like being stuck on desk duty, but it might give us a clue to what happened to her. If Konstantin Black was trailing her, her friends might have noticed, or Emma might have said something to someone.

She might have even left with Konstantin willingly—before

he'd been on the Högdragen, he'd been a tracker just like Ridley and me, and he was just as capable of talking a changeling into leaving with him as we were. And if he had done that, maybe Emma had told someone about it or where she was going.

That didn't seem likely, especially given how aggressive Konstantin and Bent had gotten with Ember and Charlotte, and given the alleged state of Emma's room. But at this point we couldn't rule anything out, and we had to work as quickly as possible to find Emma.

Ridley and I went our separate ways, and I jogged back to the hotel, holding my jacket up over my head to keep out the rain. By the time I reached the lobby, my jeans were soaked through, and the front of my shirt was damp and sticking to me.

The hotel was cool and modern, with complimentary bottled water and tea in the lobby and hipsters lounging around playing on their tablets in slick chairs and art deco sofas. We'd chosen it because of its proximity to Emma's house, and the clash between our one-bedroom suite and my loft in Doldastam was staggering.

The view of downtown Calgary from the windows was amazing, but the shades were drawn when I came in, leaving the room in relative darkness. I tossed off my soaking jacket, and then I stumbled over an ottoman in the sitting room. Ridley had offered to take the pull-out sofa, so my things were in the bedroom, and I went into it to retrieve my laptop.

If I hadn't been so distracted, hurrying in my worry that something bad had happened to Emma, I would've noticed that things weren't right—that the shades had been open forty minutes ago when we'd dropped off our things but were closed now, and that the ottoman was now out of place, rather strategically placed in front of the bedroom doorway.

I doubt I could've seen him, though—his skin had changed color, blending in with his surroundings perfectly. But if I weren't distracted I definitely would've heard footsteps behind me as I was bent over the bed, digging through my duffel bag. And I'd like to believe that I would've felt the presence of someone standing behind me.

But I didn't. Not until I felt a strong hand covering my mouth, pulling me straight back against him, and a sharp cold blade pressed to my throat.

"Don't make a sound," Konstantin said into my ear, whispering like we were lovers.

TWENTY-TWO

culpability

I stood frozen against him. I could feel the hard contours of his chest pressed against my back, warming me through my wet shirt, and I tried to slow the rapid beating of my heart so he wouldn't feel it. The whiskers from his beard tickled against my cheek and neck, and the skin of his hand felt rough on my lips. He smelled of cold, like ice and snow on the harshest days of winter.

"I know you're devising all kinds of ways that you can kill me," Konstantin murmured in my ear. "But I want to warn you that it won't do you any good."

I went limp in his arms. The blade scraped against my neck, but it didn't slice anything open. He removed his hand from my mouth to wrap around my waist, catching me before I slipped to the floor, and now the knife was aimed at the tender skin under my chin. It would hurt if he sliced across, but it certainly wouldn't lead to death.

In one quick move, I stood back up and thrust my head backward, head-butting him. He groaned, and I grabbed his wrist, twisting it sharply until he released the knife. His arm was still around me, and he squeezed tighter. I leaned forward and, pulling on his arm, I flipped him forward, and he landed on the bed on his back.

The knife was on the floor, so I grabbed it, and then I jumped on top of him. I straddled him and pressed the knife to his throat. His lip was bleeding from when I'd hit him, but he still managed to grin broadly up at me.

"You can't kill me," Konstantin said. "I'm the only one who knows where Emma Costar is."

"How did you find her?" I demanded. "What do you want with her?"

His smile fell away, and his steel eyes looked pained. "I'm afraid that I want nothing with her anymore."

"What do you mean?"

"Did you ever read *Of Mice and Men*?" Konstantin asked. "Bent has always reminded me of Lennie. He even talks about rabbits all the time, but I blame that on his fascination with the Kanin."

"I have a knife to your throat, and I'd like nothing more than to see you dead," I told him, and I pressed the blade harder against his flesh, breaking the skin just slightly. "So you should really answer my questions."

"I will. But maybe you should ask yourself a question first," Konstantin said. "Like, where is my companion? I don't usually work alone."

I lifted my head, taking my eyes off Konstantin only for a moment, and I expected to see Bent lurking in the shadows somewhere. But there was nothing, and that moment of distraction was all Konstantin needed.

He grabbed my shoulders and flipped me over so I was lying on my back on the bed, and he rolled on top of me. He grabbed my wrists, pinning them against the white comforter. My legs were trapped underneath him, and when I fought against his grip, he didn't budge.

"What do you want?" I asked, staring up at him in the dim light of the bedroom. "Why were you here waiting for me? If you have Emma, what's the point?"

"I remember you." Konstantin's eyes were searching mine, and they seemed to soften. "I'm sorry I didn't right away, but I remembered you as soon as you punched me in the stomach in Chicago. You were the plucky tracker, trying to claw your way up to be a guard. Nobody wanted you there, but you didn't care. *You* wanted to be there."

My heart pounded in my chest, and I swallowed back my anger, which was easier since he'd thrown me off my guard by remembering far more about me than I'd thought he'd ever known.

"How did you . . ." I narrowed my eyes at him. "How would you even know that? You didn't know who I was."

"Of course I did. You were that little blond girl, and that alone made you stand out, but you were always fighting twice as hard as anybody else." He paused, grinning down at me. "And I'd always catch you staring at me."

"You were on the guard," I replied coolly. "I was watching the Högdragen."

"No, you were watching *me*. You looked at me like . . . like I could do no wrong." Konstantin sounded wistful.

"I was young and stupid." I looked away.

"I'm sorry," Konstantin said softly. "For what happened with your father."

I snapped my head back to glare up at him. "What happened with my father? You tried to kill him," I snarled, and I tried to fight him off, but he had me pinned.

"Bryn!" Konstantin was calm and firm. "Stop fighting."

"What do you want with me?" I shouted. "If you're gonna kill me, then just kill me."

"I'm not gonna kill you," Konstantin said with an annoyed sigh. "I want you to . . ." He hung his head for a moment.

"Do you even know what you want with me?" I asked.

"I'm trying to protect you!" he yelled in exasperation.

I laughed darkly. "*Protect* me? Why in hell would you do that? I want to kill you, and you want to kill me. You even told Ember you're coming after me."

"What? I never told anyone I was coming after you."

"You told her to 'tell that white rabbit to watch out,'" I said, repeating what Ember had told me.

"That wasn't a threat." He shook his head. "I was warning you. You need to stop this."

"Stop what?" I asked, incredulous.

"Dammit," he muttered.

Konstantin pulled the knife from my grip, then he let go of

me. I stayed where I was, lying on my back on the bed, because I wanted to get a read on what was happening before I made a move. He sat on the edge of the bed, his back to me with the knife in his hand, and he ran a hand through his dark tangles of hair.

"I feel terrible about what happened with your father. And now everything that's happening here." He shook his head. "I made a choice a long time ago, and I'm still trying to make things right." He looked back at me over his shoulder. "But things are in motion, and there's going to be a lot of casualties, and I don't want you to be one of them."

"Why?" I asked in disbelief. I moved so I was sitting on my knees. "Why would you even care what happens to me?"

"Because you saw good in me that wasn't there." He turned away and stood up. "Forget about me. Forget about everything here. Just go back to Doldastam . . . No, don't go there. Just go. Forget about the Kanin and everything."

"I'm not forgetting about my family or friends or my people," I told him. "I can't just run off, like you did. And I'm not leaving without Emma Costar."

He rubbed his forehead. "It's better for you if you leave without her."

"Where is she, Konstantin?" I asked.

"Bent just doesn't know his own strength," Konstantin replied, almost sadly.

"What happened to her? If you hurt her, I'll—"

He groaned. "This was going so well. Can we stop with the threats?"

Amanda Hocking

"Not if you won't tell me where she is."

"I don't know where he left her, but it won't do you any good to find her," Konstantin said in a way that made my blood run cold.

"You killed her," I said, my voice trembling with barely contained rage. "You son of a bitch."

I dove at him and punched him in the face, and I think he let me at first, allowing me to hit him in the face and chest a few times before he tried to grab my wrists. Then I kicked him in the stomach, and he grabbed me and twisted my arm behind my back. I tried to buck him off, but he pushed me forward, slamming me against the wall.

"Let me go," I growled, but I was trapped between him and the wall.

"Stop, Bryn. I can't undo what's already been done."

"I'm going to kill you," I warned him.

"I'm trying to make things right. I know you don't believe me, but I'm trying." His words were low and filled with regret, and his beard brushed against my cheek. He let go of my arm, and I pressed my palms against the wall, but I didn't turn around. I didn't fight him. "I know you have no reason to trust me, but please, trust me on this."

I closed my eyes, wishing I didn't trust him, but I did. I didn't know why. Maybe it was the sincerity in his voice, or the fact that he could kill me but didn't, or maybe it was just the memory of the good I thought I'd seen in him when I was younger.

His breath felt warm and ragged on my cheek, and his hand was on my arm. He didn't have me pinned, exactly, but his body was pressed against me, holding me in place. I could push him off, but I didn't.

"I can't let you go," I told him.

"I can't let you follow me," he said softly.

I looked back at him over my shoulder. The curtain had been pulled back a bit in our struggle, and the light landed on his face, so I could clearly see the hurt and regret in his stormy gray eyes.

"I'm sorry, Bryn," he said simply, and before I could ask him why, I felt a sharp pain in the back of my head as he hit me with the butt of the knife, and then everything went black.

commiserate

When I closed my eyes, I still saw her body. On a river-bank, where ice and snow still clung to the earth, even as a cold spring rain fell around us. Her eyes were open, un-blinking as the drops of water fell into them. She was fifteen, but with her full cheeks and tangles in her curly hair, she looked younger.

Her face stared upward, but her body had been turned at an unnatural angle—her neck had been snapped. The pajamas—pink shorts and a long-sleeve top with hearts and flowers—had been torn, and her knees were scraped.

Emma Costar had put up a fight, and despite Konstantin's proclamations that he was sorry and he was making things right, this young girl had been killed and left on a cold riverbank.

Ridley had come back to the hotel later in the afternoon and found me unconscious on the bed, where Konstantin had left me. I told him that Konstantin had implied that she was dead, and Ridley had redoubled his efforts to track her. He'd gotten a sweater from her bedroom—using his persuasion to get a detective to hand it off to him. Using something recently worn by her, he'd finally been able to get a stronger sense of her.

She hadn't been dead long, and that was the only reason he'd been able to get a read on her at all. We'd finally found her along the riverbank, and I'd wanted to carry her away or cover her up, but Ridley had made me leave her just as we'd found her. He called and left an anonymous tip to the police, and soon her host family would be able to bury her.

Her real parents would get nothing. As soon as we got back to Doldastam, we went to make the notification. They seemed to know as soon as they saw us, Emma's mother collapsing into sobs as her husband struggled to hold her up. We told them everything we knew, and promised that we would bring Konstantin Black and Bent Stum to justice. I wasn't sure if they believed us, or even if they cared.

They hadn't raised her, but they still loved her. They still dreamed of the day when she would come home and their family would be united again. But now that day would never come, and they were left mourning something they had never had.

"This has been one long, shitty week," Ridley said, speaking for the first time since we'd left the Costars' house.

Our boots crunched heavily on the cobblestone road. The temperature had dropped sharply, leaving the town frigid and the streets empty and quiet. It was just as well. Neither Ridley nor I were in the mood to run into anyone.

"The last few days have been some of the longest of my life," I agreed wearily.

"I don't know about you, but I could really use a drink." Ridley stopped, and I realized that we'd reached his house. I'd been so lost in my thoughts that I hadn't noticed where we were.

He didn't actually live that far from the Costars, but his cottage was much smaller than the royals' mansions that populated his neighborhood. It was a very short and squat little place made of stone, with a thatched roof. Small round windows in the front gave it the appearance of a face, with the windows for eyes and the door for a mouth.

"I'd rather not drink tonight," I told him.

"Come in anyway." His hair cascaded across his forehead, and dark circles had formed under his eyes. He still hadn't shaved, but that somehow made his face more appealing. Though he looked just as exhausted as I felt, there was a sincerity and yearning in his eyes that I didn't have the strength to deny.

Ridley saw my resistance fading, and he smiled before turning around and opening the door. His cottage was built half in the ground, almost like a rabbit burrow, and that's why it had such a squat look. Only a few feet of it actually sat above the ground, and I had to go down several steps when I went in.

Inside, it was cozy, with a living room attached to a nice little kitchen, and the door was open to his bedroom in the back. As soon as we came in, Ridley kicked off his shoes and peeled off his scarf, then went over to throw a few logs in the fireplace to get the place warmed up.

"Sure I can't interest you in a drink?" Ridley asked when he went into the kitchen.

"I'll pass." I took off my jacket and sat back on his couch before sliding off my own boots.

I'd been inside his cottage a couple times before, but usually only for very brief visits to ask him a question about work. This was my first real social call, and I took the opportunity to really take his place in.

The coffee table was handmade from a tree trunk, made into an uneven rectangle with bark still on the edges. The bookshelf on the far wall was overflowing with books, and next to it he had a very cluttered desk. On the mantel, there was a picture of a grade-school-aged Ridley posing with his father, who was all decked out in his Högdragen uniform.

"Have you ever had to make a notification before?" Ridley came back into the living room, carrying a large glass mug filled to the brim with dark red wine.

"This was my first," I said. "It's the only time I ever came back without a changeling."

He bent down in front of the fireplace, poking a few logs to help get it going. "I've done it once before. It's never any fun."

"This time must be worse."

"Why do you say that?" Ridley sat on the arm of the couch at the far end from me and sipped his wine.

"This time it's kind of our fault."

"It's not our fault," he said, but he stared down at his mug, swirling the liquid around. "We left as soon as we got our assignment, but she was dead by the time we even got to Calgary. There was nothing we could've done."

"No, there's nothing more *you* could've done," I corrected myself. "But I should've taken care of Konstantin when I saw him in Chicago."

I said that, but I wasn't sure if I meant it anymore. Even after we'd found Emma dead, I felt more conflicted than ever. I didn't know what Konstantin's role had been in her death, and although I was certain he carried some culpability, I also thought things were far more complicated than either Ridley or I had realized.

"What happened with him, exactly?" Ridley asked carefully, giving me a sidelong glance. "Back in the hotel."

I pulled my legs up underneath me, leaning away from him. "I already told you."

"No, you didn't. Not really." He slid down off the arm of the couch so he could face me. "You told me that he'd been in the room, you'd fought, and that he must've knocked you out. That was about it."

"That's about all there is to tell."

"But what I don't understand is, why was he there?" Ridley paused. "Was he waiting for you?"

"I don't know." I ran my hand through my hair.

"Did he hurt you?" he asked with an edge to his voice.

"We fought, and he knocked me out, so yes." I gave him a look. "But other than that, I'm okay, and I got in a few good punches."

"Why didn't he kill you?" Ridley asked. "Don't get me wrong, I'm glad he didn't. But . . . he's tried to kill your dad, he killed

Emma. He obviously doesn't care if he gets blood on his hands, so why did he leave you alive?"

I lowered my eyes. "I think he does care if he gets blood on his hands. And I think Bent killed Emma, not Konstantin."

"Are you . . ." Ridley's expression hardened, and he narrowed his eyes. "Do you have feelings for him?"

I groaned, but my cheeks flushed. "Don't be gross, Ridley."

"There's clearly something going on between the two of you—"

"Why?" I snapped. "Why is there 'clearly something'?"

"Because he should've killed you, and he didn't. And you should've killed him, and you didn't. So something's going on, and I want to know what it is."

"It's not like that." I shook my head.

"Bryn." He set his mug down on the table and moved closer to me. "I'm just trying to understand." He put his hand on my thigh, and I chewed my lip.

"Konstantin Black is a bad man who has done bad things, who will do bad things again," I told him, willing myself to meet his gaze as I spoke. "I know that. But there's something more going on, something much bigger at play."

"I know that you think he's working for someone else, and you're probably right," Ridley said. "But that doesn't mean he deserves your sympathy."

"I'm not sympathetic." I sighed. "At least I don't want to be. But I'm not ready to completely distrust him. Not yet."

"He's done terrible things. He's not to be trusted," Ridley implored me to understand, his eyes dark with concern.

"I know. I will take care of Konstantin. I promise." I put my hand on his, trying to convey that I meant it. "But please, for now, can you not tell anyone that I saw him in Calgary?"

"You want me to lie to the King and Queen?" Ridley asked with exaggerated shock.

"You've done it before," I said with a hopeful smile.

"No, don't look at me like that." He shook his head, then sighed. "Fine. I'll keep this between us. But Bryn, this is a very dangerous game you're playing."

"I know," I admitted, and squeezed his hand. "Thank you for keeping my secret."

"You can always trust me with your secrets," he said with a crooked smile, and the look in his eyes made my heart ache. "You know, that's the real reason I went on this mission."

"What is?" I asked.

"I was afraid you'd run into Konstantin, and I didn't want you to go up against him alone. And then I wasn't even there when you fought with him," he said, and guilt flashed across his face.

"I was fine. I took care of myself," I insisted.

"No, I know." He lowered his eyes for a second, taking a fortifying breath, as if he were building up to something. His hand was still in mine, and he ran his thumb across it. Finally, he lifted his head, meeting my eyes willfully. "On the train, you questioned my commitment to the mission."

"Ridley, I didn't mean it. I know you did everything you could in Calgary—"

He held up his other hand, silencing me. "I know, and I'm

sorry that things didn't work out better for Emma and for you in Calgary, and I'm sorry that we didn't arrive sooner. But I'm still glad I went. For you, I would lay down my life any day."

If he'd leaned in to kiss me then, I would've let him. I would've gladly thrown my arms around his neck and pulled him tighter to me as his lips pressed against mine.

But he didn't. He just stared into my eyes for a moment, filling me with a heat that made me feel light-headed and nervous and wonderful all at once.

Then there was a knock at the door, and he pulled his hand away from me, and the moment was shattered, and I could suddenly breathe again.

As Ridley got up to answer the door, I looked up through the small windows near the roof and tried to peer through. I got a glimpse of a girl, and I was hit by the painful realization that I'd stayed here too long. That I shouldn't have come to visit at all.

"Oh, good, you're home!" Juni said in relieved delight when Ridley opened the door, and I was already hurrying to pull on my boots. She threw her arms around him, hugging him tightly, and my cheeks flushed with guilt at the fantasy I'd just been having in which I would hold her boyfriend in much the same way.

"I was so worried about you," she said as she held him.

"I'm okay, I'm fine," he tried to comfort her.

I cleared my throat as I put on my coat, since they were standing in the doorway, blocking my exit.

"Oh, Bryn, I didn't realize you were here." Juni let go of Ridley and gave me a wide smile. "I'm glad to see you made it back safely, too." Her smile gave way to sadness. "I heard about the poor girl in Calgary."

"Thank you, but I should really be going," I said, returning her smile with a lame one of my own.

"You don't need to go." Ridley pulled away from Juni so he could turn to me.

"No, I do. You two need to catch up anyway."

I couldn't force a smile much longer, so I slid past them as politely and quickly as I could. With hurried steps, I walked back to my loft, feeling more conflicted and lost than I ever had before.

TWENTY-FOUR

oath

D o you wanna talk about it?" Ember stood over me look-ing down, so her bangs were falling into her eyes. Her arm had a brace on it, but otherwise the medic had almost completely healed her, and she spotted me as I did bench presses.

"Nope," I said through gritted teeth and pushed the bar above my chest before slowly lowering it back down.

"Well, I think you should," Ember persisted. "You and Ridley got back from Calgary yesterday, and you've hardly said anything." She paused, waiting until I finished my rep and racked the bar. "I know you must feel terrible about what happened with that girl."

I sat up, wiping sweat off my brow with the back of my arm. "I know you mean well, but I really don't wanna talk about it."

"Okay," she relented. "But I'm here if you need me."

"Thank you." I smiled up at her, but it fell away when I saw Ridley enter the gym behind her.

I'd been avoiding him since yesterday, and I had planned on avoiding him for as long as I possibly could. But since he was walking toward where Ember and I were working out, it seemed like my time was up. He wore slacks and a suit vest, so he definitely wasn't here for exercise.

Ridley stopped when he was near enough that he wouldn't have to shout, and then he motioned to us. "Bryn, Ember, you're needed in classroom 103."

"What do you mean, we're needed in a classroom?" I asked.

"Yeah, and by who?" Ember added.

"It's an impromptu meeting," he said without elaborating, then turned to walk away.

"A meeting? With who?" Ember asked.

"Just come on!" he called without looking back to see if we followed.

Ember exchanged a look with me, and I just shrugged and took a swig from my water bottle. My tank top was sweaty in a couple places, and my yoga pants were frayed and old. I hoped whoever we were having our meeting with wasn't super-important, because Ridley didn't imply that I had time to change.

We walked down the hall out of the gym, past the classrooms where trackers-in-training were studying proper techniques, social etiquette, and human history. Room 103 was one of the larger classrooms and was located right next to the Rektor's office.

When we reached it, Tilda and Simon Bohlin were already seated at desks, along with half a dozen other top trackers who had already returned with their changelings. Ridley stood near the front of the room, and leaning against the teacher's desk with his arms crossed was King Evert.

He was dressed somewhat casually, in a suit with a black shirt and no tie. He hadn't worn his crown, but he rarely did, except for special occasions. Still, I regretted not hurrying to the locker room to change.

"Are these the last two?" Evert asked as Ember and I slowly took our seats at two empty desks near the front.

"Yes." Ridley went over to shut the door behind us, and then he took his spot next to the King. "This is every tracker that's back."

Evert stared out at the room. The light glinted off his slicked-back raven hair, and one ankle was crossed over the other. I'd rarely seen him without his usual smirk, but the expression he wore now was decidedly grim.

"My wife doesn't want us to go to war," he said finally, his words carrying a weight they usually lacked. He looked as if he felt much more resigned to being a leader than he ever had before. "She wants us to solve things peacefully and quietly, sneaking changelings in during the night. And that's why she doesn't know about this meeting.

"An accused traitor killed one of our children, and if he has his way, I'm sure he'll kill more," King Evert went on.

I lowered my eyes, but I could feel Ridley's gaze on me, almost willing Evert's words to take hold in me.

"I agree with my wife on many things. She tries to be kind and fair." Evert uncrossed his arms and put his hands on the desk behind him. "But when someone is shedding the blood of our people, that's where I draw the line. That's when I say fuck it. Let's go to war."

"We're going to war?" Tilda asked, too surprised to be afraid to speak out to the King. "Against who?"

"Konstantin Black and Bent Stum and anyone they might be working with," Evert explained. "There's no point in going after the changelings, because he's one step ahead of us every time. He's anticipating our moves. So now we're going after him."

"How will we find them?" Ember asked.

"We're coming up with a plan now." Evert motioned between himself and Ridley. "But since Konstantin seems to somehow be intercepting our highest-ranked changelings, we're going to set a trap. We'll send all of you to one place, where one changeling is supposed to be, and when you see Konstantin and Bent, you'll swarm them."

"When we catch them," I began, choosing my words carefully and hoping that I didn't look as sick as I felt, "we're supposed to bring them in to stand trial, right?"

"I've thought about it, and I don't see the point. Why waste resources and time?" Evert asked. "He's enemy number one. You find him, you kill him. He hasn't shown us any mercy, and we won't show him any."

Ridley met my gaze, and the fear flickering in his eyes made me bite my tongue even harder. I couldn't tell the King about my fight with Konstantin, especially not now, not if I didn't want to end up in jail for aiding the enemy. But I could tell Ridley was afraid that I would risk my own neck to defend Konstantin.

While the idea of killing Konstantin made my heart twist, I

couldn't argue with the King. Konstantin was still the enemy, and he was complicit in the attempted kidnappings and murder of our people. Something had to be done. I may disagree on what that "something" might be, but arguing with the King would get me nowhere.

"We're coming up with the specifics now, but the plan is to send you out early next week," King Evert went on.

"Excuse me, sire?" Tilda raised her hand timidly. "Is there a way that we can opt out of this mission?"

I looked sharply at her. Her long chestnut hair hung in a braid, and her skin had begun to shift color when everyone looked at her, paling to match the beige of the walls and the tan of the desk, so she could blend in and disappear—a side effect of her embarrassment.

"Opt out?" Evert's brow furrowed and he crossed his arms again.

"This mission of going after traitors sounds particularly dangerous, and . . ." She stopped and took a deep breath. "I'm fourteen weeks pregnant."

"You're *what*?" I asked, unable to contain myself, and she lowered her head.

Beneath the desk, I saw her hand pressed against her stomach. Tilda had always been so toned, and while lately there had been a very subtle bump to her normally taut stomach, I had barely even registered it, let alone considered that she might be with child.

"Of course, in your condition, you don't need to be on active duty," King Evert said.

"When this meeting is over, I'll have you come into my office to fill out some paperwork," Ridley added, then gave her a smile. "Congratulations."

"Thank you," Tilda said softly and smiled at him.

The King spoke for a few minutes longer, summarizing what he'd already told us, and saying that we should all be ready to move next week. He ended the meeting by saying that he'd be in contact with Ridley later on, and then reminded us all to keep everything he'd said under wraps.

After King Evert left, Ridley dismissed the rest of us, and while the other trackers left quickly, talking among themselves, Tilda, Ember, and I were slow to get up. Ridley was at the main desk, gathering up some paperwork he'd apparently brought in with him for the meeting. I sat hunched over my desk, trying to absorb the newfound revelations.

"You're pregnant?" Ember asked Tilda, echoing my own disbelief. She'd gotten up from her desk to walk over to where Tilda still sat at her desk. "You're one of my best friends. How could you not have told me this?"

"I wanted to tell you," Tilda said emphatically, and she looked over at me. "Both of you. I was just waiting for the right time."

"How could you have let this happen?" I asked. My voice was quiet, but the accusation in my tone was unmistakable, and Tilda sat up straighter, her eyes widening with indignation.

"*Let* this happen?" Tilda asked incredulously.

"You should've been more careful," I went on, unabashed. "Weren't you and Kasper using protection?"

"My sex life with Kasper is none of your business," Tilda snapped.

"I just can't believe you would do this." I shook my head. "Just throw your career away."

"Bryn!" Ember admonished me, but I ignored her.

"I'm not throwing away anything," Tilda said, growing more defensive. "I just don't want to fight while I'm pregnant. Once I'm done with maternity leave, I'll go right back to work."

"Yeah, that's what they all say, and then they never come back," I muttered.

"Things are getting a little heated," Ridley interjected, attempting to be a voice of reason, but both Tilda and I were staring daggers at each other. "Everyone should calm down, and talk about things later."

"They all who? And who gives a damn what other people do?" Tilda was nearly shouting by now. "I'm talking about me. And this is about *me* and *my* baby. Not you. It's not like I did this to you."

"I just can't believe this." I stood up, pushing the chair back from my desk so hard it tipped over. "I always thought you were better than this."

"Wow, Bryn." Tilda's voice was cold and flat, but hurt flashed in her gray eyes. "I could say the same thing about you."

Ember rushed to defend Tilda, but I barely heard her. I just turned and stormed out of the room, dimly aware that Ridley was calling after me. But I just kept going. The muscles in my arms felt tight and electric, and I nearly punched in the door to the girls' locker room. My breath came in angry, ragged gasps, and it was hard for me to think or focus. I wanted to hit something, and I didn't even know why.

"Bryn!" Ridley shouted, busting into the locker room without knocking. I stood next to my locker, my fists balled up at my sides, and I cast an annoyed glare at him. "What the hell was that about?"

"You're in the girls' locker room," I pointed out lamely and struggled to get hold of my temper.

"No one is here, and it's not like they have anything I haven't seen." He put his hands on his hips and stared down at me. "Everything you said in that classroom was totally uncalled-for. You were being a huge asshole."

"I'm the asshole?" I rolled my eyes and laughed bitterly. "She's the one that was negligent and immature! She's abandoning her job for some stupid boy!"

"No, she's not," Ridley corrected me as reasonably as he could. "She's an adult woman starting a family with someone she loves. That all seems relatively normal and healthy to me."

I slumped back on the bench and took a deep breath to calm myself. "Our priority is to this kingdom and these people. We took an oath when we were sworn as trackers, and now there's something major going on, and she's going to be off playing house."

"We're allowed to have lives, Bryn." His tone softened, like he was sad that he needed to explain this to me, and he sat down on the bench across from me. "We can date and have fun and raise families and fall in love."

Running a hand through my hair, I refused to look at him and muttered, "You would say that."

"What does that even mean?" Ridley sounded taken aback.

"Because you're in love with Juni," I told him pointedly, as if I were accusing him of a crime.

"I never said that. I just started dating her, and that doesn't even matter." He brushed it off. "The point is that you're acting insane right now." I scoffed, so he continued. "Tilda is your friend, and you're scared and pissed off and you're taking it out on her for no good reason."

I bristled. "I am not scared."

"You are," he insisted. "You're scared of losing her, that she won't be able to work with you as much anymore. But what I think is really bothering you right now is that the King wants you to go kill Konstantin, and you're not sure if you can."

"That's . . ." I shifted on the bench and shook my head. "You don't know what you're talking about."

"I know exactly what I'm talking about." He leaned forward, trying to get me to look at him, but I refused. "I know you, Bryn."

My shoulders sagged, and I hung my head low, staring down at the cracked tiles of the locker room floor. I put my head in my hands and let out a long, shaky breath.

"I don't want to kill him. I should, and I know I should, but I don't."

"I know," he said. "I may not understand why, since I'd give anything to kill the man that killed my father, but I know that this is how you feel."

I lifted my head to meet his gaze, so he could see that I meant it. "I just want to make sure the right person pays for the right crime, and . . . I don't think that's Konstantin." I groaned, realizing how foolish it sounded. "What's wrong with me?"

"Nothing," Ridley assured me. "You just have strong convictions, and you want to do the right thing."

"Are you going out on the mission?"

He shook his head. "No. The King wants me to stay back." He studied me for a minute, then asked, "If you were to see him, would you kill Konstantin?"

Without hesitation, I answered, "The King ordered me to do something. I am a tracker, a member of the King's court, and I took an oath that I would follow all the orders he gives me. So yes, I will do what's required of me."

motives

Konstantin's gray eyes stared back at me, unyielding, unforgiving. It was his first official photo when he'd joined the Högdragen, in full color on the top page of his file. He'd been younger then, clean-shaven, skin smooth, but unsmiling. The Högdragen were never supposed to smile, not when they were working.

It was strange because in the picture he looked harder than he did now. The years on the run had taken their toll on him, definitely, but he'd softened somehow.

I wish I could know what had changed between the time that proud young man had been photographed in his crisp uniform, and the night he'd run my father through with his sword.

After Ridley had confronted me in the locker room, I'd changed and gone back to apologize to Tilda, but she was already gone. But that might be for the best. She could probably use some space before I went to her and owned up to how unfair and cruel I'd been.

Ridley had gone off to take care of some pressing Rektor business with another tracker, so I took the opportunity to sneak in and grab Konstantin Black's file from the cabinet behind his desk. Technically, anybody was allowed to look at Konstantin's file, since he was a wanted man, so I had no need to sneak, but I didn't want to talk to Ridley about it. At least not right now.

I sat cross-legged on my bed with Konstantin's file spread out before me, hoping that it would give some kind of insight that would help me figure out what happened and what was going on.

But so far there wasn't anything that I didn't already know. His father had died when he was very young, and he'd been raised by his mother, who died around the time he joined tracker school. He'd graduated at the top of his tracker class, and he went on to successfully bring in 98 percent of the changelings he was assigned to in the eight years he worked as a tracker.

He joined the Högdragen at the age of twenty-three immediately following his retirement from tracking. He'd transitioned seamlessly into their ranks, rising quickly because of his diligence and charm. Shortly after Mina married the King, she'd appointed Konstantin as her guard, where he'd risen to even greater prominence.

Everything in his file showed him as a loyal, intelligent hard worker, even if he was occasionally noted for his pride. If he was arrogant, it seemed justified. He gave a superior performance at his job, and he was beloved by the people.

In every one of the King's Games Konstantin had competed in, he'd walked away with top honors. He was a hero to the people, and a loyal servant to the King and Queen.

That was it. That was all that was in his file. Just accolades and praise, up until the night he attempted to kill my father. Then there was a report explaining the incident and that Konstantin had disappeared in the night's snow.

But there had to be something more. Something I was missing that would make him change so drastically. From a guard full of swagger and promise to a traitor on the run, humbled and worn.

Ember's footsteps pounding up the stairs to my loft interrupted my thoughts, and I scrambled to put everything back in the file. I'd just shoved it underneath my blankets when Ember threw open the door.

"I know, I know," I said as soon as I saw her glaring down at me. "I acted like a jackass toward Tilda today."

"You certainly did." She trudged over to me, her boots leaving snowy prints on the creaking floorboards. "You really hurt her feelings."

"I'll apologize to her later," I promised Ember. "I just thought I'd give her some space."

"Good." Ember kicked off her boots, then flopped back on the bed beside me. She wore thick leggings under a skirt that flounced around her. "It will suck not having Tilda to train with or work with around Doldastam. But she says she's coming back after the baby's born."

"I know," I said, without much conviction.

"I mean, my mom didn't go back to tracking after she had my older brother." Her eyebrows pinched together and her mouth turned down into disappointment. "And that other tracker Sybilla had her baby two years ago, and she still hasn't come back."

"Maybe Tilda will be different." I tried to cheer Ember up. "And even if she doesn't come back, she'll still be in town, and we can still see her."

"You think she's wrong, though." Ember leaned back on the bed, propping herself up with her elbows and looking at me. "You don't think she should have a personal life, that any of us should."

"I have friends, and I've dated, and I thought it was great when Tilda and Kasper started dating. So it's not that we shouldn't have personal lives," I said, trying to explain my position. "I just think we made an oath to make this job our priority, and having strong attachments can interfere with that."

"Is that why you and Ridley never hooked up?" Ember asked.

"What? I—we—we never . . ." I sputtered, and sat back on the bed, moving farther away from her. "We never did anything because neither of us wanted to. I don't have those feelings for him, and I'm sure he feels the same way. He's my boss, and both of us could lose our jobs, and now he's dating Juni, and besides, we didn't want to. So. I don't know what you're talking about."

Ember raised her eyebrows and smirked at me. "Whatever you say, Bryn."

"Nothing good ever comes from falling in love," I told her

definitively. "You act ridiculous and lose your mind and you forget what really matters to you, and then you end up side-lined and married or heartbroken and destitute, and neither of those are good options, so it's better if you just avoid relation-ships altogether."

"Gosh, I really hope you don't mean that, because that just sounds sad," Ember said, staring up at me with pity in her dark eyes.

I let out an exasperated sigh. "Just never mind." I stood up, grabbing a sweater off my bedpost, and pulled it on over my tank top.

"What are you doing?" Ember sat up straighter, alarmed.

"I should probably head out. I'm supposed to go over to my parents' for supper." If I left now, I'd actually be a little early, but I'd grown tired of talking about romance and Ridley.

"Oh." Her face fell. "Okay." She slowly pulled on her boots and got to her feet. "Sorry if I said something to offend you."

"No, you're okay." I brushed it off. "You're fine. I just have stuff to do."

Ember left, not seeming totally convinced that I wasn't mad at her, so tomorrow I'd probably have to spend some time making up with both her and Tilda. But for now I had other things on my mind. Once she'd gone, I moved Konstantin's file, preferring to hide it in the bottom of my nightstand drawer, underneath odds and ends.

The dinner with my parents had actually been my idea. After I'd read the incident report, going over what had happened with Konstantin in black-and-white, I realized that I needed to talk to my dad and find out what had actually happened that night before I came into the room.

The sun had nearly set by the time I reached my parents' cottage in the town square. It had been a rare day without a cloud in sight, and the sky was darkening from pink to amethyst as the sun dipped below the horizon.

Before I even opened the front door, I could hear my mother, singing an old Skojare seafaring hymn. I paused, peeking through the kitchen window to see her standing in the kitchen, an apron around her waist and flour everywhere. She always sang when she baked, usually Skojare songs in a mixture of heavily accented English and Swedish, or occasionally Barbra Streisand. My mom had always been a sucker for Streisand.

When I came inside, I closed the door quietly behind me, and she didn't hear me as I took off my boots and hung up my jacket. As a tracker, I'd been trained to tread lightly, to move about without making a sound, and I'd made it all the way into the kitchen before she turned around and saw me.

"Bryn!" Mom gasped and put her hand to her chest. "You scared the daylights out of me!" She smiled and swatted me playfully with an oven mitt. "Don't give your mother a heart attack. It's not very nice."

"Sorry," I said, but couldn't help laughing. "What are you baking?"

"Just a gooseberry pie for dessert."

"I'm sure it'll be delicious." I grinned. "Where's Dad? I wanted to talk to him before dinner."

"He's in his study," Mom said, but she stopped me before I turned to go. "Listen, Bryn, I need to talk to you for a second."

"About what?" I asked, and even though I was an adult living on my own, I still felt like a little kid about to be grounded for staying out too late.

"Well." She took a deep breath and tucked a few errant strands of hair behind her ear, unmindful that she was getting flour in it, and her eyes were grim. "I know that Konstantin Black is the one causing all the trouble."

I took half a step back from her and straightened my shoulders, preparing for a fight, but I waited until she'd said her piece before saying anything.

"I know that you have a job to do, but . . ." She pursed her lips. "He nearly took your father and you away from me already. I don't want you messing around with him."

"Mom, he barely hurt me before," I tried to deflect her concern. "It was little more than a scratch, and I was just a kid then. I can handle him now. You don't need to worry."

"Bryn, you are my daughter, my *only* daughter." She walked closer to me and put her hands on my shoulders. "I know how brave and strong you are, but I need to know that you're safe. And I can't know that if you're chasing around after this madman."

She put her hand to my cheek, forcing me to look up at her, and the aquamarine in her eyes was filled with pleading. "Bryn. Please. Promise you'll stay away from him."

"I'll stay away from him if I can," I told her honestly. "But

I'm going to protect myself and this kingdom. I'll do what I need to do, and that's the best I can give you."

Her shoulders slacked, but her hand lingered on my face. "Be safe. Don't be reckless or brave. If you must go out after him, then come back safe."

"I will," I assured her, and she leaned forward and kissed my forehead.

"Okay." She stepped back and smiled at me, trying to erase her earlier seriousness. "I need to finish with the pie. Go ahead and see your father."

remnants

Dad sat at his desk, his head bowed over paperwork and his reading glasses resting precariously on the end of his nose. The only light came from a small lamp next to him, and it made the silver hair at his temples stand out more against the rest of his black hair.

"Can I talk to you for a second, Dad?" I asked, poking my head in his study.

"Bryn." He smiled when he saw me, and pulled off his glasses. "Yeah, of course. Come in."

I closed the door behind me, and then sat down in the chair across from his desk. The walls of his study were lined with shelves filled with old books and Kanin antiquities. On his desk, he used an old artifact —a rabbit carved out of stone—as a paperweight. I'd always felt that in another life, my dad would've made an excellent history professor.

"Is something wrong?" He leaned forward on the desk, and his brow furrowed in concern.

"Not exactly." I crossed my legs and settled back in the chair. "But I need you to tell me about the day that Konstantin Black tried to kill you."

"I'd be happy to tell you anything you want to know, but I don't know how much there is to tell." Dad shook his head. "I mean, you were there and witnessed most of it. What you didn't witness, we've already talked about."

And we had. Dad had been interviewed by multiple Högdragen and even the King himself, as they tried to get to the bottom of what had happened with Konstantin. Beyond that, Dad and I had talked about it after it had happened. I'd been just as confused as everyone else, if not more so.

"It's been a long time, though. I need a refresher," I said.

"All right." Dad set his glasses aside on the desk and leaned back in his chair. "We were at the celebration that night, and everyone was there. Lots of people were drunk. We were all in good spirits about the Vittra King being killed. Konstantin was working, but I don't even really remember seeing him. You probably had a better view of him than I did."

I had had my eyes on Konstantin most of the night. While my duties were to stand at attention during formalities and help keep inebriated townsfolk from causing a ruckus, most of that really meant standing at the side of the room and watching. So my gaze frequently went to Konstantin, who smiled much more than a member of the Högdragen was supposed to.

That was honestly what I remembered most about him that

night. Him standing proud and confident in his lush uniform, smiling and laughing with anyone who bumped into him as he stood by the King and Queen's side. Konstantin had seemed like a man in good spirits—not like one plotting murder.

"I grew weary of the party, probably fairly early in the evening. At least by your standards. I am an old man, after all." Dad offered a small smile to lighten the story. "I headed back to my office, where I worked on a letter to the Trylle. I fell asleep briefly at my desk, I believe, and I kept periodically peeking out so I could catch you before you left."

"You were kind of stalking me that night?" I asked, raising a bemused eyebrow.

"You were only fifteen and it was your first night on the job, and there were far too many drunk idiots dancing around." He shrugged. "I wanted to make sure it went okay for you."

"Thank you." I smiled, warmed by the thought of my dad watching out for me, whether I'd needed it or not.

"You're very welcome," Dad said. "And when you were done, Konstantin found us in the main hall, and that was the first time I'd spoken to him all night."

"When was the last time you'd spoken to him before that?" I asked.

"Um, I'm not completely sure." He scratched his temple. "I think probably the day before. Konstantin had come to get me to ask me something on the Queen's behalf about the celebration. I don't remember exactly what it was, but I think it was just basic palace party stuff. Nothing out of the ordinary, really."

"Had you ever fought with Konstantin?" I pressed.

"No." Dad shook his head. "No, we barely spoke. I saw him around the palace from time to time, but the only times we ever talked was if he was passing along a message from the King or Queen, or vice versa.

"I know he was something of a star to folks around here," he went on. "And I never really bought into the hero worship, but I'd never had a bad word to say about him. He could be cocky, but he was polite and efficient, and he seemed to do his job well, so I never had reason to complain."

"Did he say anything to you?" I asked. "After you left me in the hall, and you and Konstantin walked back to the Queen's office."

"We chatted a bit on the way to the office, talking about the party and how late it was." Dad shrugged. "We were both tired, but it was all basic, nothing giving any indication that he was unhappy with me." He leaned forward, resting his elbows on the desk, and then rubbed the back of his neck. "That's why I never thought it was personal."

"He wasn't mad at you. He was trying to get rid of the Chancellor," I said, surmising what I'd long suspected.

Dad nodded. "Right. I don't know why he went after me and not the King or Queen. Obviously, they have more power than me. But maybe he planned on going after them next. I don't know."

"What did he say to you once you got to the Queen's office?" I asked.

"First he had me looking around for the Queen's document I was supposed to go over, which now I know doesn't exist. I don't know why he was having me search around her desk for something that wasn't real, unless he was stalling for time, but I don't know why he'd do that." He rubbed his chin, contemplating.

"You think he may have been putting off his assassination attempt?" I asked when Dad didn't say anything for a moment.

He shook his head, as if clearing it. "Honestly, I don't know. Maybe. Or maybe he was just waiting for the right moment."

"Did the right moment ever come?"

"Yeah, it must've." He leaned back again, his eyes far away as he was lost in his memory of that night. "When I was bent over, digging through a drawer in the Queen's desk.

"Then Konstantin said, 'Chancellor, I am very sorry.' And I turned around, thinking he was apologizing for misplacing the paper, and I started to tell him it was all right. Then I saw that his sword was drawn.

"I held up my hands, and I said, 'You don't have to do this. We can talk about it.'" Dad fell silent, letting out a heavy breath. "Konstantin shook his head once, and he said, 'I have nothing I can say.' And that was it."

"And then he stabbed you," I supplied quietly.

"I dodged to the side, not enough to miss his blade entirely, but enough so it missed my heart by an inch." He touched his chest, rubbing the spot where his scar was hidden beneath his shirt. "I cried out, and I fell to the ground. And you came running in."

I knew how the rest of the story played out. With Konstantin apologizing to me. Then I charged at him and he stabbed me through the shoulder before escaping into the night.

I leaned forward, looking up at my dad intently. "I need to ask you something, and it's going to sound weird, but I want you to be honest with me."

"I always try to be honest with you," Dad replied.

"Do you think Konstantin wanted to kill you?" I asked him directly.

He ran his hand through his hair, pushing it back from his forehead, and took a minute before speaking. "You know, I thought about that a lot then, and I didn't tell anybody the truth, because it sounded insane. And then after he stabbed me, he'd hurt you, and I couldn't forgive him for that. He had no business going after you. You were just a kid."

"Dad. You didn't answer the question."

"The truth is . . . no." He answered almost sadly. "I don't think Konstantin wanted to kill me. I don't even think he wanted to hurt me. It doesn't make it any better that he did. In fact, it makes it worse. He nearly killed me and hurt you, for no good reason."

"Do you think . . ." I licked my lips, choosing my words very carefully. "Do you think maybe he had a good reason, and we just don't know what it was?"

"He could've killed you, Bryn, and there is no reason in the world that would've been good enough for that," Dad said simply, and I couldn't argue with him.

If Konstantin had killed my dad, I wouldn't even be asking what his reasons were. They wouldn't have mattered. But since he hadn't succeeded, I allowed myself to entertain the idea that something much larger was in place, something that made Konstantin an unwilling agent of evil.

Even though I should only have vengeance in my heart, I found myself struck by something my dad had said. Or, more accurately, something Dad had said that Konstantin had told him right before he stabbed him: *I have nothing I can say.*

Not *there's nothing to say* or *we have nothing to talk about.* No, there was nothing that Konstantin *could* say, as if he hadn't been allowed to.

The more I researched Konstantin, the less I seemed to know. For the past four years, I'd been haunted by the fact that I had no idea why he'd gone after my father, and now his motivations left me even more baffled than ever before.

He hadn't even known my father would be there that late. Konstantin happened to stumble upon us in the hall. If Dad hadn't been waiting for me, Konstantin wouldn't even have had a chance to do anything.

So why that night? Why that moment, when it wasn't something he could've planned for? And why try to kill the Chancellor, and not the King or Queen?

borealis

My mind was still swimming with what my dad had told me as I made the trek home in the darkness. The air was crisp and clean, even if it did leave my face icy, and I shoved my hands deeper in my pockets. The moon had begun to wane, but it was still bright and rather fat, illuminating the clear sky.

It was late enough that the cobblestone roads leading away from my parents' house were empty. Even the chickens and goats that frequently wandered the area had gone home to rest for the night.

I heard another set of footsteps, echoing off the stone, coming toward me from a cross street, but I didn't really register them. I was too lost in my thoughts, trying to figure out what I was missing with Konstantin.

"You don't see enough of me already, so you've resorted to stalking me?" Ridley asked, and I glanced up to see him walking over to me, grinning crookedly.

"What?" I was startled by him, and it took a second for me to realize he was joking. Then I smiled back and motioned toward my parents' place. "No. I was just coming from my parents' cottage."

"Likely story." He'd reached me, and we both stood in the middle of the empty road. "Care if I join you?"

"Sure." I shrugged and started walking north again, and he fell in stride beside me. "We're gonna have to split off soon, though. Your place is west, and mine is east."

"We'll worry about it when we come to it. For now, let's just enjoy the time we have together," he said simply.

We walked for a little while, neither of us saying anything. I wished that silence had felt comfortable and easy between us, like it used to. But now it felt thick and heavy, filled with things that I didn't want to say.

"Aren't you gonna accuse me of being the one stalking you?" Ridley asked finally, and he'd fallen a bit behind, so I slowed to meet his steps.

"No." I stared down at the road, watching pebbles crunch underneath my feet, and I found myself saying something I'd been trying to pretend wasn't true. "I assumed you were coming from Juni's."

"I was," he admitted. "You don't like her very much, do you?"

"No, of course I like her," I said, probably too quickly and too enthusiastically, but that had to be better than confessing how I really felt. "She's fantastic and probably the nicest person that's ever lived. What's not to like?"

"You say that, but you sound annoyed."

"I don't mean to. I'm not." I looked over at him, forcing the brightest smile I could manage. "She's great. I'm happy for you. For both of you."

"Thanks," he said, sounding as halfhearted as I had.

"Just . . ." A lump grew in my throat, thick and suffocating, and yet I continued to talk around it, asking a question that I knew I shouldn't ask. Even as the words fell out of my mouth, twisting my heart painfully, I wished I hadn't said anything at all. "Why her?"

"Why her what?" Ridley asked.

"You dated all these girls for so long, and when I say 'dated,' I'm using the word very liberally." Words kept tumbling out as I struggled to explain away what I really meant. "Because you had a string of girls you saw maybe once or twice, and I get that Juni's perfect." I paused, remembering that she was actually amazing. "I mean, she is *perfect*. But . . ." I trailed off. "I don't know. I don't even know what I'm asking."

He didn't answer right away, which only made me more nervous. My stomach churned, and my heart had begun to beat so rapidly, I'd begun to feel weak. Why had I said anything at all? Why couldn't I just forget that I felt anything for Ridley? Why was it so hard not to want something I knew I could never have?

"Things changed," he said at length. "I'm getting older, and running around doesn't have the same appeal. I realized that I don't wanna do that anymore. That I don't want to be that guy, and I'm sick of living like I'm just a kid without a care in the world. I care about things, I have responsibilities, and I want just *one* girl."

"That all makes sense," I said, even though I wasn't sure if it did or not. I just wanted to end the conversation and move on to something that felt much less terrifying and painful.

"Does it? I hoped it did. Sometimes I just ramble."

"I've long since suspected that." I tried to keep my tone light, to make a joke of things, but I wasn't sure if it worked.

Either way, we didn't say anything more, and we'd finally reached the fork in the road. A small, triangle-shaped sweets shop diverged the road into two paths—one going to the west end, where Ridley lived among the mansions, and one to the east end, where I lived in my loft above the barn.

"Here we are." I stopped and turned to face him, since it seemed rude to just walk away, even though I really wanted to.

Ridley looked around, as if expecting to find something exciting. "Where are we?"

"The point where we should split off." I gestured to the two roads.

"Why here? Why not keep going a block that way?" He stuck his thumb back behind him, at the road that led to his house.

"The road splits here, and that'll take me a block out of my direction."

"Then I'll go that way," he offered and pointed to my road.

I shook my head. "That'll take you a block out of your way."

"Maybe I don't mind going out of my way. Maybe I like the extra detour." He was smiling, but his eyes were serious. "Would it be so bad if I wanted to spend a few more minutes with you?"

"It's not bad. It's just . . ." I stopped when I saw color splashing on his face, and I turned my gaze up at the night sky to the aurora borealis shimmering above us. "Look at that."

Vibrant blue shifting to brilliant violet light illuminated the ether in winding arcs. Stars glimmered like diamonds in the indigo sky as pulsating hues washed across the night sky in luscious waves.

"Oh wow," he whispered.

"It's amazing." I stared up in awe at the dazzling colors dancing across the clear night sky. "No matter how many times I see the northern lights, I'm still stunned by how beautiful they are."

"Yeah, I know exactly what you mean," Ridley said. There was something low and meaningful in his voice that made me turn to him, but he was already looking at me.

"What?" I asked, confused by the somberness in his expression.

"Before when we were talking, were you asking why *her*?" The aurora above us reflected on his face, and his dark eyes were filled with heat. "Or were you asking why *not* you?"

"No. No." I avoided his gaze and ran my hand through my hair. "I would never. No." I swallowed hard. "I know why not me."

"Why not you?" he repeated.

"Because it's wrong." I finally met his eyes and tried to smile at him, trying to play off the growing pain in my chest. "There's a million reasons why not me, and you know them all. And you don't . . . you don't even want to anyway."

He smiled in disbelief at me. "I've wanted to kiss you practically since the day I met you. But I knew you would never let me."

"How would you know that if you never tried?" I asked, and then I was too nervous to even breathe, terrified of what might happen next.

For a second he only stared at me, and I wished I'd never said anything. I wished I'd left my parents' house five minutes sooner so I wouldn't even have seen him at all tonight, and I wouldn't be playing this stupid game where I pretend that we like each other or that we could ever be together. Because I know we can't, and he knows we can't, so it's better if he just walks away. If he just turns around and leaves me here alone, but my heart is thudding painfully in my chest, begging him to kiss me.

And just when I'm certain he won't, and I'm about to turn and hurry away in shame, he's there. His lips are cold, pressing hungrily against mine. His fingers knotting in my hair, pulling me to him. His stubble scrapes against my lips and cheeks, but I don't mind, I like it. I love everything about him that feels so real, touching me, holding me.

I wrap my arms around his neck, and I bury my hands in his hair. It's longer and thicker than I thought it would be, and I feel the curls at the nape of his neck wrapping around my fingertips.

He's strong, stronger than I thought he'd be, and his arm around my waist is crushing me to him so hard that I can barely breathe. But I don't care. I don't want to breathe. I just want to kiss him forever, tasting him on my lips, feeling him against me.

But then he pulls away, gasping for breath, but he keeps his face close to mine.

And then suddenly, as oxygen fills my lungs, my senses take

hold of me, and I realize exactly how wrong that was. I let go of him and step back, even though it kills me a little to do it.

Ridley stands there, his arms falling to his side, as he watches me back away from him.

"I have to go," I say, because I can't think of anything better, and then I turn and I'm running as fast as my legs will carry me, as far away from Ridley as I can get.

TWENTY-EIGHT

contrition

I didn't expect to see you," Tilda said with ice in her voice, but she'd let me into her place, so it couldn't be all bad.

She lived in a small apartment above an electronics store. On the outside, the store appeared to be an ordinary shop, like a haberdashery from a village in a fairy tale. But inside, it was filled with slick gadgets—all of them a model or two behind whatever was most popular with the humans, since we did a horrible job of stocking and ordering things. Besides, there wasn't *that* much of a demand for them in Doldastam.

Still, Tilda's apartment had to be one of the more modern spaces in town. Her furniture reminded me of the hotel I'd visited in Calgary, and she had a stainless steel dishwasher next to her sink—the only one I'd ever seen in Doldastam. A flat-screen TV sat across from her sofa, and while TV wasn't unheard-of here, it wasn't exactly a staple in every home.

"So what is it that I can do for you?" Tilda folded her arms over her chest, and the loose fabric of her tank top shifted, showing the slight swelling of her belly that I should've realized the significance of sooner.

"I just wanted to talk to you." I shoved my hands in my pockets and tried not to visibly recoil under the scrutiny of her glare. "I needed to apologize for the things I said yesterday. I was out of line."

"Damn right you were," Tilda snapped, but she stepped back from me, giving me room to move in from the entryway. She sighed and rolled her eyes before turning to walk into the kitchen. "Do you want anything? I was gonna make some tea."

"Sure. I'll have whatever you're having," I said, following behind her.

"Blackberry and hibiscus it is." Her long chestnut hair was pulled back in a ponytail, and it swayed behind her as she moved around, putting the kettle on the stove to boil, and getting the tea and cups out from the cupboard.

Then she turned back to face me, her arms once again crossed over her chest, her gray eyes staring at me expectantly. "So? Where's the apology?"

"I am really and truly sorry for everything that I said to you at the meeting yesterday," I told her emphatically. "I was upset about things that weren't your fault and really had nothing to do with you, and I shouldn't have yelled at you. You're my friend, and I should've been happy for you."

"That's true." She relaxed a bit. "You have your own bag of issues with love and relationships that I don't even wanna get into, but that is *your* deal, and you had no right to take it out on me."

"No. You're absolutely right," I agreed. "I acted like a jerk for no reason, and I'm sorry. Honestly, I'm very happy for you. If you're happy and this is what you want."

"I am happy, and this is what I want." Her whole face lit up when she put her hand on her stomach. "I love Kasper, and although this baby wasn't exactly planned, I'm happy about it."

"You'll make a great mom," I said, and I meant it.

She smiled gratefully at me. "Thank you."

The kettle whistled, so she turned away and poured the hot water into cups. Carefully, she scooped the fresh tea leaves from the tin, and filled two acorn-shaped infusers with the leaves before dropping them in the cups.

"Now, what's going on with you this morning?" Tilda asked as she handed me a cup.

I leaned back against the counter and sipped my tea before replying. "What do you mean?"

"Bags under your eyes, your hair isn't brushed, and you look like hell," she said bluntly. "Did you get any sleep last night?"

I ran my fingers through my tangles of hair, trying to smooth it out, before giving up. "I got some sleep."

"So what was keeping you up?" she asked.

Last night, I kissed Ridley, and then ran away so fast that by the time I got home I could barely breathe. It was a horrible, terrible mistake that I had no idea how to correct, but it was also wonderful and magical, and part of me—too large of a part, really—kept trying to figure out how to make it happen again.

"That might be too much to get into right now," I said, because it was much easier than explaining anything else, and I bobbed the infuser up and down in my cup.

A key clicked in the lock, and both Tilda and I looked at the front door to her apartment. Her boyfriend Kasper pushed open the door, dressed in his Högdragen uniform. The fabric fit snugly on his broad shoulders, and his black hair was cropped in short, neat curls.

"I didn't expect you home so early," Tilda said. "I thought you were working today."

"I am, but I'm actually here looking for Bryn." He motioned to me, and I straightened up and away from the counter.

"Me? Why? And how did you even know I'd be here?" I asked.

"I stopped by your place, and you weren't there, so I thought maybe Tilda might know where you were," Kasper explained. "There's urgent business at the palace."

I set my cup of tea down. "What do you mean?"

"Is something wrong?" Tilda asked.

"I don't know." He gave her an apologetic look and shook his head. "They just sent me to get Bryn, and said the King and Queen want to see you immediately."

"I'm sure it's fine." Tilda smiled at me, but worry filled her eyes. "And when you're done, just let me know if you need anything, okay?"

I nodded, and then waited as Kasper kissed her briefly on the lips. Tilda walked us to the door, and I followed Kasper down the stairs and out to the street. He took long, deliberate steps, the way all the Högdragen were taught to. I tried to match my pace to his, but he was much taller than me, which made it a bit harder.

"I don't know what it's about, but I don't think you're in trouble." He glanced back at me, making sure I was keeping up.

"Then what is it?" I pressed.

"I really can't say more, Bryn."

He shook his head, and looked ahead again, quickly weaving through the busy marketplace as we made our way toward the palace. People parted for him out of respect for his uniform, and some of the younger kids even stopped to stare.

I had no idea what could possibly be going on, but the King and Queen had a sent a member of the Högdragen to personally retrieve me. That did not bode well.

departure

The King sat in his high-backed chair beneath the massive portrait of himself as a younger man at his coronation. His wife paced the meeting room, and this was the least formal I'd ever seen the Queen. She wore a simple white dress underneath a long silver satin robe that billowed out around her as she moved, and the length of her hair lay in a braid down her back.

My father stood at the end of the table near the King, with a piece of paper before him. The paper had been rolled, and the ends kept trying to curl back up, so I could see the wax seal at the top. It was blue, imprinted with a fish—the seal of the Skojare.

"Your Majesties, Chancellor." Kasper bowed when he entered the room, and I followed suit before he introduced me. "Bryn Aven has arrived to see you."

"Thank you." King Evert waved at him absently, the heavy rings on his hand catching the light from the chandelier above us.

Kasper left, closing the door behind him, and I stood at the end of the table, opposite the King, and waited to be told why I'd been brought here.

"Thank you for coming here so quickly." Evert spoke to me, but his eyes were elsewhere and he shifted in his seat.

"This is unnecessary," Mina hissed. She'd stopped pacing to glare down at her husband.

"I really do think this is the best course of action," my dad said, looking between the two of them. "Given this letter, and the situation we've been dealing with, it does make sense."

"Sorry for interrupting, Your Highness," I began, and they all turned to look at me, as if they'd forgotten I was there even though I'd just arrived. "But why have you summoned me?"

"Tell her about the letter," the King directed my dad with a heavy sigh.

"This morning we received this letter from Mikko Biåelse, the King of the Skojare." Dad held up the paper. "His wife Linnea, the Queen, has gone missing."

"Missing?" I asked.

"She's only a child. Perhaps she found being married to an old man unbearable and ran away," Mina argued. "I've heard of far stranger things."

It had only been a week ago that I'd met with Linnea, her husband, and her brother-in-law in a neighboring room for brunch. She'd been poised but friendly, and there had been a loneliness about her. And she'd been very young, with an aloof husband, so Mina's claims didn't seem unreasonable.

"In light of the current situation with our own changelings, I think we need to consider kidnapping," Dad reasoned. "Mikko seems convinced that Linnea didn't leave of her own accord and he's asked for help in recovering her."

"Husbands know so little of what their wives are up to," Mina sneered, and Evert gave her a hard look, causing her to roll her eyes. "Oh, you know what I mean."

"I agree with the Chancellor on this one," Evert said, and Mina huffed and began to pace again. "With Konstantin Black out for blood, we need to take all of this seriously."

"It's because of Konstantin Black that we shouldn't get involved!" Mina insisted. "We don't know where he is or when he may strike again."

"Our involvement will be very minimal," Dad said. "Bryn would go to Storvatten, working as liaison for us, and would help if she can. There's a good chance she won't be able to do much more than offer condolences, but that will be enough to secure our position as their friend and ally."

"I'm to be a liaison?" I asked, and though I should've been nervous, my initial reaction was one of pride. I let out an excited breath and tried my best to suppress a smile, but I still held my head up higher.

"Yes. With your Skojare blood, we thought you'd be the best tracker for the job," King Evert informed me.

While I felt a little deflated upon learning I'd been chosen for the job because of who my mom was and not because I was the most qualified, I decided that being Skojare counted as a qualification, and whether the King knew it or not, I was the most capable for the job.

Being the liaison was a very high honor, and one that would

certainly look outstanding on my résumé when I applied to join the Högdragen. But even in the immediate future, this role could lead to other important tasks. It could be the beginning of the career I'd spent my whole life working toward.

Mina shook her head, then looked over at me. "Have you ever even been to Storvatten, tracker?"

"No, my Queen, I have not," I admitted, bristling slightly at being called *tracker* instead of my name, since I knew she knew it. "But my mother grew up there, and she has told me many stories about it and her family."

Dad gave me a look, since I'd exaggerated. Mom very rarely spoke of her hometown, but I would say nearly anything at this point so I wouldn't lose my chance at being liaison.

"See?" Evert gestured widely. "Bryn's perfect for the job. She'll make nice, and everything will be fine."

"She may be the best one for the job." Mina stopped walking and wrung her hands together. "I just think it would be very unwise to send away help when so much is going on here. The Skojare have done nothing for us, and we don't need to risk our kingdom for them."

"They need our aid." Evert held his hand out to her, and reluctantly, she took it, letting him comfort her. "This will go a long way to furthering an alliance with them."

"We don't need an alliance with them," Mina said. "Perhaps this is the beginning of their death rattle, and we shouldn't interfere."

"You say that as if their stockpile of sapphires means nothing to you." The King gave her a knowing look, and Mina's lips pressed into a bee-stung pout. "We are working toward a new era of peace, and they've asked for our help. We can spare one tracker."

"Pardon, Your Highness," my dad interrupted. "But given the state of things, wouldn't it be prudent to send two trackers out on the mission? Just to be safe."

"I've agreed to send this *one* tracker!" Mina pointed at me. "Not anyone else!"

"If I may offer a suggestion, My Queen, Ember Holmes is only on partial duty because of her injury, but she would still be a great asset to me," I said, hoping to ease her anxiety.

"She's suffered a fracture." Dad dismissed the idea with a shake of his head. "It's unfair to ask her to risk further injury by sending her out to work again."

"The Chancellor is right, but so is Mina." Evert still held her hand and offered her a sidelong glance. "I'd rather not spare another good set of hands when we're not sure when Konstantin may strike again."

"What about the Rektor?" Mina asked. "He adds little to our security, doesn't he?"

"Ridley Dresden?" Dad considered this, and my heart dropped. "He's a capable tracker."

"Sire, I don't think that Ridley is well suited for this," I interjected, wanting to put an end to the idea before it got started. I didn't really have any reason other than it sounded like an awkward hell traveling with him after our kiss last night.

Dad raised an eyebrow, surprised by my protest, and he continued on with his support for Ridley. "He's actually more skilled in relations with other tribes than Bryn is, so he'd be a great addition to the mission."

"I had asked him to stay back from the field for a while to focus on paperwork here . . ." Evert shrugged. "But we could spare him for a few days to go on this fact-finding mission with Bryn."

"Your Highness, with all due respect, there are other trackers that may be better," I tried again. "Simon Bohlin is—"

But Mina cut me off. "If they're better, then we need them here, protecting us."

"The Queen has spoken," King Evert decreed. "Now I suggest you pack your things and get on your way as soon as you can. They are expecting you in Storvatten by tomorrow morning."

"Yes, Your Majesty." I bowed before him and the Queen. "Thank you for the opportunity."

THIRTY

shamed

I'd offered to drive, but Ridley had insisted he could do it. That was the last time we'd spoken to each other, and that had been over ten hours ago. We'd stopped for gas, bathroom breaks, and cheap gas station food, and we had managed to do it all without exchanging a word.

Our conversation before we left had been quick and to the point. My dad had been there—either fortunately or unfortunately, I wasn't sure which—and he'd relayed the parameters of the mission to Ridley, so there had been little need for us to speak.

Ridley occasionally hummed along to whatever song was playing on the stereo, but that was it. I stared out the passenger window, watching the barren landscape change from snow-covered plains and lakes to green tree-covered forests the farther south we went.

"It's getting dark," I said finally and turned to look at him.

Ridley's hand tightened on the steering wheel, and he kept his eyes locked on the empty stretch of highway before us. "So it is."

"We can switch. I can drive through the night," I offered.

"No need." He tilted his head, cracking his neck. "You haven't slept this whole time, so it doesn't matter if I drive or not. We'll be in the same boat."

"Do you want to stop for the night?" I asked, even though I thought I already knew the answer.

"We're expected in the morning. We don't have time to stop."

I sighed, and then gave up on talking. I slumped lower in my seat and pulled my knees up, resting my bare feet against the dashboard. But now the silence somehow felt even more unbearable, so I looked over at him.

"I'm sorry."

His jaw tensed, and he waited a beat before asking, "For what?"

"Whatever it is that has you so pissed off at me," I said, because I really didn't know why he was mad. Something to do with us kissing, obviously, but I didn't know what, exactly.

"I'm not mad at you," Ridley said, but he sounded exasperated. "I just . . ." His shoulders sagged, and his hand loosened on the steering wheel. "I don't know what to say to you."

"Things are . . . awkward," I agreed. "But maybe if we talk, it'll be less awkward."

"All right." He rubbed the back of his head and took a deep breath. "That kiss last night was a mistake."

I knew it was. Deep down, I knew it was a mistake. But still, after hearing *him* say it, my heart felt like it had been torn in half. The pain in my chest was so great, I wasn't sure I'd be able to speak. But I did, and I did it while keeping my voice and my expression blank.

"It was," I said, sounding astonishingly normal, and I pushed the heartache down.

He was right, so I had no reason to feel bad about it. And if he hadn't said it was a mistake, I would have. Because we both knew it was. We both knew it was something that could never happen again.

"It happened . . ." He trailed off, like he didn't remember what he wanted to say for a second. "I don't know why it happened, I guess, but it did."

"It did," I said, unsure of what else to say. "But it's over now, and it's probably for the best if we just pretend it never happened."

"Right," he said under his breath. "That'll make everything okay again."

"Do you have any better suggestions?" I asked him pointedly.

He pressed his lips together in a line, and his eyes darkened. "Nope. Your plan will work great."

I ran both my hands through my hair, pushing it back from my face, and I wished he wasn't being so difficult. "Did you tell Juni about it?"

"No. I haven't yet."

I rested my head against the seat and watched as the first

stars began to shine in the darkening sky. "Maybe you shouldn't."

"Why not?" Ridley asked.

"I just think maybe it'd be better if nobody knew about it."

"Okay," he said after a pregnant pause. "I mean, if that's what you want."

"With me being the liaison for the King and Queen, and you coming with and being my boss, I just don't think it would look good. Especially now that I'm getting more responsibility."

"Right. Of course," he said, and the edge to his voice was unmistakable.

"How about some music?" I suggested, since the conversation hadn't gone as well as I'd hoped.

Instead of waiting for him to answer, I leaned over and turned up the stereo. It was Bastille's song "Pompeii," one that I normally loved to sing along to, but now I just wanted it to blanket the silence between us, so I could go back to staring out the window and pretending that it didn't kill me to be this close to Ridley.

We drove all night, and with the aid of energy drinks that Ridley really hated the taste of, he managed to stay awake. I slept some in the very early morning hours, with my head resting against the cold glass of the window, but he refused to let me drive, so I didn't feel guilty about it.

The name *Storvatten* when translated roughly meant "great water," which was fitting, since the Skojare capital was located on the northern coast of Lake Superior, not far from where the province of Ontario met Minnesota.

When we were about twenty minutes away, Ridley pulled

over to the side of the road so we could freshen up. It wouldn't be proper for us to meet with the royalty looking all disheveled and unkempt. He stood to the side of the Land Rover, changing from his jeans into a sharp suit, while I crawled into the way-back of the SUV.

I'd debated whether to wear a pantsuit or a dress before finally deciding that a dress would probably be more fitting, and then hurriedly applied makeup and fixed my hair. Ridley had already gotten back in the driver's seat when I climbed into the front, carefully so he wouldn't get a look up my skirt. With dresses, I never wore anything with a hem that went past my knees, so it wouldn't restrict my movement if I needed to fight.

The Skojare palace was supposed to be quite beautiful, and as we approached it, with the rising sun backlighting it with pinks and yellows on the lake, it did not disappoint. The palace was half submerged in water, with the top half sitting on the lake like an island. The entrance was on land, a docklike walkway made of rocks and wood that led to the front door.

Ridley stopped at the end of the dock, where a footman told us he'd alert the King to our arrival, before taking our SUV to park in a nearby garage. As we walked out on the dock—stretching nearly a mile out to the palace—I raised my hand over my eyes, shielding them from the sun, so I could get a better look at the palace.

It was astounding, unlike the palace in Doldastam or the Trylle palace in Förening that I had visited once. Those were beautiful, but they looked like mansions or castles. This was otherworldly, with glass walls shaped into swirls and spirals that pierced the heavens.

When we reached the doors—made of heavy iron—Ridley knocked loudly, and I stared up at the fantastic structure that towered above us. The Skojare must've had a very strong power of persuasion, so they could convince locals around here that they weren't seeing this majestic castle. It was translucent blue, which helped camouflage it with the lake, but the only real way to get humans from interfering was to trick them with psychokinesis.

"You look really nice," Ridley said, pulling my attention back to him. His hands were folded neatly in front of him, and he looked straight ahead at the door. "I always thought you looked good in dresses. You've got the gams for them."

"Gams?" I asked in surprise.

He smirked. "It's a cooler word for legs."

I gaped at him, trying to think of a way to respond, but then the palace door swung open, and we stepped inside.

THIRTY-ONE

great water

Inside, the palace reminded me of ice. Many of the walls were made of frosted glass several feet thick. The glass itself appeared bluish, but it had been sandblasted to make it opaque. The other walls were covered in a silvery blue wallpaper that looked like frost.

The glass walls that surrounded the spacious main hall had been shaped to look like waves, making it seem as if we were standing in the center of a whirlpool. The floor was made of several large panes of glass, allowing us to see down into the pool below.

"Look at that," Ridley whispered, and pointed to a girl in a bathing suit as she swam beneath us.

We'd been left here by the footman who greeted us at the door, while he went to retrieve the King. That gave us plenty of time to admire the unusual and lavish décor of the Skojare palace.

"So good of you to make the trip," a woman said, startling us from our admiration.

As she strode across to meet us, a length of her elegant sapphire dress trailed on the floor behind her, and her lips pressed into a thin smile that didn't quite reach the ice-blue of her eyes. Her porcelain skin had been softly lined by age, and I suspected she was in her early sixties, although she still held all of the beauty she had certainly had in her youth.

"We're very glad to help," Ridley told her.

"And you are . . . ?" She turned to Ridley, her sharp eyes now fixed on him.

"Ridley Dresden. I'm the Rektor for the Kanin."

"Hmm." She considered us both for a moment, then let out a resigned sigh. "I am Marksinna Lisbet Ahlstrom. My granddaughter is the Queen, Linnea."

"We're sorry for your situation, and we will do our best to help you find her," I said.

Her eyes rested on me. "You must be Bryn Aven. You look so much like your mother." She smiled when she said it, but there was something about her voice that made me believe it wasn't a compliment. "Runa was my niece." She corrected herself. "She still is, of course, but since she defected so many years ago, I've gotten in the awful habit of referring to her in the past tense."

"That's understandable," I said evenly.

"Anyway, to the business at hand." Her smile twitched, betraying the sadness underneath, and she absently touched her blond coif. "Linnea is my granddaughter. A tragic car accident left her orphaned eleven years ago, and I've been raising her ever since." Tears formed in Lisbet's eyes, but she blinked them back. "She's all I have."

"Do you have any idea where she might have gone?" Ridley asked. "Was there any indication that she might be unhappy, or that she'd wanted to leave?"

A massive door on the other side of the hall was thrown open, the heavy wood slamming loudly into the wall, and King Mikko burst through, accompanied by his brother Kennet. Like Lisbet, Kennet was dressed formally. He wore a gray suit made of a material that reminded me of shark's skin.

Mikko, on the other hand, looked like an absolute mess as he hurried over to us. One of the tails of his shirt had come untucked, the top few buttons were undone, and his suit jacket didn't match his pants. But beyond that, he was unshaven, his eyes were red-rimmed, and his hair was disheveled.

"You need to find my wife," he insisted, his voice a low rumble. Kennet put his hand on his shoulder, trying to calm his brother.

"They're here to help," Lisbet told him, speaking to him the same way one might speak to a frightened child. "But they've only just arrived."

"She's . . ." Mikko shook his head, then gave me the most demanding, panicked look. "Something bad has happened. She wouldn't just leave. You need to find her before . . ." He choked up, and Lisbet put her arm around him.

"This has been very hard on the King," Lisbet said. "Perhaps it's best if I take him to lie down while the Prince fills you in on the details."

"I want to help," Mikko insisted, but though he was much bigger and invariably stronger than Lisbet, she pulled him away from us without a struggle.

"You need to rest now. That will be a great help to us," Kennet assured his brother.

He watched as Lisbet led Mikko away, and turned back to us once they'd disappeared through the doors that Mikko had burst in through.

"The King seems to be taking it very hard," Ridley commented.

"I'm a little surprised by his display," I said, choosing my words as carefully as I could. "When I met him before, he seemed somewhat . . . aloof."

Kennet gave me a knowing smile. "My brother is a very complicated man."

"What exactly has happened with the Queen?" Ridley asked. "What do you know of her disappearance?"

"The King and Queen retired to their chambers two nights ago," Kennet explained. "Linnea couldn't sleep, so she told the King she was heading down for a swim. He went to sleep, and when he awoke at three in the morning and realized she hadn't returned, he alerted the guards and began a search for her." Kennet gave a helpless shrug. "She hasn't been seen since."

"We would like to speak to the guards who conducted the search, if that's possible," Ridley said.

"Definitely." Kennet nodded. "We'll have a meeting to brief you with the details as soon as the others arrive."

"The others?" I asked.

"Yes. The Trylle have offered to send help as well, and they should be arriving shortly," Kennet said, and though his expression was somber, a light played in his aqua eyes as he looked down at me. "But we very much appreciate you coming. I'm not sure what we would've done if you hadn't."

"We're always happy to help our allies," Ridley said rather brusquely, and Kennet glanced over at him.

"I'm sure you've had a very long drive here." Kennet's expression shifted instantly from grave to megawatt smile. "I'll show you to your rooms, so you can rest and freshen up for a bit. As soon as the Trylle arrive, we'll have the meeting."

"Don't you think it's best if we start the search now?" Ridley asked. "Whether the Queen has left of her own volition or been forced away against her will, the trail to find her will only get colder as time goes on."

"The Trylle are set to arrive within the half hour." Kennet still had a smile plastered across his face, but his tone didn't sound pleased. "The trail won't have frozen over by then. Besides, this was as the King wanted it, and I'm certain you know how to properly follow the King's orders."

Ridley smiled back. "Of course."

"Now." Kennet faced me. "Let's go to your rooms."

He turned and led the way out of the main hall, speaking in slightly bored tones about the history of the palace. The main floor was entirely above the surface of the lake, while the private quarters and the ballroom were located underneath the water. It had been specifically built so from anywhere in the palace, anyone could access the lake within five minutes.

As we went down a spiral staircase to the lower level, I noted that despite the recurring marine theme, the Skojare palace was decorated similarly to other palaces. A sculpture that appeared to be a Bernini sat in the center of the great room at the bottom of the stairs.

"That's Neptune and Triton," Kennet said offhandedly as we walked past it.

The floors were marble tiles, alternating between white and navy, and the walls were covered in the same paper as upstairs — blue with an icy sheen. Crystal chandeliers lit the hallway that led to our rooms.

We reached Ridley's room first, with Kennet opening the door and gesturing inside before quickly walking away. I gave Ridley a small smile, then hurried after Kennet to my room at the other end of the hall.

"And here you are." Kennet held the door open for me, and I slid past him. "I'll let you get settled in a bit. There's a bathroom across the hall. My room is at the other wing of the palace." He pointed toward it. "But if you ask any of the servants, they will tell you where to find me.

"If you need anything," he said, his voice low and deep, "anything at all, don't hesitate to find me."

"Thank you," I said, and he smiled at me in a way that I was sure plenty of girls had swooned over before, but I was not the swooning kind, so I merely smiled politely back.

Once he left, shutting the door behind him, I turned to check out my room, and I realized that an underwater palace sounded much nicer than it actually was. The walls facing outside were rounded glass, making me feel more like I was in an aquarium than a luxury bedroom.

The bed and the furnishings were nice, all silks and velvets in blues and silver, but through the windows the lake looked dark and murky. I pressed my hands against the glass and peered upward through the water at the few rays of sunlight that managed to break through.

A small tuft of dark green mold grew where the window met the frame. That explained the smell. As soon as I'd stepped downstairs, I'd noticed the scent of moisture and mold. It reminded me of a dank old basement.

I noticed a small puddle of water dripping down from a leak somewhere near the ceiling. I looked closer and saw water dripping down the wall, leaving a patch of wallpaper faded and warped.

Once upon a time, I was sure, this palace had been absolutely magnificent, but the Skojare's wealth—and thus their ability to maintain a palace of this caliber—had begun to diminish. Since most of the royalty had gills, the Skojare were often unable to leave their offspring as changelings. Humans might overlook an ill-tempered child with odd habits, but they would definitely notice a set of blue gills on their baby.

If they were to reverse the situation, leaving common gill-less Skojare as changelings, the commoners would inherit the wealth, which the royalty did not approve of. Titles and rankings were determined by abilities, so most of the gilled Skojare were in positions of royalty, leaving the entire system to stagnate.

Those born with gills were trapped in Storvatten, unable to

live or work among the humans, while those born without them were left doing the brunt of the work. Fishing was the main source of income for the Skojare, with the gill-less being forced to do the trading with the humans, and the royalty survived through insane amounts of taxes. The ones who could leave and get jobs with the humans often did, so the population of the Skojare had dwindled.

"Bryn?" Ridley asked, rapping on the door once before pushing it open. "How are you doing?"

"Fine." I turned around to face him. "What do you make of all this?"

"I don't know." He flopped back on my bed and folded his hands behind his head. "It was in poor taste for that Prince to flirt with you while we're supposed to be looking for his missing sister-in-law."

I scowled down at Ridley. "He wasn't flirting."

"You never know when anyone is flirting with you," he muttered.

"I do agree that everyone's behavior feels a little . . . *off*." I sat down on the edge of the bed. "When I met Mikko last week, he was cold and barely spoke. Now he's falling apart?" I shook my head. "It doesn't quite add up."

suspicion

The meeting room was even more like a fishbowl. It stuck out from the rest of the palace in a bubble, with one interior wall and one extra wall of glass domed out around us. Half the room was still under the palace, with a white antique tin ceiling and plenty of lighting to keep the darkness of the lake around us at bay.

A very long table sat in the center of the room, but there were only three other people in there when the footman showed Ridley and me in. Papers were spread out over the table, but nobody was looking at them. Prince Kennet stood at the far end of the room, and the other two men had their backs to us.

"Come in!" Kennet waved for us to join them, and then the young men turned to face us as we approached. "These are our allies from the Trylle."

The first had unruly chestnut hair that landed just above his ears, and his tanned skin had an almost greenish hue, subtle but noticeable enough that it meant he had strong abilities for the Trylle. The more powerful a Trylle was, the greener he or she was in coloring. He was dressed the less formally of the two —wearing only jeans and a button-up shirt, while his companion wore a suit.

His companion had short dark brown hair, kept smooth and neat. His features were delicate, almost feminine, with a small nose and smooth skin. It was his eyes that stood out the most to me—they were a bright blue, which meant that although he came with the Trylle, he must have Skojare blood in him, too.

"I'd like you to meet our friends from the Kanin," Kennet told them, motioning to us. "These are two of their finest trackers, Ridley Dresden and Bryn Aven."

"It's nice to meet you," the blue-eyed one said, leaning forward and shaking our hands.

"This is the Trylle Chancellor, Bain Ottesen," Kennet gestured to Blue Eyes. "And this is Markis Tove Kroner, adviser to the Trylle Queen."

"Pleasure to meet you both," I said, bowing slightly to them, since they were both apparently my superiors.

The Trylle were peculiar, and growing more so since their new Queen had begun her reign four years ago. They sent white-collar advisers and Chancellors—high-ranking members of their society—while the Kanin had sent blue-collar trackers. Not only because it made sense for us to go, since Ridley and I knew more about going after missing people than an adviser would, but also because our Markis never would do something like this.

But maybe the Trylle just viewed the situation differently.

They may have sent Bain and Tove more as figureheads to lend support rather than actual aid, while King Evert had sent Ridley and me because there was a real fear that something dangerous might be afoot.

"If we're all here, maybe we should get into it, then?" Tove asked, tucking his hair behind his ears.

"Yes, I was saying before, we have the reports from the guards that night, and I have the layout for the palace, if that will help you." Kennet stepped back and motioned to the papers on the table.

"So will we actually be able to interview the guards that searched for the Queen?" Ridley asked.

Kennet shook his head sadly. "The King thought the reports would be adequate enough."

Tove stepped over to the table and started going through the papers until he found the report. I stood next to him, peering over his shoulder so I could read it. It was handwritten, and I couldn't make out every word. But the general gist seemed to be that the guards had looked everywhere and found no trace of her.

"So the King was the last person to see her?" Tove asked as he reached the end of the report.

"Yes," Kennet said. "They were in their chambers together getting ready for bed when she went for a swim."

"Or at least that's what he told you." Tove looked up from the report, fixing his mossy green eyes sharply on Kennet.

Kennet met his gaze evenly and replied, "Yes. That is what he told me."

"This must be a terrible hardship for the King," Bain said, rushing to soften his companion's veiled accusation. "How is he holding up?"

Tove set down the file and moved on to rummaging through the rest of the papers. I'd turned to face Kennet, wanting to see his reaction about his brother, but I kept half an eye on Tove.

"He's very broken up about it," Kennet said.

"Will we be able to speak with him again?" I asked. "I think it would be a great help to get more details from him directly."

"Perhaps later on this evening." Kennet appeared regretful. "But you saw him this morning. You know he's in no condition to see anyone."

"We understand," I said. "But you will let us know when he's feeling better?"

Kennet smiled easily. "Of course."

"There's at least a hundred rooms in here," Tove announced. He stood hunched over the blueprints for the palace. "Are they all occupied? How many people live here?"

"Storvatten is a very small town, so many of the Markis and Marksinna are invited to live in the palace with us," Kennet explained. "At the present time, there are seventy-eight royal members living here, not including servants."

"There's not enough time to interview them all," Tove mumbled.

"On a related note, *who* exactly can we interview?" Ridley asked, doing his best not to sound harsh. "The King and the guards are off the table, which is disappointing, since they're the closest thing we have to eyewitnesses."

"The guards did interview Mikko that night, and it's all in the report." Kennet pointed to the discarded report on the table, which Bain picked up and began to leaf through. "The guards also interviewed everyone in the palace that night, and came up with nothing."

"But we can't interview them?" Ridley asked.

"The King thinks it would be unnecessary to bother them," Kennet explained.

Ridley sighed and folded his arms over his chest. "I don't mean to speak out of place, but with these limits, the King is greatly hampering our investigation. I'm not completely sure what you're expecting us to do here."

Kennet shrugged his shoulders. "I'm not really sure, either."

"Is this the exit?" Tove tapped the blueprints on the bridge that led from the palace to the dry land. "This is the only way to get out of the palace, right? And it's got guards at the end that we had to speak to before we could enter."

"How could the Queen get by without the guards noticing her?" I asked, drawing the same conclusion as Tove.

"That is the only direct way," Kennet allowed. "But there are doors all over that lead right out to the lake. If she walked out, or anyone walked out with her, the guards would've spotted her, and they made no mention of it in the reports."

"But she could have swum away?" Bain asked.

Abruptly, Tove straightened up. "Can I have a moment alone to consult with the others?" he asked Kennet.

"Um, yeah, yes, of course." He fumbled for a moment, then smiled at him. "Take all the time you need."

Kennet took long, fast strides toward the door, his bare feet slapping on the cold marble tiles and echoing through the bubble. None of us said anything until he'd gone, leaving us in a somewhat strained silence.

"What are you thinking?" Bain set aside the file and looked up at Tove with a mixture of affection and concern.

"There seem to be three clear options." Tove leaned back against the table and crossed one foot over the other. "One, someone kidnapped the Queen, somehow bypassing the guards and all the people in the palace. Two, she snuck out that night and decided to run away. Or three, which seems the most likely to me, is that the King killed her and disposed of her body somewhere nearby."

"You can't accuse the King," Bain said quickly, while both Ridley and I stood in silence, processing what Tove had said.

It really wasn't that surprising, and honestly, I'd been thinking of it myself. Based on everything Kennet had told us, it sounded like the King was feigning grief to stonewall our investigation. Combine that with his marriage to a lonely child bride, and contrast his indifference at the meeting with his overt distress at her disappearance, like he was overcompensating, and something didn't add up.

"No, of course not." Tove shook his head. "If the King did kill her, there's nothing we can do about it. If we were to say anything, it would only start a war between our kingdoms. The only ones who could lobby accusations without the risk of treason would be the Prince or maybe Marksinna Lisbet."

"But if King Mikko did kill her, why call us here?" I asked, deciding to play devil's advocate in all of this. "He'd already gotten away with it. Why draw more suspicion on himself?"

"You know why," Ridley said, making me look back at him. "Konstantin Black."

"What would he have to do with this?" I asked.

"The King has to blame his missing wife on someone, and with everything Konstantin has been up to lately, he would make an excellent scapegoat," Ridley said. "And of course, there is the chance that Konstantin *is* actually the one behind the Queen's disappearance."

"Who?" Tove asked.

"The Kanin traitor," Bain reminded him. "He's been kidnapping Kanin changelings."

Tove grimaced. "Right. Sorry. I'm bad with names."

"You really think Konstantin had something to do with this?" I asked Ridley and shook my head. "It doesn't make sense. It's a totally different MO."

"I'm not saying he did it. There's no evidence supporting he has anything to do with this," Ridley said. "But everyone's a bit jumpier with him and Bent Stum running around, especially since we don't really know why they're doing any of this."

"A Queen is a big leap from changeling, though," Tove reasoned. "Especially the Queen of another tribe."

"Bent Stum is Omte and he's been going after Kanin," I argued. "Maybe their plan is to hit all the tribes. The Skojare don't have changelings, so maybe this is his way of attacking them."

Bain and Tove exchanged a look. Bain pursed his lips, then shifted his weight from one foot to the other.

"That traitor guy probably has nothing to with this." Tove put his hand on Bain's arm, and he seemed to relax a bit.

"Tove is right, and number three is the most likely choice," Ridley said. "But if the King did kill her, or even if she ran away, there's probably not a lot we can do. So while we're here, we might as well go on the assumption that someone kidnapped her. It's the only way we can actually help."

"Even if she was kidnapped, what can we do?" I asked. "We've read over the guards' report, and there's nothing there."

"There was something I saw in the file." Bain turned around and grabbed it, flipping through it quickly. "It caught my eye, then Tove asked Kennet to leave, and I forgot for a moment, but . . . yep. Here it is. The Queen had gone down to the pool area to swim, and she'd discarded her robe, which they found at the side of the pool. And in the blue satin of her fabric, they found a solitary black hair."

"Oh, shit," I said under my breath, and my heartbeat sped up.

"Now, I haven't met everyone in the palace, but the Skojare have always been very picky about mixing bloodlines," Bain said, explaining something I already knew. "If you marry out of your tribe, you're gone. So I sincerely doubt that anybody in this place has hair darker than blond."

He was very right. There was absolutely no way my father would've been allowed to live here after he married my mother. In fact, he'd never been allowed to even visit. For a black hair to get on Linnea's robe, it had to come from someone outside of the Skojare.

And although I couldn't say for certain who it came from, I did know for sure that Konstantin's hair was charcoal-black.

pursuit

The rocks stung my bare feet, but I paid them no mind as I walked with Tove Kroner along the shore of Lake Superior. I had changed into jeans and a sweater before heading out, since a dress didn't seem appropriate for scouting the area for signs of Konstantin Black, Bent Stum, or Queen Linnea herself. The weather was warm enough to go without boots, and I always felt better with my feet touching the earth, so I'd forgone footwear.

During our meeting, we'd come to the conclusion that the only way for anyone to make off with Linnea was through the water. The pool in the lower level of the palace was freshwater, with a tunnel that led out into the lake. Someone could've come inside and taken her out that way. Admittedly, it would be harder for someone who didn't have gills and couldn't breathe underwater, but not impossible.

If Linnea had been taken that way, she would've come out

on the nearby shore of the lake. So we'd decided to split up and search the shore. Ridley suggested that we mix the search parties, with him pairing with Bain, and me with Tove.

I couldn't help but think he was looking for a reason to avoid me. We'd been getting along well since we'd gotten to Storvatten, but I was sure it was because there was work to be done.

Ridley and Bain had gone east, starting at the bridge and moving outward, and Tove and I went west. Thick evergreen forests lined the shore, going right down to the rocky banks of the lake.

Storvatten was more of a village, with scattered cabins and cottages hidden in the trees. There were no paved roads—only dirt and gravel paths connecting them. As Tove and I walked along the lake, I'd glance over and only occasionally get a glimpse of a house. Most of them were overgrown with moss, making them nearly invisible among the trees, but they were all within feet of the lake.

"Should we ask them if they've seen anything?" I asked Tove, and motioned to nearby house.

It was built very low to the ground, so I assumed it was more of a burrow, like Ridley's house. Moss covered the thatched roof, and low-hanging branches shaded it. But in the small front window I saw a face staring out at me—the bright blue eyes locked on me and Tove.

Tove considered my suggestion, then shook his head. "If they'd seen something, they would've told the guards. And if Linnea was kidnapped, her captor was smart enough to get in and out of the palace without being seen, so they were probably smart enough to bring her to the shore outside of the Storvatten city limits, past the prying eyes."

"Do you know how much farther that is?" I asked. Before we left, we'd all looked at a map of Storvatten, but it had been hand-drawn and rather vague on detail and distance.

"Not that much farther, I don't think." He climbed on top of a large rock nearby so he could get a better gauge of the distance, and looked back toward the palace. "Storvatten isn't that big. We must be almost out of it by now."

An engine revved, and it was hard to tell the distance with the sound echoing off the trees, but based on the birds taking flight and scattering in the sky, it couldn't be that far.

"The road must be that way." I pointed toward where the birds had fled from, and Tove slid down the rock and followed me.

We went into the woods, ducking under low branches, and the pine needles stung my feet. Through the trees, I could see a highway, and I could still hear the car. When I glimpsed the black sedan through the branches, I picked up my pace, starting to run toward it.

I broke through the trees and ran onto a worn, deserted stretch of highway. Several feet down the road from me, the car sat idling on the side of the road. The car door opened, and in the seconds before the figure stepped out from it, my heart stopped beating.

Then Bent's lopsided head rose above the door. His left eye appeared slightly larger than the right, and his massive hand gripped the door as he scowled at me.

"What the hell are you doing here?" he shouted. "I thought Konstantin took care of you."

"Where's the Queen?" I asked him and ignored his question.

He laughed, a dumb, heavy sound that bounced off the trees and startled the birds that hadn't left yet. He stepped around the door, lumbering, really, and I realized that he was much taller and larger than I'd originally thought.

"You tell me. You're the one with all the answers." Bent grinned as he walked toward me, his steps large so he'd reach me quickly, but I refused to step back. I never backed down from a fight.

The trees rustled behind me, and I glanced back, expecting to see Konstantin, but it was only Tove finally catching up to me. He hadn't started running when I had.

"You better run while you can, little girl," Bent said, and I turned back to face him. He'd nearly reached me, and I squared up, preparing to do whatever I had to do to take him down. "And this fight ain't going like last time."

Just before he reached me, he suddenly went flying back— soaring through the trees, with branches cracking as he hit them. I stood frozen and stunned, and then looked over to see Tove standing with his arm extended and his palm out.

I knew that the Trylle had the power to move objects and people with their minds, but I'd never actually seen it in real life before. But Tove had just picked up Bent and thrown him through the trees, and honestly, it left me breathless for a moment.

"I'll take care of him," Tove said and nodded toward the trees. "You look for the Queen."

"Okay," I said, and as he started jogging into the woods to go after Bent, I added, "Be careful." Though I wasn't sure if he needed that.

I ran over to the sedan and looked in through the open door. I hadn't exactly expected to see Linnea sitting in the backseat, but it was still disappointing to find it empty. Hurriedly and without really knowing what I was looking for, I searched through the glove box and around the seats—but other than empty food wrappers and water bottles and a pair of jeans and a black T-shirt, there wasn't really anything.

I popped the button for the trunk and I lifted it very slowly, steeling myself in case I found a body. But there was nothing.

Out of the corner of my eye I saw movement, but when I looked over, there was nothing. Dark clouds hovered overhead, but there was no wind, so the branches were still.

Then I saw it again, just in my peripheral vision—something was moving. But when I turned to face it, there was nothing.

And then, intrinsically, I knew it. His chameleonlike skin let him blend in with the trees, and I had no idea where he was exactly, but I was certain of it—Konstantin was here, stalking me.

relinquish

I stood in the middle of the highway, not moving—just listening. Twigs snapped, but I didn't look toward them. I didn't want him to know that I had heard. I just listened, following the sounds of his movement.

He was coming closer, trying to sneak up behind me. I kept my head forward, but from the corner of my eye I saw him. The briefest shadow of movement and the dark tufts of his hair, and then I knew exactly where he was.

I waited a second more, letting him take a step closer to me, and then I turned and sprang on him. I swung and my hand connected firmly with his face, and it felt a bit strange, like the air had suddenly become solid matter.

His color instantly began to change, hurrying to blend in with the surroundings, but in his panic ended up more of a mottled gray. I grabbed his hair and I whirled him around, slamming him against the car.

I had no interest in repeating our fight in Calgary, and when he tried to move, I just slammed him harder against the car.

"You don't have to be so rough with me." Konstantin groaned, with his face pressed in the glass.

His skin changed back to flesh tone, and I held his arms, twisted them up behind his naked back. He'd taken off his clothes so he could blend more easily into his surroundings—fabric didn't change color—and his well-toned arms and torso felt cold under my touch.

In my back pocket I had a length of leather strapping that I'd brought with in case of just such a situation. Now I tied it around his wrists, binding him tightly.

"What did you do with the Skojare Queen?" I demanded, once I was certain that he was secure.

"Just because you've got me doesn't mean that I'll confess." He looked back at me over his shoulder. "Now I'm assuming you've taken me prisoner, so you might as well take me to my cell. Because I am done talking, white rabbit."

Still catching my breath from the fight, I met his gaze, trying to get a read on him, but his gray eyes were stony and cold, giving up nothing.

"Why did you come here?" I asked breathlessly. "What are you trying to do?"

"I could ask you the same thing," Konstantin replied. He tried to turn around, so I slammed him harder against the side of the car, letting him know that things were going to go much differently than they had last time.

"I'm trying to make sure that you don't kill anyone else," I told him through gritted teeth.

Konstantin smirked at me, but before he could say anything more, Bent came soaring through the trees and landed on the pavement behind the car, skidding roughly on his stomach. He groaned loudly, but he didn't move.

Tove came charging through the woods behind him. He leapt on Bent's back and, using a heavy leather strap like what I'd used, he hurriedly tied up Bent's wrists. We had heavy chains and shackles that we used in jail cells, but for quick handcuffing, the leather straps were easier to carry and use.

"He put up quite a fight." Tove stood up, wiping sweat from his brow with the back of his arm. "But I think he's done now."

susceptibility

W here is she?" King Mikko shouted, and his deep voice boomed through everything like a terrifying thunder. Tove actually covered his ears, and I didn't blame him.

He stood at the end of the table, and Lisbet was beside him, rubbing his back and trying to calm him. Prince Kennet sat near him, his hands folded in front of his face. The gills underneath his jawline flared violently with each breath he took.

Ridley, Tove, Bain, and I sat farther down the table, all of us cowering slightly under the King's visible rage. His hands were balled into fists, and his jaw clenched tightly as he glared at us with icy blue eyes.

"They won't say," I said quietly, since it appeared that nobody else would speak up. "We've put them in the dungeon, and right now Konstantin is refusing to say anything without immunity."

"*Immunity?*" Mikko scoffed. "He probably killed her! Why would I give him immunity?"

"My King, Linnea may yet be alive," Lisbet reasoned. "We must do what we need to in order to find her."

"Bent Stum is strong but he's not very bright," Tove said. "I broke him down some so I could subdue him enough to get him here. I don't think he'll hold out for much longer. The Omte aren't known for their willpower or their loyalty."

"You think he'll tell us where my Queen is?" Mikko asked.

Tove sighed, reluctant to promise anything, and he turned to Ridley and me for help.

"The Omte are stubborn," Ridley said, choosing his words with care. "And Bent seems to fit the mold."

"Can you get him to talk or not?" Mikko began to raise his voice, and Tove flinched.

"We'll do our best, but we can't make any guarantees," Ridley said.

"All I want is to find my wife, and to see the men that took her hanged," Mikko growled. "I brought you here to help, and now you're telling me you're not sure if there's anything that can be done?"

"No, no, we're not saying that." Bain held up his hands.

"Find her, so I can punish the men that hurt her, or there will be hell to pay!" Mikko shouted, and he slammed his fist down on the table so hard, the wood cracked.

Lisbet started to say something to him, but he ignored her and stalked out of the room. We all sat quietly for a few moments after his outburst, then Kennet sighed and pushed out his chair.

"I'll go check on my brother," he said, and made his exit.

"The King is just very worried," Lisbet said, making excuses for Mikko's anger. "We all are."

"That's understandable," Bain said.

Lisbet took a deep breath, making the large sapphires on her necklace rise and fall heavily, and she folded her hands neatly over her stomach. Her eyes were fixed on the water behind the glass dome around us. The afternoon sun was bright above us, making the water appear clearer than it had this morning.

A small fish swam close to the glass; then, out of the darkness, a large muskie attacked it. Its razor-sharp teeth sank through the prey, leaving the faintest trace of blood in the water, before it disappeared back into the depths of the lake to eat its meal.

"I know that while you are in our kingdom you are supposed to follow the law of our King," Lisbet said at length. "He has made his wishes very clear—he doesn't want anyone to offer Konstantin or Bent anything that would allow them to go unpunished for their crimes.

"While I share his sentiment, justice is a secondary concern for me," Lisbet continued and turned her gaze upon us. "Linnea's return is my only priority. I want you to do anything and everything you need to do to get them to tell you where she is. Do whatever it takes to bring my granddaughter back to me."

With her direct instructions, Lisbet smiled thinly at us, and then left us alone to discuss our course of action. Bain was reluctant to go against the King's orders, but we all agreed that if we could find Linnea, he'd probably overlook our transgression.

But since Bain was hesitant, Ridley and I offered to talk to Konstantin and Bent first. We could do kind of a good cop/bad cop thing, with Ridley and me both playing the good cop and then Tove taking over as the bad cop, since he'd already taken his toll on Bent.

The King's guards had attempted to interrogate Konstantin and Bent, but their guard wasn't quite the same as that of other tribes. The Skojare were small, isolated, and quiet. They had no changelings or trackers, and they rarely interacted with others. That left them with an underdeveloped and somewhat lazy and inadequate guard, since they had no need for anything better.

Now, with a genuine crisis on their hands, the guard had rather wisely turned the investigation over to Ridley, Tove, Bain, and me, since we had far more experience handling criminals than they did.

Despite their low level of crime, the Skojare had a superior dungeon. It was actually buried beneath the bottom of the lake, so escape would require breaking through concrete, then digging through ten feet of earth before swimming up through the lake. A rusted spiral staircase led down to a small, dank tunnel that connected the palace to the dungeon.

Water dripped down through cracks in the tunnel, and most of the stones were slick with water and mold. The path was lit with dim lanterns, just like the dungeon itself. It was a rather small place, with only four cells shut with heavy iron bars.

Konstantin sat on the floor with his back against the bars

and his head slumped forward. After I'd captured him, I'd given him the black T-shirt and jeans from the car to put on so he wouldn't have to stay here naked, and the bars left rusty lines on his shirt.

Across from his was Bent's cell. Bent was covered by a sheet, lying on the plank of wood that served as a bed. These were bare cells, with stone walls and metal toilets in each corner.

"Wake up." Ridley kicked the bars behind Konstantin's back, and he lifted his head. "We're here to talk to you."

"Don't bother trying to raise Bent," Konstantin said without looking at us or standing up. "He won't get up."

"What do you mean?" I asked, and turned my attention to Bent's cell. "Bent? Bent! Get up."

He didn't stir, so I walked over to his cell, pressing my face against the bars to get a better look. I shouted his name again, and then I saw the dark stain at the top of his sheets. The lanterns didn't give off much light, but it was enough that I could see that the stain looked red.

"Ridley, get the keys," I said.

"What? Why?" he asked, coming over to have a look.

"Just get them now," I commanded, and he did as he was told, jogging down the hall away from me.

There was a long stick with a hook at the end leaning against the wall in the tunnel, and I assumed it was used for handing prisoners things from a distance or perhaps poking an unruly inmate who didn't want to get out of bed.

I grabbed it, and then carefully I angled the stick so I could hook the edge of Bent's sheet. I was saying his name, telling him he'd better not being playing any games, but he never replied. As I pulled the blanket back, it became obvious why.

His eyes were open wide, staring vacantly at the ceiling above him, and his throat had been torn open, leaving a jagged gaping wound. By the looks of the bent shackle in his hand, I guessed he'd used the rusted sharp point on the end to do the job, but it couldn't have been easy. The blood still looked wet and bright dripping from his throat, so he couldn't have done it long ago, but it didn't matter. Bent Stum was dead.

penitence

B ryn," Konstantin whispered, and I turned away from Bent's bloody corpse to see that Konstantin was standing now, his hands gripping the prison bars in desperation as he looked out at me.

"Did you just stand there, watching him while he killed himself?" I asked coldly. "Or maybe you talked him into it?"

Konstantin laughed darkly. "You can't really believe he killed himself."

"You're saying that you somehow got out of your cage and did it yourself?"

"No, of course not." He shook his head. "Bent was a dumb oaf. I know I shouldn't speak ill of the dead, but he was. He would talk soon, so somebody silenced him."

"Who?" I stared down at him dubiously. "Who would've come down here to do that?"

"I'll tell you, white rabbit, but you have to let me out first,"

Konstantin said with a sly smile. But beneath the steely gray of his eyes, I saw fear flickering.

"Not a chance," I replied immediately.

"I can't stay here locked up, or they'll come for me next."

"Good." I folded my arms over my chest. "You're a murderer. It's about time you get your comeuppance."

"I've never killed anyone!" Konstantin sounded exasperated. "I know I hurt you and your father, and I've hurt plenty of other people. But I haven't killed any of them."

"Tell that to Emma Costar," I said, and the image of her lying dead on the bank of the river flashed in front of my eyes again.

"That was Bent. He's clumsy and stupid, never knowing his own strength." He rested his forehead against the bars. "I shouldn't have left him alone with her. That is my fault, but I never laid a hand on her."

"Where is Linnea?" I asked. "If you tell me where she is, I'll let you go."

Konstantin groaned and threw his head back. "I don't know where she is."

"Someone is trying to kill you, and they have access to your cell. I suggest you start talking if you want to live."

"I swear, I don't know where she is," he insisted fiercely.

"You're lying. I know you're lying. You wouldn't even be here if it wasn't for her."

"We came here for her, that's true," Konstantin admitted. Then he pursed his lips, pausing before going on. "But things are very complicated."

"Why the Skojare?" I asked. "You've been targeting the Kanin for so long, then why suddenly hit the Skojare?"

"It wasn't my idea. *None* of this was my idea." His shoulders sagged and he let go of the bars. "But I'm not sure that makes any of this any better."

"Whose idea was it?" I asked. "I know Bent wasn't the brains of the operation."

He looked up at me, tears resting in his eyes and a sad smile on his face. "Have you ever been in love?"

I tensed. "That's none of your business."

"No, you haven't." His smile widened and he shook his head. "Lucky you."

"What does this have to do with Linnea?" I asked.

"Everything. And nothing." He stepped back from the bars with a resigned expression on his face. "I've done so many things in the name of love. And lately I've begun to wonder, is it still love if it makes one do terrible things?"

"That just sounds like an excuse to be evil," I told him honestly.

"I would agree with you, but I regret a lot of it." He sighed and sat back on the wooden bed behind him. "I regret most of it, really, but still, I can't bring myself to regret falling in love. Even though I died. The real me, the me I'd once been, the me that you admired so much. He died the instant I fell." He stared intently at me. "But for love, I'd gladly kill myself again."

"If you don't tell me what's going on and where Linnea is, you're going to die in that cell," I warned him, trying to reason with him. "Not metaphorically die, but literally die, the way

Bent did, and as unpleasant as that had to be to watch, it's going to be much worse to experience for yourself."

"Then that's the price that I'll have to pay," he said simply. He laid back on his bed and rolled over so his back was to me. "But you can still heed my advice, white rabbit. Get away from all of this before it's too late for you."

justice

Ridley sat on my bed, hunched over with his fingers tangled in his dark hair. I pulled my own wave of hair up in a ponytail, as if tugging my hair back would help me think more clearly.

"I don't know, Bryn," he said finally and lifted his head so he could watch me walk back and forth, pacing along the window that faced the dark water outside. "Trusting Konstantin might be your downfall."

"I don't trust him." I shook my head adamantly. "I could never trust him."

"You're saying that you believe him about some weird conspiracy going on here?"

"It's not a conspiracy," I corrected him.

"You're saying that somebody in this palace killed Bent Stum and made it look like a suicide to cover up something to do with the missing Queen." He gave me a hard look. "That sounds like a conspiracy to me."

I stopped walking to argue my position. "Bent was gonna talk. Tove thought so."

"No, Tove thought he was most *likely* to talk, but you saw him at that meeting. He was resistant to giving any form of a guarantee on that."

"Konstantin *knows* something, though."

Ridley rolled his eyes. "Of course he does. He knows everything! He's behind it all."

"No, I mean . . ." I chewed my lip. "Just bear with me for a moment. Let's say Konstantin was telling the truth and that someone did kill Bent. Who had access to his cell?"

"I ran upstairs and got the keys from one of the guards, but you know how lax their security is around here." Ridley shrugged. "Any one of their guards had access to the keys, but it wouldn't be that hard for any of the *seventy-eight* other people who live in the palace to get the keys. They just have them hanging up in the guards' station at the top of the stairs."

I groaned. "I just feel like we're missing something. There has to be a connection that we're not seeing."

"All of this is based on something a known traitor said while pleading for his freedom." Ridley stared sadly at me. "I hate to say it, Bryn, but I think you're being naïve."

"No, I'm not. This all just doesn't add up!" I shouted, then lowered my voice so I wouldn't disturb anyone.

After we'd called the guards and dealt with Bent's body, it

had been rather late by the time we got back to our rooms. We'd talked briefly with Tove and Bain before they retired to their rooms, and now we were left rehashing the same ideas over and over again in the dim glow from my bedside lamp.

"Bent is out of the picture, we've got Konstantin, Linnea is probably dead," Ridley said. "There's nothing left to deal with. You may not want to admit it, but it's over, Bryn."

"We don't know that Linnea is dead," I reminded him.

"If you believe Konstantin, then all signs point to her death," he reasoned. "Konstantin says that Bent was an uncontrollable idiot that killed Emma, so he probably killed Linnea, and maybe he didn't tell Konstantin where he dumped her."

"What if Konstantin came here to kidnap Linnea, but she was already missing?" I asked. "Or dead?"

"Who killed her, then?"

"Mikko." I kept my voice low, in case someone might be listening. "He had opportunity, since he was alone with her that night, and he stormed out of the meeting, so he had a chance to kill Bent, too."

Ridley brushed off the theory as soon as I proposed it. "That leaves more questions than answers. If he killed her, why did he call us here? And what would his motive for killing Bent be? Not to mention that he doesn't even have a motive for killing his wife in the first place."

"I don't know," I admitted softly.

"And why were Konstantin and Bent even here in the first place? If this is a simple domestic dispute gone bad, then why would they even come here?"

"I don't know!" I shouted, growing frustrated. "Why is Konstantin everywhere we go?"

Ridley's eyes darkened, and he stared grimly at me. "He's not everywhere *we* go, Bryn. He's everywhere *you* go. And that is a very good question."

"You don't think I have something to do with this."

"No, of course I don't." He sighed. "But . . . once is a fluke. Twice is a coincidence. But three times? That's a pattern. There's some connection I don't understand, but I think you need to start taking a hard look at what's happening here."

"I am, Ridley! I'm looking at this constantly. You think I'm not always worrying about this, and thinking about Konstantin? That for even one second I'm not terrified that I'm missing something or screwing this up somehow?"

I knew I was yelling and I should stop, but I couldn't control myself. Everything with Linnea and Konstantin and the missing changelings, it was all making me feel crazy and helpless. Everywhere I went, I was one step behind, and I didn't know how to fix it. I didn't know how to fix anything.

"I'm sorry. I know." Ridley stood up and put his hands on my shoulders. "Hey, calm down." Roughly, he pulled me into his arms, and I let him, resting my head against his chest. "I know you're doing everything you can, and if anyone can figure this mess out, it's you."

"But I can't, Ridley," I whispered.

He put his hand under my chin, lifting it so I would look up at him. "You can do anything."

Ridley leaned down, his mouth brushing against mine, and

I wanted nothing more than to give in to the moment, to give in to the passion of his embrace and the icy taste of his lips, but I couldn't. As desperately as I wanted to feel nothing but him, the nagging inside my heart pulled me away.

"I can't." I lowered my eyes and stepped back from him. "There's too much to lose. You should probably go."

"Right. You're right," he muttered and rubbed his neck before turning away from me. "You're always right."

When he reached the bedroom door, he paused, half looking back at me. "The right guy is behind bars right now, Bryn. No matter what's going on with us or anything else, you should find some comfort in that."

Ridley left me alone then, and I felt many, many things, but comfort wasn't one of them.

THIRTY-EIGHT

entrapped

The staircase had rusted and weakened so much from lack of use that it felt precarious under my feet. But everything felt precarious at that moment. The iron keys were heavy in my hand, and though my stomach twisted painfully, I didn't turn back.

I wasn't sure if this was the right thing. But it was the only thing I could think to do. I had to find out who Konstantin was working for and what had really happened to Linnea. Until I had that information, this would never feel over to me.

Ridley had been right, though, and getting the keys from the guards had been comically easy. The station was completely unmanned, and the keys were sitting on the desk. I grabbed them quickly, then hurried down to the dungeon.

As I walked slowly through the tunnel, I reminded myself that the keys were only a decoy. I would promise Konstantin that I would set him free if he divulged the truth to me. But I would never let him go free again. I couldn't.

As I approached the dungeon, the hair on the back of my neck began to stand up. The door to Konstantin's cell was wide open, and as my heart thudded in my chest, I feared I'd come too late. Somebody had already taken care of him.

Then he emerged from the shadows. He stepped out slowly, deliberately, with his eyes locked on me. But my eyes went down to the sword in his hand, the long blade battle-worn but sharp.

"You shouldn't be here," Konstantin said when he saw me, and he wore the same expression he had when he'd raised his sword on my father.

"I came to set you free." I raised the keys to show him, and he flinched like he'd been punched.

"Run," he whispered. "Run, white rabbit, as fast and far as you can."

"Not until you tell me what's going on." I stood tall despite my fear.

"This has gone on long enough," a voice grumbled behind me, and I whirled around.

He'd been standing in the shadows, along the wall of the tunnel by the mouth of the dungeon. He wore all black, helping him blend in, and his skin had shifted color, completely matching the stones around him. But now as it shifted back, it was like watching a mirage come to life.

Then I realized that not quite everything had changed color. The scar that ran across his face from just above his left eye down to his right cheek, that had stayed a dull red. His black hair was greasy and landed just below his shoulders, and his beard was more unruly than I'd seen in pictures.

But I knew exactly who he was. I saw his face glaring down on me every time I stepped into Ridley's office. It was Viktor Dålig—the most wanted man of all the Kanin.

"Finish her!" Viktor commanded, and that was enough to snap my senses into motion.

With the keys still in my fist, I swung at Viktor. But he was too fast, and he grabbed my arm, bending it back. He grabbed my ponytail, yanking my head back. I kicked him, but he was unfazed, and then Viktor slammed my head into the stone wall.

The first time, I felt it. A blind searing pain that blotted out everything. Somewhere in the background, I thought I heard Konstantin yell out. But the second time Viktor slammed my skull into the stone, the world fell away, and I collapsed into darkness.

retreat

I shoved my clothes roughly into my duffel bag, and Ridley knocked on the open door to my bedroom.

"How are you holding up?" he asked when I didn't reply.

"I've been better."

My right temple had a scabbed-over gash and a dark purple bruise, but the worst of it was under my hair, where I'd needed six stiches. Viktor had meant business, and the medic that had fixed me said I was lucky that he hadn't actually smashed my skull in.

Twelve hours later, I had a killer headache, and the vision in my right eye still didn't seem quite right. Whenever I looked to the left, I could see a blinding white spot out of the corner of my eye.

"If it hurts, they can give you something for the pain." Ridley leaned forward, inspecting my injuries. He reached out tentatively to brush back my hair from the wound, but I pulled away before he could, so he dropped his hand and straightened up.

"I'm okay. I just want to get out of here and get home."

"Well, I'm all packed up. We can head out whenever you're ready."

My jeans were blocking the zipper, so I pushed my clothes down deeper and continued my fight to get my bag zipped. "I'm just about done."

"You know, you shouldn't blame yourself for what happened," Ridley said. "You went down to reason with Konstantin, who was in a cell. You had no reason to think he could break out and attack you. If they had any kind of security here, they could've stopped him. But they think he went through one of the doors out into the lake, and he has to be long gone by now."

In the morning, Ridley had come to my room to see how I was doing, and when I wasn't there he'd gone down to the dungeon, where he'd found me unconscious and bleeding on the floor. When I first awoke, I remembered nothing of the attack. I only knew that Ridley was holding me in his arms, his eyes filled with fear and affection.

But as the morning had gone on, my memories had been slowly coming back. A hazy blur of the dungeon. Konstantin telling me to run. Viktor Dålig emerging from the shadows. Then the blinding pain.

I knew I would tell Ridley about seeing Viktor, but I wanted to wait until I was certain that Viktor was involved. Everything felt too hazy and blurry, and I wasn't even sure I could trust my memories.

Viktor had killed Ridley's father, and he'd been on the run for years. I'd had the chance to stop him, but I'd let him get away, and I couldn't tell Ridley about it unless I was sure it was true.

"If don't blame myself, then who should I blame?" I asked, sounding much harsher than I meant.

"Konstantin," he said simply, and I let out a deep breath that I didn't even realize I'd been holding.

"Ah, good." Lisbet smiled, entering my room without knocking, and Ridley and I stood at attention. "I'm glad to see you're both here. How is your head doing?"

"Better, Marksinna," I told her politely.

"Good." She walked around my bed, the long train of her gown filling up the floor as she went over to the window. Her gills fluttered lightly, and she glanced down at the bed. "What are you doing? Are you packing your things?"

"Yes, Marksinna," Ridley said. "Bent is dead, and Konstantin is gone."

"You weren't invited here to find Bent or Konstantin," Lisbet said. "You're here to find my granddaughter, and I don't see her anywhere."

Ridley exchanged a look with me, but I lowered my eyes. I didn't agree with the conclusion that Ridley and the Trylle had come to, but I had been outvoted. As soon as I'd been well enough this morning, Ridley had informed me that the Trylle were moving on, and so would we, and that had been the end of the discussion.

"We believe . . ." He stopped, clearing his throat. "We believe that the Queen is no longer alive. We think that Bent or Konstantin killed her. I'm very sorry. Please understand that you have the deepest sympathy of the Kanin people, and you will always have our full support. But our mission here is complete and, like our Trylle allies, duty requires us to return home to serve our own kingdom."

"I see." She lowered her eyes and swallowed hard. After a moment, she said softly, "Then there seems to be no reason for either of you to remain here. Send my gratitude to your King for your aid, and I trust that you can see yourselves out."

Ridley opened his mouth as though he meant to say something, but there was nothing he could say. Lisbet left us alone in the room with a heavy silence covering us.

"So that's it then?" I asked. "We just leave?"

Ridley let out an exasperated sigh. "What else would you have us do?"

"Finish our job!" I snapped.

"We have!" he shot back, then lowered his voice. "The Queen is dead, Bent is dead, and Konstantin is gone, leaving without a trace, and he's almost certainly moving on to his next target. We can't help the Skojare any longer. We need to get back and protect our own people."

He softened and stepped closer to me. "As a tracker, you know that you don't get to pick where your job is or when it will begin or end. You just do the work that is given to you, and then you move on." He put his hand on my arm. "This job didn't work out the way either of us had planned, but it's time to go home."

I nodded, hating that Ridley was right. There was nothing left for us in Storvatten. The only thing we could do was head back to Doldastam. I finished gathering my things so Ridley and I could start the long journey home.

Ice Kissed

ONE

retention

Fresh snowflakes stung my face, so I closed my eyes and lowered my head and urged Bloom to run faster. For being one of the largest Tralla horses in Doldastam, Bloom was surprisingly quick, and his heavy hooves plowed through the snow as he raced beside the stone walls that surrounded the town.

My head had begun throbbing again—a dull pain that radiated out from the gash just under my hairline along my right temple, held together with six stitches. I tried to ignore it, the same way I had any time the pain had flared up over the last two days, and gripped Bloom's reins tighter.

Late last night, Ridley Dresden and I had arrived back home from our job in the Skojare capital of Storvatten. Though we'd been released from our duties since the mission was declared complete, I would hardly call it over. Konstantin Black had escaped, and the Queen we'd gone to find was still unaccounted for.

All the royals were resigned to the fact that Queen Linnea Biâelse was probably dead, most likely killed before Ridley and I had even arrived in Storvatten, so none of them held her persistent absence against us. In fact, the missing Queen's brother-in-law, Prince Kennet Biâelse, had seen us out, and he seemed concerned that we didn't judge ourselves too harshly.

In the majestic hall of the Storvatten palace, with its frosty glass walls shaped to look like waves encircling us, Kennet had stood with Ridley and me by the door.

"I'm very sorry we weren't able to do more," I apologized once more before we departed.

"You did all you could." Kennet stared down at me, his aquamarine eyes sparkling like jewels, and sighed heavily, making the nearly translucent gills just below his jaw flutter.

Then he took one of my hands, holding it warmly in both of his. While I was surprised by the heat and strength of his large hands encircling mine, I felt too numb to really register it. The failure of the mission left me distraught and defeated, and after the previous night's attack my head was still in a painful fog.

"Don't be too hard on yourself, Bryn," Kennet said in a voice like rolling thunder. "You're better than you give yourself credit for."

"We should get going," Ridley interjected, "if we want to make it back to Doldastam by nightfall."

"Yes, of course." Kennet smiled wanly and seemed reluctant to let my hand go. I tried to smile back at him, but I couldn't muster it in my current state.

Ridley had the front door open for me. As we stepped out

of the palace of glass, Kennet called after us, "I hope to see you again. You're both always welcome here."

I said nothing in reply, because I had no intention of ever returning to Storvatten or to that palace. With no sign of Linnea or Konstantin, there would be no reason for me to ever come back.

When we'd left Storvatten, my memory of Konstantin Black's escape from the prison was still a bit of a blur. My head injury made it difficult for me to think clearly or recall the incidents surrounding my skull being smashed into the stone wall of the dungeon.

Ridley had scoured Konstantin's cell before we left Storvatten, hoping to find a few hairs or a bit of cloth that he could use to track him. But Konstantin was smart—long before he'd become a traitor to the Kanin, he'd been a tracker. He knew how our world worked, so he hadn't left a trace of himself behind for Ridley to get a read on, making it impossible for us to know where he had gone.

On the long ride back home, Ridley drove, and I lay with my head pressed against the cold window of the SUV, trying to force my mind into clarity.

I told Ridley the truth about Konstantin's escape—that I had gone down to the dungeon to reason with him and find out what happened to the missing Queen Linnea, and that Konstantin had already gotten out of his cell. I'd been overpowered, and he'd escaped. But I had left out one glaring detail—it wasn't Konstantin who had smashed my head into the wall until I was unconscious.

That had been Viktor Dålig.

Fifteen years ago, Viktor had tried to overthrow the Kanin King Evert, and in the process, he'd killed Ridley's father. Since that attempted coup, no one had seen or heard from him.

Then, out of the shadows, he'd appeared in the Storvatten dungeon to help Konstantin Black escape.

I knew I needed to tell Ridley, but I was terrified that my memory was playing tricks on me. The attack still felt jumbled and hazy. What if the head trauma made me recall Viktor's face when he'd never been there?

But now as I rode Bloom through the falling snow, pushing him hard as though I could somehow escape the truth, I realized I was more afraid that my memories were right. That Viktor Dålig had been there, and I hadn't stopped him. I'd let the two greatest enemies of our kingdom get away.

TWO

concession

The King stood with his back to us, warming his hands over the crackling fireplace. A cold snap had descended on the kingdom, and even in the palace we could hear the icy wind beating against the stone walls.

None of us said anything as we waited for King Evert Strinne to take his seat at the head of his table next to his wife, Queen Mina. The Queen sat rigidly in her seat, and Ridley and I sat across from her at the other end of the long table. Though she looked in our direction, her gaze seemed to go right through us.

Normally she had a softness to her—in the way her body leaned toward you, as if she really cared about what you were saying—and her gray eyes had a warmth in them. But it was as though the cold had somehow gotten deep inside her, and she sat frozen in her chair with a white fur cape draped over her slender shoulders.

In her lap sat a small, white Gotland rabbit, Vita. It was the Queen's personal pet, and she sometimes brought her with her to meetings, although I hadn't seen Vita much lately. As we spoke, Mina pet the rabbit absently.

"So." Evert finally turned away from the fireplace. His dark blazer had a bit of a shimmer to it, making the light from the flames dance across it as he walked over to his high-backed chair. "I take it from Bryn's injury that things did not go well in Storvatten."

I lowered my head, hoping my blond hair would fall forward enough to cover the bruise on my temple, but it was an awful dark purple and extended to my eyebrow. It was hard to hide. Fortunately, my worst injury was behind my hairline. Stitches mended the nasty gash, and my waves of hair helped to mask the swelling and discoloration.

"It could've gone better," Ridley admitted. "But overall, it wasn't terrible."

"Evert spoke with Prince Kennet on the phone yesterday before you arrived back in Doldastam," Mina said, and her voice lilted with the subtle British accent she used on occasion, usually to impress visiting dignitaries or other royals. "We know *exactly* how everything went in Storvatten."

I stiffened in my chair, instinctively pulling my shoulders back, but I kept my expression even. While I was disappointed in my own performance, I also knew that the failings in Storvatten weren't entirely my fault. The Skojare had inadequate guards and security, not to mention a weakly protected prison.

King Evert held up his hand, the gaudy diamonds on his

platinum rings catching the light, and silenced his wife. "I want to hear how you think it went in your own words."

"Well." Ridley shifted his weight in his seat and cleared his throat. "We were tasked with locating the missing Skojare Queen, but all our efforts for gathering information were stonewalled. The Prince refused to tell us anything or let us speak to any possible witnesses."

Mina raised her chin haughtily, and her eyes were hard. "I didn't realize the Prince had that much power."

"He got his orders from the King, but we were almost solely in contact with the Prince. He was the one who directed us," Ridley elaborated. "We went out to search the area for possible clues as to what happened to the Queen, and that's when Bryn and a Trylle ambassador managed to apprehend Konstantin Black and Bent Stum."

"You overpowered Konstantin?" Evert appraised me, appearing impressed for a moment.

"Yes," I said. "I subdued him and brought him back to the palace, where he was placed in the dungeon, along with Bent Stum."

"It's my understanding that Bent killed himself?" Evert asked.

"Yes, we believe he took his life shortly after being placed in the cell," Ridley answered. "Later, Bryn went down to question Konstantin further, and he'd gotten free from his cell. He assaulted her and knocked her unconscious, and then he fled."

"That . . ." I took a deep breath, steeling myself for their reactions. "That's not entirely accurate."

From the corner of my eye, I could see Ridley turn to look at me, but I refused to look back. I kept my gaze fixed on the King.

"Oh?" Evert sat up straighter. "What did happen then?"

"I went down to question Konstantin, and he was already out of his cell—that part was true," I said. "But what I didn't realize initially was that he wasn't alone. It wasn't until it was too late that I saw that Viktor Dålig was also there."

Mina breathed in sharply, and Ridley swore softly next to me. King Evert's expression faltered, but only for a second, and then he narrowed his eyes at me.

"Viktor Dålig?" Evert asked. "You're sure it was him?"

"I've been training as a tracker since I was twelve," I said. "I've seen his Wanted poster hundreds of times. I'm sure it was him."

Evert turned away, toying with his rings as he stared into the distance thoughtfully. The Queen looked like she had been punched in the stomach. Ridley's hands were on the table, balled up into fists, and his breath came out in angry bursts through his nose.

"Why didn't you say anything sooner?" Evert asked finally, still looking away.

"Viktor slammed my head repeatedly into the stone wall of the dungeon," I explained. "I couldn't remember things very well at first, and I wanted to be absolutely certain before I said anything."

Evert turned to look at me, his dark eyes on mine. "And you're certain now?"

"Yes, I am," I told him honestly.

"Did he say anything?" Evert asked.

"He just told Konstantin to kill me, and when Konstantin didn't act fast enough, Viktor grabbed me and attacked me."

"This changes everything," Evert said with a heavy sigh. "We must prepare for war."

"Based on the word of a tracker with brain damage?" Mina nearly shouted in disbelief, and I bristled.

"Viktor Dålig has already tried to kill me once," said King Evert, "and he's been on the run for well over a decade. I have no idea what he's been up to in that time, but if he's been working with Konstantin Black I must assume he's grown even more dangerous. I will not let him make an attempt on my life again."

"These are all assumptions." Mina shook her head. "You can't prepare for war on assumptions, especially when we don't know what we're up against or where our enemy might be."

"Mina, I value your counsel, but on this matter, my decision has already been made," Evert told her firmly. "We will find him, and we will destroy him, and that's final."

Mina lowered her eyes, holding Vita more closely to her, and she said nothing more after that. Evert stood up, saying he needed to meet with advisors, but he'd be calling on Ridley soon. If we were preparing for war, Ridley would have to gather the trackers and start readying them to be soldiers.

As soon as we were dismissed, Ridley stood up and stormed out of the meeting room. I followed quickly, but his strides were long and angry and it took me a moment to catch up with him.

"Ridley," I called after him as we walked down the palace hallway, empty apart from a few maids with their hands full of cleaning supplies. "Wait."

He whirled on me then, his dark eyes blazing, his lips pressed together. I couldn't help but think back to when his eyes had blazed in an entirely different way a few days ago, when he'd pulled me into his arms and pressed his lips passionately against mine.

But whatever desire he'd held for me was gone, replaced by barely restrained anger. "You should've told me, Bryn."

"I wasn't sure—"

"That's bullshit!" he roared, and I flinched. The maids were at the other end of the hallway, and they glanced back at us before hurrying on. "That may be why you didn't tell the King right away, but you should've told *me*."

"I'm sorry," I said, since there was nothing else I could say.

He ran his hand through his dark hair and looked away from me, his jaw set hard. "I know things have been . . . complicated between us lately, but that's no excuse not to tell me this."

"That's not why." I hurried to reason with him. "I just had to be sure. I couldn't tell you something this big without being absolutely certain."

He smirked darkly at me. "So you thought it would be better to blindside me in a meeting with the King and Queen?"

"No, I . . . I wasn't thinking." And that was the truth. Everything had been such a mess lately, and I hadn't been able to think clearly—especially when it came to Ridley. "I screwed up. I'm sorry."

"No." Ridley waved his hands and took a step back from me. "I don't need your apologies, Bryn. And I think for right now it'd probably be best if we stayed away from each other as much as we can."

"Ridley," I said lamely, but I didn't argue with him.

Then he turned and walked away, his footsteps echoing heavily in the empty hall, and as my head began to ache again I felt more alone than I had in a long time.

militia

W hen I stepped into the gymnasium, the noise from training fell to a dull murmur, and I could feel eyes turning toward me as the door groaned shut behind me. Thanks to my Skojare-esque appearance, I was used to being stared at in Doldastam—my blond hair and pale skin had always stood out in stark contrast to the tan skin and dark hair of the rest of the Kanin. But this was way beyond normal.

Since the King had officially declared war on Viktor Dålig, Konstantin Black, and all of their associates yesterday afternoon, the tracker school had been turned into an army training camp.

The changes had fallen over the city swiftly and quietly. As I'd walked to the tracker school in the blowing snow, I'd noticed Högdragen standing guard in front of houses—two in front of the more important Markis and Marksinna homes, while one was enough for the less notable families. In the least prominent neighborhoods, one guard would be enough for a whole block.

Even this room full of trackers seemed different: some stood in rows listening to an instructor, while others ran laps and still others did combat drills. Yesterday they had been merely trackers, but now they were soldiers, preparing for a war with an enemy that they might never encounter.

All these changes had taken place because of me, because of what I'd told the King, and because I'd let Viktor Dålig and Konstantin Black slip through my fingers once again. That's why everyone looked at me, their expressions ranging from respect to skepticism to annoyance.

Ember Holmes broke through the trackers practicing combat drills. Her dark hair bounced in a ponytail behind her, but her bangs were damp with sweat, making them stick to her olive skin.

Boxing tape bound her hands, but her knuckles were still red and one of them was bleeding. To make up for her petite size, she fought twice as hard as anybody else, and I'm sure she'd given her training opponent a run for his money today.

"Haven't any of you ever seen another tracker before?" Ember asked over her shoulder, casting an irritated glare at everyone in the gym as she walked toward me.

The teacher instructing the trackers barked an order, and that seemed to get everyone back in motion. The volume in the room returned to normal, and I could feel eyes shift away from me.

"You're late," Ember pointed out, as if I weren't aware. "I thought you might be taking the day off to recuperate."

"I had considered it," I told her, but that was a lie. The headaches still flared up intermittently, and occasionally the vision in my right eye blurred for a few minutes. But I didn't need any more time to rest. I was ready to get back to work.

I just hadn't wanted to come here and deal with all this. Especially when I didn't know what the point of the heightened security was. Viktor Dålig and Konstantin Black were dangerous, but we didn't know where there were, and there were only two of them. It wasn't like we were planning to invade another tribe or country. An army felt unnecessary.

"Bryn Aven." Tilda Moller smirked down at me, but there was a playful gleam in her smoky eyes. "Nice of you to join us."

Unlike the other trackers who were dressed in workout clothes, Tilda had on a tailored black linen jacket with epaulets on the shoulders and matching trousers—our army uniform. The jacket hung open, revealing a white shirt and the subtle curve of her belly. Her hair was pulled back into a smooth ponytail, and with a clipboard and papers in hand Tilda looked every bit the part of an officer.

"I didn't expect to see you here." I smiled up at her. "I was afraid you were on leave."

"Modified duty," she corrected me. "I won't be fighting, but I can help organize and make assignments."

"Where do you want me then?" It didn't really matter where Tilda put me, as long I was doing something. I had plenty of frustration I needed to get out.

As Tilda ran her finger down the clipboard, I caught sight

of a shiny new silver band wrapped around the ring finger on her left hand.

"Whoa, what's that?" Ember asked, noticing the same thing I had.

"Oh, this old thing?" Tilda laughed, and her cheeks reddened as she held up her hand for us to get a better look. "Kasper actually proposed to me at the beginning of the month, but I've been waiting to tell anyone until after I'd told you about the baby. Since you guys know, I thought I ought to start wearing the ring."

"Oh my gosh, Tilda! Congratulations!" Ember squealed and threw her arms around Tilda, giving her an awkward bear hug.

I smiled. "Yeah, congrats. That's great news."

"I'm glad you're both so excited," Tilda said, carefully prying herself out of Ember's hug. "Because I was going to see if you two wanted to be my bridesmaids?"

"Are you kidding me?" Ember asked, and she was so excited I feared she might actually explode.

"Yeah, of course," I said. "It would be an honor."

"When is it? What do you want me to wear?" Ember asked in one quick breath.

"Well, that's another thing," Tilda said, appearing sheepish. "We were originally thinking we'd get married in a couple months, before the baby was born. But with everything that's going on right now, we decided we want to do it sooner rather than later. So we're thinking the third of May."

"That's only a little over a week away," I said in surprise.

"I know, I know, but we're all here, and you and Ember could get sent off on a mission at any moment," Tilda explained. "We just wanted something small and intimate anyway, and we love each other, so why not do it now?"

She looked at me hopefully, almost asking for my approval. After the way I'd botched the news about her pregnancy, I knew I had to handle things much more maturely this time.

I smiled. "You're right, and that sounds really great, Tilda. I'll be happy to help you celebrate your day whenever you want me to."

"Thanks." She looked relieved then waved her hand. "Anyway. We can talk about all the wedding stuff later. Right now, we should all get to work."

"Right. So what should I be doing now?" I asked again and cast a glance around the room to see what my options were.

"If you're up to it, you could work on combat training with Ember," Tilda suggested, apparently deciding to go with her gut instead of the clipboard.

"Good. The guy I've been going against could use a break anyway," Ember added with a laugh.

That did sound like the best possibility, but my attention was elsewhere so I didn't immediately reply. While I was scanning the room, I'd spotted Ridley in the far corner, nearly hidden behind the boxing ring. A group of maybe twenty trackers sat on the floor around him, staring up with rapt interest as he paced in front of them.

I was too far away to hear him over the noise of the gym, but his arms were clasped behind his back and he spoke with a kind of intensity. He wore the same uniform as Tilda, though his jacket was buttoned up and he had a large silver rabbit pinned to his jacket—the sign that he was the Överste.

In times of war, the Rektor took on the role of the head officer overseeing the army. The head of the Högdragen, the Chancellor, and the King all ranked above him. The Överste made no decisions in terms of battle, but the position still had great responsibility in commanding the trackers/soldiers and preparing them for their orders.

"Bryn?" Ember was saying my name, but I didn't look back at her.

"What's going on over there?" I asked and motioned toward Ridley.

"Ridley's training the scouts," Tilda answered.

I turned back to her. "Scouts?"

"They're going to go out and find Viktor Dålig and Konstantin Black," Tilda explained. "They're supposed to find the base camp, get a rough idea of how large Viktor's operation is, and then report back to us. Based on the scouts' information, we'll send out troops to find Viktor and everyone that works for him, and destroy them.

"The Högdragen will stay behind, so Doldastam's not left unprotected while all the trackers—sorry, troops—are off to war," Tilda finished, and I remembered the guards I'd seen stationed at doorsteps.

Until—and if—scouts found Viktor Dålig, we had no idea when or where he would strike again. That meant everyone here would be on high alert as a precaution, especially since we still didn't understand what he or Konstantin wanted.

"And before you ask, no, you can't join the scouts," Tilda said, her eyes apologetic. "Ridley told me to tell you."

"It's probably just because you're injured," Ember said. "Just like how I didn't go on the last mission, because I'd broken my arm." She swung her arm around now, fully healed by medics since Bent Stum had broken it.

Tilda looked down at me, her full lips pressed together and her eyes grim, and she didn't say anything. Like me, she knew my injury wasn't the reason I was being held back. I'd already let Viktor Dålig get away once. They weren't about to let me make that mistake again.

"We should get training," I said, because I was tired of talking.

Tilda nodded then walked away, checking over the papers as she did. Ember led me to a spot on the mats where she'd been practicing. Her partner had moved on to work with someone else, and when he saw that Ember would be training with me and not him, he appeared relieved.

I wrapped my hands with boxing tape while Ember explained what specific moves she'd been instructed to focus on today. When I finished, I tossed the tape aside and glanced over at Ridley. He happened to look up at the same time, and his eyes met mine.

Even across the room, I could see the anger still burning in them. He hadn't forgiven me yet, and I wasn't sure if he ever would.

Then Ember's fist collided painfully with my jaw, and I swung at her instinctively. She blocked her face, so I went for her stomach—connecting solidly with the firm muscles of her abdomen.

She gasped in pain, but smiled broadly at me. "Now that's more like it."

FOUR

compunction

The wind had calmed down some, so I left my jacket open, letting the air freeze the sweat that still stuck to me. After we'd finished training for the day, Ember had insisted that I join her for a treat at the bakery in the town square, saying we'd earned it. Tilda had to finish up some paperwork, and then she planned to meet us so we could talk more in depth about her wedding plans.

My muscles already ached and my right wrist cracked loudly every time I moved it, but I wasn't sure I felt like I'd earned anything. The day left me feeling more like a failure than I already had.

Several inches of snow had piled up while we'd been working. Although there were still tracks from people and animals braving the weather, the streets were mostly deserted. The Kanin could handle whatever the weather threw at them, but that didn't mean they were masochists. Most of us knew when it was worth it to stay in by the fire.

But Ember didn't seem to mind. She just pulled her hat down over her ears and trudged through the snow banks.

"You were awfully quiet today," Ember commented as we made our way down to the bakery.

I shrugged. "I was just training."

"It's more than that." She paused before adding, "You know no one blames you."

"Some people do."

Ember scoffed. "Those people are stupid. Everyone who knows you knows that you did everything you could to stop Viktor Dålig and Konstantin."

We'd been outside long enough that the cold had started to get to me, but I didn't zip up my jacket. I just clenched my jaw, refusing to let my teeth chatter.

An oversized white husky was digging through the garbage outside the butcher shop. Large snowflakes clung to his thick fur. He looked at me as we passed by, his bright blue eyes seeming to look straight through me, and a chill ran down my spine. I quickly looked away.

"What if I didn't do everything I could?" I asked.

Ember was so startled that she halted. "What? What are you talking about?"

"I mean, I did." I turned back to face her, since I had walked a few steps after she'd stopped, and behind her I saw the husky had returned to rooting through the trash buried beneath the snow.

Ember narrowed her eyes. "Then what are you saying?"

"I don't know." I let out a deep breath, and it was shaky from the cold. I turned my head toward the sky, blinking back the snowflakes that hit my lashes. "I did everything I could, but it wasn't good enough. So then . . . what does it matter?"

There was something more to it than that, though. Something I couldn't explain to Ember.

Viktor Dålig had beaten me, that was true. The sight of him had been like encountering a ghost, and I'd been in shock, so he'd been able to get the best of me. That didn't mean I hadn't wanted to stop him, but it had been my fault for letting myself be caught off guard, even for a moment.

But Viktor had wanted to kill me. When he'd smashed my head into the stone, he'd been trying to execute me—I knew that with absolute certainty. But he hadn't succeeded, and I had a feeling that I had Konstantin Black to thank for being alive.

Run, white rabbit, as fast and far as you can, he'd whispered when I came upon him in the dungeon. Even though he'd been escaping, he'd looked so defeated then—his gray eyes soft and mournful, his entire body sagging, his olive skin going pale beneath the shadow of his beard. Konstantin hadn't wanted me to get hurt.

I'd been convinced that Konstantin had been working for someone, that his attack on my father and his plots to go after changelings weren't his idea. In Storvatten, he'd even said as much to me, telling me that he'd done it all for love. Whatever that meant.

"What happened in Storvatten?" Ember stepped closer to

me. "You never even told me about Viktor Dålig. I've had to hear everything through other people," she added, trying not to sound hurt that I hadn't confided in her more.

"What have you heard?" I tilted my head, curious to know what people were saying.

"That he surprised you and overpowered you, and then he escaped with Konstantin," she explained with a weak shrug. "Is there anything more to it than that? Did Viktor say anything to you?"

The butcher leaned out the back door of his shop and banged loudly on a metal pan, scaring the husky. The dog gave one hungry glance in my direction before running off and disappearing into the snow.

"No. He didn't say anything." I shook my head. "But . . ."

"But what?"

The wind came up a bit, blowing my blond waves of hair in front of my face, and I brushed them back absently. Ember pulled her jacket tighter around her, but she kept her dark eyes locked on me.

"I can't help but feel like if I'd found the Queen, I'd have some answers," I said finally, deciding that part of the truth was better than admitting that I didn't think Konstantin was as evil as I once had.

"The Skojare Queen?" Her brow pinched, not understanding. "I thought she was dead."

"That's the theory," I said. "I wanted to look for her more, but the Skojare King called off the search, and Ridley said there wasn't anything left for us to do."

"If the Skojare King doesn't want you looking anymore, then Ridley's right," Ember said.

"I know, but . . ." I chewed my lip. "If I could find Linnea, I think I could find out what Konstantin is up to."

"*If* you find her, and that's assuming she's even alive," Ember pointed out. I lowered my eyes but didn't say anything. "And you have direct orders to stay here and prepare for war. You can't go off on some kind of wild-goose chase at a time like this."

"I know." I let out a reluctant sigh. "I just hate feeling so useless."

"Everything that's happened lately has to have been rough on you." Ember looped her arm through mine and started leading me away, toward the bakery. "But that doesn't mean you're useless. You're strong and you're smart. You're a great soldier, and that's important too."

We rounded the corner, and the sweet scent of pastries wafted through the air. My stomach rumbled, and I realized I'd skipped lunch that day. I'd been so focused on my training that I'd completely forgotten about it.

I began fantasizing about a delicious blackberry tart—a wonderful combination of sweet and bitter, with an emphasis on the bitter. But my momentary good mood immediately soured when the door to the bakery opened, and Juni Sköld stepped out into the snow.

It wasn't exactly the sight of her that made me freeze in my tracks. Juni worked at the bakery, so I shouldn't have been that surprised to see her here. She had to be one of the nicest people in all of Doldastam, and her luminescent skin literally radiated with happiness and kindness.

It was who she was with, and what she meant to him, that made me stop cold. Following right behind her was Ridley Dresden. He still wore his uniform, so he'd come here right from work to walk his girlfriend home.

"What's wrong?" Ember asked. Since her arm was looped with mine, she'd been forced to stop alongside me.

Juni was laughing at something Ridley had said, but then she turned, and as soon as she spotted us her smile widened. Ridley, on the other hand, looked stricken at the sight of me.

I'm certain that part of it was because he was still angry at me. But another part was probably because he'd kissed me— *twice*—since he'd been dating Juni. The first time was only a few short blocks from here, and it had been so passionate and so intense that even thinking about it now made my pulse race and my stomach swirl with butterflies.

"Bryn!" Juni exclaimed, walking over to me while Ridley trailed several slow steps behind her. "It's so good to see you! How are you holding up?"

"I'm . . ." I couldn't even muster a fake smile.

Seeing her sheer delight and genuine concern for my well-being made me recognize that I had to be one of the worst beings who ever lived. And that was combined with the way Ridley was acting right then—shoving his hands in his pockets, avoiding looking at me at all costs. When his eyes finally did manage to land on me, his gaze was so harsh I felt about two inches tall.

"We've had a long day," Ember supplied, since it seemed that I would stand there forever without saying anything.

"I'm just cold," I said suddenly. "I think I should get inside."

"Well, you stay warm," Juni said, but she looked puzzled. "And take care."

"Thanks, you too." I ducked my head down and hurried toward the bakery as fast as I could.

"Why didn't you say anything to her?" I heard Juni ask Ridley as I pulled open the door. "Are you two fighting?"

I practically ran inside the bakery so I wouldn't have to hear his answer.

archives

The day started rough, and it ended with me falling asleep among stacks of books in the palace library. It began with a five a.m. run around the outside of the school, shoving through the massive drifts of snow with all the other trackers. Ridley walked alongside us, barking orders and demanding that we push ourselves harder.

And I did. I pushed myself all day, through every workout and obstacle course and combat training session. The hope was that eventually I would be too exhausted to think. If I drove my body to the very brink, all my concerns about Konstantin and everything that had happened in Skojare would finally die out. Not because I wasn't still worried, but because I no longer had the strength to worry.

It didn't matter, though. My entire body ached from the strain, but the thought wouldn't stop gnawing at the back of my mind—I had left unfinished business in Storvatten. I'd been sent to find Queen Linnea, and I hadn't. And with all the signs pointing to the fact that Konstantin Black had to have had some part in her disappearance, Linnea had to know *something*. She might even be able to shed light on his connection to Viktor Dålig.

But since I had no idea where she was or if she was even alive, I had to move on to other sources. After training had finished up, Ember invited me to go out with her and a few other trackers to the wine bar in the town square. I declined, telling her that I needed to get some rest, but that was a white lie. Ember would offer to join me if I explained what I was up to, but she'd worked hard all day. She deserved to have fun instead of helping me to try to work off my guilt.

The library in the palace was always open to the public, but by the looks of it it had been at least a day or two since anyone had visited. It was an immense room with bookshelves lining the walls from floor to ceiling, nearly two stories above.

The room was dark and freezing, so the first thing I did was get a fire going in the hearth. A large window lined one wall, and all the panes had been frosted over. When I walked past it on my way to search for books, a cold draft blew in through the cracks.

The Kanin took their history very, very seriously. There were shelves upon shelves of tomes on lineage, public records, and accounts of events dating back hundreds of years. Fortunately, the ones I wanted were more recent, so they were located on the lower shelves, which meant I didn't have to use the precarious ladders to reach them.

In trying to find a connection between Konstantin Black and Viktor Dålig, I decided to go to the most obvious place—family lineage. Before he had been condemned as a traitor and stripped of his title, Viktor had been a Markis, so his bloodlines were recorded in great detail in a fine, black leather-bound volume with gold lettering on the spine and cover.

Although Viktor had been a fairly high-ranking Markis, his wife had actually been higher—a Kanin Princess, with both her father and her brother holding the crown. Had she not died in childbirth twenty-two years ago, she would've most certainly been Queen after her brother King Elliot Strinne's death, which meant Viktor would've been King.

But that was not how things had gone.

I went back several generations, trying to see if there had been overlap with any nonroyal Kanin, but Viktor's bloodline remained unsoiled. He shared ancestors with my father, but that wasn't a surprise to me. If I went back far enough, every Markis and Marksinna in Doldastam shared an ancestor.

While tracker lineage is important—the purity of all bloodlines is important to the Kanin—it's valued less than that of the royalty. The book detailing Konstantin's lineage wasn't as well made, so it was more worn, with the older pages in the front coming loose.

Konstantin's family records were just as detailed as Viktor's, but his family was much smaller. He'd been an only child orphaned at an early age, and his parents had come from small families of trackers. Especially in the past, when medical treatment had been harder to come by, the infant mortality rate had been very high for trackers, and it showed in Konstantin's family tree.

But he had come from a long line of trackers who had survived against the odds, which probably explained his determination and strength. He was the very best many generations had to offer.

Nowhere in Konstantin's past did the records show any familial mingling with Viktor Dålig. The two were of no relation, classes apart. They should have no connection to each other.

When the bloodlines proved fruitless, I moved on to the records of recent history—most notably Viktor's attempts at overthrowing the King. Much had been written about them, and I'd had to read about them often while I'd been in school, but I needed a refresher.

King Elliot Strinne had become very ill, very fast. It started with a severe headache, and within a few days he was dead. His death was eventually attributed to complications due to meningitis, and that winter there were three more cases of meningitis in Doldastam—including Chancellor Berit Abbott—although thankfully, no one else died from the disease.

The panic of the illness was also quickly overshadowed by the controversy surrounding the King's death and the appointment of his heir. The most direct heir to the throne at the time was been his niece, but she was only ten.

There also hadn't been a Queen in power without a King by her side in well over two hundred years, and while I would have liked to believe the patriarchal nature of Kanin society hadn't affected the decision to pass over the King's niece, that was most likely wishful thinking.

Chancellor Berit—along with a board of advisors—had decided to appoint Elliot's cousin Evert Strinne as King, despite Viktor Dålig's protests that his daughter should be next in line. On January 15, 1999—two weeks after Elliot's death—Evert was crowned as the King of the Kanin.

It was then, while I was reading the passage about Evert being sworn in, that my heart froze.

At 1:08 p.m. on the fifteenth of January in the year nineteen-hundred-ninety-nine, Evert Henrik Strinne took the oath of the King, with the acting-Chancellor Iver Aven officiating.

In the late 1990s, my father, Iver Aven, had been working his way up the political ladder, and eventually he worked underneath the Chancellor. When Berit Abbott had become ill with symptoms of meningitis, he'd had to take a step back from his duties to focus on his recuperation. That left my father to fill in as the Chancellor.

When King Evert had been sworn in, I had just turned four, so I have only vague memories of the time—mostly the dark colors of the funeral and the bright colors of the banners and flowers at the coronation. I had known that my father worked for his predecessor, Chancellor Berit, and I had heard that Dad had sworn in the King, but that fact had never seemed important.

In history class, that bit had always been glossed over—the King was sworn in by the Chancellor, blah blah blah, and since my father was acting under the umbrella of Berit Abbott's authority, it was Berit who had signed the official document. My dad acting in the Chancellor's absence was perhaps the most benign part of how Evert had become King, but now I realized it might hold extreme weight: it was the connection between Konstantin Black and Viktor Dålig.

Two days after Evert was crowned, Viktor Dålig had led a coup trying to overthrow Evert in an effort to get the "rightful" monarch—his daughter—on the throne. He'd killed four members of the Högdragen before being captured. Over the next week, a brief trial was held, with the King presiding. Viktor was convicted of treason, stripped of his title, and sentenced to be executed the following day.

In a move that many believed extreme, King Evert also stripped Viktor Dålig's three young daughters of their titles and inheritance, and banished them from Doldastam and Kanin society. This enraged Viktor, leading him to swear vengeance on anyone who had anything to do with the verdict.

At the time, Evert had laughed it off, but during the night Viktor Dålig managed to escape from his cell, and he had been on the run for the past fifteen years.

My father had nothing to do with Viktor's conviction, since it was King Evert's decision and his alone. But Viktor had been in attendance at the coronation, as had everyone in Doldastam, when Evert was crowned. He had to have seen my father swearing him in, and with Berit Abbott's illness, it was easy to believe that my dad had helped the council decide that Evert should be crowned over Viktor's daughter.

This could finally be the explanation for Konstantin Black's attempt on my dad's life four years ago. It was just an extension of Viktor's revenge.

The actual Chancellor at the time of Evert's ascension to the throne, Berit Abbott, had succumbed to the damages of his disease, forcing him to step down in 2001 when my dad took over his job. Berit died not much longer after that. Time had already gotten its vengeance on Berit, so Konstantin had moved on to the next guilty party—my dad.

But why would Konstantin care? He'd been seventeen at the time of that whole mess, a tracker with aspirations of becoming a member of the Högdragen, but no affiliations with the royalty. By all accounts, he was a loyal servant of the kingdom, with no hints of rebellion or mutiny.

How would Viktor have recruited Konstantin to join him for his vengeance? And why wait so long to get started on it? When Konstantin had attempted to kill my dad, it was eleven years since Viktor declared vengeance on the King.

And what did any of this have to do with Konstantin going after the changelings? Perhaps he was attempting to be some kind of Pied Piper—taking all the children until he received his payment, which in this scenario I could only imagine would be the King's head.

But that didn't explain Viktor's interest in the Skojare. They had nothing to do with the perceived slight against Viktor or his family, so they did nothing for his for retribution.

I could see connections that hadn't been clear before, but there were still pieces missing, leaving me feeling more frustrated than ever. Surrounded by books and all the information of my people, I could find no answers.

The fire was now only embers, but I preferred the cold, hoping it would help keep me awake as I sat hunched over the old books. Eventually, though, my body collapsed with exhaustion. I don't even remember falling asleep.

One moment I was reading, the lines of text blurring in the dim light, and the next I was dreaming nothing but white. Then, slowly, I saw a face begin to take shape, and eyelids fluttered open, revealing startling sapphire eyes.

Somehow, I knew it was Linnea, the missing Skojare Queen.

Her lips appeared, bright red from the lipstick she wore, and her face was fully visible, surrounded by a halo of platinum blond curls and backlit by a bright white light. And then, as if she were whispering right in my ear, I heard her.

Come find me.

tonåren

As I approached the house where I'd grown up, I could see my mom shoveling snow off the front walk.

Her long blond waves of hair were falling free from their loose bun, and the cold had left a bit of rose on her fair cheeks. Mom was on the tall side, and while her beauty and lithe figure appeared deceptively delicate, she was athletic and strong, able to toss away shovels full of heavy, wet snow with ease.

"Bryn!" Mom smiled broadly at me. "I wasn't expecting you today. I would've thought you had training today."

"It's Saturday, so we have a break," I lied.

While preparing for war, there were no breaks. On Sundays, our training would be slightly more relaxed, but we never had a day off. I was skipping today—and probably tomorrow, and the day after that—but I didn't plan on telling my mom that. At least not yet.

After I'd woken up in the library with a horrible crick in my neck, my dream had haunted me. It felt ethereal but all too real. I was positive it was a lysa, even though I'd never had one before. While lysas were more common among the Trylle, who had the strongest gift of psychokinesis, they weren't unheard of in the Kanin, the Skojare, and even the Vittra.

A lysa is something between shared dreaming and astral projection. It's the ability to psychically enter someone else's thoughts through a vision, usually a dream. Unless the troll giving the lysa is very powerful, it's usually brief, and in tribes like the Skojare who aren't known for their psychic abilities, it only works in an emergency. Necessity and fear tend to strengthen telekinesis enough to enable a lysa.

I didn't know why Linnea had picked me to receive her lysa, but now that I had proof she was alive, I knew one thing for certain—I had to find her.

I'd wanted to rush out and talk to my mom immediately, but if I was unkempt and unshowered, that would alarm her. So I'd hurried back to my apartment and gotten cleaned up before trekking to my parents' house. I had to be as careful and discreet as possible, since I was supposed to be working today. If someone saw me—especially Ember or Tilda or Ridley— things would get unnecessarily complicated, and I didn't have time for that.

"Is something wrong?" Mom asked, narrowing her eyes in concern. She reached out, gently touching a gloved hand to the fading bruise on my temple. It had been worse the day I'd returned home after the attack, and when she had seen it then, she'd been frantic.

"I'm fine," I tried to assure her with a smile. "I was hoping we could talk for a minute, though."

"Yeah, of course." She dropped her hand and motioned to the house. "Let's go inside."

I waited until after we'd both peeled off our winter jackets and heavy boots, and I even waited until after my mom made us cups of hot blackberry tea. All I wanted to do was rush through, asking my questions, but I did the best I could to make this seem like a normal visit.

"Your dad's at a meeting in the palace," Mom said as she set a cup of tea in front of me at the kitchen table, and then she sat down across from me, sipping her own tea.

"It has to be so hectic for him, with everything's that's going on," I said.

She nodded. "I'm sure things are just as crazy for you."

"Yeah, things are busy," I said before lapsing into an awkward silence.

"Just spit it out." Mom leaned back in her chair, appraising me with a bemused smile. "You came over here to talk about something, and there's no point in dancing around it."

I took a deep breath before launching into it. "Konstantin Black went to Storvatten to take Queen Linnea, but he didn't. He swore on his life that he had no idea where she was, and it didn't appear that anyone in Storvatten knew where she was either. At least not the people who cared the most about her."

Mom considered this for a moment. "And you believe Konstantin?"

"I do," I told her, and she inhaled sharply but said nothing.

"There are three options—Konstantin took her and killed her, someone in Storvatten killed her and tried to frame Konstantin, or she ran off. In the first two scenarios, she's dead, so the only one that's really worth following up on is the third option."

"You think she ran away?" Mom asked, her interest piqued. "Why would she run off?"

I pursed my lips, wishing there was another way to say it. My mom was not a particularly hateful or vengeful person, but I couldn't blame her for the anger and distrust she still felt toward Konstantin. After all, he had nearly killed both her husband and her daughter.

"I think Konstantin warned her," I said finally. Mom lowered her eyes and shifted her weight in her chair, growing irritated, but I pressed on. "After what happened with Emma Costar in Calgary, when Bent Stum killed her, I think Konstantin didn't want anybody else to get hurt."

"Bryn." She raised her eyes so she could stare harshly at me. "You can't possibly believe that."

"There's something really weird going on in Storvatten," I said, ignoring my mom's challenge. I couldn't win that argument, so I didn't engage it. "It doesn't fit Konstantin's pattern—he had been targeting Kanin changelings still living with humans. Linnea was a Skojare Queen in her palace, and she'd never even been a changeling."

Mom fidgeted with her tea cup, twisting it on the table and staring down at it. Her shoulders were rigid, her entire body held at nervous attention.

"Let's say I believe you," she said, almost reluctantly. "Why are you here? What light do you hope I can shed on any of this?"

"If I'm right, and somebody warned Linnea that she had better get out of Storvatten, where would she go?" I asked.

Like my mother, Linnea had been born and raised in Storvatten. She had probably never met a human and hardly stepped out of the palace, except to go for a swim or visit other royalty. Thanks to her Skojare gills, she would never be able to blend with human society.

The Skojare didn't have that much money anymore, and most of what they did have of value were jewels locked up in safes. None of it had been reported missing when Linnea had disappeared, so if she was on the run, she had no money with her.

Her options as a penniless, sheltered, beautiful but mutated teenager were extremely limited.

"When I was growing up in Storvatten, locked up in that frozen palace while my parents tried to sell me off to a suitor for the highest price, I often dreamed of running away," Mom admitted quietly. "I finally did when I ran off with your father, but I hardly imagine that Linnea is hiding among us in Doldastam. We Skojare tend to stand out here."

She offered me a weak smile then, and I knew how painfully true her statement was. Thanks to the unique fair skin of the Skojare, Linnea would be unable to blend in with any of the other tribes of trolls.

"There's nowhere?" I pressed. "Didn't you tell me once

about how you and some of your friends took off somewhere for a week when you were a teenager?"

A look of wistful surprise passed across her face, and the corner of her mouth curled up slightly. "The tonåren. I'd nearly forgotten about that."

"Yeah, the tonåren," I said, trying to remember what she'd told me about it.

"It wasn't an official thing," Mom explained. "That's just the word we used for when the royal teenagers grew restless and didn't want to stay cooped up anymore. Those without gills would sometimes try to make a break for the human world, heading out to cities for a week or two before coming back.

"But my best friend had gills, and I didn't want to leave her behind, so we had to choose another option." Mom took a long drink of her tea. "Lake Isolera."

"Lake Isolera?" I asked. "You never told me about that."

"I'd nearly forgotten, and it feels like a half-remembered dream." She shook her head. "It was a story we'd heard from our childhood. A magical place that an ancient powerful Queen had a put spell on, so it would always be warm and private. An oasis to swim in when the harsh Canadian winters bore down on us.

"But it had an enchantment on it, to keep humans or unwanted trolls from stumbling upon it," Mom went on. "Everyone who says they've been there is never entirely sure if they really went or if they only imagined it."

"So, is it real?" I asked her directly.

"I . . ." She furrowed her brow in concentration and sighed.

"Honestly, I can't say for certain. But if Linnea was running from someone, and she believed Lake Isolera was real, the same way I believed it was real when I was her age, then that's where she would head."

"Where is it?" I asked, stifling my excitement.

"Swim one day along the shore, and then walk half a day due north, and you'll find it under the brightest star if you've followed the right course," Mom said, sounding as though she were reciting an old nursery rhyme.

"You don't have more accurate directions than that?" I asked hopefully.

She raised an eyebrow at me. "For a magical place that probably doesn't really exist? No, I'm sorry, I don't It's like asking for specific directions to Narnia."

"You just go through the wardrobe to get to Narnia. That's pretty specific."

Mom rolled her eyes, but she pushed her chair back and stood up. "Let's go to your dad's study. If we look at a map, I might be able to figure it out better."

I followed her back to my dad's cluttered office, and she pulled down his heavy, worn atlas from a shelf and spread it out on his desk. Unlike the atlases humans might find in their world, this one was marked for troll territories, major cities, and places of importance, all overlaid atop the human landmarks so we could find the troll locations when we ventured out into the human world.

As Mom bent over the atlas, she mumbled to herself. I stood beside her. I didn't catch every word she said, but from what I gathered she was trying to remember how fast she could swim.

Then finally, after some deliberation, she took a pen off my dad's desk and circled a blank spot on the map in Ontario.

"There. That's Lake Isolera," she proclaimed rather proudly.

I leaned forward, squinting at the map. There were plenty of blue splotches covering the area, indicating all of the lakes. But the spot Mom had circled was completely devoid of water, an odd dry patch in an otherwise watery land.

"Are you sure that's the right place?" I asked. "There's nothing there, but there are tons of lakes around it."

"Well, either it isn't real or it's hidden under a magic spell, so of course there wouldn't be anything on the map." She straightened up and folded her arms over her chest. "But if it does exist, that's where it is."

"If Linnea ran away, you think that's where she would be?" I looked up at her.

"Either at the lake, or trying to find it." Mom nodded, her lips pressed into a grim line. "Assuming she isn't dead, of course."

SEVEN

abscond

You have to talk to Ridley," Tilda told me firmly, and I groaned and slumped back against the wall.

After talking with my mom, I'd snuck into the school, barely managing not to be seen, and then lay in wait in the locker room that doubled as a women's restroom. Thanks to her pregnancy, Tilda had to use the bathroom rather frequently—as she had lamented several times—so I knew it wouldn't be too long before she came in.

In fact, I'd only hidden in a stall for fifteen minutes before she entered. I waited until she'd finished, and when she came out of the stall she nearly screamed at the sight of me. Once she calmed herself, she gave me a hard look—one that could cut twice as deep as any lecture.

I hurriedly explained my absence from training today, and my plan to find Linnea and why I thought it was so important.

As she listened, the steel in her gray eyes began to soften, but she didn't exactly look at me with approval either.

"But you're my commanding officer," I insisted. "You should be able to give me the go-ahead."

Tilda shook her head. "You know I have no authority to release you from your duties. Even if I did, it would mean nothing. Unless you get Ridley's approval, you'll be considered AWOL."

I leaned my head back against the wall and stared up at the ceiling, weighing my options. On one hand, if I left without permission, not only would I lose any hope of being on the Högdragen, but I'd most likely be fired as a tracker. I'd still have to stay in the army until after this "war" was over, but as soon as it was, I'd be out of work.

And on the other hand, getting permission meant I'd have to talk to Ridley.

"If you think this is the right thing to do, and it seems that you really do, then you need to talk to him," Tilda said, her voice low and comforting. "Whatever is going on between the two of you, he'll still be fair and hear you out."

I looked up at her hopefully. "Will you get him for me?" She started to scoff, so I quickly explained. "If I go out there now, it'll be a big spectacle because I've already skipped half a day. I just wanna get this over with and get out of here."

Tilda sighed but smiled crookedly at me. "Fine. Wait here."

While she went to retrieve Ridley, I sat down on one of the benches by the lockers. It may have seemed strange talking to the Överste in the girls' locker room, but with so few female trackers, odds were that no one would use it. In fact, it was probably the least used area in the whole school.

Ridley pushed open the door hard enough to make it bang against the wall, and I hopped to my feet. He didn't look at me when he came in, instead preferring to stare off at some point directly to the right of me, but finally, he forced his dark eyes to rest coldly on me.

His uniform looked good on him; like always, he'd left the top button undone, revealing just a hint of his chest. If the King or members of the Högdragen came around, he could get in trouble for that, but by the hard look on his face, I didn't think he gave a damn.

"What the hell is so damn important that you think you can just blow off your job?" Ridley demanded.

"Queen Linnea."

"We already went over that—"

"I think I know where she is," I cut him off, and that got his attention.

For a brief second, he looked at me the way he always had—his mask of anger momentarily displaced. A wave of heat flushed over me, reminding me of the way I felt about him, but I pushed it away. I didn't have time for that, even if he didn't hate me right now.

"What are you talking about?" Ridley asked.

"She came to me in a lysa," I said, and skepticism flashed in his eyes. "I know how rare they are, especially coming from a Skojare. But I also know that it was real. Linnea is alive, and she told me to come find her."

He arched his eyebrow and folded his arms across his chest. "Did she happen to tell you where she was?"

"No, not exactly," I admitted.

"If this was a true lysa, and Linnea really wanted you to come find her, why wouldn't she tell you *exactly* where she was?"

"I don't know." I shook my head "The Skojare don't have a ton of psychic powers, so it most likely took all she had to get out that one quick message, like an SOS."

Ridley narrowed his eyes slightly. "That leads to another question—why you?"

I let out a frustrated sigh. "I don't know. When I find her, I'll ask."

"How do you plan to find her if you don't know where she is?" Ridley asked, and I hurried to explain my conversation with my mom about Lake Isolera.

When I finished telling him my plan to find Linnea, reiterating why it was so important, Ridley didn't say anything. He stared down at the floor, breathing in deeply through his nose, and then he closed his eyes and rubbed his forehead.

"How far away is it?" he asked finally.

"Based on the point on the map, I'd guess around a hundred to a hundred and fifty miles from Storvatten. So that puts us at about a day's journey from here."

He considered it, then nodded once. "Okay." For a second I was so relieved that I almost hugged him, and then he added, "But I'm going with you."

"What?" I asked, and I'm sure I sounded as shocked as I felt. "You—you . . . you're running the army."

I'd stumbled because I wanted to say, *you hate me.* But I couldn't say that, so I pointed out the next logical reason why he wouldn't be able to go.

"Tomorrow is Sunday, and that's a light day. If we head out now, taking shifts driving, we should find the place and be back by Tuesday," Ridley reasoned. "The scouts left this morning to search for Viktor Dålig and Konstantin Black. We'll just be doing basic drills back here. Tilda can handle it until we get back."

I opened my mouth, trying to think of protests, but I merely ended up gaping at him.

"You don't need to come with," I finally said.

"If Linnea knows *anything* about Viktor, I want to be there when you find her," he said, and by the resolve in his eyes I knew he wouldn't back down. Not that I blamed him.

I swallowed hard, as if my guilt had taken physical form as a painful lump in my throat. "Understood."

"Go pack and get the things you need," Ridley instructed me. "I'll talk to Tilda and the King and get everything arranged. When I'm finished, I'll meet you at your place, and we'll head out."

skirmish

W hat had started as light snow an hour ago had switched to an icy sleet that sounded like pebbles hitting the windshield. To Ridley's credit, he slept through it—his head lolled to one side, bouncing along with the Land Rover as it navigated the worsening terrain of the back roads.

It was over twenty hours into our journey to the mythical and possibly nonexistent Lake Isolera, which had begun with an awkward train ride during which we both struggled to fill the silence by inspecting maps of Ontario.

Before we left, I'd borrowed a Skojare book from my mom. She kept a few artifacts from her past life in Storvatten, and this was a book of fairy tales that her beloved grandmother had read to her. It had a few poems and stories that mentioned Lake Isolera, and since that was the only thing we had to go on, I took it.

On the train, Ridley had read the stories about the lake

aloud. They had a tendency to switch between English and Swedish mid-sentence, and his pronunciation was much better than mine. Out of the five tribes, the Skojare were the most isolated, and therefore, most attached to the ways of the old world—including the original language of all the troll tribes.

"Through the trees and past the *slinggrande flod*, in the depths of snow that no human would trod," Ridley read aloud. "There is a land of *trolleri* and beauty, the most wonderful place that ever you'll see."

I closed my eyes, listening to the comforting baritone of Ridley's voice. When he was reading from the book, he spoke like he normally did—no hint of anger or unease. My chest ached with regret and longing. He was so close to me. Our arms brushed up against each other on the armrest. But he was still so far away.

If I looked up at him, I would see an icy wall in his mahogany eyes where once there had only been warmth.

All I wanted was to take back everything that had happened—not telling him about Viktor right away and even kissing him. I just wanted things to go back to the way they used to be between us, but I didn't have the words to erase what had happened. So I just closed my eyes and listened to him read.

Once we'd picked up a rental car at the train station, things had actually gotten easier. We needed to take turns driving, and Ridley had offered to take the first shift. I hadn't slept well, but at least it wasn't tense or weird that we weren't speaking.

I'd taken my shift a few hours back, and Ridley had been sleeping soundly the whole time. Most of the drive had been easy and relatively uneventful, but gradually the clouds had moved in, growing darker and blotting out the sun. Then the snow had begun, which wasn't bad when compared to its icy counterpart that pounded down now.

The windshield wipers could barely keep up at this point. The SUV slid on a slick patch. I managed to catch it before we went off the road, but it jerked hard when it hit a dip on the pavement.

"What's going on?" Ridley asked, waking up with a start.

"Everything's okay."

He sat up straighter, blinking back sleep, and looking out the window at the mess the sky was pouring down on us.

"Do you want me to take over?" he asked, eyeing my hands gripped tightly on the wheel.

I shook my head. "No, I've got it. You just woke up."

And at that moment, the Land Rover decided to skid again. It wasn't bad, and I recovered easily, but it hadn't eased Ridley's concerns.

"Are you sure?" he asked. "Because I got plenty of sleep, and I'm feeling alert now."

"Yeah, I'm sure," I insisted. "Besides, I think we're getting close."

He waited a beat before adding, "Because sometimes you say you're sure, and you're not."

"What are you talking about?" I gave him a sidelong glance, since I didn't want to take my eyes completely off the road. "I never say I'm sure unless I am."

He laughed dryly. "Whatever you say."

"What's *that* supposed to mean?" I asked.

"It means . . ." He ran a hand through his wavy, sleep-tousled hair. "Nothing. I shouldn't have said anything."

"But you did."

Ridley let out a long breath. "It's just . . . you sure kissed me like you meant it, and then you told me that you didn't."

At first I was too stunned to say anything. I couldn't believe he was even bringing it up. Finally, I managed a plaintive "That's not fair."

"Life isn't fair, Bryn," he muttered dryly, and for some reason that set me off.

"You kissed me like you meant it too," I shot back. "And you have a girlfriend!"

"Juni's not my girlfriend," he nearly shouted, shifting in his seat. "We've gone on a few dates is all."

I scoffed. "That's bullshit, Ridley."

"And it doesn't matter," he said, instead of arguing my point. "You've made it perfectly and repeatedly clear that you have no interest in dating anyone ever, so I don't know why it bothers you if I'm seeing someone or not."

"It doesn't bother me. Do whatever you want."

He mumbled something, but I didn't ask what. I just let him lapse into silence and stare out the window, not that there was much to see. The sleet was coming down so heavily that visibility was completely shot.

That's how the tree appeared out of nowhere. It had been

uprooted by the excessive weight of the snow-sleet mixture, and it tipped across the road, angling upward with branches sticking out haphazardly.

I jerked the wheel, attempting to swerve around the tree, but there was nowhere to swerve to. This was a narrow road, barely wider than a lane, and the tree had it blocked entirely. The tires slipped on the icy mixture, and we careened off the road.

collision

Ridley cried out in surprise as the SUV spun ninety degrees, and bounced down the shallow embankment next to the road before slamming into a tree and coming to a hard stop.

We both sat there panting, neither of us saying anything. The dashboard console began to beep angrily, letting us know that we'd collided with something—as if we couldn't figure that out already.

"You okay?" Ridley asked.

"Yeah. You?"

He nodded. "You should've let me drive."

"There was a tree in the road!" I gestured back toward the road several yards behind us. "That wasn't my fault."

"Right." Ridley rolled his eyes. "Of course. *Nothing* is ever your fault."

I didn't want to argue with him, so I got out of the SUV under the ruse of inspecting it for damage. Fortunately, the Land

Rover had hit a massive pine tree, and its long branches covered with thick needles helped to keep back the sting of the sleet.

We'd been going relatively slowly when I swerved on the road, so thankfully the SUV hadn't been going that fast when it hit the tree. Other than some minor bumper damage, it didn't seem like the Land Rover was any worse for wear.

Ridley got out of the vehicle and walked over to where I was standing near the tree. The branches mostly sheltered us, but it was warm enough that when the sleet rested on the pine needles they eventually began to melt, dripping through the branches in a light shower that sprinkled down on me.

"I've never said nothing is my fault," I said. The adrenaline from the accident left me feeling sharper, pricklier, and I know that my words came out harsher than I meant them, but I didn't care. "I've never even thought that."

"You sure as hell act like that," Ridley snapped back, matching my intensity, and I turned to glare up at him.

"If you think I don't constantly blame myself for letting Viktor get away—"

"I don't blame you!" he shouted, then he stopped. As quickly as that, the fight had gone out of him, and his whole frame seemed to sag. The icy mask he'd been wearing melted away, and he just looked hurt and a little lost. "Why can't you just tell me things?"

"I'm sorry I didn't tell you about him." I was surprised that my voice quivered with my sincerity, and I hastily steadied it. "I just had to be certain about what I saw. After all you've been through with Viktor, I didn't want to get you upset for nothing. But now I realize it would've been better if I had told you sooner, and I'm sorry. I can never tell you how sorry I am."

"I don't need your apologies." He shook his head. "And I'm not even really mad at you."

"You're not?"

He shrugged. "I mean, you should've gotten me before you went down to talk to Konstantin."

"I thought he would be more likely to open up if it was just me." I tried to explain my reasoning, and I couldn't tell if he accepted it or not.

Hesitantly, Ridley said, "I know that makes sense."

"But?" I prompted, since he'd left that statement hanging in the air.

"But Viktor almost killed you, Bryn." He looked at me for the first time since he'd gotten out of the SUV, and the heat had returned to his eyes, burning darkly within him. "I was asleep a few floors above you, and the man who killed my father came back after being gone for years and nearly killed the person . . ."

Ridley trailed off, and I didn't push him to finish. Whatever he was going to say, I didn't think I wanted to know. The pounding of my heart would argue with that, but I knew logically it was better for us if he didn't finish that sentence, if I don't know what I really meant to him.

"I don't know what's going on between us," he said finally. "But I do know that I don't want to lose you."

I swallowed hard. "I don't want to lose you either."

"Then you need to confide in me, okay?" Ridley asked. "You can't go running off without letting me know. I told you before that we're in this together, and with Viktor back, I mean that now more than ever."

"I can do that," I agreed. "And I promise not to keep secrets from you anymore."

"Friends again?" he asked with a hopeful smile, holding out his hand to me.

"Friends."

He'd had his hands shoved in his pockets, but mine were cold and damp from touching the vehicle to check for damage. When I took his hand to shake it, the warmth that enveloped me was astonishing. Instantly, I knew this was a bad idea, but I didn't let go of him.

The air smelled of snow, water, and fresh pine needles. The dripping water had dampened our hair, making his a bit wavier than normal, and for some reason it made his mahogany eyes appear brighter. I was cold and wet, and I imagined how much warmer it would be in his arms.

And then I wasn't imagining it. We'd both moved forward, filling in the gap between us, and he let go of my hand.

"We should, um, probably get going," he said in a low voice.

"Right," I agreed, forcing a smile when I stepped back from him. "We should check the GPS and find out how close we are."

Pushing down all the conflicting emotions I had swirling inside me, I turned to the job at hand and got back in the car.

The coordinates for the lake weren't exact, so we'd made our best guess with longitude and latitude on the GPS app on Ridley's tablet. I grabbed the tablet off the dashboard, but it was updating slowly. Service could be sketchy out here, blinking in and out. At least it was working now.

"What's it say?" Ridley asked when he got in the SUV. He shook the water from his hair then peered over at the tablet in my hands.

"According to the GPS we're not that far anyway, and there isn't a road going directly to Lake Isolera. Want to try walking it?"

"Sure. Why not?"

I started the Land Rover and carefully drove it back up to the road, parking it near the tree that had diverted our course. It ran normally, which was a bit of a relief, and parking it along the road would make it easier to find when we came back.

We added ponchos over our winter gear, then grabbed our packs and locked up the vehicle before making the trek out into the wilderness. Ridley had a waterproof case for his tablet, which was good because the weather showed no signs of letting up.

The first hour we wandered through the trees was the worst. We went where the GPS directed us, and when we found nothing, we began circling out further. Every time I had the chance, I broke branches and tied red string to trees, trying to leave some signs so we wouldn't get lost, and we'd be able to find our way back to the SUV.

Though we had put on boots, hats, and gloves, it had all soaked through. We were used to the cold, but it seemed to permeate everything, making my bones ache. Every step had become painful, but neither Ridley nor I were willing to give up so easily.

Just when I was getting to the point where I wasn't sure I could take the cold much longer, I saw an odd shimmer through a patch of pine trees. A subtle change in the snow falling down, like it was bowing around the side of a snow globe, but it only lasted a moment. When I tilted my head, though, I was almost certain I could see rays of light spilling out through it.

I started walking forward, moving more quickly than I had before, with Ridley following.

"What's going on?" Ridley called from behind me.

I stopped long enough for him to catch up, and I pointed at the trees in front of us. "I think I see something." I tilted my head again, and for a split second, I saw it—a shimmer across the air. "When I look just right, I can see it."

Ridley squinted and brushed back the snow that clung to his eyebrows. "I can't see anything."

I knew that I might be crazy, that this might be some cold-induced insanity causing me to see a mirage, but deep down, it just didn't feel that way. The closer we got, the more certain I became. Ridley continued to echo his inability to see what I was chasing, but he never suggested we turn back.

Maybe it was my Skojare heritage. My mom had said that the lake had been cloaked in enchantment so that even other tribes wouldn't be able to find it. I must've had just enough Skojare blood in me that I could see the faintest hint of it.

The pine trees were growing closer together, so I had to bow my head and physically push branches out of the way to get through them.

When I finally made it through and lifted my head, the sun was shining so brightly I had to squint. I held up my arm to block the light, and it was a few seconds before my eyes adjusted enough to really see anything.

The first thing I saw, sparkling like a massive sapphire, was a lake spanning several miles. It sat in the center of a clearing surrounded by a thick barrier of pine trees, and it had to be the most beautiful body of water I'd ever seen.

"Lake Isolora," Ridley whispered behind me, sounding in awe. "It does exist."

isolera

In the bright light, the grass that framed the lake appeared almost lime green, sprinkled with brightly colored wild-flowers in shades of pink and purple. The grass gave way to fine white sand that sparkled as if it were mixed with diamond dust, and the water lapped gently against it.

It was so warm that all my winter gear felt unbearable. I shed my hat and poncho first, then I kept going until I was left in the black leggings and tank top I'd worn underneath my sweater and jeans.

"How is this even possible?" Ridley asked.

I glanced back at him, pulling my eyes away from the lake with some difficulty. He'd taken off his boots and jacket but apparently moved much slower than I did. A bright blue but-terfly fluttered past him, and his eyes followed it, transfixed for a moment.

"The Skojare must've had power unlike anything we've ever

seen if they could cast a spell like this and keep it going for years," I said, then turned back to the water. "Hundreds of years, if my mom's book is to be believed."

In Doldastam, it took half a dozen gardeners working in special "greenhouses" to keep the garden up and running. Growing grapes and tomatoes couldn't be anywhere near as difficult as this oasis, even if the gardeners' psychokinetic abilities were working against subarctic temperatures to keep fruits and vegetables alive. On top of that, we'd had to poach several of the workers from the Trylle, since their powers were stronger than ours.

"Our ancestors used to be more powerful," Ridley reminded me, but he sounded as if he was in a bit of a daze. "We've lost our abilities over the centuries. I mean, we've heard that our whole lives, but if another tribe could do this, then we've lost so much more than I ever imagined."

The grass felt like soft downy carpet under my feet as I walked toward the lake. I expected the sand to be scorching hot, the way beaches always seemed to be under the glaring sun, but instead it felt perfect—silky and warm against my frozen toes.

"Have you ever seen anything like this?" I asked Ridley.

"No." When he spoke again he sounded closer to me, so he must've been walking up behind me, but I didn't look back. "I sorta feel like I'm in a dream."

I nodded slowly. "I know exactly what you mean."

While my mom literally felt the water calling to her when she'd been away from it too long, thanks to her Skojare blood,

I'd never felt such a strong pull. I enjoyed the water a little more than the average Kanin, but it wasn't exactly a *need*.

But now I felt it. Tugging at something inside me, like I was connected to the lake by an invisible thread wrapped around the very core of my being, and now the thread had pulled taut. I stepped close enough that the water lapped against my toes. A delicious wave of relief rolled over me, and I hadn't even noticed how apprehensive I'd been feeling.

I crouched down and cupped the water in my hand. At first, I just watched it drip through my fingers, running clearer than any river or lake I'd seen. Then I held my cupped hands to my mouth, taking a long sip, and it tasted crisp and pure and luscious. Almost instantly, I felt refreshed in a way I never had before, even after the deepest night's sleep.

"Bryn?" Ridley said in a way that made me realize he'd been calling my name, and I looked back over my shoulder at him. He stood at the edge of the beach behind me, and his expression had a lax, dreamy quality to it, but anxiety had edged into his eyes.

"Yeah?"

"We still have a mission," he reminded me. "We need to find Linnea, and I'm not even sure if she's here."

I turned away from him for a moment to stare out at the lake before me. I wanted nothing more than to submerge myself in Lake Isolera, letting it wash over me, warm and cool all at once. But Ridley was right. We had a job to do.

I stood up and stepped back, so the water wasn't lapping at my toes any longer.

"Where should we look?" I asked, but my eyes were already scanning the clearing.

Other than the thick evergreens that walled out the cold reality beyond the magic of Lake Isolera, there were no trees. There wasn't even much land in the clearing. It was mostly the lake. If I didn't see Linnea now, I had no idea where she could be hiding.

"If she's here, she's in the lake," Ridley decided. "We should swim."

And I didn't need any more convincing than that. I knew I couldn't let the water enchant me the way it had a few moments before, but I would still be more than happy to swim in it. I just had to keep my wits about me.

Ridley stripped down to his boxers, and while part of me wanted to appreciate the taut muscles of his chest and abdomen, I deliberately did my best not to look at him. Not only because we had a job to complete, but because we'd just agreed to be friends, and I didn't want to muck that up by fantasizing about what it would feel like to run my fingers down the hard contours of his chest and stomach until . . .

I shook my head and waded out into the water, hoping that it would wash away my thoughts. As soon as I was out far enough, I dove under, letting the lake completely cover me, and I honestly can't remember a time when I ever felt better. It was like enveloping myself in unadulterated bliss.

For a few moments, I did let myself just swim and relish the feeling. But then my lungs began to demand oxygen, and I surfaced. I breathed in deeply, staring up at the blue sky above me, until Ridley came up a minute later, gasping for breath.

"Are you okay?" I asked, swimming closer to where he'd emerged a couple yards from me.

"I'm fine," he insisted and wiped the water from his eyes. "How long can you hold your breath?"

I shrugged. "I don't know. Maybe five minutes."

During grade school, I had frequently shown off my ability to hold my breath for extended periods of time. I thought it would make the kids think I was cool, but it turned out I was nothing more than a circus sideshow. The average Kanin could hold their breath for roughly thirty seconds, so my feat seemed quite impressive and a little freaky. But by comparison, my mom could hold her breath under water for nearly a half hour.

"Yeah, I can't do anywhere close to that." Ridley shook his head. "I tried to go down to the bottom of the lake, but it's way too far for me. If Linnea has gills, she could be hanging out in the depths of it."

"That makes sense," I agreed. "I'll see how far down I can go and look for her. You wanna stick to the shallower areas?"

"Works for me."

I took a deep breath, then plunged under the water. I went straight down, thinking that I would find the bottom and search along there. If this was a hidden paradise built for gilled trolls, it wasn't a stretch to guess that there might be something at the bottom.

Ridley wasn't kidding about how deep it went. Even with the water being totally clear, it soon became too dark for me to see well. When a small silver fish swam by, I caught just a glimmer of light on its scales.

Even as a dull ache in my head and chest began to build, the delirium of the water overtook me. It seemed to flow through me, filling me with pure elation, and I swam deeper. I'd like to say I was more determined than ever to find Linnea, but really, that came in second to the way the lake made me feel.

But slowly that was beginning to give away to pain and panic as my body struggled with a buildup of carbon dioxide. My lungs started to burn. I looked up toward the rays of light barely breaking the water, and it occurred to me too late that I had gone down too far.

I had swum down for almost five minutes, which meant that it would take me almost five minutes to surface. That was twice as long as I could hold my breath. I was in trouble.

With my eyes fixed on the sun above me, I kicked my legs as fast as I could, racing against the clock. My lungs felt like they were going to explode, and the muscles in my abdomen began to painfully spasm.

But the light above was growing brighter, and if I pushed myself, I could just make it. The pressure aggravated my head injury, making the vision in my right eye blur and my head throb. A fog was descending on my brain. Then everything faded to blackness, and my legs went limp underneath me, despite my demands that they swim on.

delusion

The good news was I was breathing. I could feel it—oxygen filled my lungs with ease. Beyond that, my stomach ached as if I'd been punched, and my head throbbed dully. But all that pain meant I was alive.

"I think she's coming to," a female voice was saying softly.

"Bryn!" Ridley shouted in a panic, slapping me on the cheek.

"Stop hitting me," I mumbled and weakly pushed his arm back. The ground felt soft beneath me, so I assumed I was lying on the grass, safely out of the dark clutches of drowning.

He exhaled roughly. "You scared the crap out of me, Bryn."

"Sorry." I opened my eyes to see Ridley and the missing Queen Linnea bent over me. "Hey, I found her."

Linnea smiled—there was no lipstick out here, so her lips were a pale pink, in line with the porcelain tones of her skin.

Strangely, without the makeup she actually looked older than when I'd seen her before.

She was sixteen but a young sixteen, with an innocence about her. The too-bright red lipstick had reminded me of a little girl playing dress-up, whereas now she simply appeared to be her age. It probably didn't help that with her ringlet curls and wide blue eyes, she bore a remarkable resemblance to Shirley Temple.

"Actually, I found you," Linnea correct me. "You were about to drown when I spotted you and pulled you to the shore."

"Thank you."

I sat up, and a wave of dizziness nearly knocked me back, but I fought it off. It didn't help waking up in this place, where everything felt like a dream. Everything had a shimmery edge to it, like it wasn't quite real.

"You okay?" Ridley put a hand on my shoulder to steady me, and his strength reassured me the way it always did.

For a moment, with the sun backlighting him and the water dripping down his bare chest, Ridley appeared absolutely dazzling. He'd leaned over when he touched me, and the very nearness of him took my breath away. That only made his chestnut eyes darken in concern, and I hurried to shake off the feeling and pull my attention away from him.

"Are y-you okay?" I asked Linnea, stuttering a bit as I composed myself.

She nodded. Other than the lack of makeup, she looked the

same as she had when I saw her last—no signs of injury. She wore a blue bikini, revealing her slender figure, so any bumps or bruises would have been visible.

"What are you doing here?" I asked, deciding to cut to the chase. "Why did you leave Storvatten?"

"I couldn't stay there anymore." She shook her head, and her translucent gills flared beneath her jaw. "Something is going on there."

"What do you mean?" Ridley asked.

"The guards at the palace have been acting strangely," she explained. "They were normally aloof and careless, but lately I've felt like they were watching me too closely. I don't know how to explain it, but everywhere I went, I felt like I had eyes on me."

"Did you tell anyone about it?" I asked.

"Not right away," Linnea went on. "At first I thought I was only being paranoid, so I waited a few weeks before bringing it to my husband. Mikko wasn't overly concerned, but he tried to ease my fears by saying he would talk to the guards."

"Did anything change after that?" Ridley pressed her, and I could tell he was doing his best not to sound accusatory.

We'd long suspected that Linnea's husband, the Skojare King Mikko, had had some involvement in her disappearance. Even with Konstantin Black's presence, there still seemed to be something odd about Mikko and the guards in Storvatten. They had blocked our attempts at gathering information and doing a proper investigation, not to mention that Mikko had shifted from indifferent about his wife's disappearance to devastated rather quickly.

There was also the matter of his marriage to Linnea. It had been arranged by their families, as most royal mergers were, and Mikko was twice her age. They'd been married for less than a year, and I had to wonder what exactly those kind of nuptials were like.

"Things didn't really have a chance to change," Linnea elaborated. "I told Mikko about my suspicions, and two days later the dark man was telling me that I had to get out of there."

"Wait." I waved my hand. "What man?"

"He never said his name, but he had a darker complexion, like you." Linnea pointed to Ridley, referring to his dark olive skin. "Black wavy hair, a beard, and gray eyes."

I hadn't really needed her to describe him, but I wanted to be absolutely sure. It was Konstantin Black.

"What were you doing when he approached you?" Ridley asked.

"I'd gone to bed with Mikko, the way I always did, but I couldn't sleep." Linnea sat back and pulled her knees up to her chest, wrapping her arms around them. "I've been a bit on edge lately, since I've been getting this weird vibe from everyone at the palace. So I went down to the pool to swim, hoping to burn off some of my anxiety.

"I actually snuck down to the pool," she went on. "With the guards acting so strangely, I didn't want any of them following me. But as soon as I got there and slipped off my robe, that man emerged from nowhere.

"It was almost like Mystique from the X-Men," Linnea continued with wide eyes.

With the Skojare spending most of their lives locked inside the palace, hidden away from humans and the rest of the world, they spent a great deal of time watching movies and reading books. It was a way to make the time go by faster.

Konstantin appearing out of thin air had to be an amazing thing for her to see. Even though Linnea had been exposed to some of the magic of our world, she had limited interactions with other tribes. Like many Kanin, Konstantin's skin could change color, so he could blend into the background. It was disorienting to witness in real life.

"Did he hurt you?" Ridley asked, since he was more fixated on the idea that Konstantin was a villain. I hadn't completely ruled him out as one yet, but my certainty was wavering. "Did he threaten you at all?"

"No. I mean, I don't think so." Her brow furrowed, and she pursed her lips. "He didn't hurt me, but he said, 'You must leave. If you want to live, you must get as far away from the palace as you can, and never come back. And you must tell no one.'"

"Did he say why?" I asked.

"No." Linnea shook her head, making water spray lightly from the wet curls that framed her face. "I tried to ask him why I had to leave and who he was, but he just became more insistent and said there wasn't any time."

"And you listened to him?" Ridley asked, unable to hide the incredulity in his voice. "Why?"

"Because he voiced what I'd already been feeling," Linnea

explained with a half-shrug. "I didn't feel safe in the palace, and he'd confirmed my fears."

"And you told no one?" I asked.

"No." She frowned. "I didn't think I had time. I wanted to tell Mikko and my grandma. They must be worried sick." She perked up then. "Have you talked to either of them? How are they doing?"

"We were in Storvatten helping the search for you, and we saw them both. They're doing fine." I glossed over it. I didn't want to share my concerns about her husband, at least not until I heard everything she had to say.

"How did you escape from the palace without being seen?" Ridley returned to the subject at hand.

"The palace has a freshwater pool that connects to Lake Superior by a tunnel, so I just swam out that way. Since no one had spotted me coming out of my chambers, it was fairly easy," Linnea said. "Once I was out in the lake, I had no idea where to go, so I just kept swimming. Then I remembered the stories my grandma had told me about Lake Isolera, so I decided to try to find it."

"So you've been out here for . . ." I paused, trying to remember when Linnea had gone missing. "Ten days? How have you survived? What have you eaten?"

"I don't know." That seemed to puzzle her too. "I haven't been hungry. I didn't even realize it had been ten days. I thought maybe two or three."

I glanced out at the lake behind her and remembered a line

that Ridley had read from the fairy tale book on the train. *The water of Isolera will sustain all who dream of it.* There was some serious magic here. Maybe it was the near drowning, but its power had begun to unnerve me.

"Did you call for me?" I asked Linnea, pulling my gaze from the lake back to her. "In the lysa?"

"Yes!" Linnea beamed. "And I am *so* happy it worked! My grandma had trained me to use it in case of an emergency, but I'd never been very good. It uses so much energy, but I think the magic of this place helped strengthen me."

"But why me?" I shook my head. "Why not your grandma or your husband?"

"I was afraid that if I got to Mikko or Nana, they would mistakenly alert the guards to search for me, and I don't trust the guards," Linnea explained. "I wasn't sure if anyone without Skojare blood would be able to find Lake Isolera, and you were the only Skojare I knew who wasn't connected with Storvatten."

"So what do you want to do now?" Ridley asked. "Do you plan to go back to Storvatten?"

Linnea let out a heavy sigh, and for a moment she looked much older. "I don't know. I know that I can't stay here forever, and I miss Mikko desperately."

She was staring down at the sand beneath her toes, which allowed Ridley and me to exchange a look. We were both surprised to hear that she missed Mikko. So far, our impression had been that she was in a marriage of obligation.

"Why don't you come back with us to Doldastam?" Ridley suggested. "Once we get there, we can contact your family and decide what to do."

I was eager to get going, so as soon as Linnea agreed, I went over to gather our winter clothes. They had completely dried, and when I looked up, I realized the sun had moved all the way across the sky. It felt like we'd been here for maybe 15 minutes, but it must've been much, much longer than that.

Linnea had swum here from Storvatten, so she had only her swimsuit. Fortunately, when she'd made the trek across land a week and a half ago, the weather had been a bit warmer, but I still wasn't sure how she had made it.

I supposed she was like my mother—much tougher than she appeared. Skojare like my mom and Linnea had to be in order handle the harsh temperatures of swimming in a freezing lake during the winter.

Ridley gave her his jacket, and I gave her my jeans. That meant I'd be venturing out in only my leggings, which wasn't ideal, but I would make due.

When we pushed through the branches the way we had come in, it was the strangest feeling. It was almost like a dream within a dream, where even after you awake, you're still dreaming. It was totally dark when we emerged from Lake Isolera, which was very disorienting since the sun had somehow still been up there.

Fortunately, the snow had stopped. The moon was only a sliver, but the fresh snow reflected it, making it appear brighter.

Thanks to the strings and broken branches I'd left behind on our trail, we were able to make it back to the SUV with relative ease.

But by the time we reached it, I could barely remember what Lake Isolera had looked like.

repatriation

It was very late on Monday night when Ridley pulled the SUV in front of the palace in Doldastam. Ridley and I had taken shifts driving on the way back, the same way we had on the way there, but we were both tired and sore from the long journey. Linnea, on the other hand, sat up in the backseat, wide eyed and excited the whole time.

She'd hardly seen any of the world outside of Storvatten, and even though most of our trip involved empty roads and wide open spaces, Linnea still watched out the window with rapt interest. For what little interaction she had with the human world—when we'd stopped at gas stations and boarded the train—she almost exploded with delight.

We'd disguised her gills as best we could by giving her a scarf to wrap around her neck, and she'd worn one of my hoodies and a pair of jeans. My clothes were a bit big on her, but that worked in the case of the sweatshirt. It gave the hood ample room to cover her curls and drape over her gills.

Two Högdragen stood guard just outside the front door of the palace—a new feature since the whole "war" had started—and they stopped us, as if Viktor Dålig would knock politely on the front door if he came to assassinate the King.

One of the Högdragen was Kasper Abbott, Tilda's boyfriend—well, fiancé now. The streetlamps made the silver flourishes on his black uniform shimmer. His black curls were gelled perfectly into place, and his beard was immaculately groomed. He stood at attention, but he gave me a quizzical look as Ridley, Linnea, and I approached them.

"The palace is closed for the night," the first guard informed us.

"We have business with the King," Ridley replied.

"What business do you have with the King?" Kasper asked, and he glanced away from me over to Linnea, who was still hidden in the oversized hooded sweatshirt.

The other guard glared at Kasper, and then before Ridley could answer, the guard told us, "The King and Queen have retired for the night. Come back in the morning."

"Elliot, this is Ridley Dresden, the Rektor and the Överste," Kasper said, doing his best not to chastise his comrade in front of us. "If he wants to see the King, it must be important."

"I have orders from the King not to disturb him." Elliot kept his head high and his shoulders back.

I could see this was going to get us nowhere, so I turned to Linnea, who had been staring up at the massive stained-glass window above the front door to the palace. When she looked back down at me, I nodded, encouraging her. Linnea pushed back her hood and pulled the scarf from around her neck, then smiled up at the guards.

"You may recognize Linnea Biâelse, the missing Queen of the Skojare," Ridley explained with a hint of snark. "I think that King Evert will make an exception for us now."

"Elliot," Kasper said in a voice just above a whisper. "Get the King. I'll take them to the meeting room to wait for him."

"Yes, of course." Elliot quickly bowed before Linnea. "Sorry, Your Highness." He took a step back, stumbling on the cobblestones, and then hurried inside to get the King.

"I'm sorry about that." Kasper relaxed his demeanor after Elliot left. "He's a good guard. He can just be overzealous sometimes."

Kasper led us inside the palace and down the hall to the room where I usually met with the King. Since nobody had been expecting us, the hearth was dark, and it was rather chilly. The cold front that had descended upon Doldastam last week showed no signs of letting up.

Linnea shivered involuntarily, but I wasn't sure if it was because of the cold or something else. When Kasper rushed over to start a fire for us, she smiled as she thanked him, but it didn't quite meet her eyes.

"Are you okay?" I asked her, and she nodded and met me with the same smile she'd given him—thin, forced. There was a hardness to her expression, making her appear like a china doll.

While Ridley brought more logs over to the fireplace to help Kasper get it going faster, I walked over to Linnea. She stood at the edge of the room, her arms wrapped around herself, and when I put my hand on her shoulder, she jumped a little.

"What's wrong?" I asked softly.

"I'm just nervous." Linnea tried to force a smile at me, but she gave up and let out a panicked breath. "There's no going back now, is there?"

"What do you mean?" I asked.

But before she could answer, King Evert threw open the doors to the meeting room with Queen Mina following right behind. His black hair was disheveled from sleep, and he wore a silver satin robe lined with fur, while his wife wore a matching feminine version. Her hair hung down her back in a thick braid, and though both of them appeared to have just been roused from sleep, Mina had managed to put on her crown and a necklace before coming down here.

I walked over to the end of the table with Ridley to greet them, while Kasper took his post next to the fireplace, presumably leaving Elliot to guard the front gate by himself.

"What's this I hear about the Skojare Queen?" Evert asked and put his hands on his hips, managing to sound both concerned and irritated.

Mina had already spotted Linnea, gasping when she did. "It's true."

While the King demanded to know what was going on, his wife strode over to Linnea. Mina put her hands on Linnea's shoulders in a gesture of reassurance, and when she spoke in her faux-British accent the way she did whenever she was around royalty, her words were filled with soft comfort.

"How are you doing?" Mina asked her. "I can't imagine the ordeal you've been through."

"I'm all right," Linnea said, but her voice cracked a little.

Mina put her hand on Linnea's cheek and bent down to look her right in the eyes. "You're safe now. And that's what matters."

Linnea smiled gratefully at her and wiped at her eyes before a tear spilled over.

Ridley had been filling the King in on our adventures in finding Linnea, but I'd only been half-listening since I wanted to keep an eye on her. Mina looped her arm around Linnea's waist, and they turned their attention to Ridley and King Evert, so I did the same.

"Once we found Queen Linnea, we drove back here," Ridley said, finishing up the story.

Evert sat in his high-backed chair, and he scratched his head for a moment, taking in everything Ridley had said. Ridley and I stood across the table from him, waiting for his response.

"This is all well and good, and I am glad the Skojare Queen is safe"—he paused to look over at her—"I truly am. But Ridley, if I recall correctly, you asked to be relieved from your post for a few days to help the scouts track Viktor Dålig. You made no mention of the Skojare Queen."

Ridley cleared his throat and shifted his weight. I'd wondered what exactly he'd told the King so that both Ridley and

I had been able to get out of our duty here in Doldastam. Since we were on lockdown, I knew it couldn't have been easy.

"I believed that Queen Linnea may have had some information on the whereabouts of Viktor Dålig," Ridley explained.

Evert arched an eyebrow at Linnea. "Do you?"

"I don't—don't know who Viktor Dålig is." Linnea shook her head. "Should I?"

"No, you haven't had a reason to before." Evert held up his hand to her and turned his hardened gaze back to Ridley.

"It is unfortunate that she doesn't know anything, but it was a risk I thought was worth taking." Ridley stood firm. "Besides, she is the Skojare Queen. Her whereabouts are important to our people as a whole."

"My King, he's right," Mina chimed in. "Ridley and Bryn found Queen Linnea safe and sound. They did a commendable thing. You should not be yelling at them for it."

He let out a sigh, then nodded. "I'm sorry. My sleep-deprived brain is not functioning properly. This should be a time for celebration." Evert straightened up and smiled. "We'll call the Skojare King to retrieve his young bride, and when he does, we'll have a party in Queen Linnea's honor."

"Must I go back?" Linnea blurted out suddenly, and everyone turned to look at her.

"Don't you want to go home?" King Evert asked her.

"I miss my husband terribly, and my grandmother," Linnea hurried to explain. "But there is something going on in Storvatten. I don't feel safe there."

Evert shifted uneasily in his chair, unsure of how to deal

with a frightened teenage queen. "You have guards, and you have your husband. Talk to them, and I'm sure you'll sort it out."

"I don't trust the guards there." Linnea shook her head.

"Speaking from experience, I would say the guards in Storvatten are rather inept," I added. When we'd been at the palace right after Linnea had gone missing, I'd found the guards to be lazy, incompetent, and entirely unfit.

"That may be." Evert cleared his throat. "But this is something you must talk about with King Mikko. We have no control over the happenings in your kingdom."

Linnea lowered her head and nodded once. The last thing I wanted to do was send Linnea someplace where she was unsafe, but I couldn't think of a way to disagree with the King. He couldn't control the guards in another kingdom. That was up to Linnea and her husband.

"What if we send a couple guards with her, to help keep her safe?" Mina suggested. "At least until she and her husband get the situation sorted out in Storvatten."

Evert shook his head. "My Queen, you know we can't spare anyone right now."

"Surely we can spare one or two," Mina insisted, and I was aware that this was the exact opposite position she had held the last time I went to Storvatten. Then, she'd been fighting the King who wanted to send aid to the Skojare, saying we couldn't spare anyone.

It was also surprising how kind Mina seemed to be tonight. When I'd returned a few days ago, she'd been cold bordering on mean, which really wasn't like her. But now she seemed to have returned to her normal self.

I wondered if something had happened, or maybe her current disposition was simply because Linnea was here. I couldn't tell if Mina was genuinely concerned for her, or if our queen just wanted to save face in front of foreign royalty.

"What about Bryn?" Mina gestured to me. "She's familiar with the Skojare, and she's already proven herself to be a great help to Queen Linnea."

King Evert considered it for a moment, then nodded with some reluctance. "Bryn can go to Storvatten, if it's as Queen Linnea wishes, but we cannot spare Ridley. He's too important here."

"What about him?" Linnea asked, pointing to where Kasper stood next to the fireplace, and he appeared as startled as the rest of us. "I'd feel better going with someone I've already met, even if it's only briefly, than someone chosen at random."

"A member of the Högdragen would be good," Mina decided. "He can help retrain the guard in Storvatten."

"It's settled then," King Evert declared, probably before either Mina or Linnea suggested that anyone else tag along. "Bryn Aven and Kasper Abbott will accompany Queen Linnea back to Storvatten." He stood up. "Now, I will call her husband to let him know she's safe, and then I will return to bed since it's very late."

THIRTEEN

tutoring

I f you're going to represent the Högdragen, then you need to act like one."

Kasper stood in the center of the Högdragen training hall. Since he'd taken time out of his busy schedule specifically to work with me this morning, I knew that I should be paying attention to him, but I couldn't help but look around in awe.

The Högdragen area was located off the back of the palace, so I'd only ever caught glimpses inside it when I'd been in school, touring the palace. Attached to the training hall was a gym fully loaded with all kinds of equipment and a small dormitory, where the unmarried guards lived.

The training hall itself had less square footage than the tracker gymnasium at the school, but the ceilings seemed to go on forever, with iron lighting fixtures hanging from exposed beams and skylights above them. Tapestries of silver and black—the colors of the Högdragen uniform—adorned the walls. The floors were a glossy black walnut hardwood.

A few black wrestling mats were spread out in the center of the room, and Kasper stood on one. His dark tank top revealed the thick muscles of his arms, which were crossed over his chest. He was tall and broad-shouldered, especially for a Kanin, who tended to be on the slight side.

"I have had training before, you know," I reminded him as I walked out to meet him. We were the only two in the room, and my footfalls echoed through the cavernous space.

He smirked. "Not like this."

Since I would be going to Storvatten to help guard Linnea and I'd be accompanying Kasper, I'd technically be working as a liaison for the Högdragen. King Evert hadn't sorted out all the details before he'd gone to bed last night, but we'd gotten enough of them for Kasper to feel that some Högdragen training would be good for me.

For as long as I could remember, it's been my dream to be a member of the Högdragen, so I was doing my best to hold in my excitement and act professional. Ridley said it wasn't absolutely necessary, but I wasn't one to turn down doing anything that might help me join the Högdragen someday.

So I'd helped get Linnea settled in last night—along with Queen Mina, who insisted on personally seeing her to the guest chambers—and then I'd gone home, gotten a few hours of sleep, and woken up bright and early to meet Kasper for training.

"So what are we working on?" I asked.

"Since I probably only have about a day to get you ready, it's gonna be a crash course," he said grimly. "I wanna see where you're at, and we'll take it from there. And I want to work on how you carry yourself."

"How I carry myself?" I bristled. "There's nothing wrong with that."

One thing I took pride in was how I carried myself. Trackers had to learn to stand tall, shoulders back, chin up, feet together. We were slightly more relaxed than the Högdragen, who tended to stand and march like toy soldiers, but because of my aspirations, I mimicked the Högdragen the best I could.

"We'll talk about it when we get to it." Kasper held up his hand, silencing my argument. "But we should get started." He lowered his arms and stood with his feet shoulder length apart. "Show me what you've got."

I shook my head, not understanding, and my ponytail swayed behind me. "What do you mean?"

"I wanna see how you handle yourself in a fight. If we're going to protect the Skojare Queen from possible attempts on her life, I need to see how well you can do that."

For a moment, I hesitated out of a strange sense of intimidation. I'd fought guys as big as Kasper before, and Bent Stum had actually been much stronger than him. So that wasn't the issue. It was reverence for his title, and my fear that I wouldn't live up to the expectations of a proper Högdragen.

But Kasper had decided that it was time to start, so when I didn't move, he did. He came at me, and I quickly slipped out of the way. I was stocky and strong, but not as strong as him, so I knew that I'd have to use my agility and smaller stature to my advantage.

I swooped around him and crouched on the ground, preparing to kick out his legs from under him. As soon as I crouched, he grabbed my leg and flipped me back, so I landed on my back on the mat with a painful *thwock* that echoed through the hall.

The vision in my right eye blurred again for a moment, and I was beginning to wonder how long I'd have to deal with the aftermath of my injury. But within a second, I had jumped to my feet.

"The true testament of a good fighter isn't the ability to not get knocked down, but in how fast they can get back up," Kasper commented as I dusted myself off, then he grinned. "Though I've found it never hurts to avoid getting knocked down in the first place."

"Want me to go again?" I asked.

He nodded, and that was all the incentive I needed this time. I ran at him, and when he grabbed for me, I dodged around his side. This time, I jumped on his back and wrapped my arm around his neck, hoping that either my weight would throw him off balance or I could put him in a kind of sleeper hold.

But neither of those things happened. Instead, he threw himself back with all his might, crushing me against the floor before he hopped to his feet.

I got up again, just as quickly as I had before, even though that fall had hurt twice as badly, and it took longer for the vision in my eye to correct itself. As soon as I did, Kasper commanded, "Again."

So I went at him again. And again. And again. Sometimes our skirmishes went for longer, while others were over in a matter of seconds. I got the best of him a few times, knocking him down or pinning him.

By the time Kasper had knocked me on my back for the twentieth time that morning, I was not getting up so fast anymore. I lay on my back, staring up at the overcast sky through the skylights, and catching my breath.

I expected Kasper to tell me to go again, but instead he sat down on the mat next to me. Sweat glistened on his brow, and he appeared a little winded himself. I might not have beaten him as often as I'd have liked, but he was on the Högdragen. He was supposed to be a much better fighter than me, and the fact that he was tired at all showed I was doing something right.

"What do you think?" I asked.

His hair was cropped rather short, and he usually kept it back with gel, but the sweat had loosened a few curls so they fell forward. Kasper leaned back, propping himself on his arm, and absently pushed back the locks from his forehead.

"You're good for a tracker," he said with a light laugh. "We'll take five, and then I'll show you a few moves that I think can help you out where you're getting stuck."

The door at the end of the hall opened, and I craned my neck to see who was disturbing our practice. If it was somebody important, like another member of the Högdragen or the King,

I'd have forced myself to my feet, but it was only Tilda, carrying two bottles of water, so I could keep relaxing.

"I thought you two could probably use a bit of a break by now," Tilda told us with a smile and she sat down cross-legged on the mat.

"Thank you." I sat up so I could take the water from her and quickly guzzled it down, while Kasper gave her an appreciative peck on the mouth.

"Aren't you working this morning?" Kasper asked, motioning to her uniform.

"I am, but they're just running drills, so I snuck out for a few minutes." She smiled when she looked up at him, but it was bittersweet. "If you're leaving soon, I want to get in as much time with you as I can."

Kasper slid across the mat, moving closer to her. He wrapped an arm around her waist and leaned in even closer. "I'm sorry. You know I wouldn't leave if I didn't have to."

"I know." Tilda let out a heavy sigh and stared down at her lap. "I'll miss you, but I understand. I just wish that this didn't mean we'd have to postpone our wedding."

As a member of the Högdragen, Kasper really had no choice. King Evert hadn't consulted with him last night about whether he'd be willing or able to go, and he hadn't needed to. Being on the Högdragen was essentially like being property of the kingdom. Everyone in Doldastam had to follow the King's orders, but none so strictly as the Högdragen. If the King said jump, they didn't ask how high—they just jumped.

"I shouldn't be gone for very long," Kasper assured her.

"We just have to make sure the Queen is safe and help set up a more functional guard, and then we'll be home. And as soon as I get back, we'll be married."

He put his hand on her stomach, rubbing the bump where their child grew, and Tilda smiled at him. They kissed again, more deeply than the last time, and while it wasn't a crazy makeout session, it was enough that I began to feel uncomfortable.

And not just because I felt like a creepy voyeur. They were so clearly in love—evident in the way they looked at each other and touched one another. For a fleeting second, it made me think of Ridley and wonder if I had made the wrong choice pushing him away.

But then I remembered why they were kissing in the first place. Kasper was comforting Tilda because he was leaving her, because he wasn't in control of his own life. He'd given himself to the Högdragen, and no matter how much he loved her, she'd have to come second to the job.

I didn't want to do that to anyone else, and I never wanted to be forced to choose between love and duty. So it was best if I just avoided love altogether.

"I can give you two a minute alone, if you want," I offered.

"No, we're fine." Tilda laughed and blushed before putting some distance between her and Kasper. "I should probably get back soon anyway."

"And we should get back to training," Kasper agreed.

"How is that going?" Tilda asked me. "He's not being too rough on you, is he?"

"No. He's not dishing out anything I can't take."

"I'll have to try harder then," Kasper said, and Tilda laughed.

"You two just better not hurt each other," she warned us. "Or you'll have me to deal with."

"Yes, ma'am." I saluted her, and she rolled her eyes.

"I really should get back," she said, and she kissed Kasper before getting to her feet. "I'll see you tonight?"

"As soon as I'm done working the dinner for the Skojare King and Queen," he said. "Then I'll be over."

"I love you." Tilda looked between the two of us. "Both of you. So play nice."

As soon as she was gone, Kasper and I got up, and he told me to come at him again like I had before—only this time, he would teach me how not to end up flat on my back.

beholden

Even though there were only eight of us attending the celebratory dinner, we still waited in a line to be announced by King Evert's personal guard, Reid Kasten. It was a meeting of royalty, which called for formality. King Mikko Biâelse of the Skojare, and Linnea's grandmother, Marksinna Lisbet Ahlstrom, had arrived to retrieve Linnea.

They were so grateful that Ridley and I had found her that we were invited to attend the dinner as honored guests, which felt a bit odd for us. I would always have rather been working than making awkward dinner conversation, but I would be lying if I said that I didn't enjoy a reason to put on the new dress I'd gotten from the town square.

As much as I loved working out and showing my strength—the way I had been all day with Kasper—I loved getting dressed up almost as much. For most of my life, I'd been pigeonholed as purely a tomboy, but that wasn't accurate. I could hold my own wrestling in the mud with boys, and I could hold my own in a gown in the ballroom.

The dress I wore today was silvery white with a damask design in pale blue velvet over it. The front hem of the dress fell just above my knees, on the off chance I'd need to fight or run, and the back flowed out much longer behind me, trailing on the ground.

As strange as I felt waiting beside Ridley in line to enter the dining hall, Kasper seemed even more awkward. He'd only planned on working the party—standing at attention by the door. Instead, Markisinna Lisbet had insisted he join as a guest, and he stood behind us, fidgeting with his uniform and muttering anxiously.

Reid loudly announced King Mikko and Queen Linnea, and they entered the dining hall to formally greet Evert and Mina before taking their seats at the long table. Since Lisbet was of a lower rank than them—a Markisinna is a step below Princess—she would be introduced after them. While waiting, she took a moment to turn to Ridley and me.

Her golden hair was carefully coiffed on her head, and her elegant gown easily surpassed mine in loveliness. Large diamonds and sapphires adorned heavy rings on her fingers. Even though she had to be in her sixties, she still had an incredible, refined beauty.

"I am so sorry about the way things went in Storvatten when you were there before," Lisbet said, her brilliant blue eyes moist with tears.

"There is no need to be," Ridley assured her.

I wasn't completely sure what she was apologizing for, other than when Victor Dålig had slammed my head into the wall. But that wasn't her fault. That was mine.

She smiled and took my hand and Ridley's in each of hers—her skin soft and warm like thin velvet. "I cannot thank you enough for bringing my granddaughter safely back to me. Anything—*anything*—either of you ever need, let me know."

"Marksinna Lisbet Ahlstrom of the Skojare," Reid announced.

Lisbet squeezed our hands and mouthed the words *thank you* again before letting go. She gathered up the length of her dress, then entered the dining hall.

Since Kasper was a member of the Hogdragen, it meant he outranked us, so he was called next, leaving Ridley and me alone in the foyer. As the Överste, Ridley could've worn his uniform the way Kasper had, but instead he'd chosen a well-tailored suit.

As we waited, he readjusted the cuff links in the sleeve of his black dress shirt. I stood with my hands clasped neatly in front of me, watching as Kasper stiffly greeted everyone in the room.

"Are you heading out tomorrow?" Ridley asked, still fixing the diamond cuff link.

"I believe that's the plan. We're leaving first thing in the morning to head back to Storvatten."

"It's a really good opportunity for you." He'd finished his readjustment and folded his hands behind his back, standing tall and proper. "Working with the Högdragen like this. And you've earned it. Nobody has worked harder for recognition than you have."

"Thank you."

"But I have to be honest," he said in a low voice. "It's not gonna be the same here without you."

He looked at me then, his deep-set eyes under a veil of thick lashes. The heat I'd been longing to see in them had returned, and for a moment, there was nothing else. It was only me and him, and the warmth growing in my belly, and the way he made me feel so light-headed and wonderful all at once.

And then, "Ridley Dresden, the Överste of the Kanin," Reid announced so loudly it almost felt as if he were shouting inside my head.

Ridley walked away from me, leaving me behind to catch my breath. Which was just as well, because I'd never have made it through the introductions without a moment to gather myself.

I was seated next to Lisbet, and after I'd gotten settled in I realized that must've been a deliberate choice. All the Skojare—me, Lisbet, Linnea, and Mikko—were on one side of the table, a row of pale blonds across from the darker complexioned Kanin: Ridley, Evert, Mina, and Kasper.

For a second, before I got myself under control, I felt a wave of anger wash over me. I hated being singled out or deemed as "other" simply because of the color of my hair and skin. Even though this hadn't been done out of malice, it still stung every time I was deemed "un-Kanin."

But then I reminded myself that it was an honor to even be here, that I was still seated next to royalty. And maybe the decision had to do with ranking, and since I was the lowest one here, I was seated with our guests instead of next to our King.

Maybe. But I didn't really believe that.

Mikko started off dinner with a toast, standing and raising his glass of sparkling wine. The last time I'd seen him in Storvatten, he'd been a wreck—an overacting wreck, I'd suspected. But now he showed no signs of wear. His handsome face was unreadable, even when he looked down at his wife.

"I want to thank you all for returning my wife to me and for showing her so much hospitality," Mikko said, his deep voice betraying no emotion. "Your kindness and bravery will not soon be forgotten, and the Skojare are indebted to you." He raised his glass higher. "*Skål!*"

"*Skål!*" We all cheered in unison, then took a drink of our wine.

"I would also like to extend a special thanks to both Kasper Abbott and Bryn Aven," Mikko went on, still standing and taking turns looking between Kasper and me. "You are taking on the responsibilities of another tribe, which goes far beyond your duties. While I don't know if the Skojare *need* you, it will provide my wife great comfort, and it is as she wishes."

"It is." Linnea smiled up at her husband, and then she got to her feet.

It was a faux pas for her to speak while another person was toasting, and it was especially unheard of for her to stand up and join him. But when she looked out with sparkling eyes at the table, beaming with such wild delight, it was obvious that her excitement would not be held back by propriety.

"We both want to offer you our immense gratitude," Linnea said. She lifted her glass high in the air, spilling a few drops in her haste, but she didn't seem to notice or mind. "So to Kasper Abbott and Bryn Aven, I'd like to drink to you!"

She quickly took a drink from her glass, but everyone else was slower to follow suit. Kasper reddened and smiled thinly at her before taking a very quick sip. A King and Queen were never supposed to drink to their staff, but since Queen Linnea had suggested it, everyone had to do it or they would seem rude.

I finished my glass in one long swig because I had a feeling that it was going to be the kind of night where I'd want the wine to take the edge off, and as the dinner progressed, I was repeatedly proven right.

Linnea was almost giddy, and while Lisbet was much more composed and reserved than her granddaughter, she was also brimming with happiness. The two of them talked and giggled, steering most of the conversation. Queen Mina was determined not to be left behind, so she laughed louder and spoke quicker than she normally did.

King Evert, for his part, tried to look amused and interested, but he'd never been a good actor. I always thought that being a leader meant having a good poker face, but Evert proved me wrong in that regard.

Despite the antics of Linnea, it was her husband that kept drawing my attention. He didn't seem annoyed or embarrassed by her behavior, nor did he seem to enjoy it. He rarely spoke, instead sitting quietly and eating his food without reacting much to what was happening.

He seemed so cold and distant. I couldn't imagine that

Linnea actually loved him or missed him the way she claimed to have.

And even as the happy haze brought on by several glasses of wine settled over me, I found myself once again wondering what exactly Mikko was hiding behind his blank stare.

intemperance

My boots came up to my knees, and my jacket went down to the ground, but the cold air still managed to get through, sending a chill down my spine. Not that I minded. As the evening dragged on, the dining hall had grown increasingly warm and stifling.

Just beyond the palace door, I breathed in deeply, relishing the icy taste of the air as it cooled my flushed cheeks. The combination of being free from the dinner, the minor promotion in job duties, and the buzz from the alcohol all seemed to hit me with the exhilarating headiness of the wind. The night suddenly felt so very alive.

"I'll meet you at the garage at seven in the morning," Kasper reminded me. He and Ridley had been standing just behind me, making small talk about the dinner, and now Kasper had begun to say his good-byes.

"I'll be there," I said with an easy grin.

Ridley waved at him as Kasper left, watching as he walked away—nearly jogging in his hurry to get to Tilda's apartment. It was less than eight hours until he would have to be up, getting ready to depart for Storvatten, so I'm sure he wanted to make the most of their last evening together for a while.

"I'm surprised you're in such a good mood," Ridley said, turning his attention to me. He moved a few steps closer, filling in the gap that Kasper's absence had left. "After that *interesting* evening we had."

I laughed. "Yeah, but it's over now."

"It makes me glad we're not royalty. I'd hate to sit through those all the time."

"It's getting late." I exhaled deeply, letting my breath fog up the air. "I should be heading home and to bed, since I have a long day tomorrow."

"Yeah, I suppose." Ridley glanced up at the night sky, then back at me. "You be careful this time, all right?"

"I will," I promised him.

Then, since there really wasn't anything more to say, I gave him a small wave before turning to walk away. I'd only made it four steps before he stopped me.

"Bryn," he said, and I looked back over my shoulder at him. "Let me walk you home."

They were five simple words that sounded almost inconsequential, especially since Ridley had walked me home on several occasions. But somehow tonight they felt like so much more. There was a weight to them that had never been there before.

It was in Ridley's tone, which held a hint of urgency, his voice low but strong enough to carry. In his eyes that burned so intensely, I could almost see the hunger hidden in the darkness.

Finally, I answered him, and I didn't even know what I would say until the word came out of my mouth. "Okay."

He looked relieved, and then he walked over to meet me. His steps matched mine easily. I wrapped my arms around myself to keep from shaking—if it was from nerves or the cold, I wasn't sure—and he kept his hands in his pockets. The night was quiet, the streets were empty, and neither of us was saying anything.

It was a two-minute walk from the palace to the stables, and it had never felt so strange. My heart was racing, quickly pumping blood that felt too hot in my veins, and it caused a delirious heat to wash over me.

It was really the strangest feeling. Like teetering on the edge of a precipice. I *knew* something was going to happen. And the anticipation was killing me.

My apartment was a loft above the stables, and when we reached the staircase that ran alongside the building, I started to go up. But Ridley had stayed behind. I turned back to face him, standing at the bottom of the stairs and staring up at me with the same look he'd had outside of the palace.

"Aren't you coming up?" I asked, and for one terrifying moment, I was certain he wouldn't. And then he began to climb the stairs.

At the landing, I unlocked the door, acutely aware of Ridley's body behind me. My hair had been pinned up in a loose updo, and I could feel his breath warming the back of my neck.

We went inside, pretending this was normal, that this was like every other time he'd been in my loft, but the air felt electrified. He commented on the dirty laundry overflowing my hamper, and I apologized for the cold while starting a fire in the woodburning stove.

I kicked off my boots and jacket then lit a few candles while he set aside his own jacket and shoes. Now we stood in the center of the room, a few feet of empty space between us, gawking at each other. The floorboards felt cold underneath my feet, and I kept staring at the few buttons of his shirt that had been left undone, showing off the smooth skin of his chest.

I opened my mouth, planning to ask him if he wanted to sit down or have a drink, but the words suddenly felt like a waste. I didn't want to sit down or have a drink. I only wanted *him*.

I went over to him, and without hesitation, without thinking, without worry, I kissed him, knowing he would kiss me back just as hungrily. And he did not disappoint. He wrapped his arms around me, pulling me to him, but I didn't feel close enough. I pushed him back until he hit the wall.

Ridley stopped kissing me long enough to smile crookedly as I started to undo the buttons of his shirt, but even that quick separation felt too long. Then his fingers were in my hair, and his lips were on my mouth, and I didn't know if I'd ever wanted anything as badly as I wanted him. My body literally ached for him, starting in my chest and working its way down to a desperate longing between my legs.

His shirt was gone, and I'm not sure if he pulled it off or I did, but either way I was grateful. I ran my hands over the firm ridges of his chest and stomach, surprised by how warm his skin felt against mine. Then I felt his hand on my thigh, curious and strong.

Just as his fingers looped around the thin waistband of my panties, Ridley pulled his mouth from mine and looked me in the eyes. "Are you sure—"

But I silenced his question by kissing him again, and I put my hand over his and pushed down, helping him slip off my panties. I stepped out of them and back from him. As he watched me, I pulled my dress up over my head and tossed it to the floor.

His eyes widened in appreciation, and he whispered, "We should've done this a long time ago."

Ridley started to unbutton his pants as he stepped closer to me. He reached out for me, but I pushed him on the bed so he was lying on his back. Grabbing his pants with my hand, I yanked them off in one swift move, and then I climbed over him, letting my body hover just above his.

I leaned down, kissing him again, savoring the moment. Our bodies were so close, I could feel the heat from his. He put one hand on my hip, his fingers gripping me desperately, begging for more.

And then finally, I lowered myself on him, and my breath

caught in my throat. He gasped, almost in relief, and closed his eyes at first until we found our rhythm together.

I sat up, taking more of him and moving faster. He was breathing heavier, and just as the delicious heat exploded deep within me, Ridley sat up, still inside of me. He wrapped his arm around me, holding me against him at the moment he finished.

We both leaned against each other, panting, and my body felt like jelly. As if all my bones and muscles had melted into this wonderful, contented goo, and all I wanted to do was stay melded to Ridley like this forever.

But I couldn't. I leaned back a bit, trying to catch my breath. My hair had come free, and Ridley brushed away a lock that had fallen in my face. He let his hand linger, warming my cheek, and by the look in his eyes, I knew he wanted to say something he wouldn't be able to take back.

"Don't," I whispered.

He shook his head. "Don't what?"

"Don't say anything that would spoil this. Let's just leave this as it is."

He let out a deep breath. "Okay."

I smiled at him, pleased that he wouldn't push anything, and I climbed off him. I blew out the candle on my table and the one next to my bed, so the loft was in near darkness with only the fire in the stove casting light.

I climbed back in bed, lying on my side with my back to Ridley. He waited, sitting on the bed where I'd left him, but now

I felt the bed moving as he settled in behind me. I scooted back on the bed, moving closer to him, and he put his arm around my waist, strong and warm against my bare skin.

His body felt wonderful against mine, spooning me to him. I closed my eyes, wishing I could fall asleep like this every night, but knowing I never would again.

annul

The fire had gone out in the stove, so it was cold and dark as I scrambled around my loft. I'd pulled on a sweater and moved onto digging through my top drawer for a clean pair of panties and a bra, but I kept coming up with mismatched socks instead, making me curse myself for not doing laundry more often.

The bed creaked behind me, and I hurried to yank on my underwear. I could make out the dim outline of Ridley as he sat up, and my whole body tensed up as my stomach dropped. I'd been hoping to sneak out of here before he woke up, so I could avoid an awkward morning-after conversation.

"Sorry if I woke you," I said, since standing in tense silence wasn't making the situation any better.

"No, it's no problem." He leaned forward and clicked on my bedside lamp, bathing the room in dim light.

Ridley sat at the edge of my bed, the covers draped across

his lap and covering the more intimidating parts of his naked body. He was hunched forward slightly, staring down at the worn floorboards, and he ran his hand through his tangles of sleep-messy curls.

I waited, hoping he would say something, *afraid* he would say something. But when he didn't, I burst into motion. As uncomfortable and even painful as this morning was, I still had a job today. I had twenty minutes to pack and meet Kasper at the garage before heading out to Storvatten.

"Sorry, I have to get going," I tried to explain so he wouldn't think I was rushing out on him, even though I would've wanted to rush out on him whether I had somewhere to be or not.

"No, I get it."

Throwing my duffel bag on my old couch, I quickly made trips from my dresser and armoire, loading it up with everything I thought I might need. It was a little tough packing, because I wasn't entirely sure how long I'd be gone. It could be a few weeks—maybe even longer.

Plus, I need clothing for every occasion. Jeans for working, suits for meetings, uniforms for formal affairs, and even a couple of dresses. Thankfully, in tracker school, we'd actually had classes on learning to pack quickly and efficiently.

"Listen," Ridley said.

I paused long enough to look at him, and I realized that I'd been so focused on packing that I hadn't noticed him getting out of bed and dressing. His shirt still wasn't buttoned, and he was fixing the collar as he spoke. Still only wearing a sweater and no pants, I suddenly felt exposed.

"We don't need to talk about last night." I tried to brush him off and run back to packing, but he put his hand on my arm as I darted by, stopping me.

"I want to, though," he insisted.

Swallowing hard, I looked up at him. "Okay."

"Last night . . ." Ridley's eyes were slightly downcast, so he wasn't looking directly at me. He took a deep breath. "Last night was kind of amazing."

"Yeah," I said, since I couldn't think of anything more to say.

Last night actually had been amazing. I could still taste his lips on mine and feel his hands on my skin. In the moment afterward as I lay in his arms, my head against his shoulder, both of us gasping for breath, our bodies entangled—I'd never felt closer to anyone. I'd had this sense of utter completion that I'd never felt before.

Now, I felt a strange, cold emptiness inside me, an absence where he'd been.

"I don't know why it happened. I mean, I'm not complaining." He gave a weak smile that quickly faded away. "But it doesn't matter why, I guess. It just . . . We both know that it can't happen again."

"It can't," I agreed, somehow managing to force out the two most painful words I'd ever spoken. My throat wanted to close up around them, swallowing them completely, but I had to say them.

I knew that Ridley was saying this so I wouldn't have to. He was doing this to spare me the discomfort of actually having to form the words. But that didn't make this conversation any less painful.

"It's too much of a risk for you." Then Ridley shook his head, correcting himself. "For both of us, really. I could lose my position as the Överste, and before I honestly wouldn't have cared that much. But with us going after Viktor Dålig, I want to be there on the front lines."

"As you should be," I said. "Working with Kasper, this is my big chance to make a good impression for the Högdragen. I can't blow that by giving anyone any reason to think I might have gotten where I am by sleeping with my boss.

"And you'll be busy with your work," I continued. "And I'll be gone for a long time. There's not even any point to us, even if we wanted there to be."

Ridley looked me in the eyes for the first time since we'd woken up. There was so much unsaid, so much hanging be-tween us, the air felt thicker. All I wanted to do was kiss him one last time, but I knew that would only make things harder.

"And there's Juni," Ridley said, breaking the moment, and I lowered my eyes. "She's not my girlfriend, but she deserves bet-ter than this."

"She does," I said, and I meant it. Juni had to be one of the nicest people I'd ever met, and I sincerely doubted she would approve of Ridley spending the night with me.

"Whatever has been going on with us lately . . ." He trailed off, waiting several moments before finishing. "It has to be over now. Last night was it. That was the last time."

I nodded, because I was afraid I wouldn't be able to speak if

I tried. He was right, and I agreed with him entirely. If he hadn't said it, I would've.

But it still broke my heart. The intensity and the severity of the ache in my chest was something that I hadn't been expecting. It hurt so badly it almost took my breath away.

So I bit the inside of my cheek, focusing on the pain, and stared down at the floor, waiting for this moment to be over. Ridley finished gathering up his things, and I didn't look at him or say a word. I didn't even move until I heard the door shut behind him.

Then I ran a hand through my hair, took a deep breath, and finished packing. It was the only thing I could do to keep from screaming.

recrudescence

Under the twilight sky, the palace in Storvatten left me just as awestruck as when I'd first laid eyes on it. Its walls were made of luminous pale cerulean, curved and molded to look like waves swirling around the palace. Several spires soared high into the air, and in the fading light, set against the amethyst sky, the glass always seemed to glow.

Kasper and I walked along the long dock that connected the palace with the shore, since it sat like an island fortress several miles out into Lake Superior. It was a long walk, but it gave us plenty of time to admire the beauty of the fantastical structure that rose from the water, leaving a mirrored reflection beside it.

It was much warmer in Storvatten than it had been in Doldastam, with all of the snow melted. There was no ice on the lake near the palace, but I suspected that had more to do with Skojare magic than it did with the temperature. A lake frozen through is no place to swim.

When we reached the doors of the palace, Kasper paused to smooth out his uniform, even though it didn't need smoothing. For our long journey south, we'd worn comfortable attire, but to greet royalty we couldn't look like we'd been traveling all day.

At the end of the dock, before we left our SUV with a valet, Kasper had put on his uniform, and I'd changed into a simple but elegant white dress. On the drive, I'd already touched up my makeup and put my hair into a cascading side braid. Fortunately, the bruise on my temple had faded enough that I was finally able to mask it entirely with concealer.

Kasper used the large, heavy knocker, which commanded a low booming sound that seemed to resonate through everything. While we waited for the footman to answer, I took a moment to admire the massive iron doors. The last time I was here, I hadn't noticed the intricate designs carved into them. They showed Ægir—the Norse god of the sea—with waves crashing around him.

As soon as the footman opened the door, I heard a voice booming behind him. Despite its cheery tone, it had a thunderous quality, much like King Mikko's, so I knew it had to be Mikko's younger brother, Prince Kennet Biâelse.

"Let them in, let them in," Kennet commanded. He shooed the footman away and opened the door wider, smiling broadly at me. "You've had a long journey. Come inside."

I returned his smile and stepped inside past him, noting that he smelled faintly but rather deliciously of the sea. But the scent was mixed with something else, something refreshing and cool, like rain on a spring day or an arctic breeze. I wasn't sure exactly what it was, but I couldn't help but breathe in more deeply anyway.

"The King, the Queen, and Lisbet arrived about fifteen minutes before you did," Kennet explained. "They extend their apologies, but they're exhausted from their trip and have retired for the evening. So I'll be showing you to your rooms and getting you anything you'd like."

"Showing us to our rooms will be enough," Kasper said as he admired the main hall.

The rounded walls were sandblasted glass—opaque with a hint of light turquoise showing through. Like the outside of the palace, they were shaped to look like waves. They curved around us, making it feel as though we were standing in the center of a whirlpool.

Beneath our feet, the floors were glass, allowing us a glimpse of the pool below. It was empty now, but when I'd been here before, I'd seen royalty swimming in it. Above us, chandeliers of diamonds and sapphires sparkled, splashing shards of light all around the room.

"To your rooms it is," Kennet said with a bright smile, and he turned to lead us out of the main hall down to the quarters where we'd be staying.

Even though it was late, Kennet still wore a suit, and I'd never actually seen him in anything else. This time it was a frosty gray that shimmered silver when the light hit it right, and it was perfectly tailored for his well-toned frame.

Both Kennet and his older brother, Mikko, were very handsome: golden hair, dazzling aqua eyes, strong jaws, perfect complexions, and deep, powerful voices. Kennet was slightly shorter and more slender than his brother, but he didn't appear any less muscular.

"I didn't expect you back so soon," Kennet said, lowering his voice as though he were confiding in me. He walked beside me down the corridor, while Kasper followed a step behind. "But I have to admit, I'm happy you are."

"I'm just happy it's under much better circumstances," I replied carefully.

"Ah, yes. With the Queen back, it is a time of much celebration." His voice rose with excitement when he spoke, but then he looked down at me, smiling with a glint in his eye. "Hopefully that means our time together will be much more fun this time around."

It occurred to me that Ridley had been right when we were here before (as painful as it was to think of Ridley in any capacity right now). He'd thought that Kennet had been flirting with me, and I'd brushed it off as nonsense. But now I was beginning to see the merit in the idea.

Ordinarily, I would consider it a bad idea to flirt with a Prince. It could be rather dangerous, in fact. But considering that something very strange was going on in this palace, having another member of the royal family on my side wouldn't be a bad thing.

"I'm certain it will be," I said, attempting to match Kennet's playful grin with my own, and he laughed warmly.

Kennet led us down the spiral staircase toward the private

quarters. The main floor was entirely above the surface of the lake, while the private quarters and the ballroom were located underneath the water. As soon as we went downstairs, the musty scent grew stronger.

While an underwater palace sounded like a magical and grand thing, the impracticality of it seemed to have taken its toll. Wallpaper lined the hallway—blue with an icy sheen—but it had begun to peel at some of the corners. Even the navy-and-white checked tiles on the floor had begun to warp in a few places. All damage from the constant moisture of being in a lake.

As I suspected, Kennet led me to the room I had stayed in before, after first dropping Kasper off several doors away. The valet had already carried my bags down, and I was pleased to find them sitting on the lush bedding.

The wall to the outside bowed out, like a fishbowl, and the darkness of the water seemed to engulf the room. Despite all its luxurious trappings, the room filled me with a sense of un-ease. Like I was a dolphin on display at a zoo.

"In case you don't remember from last time, the bathroom is across the hall," Kennet explained; he'd followed me inside the room, standing directly behind me as I stared out at the lake. "My room is in the other wing, should you need me for any-thing at all."

I turned back to face him, and despite the gnawing ache in my heart over Ridley, there was something in Kennet's smile that made it . . . not exactly easy to smile back, but at least not so hard and not quite so painful.

"I trust that the room is in order for you," Kennet asked, and I realized he hadn't taken his eyes off me since we'd entered the room.

Smiling, I gestured around me. "It's perfect, thank you."

"If there's anything you desire, I'll be happy to get it for you." And there it was again. A glint in his eye that somehow seemed both dangerous and a bit charming.

"Thank you, but right now the only thing I desire is a good night's sleep," I told him politely.

He arched an eyebrow. "You will let me know if that changes?"

"Of course."

When he left, shutting the door behind him, I let out a deep breath and collapsed on the bed behind me. The day had left me exhausted in ways I didn't even know were possible. It still felt as if a hole had been torn inside me, as if my very insides had been ripped out, leaving a cold shell.

But there was no time to cry or mourn what might have been between Ridley and me. It was over, the way it should've been a long time ago, and the only thing I could do was push past it and hope that eventually the pain would get more bearable.

exchequer

First thing in the morning, Kennet took Kasper and me down to the guard station. The last time I'd been here, when Ridley and I had been investigating Linnea's disappearance, we'd been denied access to the guards.

This time, Kasper and I were here specifically to see if there was any truth to Linnea's concerns and to implement new standards for the guards so they'd be better protection for the royalty. That meant we had to be directly involved with the guards.

The guard station was a small round room at the center of the lower level of the palace. It was sparsely decorated, with three large paintings of the royal family the only adornments on its white walls. Four large desks were placed at odd angles, along with several filing cabinets.

Much like the rest of the palace, everything in this room looked as though it had seen better days, save for the steel vault on the other side of the room. It appeared to be sterling and new, as though it would fit better in a bank vault than an old office.

Hunched over one of the desks, a guard scribbled something down on a notepad. His golden hair was slicked back until it curled at the nape of his neck, with just a hint of silver at his temples revealing his age. Under the tailored sleeves of his dress shirt, his shoulders were broad and his biceps were rather thick.

Another man—younger than the first, closer to my age—with a slender build and a slightly upturned nose, sat perched on the edge of the desk. He'd been leaning over, watching what the older man was writing, but he instantly hopped to his feet when we walked into the room.

"Your Highness," he said, bowing before Kennet.

The other man, who had been working on something, rose more slowly.

"No need for the formalities." Kennet brushed them off and glanced back at Kasper and me. "Bayle can be old school at times. He's a relic from Father's reign." The older guard grimaced, not that I blamed him, but Kennet turned back to him with a smile. "I'm just here to make the introductions. These are our friends from the Kanin, Bryn Aven and Kasper Abbott."

"Nice to meet you," the younger man said, but he didn't really looked pleased to meet us, nor did he introduce himself.

"I'm Bayle Lundeen." The older man came around the desk to shake our hands. "I'm the head guard. Anything you need, I should be able to help you."

"They're actually here to help *you*," Kennet reminded him.

"We need to revamp things so the Queen feels safe in her own home."

"Yes, of course." Bayle smiled wanly at us. "I'll do my best to implement any changes that the King and Queen see fit to impose."

"I just hope a uniform isn't one of them." The younger guard snickered, and Bayle shot him a glare.

Kasper had worn his Högdragen uniform, the way he did any time he was working. Since I wasn't officially on the Högdragen, I wasn't allowed to wear one, so I'd gone with a modified version of a tracker solider uniform: tailored black linen with epaulets, but not nearly as flashy as the silver and black velvet one Kasper wore.

"I'm sorry. I didn't catch your name," Kasper said, his tone even and polite.

"Cyrano Moen." The younger man straightened up, raising his chin. "I'm the Queen's personal guard."

"Well, Cyrano, it's funny that you mention uniforms, because I was actually going to suggest them," Kasper said, causing Cyrano to scowl.

"We've always had a dress code here." Bayle gestured to his and Cyrano's outfits, which were very businesslike—dark trousers, dress shirts, ties. Cyrano even had a suit jacket.

"A dress code isn't the same as a uniform," Kasper explained. "The Kanin have found that not only do those wearing a uniform tend to exhibit more pride and integrity on the job, but they also have more of a presence since they give the guard greater visibility. Ultimately, we've found that a uniform provides a sense of security and helps curb assaults."

Cyrano looked at Kennet, almost pleading with him to stop Kasper, but Kennet shrugged and smiled.

"We actually do have uniforms," Bayle said. "We only wear them for special occasions, like weddings or coronations, but it wouldn't be unthinkable for us to start wearing them on a daily basis."

"You're all working together!" Kennet beamed and clapped Bayle on the back. Still grinning, he looked at me. "Is there anything more you need from me before I leave Bayle to show you around the place?"

"No, I'm certain Bayle will be more than helpful," Kasper replied.

I didn't say anything, but my gaze had wandered back to the strange vault door at the other side of the room. It stood in stark contrast to the worn look of everything else. I wondered if the armory was behind it, but I doubted the Skojare had much in the way of weapons.

"You wanna see what's behind that door?" Kennet asked with a wag of his eyebrows.

Bayle cleared his throat. "My Prince, I'm not sure if that would be wise."

"Nonsense!" Kennet strode across the room. "There are several guards here. Nothing will go wrong."

I shook my head. "I don't need to see anything if it will cause trouble."

"It's no trouble at all." Kennet punched a few numbers on a state-of-the-art keypad next to the door, then scanned his thumb—both of which were light years ahead of the lock-and-key system the Skojare had for the dungeon.

Kasper pursed his lips and glanced over at me, as if I had intentionally brought this on. While Bayle seemed to have misgivings about Kennet opening the door, Cyrano had walked up behind Kennet, almost standing on his tiptoes so he could peer inside the second it opened.

There were several loud clicks, followed by a strange wooshing sound, and then the door slowly opened a bit. Kennet glanced around and, seeing that I wasn't beside him, he waved me over.

"Come have a look," he insisted with a smile. As soon as I'd reached him, he threw open the door, and I was nearly blinded by the sparkling inside.

I wish I could say that it didn't hit me the way it did—that my jaw didn't drop and my heart didn't skip a beat for a moment. But despite my education, and even my career in service, I still had troll blood coursing through my veins, and if there was one thing trolls desired in life it was gems.

The round room behind the vault door wasn't very large—maybe the size of standard swimming pool. White lights from the ceiling were aimed perfectly so there could be no shadows. Nothing could hide in here.

But the space was packed with sapphires. It actually seemed like a rather childish way to store them, with jewels simply piled up around the room. There were a few shelves where larger, more precious stones were displayed, but mostly they were just strewn about. Millions of dollars in gemstones were lying around the way a messy child might leave toy cars.

While most of the sapphires were a darker blue, they came in all shades ranging from pale turquoise to nearly black, not to mention some that were pink or red. Some were translucent, like diamonds, while others were opaque, like opals. But all of them sparkled like the night sky.

I didn't know enough of Skojare history to say for certain where they'd gotten all of these, but I knew they had once traded with humans for jewels. If I went far enough back in their history, I'd heard tales of them stealing, some of their ancestors even taking to the sea and pirating.

But really, it didn't matter how the Skojare had gotten the sapphires; they were here now, and I realized they were the only things in the palace that were safely guarded.

The gems also didn't completely mesh with what I'd seen of the palace and what I knew about the Skojare tribe. My understanding was that their funds were drying up. I'd heard they still had some jewels, but they were hoarding them so they wouldn't go completely broke.

The hoarding definitely did appear to be true, but apparently the term *some jewels* was very subjective.

"Beautiful, aren't they?" Kennet asked, breaking my trance, and I turned back to him, forcing myself not to admire the gems anymore.

"Yes, they're quite lovely," I admitted.

"I suppose that's enough for today then," Kennet said, and

he closed the door almost reluctantly, locking the treasure back up.

After that he left, allowing Bayle and Cyrano to give Kasper and me a tour of the palace and explain its inner workings.

The palace was filled with the wealthiest members of the Skojare, living in small apartmentlike spaces, and the guards, who lived in smaller dormitories on the second floor. The guards in their suits were nearly indistinguishable from the rich, and in part, I think that was because the lower-class didn't want it to be obvious who worked for whom.

Eliminating class distinctions was commendable, but somebody had to protect the royalty. Even public leaders in the human world had a secret service. Everybody couldn't run around and play together. Somebody had to do the work, but here in Storvatten, it seemed that nobody wanted to.

It could even be seen in how rundown everything was. But as I saw the cracks in the walls, the warped floor tiles, and even the broken locks, I couldn't help but think back to the vault filled with sapphires.

Why did the Skojare let the palace fall to disrepair when they had so much money? Was their greed so strong that they would rather sit on the gems and let everything fall apart around them than spend the money on necessary repairs? It was like one of Aesop's fables, where the outcome couldn't be good for them.

NINETEEN

de rigueur

I t's insane to me that they've lived like this for so long," I said
for the hundredth time.

After Kasper and I had spent a long day going over the palace with Bayle and taking notes, we'd retired to my room to
start making a plan for how we would improve things. The
problem was that there were *so* many areas that needed improvement, it was hard to know where to begin.

Bayle had provided us with all kinds of paperwork on training processes, job descriptions, schedules, dress codes, pretty
much everything we might want to look at, and it was spread
out all over my bed.

I had a notebook on my lap so I could jot down ideas, and
Kasper was pacing the room, looking over a training sheet and
shaking his head. He'd taken off his uniform jacket, so he wore
only the T-shirt underneath.

"They have zero combat training." Kasper hit the paper in

his hand. "How can you be a guard if you have no ability to protect anyone?"

"I don't know." I shrugged. "I can't believe that something bad hasn't happened already."

"Everyone here is almost completely unprotected!" Kasper was nearly shouting in his frustration. "The only things they've got properly secured are those ridiculous sapphires, and I can't believe they even thought of that."

I was about to join in Kasper's rant about the severe inadequacies of the Skojare guard when a small knock at the door interrupted us. Pushing the papers aside, I got up and answered it to find Marksinna Lisbet, dressed in a flowing gown.

"Dinner starts in twenty minutes, and we'd be so pleased if you both could join us," Lisbet said, smiling in her aristocratic way that I'd begun to find charming.

I glanced back at Kasper, even though I knew exactly how he'd respond. Even more so than me, he had a strong sense of propriety. When he was on duty, he took his work very seriously, and I admired that about him.

"We would be honored to, Marksinna," I told Lisbet. "But since we're working for your kingdom now, it wouldn't be appropriate for us to share a table with you or the King and Queen."

Lisbet laughed, an effervescent sound that nearly matched her granddaughter's. "It's never appropriate to turn down the King and Queen's request, and they've invited you to join us for dinner. So I suggest you get dressed and meet us in the dining hall in twenty minutes. We're excited to hear your thoughts on the kingdom."

Since she'd really left us with no choice, I scrambled to get dressed and fix my makeup. Kasper should've had an easier time, because he only had to put his jacket back on, but he ended up spending roughly fifteen minutes reapplying gel to his dark curls to keep them perfectly in place.

"When they ask us how we think their palace is, what should we say?" Kasper asked in a hushed voice as we made our way down a long corridor toward the dining hall.

"We'll just have to be as vague as possible," I suggested. "The truth is too brutal to say all at once over dinner."

"I just hope we can make it through the meal without someone saying, 'Off with their heads,' " he muttered.

"Even if they did say that, who do they have to enforce it?" I asked dryly.

Kasper laughed. "Good point."

We reached the hall to find Mikko, Linnea, Kennet, and Lisbet already seated around the table. Four guards were standing at attention in the corners of the room, including Linnea's personal guard, Cyrano, and they were all wearing matching uniforms—a frosty blue satin number that rivaled the Högdragen uniform in style and flair. They weren't exactly practical, although the guards did have swords sheathed on their hips in flashy metallic sashes, but the uniforms did identify their station.

As I made my way over to the table, I couldn't help but notice the icy glare from Cyrano. I wasn't sure if it was because of the uniform, although I was certain he wasn't happy about that, or because he had to stand guard while Kasper and I got to eat at the table.

Kennet stood up. "Bryn, why don't you take the seat next to me?" He pulled out the chair beside his. I'd been planning to sit next to Kasper at the end of the table, but I didn't want to seem rude by denying the Prince's request.

"Thank you." I smiled at him and allowed him to push my chair in for me, even though that was definitely not proper etiquette.

"So, how are you enjoying the palace?" Linnea leaned forward to speak to me, not minding if her elbows were on the table, and pushing elegant dinnerware to the side to get a better look at me.

"I can honestly say there's nothing else quite like it," I said.

"It is truly magnificent," Kasper said, echoing my sentiments.

A butler came around to begin serving the first course. Before I had the chance, Kennet slipped my silk napkin off the table and dropped it artfully on my lap. His hand brushed my thigh when he pulled it back, but neither of us acknowledged it.

"This is your first time here, isn't it?" Linnea asked, turning her attention to Kasper.

He nodded. "Yes, it is."

"My husband and I are *dying* to know what you think of our security here." Linnea leaned back in her chair so the butler could place her napkin on her lap, then he set a bowl of tomato bisque before her. "We already love the suggestion about the uniforms."

Behind her in the corner, Cyrano snorted a bit. He was doing a horrible job of keeping his expression blank, the way any good guard would do when they were working. Tomorrow, I knew that Kasper would have a long talk with him about the appropriate way for guards to behave.

"I've been saying they should be back in uniform for years," Lisbet commented between spoonfuls of her soup.

"They used to be?" I asked in surprise.

Lisbet dabbed at her mouth with her napkin before answering. "Yes, when I was a young girl, things were different. Much stricter."

"Things change, Nana." Linnea chose her words deliberately, looking over to Lisbet. "Mikko is leading us into a more equitable era."

Since she was home, the Queen had begun to wear lipstick again. Fortunately, she'd gone with a dark pink instead of the usual bright red, which suited her pale complexion much better. Her shoulder-length ringlet curls sprang free around her head, and her wrists were draped in several jeweled bracelets.

Everyone at dinner was dressed formally, including Kennet, whose steel-gray suit appeared to be sharkskin, since it had a subtle sheen to it. I'd like to say I didn't notice how striking he looked in it, but it would be impossible not to.

"Equity should never come at the cost of safety," Lisbet said, and her tone challenged anyone to disagree with her.

"Safety should never come at the expense of fun." Kennet

Amanda Hocking

defied her with a broad grin, which caused Mikko scowl at him from across the table.

"Forgive my brother. He has never been known to take things seriously," King Mikko said, speaking for the first time since dinner had started. It always startled me a bit when he spoke—in part because he rarely did, and in part because of the sheer gravity of his voice.

"Forgive *my* brother," Kennet countered. "He has never been known to take a joke."

"Both of you, behave," Linnea said in a firm but hushed tone. In that moment, she had a weariness beyond her years, and I suspected this hadn't been the first time she'd had to remind the brothers to act appropriately. "We have guests."

"You spoke of making changes," I said, trying to change the subject. "Have there been changes to the guard in recent years?"

"Not dramatic ones." Mikko pushed the soup bowl away from him, having only eaten a few bites, and a butler hurried to take it away. "Most of the alterations were under my father's reign. He streamlined the guard and appointed Bayle Lundeen to implement the changes."

Kennet took a drink from his wine and smirked. "The kingdom says it was out of his strong sense of justice and commitment to an egalitarian society, but the truth was that our father was a tremendous cheapskate. He'd much rather have kept the vault full than paid the guard their rightful due, which meant we needed a smaller guard."

From behind Linnea, I saw Cyrano nod his head in agreement.

"Kennet!" Linnea gasped. Her level of shock was almost comical, especially considering that Mikko and Lisbet seemed unfazed. "It's not right to speak ill of the dead, especially your King."

"Perhaps it's best if we don't discuss business over dinner," Mikko said. I wasn't sure if he was coming to the aid of his wife, or if he also disapproved of Kennet's statement. It was impossible to tell since Mikko's face was an unreadable mask.

"I've always found that to be the best policy," Kennet agreed amiably.

Looking at Kennet and Mikko staring at each other across the table was a bit like a funhouse mirror. They looked so much alike, even though Kennet was younger and slimmer. But Kennet was very expressive, often grinning and raising his eyebrows, while Mikko rarely seemed to emote at all. Not to mention that Kennet was talkative and flirtatious, and Mikko barely said a word.

The waitstaff began to clear the first course before bringing in a massive salad of arugula, pressed melon, and goat cheese. While they exchanged our dishes, nobody spoke, and the only sound was the clearing of silverware and the setting down of plates.

"There are so many other things we have to talk about," Linnea said, since no one else seemed eager to pick up the conversation. "I am disappointed that I wasn't able to see either of you more today."

"Tomorrow you should make time for a little fun, Bryn," Kennet said. "You must take a break and have lunch with me."

I paused, trying to find a polite way out of it, until I came up with the perfect solution. "If you insist, then Kasper and I would be happy to join you."

But Kennet would not be appeased. "Unless of course Kasper has more pressing business to attend to?" He raised an eyebrow at Kasper.

"Kennet, you've met beautiful girls before," Lisbet said in exasperation. "Certainly you know how to contain yourself around them."

For once, Kennet didn't have a snappy comeback, and I just kept my head bowed, focusing on the salad before me. Even though I wasn't the one putting on the display, I still felt the maddening urge to blush, but I suppressed it as best I could.

"What is on your agenda for tomorrow?" Linnea asked, doing her best to keep the conversation flowing.

"I believe Bayle has a few more things he'd like to show us," Kasper said. "We haven't seen the towers yet."

"How exciting! The towers are my *favorite* part of the palace," Linnea enthused.

"When do you think you'll be ready to brief me on the changes you'd like to make?" Mikko asked, surprising me by showing an actual interest in what we were talking about.

"A few more days, I think," I said.

He nodded. "Let me know when you're ready, and we'll get something on the books."

"We're all excited to hear what recommendations you have," Linnea said.

"We'll certainly be honored to share them with you," Kasper said.

"Queen Linnea, how are you finding being back in the palace?" I asked her.

Since we'd gotten back, I'd had hardly a moment to check in with her, and I was curious to find out if she still felt out of sorts. I'd have preferred to ask her when we were alone in hopes of getting a more honest answer, but since I wasn't sure when that would be I thought now was better than never.

"I couldn't be happier to be home. I'm a bit embarrassed for all the trouble I caused for disappearing like I did. That strange man spooked me, I suppose, but I'm glad that you brought me back where I belong." She reached over and squeezed Mikko's hand on the table, looking up at him in adoration, but he barely glanced at her.

"We have already tried to make a few changes to keep her safe," Mikko said, lifting his eyes briefly to look at me. "Her personal guard was sent away and replaced with a new one."

"I graciously offered her the use of Cyrano until they find a more permanent solution," Kennet said. "I am a very generous man. In every aspect of my life," he added, winking at me.

"I do already feel safer," Linnea said, turning the conversation back and smiled brightly at me. "But it does help knowing that you and Kasper are here."

I wanted to reassure her that she was indeed safer with us, but honestly, I wasn't sure who exactly she needed protection from, so I remained quiet.

TWENTY

belfry

With the icy wind blowing through my hair, I leaned farther out the window than I knew I should have, but I couldn't help myself. We were in the highest room in the tallest tower of the castle, and the lake had to be at least a hundred meters below us.

"I think that's far enough, Bryn," Kasper said, doing his best not to sound nervous.

"He's right," Bayle Lundeen agreed, and that's when I reluctantly pulled myself back inside.

I wasn't sure what it was about being here, but the power of the Skojare in my blood seemed to be stronger. The water seemed to call to me more than it normally did, and when I'd been in the sapphire room yesterday, I'd felt an uncharacteristic moment of greed.

Maybe it was being around Skojare people that amplified

something inside me. Or it could simply have been the room we were in, since it was full of magic.

The tower rooms themselves weren't overly spectacular. They were somewhat small, cylindrical spaces at the top of about a thousand stairs. (There were actually several landings along the way with couches, water fountains, and restrooms, since you'd inevitably have to take a break getting up there.)

The walls were iridescent, reminding me of the inside of clam shells, and there were two windows: one facing the shore in front, and one facing the lake to the back. Both windows opened outward, with no screen. Kasper pointed out that it seemed dangerous, but Bayle assured us there'd never been any accidents and only three suicides over the past century.

A bed curved along the wall, covered in soft blankets and plush pillows. To one side of the room was what appeared to be a large white armoire, but when Bayle showed us the inside, it contained a small toilet and pedestal sink.

Across from it was a desk made of marble, also built to curve right against the wall. Ornate designs were carved into the legs and edges, and rising from the desk was a tall bookcase, lined with all kinds of books ranging from tomes dating back hundreds of years to the latest novel by George R. R. Martin. It was a small yet varied library.

This room was a self-contained little unit meant to house the tower guards.

"So this is how you keep the palace hidden?" I asked, admiring the room around me.

Bayle nodded. "We used to have a guard in each of the five towers, but with the cloaking abilities dwindling, we don't want to run the risk of burning out the guards we have, so we only have three on duty at all times. Since this is the tallest tower, it's the least used."

That made sense. If I had the choice of walking up several hundred stairs instead of a thousand to go to work, I would gladly choose the smaller tower. But Bayle had wanted to show us the full breadth of the kingdom, and we weren't disturbing anyone by checking out this one.

The tower guards were more like trackers than they were like the Högdragen. The Skojare might not have had changelings, but like trackers, the tower guards had special abilities that were specifically nurtured in their bloodlines.

Most of the Skojare lacked psychokinesis. Like all the tribes, our abilities had begun to wane over time. The royalty tended to blame this on diluting bloodlines. I suspected there was truth to that, but I also wondered if declining use and losing touch with our heritage impacted it.

Regardless, there were still some Skojare who possessed the ability of cloaking. They couldn't make themselves invisible, only objects and places. The power didn't seem to work as well on trolls as it did on humans, meaning a troll could see their tricks while a human would be fooled into seeing nothing.

But that was really who they needed it for. It was how they kept humans from spotting their massive palace on the lake, and it was how they kept Lake Isolera hidden.

Unlike the palace, though, which required upkeep from

tower guards, Lake Isolera had been placed under a spell long ago by one of the first Skojare queens. Her power had to have been incredibly strong, since her enchantment was the only thing that kept it cloaked. Eventually, the spell would fade, and Isolera would become an ordinary lake in the Canadian wilderness.

From what I understood, the tower guards would sit in the room and project the idea of a force field—thinking of an invisible wall that would hide everything behind it, and pushing out with their mind the way I would push against a boulder with my hands. It was a very taxing job, one that could burn people out quickly, so the guards worked in shifts and took frequent breaks lying down or reading a book.

It was necessary work, if the Skojare didn't want to be discovered by humans, and I couldn't imagine that discovery would go for well them.

"Since this tower isn't used for anything else, you could have two guards up here, watching the perimeter for enemies," Kasper said, motioning to the windows on either sides of the room. "I know the tower guards are too busy to be able to do that, but regular guards would work."

"We could, but that seems unnecessary," Bayle said. "The tower guards are protecting us from outsiders."

"What about Konstantin Black?" I asked, and he stiffened.

Bayle cleared his throat. "He was an exception, and I doubt he'll be coming back."

"You can say that, and you may be right," I allowed. "But do you know why he was here? How he got in? What he was hoping to achieve? Or why he warned the Queen to get out?"

"Of course not," Bayle replied icily. "We don't know that any better than you do."

"Then how can you possibly know that he or someone else like him won't strike again?" I asked.

Bayle inhaled sharply through his nose. "I suppose I don't." Then he lowered his dark blue eyes to gaze at me. "But from what I gather, Konstantin Black is Kanin, and he was *your* problem first. Whatever he was doing here, it was your people that brought him upon us, and it was you who lost him."

"I wouldn't have lost him if you'd been doing your job!" I snapped. "If you had even a halfway decent guard set up, he never would've gotten inside the palace in the first place."

"I work with the guard that I am given!" Bayle shouted. "You think I wouldn't want a guard as well trained and dedicated as the Högdragen? Of course I would! But that's not what King Rune designed."

King Rune was Mikko and Kennet's father, who had apparently decided to tie the purse strings much tighter than they needed to be.

"King Mikko refuses to undo his father's changes, which means we have no money, no training, nothing for any of that," Bayle continued in frustration.

"And that's why we're here!" Kasper spoke loudly in order to be heard, but there was no anger in his voice. He stepped between Bayle and me, holding his hands palm out toward each of us. "We're here to help, and to make sure that somebody like Konstantin Black can never get in here again. We're on the same page here."

Bayle huffed, but he seemed to relax a bit. He smoothed the satin of his uniform. He looked much more like a leader in it, and he even carried himself better. Kasper had definitely been right about the effect clothing had on the psyche.

"Kasper is right," I said. "I'm sorry."

Bayle nodded, and I suspected that was as close to an apology as I would get.

"It has been a great shame that the Queen went missing on my watch," he said finally. "I've tried to pinpoint how exactly Konstantin got in here, but the truth is that there are too many holes in our fence for me to know for sure."

"The Queen had begun to fear for her safety before Konstantin even arrived," I said. "There's a chance someone on the inside was working with him."

Bayle lowered his eyes. "I have considered this."

"And do you have any idea who it could have been?" Kasper pressed when Bayle didn't go on.

"No." He shook his head. "I simply don't know how any of the guards could benefit from the disappearance of Queen Linnea. She's kind and fair to everyone. The kingdom has a policy that doesn't allow us to pay ransom, and I doubt King Mikko would go against the rules of his ancestors, so no one could profit from her kidnapping."

"What if she had been killed?" I asked. "Would anything have changed?"

"I can't see how," Bayle said. "The crown follows the Biâelse bloodline. There would be no transfer of power, since Queen Linnea only has the title by marriage."

My thoughts circled back to where they'd started—the only person who could benefit from Linnea being gone was the one who didn't appear happy to be married to her.

"As the head guard, who are your official bosses?" I asked.

"The King has final say in all matters of the kingdom, but to a lesser extent, I am sworn to obey the entire royal family, including the Queen, the Prince, and Marksinna Lisbet as the Queen Grandmother," Bayle answered.

"What would you do if any of them asked you to commit murder?" I asked, and both Bayle and Kasper stiffened. It was a taboo topic among guards.

"In times of war, I am to defend the kingdom and fight our enemies," Bayle said, practically reciting the answer from a textbook. "In times of peace, I am to protect the King at all costs. It is my duty to kill if necessary, but never to murder. Taking a life must only be done in preservation of the kingdom."

"I know what you're supposed to do, but I'm asking you what you would personally do," I said.

"I would follow the tenets of my position, and I would not murder anyone," he said, but his eyes darted just slightly when he spoke.

"Would you tell the person you'd been instructed to kill?" I pressed. "Because if you turned down the King, I'm sure he could keep asking until eventually he found a guard who would do as he asked."

"I . . ." Bayle stopped for a moment, thinking, and when he spoke again, his shoulders had sagged. "I would like to believe that I would do the right thing."

Later, when we were walking down the spiral stairs to the main floor, Bayle had gotten quite the lead on Kasper and me, and he was well out of earshot. Just the same, Kasper slowed his steps and lowered his voice.

"There is no right answer to that question, you know," Kasper said, and I looked sharply at him.

"Of course there is. Murder is always wrong."

"When you're a civilian, that's true," he conceded. "But the King has the power to declare war and name anyone a traitor, worthy of death. He decides what is and what isn't murder. When you swear to serve him, you give up your own individuality; you forsake your own beliefs and morals in the name of the higher calling of serving the kingdom, for honor and duty."

I shook my head. "You can serve the King without betraying your own morality. They don't have to be mutually exclusive."

"I would like to think so, and I like to live my life that way," Kasper said. "But if the King commanded me to do something, and I denied him, he could have me locked up or banished. Even executed. So it's not just morality that would influence my decision. It's also self-preservation."

I stopped, and Kasper walked down a few more steps before pausing to look back up at me. Until this moment, I'd viewed him as one of the most upstanding people I knew, worthy of admiration. He was honorable, noble, and seemed to embody every quality that a member of the Högdragen was supposed to possess.

"But you wouldn't do it," I persisted, almost begging him

to agree with me, to pretend that this was all a misunderstanding. That the most virtuous members of the Högdragen couldn't be as fallible as everyone else.

Kasper sighed heavily. "I believe I would do my best to sway the King to the correct course of action and to protect the innocent. But in the end, I am nothing more than a sword at the end of the King's arm. I do as he directs."

TWENTY-ONE

entanglement

From out in the hall, I could hear Kasper talking, followed by the fainter sound of Tilda's laughter. His bedroom door was open, so I peered around to see him holding his cell phone out toward the dome glass wall that held the murky water at bay. He was video chatting with Tilda and giving her a tour of our accommodations.

"The water is so dark," Tilda was saying, her voice coming out weak and metallic from the phone. "I'd expected it be clear and bright."

"Everything here is darker and dingier than you might guess," Kasper admitted.

"Well, good. I was afraid you'd get too enchanted with Storvatten and not want to come back to me, so I'm glad it's not all that magical," Tilda said, laughing a little.

Kasper turned the phone back around to face him, so she

could see him again. "There's nothing in this world that can keep me from coming back home to you."

Since I'd accidentally eavesdropped on a private moment, I cleared my throat and knocked on the open door.

Kasper turned back to me with a start, so Tilda asked in concern, "Is someone there?"

"It's Bryn." Kasper pointed the phone toward me so I could see Tilda's smiling face on the small screen.

"Hey, Tilda." I waved toward the tiny camera on the phone, causing her to laugh.

"How are you enjoying the palace?" Tilda asked.

"I'm enjoying it as much as I can, I guess." I shrugged.

"Good." She paused, seeming to hesitate. "Ridley asked me how you're doing, and he'll be happy to hear that you're looking well."

"Thanks." I swallowed back a lump in my throat and looked away from her. "I didn't mean to interrupt your moment here, but I was just checking to see if Kasper wanted to join me for lunch."

After we'd toured the towers, Bayle had shown us around the palace for the rest of the morning, but he'd given us an hour on our own for lunch. Kennet had said that he'd meet me at my room at noon, but I was getting hungry and decided it would be better if I got something on my own.

"I thought you were having lunch with the Prince?" Kasper asked.

"Lunch with the Prince?" Tilda raised an eyebrow that

others might have misinterpreted as intrigue, but I knew it meant nothing but disapproval.

Tilda had already witnessed my out-of-class dating once, and heard me vow that I'd never do it again. Back when I was sixteen and freshly graduated from tracker school and I thought I knew everything, I'd pursued a crush with a slightly older Markis.

Even though I was determined to be a Högdragen, and inter-dating between a tracker and a Markis was forbidden, I was at a stage in my life where I thought I could do what I wanted—that I was smart enough to play around the rules.

I hadn't been in love with him, but initially I had been enamored by his charm and good looks. He seemed to enjoy me too, and there was something about the danger of getting caught that made it all the more exciting.

After we'd been sneaking around for a few weeks, I began to detect an arrogant, mean streak to him. Once when we were fooling around in his room, I noticed a polar bear rug on his floor. Hunting wasn't prohibited by the Kanin, but doing so purely for sport was frowned upon.

I asked him about it, and he proudly boasted of killing it himself. Not long after that I began to realize that thanks to my exotic blond hair and blue eyes, I was just like the polar bear—a trophy from a conquest.

When it was all over, Tilda did her best not to say "I told you so," even though she had repeatedly warned me this was a bad idea and expressed her disapproval. But she was more than relieved when I told her that it would never happen again, and I swore off romance with royals forever.

Of course, I did have this awful habit of breaking promises I'd made to myself.

"I've been waiting in my room for fifteen minutes, and the Prince hasn't shown up," I told Tilda, doing my best to display a lack of interest in him. "I thought I'd head up to the kitchen and grab something."

"I already called up to the kitchen and had them bring me something." Kasper pointed to a half-eaten sandwich on a silver tray next to his bed. "Otherwise I would."

"No problem." I waved it off. "Enjoy your lunch with Tilda."

"Take care of yourself, Bryn," Tilda called after me as I turned to leave.

With nothing else to say, I preferred to hurry out with my head down, trying to pretend it didn't hurt to hear that Ridley had been concerned about me. It hurt because he cared, and it hurt because he shouldn't, and it hurt because things with us would never be the way they were with Tilda and Kasper.

I had my eyes on the floor, my mind desperately trying to push away any thought of Ridley. My heart throbbed painfully in my chest. That was how I didn't notice Prince Kennet until I'd run right into him—literally hitting my head against his chest.

"Sorry, Your Highness, I'm sorry, I didn't see you there." Apologies tumbled out of my mouth.

"No need to be sorry," Kennet said, his deep voicing lilting as he smiled. "In fact, I should be the one saying I'm sorry."

"Don't be ridiculous." I brushed my hair out of my face and looked up at him. "I'm the one who ran smack into you."

"You did do that," he agreed. "But running into you is never all bad. Especially when I've left you waiting so long for our lunch date."

"Oh, right, that." I hurried to think of a way to contradict him on the term *date*.

"You must be ravenous by now," Kennet went on before I could correct his statement. "The good news is that lunch is waiting for you." Then he frowned. "The bad news is that it won't be with me. Queen Linnea has requested that you join her instead, and since the Queen outranks me, I am obligated to step aside. This time."

"She and I do need to talk about the things going on in the kingdom, so it's just as well," I said.

"A working lunch?" Kennet wrinkled his nose. "That sounds terrible."

"I enjoy the company of the Queen, and this may come as a shock to you, but I enjoy my job a great deal."

Kennet put his hand over his heart in mock surprise. "I can hardly even fathom the idea."

"I thought as much," I replied with a laugh.

"There is some good news though," Kennet said. "I get to escort you to the Queen's tea room."

"She has her own tea room?" I asked, following Kennet as he started to walk away.

"She's the Queen. She has her own *everything*."

"Do you think that's why she was targeted?" I asked.

He shrugged. "I don't know why anyone went after her. I know I just said she has everything, but in truth it all actually belongs to my brother. She just has access to it."

That was essentially what Bayle had already told me. There wasn't really any reason for anyone to go after Linnea, unless it was personal. But I'd been hoping that Kennet might be able to shed a different light on things.

"Do you share any of the Queen's concerns?" I asked.

"You mean do I feel that someone is lurking around the corner waiting to nab me?" Kennet seemed to consider it, but when he looked down at me he was grinning. "How could I feel unsafe when I know I've got you here to protect me?"

"I'm here to protect the Queen."

"Technically you're here to help the royal family, which does include me."

"You didn't really answer my question though," I said. "Do you think something is going on here?"

"I think that our guards have been horribly trained and commanded for years now," Kennet said, and he seemed to be choosing his words with an unusual level of care. Normally, he'd say any little thing that flitted into his mind, but for once he appeared cautious.

"As a result of the guards' ineptitude," he went on, "it's entirely plausible that something troublesome is afoot. But it would be near impossible to discern what is due to incompetence and what's due to actual nefarious intentions."

"Bayle told me your brother has been reluctant to make

changes," I said. "If the guard is awful, do you know why that is?"

"The exact machinations of my brother's mind have always been a mystery to me," Kennet said with a sigh. "I do know that during his coronation speech, he promised to continue our father's reign, upholding everything that he'd put in place. But why the King refuses to change in the face of all the evidence telling him it's necessary . . ." He trailed off.

He stopped and turned to me, his blue eyes softening. "You have to understand. Our father was a very difficult man, and Mikko got the brunt of Father's . . . *difficulty*. Mikko never learned how to stand up for himself, and he's uneasy about change or responsibility."

"That doesn't sound like a good combination in a King," I pointed out.

"No, it doesn't." Kennet smiled bitterly for a moment, but it quickly fell away. "Anyway, it's not my place to speak ill of the King—either my brother or my father."

"Thank you for being so candid with me, my liege," I said, since Kennet had been more honest with me about his family than many other royals I had encountered would be.

He stopped, turning to face me, so I did the same. "You know, you really don't have to do all that. You can just call me Kennet. I feel like we are on a first-name basis."

"That seems like a very dangerous territory to venture into," I said. "You are the Prince. I am a tracker from a neighboring tribe. It would be very unwise for the two of us to mingle, which is why it is for the best that we don't reschedule our lunch . . . meeting."

"That hardly seems fair." Kennet scoffed. "I see absolutely no reason the two of us can't be friends."

"There is that whole business where I could be jailed and you could be stripped of your title," I reminded him. "That seems like a good reason."

"It's only if we procreate and dilute the bloodline that the offense is punishable by incarceration." Kennet brushed it off, as though it weren't a big thing. "There's no law against us fraternizing."

"Perhaps I don't want to fraternize," I countered.

"Are you asking me to procreate then?" Kennet asked with a wag of the eyebrow.

"I think it's best if we stop this conversation, and I get to my lunch with Queen Linnea," I said. "It's never good to keep the Queen waiting."

"Right you are." Kennet smirked, but he started walking again.

"Thank you, Prince," I said as I followed him.

"Anytime, tracker," he replied.

TWENTY-TWO

doubts

Sunlight flooded the tea room. The outside wall was domed glass, starting in the middle of the ceiling and curving down until it met the floor at the surface of the lake. The windowed wall was divided into three pie-shaped panes of glass, separated by ornate golden sash bars.

Since it was on the main floor, it was one of the few rooms in the palace that let in the warm spring sun. It shimmered on the lake outside, casting shards of light through the tea room like a disco ball.

The walls had wainscoting halfway up, where it met wallpaper covered in pale blue roses and light green vines. A chaise sat against the wall with an antique coffee table surrounded by several tufted chairs.

In the center of the room was a round table, directly underneath an elegant gold chandelier that hung where the glass met the ceiling. Piles of fresh fruit, trays of pastries, and an array of tea bags were spread out on a lace tablecloth. Delicate saucers and cups were hand painted with roses of pink and blue.

Linnea sat at the table with a raspberry tart in her hand, smiling at me as I came in. In her knee-length azure sundress, she reminded me of a little girl playing tea party and pretending to be a princess. But of course, she wasn't playing pretend—all of this was real life for her.

Kennet had dropped me off at the door, promising to see me later, and then left me alone with the Queen. Her personal guard—who should've been in the room with her, or at the very least standing at the door—was nowhere to be seen, and I would have to remember to make a note of that when I returned to Kasper. The King and Queen should never be left unguarded.

"I'm so glad you could make it!" Linnea said effusively and gestured to the empty seat across from her. "Sit, sit. Eat and drink, and we have so much to talk about!"

"Thank you, Your Highness." I sat down and added fruit and a cucumber sandwich to my plate, while Linnea began to rattle off all the reasons it was so great to have me there.

"Everyone here is *so* stuffy and dull," she said with a dramatic eye roll and took the last bite of her tart. Today she'd gone for minimal jewelry, wearing only her large diamond wedding band along with white lace fingerless gloves. "Even the ones my age."

Since I'd known Linnea, she seemed far more excited about the idea of having a new friend to talk to than having a guard to watch her back, and I wasn't exactly sure how I felt about that.

While I liked Linnea just fine, I didn't want to be chosen for a job because she thought we'd make great pals. I was here to show my merits as a guard and to get to the bottom of what Konstantin had been doing here in the first place. But perhaps I could use the Queen's need for a friend to get her to confide in me about what was really going on around here.

When Ridley and I had been looking for her before, we had suspected that she might be too demanding or childish for Mikko. Maybe she annoyed him, or he simply didn't want to spend the rest of his life trapped in a loveless arranged marriage to her.

How Konstantin tied into a possible plan to do away with her, I had no idea. But maybe she knew something that could help.

"The King must be happy to have you back." I poured myself a cup of tea and watched for her response out of the corner of my eye.

"Yes, he's thrilled!" Linnea laughed. "The first night we were back together, I didn't think he'd ever let me go. He held on to me for hours and made me promise that I'd never leave him again."

"*Really?*" I asked, then hurried to correct myself so I didn't sound quite so shocked. "I mean, he seems so . . . in control of his emotions."

"I know, I know." She laughed again. "It's the craziest thing, because he's such a big strong man, and he's the King of an entire kingdom. A small one, but a kingdom nonetheless. You'd think he'd be so brave and tough, and oh he tries to be. But do you want to know a secret?"

I nodded. "Yes. I would."

Linnea leaned forward over the table, so I did the same, and even though we were alone, she whispered. "Mikko is terribly shy. Almost pathologically."

"Really?" I asked.

"Yes, it's really so sad." She leaned back in her chair and returned to her normal volume. "That's why whenever he's at dinner with people, he's so quiet, and he seems so cold and stoic, but that's not who he is at all."

"I never would've guessed that." I settled back in my chair, trying to run through all my encounters with the King.

"Before we were wed, I did *not* want to marry him," Linnea confessed. "It had all been arranged since I was twelve, but with the age gap, we'd hardly spent a moment together before the wedding, and when we did he said nary a word to me."

"That sounds dreadful," I said.

"It really was." She nodded, her transparent gills flaring slightly under her jawline. "I mean, it was just after my sixteenth birthday, and I wanted to fall in love, and I thought there was absolutely no way I could do that with this cold brute of a man.

"But the truth is that Mikko is one of the kindest, most loving, most caring men I've ever met." Linnea smiled, the soft, wistful kind that barely graced her lips—and her aqua eyes sparkled. "And as I got to know him—the *real* him—I began to fall madly in love with him."

"That's . . . amazing," I said, unsure of how else to respond.

She leaned forward again and lowered her voice. "It wasn't until we'd been married for four months that we even, you know . . . *shared* a bed together. Mikko wanted to wait until I was completely comfortable with it."

"He sounds like a very honorable man," I said.

If what Linnea said was true, then he definitely was. But I was having a hard time reconciling this information with the cold, aloof King I'd considered him to be.

Although, when the Queen had been missing, a different side of Mikko had emerged. He'd been visibly distraught and inconsolable. At the time, I'd thought it was all a melodramatic act, but if Linnea was telling the truth, he might have been so afraid of losing her that he'd let his guard down and shown his real feelings.

Of course, that made everything even more confusing. If Mikko hadn't grown tired of or irritated with his wife, then why had anybody wanted to get rid of her?

Not to mention the fact that Mikko had thwarted our investigation when Linnea was missing. We'd wanted to interview guards and look at reports, but we were denied access.

"Have you talked to Mikko about what happened before you went missing?" I asked.

"I talk to Mikko about everything," Linnea said, and with her love of chatting, I had a feeling that was very true.

That probably made them very compatible. She enjoyed talking, and Mikko was more of a listener, so they balanced each other out.

"Did he say anything about Konstantin Black?" I asked. "Does he know anything about him?"

"Everything he knows, he's heard from you." Linnea shook

her head. "He is grateful that Konstantin warned me to run away, though, and Mikko is relieved he wasn't executed. Konstantin may have saved my life."

I rested my arms on the table. "From whom, though? Does Mikko have any idea who might have wanted to hurt you?"

"No. He's tried talking to the guard, but the unfortunate truth is that he's been very hands-off about most things," Linnea admitted, frowning. "His social anxiety makes it so hard for him to interact sometimes, so he's really left Bayle Lundeen to handle everything."

"Do you trust Bayle?" I asked.

"I don't know." Her eyes widened, as if it had just occurred to her that she shouldn't. "Do you?"

"Honestly, I'm not sure I trust any of the guards around here. It's hard to tell who knows what," I said.

"I know." She nodded. "What I said the other night about overreacting and running away, that was for the benefit of the guards. I have no idea who we can trust anymore. But to tell you the truth, I'd never considered that Bayle might be involved."

"He's the head guard, and this is all happening on his watch. Either he's involved, or he's too incompetent to stop it."

Linnea exhaled deeply and rested her chin on her hand. "Rune trusted Bayle and appointed him, and both Mikko and Kennet are loyal to him and seem to trust him. Their father was a terrifying man, and even after his death neither of the boys wants to defy him. But . . ." She chewed the inside of her cheek, pondering the situation. "You're right, and I know you're right."

"I know it's tough for the King to go against what he believes his father's wishes were, but the guard needs an overhaul to keep you all safe," I said. "Whether your husband is comfortable with it or not, he needs to start taking control of his guards. If he wants to keep you safe, the King needs to be in charge."

Linnea nodded. "He needs to hear it from you though."

"What?" I asked.

I'd gone into this luncheon thinking that Mikko might be the one behind everything, or at the very least a participant in Konstantin's plot. But Linnea had just turned that theory on its head, and now she wanted me to go to Mikko and tell the King he needed to get rid of his top guard.

"You're an expert on these matters, and you're right." Linnea pushed back her chair and stood up. "We should go now. He's down in his office. It's the perfect time for you to go tell him what you think."

"We should set up a meeting with Kasper, maybe even your grandmother and the Prince," I suggested, since I felt unprepared to present my case to the King—especially considering I didn't completely know what my case was.

"We'll have a proper meeting later." Linnea waved it off. "Let's go."

The Queen had given me an order, so I had to obey. As we walked downstairs toward the King's office, Linnea chattered the whole way, although I'm ashamed to admit that I'm not entirely sure what about. My mind was focused on trying to figure out what exactly I would say to the King, and how I should phrase everything.

Linnea pushed open the door to her husband's office without knocking. I was still lost in thought, but Linnea's scream pulled me into the moment instantly.

Mikko's desk faced the water, so his back was to the door. He was hunched over his desk, hard at work on something, so he didn't see the man standing behind him with a sword raised above his head, about to strike and cut off the King's head.

TWENTY-THREE

impact

Training kicked in, and I didn't have to think —my body just sprang into motion. I ran at the man, knocking him to the ground and grabbing his wrist. I slammed it into the floor, forcing him to drop the sword.

He tried to crawl toward it, and the satin of his uniform made it easier for him to slip out from underneath me. But I knelt on his back, pressing my knees into his kidneys as I pinned him in place.

With one swift move, he tilted to the side and thrust his elbow up, hitting me squarely in the chin. It was just enough to throw me off balance, and he scrambled out from under me. He grabbed the sword, but I was already on my feet when he jumped up and pointed it at me.

There was a split second of shock when I realized who it was—Cyrano Moen, Linnea's personal guard.

Cyrano tried to run at me. I dodged to the side, avoiding the blade of the sword, then I grabbed his arm. I turned him around, bending his arm at a painful angle, and he let out a yelp. If I applied more pressure, I would break his arm, and that caused him to release his sword again.

I took it from him this time, letting him go so he fell on the ground. Cyrano lay before me, panting, and I hoped this meant the fight was over. In the background, I heard Linnea crying and demanding to know why he would do this.

But he didn't answer. Instead, he reached for the spare dagger in his boot.

"Drop it," I commanded, and his hard blue eyes were locked on mine. He had to know I meant it, but there was a determined mania in his gaze that I didn't understand.

He slowly got up, still holding the dagger, so I repeated, "Drop it."

"Cyrano!" Mikko's voice boomed from somewhere behind me. "Do as she says!"

"I'd like her to make me," Cyrano snarled, and then he lunged at me.

In my days of training as a tracker, I had run a sword through hundreds of dummies. They were built to have the same feel as a troll, so we'd know how much resistance a body would give and how much force we'd need to get the sword through.

Still, I can't explain how different it felt, or even what the difference was, when I pushed the blade straight through Cyrano. It was easier than I expected—the flesh gave way, and when the bell of the sword handle pressed against his stomach, I felt the warmth of his blood as it spilled over.

The only light came from a desk lamp, casting too much of the room in shadows. Everything seemed to have an eerie, yellow hue to it, thanks to the way the light played off the reflective glass and the water outside.

We had turned, so the window was behind me, and the light bounced onto Cyrano's face. It cast a shadow across his mouth and body, but his eyes were wide and I could see the yellow dancing in them, like fiery waves.

His eyes stayed locked on me still, filled with that strange mania. Not until the final seconds, when I was lowering him back to the ground and pulling the sword out of him, did the frenzied look finally give way. A glassy peace seemed to come over him, and he was dead.

Linnea ran over to Cyrano's body, pounding on his chest and screaming, demanding why he'd want to hurt her husband. She'd never been anything but kind to him. How could he betray her like this?

Her words eventually seemed to fade away, becoming a distant foggy sound, like something from a dream. Mikko came over and pulled her off.

I don't remember letting go of the sword, but I remember the sound it made, clattering against the floor. I didn't move or speak until Bayle Lundeen came in, asking me questions.

I answered them as directly and simply as I could, but the words felt detached from me, as if they were coming from someone else. It was my voice, it was the truth about what I'd done, but it wasn't me.

Nobody told me that I was acting strangely or that I didn't seem present, so I must've been performing normally. I have no idea how long I talked to Bayle and King Mikko. It might have been minutes. It might have been an hour.

Eventually, Kasper came and took me back to my room. He suggested I shower, since I had Cyrano's blood all over me, and then he headed back upstairs, promising to help with the investigation.

The shower lasted a very long time. I know this because it started out hot, but when I'd finished, the water was icy cold. I walked across the hall from the bathroom, wearing only a white robe. I'd thrown my clothes away in the trash can. I didn't need them anymore.

When I went into my room, I still felt vaguely as though I was in a dream. I just couldn't seem to feel my body. It was as if I were floating above everything, not a part of this world, and I wondered if this was what it felt like to be a ghost.

"Bryn?" Kennet asked, and I looked over to see him sitting on my bed. His usual smile was gone, and his eyes were dark.

"How long have you been there?" I asked.

"Long enough," he said, like I would know what that meant, and he stood up so he could walk closer to me. "Are you okay?"

"I don't know," I admitted, and I wasn't sure I had the ability to lie right then. It seemed out of the realm of my abilities to make things up. "I just killed a man."

"I know."

I waited a beat before adding, "I've never killed anyone before."

It was so much simpler than I expected. Taking a life seemed like it should be a much greater challenge, but my sword had gone through him just like it would through anything else. And then he was dead.

There was a weight to that that I hadn't expected. No amount of training or even belief that I had done the right thing could change the way it felt. A man had been alive. Now he wasn't. And it was because of me.

"You were doing your job, what you needed to do," Kennet said. "That's why I came here. To thank you for saving my brother's life."

"Is the King okay?"

I tried to collect myself, realizing that I had a job to do. I was a tracker. I'd been training for years to do what I'd just done. I just needed to get through the shock of it all.

"Yes, he's fine, thanks to you." Kennet smiled. "Mikko wanted me to extend his gratitude to you, and I'm certain he'll do it personally later on. He thought you might need time to collect yourself."

"No, I'm fine." I brushed my fingers through my tangles of wet hair and turned, walking away from Kennet and toward the window. It was still daylight out, and a few rays of light managed to break through the murky water. "I'll do whatever they need me to do."

"No one needs you to do anything right now." Kennet followed me, his steps measured to match my slow place, before stopping behind me. "The King has given you the night off to do as you wish."

"But isn't there an investigation to be done?" I turned back to face him.

"The King, Kasper, and Bayle are handling it right now," Kennet reassured me. "You can join them tomorrow. But for now, I think it's best if you get some rest."

I shook my head. "I'm fine. I don't need rest. I need to figure out what's going on."

"Bryn, take a break when you've earned it." Kennet sounded weary, probably growing exhausted from trying to convince me that there was more to life than work. "And by Ægir's might, you've earned it."

I closed my eyes and took a deep breath. Kennet was close enough that I could breathe him in again—the heady scent of the sea and fresh rain and ice. He smelled of water in all its forms, so wonderful and soothing.

Without thinking, I leaned into him, resting my head against his chest, and he responded by wrapping his arms around me and holding me to him.

"I'm sorry if I come on too strong." His words were muffled in my hair as he spoke. "It's just that this palace can be awfully lonely day after day. But I don't want anything from you that you don't want to give."

I buried my head deeper in his chest.

"You smell like home," I whispered, realizing too late that my inability to lie had also become an inability to filter. Words were tumbling out without hesitation. "But not like the house I grew up in."

"It's water that you smell," he explained, his words muffled in my hair. "And water is your home."

Home. It was the last word that echoed through my mind when sleep finally overtook me that night.

TWENTY-FOUR

afflicted

I remembered nothing from my dreams, but I couldn't shake the fear. I was sitting in my bed, in the strange darkened room of the Skojare palace, covered in a cold sweat and gasping for breath, and I didn't know why I was so terrified.

Kennet had slipped out after I'd fallen asleep, which was only proper. But I missed the comfort of his presence, and I realized that in spite of all my best intentions, I now considered Kennet a friend.

"Bryn?" Kasper cautiously pushed open my bedroom door and looked in. "Are you awake?"

"Yeah." I sat up straighter and used the blanket to wipe the sweat from my brow. "Yeah, you can come in."

"Are you okay?" Kasper asked. Even in the darkness, my distress must've been apparent.

"Yeah, I'm fine." I brushed it off. "What do you need?"

"I know I told you to rest, and I understand if you want to—"

"Just tell me what's going on," I said, rushing him along.

"We're going to check out Cyrano Moen's house, and I thought you'd want to join us."

The clock on my nightstand said it was nearly midnight. "Now? Why haven't you already gone?"

He let out an irritated sigh. "I don't know. Bayle insisted that we do all this other pointless stuff first." He shook his head. "Honestly, I want you to join me so I can have another set of eyes that I can trust."

"I'll go with you."

I hopped out of bed, and Kasper turned away since I'd been sleeping in just a tank top and underwear. I hurried to throw on a pair of jeans and a shirt, and then we left my room.

Cyrano Moen's house was three miles from the palace, counting the long walk on the dock that connected the palace with the mainland. Storvatten itself was a strange, quiet village with no street lights and no real roads to speak of, just dirt paths meandering through the darkness.

Most of the houses were burrows—squat little houses half-buried in the ground with thatched roofs and moss growing up over them. Cyrano's was no different, but unlike the other houses surrounding it, his actually had the lights on.

The front door was open, and five steps led into a living room. Bayle was already inside when Kasper and I arrived, looking around the small space. The house was round, and everything inside it was visible from the front door—the living room, the kitchen, even the bedroom in the back corner where a crib sat next to a full-size bed.

"Cyrano had a family," I realized, and guilt hit me like a sledgehammer.

"Neighbors said they left earlier today," Bayle said, then motioned to discarded clothes on the bed and a pacifier on the dirt floor. "By the look of things, I'd say they went in a hurry."

A picture hung on the living room wall of Cyrano with a lovely young wife and a small, pudgy baby with a blue ribbon in her hair. She was an adorable baby, but there seemed to be something off about her eyes, something I couldn't place.

That wasn't what struck me, though. It was that this man had a family, one I'd taken him away from.

"Bryn." Kasper touched my arm, sensing my anguish. "You were protecting the King."

"What was that?" Bayle asked, looking over at us.

"How old is the little girl?" I asked, not wanting to let Bayle in on my private feelings, and pointed to the picture.

"A little over a year, I think," Bayle said. "Cyrano talked about her from time to time. Her name was Morgan, and I think she was diagnosed with some sort of disorder a few months ago."

"Disorder?" I looked at him. "What do you mean?"

"I can't remember what it was." Bayle shook his head. "Something with her brain. She started having seizures, and she couldn't crawl because she didn't have any strength. And there was something with her eyes. They kept darting all around."

"Salla disease," Kasper said, filling in the name Bayle had forgotten.

Bayle nodded. "Yeah, that's it."

I'd heard of Salla disease before. It was some kind of genetic disorder that affected a small percentage of the troll population, but it wasn't common enough that I knew much about it.

"My little sister Naima has it," Kasper said, and his whole face softened when he mentioned her.

"What is it exactly?" I asked.

"It affects the nervous system, and it made it hard for Naima to talk or move, not to mention the seizures," he said. "Fortunately, my parents caught it early with Naima, and they got the medics involved right away. With a combination of medication and their healing powers, along with a couple other things, they really helped her."

Our medics had the ability to heal with psychokinetic powers, but they weren't all powerful. They couldn't undo death, and they couldn't eliminate most diseases. They could take away some symptoms, but they couldn't eradicate disease entirely.

"I mean, she's not cured, and she never will be," Kasper elaborated. "But Naima's ten now, and she can talk, and she *loves* to dance." He smiled. "She's really happy, and that's what counts."

"I'm glad she's okay now," I said.

"Me too," he agreed. "But the treatments my parents got for her cost a fortune. My dad had to get a second job to help cover them."

"That's terrible, but if the two of you are done talking about your families, do you wanna start looking around to see if we can find any clues about Cyrano?" Bayle asked, sounding awfully patronizing for someone who had hired Cyrano in the first place.

"Yes. Of course." I saluted him, which made him scowl, and I started to look around the room.

In reality, there wasn't much to investigate. The house was small and ordinary, and it didn't appear that Cyrano had left behind a manifesto. But since Bayle had been condescending, I wasn't going to leave a single stone unturned.

I lifted up the blankets on the bed, riffled through the baby's toys in the toy box, and leafed through the few books on the shelf. None of them were too exciting—there were a few books on parenting and Salla disease, a dog-eared copy of *Atlas Shrugged,* and a book by Jordan Belfort.

While I dug around their living room, Bayle walked around not doing much of anything, and Kasper scoped out the kitchen. I was flipping through one of the books when I glanced over at the kitchen to see that Kasper had dropped to his knees and was reaching underneath the stout wood-burning stove.

"What are you doing?" I asked, setting aside the book to check it out.

"I thought I saw the light catch on something." He squeezed himself against the stove, reaching all the way to the back, then he scooted back out.

"What is it?" I asked, and Bayle came to look over my shoulder.

Kasper sat back on his knees and opened his hand, revealing two blue stones each about the size of a marble but not quite as round. Their dark blue color sparkled as Kasper tilted his hand.

"Those are big sapphires," I said.

Kasper looked up at me. "This has to mean something."

incentives

W hat is going on in my kingdom?" Marksinna Lisbet
asked, and for the first time since I'd met her, she
truly appeared her age.

Her golden hair fell in loose curls down to the middle of her
back. Her satin dressing gown flowed around her, creating a
half-circle of shimmering fabric on the marble floor of her
chambers. She sat at her vanity, her makeup and jewels spread
out on the table beside her.

The only jewelry she wore was the large sapphire wedding
ring from her long-deceased husband, and even though it wasn't
yet six in the morning she'd already applied a coat of mauve
lipstick.

"Nana, it's not so bad," Linnea said, attempting to comfort
her. She sat on a plush chaise behind her grandmother, and
based on her lack of makeup and loosely tied robe that revealed

a lace-trimmed camisole underneath, I suspected she hadn't been awake long either.

Lisbet had summoned Kasper and me very early this morning to have a private meeting in her chambers, with only her and her granddaughter. When we arrived, she apologized for the early hour, but said she thought it was the only way a meeting among us would go unnoticed.

"It's not so bad?" Lisbet shot a look over her shoulder at Linnea and scoffed. "Just two weeks ago someone attempted to kidnap you, and last night *your* guard tried to murder your husband! How can you say it's not so bad?"

"Well . . ." Linnea faltered for a moment, frowning. "Both Mikko and I are alive and well. So it can't be *that* bad."

"My child, you know you are the world to me, but things are very bad indeed when the only positive thing you can say is that you're simply alive," Lisbet said. "You're a vibrant, healthy, young Queen. You are *supposed* to be alive!"

"Kasper and Bryn are here," Linnea tried, gesturing toward where we stood at attention near the door. "They'll help us sort out this mess."

The Marksinna looked toward us, an unsettling weariness and fear in her eyes, and she nodded once. "You are here, and I am very grateful for it, because without you I have no idea what would have become of my grandson-in-law. But what do we do about all this?" Her gaze fell heavily on Kasper and me. "Who is behind these attempts on my family's lives? And how do we stop them?"

"Bayle Lundeen has launched a full-scale investigation—" Kasper began, but Lisbet immediately held up her hand to stop him.

"I don't trust that man." Lisbet grimaced. "I haven't trusted him for so long, but Mikko refused to hear anything about it. Lundeen was his father's lackey, which really tells you something about him. Rune Biâelse was an awful, cold tyrant, and anybody he trusted can't be good news."

"Nana!" Linnea exclaimed.

"I'm just stating a fact, my dear," Lisbet said, brushing her off. "And worse still, Rune left his son too terrified to act even long after his death."

"I don't trust Bayle Lundeen either," Kasper agreed. "But now I'm a part of the investigation, and I'm hoping to steer it in the right direction."

"A noble intention, but I'm not certain it will bear any fruit," Lisbet said. "That is why I called you both here. You have no connection to this guard, and you've already proven yourselves to be far more intelligent and capable than anyone we have here. I want you to look into it, separate from whatever farce it is that Bayle Lundeen is spearheading."

I exchanged a look with Kasper, who nodded his encouragement.

"That was already our intention, Marksinna," I said. "We did not trust the guard when we arrived, but after the incident with Cyrano, we trust them even less. Now we must determine how widespread the betrayal is, and who is behind it."

"Excellent." Lisbet smiled at us. "What have you uncovered so far?"

"Cyrano was supposed to be guarding Queen Linnea over the lunch hour, but he informed her that he had a meeting with Bayle he needed to attend," Kasper began.

"I already know that," Linnea said. "I'm the one who told you that."

"Right." Kasper gave her a look but kept his voice even. "We have confirmed that the meeting did exist and that Bayle was there with ten other guards who all vouch for him, along with the kitchen staff and footmen. Cyrano wasn't supposed to attend because he wasn't allowed to leave the Queen unguarded, which he did."

"He told me I would be fine because I would be with Bryn," Linnea said. "And as it turns out, I was much safer with Bryn than I would have been with him."

"So Cyrano lied to get a moment alone with the King so he could kill him?" Lisbet shrugged. "That doesn't tell us *why* he wanted to."

"No, but it does suggest that Bayle wasn't directly involved," Kasper said.

"It's also worth mentioning that Cyrano had a wife and a young child," I said, and by the surprised looks Lisbet and Linnea gave each other, I guessed this was news to them. "His daughter has a rare disease that requires costly treatment, which makes money an excellent motivator. Both the wife and the child appear to have left in a hurry."

"Clothes were scattered over the beds, but there were no signs of a struggle," Kasper said. "They seem to have left very suddenly but of their own accord."

"That's not that surprising if they heard Cyrano was a traitor who'd been killed," I continued, not letting the darkness of his death cloud my words. "We would expect them to run away lest they be punished for his crimes."

"If they are innocent, they have nothing to fear," Linnea piped up, and that was her naiveté showing.

Another time, I would have to explain to her how Viktor Dålig's young children had been punished for his transgressions. The world was not a fair place, and a Queen needed to know that if she wanted to help rule a kingdom.

"We did find something odd, however," Kasper went on. "Under the stove were two sapphires, a little smaller than a marble. We suspect that in the commotion of leaving, they fell out and rolled under the stove, and Cyrano's wife either didn't notice or was in too much of a hurry to be bothered with them."

"Sapphires nearly as large as a marble?" Lisbet shook her head. "Are you certain they were real?"

Kasper nodded. "Based on the color and size, Bayle estimated they were worth at least twenty thousand dollars apiece."

Linnea gasped. "How could a guard have sapphires worth that much? And how could his family be so careless as to leave them behind?"

"That is an excellent question," I said. It was one that Kasper and I had been quick to answer last night. "The only way Cyrano's wife wouldn't have noticed or wouldn't have cared about leaving behind nearly fifty thousand dollars was if she had a lot more."

Queen Linnea shook her head with her forehead scrunched up, clearly still baffled by what I was saying. "We pay them a decent wage, but it's nowhere near enough to have that kind of money. Was Cyrano stealing them?"

"That is one consideration," Kasper allowed. "The other is that Cyrano was paid off."

Lisbet rested her chin on her hand, staring off at nothing, but her eyes darted back and forth as she thought. The Marksinna had most likely come to that conclusion long before her granddaughter had and was trying to make sense of it.

"With his daughter's illness and the rising cost of medical bills, Cyrano was very vulnerable to bribery," I said. "He probably believed that it was worth risking his life to take care of his family."

That would explain the intent mania I saw in Cyrano's eyes. He'd had no reason not to drop his sword yesterday, but after talking with Kasper, we'd both begun to suspect that Cyrano planned on going after me until I killed him. In fact, the payment to his family might have been contingent on his death. It would be the only way that whoever had paid him off could be certain that Cyrano would never talk.

I wasn't sure if that made me feel any better about what had happened. Killing a desperate man intent on dying to save his family didn't exactly sound like justice.

"Who here has that kind of money?" Kasper asked.

"Well . . . nobody." Linnea shrugged her shoulders. "I

mean, the women have jewels." She motioned to her grand-mother's table, covered in gaudy necklaces and rings. "One of my necklaces might cost ten thousand dollars, but it would have to be filled with sapphires and diamonds. We don't have massive gems like that floating around."

"They came from the vault," Lisbet said, looking at Linnea in the mirror. "That's the only place where we have stones of that caliber."

"Those belong to the kingdom," Linnea said, trying to dissuade her grandmother. "They belong to everybody. Why would Cyrano steal from himself?"

"He didn't steal it—he was paid off," Lisbet corrected her, and Linnea sank down in the chaise. "And it may 'belong' to the kingdom, but only the royal family has access to it. Only the King is allowed to spend it."

"But Mikko's saving it," Linnea argued weakly. "He's trying to do what's best for the people."

Lisbet closed her eyes and sighed. "You can't have a room full of precious stones and expect no one to get greedy."

"Who has access to the vault?" I asked. "Who could have gotten in there to take the sapphires?"

Lisbet turned back toward Kasper and me and looked up. "The system requires thumbprint recognition that you need to get the door open, and that's calibrated for only four people—the royal family. That would be myself, Linnea, Mikko, and Kennet."

"There must be some mistake," Linnea said, disputing Lisbet's assertion. "None of us would do this. I know I didn't, and of course you wouldn't do it. Mikko didn't try to kill himself, and Kennet would never do anything to hurt his brother." She shook her head. "This is a mistake. Someone else is behind this."

Lisbet regarded Kasper and me gravely, ignoring the Queen's insistence that it couldn't be any of the people she loved.

"Talk to the people and do what you need to do," Lisbet told us. "This must end."

stoic

The marble bench felt hard and cold underneath me, and I leaned forward, resting my arms on my legs. My mouth felt dry, so I licked my lips. I let out a shaky breath.

"You okay?" Kasper asked, his voice soft so it wouldn't echo in the cavernous round hall outside of the King's chambers.

"Hmm?" I'd been staring at the pattern of tiles on the floor, trying not to think of anything at all, and I turned to look at him.

"You seem kind of out of it." Even though Kasper worked to keep his expression neutral at all times, his face had softened and his dark eyebrows were pinched with concern.

"I'm fine," I lied, sitting up straighter.

We were waiting outside the King's chambers with the intention of questioning him about the sapphires in Cyrano's possession. After our meeting with Lisbet and Linnea, we'd gone straight down here, hoping to talk to him before Bayle or anybody else had a chance.

When we'd arrived, he'd still been sleeping, but his valet had gone in to see if Mikko would be willing to see us. A few minutes later, the valet had informed us that Mikko would, but he needed some time to wake up and ready himself, and Kasper and I had been patiently waiting for the past fifteen minutes.

"I know I've been really fortunate to have been a member of the Högdragen in a time of peace." Kasper still spoke low so his voice wouldn't carry. Not that he needed to worry, since we were alone. "I've only been on it for a little over a year, but even when I was a tracker, things were mostly quiet and peaceful."

"Konstantin Black did try to kill the Chancellor," I reminded him, not unkindly.

"I said *mostly*," he said, "I was out on a mission away from Doldastam when that happened, so I missed all the commotion surrounding it."

"You didn't miss much," I muttered. "Konstantin is insanely good at disappearing in the blink of an eye."

"My point was that I've never even had to draw my sword on someone and mean it, let alone take another person's life," Kasper said, and I involuntarily tensed up. "I can't imagine what that must be like."

"It's part of the job." I wanted to brush it off, change the subject, do anything other than actually talk about it.

"I know, and I know you did what you needed to do." He waited a moment, letting that sink in. "But it couldn't have been easy for you."

"It was surprisingly easy, actually," I said thickly. "From start to finish, it was all over in a matter of minutes."

Kasper put his hand on my back. The gesture felt awkward and a little stiff, but there was something oddly comforting about it.

"You were trained well, and you did what you were supposed to do. That won't change what happened, but maybe it can make it little easier on you."

I offered him a wan smile. "Thank you."

The valet came out and told us that the King would see us now. I stood up and straightened my clothes, and then I followed Kasper inside.

We found Mikko in the sitting area of his chambers. He was dressed but unshaven, with a blond scruff on his chin. The high-backed, tufted chair he sat on looked cushy, but he sat rigidly with his shoulders back, appearing rather uncomfortable.

His blue eyes landed on us briefly, then went back to staring at the rug on the floor. His lips were pressed together in a thin line, and as he breathed in deeply through his nose, his gills seemed to flutter in agitation.

There was a couch and several other chairs that Kasper and I could have sat in, but since Mikko made no motion to them, we remained standing. We never sat in the presence of royalty unless we were invited to.

"I'm assuming this is about the investigation," Mikko said.

"We just had a few things we wanted to talk to you about. This won't take long." I tried to keep my tone soft to calm any anxiety he might have.

Linnea had said he was painfully shy—although to be honest, he seemed more angry than he did nervous. But it was probably better for a King to seem cross all the time than afraid.

Mikko nodded once. "Go ahead."

"Do you know how Cyrano Moen could have come into possession of sapphires?" Kasper asked.

"No." Mikko's hands were resting on his lap, and he began to rub one palm against his leg anxiously. "Sapphires are the most plentiful stones in our kingdom, though. Perhaps he bartered with someone for them."

"We had considered this, but the ones he had were very valuable," Kasper explained. "Bayle estimated their worth at upwards of twenty thousand apiece."

Mikko's expression remained hard, unchanged by the news Kasper had given him, and his eyes were now locked on the floor. He sat stoically, not responding, for nearly a minute before he said, "He shouldn't have had those."

"What do you mean by that?" I asked.

"I don't know how a guard would come by those." Mikko looked up at us and shook his head. "I have no idea how he would've gotten them."

"We suspect he might have been paid," Kasper said, "for his attempt on your life."

The King lowered his eyes and didn't say anything. He'd stopped moving his hand on his leg, and aside from the subtle movement of his gills when he breathed, he was as still as a statue.

"Do you know who would have access to those kinds of

sapphires and would want to hurt you?" I asked him, speaking slowly and carefully.

Of course, Kasper and I already knew who had access to the sapphires, and that list was only four people long. The only person I'd really crossed off was Marksinna Lisbet. I believed she cared too much about her granddaughter to risk anything that might get Linnea hurt.

But even Queen Linnea—who seemed friendly and naive—could be putting on an act, and she could be behind everything. Most of what I knew about things here in Storvatten had come from her, and I really had no way of knowing if she was lying or not.

Despite my newfound friendship with Prince Kennet, I still didn't trust him farther than I could throw him. As the younger brother of the King, I could think of a very obvious motive for him to want his brother out of the way, but I had no idea why he'd have planned an attack on Linnea.

That was assuming of course that Cyrano's attack on Mikko and Konstantin's on Linnea were related, which was the theory that Kasper and I were going on at the moment.

And as for Mikko, with his hardened expression and clipped answers, I honestly had no idea what to make of him. I had been hoping that talking to him would clear things up, but he seemed even more cagey than usual.

"No." Mikko shook his head. "I can think of no one."

"According to Marksinna Lisbet, only four people can get to the vault," Kasper said, pushing Mikko a bit since he wasn't being forthcoming.

"Sapphires can come from anywhere, not just the vault," Mikko replied curtly.

I glanced over at Kasper. We had considered this too, but given how many sapphires were in the vault and how poor the rest of the community was, it seemed very unlikely that they came from anywhere else.

"The four people who can get into the vault are your grandmother-in-law, your brother, your wife, and yourself," Kasper went on as if Mikko hadn't said anything.

"Thank you for informing me of things of which I'm already aware, but I don't think I can be of help to you." Mikko stood up abruptly. "I'm sorry I don't know more, but I should begin preparing for the day. Bayle Lundeen is running a meeting later today, and I am certain that I'll see you both there."

Both Kasper and I were taken aback, and it was a few seconds before we could gather our wits. We thanked the King for his time and then left his chambers, since there was nothing else we could really do.

We saw ourselves out, and once we were in safely in the hall with the door closed behind us, I turned to Kasper. "He knows something."

"But who is he protecting?" Kasper asked. "Himself, or someone he cares about?"

augur

K asper told me to go rest, but I had other plans in mind.
After spending the morning going over our notes and
talking to anyone we could, we still had an hour left until the
meeting with Bayle Lundeen was set to start. Kasper and I had
tried to speak with him, but he kept insisting that he was busy
and he'd talk to us during the meeting.

Apparently, I still wasn't looking so hot, so Kasper had all
but commanded me to go lay down, promising he would get
me in time for the meeting. I considered it, but I knew sleep
wouldn't make me feel better. So I changed into a tank top and
leggings and headed outside.

On the back of the palace was a stone patio, curved along
the edge to mimic the waves on the outer walls. A hundred
rounded stairs led down from the patio to the bottom of the lake,
and I descended them slowly, pushing through the shock of the
cold as I waded into the water.

Even in May, Lake Superior barely got above freezing. The Skojare kept the ice at bay through a combination of practical tools and magic, but that didn't mean the water was warm by any means.

A human would succumb to hypothermia in as little as fifteen minutes, but I was no human. The Skojare thrived in the cold water. Spending their entire existence in Scandinavia, northern Europe, and Canada, they had adapted to handle the harsh temperatures of swimming in freezing lakes.

Even the Kanin had adjusted to the cold, but I doubted Kasper or Tilda would fare as well stepping into the icy lake as I would. It wasn't exactly a pleasant feeling—like an electrical current running over my skin. But I couldn't deny that there was something strangely enjoyable about it.

The chill took my breath away, and it felt as though it was waking up parts of my body I hadn't even known were sleeping. I lay on my back, floating on the surface. The sun warmed me from above, while the cold water rocked me from below.

I just needed to be able to clear my head. The last twenty-four hours had been a blur of insanity, and I couldn't seem to process any of it.

I knew that I'd killed Cyrano, and I knew that it had been the correct thing to do given my job and his actions. But I couldn't make sense of how I felt about it. Numb perhaps, the numbness was mixed with sadness and regret and pride.

Sadness because a man had died, and regret because I was convinced I could've done something differently so he'd still be alive. And pride because I had done exactly what I had been trained to do. When it came down to it, I had acted and saved the King.

It seemed nearly impossible to reconcile those three emotions.

I tried to let the water wash over me, desperate for a reprieve from constant worries about work and Konstantin and Ridley. No matter how hard I tried, Ridley kept floating back into my thoughts, leaving an ache that ripped through me.

Thinking of him hurt too much, and I pushed away my memories of his eyes and the way his arms felt around me.

I closed my eyes, trying to clear my mind of everything, and I just focused on the sound of the lake lapping against the palace, the iciness of the water holding me up underneath the contrasting warmth of the sun.

That was all that mattered for the moment. Soon, I'd have to go back inside and try to untangle the mess of who was trying to kill whom and why here in Storvatten. But right now, I just needed *this*—to have a few minutes when nothing mattered and I didn't need to think.

With my eyes closed, I could see the sun through my lids. Then the yellowish-red of my eyelids began to change, shifting into pure white bright light that filled my vision. It was disorienting and confusing, and when I tried to open my eyes, I realized they already were.

I was standing in the snow, but there was no horizon around me. Just whiteness, as if the world disappeared into nothing a few meters beyond where I stood. My heart began to race in a panic, and I turned in a circle, trying to understand where I was and what was happening.

Suddenly Konstantin Black was there, standing in front of me dressed all in black, smiling at me. "Don't be scared, white rabbit."

"What's happening?" I asked.

This didn't feel anything like a dream, but it had to be. There was no other explanation for how I could have been in the lake one second, and here in an impossible place with Konstantin the next. I didn't remember falling asleep, but it was a possibility, given how exhausted I had been lately.

"I can't stay long," Konstantin said.

Already, his smile had fallen away. This was the first time I'd seen him without his hair pushed back, and his dark curls fell around his face. His eyes were the color of forged steel, the kind used to make our swords, and he stepped closer to me, looking at me intently.

"Why are we here?" I asked.

"Here is nowhere." He shook his head. "You are in Storvatten, and you must leave."

I narrowed my eyes at him. "How do you know where I am?"

"I know a great many things, and it doesn't matter how I know. You are not safe in Storvatten, and you need to leave."

"It seems safe to me, now that you and Viktor Dålig are gone," I said.

Konstantin pursed his lips, and for a moment he looked pained. "I am glad to see you're okay after what he did to you."

"Why?" I shook my head. "Why do you even care?"

"I don't know," he admitted with a crooked smile. "I just don't want to see any more innocent people hurt."

"Then you need to stop working with Viktor Dålig."

The sky—if you could call the whiteness that surrounded us the sky—began to darken, turning gray, and the snow underneath my feet started to tremble.

"This won't hold for much longer," Konstantin said. Thunder seemed to come from nowhere and everywhere at all once, and he had to shout be heard over it. "You must leave Storvatten! They plan to kill you because you're getting too close!"

"Too close to what?" I asked, and by now the sky was nearly black. "How do you know?"

"Viktor Dålig gave the order. He wants anyone in his way dead."

Konstantin receded from me, but he didn't step or move himself. It was as though he were slowly being pulled into the darkness around us.

"Run, white rabbit," he said, his voice nearly lost in the rumbles, and then he was gone.

I opened my eyes to the bright sun shining above the Skojare palace, and even though I was still floating above the water, I was gasping for breath.

Everything seemed peaceful and still. There was no thunder, no darkness, no Konstantin Black. I tried to tell myself that it was just a strange dream brought on by stress and exhaustion, but I couldn't shake the feeling that I had really been talking to Konstantin. That somehow he'd managed to visit me in a lysa to warn me that there was a bounty on my head.

denunciation

It was in the fishbowl of the meeting room that everything went completely insane, and this was coming from someone who'd just been visited in a dream by Konstantin Black.

The meeting room stuck out from the rest of the palace in a bubble, with one interior wall and one exterior wall of glass domed out around us. It left me feeling as if the lake were engulfing us, as if it were a sea monster trying to swallow us all.

At the end of the long table in the center of the room sat King Mikko, with his Queen sitting to his right and his brother to his left. Lisbet sat next to her granddaughter. Other than Kasper and me, they were the only people in the room.

"This is Bayle's meeting, isn't it?" Kennet asked, looking over his shoulder at the large bronze clock hanging on the wall. "Doesn't he know it's rude to arrive late to your own party?"

"When you arrived late to your own birthday party, you told me that was arriving in style," Linnea reminded him.

Kennet smirked. "That's because everything I do, I do in style."

Kennet might have joked, but nobody else here seemed to be in good spirits. Bayle's making us wait—twenty minutes so far—wasn't making things any better. Kasper and I were close to the end of the table, a polite distance away from the royalty, and Mikko kept shooting icy glares in our direction.

I had a feeling if we didn't solve things quickly, we never would, because it seemed like we had begun to wear out our welcome.

"Oh for Ægir's sake." Lisbet let out an exasperated sigh. "My King, perhaps you should send someone to fetch Bayle. This is getting tedious."

"He will be here," Mikko said, apparently immune to the same tension the rest of us were suffocating under.

Fortunately for the rest of us, Bayle finally arrived, with guards in tow. They were senior guards I'd met earlier in the week, decked out in their uniforms. Bayle had added a vest made of platinum, with carvings of fish scales. It was real metal that he wore over his jacket, armor to protect against attacks.

Looking back, that was the first sign that something was going on. Who wears armor to a meeting?

"I'm glad you could grace us with your presence," Kennet said dryly.

"I am very sorry, my liege, but I had important business to attend to, which will become very clear to you all in a moment," Bayle said. To his credit, he actually sounded winded, like he'd been hurrying.

He seemed nervous, though—staring about the room, swallowing and licking his lips a lot, and stammering a bit when he spoke. The guard behind him held a thick manila envelope, and he would only stare at the ground.

"That's fine," Mikko said. "Just get on with it."

Bayle began to rehash what we all already knew—Cyrano's attempt to kill Mikko, my thwarting of it, Cyrano's wife and daughter running off, the sapphires, and the fact that the only people who had access to the vault were in this room.

"We spoke to all of you this morning, asking when and why you last accessed the vault," Bayle said, and he put his hand on the bell of his sword. "Marksinna Lisbet had been there three months ago with the record keeper, for accounting purposes. Prince Kennet was there two days ago, showing Kasper and Bryn."

Bayle cleared his throat. "Queen Linnea and King Mikko claimed it had been so long ago that they couldn't recollect when they'd last opened it."

"So?" Kennet arched an eyebrow. "That doesn't really tell us anything does it?"

"No, not by itself." Bayle turned to the guard behind him and took the envelope. "We checked the database to see if anybody else had gotten in the vault, and according to the, uh, the computer, the last person in the vault was, uh, King Mikko, two hours before the attack on his life."

Mikko didn't say anything immediately. He just shook his head. "That's simply untrue. I wasn't in there. I had no reason to go in."

"Sire, the fingerprint scanning says you were," Bayle said.

"The King is not a liar," Linnea hissed.

Lisbet held up her hand to hush her granddaughter, her eyes fixed on the guards. "What does all this mean?"

"Well, it, uh . . ." Bayle cleared his throat again. "We believe that King Mikko paid Cyrano Moen to attack him, making it appear that Cyrano would kill him but knowing that a guard would intervene and protect him."

"That's preposterous!" Linnea shouted. "Why would Mikko fake an attempt on his life? That makes no sense."

"We believe that King Mikko is the one behind your attempted kidnapping, and that to shift blame from himself, he planned the assassination attempt," Bayle explained. "He wanted us to think someone else was behind everything going on here."

Kennet sat back in his chair, almost slouching, and only glanced over at his brother once. Mikko, for his part, seemed unmoved by what Bayle was saying. He just kept shaking his head.

"Mikko would never hurt me," Linnea insisted. She leaned forward on the table, as if that would make Bayle believe her.

"It's with all that in mind that we have come here to arrest King Mikko Biâelse for the attempted kidnapping of the Queen, Linnea Biâelse, as well as hiring Cyrano Moen for a feigned assassination attempt," Bayle said, and for the first time since he'd come in the room, his voice sounded strong.

"That's treason!" Linnea was practically screaming now. "You cannot arrest the King!"

"Linnea, hush." Lisbet put her hand on Linnea's arm. "Let them sort this all out."

Technically, a monarch could be arrested for breaking any of the laws of the kingdom. And while I wasn't as familiar with Skojare history I was with Kanin, in the Kanin lore, I only knew of two monarchs ever being arrested—a Queen for poisoning her husband, and a King for stabbing the Chancellor in the middle of a party.

Kings had been overthrown. A few had been forced to step down, and a couple had even been executed. But they were almost never arrested. In theory, laws might apply to royalty, but in practice, they never really did.

"I haven't done anything," Mikko said, his voice a low rumble. "I'd never hurt my wife, and I never hired a guard to pretend to hurt me."

But he didn't threaten to have them banished or thrown in the dungeon. He simply denied the charges, and that emboldened the guards to come over and put Mikko in shackles.

Linnea began screaming at them, telling them that they couldn't do this and that they had to let him go, and Lisbet had to physically hold her back. Throughout the whole display, Kennet never said a word.

As the guards escorted Mikko out of the room, he walked with his head bowed and his broad shoulders slumped. He seemed almost resigned to the position, and since he was a King with all the power in the kingdom to fight the charges, I didn't understand why he was just taking it like this.

It did fit in line with what both Kennet and Linnea had said about him—that he would rather take what was given to him than fight back. But that made it feel all the more tragic to see the tall hulk of a man with his head hanging down as the guard he refused to depose escorted him out of the room.

Before Bayle left, I got up and ran after him, stopping him at the door. "We'd like to take a look at the records."

"In due time." Bayle was talking to me, but his eyes were directed out the door, following Mikko's figure down the hall. "There's a case we're working on, and you'll have your turn when we're done."

"No, we should be part of the case—" I tried to argue, but he cut me off.

"Excuse me," Bayle said brusquely. "I've just arrested the ruler of our kingdom. I have more pressing matters to deal with."

While Lisbet struggled to get Linnea to calm down, I walked back over and collapsed in the chair next to Kasper. He looked just as shocked as I felt, and considering Kasper prided himself on keeping his emotions hidden, that was really saying something.

"What the fuck just happened?" he asked.

I shook my head. "I have no idea."

quandary

Miss! You can't go in there!" the footman called after me, but if I wasn't going to heed Konstantin's warning of imminent death, I wasn't about to listen to a servant worrying about propriety.

I pushed open the door to Kennet's chambers without knocking and without waiting for anyone to let me in. He stood next to his bed loosening his tie, his suit jacket already discarded on a nearby chair.

"Miss!" The footman had hurried in after me. "You must leave."

"It's all right," Kennet told him, but he kept his eyes on me. "She can stay."

"If you are sure, my Prince," the footman said, eyeing me with disdain.

"Give us a moment alone. And make sure you don't let anybody get by this time."

The footman bowed then turned and left, closing the door behind him. Kennet's room didn't appear all that different from my own, except the finishings were nicer. The wallpaper wasn't peeling, and sheer silver curtains ran along the window that faced the water, giving the room a greater sense of privacy.

Kennet took off his tie and tossed it on the bed. "By the look on your face, I'm assuming this isn't a friendly visit."

"You know why I'm here," I snapped.

"No, I really don't." He sat on the bed, sounding tired, and most of his usual swagger had disappeared. He seemed world weary in a way that I hadn't thought Kennet capable of.

"Why didn't you defend your brother?" I asked.

"Why didn't you?" he shot back.

"Because he's not my brother, and I'm not the Prince. They never would've listened to me."

Kennet stared down at his satin bedspread. "They were arresting the King, Bryn. They weren't going to listen to me either." Then he shook his head. "I'm not sure he's innocent."

"You think he did it?" I asked.

He looked up at me. "You don't?"

"I don't know," I admitted.

Kennet motioned to me. "Well, there you go."

"You still should've defended him."

"Just because he's my brother? Or because he's my King? You think he should get a free pass?"

"No. Of course not."

Kennet cocked his head and narrowed his eyes. "You think I had something to do with it."

"I haven't ruled out any possibilities yet." I chose my words carefully.

"You don't trust me?" Kennet smirked a little and stood up, walking toward me.

"I think it would be unwise to trust anybody in Storvatten right now."

"That is probably very true." He stopped mere inches away, looking down at me. "Why did you come to my room, Bryn?"

"I want to find out the truth about what is going on here."

"But you don't trust me."

"Maybe I can tell when you're lying," I countered.

"Oh yeah?" Kennet raised an eyebrow. "Am I lying when I say I want to kiss you right now?"

I took half a step back, surprised by his frank declaration, and it took me a moment to figure out how to counter him. "Prince, I value your friendship, but that is all."

He stepped closer, smiling down at me. "You would deny your Prince a simple kiss?"

I looked up at him sharply. "You would order me to?"

"No, of course not," Kennet corrected himself quickly. "You know I didn't mean it like that."

"How do I know that?" I asked as I studied his face. "I don't know you, and I don't trust you."

For once, he didn't have a smart comeback. The weariness I'd seen in him earlier was creeping back in, and I felt a small pang of sympathy.

"Today has been a very long day, and the days ahead are only going to be longer," Kennet said, his voice a low, resigned rumble. "And as much as I'd usually love to play these games with you, I don't have it in me today."

"I don't want to play any games," I told him. "I just need you to be honest with me."

He let out a deep breath. "I will answer any questions you ask me as honestly as I can."

"Did you try to kidnap or hurt the Queen?"

He pulled his head back in surprise. "No. Of course not."

"Do you know who did?"

"It's my understanding that it was that Konstantin Black fellow."

"Do you know him?"

"Konstantin?" Kennet shook his head. "No. I never met him."

I narrowed my eyes, appraising him. "You're not lying?"

"No, I swear," he insisted, and for once I actually believed him. "I never met him. I never even heard of him until you told us about him."

"Did your brother have anything to do with the Queen's kidnapping?" I asked.

Kennet opened his mouth but seemed to think better of it. His gills flared with a deep breath, and finally he said, "I think my brother is involved in a great number of things that I know nothing about. He is a good man, and he tries to be a fair King, but he's been in over his head since the day he was crowned. No matter what he has done, I'm certain that he never meant to hurt anybody."

"What about you?" I asked.

"What about me?" A smile began to play on his lips.

"Are you a good man?"

"No, I would say I'm not a very good man," Kennet admitted. "But I would never do anything to hurt my brother. Despite our occasional differences, I love Mikko, and I won't let anything bad happen to him."

"You let him go to jail," I reminded him, and he flinched.

"Mikko is in jail," he contended. "But I'm not the one who arrested him, and there will be a trial. He will have the chance to clear his name, and I'll stand by him.

"Besides, there are worse things than jail," Kennet added.

"Did you hire Cyrano to kill you brother?" I asked.

Kennet rolled his eyes. "I already told you I'd never do anything to hurt Mikko. Haven't I answered enough of these questions?" He stepped backward and sat on the bed.

"I have one more question," I answered. "Do you know why anyone would want me dead?"

"What?" Kennet shook his head, appearing appalled by the idea. "No. Of course not. Who wants you dead?"

"No one. Never mind." I tried to brush it off, since that was easier than explaining that Konstantin Black had visited me in a dream to tell me that Viktor Dålig had put a hit out on me.

Kennet smirked. "I can't imagine a single reason anyone wouldn't want you around. Other than your incessant questions, of course."

THIRTY

desperation

The darkness of the water outside my window made it impossible to see if the sun had come up yet. I lay in bed not sleeping, the way I had spent most of the night not sleeping, waiting for my alarm to go off and tell me it was morning and I could get up and actually accomplish something.

Not that I was sure anything could be accomplished. Kasper and I had spent a large portion of yesterday trying to get Bayle to hand over papers to us, but he insisted that they needed to be locked up for safety before King Mikko's trial.

Bayle refused to tell us much of anything, citing confidentiality. We tried to push it, but since we didn't have much standing here, we didn't get anywhere. When we tried to talk to Mikko, his barrister shut us down.

There wasn't much more we could do for him, so Kasper suggested we go back to working on the mission we came here for in the first place—creating recommendations to help the palace guard function better. And that's what we did, staying up late into the night to write a report about the changes we thought the guards could make so the royal family would be safer.

It did seem a little like a moot point, with the Skojare King locked up and their kingdom in a panic. Not to mention that Bayle Lundeen still had more power than he should—but for the moment, things were in too much chaos to add reorganizing the guard.

Whoever stepped up in the interim for King Mikko—most likely Linnea, Kennet, or Lisbet—could replace Bayle, and that was our number-one recommendation. The guard needed a complete overhaul, starting at the top. Once Bayle was gone and the trial was over, it would be good for the Skojare if they could get a fresh start with a properly functioning security system in place.

A timid knock at my door interrupted my not-sleeping, and I rolled over to check the alarm clock. It wasn't even six in the morning yet, so I suspected that whoever was here wasn't bearing good news.

I opened the door to find Linnea. The hood of her dressing robe was up, hiding her mass of curls, and her eyes were red rimmed. Her porcelain skin somehow seemed even paler than normal, and she sniffled as she stared up at me in desperation.

"Please, you have to help us," Linnea said, almost sobbing already.

"Help who?" I asked.

"Mikko and me." Linnea came in past me, wringing her

embroidered handkerchief. "I saw him last night, and it was awful, but they would only let me stay for twenty minutes, and he can't live like that, Bryn! He can't!"

I closed the door and held out my hand. "Calm down. I know you're upset, but everything will be okay."

"How can you say that?" Linnea cried. "My husband is in the dungeon!"

"Getting hysterical won't get him out any sooner."

"I know. I'm sorry." She wiped at her eyes with the handkerchief, then she sat down on the bed. "I don't even know how this can happen. How can the King be arrested?"

"The laws apply to the King and commoners alike," I said, reciting what we were taught in school—but even then, everyone had known it wasn't true.

"They say they're doing it to protect me," Linnea went on, ignoring my comment. "But why would I need protection from Mikko? He *loves* me!"

"They're still investigating." I tried to placate her.

Her lips trembled as she stared up at me from underneath the hood. "I don't even know what's happening in the kingdom. How can I trust Mikko will even get a fair trial? What if they find him guilty? What will become of him? And what will become of me?"

I shook my head sadly, wishing I had something better to give her. "I don't know."

"I just can't believe this is all happening. I'm the Queen! I should have some say!" Linnea cried out in frustration.

"It's isn't fair," I agreed.

For the most part, both Kanin and Skojare societies were patriarchies—women could only rule in extreme cases and for a short period of time, usually after their husband the King had died and before their son the Prince came of age. Other tribes were more socially progressive than ours, allowing women to rule in the absence of a male bloodline, but the Kanin especially were much more rooted in tradition than most.

Linnea's power as Queen only came from her husband, or her son if she eventually had one while Mikko was King. If Mikko were to lose his crown, she would lose hers as well. With the King thrown in the dungeon, her power was locked up along with him.

"What's going on?" Kasper threw open the door my room, his sword in hand.

His hair was disheveled from sleep, and he wore only a pair of pajama pants, revealing a tattoo of a rabbit above his heart. I knew that many of the Högdragen had that same tattoo, but I'd never seen Kasper's before.

"Nothing." I held up my hands to calm him. "Everything is fine."

"I heard a noise," he said, probably referring to Linnea's yelling, and he looked around the room in bewilderment. "Why is the Queen here?"

"Am I even the Queen?" Linnea asked, growing more despondent by the second.

"She just needed someone to talk to," I explained to Kasper, and he relaxed and lowered his sword.

"What I *need* is answers," Linnea said.

"Your grandmother carries a great deal of weight in the kingdom," I said. "You should be talking with her. I'm sure she knows more about what's going to happen than I do."

"She does," Linnea agreed, but she didn't sound too happy about it. "She's on the committee to decide who should rule in the King's absence, but she won't listen to me. Whenever I say anything about Mikko, she just tells me to be patient and that the truth will come out."

"That is very sound advice," Kasper said.

Something must've occurred to Linnea, because she suddenly perked up, her eyes bright and excited. "But she'll listen to you. She trusts the pair of you. If you talk to her about Mikko, she'll *have* to listen to you."

"My Queen, I think you're being a bit a rash," I explained carefully. "Marksinna Lisbet is far more likely to listen to you than she is to two guards from another kingdom. As the Queen and her blood, you possess far more clout than we ever could."

"Nonsense." Linnea jumped to her feet, undeterred. "Nana still thinks of me as a child. She respects your opinions. You must come with me to talk to her at once."

"At once?" Kasper asked.

"Well, I'll give you a moment to get dressed." Linnea glanced over at his shirtless torso. "But as soon as you're finished."

I sincerely doubted that we could change the Marksinna's mind, not to mention that I wasn't convinced Mikko was innocent. Of course, I wasn't convinced that he was guilty either.

sequester

L innea held my hand as we ran down the hall, practically dragging me along behind her, and as we entered Lisbet's chambers, she continued to do so. I wanted to let go or pull free, but she squeezed so tightly I thought she needed it.

"What are you all doing here?" Lisbet asked, sounding more harried than surprised.

Despite the early hour, Lisbet was already up and getting ready for the day. Instead of her usual gowns and dresses, she wore suit pants with flowing wide legs and an elegant top, while her matching jacket lay carefully on her bed. She flitted about the room, putting in large dangling earrings, barely stopping to look at us.

"We want to talk to you about Mikko," Linnea said, summoning all her strength.

"I have a great many meetings today, all centered on him," Lisbet replied tiredly. She began rummaging through the drawer on her vanity. "I can't imagine there's anything more I have to say about him."

Linnea stepped away from me, letting go of my hand. "But Nana, he's innocent! Bryn and Kasper think so too!"

Kasper appeared startled by this declaration, since he'd never said anything indicating he felt that way.

Lisbet apparently found what she was looking for—a heavily jeweled bracelet—and she straightened up and looked over at us as she put it on. "Is that true?"

"I haven't seen any evidence that's shown King Mikko's guilt definitively," I replied, choosing my words very carefully so as not to alienate Linnea, but I need to be truthful. "But I haven't been allowed to see very much evidence at all."

Lisbet nodded. "That is an unfortunate necessity."

Every time Kasper and I had tried to get more information yesterday, we'd hit a wall. While I wouldn't go as far as to suggest that Lisbet declare Mikko wrongfully accused the way Linnea had, I did realize that now was the perfect opportunity to see if Lisbet could remove some of those walls.

"If we had more access, I'm certain we could be of help—" I began, but Lisbet held up her hand, silencing me.

"You've already been more than enough help," she said. "But I'm afraid your time here has run its course. Members of another tribe—no matter how well-meaning and how educated—cannot be involved in deciding the fate of our King."

I lowered my eyes. "Of course."

"Things are changing a great deal here, and I truly believe my granddaughter is much safer, and that is because of you,"

Lisbet went on. "Both of you have been integral in improving our way of life here in Storvatten."

"We have been compiling a report of our recommendations," Kasper said, since it seemed clear that Lisbet was about to give us leave. "What would you like us to do with it?"

"I would like you to complete it. We will definitely be taking all your recommendations under advisement," Lisbet said.

"But Nana, Mikko . . ." Linnea whined, impatient with all the talk not about her husband—which was understandable given her desperation.

"Linnea, my love, we have already gone over this many times." Lisbet spoke sweetly, but strain was visible in her face—the tight smile, the irritation in her eyes. "The inquest will decide what happens. I know you love him, but you must wait—as I must, as the entire kingdom must—to find out the truth, and then you must learn to be satisfied with whatever that may be."

"But this isn't fair! It's not right!" Linnea shouted with tears in her eyes, then turned to me. "Bryn! Tell her!"

At first, I said nothing, caught off guard at being put in such a position, but I finally came up with, "My Queen, you know my thoughts on this won't affect the outcome."

"She is right, Linnea," Lisbet said. "You must learn to be patient."

Linnea pushed back her platinum ringlets and tried to stay collected, but she'd only had the most tenuous grasp on composure all morning. It all became too much for her, and she burst out sobbing. Her grandmother reached out to comfort her, but Linnea pushed Lisbet off. Mumbling apologies, she ran into the adjoining bathroom and slammed the door shut behind her.

"I'm sorry for her outburst," Lisbet said. "She's still very young, and the past few weeks have been very hard on her."

"No need for apologies," I assured her. "But it sounds as if you're saying our time here is done."

Lisbet walked over to the bed and put on her suit jacket, a large sapphire brooch already pinned to the front. "I do think you've helped as much as you can."

"What of the Queen's safety? And your own?" I asked.

In the back of my mind was Konstantin's warning that my life was in danger in Storvatten—assuming he had actually visited me in a lysa, and it wasn't simply a stress dream. Either way, it didn't matter. If I felt that Linnea wasn't safe or that I had a job to do here, I would argue to stay.

"I am looking into it, off the radar of the guard, and I will get to the bottom of things. And I can assure you that I value Linnea's life more than my own," Lisbet told me emphatically. "Her safety will be my utmost priority."

"Marksinna, I know how much you love your granddaughter, but with all due respect, the kingdom has already been falling down around you," I said. "And I fear the both of you will continue to be in danger. At least as long as Bayle Lundeen is in charge."

"Today, I will attend a meeting where the acting monarch is declared in Mikko's absence," Lisbet said. "I am going to do all I can to ensure that I get the position, and my very first act will be removing Bayle." She stared down at me severely. "This kingdom will not fall apart as long as I'm around."

I wanted to argue with her, but the truth was that Lisbet had far more power than I did. She was much better equipped to handle the heft of the Skojare problems than I was. By removing Cyrano Moen, and by convincing Lisbet to remove Bayle, I had done all I could to keep Linnea safe.

"I'm sorry I don't have more time to talk to you, but as you can imagine, it's a crazy time here in our kingdom," Lisbet said. "Once you complete the report, deliver it to me. Then you are free to head back to Doldastam."

THIRTY-TWO

૭૦૯૭

valediction

In the week since Kasper and I had left, Doldastam had warmed up some, but it was still buried under snow, which was typical even for May. I'd gotten so used to looking out the windows of the Skojare palace and seeing the dark water surrounding us, it was a strange relief to see the overcast sky and snow-covered landscape.

After Marksinna Lisbet had told us our time was done, Kasper and I had spent the better part of the day perfecting our extensive list of recommendations. I wanted to be certain I wasn't leaving Linnea defenseless, and when I handed the list to Lisbet, I reiterated that they could call upon us should they need anything again.

My goodbyes with Linnea had been short and bittersweet. She didn't say much, instead preferring to sit with her head down and mumble her gratitude. I thought that would be it, but when I turned to go she lunged at me and hugged me fiercely as she cried against my shoulder.

"You mustn't forget about me, Bryn," she said between sobs.

I wasn't sure what to do, so I awkwardly patted her back and said, "Of course I won't."

"And you will come back, right?" She let go of me and wiped her eyes, trying to collect herself again. "If I need you?"

"Of course. I will always be here if you need me. I won't let anything bad befall either you or the King," I promised her, although I had no idea how I'd be able to keep that promise from Doldastam.

Linnea smiled at me with tears streaming down her cheeks. I didn't want to leave her like that, but Kasper insisted it was time to go. We'd been ordered to move on, so there was nothing more we could do there, and I left Linnea in the hands of her grandmother.

The Storvatten palace was in chaos, with people running this way and that down the halls. The meeting with Marksinna Lisbet, Prince Kennet, and an advisory board had been deadlocked most of the morning, and they had adjourned without reaching a decision on who would be King, in part because none of them agreed how long the King would be absent.

Usually, a footman would have carried our bags to and from our rooms when we arrived and departed, but today either the footmen were busy caring for arriving Skojare officials from other towns, or someone was too busy to instruct them. Either way, Kasper and I were left to tend to our luggage ourselves.

I didn't mind, except that the halls were inordinately crowded, making it harder to get by.

"We shouldn't be leaving," I muttered to Kasper as we made our way through the labyrinth the halls had become.

"This all comes with the Högdragen territory—you do what you're told as long as you're told to do it, and then you move on," he replied simply.

We managed to make it to the door in once piece with all our possessions. I paused, looking back at the icy palace around us.

"Do you think Linnea and Mikko will be all right?" I asked.

"I think that with Lisbet in charge, things will be safer here than they have been in a very long time," Kasper said.

He was right. We had begun to make changes to the guard, but Lisbet would be the one to finish them. Besides, Linnea could always reach me in a lysa, and I would come the second she called for me, if she did.

I had opened the front door to the palace when Kennet came running out to stop us, pushing through everyone bustling around the main hall.

"You were really gonna leave without saying anything?" Kennet asked, out of breath because he'd literally jogged over to us.

"You have a lot on your plate today," I said. "I wasn't even sure where you were, and I didn't think you'd have the time."

"I always have time for you, Bryn," Kennet assured me with a smile.

Kasper stood awkwardly next to us and cleared his throat loudly. I wasn't sure if it was to remind me that he was there, or to emphasize that openly flirting with the Prince was frowned upon. But it didn't matter. I planned on keeping things brief.

"Thank you for making time for me while I was here, Prince."

"It has truly been my pleasure." Kennet stared down at me, his eyes that brilliant blue that I'd thought only existed in movies, and a wry smile played on his lips. "Until we meet again."

And that's how I'd left Storvatten—feeling an odd mixture of pride and uncertainty. I had done the job I had been tasked with, and I had done it to the best of my ability. But leaving the palace while it was still so unstable didn't exactly make me happy.

It was midday on Tuesday when we drove through the walls that surrounded Doldastam. The gate was locked, and the two Högdragen manning it were incredibly thorough in checking our IDs and credentials. I was honestly a little surprised they didn't search the SUV at the rate they were going.

After my time in Storvatten and the long drive back, all I really wanted to do was put on something comfortable, go brush Bloom, and then maybe curl up in bed with a good book and lose myself for a while.

Of course, there wasn't time for that. At least not right away. Kasper and I had just completed a mission, which meant that we had to debrief King Evert.

Because of the added security, Elliot Väan—a Högdragen guard—met us at the door instead of a footman. He and

Kasper worked together a lot, and they were good friends. As Elliot led us down to the meeting room, he and Kasper made small talk, and I tried to adjust to being back home.

The Kanin palace definitely seemed darker after the glass walls and frosty wallpaper in Storvatten. Here the stone surrounded us, lit by kerosene lamps. Though there were elegant touches, with jewels and antiques in every corner, there was definitely something much more medieval about the Kanin palace.

As we got closer to the meeting room, Kasper asked Elliot, "How have things been while we've been gone?"

Elliot shook his head. "Things are not going well."

"How so?" Kasper asked, and I turned toward them, my interest piqued.

"It's too much to tell you right now." Elliot gestured toward the doors to the meeting room. "The King may fill you in anyway, and he should be here shortly."

I wished he would've said more, but meeting with the King took priority over small talk with a guard. As I went over to the table to take a seat, Kasper cleared his throat.

I looked back at him, standing tall with his hands folded behind his back. "What?"

"A member of the Högdragen stands."

"But we're having a meeting with the King. I always sit."

Kasper stared straight ahead. "A member of the Högdragen stands."

"Are you saying I should stand?"

"I'm not in a position to give you orders."

I rolled my eyes. "We've just spent a week working together. If you think I'm doing something wrong, tell me."

His mouth twitched, then he turned to me and said, "I think you get too familiar with people in authority."

My jaw dropped. I'd expected maybe a small admonishment about my posture or something. The only thing he'd really corrected me for in Storvatten was that I didn't stand tall enough.

"Don't look so shocked." Kasper sighed, and his shoulders relaxed. "I'm not trying to be mean, and it's good that they like you. It speaks well of how you carry yourself and interact with others, especially those in power who are generally slow to grow fond of those who serve them."

"You wouldn't have brought it up if you didn't think it was a bad thing," I said.

"I think it's a dangerous thing," he clarified. "Queen Linnea treated you more as a friend than a servant —which is what a guard is, when it comes down to it."

I lowered my eyes. "Things were strange in Storvatten. The Queen needed someone to rely on."

"It's not just there though," Kasper said. "You're too friendly with Ridley, and he's your boss. You talk back to our King and Queen."

"My job is to serve this kingdom to the best of my ability, and that means I won't stand idly by if I think the wrong thing is being done, even if the one doing it is wearing a crown." My voice grew louder as I spoke. Kasper had been speaking to me as gently as he could, but it was hard for me not to feel defensive.

"Bryn." He glanced toward the door, as if expecting the

King to come walking in, and he pushed his hand palm down in a gesture indicating that I should lower my voice. "I'm not attacking you. I know you have the best intentions, and you're good at what you do."

I folded my arms over my chest. "That's not what it sounded like."

"When I'm working, I set aside my opinions and feelings," he explained. "I simply do as I am told. My job is to follow the King's orders, and when I'm done, I'm done. My day is over, and I go home to Tilda, and soon I'll come home to a baby. There I have opinions and thoughts, because that's my life. That's where those things fit."

"You care about your job just as much as I do," I countered.

"No, I take my job as seriously as you do," Kasper corrected me. "The things that matter the most to me aren't my job or the King or the Queen. They're Tilda, and my family, and my friends. Those are things I'm passionate about. But at work, I keep my mouth shut and do my job."

I shook my head. "Well, I guess my service is more than just a job to me. I'm willing to sacrifice anything to help our people"—I couldn't help but think of Ridley, and I swallowed back the ache he always brought to my chest—"so if I overstep my role, it's only because this job matters so much to me."

"I'm not trying to upset you, Bryn," Kasper said. "I admire your devotion—everyone does. It's how you've gotten so far. All I'm saying is that it's not good when you make your job your whole life, and it's even more dangerous when you mistake the people who reign over you for your friends."

I opened my mouth to argue but stopped myself when I realized I was being defensive. Because what he'd said was true. Every night when he went home to Tilda and their future child, I went home to an empty loft.

It was the life I'd chosen for myself. But was it really the life I wanted?

operations

E ven a ride on Bloom couldn't help me shake my unease. The horse tried his best, galloping along the wall that surrounded Doldastam as fast as he could, but when I took him back to the stable I still wasn't feeling any better. He nuzzled me more than usual, his mane as soft as silk as it rubbed against me, and I fed him an extra apple before leaving.

The debriefing with the King had gone about as I'd thought it would—he'd already heard about Mikko's arrest and mainly been interested in who would be ruling the Skojare in his absence. But Evert had seemed more distracted than normal, and he left the meeting within a few minutes with brusque congratulations on a job well done.

I wanted to work off the anxiety that Storvatten and Konstantin and even Kasper's lecture had caused, but that required dealing with everything that went along with going to work. So that left me walking around town, trying to clear my head.

My path took me by the tracker school, but I deliberately gave it a wide berth in case I spotted Ridley. I definitely wasn't prepared to see to him yet.

As I walked by, I glanced over at the training yard behind the school. A split-rail wooden fence surrounded the yard, in an attempt to keep out the children who mistook it for a playground. Most of it was flat, level dirt with the snow shoveled away, but there was a climbing wall and a few other obstacles.

With the temperature just below freezing and the air still, it was a perfect day for the trackers to be out running a course. Instead, I only saw two people, and because of the distance between us it took me a few seconds longer than it should've to realize that it was Ember training with someone else.

Her dark hair was pulled back into a ponytail, and she wore a black thermal shirt and boots that went halfway up her calf. Her sparring partner was a guy, dressed similarly to her but with the addition of a thick winter cap. Even though he was taller and broader shouldered than her, Ember had no problem pushing him around.

Since no one else was outside, I decided to walk over and say hi. I'd just reached the fence when I finally recognized her combatant, and I realized with dismay that Ember had just thrown Markis Linus Berling to the ground.

"What are you doing?" I asked, but instead of a friendly greeting it sounded much more like a demand.

I'd never seen a Markis or Marksinna training before, in large part because a tracker was never, ever supposed to lay their hands on one, especially not the way Ember just had.

"Bryn!" Ember grinned at me, apparently not noticing the accusation in my tone. "I heard you were coming back today."

"Hey, Bryn." Linus smiled at me, and Ember extended her hand and helped pull him to his feet.

"What are you two doing?" I managed to sound less angry this time as I leaned on the fence.

"Since you've been gone, I've been working as Linus's tracker, helping him acclimate and all that." Ember started walking over to me, and Linus followed, brushing snow off his pants as he did.

"That's great," I said, and I meant it. Ember was a good tracker, and I was sure she'd be a great help to him. "But since when did acclimation include combat training?"

"I asked her to teach me." Linus pushed the brim of his hat up so I could see his eyes better. Freckles dotted his cheeks, and there was something boyish in his face that made him seem younger than his seventeen years.

It'd been nearly a month since I first met Linus in Chicago, when I was tracking him and first ran into Konstantin Black, which set off this whole thing. Since that time, Linus seemed to be doing well at understanding his role in Kanin society as a high-ranking Markis, adjusting quicker than most, but he still hadn't lost his friendly innocence.

"A lot of the younger Markis and Marksinna are requesting defensive training," Ember explained as she leaned against the fence next to me. "Things have been crazy since you've been gone."

I instinctively tensed up. "Crazy how?"

"You know how Ridley was training those scouts to go out and look for Viktor Dålig?" Ember asked.

My stomach dropped, fearing that something might have happened to him while I was gone, and it took me a moment to force myself to nod.

"Well, last week, one of the scouts reported that he thought he'd found Viktor," Ember went on. "He managed to report back with Viktor's whereabouts, but then all communication went silent. Ridley went with a rescue team to go after him. When they found the scout, he was dead."

"But Ridley came back okay?" I asked, my stomach twisting painfully.

"Yeah, he's fine," Ember said, and relief washed over me. "But they found an abandoned campsite, where they're assuming that Viktor, Konstantin, and at least twenty or so other people were hiding out. They were long gone by the time Ridley and the rescue team arrived, of course, but the scary part was that the campsite was only three hours away."

My mind flashed back on Konstantin Black, telling me that I needed to get out of Storvatten because Viktor Dålig wanted me dead. But if Viktor was hiding out near Doldastam, it seemed like I would be an easier target for him here.

Admittedly, we had Högdragen gaurding at every door, and the Skojare had the worst security I'd ever seen. But it wasn't like I could trust Konstantin either. He could have just been leading me down the wrong path. If I wasn't dreaming the whole thing up in the first place.

"That's when I decided I needed to be able to defend myself," Linus said, and while I admired his effort, I'd seen firsthand how clumsy he could be. I hoped the training would work for him.

"Linus has even rallied some of the other Markis and Marksinna." Ember looked at him with pride. "He's been getting everybody to realize the importance of self-reliance."

Linus shrugged and lowered his eyes, kicking at the snow absently with his foot. "I was just talking, and I thought that we should all do what we can to prepare. If you're all going off to war, you can't be wasting your time and energy on us."

"Good job," I told him. "I knew you'd be good for Doldastam."

He smiled sheepishly. "Thanks. But it's no big deal, really."

"So along with Linus, I've been, uh, tutoring this other girl." Ember tucked a stray hair behind her ear and looked down at the ground, so she wouldn't have to look at me. "Marksinna Delilah Nylen. She's my age, and she's uh . . ." A weird smiled played on her lips, and her cheeks reddened slightly. "She's good. She can handle herself in a fight."

Ember smiled wider and laughed, almost nervously. I had seen this behavior before—Ember had a crush. I would've called her out on it if it weren't for Linus standing right there. She was open about her love interests, and it wasn't a big deal—except that Ember was a tracker and the object of her affection appeared to be royalty.

I gave her a look, trying to convey that we would talk about this more later. When she caught my eyes, Ember only blushed harder.

"So does anybody have any idea where Viktor and his band of merry men are headed?" I asked, changing the subject so Ember would stop grinning like a fool.

She shook her head. "Not at the moment. Scouts are looking into it, though."

"Well, the good news is it doesn't sound like Viktor has that many people behind him," I said. "Twenty guys does not an army make."

"That's true, but Ridley is fairly certain it's only a scouting mission, that Viktor and his men just want to scope out exactly what's going on here," Ember explained. "King Evert's freaking out because Viktor's coup fifteen years ago was only him working with a few other guys. And not only did he kill a member of the Högdragen, he got *really* close to killing the King.

"Imagine what he could do with twenty guys," she went on. "And who knows how many more guys he has stashed somewhere else? Those were just the ones he had with him. He could have hundreds."

I'd never been angrier with myself than I was in that moment. If I had just been able to stop Viktor in Storvatten, none of this would be happening. Everything would've been over before it started.

"It's not your fault," Ember said, reading my expression. "Viktor's obviously been planning this for a long time, and I'm sure that even if you'd gotten him, somebody would've stepped in to take his place."

"Maybe," I allowed. "I just wish it had never come to this."

"I know," she agreed. "When this all started, I thought King Evert was overreacting. But now it looks like this war is shaping up to be a big deal."

THIRTY-FOUR

polity

I had just stepped up to my parents' house when my dad opened the door, as if he'd somehow been expecting my unannounced visit. His glasses were pushed up back on his head, holding back his thick black hair that had silvered at the temples.

Dad smiled at me in the way he did when he hadn't seen me in a while—happiness with an edge of relief that I was still alive and well. Without saying anything, I came into the house and he closed the door behind me.

He pulled me into a rough hug, and it wasn't until he did that I realized how much I needed it. I hugged him back harder than I normally did, resting my head in the crook of his shoulder.

"Is everything okay?" Dad asked. I finally released him, but he kept his hands on my shoulders and bent down to look me in the eye.

"Iver? Is someone here?" Mom asked, and she rounded the corner from the living room. "Bryn! You're back!"

She hurried over to me, practically pushing my dad out of the way so she could hug me. She kissed the top of my head and touched my face. Whenever I came back, she seemed to almost pat me down, as if checking to make sure that I was real and in one piece.

"Oh, honey, what's wrong?" Mom asked when she'd finished her inspection. "You look like you have the weight of the world on your shoulders."

"I heard your mission in Storvatten went well," Dad said. As Chancellor for Doldastam, I assumed he'd already gotten the rundown on how things went. "Did something happen that you didn't tell the King?"

"No." I shook my head and let out a heavy sigh.

That wasn't entirely true—I hadn't told King Evert about Prince Kennet's flirtation with me, or how guilty I had felt leaving Queen Linnea, and I definitely hadn't been able to tell him about the lysa involving Konstantin Black.

But I didn't want to tell my parents about any of that either. Well, at least not the Kennet and Konstantin parts. The thing with Konstantin would only frighten them.

"I did my job in Storvatten," I said finally, looking up at my parents' expectant faces. "But I don't think I helped anybody."

And then suddenly, the words came tumbling out of me— all the concerns I'd been trying to repress. How I wasn't certain of Mikko's guilt, and how Kasper and I might have inadvertently been complicit in his unjust arrest. How Linnea seemed more like a child than a Queen, and it didn't feel right leaving her there like that, where she would be ostracized and unprotected if her husband was convicted, and how I knew if Marksinna Lisbet couldn't deliver on her promise to change things, I would have to go back to help Linnea and Mikko. How I didn't trust a single person in Storvatten when it came down to it —not even Marksinna Lisbet or Prince Kennet. How everyone seemed to have conflicted motives and acted cagey at times, like they were hiding something, and I could never be sure if it was because they didn't trust me for being Kanin, or if they were up to no good.

Eventually, my mom interrupted my long rambling tale to suggest we move to the dining room. I sat at the table, across from my dad, while Mom poured large cups of tea for each us.

"You did the right thing," Dad said when I'd finally finished, and Mom set a cup in front of me before taking a seat next to him.

"Then why doesn't it feel that way?" I asked. "It doesn't feel like I've done anything at all."

"Of course you did," he corrected me. "You helped get the Skojare's security in shape, and you brought comfort to Linnea. That's exactly what you set out to do."

"But there's so much left unfinished!" I insisted.

"That's the problem with working for the kingdom, the way you and I do." He motioned between us. "We can only do what we're commanded to do. Too many times, my hands have been bound by the law, and I know how frustrating it can be. But sometimes that's all you can do."

"There are so many limitations to your job," Mom said after taking a long sip of her tea. "That's why I've never quite understood the appeal of it for you. You've always been so strong willed and independent. But you want a job that demands complete submission."

"Runa," Dad said softly. "Now isn't the time for this kind of discussion."

"No, it's okay." I slumped lower in my seat. "She's right. All I've ever wanted to do was make this kingdom better. I wanted to do something good and honorable. And the only way I knew how was to be a tracker or on the Högdragen." I sighed. "But lately I just feel no good at all. I feel like I'm often choosing the lesser of two evils."

"Welcome to politics." Dad lifted his glass in a sardonic cheer and gulped it down.

Mom shifted in her chair and leaned on the table. "You know how I feel about your job, and I'm not advocating for it. But I think you're taking this mission too hard."

"What do you mean?" I asked.

"You were working with another tribe, and if we're being honest, the Skojare are *weird*," she told me knowingly. "I lived there for the first sixteen years of my life, and I was constantly surrounded by that 'cagey' feeling you described. King Rune Biâelse practically made it mandatory.

"Did I ever tell you why my mother named me after him?" Mom asked, and I shook my head. Her name, Runa, was the feminine version of Rune. "The King could be mercilessly cruel to everyone and everything, and my mom hoped—

futilely, I might add—that naming me after him would somehow endear me to him."

"I've heard stories about him being an awful King, but I never realized how bad it was until I was there," I said.

"That's not to say the that the Skojare aren't cold and secretive and just plain odd naturally," she clarified. "Because they are. But Rune just made everything worse for everybody."

"And so they sent you, a Kanin, to a place where outsiders are always distrusted," Mom went on. "The problem isn't with you or even with your job in general, but with the mission itself. You were sent someplace where you could never really be of help, so naturally you came back feeling defeated."

"Your mom is right," Dad agreed. "You were sent there more as a gesture of goodwill than anything else. You were meant to make the Skojare feel aligned with the Kanin, so that if something happens, our King might able to get his hands on the Skojare's jewels."

I leaned my head back so I could stare up at the ceiling. Even though I knew what my dad was saying was true, and I'd really always known it, it still didn't feel good to be a political pawn.

For as long as I could remember, my mom had railed against my working for the kingdom. And that entire time, I'd been completely convinced that she was wrong, that all her concerns and criticisms about our way of life were either unfounded or didn't take into account the bigger picture—that I was helping people. I was making it better.

But now I wasn't so sure about anything anymore.

"I remember feeling frustrated when I was growing up in Storvatten," Mom said after a long pause. "My kingdom demanded silence and obedience. It left me feeling cold and isolated, and I wanted something entirely different." She cast a warm glance at my dad. "I followed my heart, and I've never once regretted the choice I made all those years ago."

I looked over at my parents, feeling more lost and confused than I ever had before. "But what if my heart doesn't know what it wants anymore?"

THIRTY-FIVE

wedlock

The greenhouse seemed unable to contain all the plant life, and vines weaved around door frames to climb over the walls in the small adjoining room. It was usually used as a break room, but it was a perfect place to get ready for a wedding.

Flowers of pink and white and purple bloomed on the vines, and flourishing potted plants sat on every available surface. Even the two sofas in the room had floral designs stitched onto their cream fabric.

A pale pink rose blossomed at the top of the full-length mirror, and Tilda took a deep breath as she stared at her reflection. Her long hair hung in loose curls down her back. Her cheeks were flushed slightly, and carnation-pink lipstick brightened her full lips.

The light chiffon fabric of her off-white dress flowed over her growing baby bump, nearly hiding it, but still managing to highlight how curvaceous and tall she was. Soft sleeves draped off her shoulders just so, revealing her well-toned arms and olive skin.

Ember and I stood to either side of her, both of us looking short and rather plain compared to Tilda's radiance. Our hair had been styled the same way: small purple flowers were weaved into braids twisted into an updo.

We wore matching dresses: pale blue chiffon that landed just above the knees, in a similar empire design as Tilda's. Her mother, Ranetta, had made all three of our dresses, and she'd done an amazing job, especially given the short notice of the wedding.

Tilda's mother stood behind her, carefully adjusting the wreath of flowers on her head—the Kanin tradition instead of a veil. When she'd finished, she looked at her daughter's reflection and smiled with tears in her eyes.

"You look absolutely beautiful," Ranetta told her.

"It's true," Ember chimed in. "I don't think I've ever seen anyone look prettier."

Ilsa, Tilda's older sister, opened the door with a quick knock, then poked her head in. "I think they're all ready for you out there."

Ranetta once again assured Tilda that she looked beautiful and that everything was perfect, then departed with Ilsa to take their seats before the processional started. We could hear the soft music from the piano, and we were just waiting for our cue—"Winter" by Vivaldi to begin.

Tilda took a deep breath and stared straight ahead. "I don't know why I'm so nervous," she whispered.

"It's a big day. It makes sense," Ember said.

Her smoky gray eyes widened, and she nodded. "It's a *huge* day."

"There's nothing to be scared of." I tried to calm her nerves. "Do you love Kasper?"

"Of course." She looked down at me, her eyes misty. "I love him with everything I am."

"Just remember that, and everything will be okay."

Tilda smiled, then she reached out and took my hand. Ember was on the other side of her, and Tilda grabbed her hand too, squeezing it tightly. The three of us stood together like that until the first notes of "Winter" began.

Ember went out first, walking down the short aisle. Tilda was getting married in the flower garden of the greenhouse, and there were flowers everywhere. Potted plants had been moved to the side to make room for a white velvet carpet to run down the center, and the twenty chairs set up on either side of it were decorated with floral garlands.

At the altar, Kasper's two groomsmen were already waiting underneath the flowered arbor. His best man was Elliot Väan, the guard he worked with, and his fifteen-year-old brother, Devin, was the other groomsman.

Devin looked just like a smaller version of his brother, but his fidgety, hyper demeanor set them apart, especially in contrast with Elliot's severe Högdragen stance.

When it was my turn, I kept my head high and my eyes forward. I knew that Tilda had invited Ridley, and I didn't want to see him holding hands with Juni, who would undoubtedly be getting misty eyed at the beauty of it all.

The carpet felt soft on my bare feet, and I kept my eyes locked on the pale lilac and white roses that adorned the arbor. I listened to the music and counted my steps, and I tried desperately not to think about the night Ridley and I had spent together and how I'd wished it would last forever.

When I reached the altar, I took my place next to Ember and turned to watch Tilda. She came out a few seconds later and met Kasper. As soon as she saw him, her eyes filled with tears and she smiled. He took her hand, then he leaned over and whispered something in her ear, causing her to smile wider. Then hand in hand, the two of them walked down the aisle together.

It was only when they made it to the front, and the officiant had begun the ceremony, that I allowed myself to steal a glance around the room.

Kasper's family sat in the front row, and by the rigid way his father sat, it was obvious that he'd once been a member of the Högdragen. His mother seemed more relaxed, hanging on to her husband's arm, her eyes brimming with tears.

Naima, Kasper's little sister, was the spitting image of him. She couldn't have been more than ten, with black corkscrew curls and a wide toothy smile, watching Kasper and Tilda with intense fascination.

But soon my eyes wandered beyond them, and it only took

me a moment to spot Ridley, sitting in the third row. He was alone, no Juni by his side, and he was looking right at me. His dark eyes met mine, and for a moment I forgot to breathe.

Then Tilda turned to hand me her bouquet so she and Kasper could exchange rings, and I looked away from Ridley, forcing myself not to gaze in his direction again.

Tilda's hands were trembling as Kasper slid on the ring, and she laughed nervously. From where I was standing I could see Kasper, and how his love for Tilda warmed his dark eyes when he looked at her.

To seal their matrimony, they kissed. Tilda put her hands on his face, and Kasper put his arm around her, and the kiss was chaste but passionate. As they embraced, I wondered if I'd ever seen two people who loved each other more.

interlude

Ember never missed an opportunity to dance, and she was out on the floor, twirling around underneath strings of fairy lights. Devin had been chosen as her reluctant dance partner, and she pulled him along with her, forcing him to keep up with her moves whether he wanted to or not.

After the ceremony, we'd moved to the reception in the adjacent party room, which was really just a small ballroom built for occasions like these. A three-piece orchestra had been set up at one end of the room, with Tilda's sister Ilsa singing with them. Ilsa had an astonishing range and an amazing voice somehow suited perfectly for the covers of Etta James, Rosemary Clooney, and Roberta Flack that she was performing.

I sat at the side of the room, trying to hide in the shadows as I sipped my sparkling wine and watched the dance floor. Since Tilda and Kasper had invited so few people, it left the floor rather sparse, even when most couples were dancing together.

Unfortunately, that made it all too easy for me to see through them to Ridley at the other side of the room. He was standing near the buffet, absently picking at the vegetable skewers on his plate, and when he looked up at me I quickly looked away.

Tilda had been slow dancing with Kasper, their arms around each other as they talked and laughed, but she stepped aside so Kasper could dance with his little sister. As she walked across the dance floor toward me, Kasper spun Naima around, making her giggle uncontrollably.

"Is your plan to hide in the corner all night?" Tilda asked with a crooked smile, as she sat down in the chair next to me.

"I'm not hiding," I lied and took another sip of my wine.

"Mmm-hmm," she intoned knowingly.

"It was a beautiful ceremony," I said, changing the subject.

Her smile turned wistful as she watched her new husband. Naima had taken to standing on Kasper's feet, and he held her hands as they waltzed around the room, both of them smiling and laughing.

"It really was," she agreed.

"I've never seen Kasper happier."

Watching him now, so relaxed and beaming, reminded me of what he'd said the day before. Work was important to him, but it wasn't his life. It wasn't what defined him, and it wasn't who he really was. This—the guy dancing with his kid sister, smiling at his wife—was Kasper.

His words had stuck with me, and as I watched him I couldn't help but wonder—if the balance of working a job that mattered and having a life outside of it was possible for him, could it be possible for me too? Had I been wrong in assuming I had to choose one over the other?

"You'll have to talk to him eventually," Tilda said, pulling me from my thoughts, and I looked over to see her gazing at me seriously.

I thought about playing dumb and asking *who,* but I knew Tilda would see through that, the way she always saw through my acts.

So instead I simply said, "I know."

"I don't know *why* you're avoiding him, but I know you are," Tilda said, and she raised her hand to silence me before I could stutter out some kind of excuse. "It doesn't matter right now. I just think you should go talk to him before it gets even harder to."

Ridley was still standing on the other side of the room. Kasper's dad had been talking to him, but the conversation appeared to be finishing up, leaving Ridley alone again.

"The bride is always right on her wedding day," Tilda added. "So you know I'm right when I say that you need to do this."

I took a fortifying breath then finished my glass of wine in one large gulp. "Okay." I stood up, smoothing out my bridesmaid dress, and looked down at Tilda. "Will you be okay here by yourself, or do you want me to wait?"

"No, go!" She shooed me away with a smile. "I just wanna sit here another minute, and then I'm sure Kasper will have me out dancing again."

My heart was pounding so hard as I walked across the

dance floor, I could hardly hear the music over it. I kept reminding myself that it was only Ridley, that I'd talked to him a thousand times before and this wasn't a big deal.

Of course, I'd never talked to him after having a one-night stand with him.

He smiled thinly at me as I approached, and I wished I'd had another glass of wine before making my way over.

"Hey," I said when I reached him.

"Hey," he replied, and then I realized in terror that I couldn't think of anything more to say. I'd thought as far as saying *hey*, and now I was trapped in an awful moment where I could only stare at him.

"The wedding was great," I blurted out suddenly, because it was something to say.

"It was." He nodded, then motioned to me. "You looked beautiful."

I lowered my eyes. "You don't have to say that."

"I know." He paused. "I wanted to."

"Well, thanks." I offered him a small smile.

I wasn't sure if I should tell him he looked good too, because he definitely did. His dark hair was just slightly disheveled, as if he couldn't completely tame it. He was clean shaven, which he rarely was, and his tan skin looked so smooth. The vest he wore over his dress shirt was fitted perfectly across his broad shoulders, and the first few buttons of his shirt were undone, showing off just enough flesh to make me crazy.

"So, listen," Ridley said, filling the awkward silence that had fallen between us. "I've been looking for the right time to talk to you since you got back, and now seems as good as any."

"Yeah?" I asked, lifting my eyes to meet his.

"I ended things with Juni."

My heart skipped a beat, and I hoped I didn't look as excited as I felt.

"It wasn't fair to her," he elaborated. "The way I was treating her. Juni is fantastic, and I did like her. But the truth is, I didn't like her enough."

"Yeah, that makes sense," I said, just to say something.

He took a deep breath. "And there's no point in dancing around things anymore. I have feelings for you, Bryn, very strong feelings, and I think you feel the same way."

"I . . . you know . . . I . . ." I was too stunned to properly form a sentence, and I wasn't even sure what I wanted to say.

Of course I had feelings for Ridley, and while part of me was thrilled to hear he felt the same way, nothing had changed. He was still my boss, the Överste, actually, which meant that we would both be in serious trouble if we were to get involved.

So what could I say to him? That I loved him, but it didn't matter because we couldn't be together? What would even be the point of admitting how I felt?

Through my shock and confusion, I realized something in the room had changed. Everyone had stopped dancing, and as I looked around the room the musicians stopped playing. Ilsa had been singing "Why Don't You Do Right?" but just stopped mid-word.

Most of the light in the room came from fairy lights and

candles, but someone flipped on the overhead light, blinding everyone. I lifted up my arm to shield my face, and I finally saw the reason for the change.

Reid Kasten, King Evert's personal guard, stood at the entrance.

"Sorry to interrupt the festivities," Reid announced, speaking loudly and clearly. "The King sent me here to retrieve Bryn Aven."

I glanced over at Ridley, as if he would have some insight as to what this was about, but he shook his head.

"I'm right here." I stepped onto the dance floor so Reid could more easily see me.

"The King wants to see you immediately."

"What's this about?" Ridley asked, stepping up behind me, and Reid regarded him with derision. "I'm the Överste. If something's going on, I should go."

"The King didn't say what it was concerning," Reid said, showing Ridley a bit more respect. "He tasked me with returning with Bryn Aven."

Ridley looked as if he wanted to say more, so I held up my hand to stop him. "It's okay."

I cast Tilda an apologetic smile, since any summons had intruded on her celebration, and she pursed her lips in worry as Reid escorted me away from the dance floor and toward the palace.

lush

The walk to the palace had been cold. I'd put on boots out of necessity, but I hadn't changed out of my light bridesmaid dress, and I'd only grabbed a violet cloak to keep out the chill. Since I didn't know what was going on, I didn't want to waste any more time than I had to.

When we arrived at the palace, I slipped off my boots and cloak by the door. I expected Reid to lead me to the meeting room, but he took a different turn. Instead of going left toward the east wing of the palace where public affairs took place, he went right, taking me toward the private quarters.

"Where are we going?" I asked him.

"The King's parlor," Reid replied in a clipped tone, so I decided against pressing him further.

I'd only been in the private wing twice before, both for training purposes when I was still in tracker school, so it had been a while. Here the floors changed from cold, gray stone to pearlescent tile, purportedly brought in from Italy. Sheetrock covered the stone walls, painted ivory with faint silver flourishes to give it an added elegance. Instead of kerosene lamps, the halls were lit with bright dome lights.

Before we reached the room, I could hear Queen Mina. Her laughter carried through the closed door, and it sounded as if she'd affected the British accent again.

Reid knocked on the door and waited for us to be granted entrance, and I tried to figure out what exactly was happening. None of this made sense or was even remotely close to how things were usually done.

"Come in!" King Evert shouted, without checking to see who we were or what we wanted.

For his part, Reid continued to act as if it were business as usual. He opened the door for me then stood next to it inside the room and announced my arrival. But I barely registered it because I was too busy trying to make sense of the scene before me.

The King's parlor was smaller than I'd expected. It only had room for a love seat, a sofa, and two sitting chairs—all of them high-backed tufted seats in a cream color. Above them hung a small but bright chandelier.

The walls were covered in wallpaper with alternating vertical bands of white and silver. On the wall opposite the door was a carved marble fireplace with a painting of Evert and Mina on their wedding day hanging it above it. To the left and pressed against the wall was an elegant bar made of mirrors with white baroque details.

The King lounged in the chair closest to the fireplace, one leg draped over the arm. The sleeves of his gray shirt were rolled up, and several buttons were undone. His black bangs hung over his forehead, and he had a highball glass in his hand, half full of a dark liquid.

Next to the fireplace, the Queen stood, still laughing as I entered the room. Her hair hung down in loose curls, and she wore a simple gown of pristine white. Even though she looked more relaxed than I usually saw her, she still wore gaudy diamond earrings, and the heavy necklace that lay on her collarbone was encrusted with sapphires. I presumed the wineglass on the mantel directly beside her to be hers.

But the big surprise was the man standing next to the bar, pouring himself another drink. His back was to me, but his broad shoulders and blond hair were unmistakable. His sharkskin jacket was discarded on the sofa, and the sleeves of his white dress shirt had been pushed up.

Prince Kennet seemed to be having some kind of weird party with Mina and Evert.

"Oh, Bryn!" Mina exclaimed when she saw me. "You look so lovely!"

Kennet turned around to look at me and smiled appreciatively, but I didn't have time for that.

"Thank you, my Queen," I replied politely. "I was called away from a wedding to—"

"Doesn't she look lovely?" Mina asked Evert, interrupting me.

Evert narrowed his eyes, as if needing to get a better look at me, and I stood up straighter and repressed an irritated groan. "Yeah, yeah, she does," he slurred.

"The Skojare good looks help with that," Kennet said with a wink, making Mina erupt in laughter again.

"If you won't be needing me for anything more, shall I wait in the hall, sire?" Reid asked, and I didn't blame him.

The King and Queen were drunk, or at the very least buzzed, both of them bordering on obnoxious.

"Yes, of course." Evert waved Reid off, and the guard bowed before exiting the room and closing the door behind him.

"Your Highness, you summoned me?" I asked, trying to find out what exactly I was doing there in the first place.

"That was all my idea, I'm afraid," Kennet admitted. With drink in hand, he effortlessly climbed over the back of the love seat and sat down, extending his legs out on it.

"Oh yes, Prince Kennet came all the way here from Storvatten to thank us personally for our help in sorting out their troubles," Mina explained, and as she spoke, her hand went absently to her lavish necklace. "He wanted to extend his gratitude and strengthen the friendship between our tribes."

"As I understand it, the troubles are still being sorted out," I said carefully. "Storvatten is in great turmoil without a leader."

"That's all been sorted out." Evert waved his hand again, nearly spilling his drink as he did. "The Prince is the King."

I shot a look at Kennet, and the hair on the back of my neck stood up. When I'd left Storvatten, Lisbet had all but guaranteed that she would be appointed the ruler in Mikko's absence.

She had assured me that she would do everything in her power to get the position in order to ensure her and Linnea's safety.

So how exactly had Kennet gotten the title? There was a chance the Skojare in charge of making the decision had thought it would be best if they stuck with the Biâelse bloodline and overruled Marksinna Lisbet.

But as Kennet barely stifled his smirk, I couldn't help but suspect he'd fought Lisbet for the title.

"Acting monarch," Kennet corrected him, which meant he had all the power but not the official title of King. "And only until my brother is exonerated."

I stared at Kennet evenly. "What if your brother isn't exonerated?"

"That would only be if he is actually guilty of everything he's accused of, and if he is, he shouldn't be the King." Kennet sat up straighter. "It is still a terrible mess in Storvatten, you're right, but we're on the right path to figuring everything out and making it a safer place.

"And that," he said, lifting up his glass, "is all thanks to you and the Kanin. So here's to you."

Mina hurried to grab her glass off the mantel and raised it in a toast. "*Skål!*"

"*Skål!*" Evert shouted, then proceeded to drunkenly spill his drink all over himself.

Mina looked at her husband with pity as he tried to wipe the alcohol off his shirt. "Oh, Evert, my love. Let me help you." She rushed over, using the length of her dress to help dry him off.

"I don't even know how that happened." He shook his head in disbelief. "I don't . . . I think I'm drunk."

"I think you are, too, my King," Mina said with a bit of a laugh and smiled up at him. "Why don't we get you up to bed and into something dry?"

He reached out, stroking her face in a moment of tenderness that I hadn't even known the King was capable of. "You're so patient and beautiful. What did I ever do to deserve you?"

"All the right things," she assured him, and then she stood up. "I'm sorry, but I hope you can excuse us both."

"Yes, of course." I bowed slightly.

"I'm sure Bryn and I can entertain ourselves in your absence," Kennet said, wagging his eyebrows at me.

idyll

The very moment the King and Queen left us alone, Kennet leapt up from the sofa and bolted toward me. I had hardly a second to react before his arm was around me and his lips were on mine, but I put my hand on his chest and pushed him back.

"What are you doing?" I demanded, looking up into his startled blue eyes.

"Kissing you. Isn't it obvious?" he asked like a guy who was used to taking what he wanted without any protests.

I pulled myself from his arm and stepped back from him. "I already told you. We're only friends."

"You're saying you don't want to kiss me, then?" Kennet asked with raised eyebrows. I turned away, walking toward the love seat. "Why not? You should at least offer me a reason."

For one thing, I didn't trust him. Not that I ever really had, but now with his new appointment as ruler of the Skojare and his bizarre drunken celebration with the King and Queen, I trusted him even less.

There was also the business of Ridley confessing his feelings for me, and the fact that I felt the same way, with the chance that something might be possible in the future—even the distant future. I didn't want to muck it up by fooling around with a Prince, especially a Prince who was now acting as a King.

But the biggest reason was that I simply didn't feel that way about Kennet. I liked him well enough, and he had been a good friend to me in Storvatten. But that didn't mean I wanted to make out with him.

Not to mention all the other huge reasons why it was a bad idea: I could be demoted, fired, or even banished, and the risk of that was very high in Doldastam, since we actually had a functioning guard that would be able to catch us in the act.

"Well, you're King, for one thing." I turned to face him, offering the reason that seemed least likely to offend him. "Do you really wanna blow it all by messing around with some Kanin girl?"

"Technically, you're not really Kanin," Kennet corrected me, moving closer. "And you're even technically royalty, since both your parents are. It'd be worth the risk."

I stepped back from him. "You don't even like me that much."

Kennet bristled. "Don't tell me how I feel." He softened a little. "But I'd like to spend more time with you. You could come back to Storvatten with me."

"For what?" I shook my head in disbelief. "What are you even doing here?"

"I came here to see you." Kennet tried to touch my arm, but I pulled back from him.

"Bullshit." I wasn't buying any of it.

"I was sent here to help ensure peace between our tribes," Kennet said wearily. "Without a true King right now, and with such a shitty guard, this would be the perfect time for someone to attack us. So I'm supposed to make sure the Kanin like us, so they can defend us if we need them to, and also so they don't attack us themselves."

I eyed him up, still not sure what to believe. "Who sent you?"

"Well, since I'm the acting ruler, I suppose you can say I sent myself." He offered a small smile. "But everyone, including Marksinna Lisbet, thought it would be a good idea to make nice with you all. I gave Mina that necklace as a gesture of our goodwill.

"I did also think it would be fun to spend more time with you, but apparently I was wrong about that," he added dryly.

"Sorry." I relaxed and let my arms fall to my sides, trying not to look as suspicious as I felt. "You just seem a little too cavalier about everything."

He rolled his eyes and went over to grab his drink from where he'd left it on a small side table. "You're really great at knowing how I should act and how I should feel, Bryn."

"How is Mikko?" I asked, switching from one touchy subject to another. I'd dropped the formal titles, since I had no idea if Mikko was even King anymore.

"I don't know." Kennet had his back to me as he took a drink, and I watched his shoulders rise and fall with heavy resignation. "He won't let me see him."

"Why not?"

"You'd have to ask him that yourself." He swirled the alcohol in his glass around, watching it. "I do love him. I know a lot of people don't believe that now, maybe you included, but he is my older brother. I don't want to see him hurt."

"I'm sure it's hard for him," I said gently, trying to offer Kennet a bit of comfort. "With everything that happened, and now with you being the King Mikko is going through a very difficult time."

"He never even wanted to be King," Kennet muttered, still staring down at his glass. "I offered to take the crown in his place, but Mikko refused to go against Father's decree." He shook his head and took a long drink.

"When I left, Marksinna Lisbet told me she thought she'd be placed as acting monarch," I told him.

"Did she?" Kennet laughed. "She is one crazy old bat."

The sharpness of his words startled me, but I quickly recovered and asked, "What do you mean?"

"I'm next in line for the throne." He looked at me like it should have been obvious. "If anything happens to Mikko, it goes to me. There's no way that a Marksinna with no ties to our bloodline would ever be in charge, even for a moment."

"Maybe it was just wishful thinking on her part," I said. "She was just worried about Linnea's safety."

Kennet scoffed. "I can keep the kingdom safe."

"Her biggest concern—and mine too, really—was continuing to allow Bayle Lundeen to remain in charge of the guard."

"Then you can both rest at ease," he smiled at me. "The first thing I did after being appointed was dismiss Bayle."

"You fired him?" I asked, almost breathless in my relief.

He nodded. "I did, but I think he feared an investigation, so he immediately took off. We have a few guards looking for him, but I'm not sure what a guard like ours will really turn up."

"So then are the charges against Mikko dropped?" I asked.

Kennet shook his head. "It's not quite that simple. There's still evidence against him, and we do have to wait for a trial. I'm sure this will all be sorted out soon." He walked over to me, probably because I'd softened since our conversation had started.

"Is Linnea holding up okay?" I asked, since I didn't know what to say to that.

"About as well as you'd imagine."

"But you'll keep her safe, won't you?" I asked, and I tried to play on his pride to ensure that he would do everything in his power to protect her. "As long as you're the acting King, you wouldn't let anything happen to her, would you?"

"No, of course not," he said, and a sparkle had returned to his eyes. "But if you're really concerned about her, why don't you come with me?"

"Prince—" I started to decline, but he silenced me.

"I know I was a little overzealous before, and I am truly sorry about that," Kennet said, his voice low and apologetic. "But I like having you around, and Linnea would love to have you back. You can help us, and honestly, we do need you."

"I appreciate the offer, I really do," I said. "But as much as I enjoy your company and Linnea's, I just don't think can. There's too much going on in Doldastam."

Kennet frowned. "So that's a no?"

"No." I shook my head. "My place is here."

"Oh, Bryn." He let out a sigh, and he reached out to fix a lavender flower that had come loose from my hair. When he finished, he looked down at me sadly. "I don't think you really know your place at all."

conciliation

It was time to get back to reality.

That's what I told myself after I'd finished getting changed in the locker room. I pulled my hair up in a ponytail and headed out to the gym, determined to head back to work.

With everything going on—Storvatten preparing for war, Viktor and Konstantin, not to mention things with Ridley, and Kennet's bizarre invitation last night, and Tilda's wedding, which was a good thing but still out of the ordinary—my life had been completely devoid of routine.

Since I'd joined tracker school when I was twelve, this place and this job had been my one constant. I was sent out on missions where I had to encounter changelings and deal with unique obstacles, but I always came back here.

And right now, when everything felt like it was crumbling down on me, I needed this more than ever. I needed to disappear into my work until I was completely gone.

So when I stepped into the gym, expecting my tiny little haven in the chaos of the world, I was caught off guard to see that things had been completely turned upside down.

All the trackers were training at once—some doing combat or sword fighting, others lifting weights, while still others were running laps—which filled the gym with far more people than I would've preferred. On top of all that there was also a group of around twenty-five Markis and Marksinna standing in formation as Ember commanded them.

I recognized a few of them, like Linus Berling, but the rest of them stood out thanks to their designer workout clothes. One girl was even training while wearing a diamond tennis bracelet and chandelier earrings.

"Down!" Ember shouted as I walked over to her, and her ragtag troops dropped to the floor.

Some of them moved more quickly than others, and I wasn't surprised to see that Marksinna Tennis Bracelet had trouble keeping up. Linus did relatively well, but he relied more on effort than skill. A girl in the front was doing astonishingly well, though, as if she had been training for years.

When she hit the ground, I noticed a subtle change in her skin color—the deep olive darkening to match the black of her workout clothes for a second. Her long dark hair was in a loose braid that bounced when she dropped. Her large eyes were almost almond shaped, and she kept them locked on Ember as she awaited her next order.

"Up!" Ember commanded almost as soon as they hit the floor, and they hurried to get back on their feet. When Ember saw me, she smiled. "Why don't we all take five? You've been working hard."

"How's it going?" I asked Ember as her troops took a breather or got something to drink. Linus offered me a quick wave before jogging over to the drinking fountain.

"Good." She nodded. "They're shaping up really well."

"That's only because we have such a good teacher." The girl in the front wiped sweat from her brow, and she had a water bottle in her hand.

"Thanks." Ember smiled, maybe a little too widely, and they looked at each other for what was beginning to feel like an uncomfortable amount of time. "Uh, sorry. Bryn, this is Delilah, I mean, Marksinna Delilah Nylen."

Delilah rushed to fill the gap between us so she could shake my hand, and I noticed she was a little taller than Ember. "I've heard so much about you. You're a real hero."

"I'm not even close to being a hero, but thank you," I said.

"Sorry, sure." When she released my hand, she stood up straight with her shoulders back, the way I knew Ember had taught her. Then she tapped her water bottle. "I need to refill this, so I should do that before we start up again."

"Go ahead," Ember told her, and the second Delilah was out of earshot, Ember turned to me and asked in an excited whisper, "What do you think?"

"Well, she has good posture," I said.

"That's it?" Ember stared up at me. "That's all you've got?"

I glanced over to where Delilah was refilling her bottle at the fountain at the edge of the gymnasium. "She's obviously a hard worker, and she seems to know her stuff." Ember kept staring at me, so I added, "And she's very pretty."

Ember practically beamed. "She's great, right?"

"She is," I admitted hesitantly.

But not only was Delilah a Marksinna, she was one who could change her skin color, meaning she had an important bloodline. No one in a position of authority would look kindly on Ember messing with that.

"Just be careful," I advised.

"I always am." Ember looked so pleased that I didn't want to completely spoil her mood.

By then it was time to start training again, and Ember began barking commands. Delilah seemed more than happy to follow them, which boded well for their burgeoning relationship. Even though Delilah was nobility, she seemed to respect Ember's experience and leadership.

I realized I had my own forbidden romance that I needed to deal with, and before I could really head back to reality, I needed to talk to Ridley.

Over at the other end of the gym, Ridley held a clipboard, reading the papers attached to it. Since Tilda had gotten married last night, she was off today, which left him working her job for the day.

His brow was furrowed in concentration when I reached him. I didn't want to disturb him, so I waited next to him until he noticed me, which thankfully didn't take long.

"Tilda is *really* good at her job, but her handwriting is atrocious," Ridley said, telling me something I already knew. "I will be so relieved when she gets back from her honeymoon in a couple days."

"They're taking a short honeymoon, so it won't be too bad."

He finally looked up at me, and I suddenly felt sick. I didn't know what to say to him. All I wanted was for him to pull me into his arms, but I knew he couldn't.

"Now probably isn't the best time for this conversation," I began, swallowing down my fear. "I just wanted to tell you that I, um, want to talk to you, I guess."

"About what I said last night?" he asked.

I nodded. "Yeah."

"Now's perfect," he replied instantly. "Come on."

A gym filled with people obviously wasn't the best place to have a private conversation, and Ridley walked away. I followed him out into the hallway, which was quiet and deserted. Trackers-in-training should've been in class, but they were all either in the gym doing drills or out in the yard doing obstacle courses.

"So?" Ridley folded his arms over his chest and stared down at me expectantly.

"Well . . ." I exhaled shakily. "You know how I feel about you."

"What if I told you I don't?"

I looked up at him, his eyes filled with that dark intensity that made my heart race. "Ridley."

"I said it. Would it be so bad if you said it too?" he pressed.

"I care about you," I admitted, saying it aloud for the first time, and there was something terrifying and exhilarating in that. "I care about you a lot."

One corner of his mouth pulled up in a crooked smile. "Good."

"But you know the deal," I said, and his smile fell away. "We would both lose our jobs, and as much as I do care about you, I'm not willing to do what my parents did. My dad sacrificed a lot, but my mom gave up *everything*. I know she loves my dad and she loves me, way more than she ever cared about Storvatten, but that doesn't mean she wants this life that's been thrust upon her either. And unlike my mom, I do really care about Doldastam and my job, even as imperfect and insane as it has been lately."

"You're not your mom, and I'm not your dad," Ridley countered. "I would never ask you to give up the life you've chosen. I know how much your job means to you, and I wouldn't let you sacrifice it for me, even if you wanted to."

"But that goes for you too," I argued. "You have to go after Viktor. I can't let you lose your position as the Överste, not when it's so important to you, and the kingdom needs you. But where does that leave us? Neither of us can give up the things that are standing in our way."

"I can," he said simply.

"No, Ridley, you can't."

"Not right now, that's true. But as soon as we have Viktor, and I mean the very second, I'll quit."

I shook my head. "I can't ask you to do that."

"You don't have to. I *want* to," he insisted. "I've done this job long enough, and I'm sure that Tilda would be twice as good as me, and she'll probably want a desk job soon. So I'll find something else."

"What else?" I asked.

"*Anything* else." Ridley grinned. "That's the point. I don't care. I can do whatever I want. But the thing I want most is to be with you."

Suddenly, I felt dizzy. It almost sounded too good be true.

"You really wanna do this?" I asked breathlessly.

"Yes. Once we catch Viktor, I want to give us a real shot." He took my hands in his. "What do you think?"

I nodded, too excited to speak at first. "Yes."

Ridley stepped away from me to look through the narrow windows in the gymnasium door, checking to see if anyone was watching. They must not have been, because he rushed back over and pushed me back against the wall, so we were more hidden if anyone decided to pry, and he kissed me full on the mouth.

It ended much too soon, with him pulling away from me as he tried to catch his breath. "I have to get back. And so do you. And right now I'm still your boss, so that's an order."

honeymoon

Lunch usually meant hurriedly devouring salads and hard-boiled eggs in the cafeteria at the school, all the trackers crammed in together like sardines since we were working at full capacity.

So that was why I didn't mind skipping out on lunch to head over to Tilda's apartment. Yesterday, while we'd been getting ready for her wedding, she had asked me if I could come over to get the keys to her place so she could show me how to feed her goldfish while she was on her honeymoon. She and Kasper were leaving this afternoon, so this was the last chance to do it.

I left the school feeling lighter than I had in days. After the conversation with Ridley, the future felt like it actually held the promise of something good. The dark days that had been surrounding me might actually be making a turn for the better.

We were still at war, and things weren't over yet, but for the

Amanda Hocking

first time in a while, I felt optimistic. As I walked downtown, I caught myself humming.

A Land Rover was parked in front of the electronics shop below Tilda's apartment, presumably rented from the King's fleet, since other than a few of the very rich, nobody owned a vehicle in Doldastam. The tailgate was open, and Kasper was loading up two large duffle bags in the back.

"I thought you guys were only gonna be gone for a couple days," I said and motioned to the overstuffed bags in the back.

"Three days, two nights at a bed and breakfast in Churchill." Kasper shut the back of the SUV and turned to me with a look of resigned exasperation.

With everything that was going on, the King didn't want them to be gone for very long, and for their own safety, Kasper and Tilda had chosen a human town only an hour's drive from Doldastam.

"And Tilda actually has a bag upstairs still. But the pregnancy is making her worry more, and if what she needs to relax on this honeymoon is everything and the kitchen sink, then I'll be more than happy to load it up."

I smiled at him. "You're gonna make a great husband."

Kasper laughed. "Just remind Tilda of that when she gets mad at me, okay?"

We went down a narrow alley squished between the electronics shop and the taxidermist next door. Around the back of the shop was a doorway that opened to a set of stairs leading up to the small two-bedroom apartment. Tilda had lived there for two years by herself, and it had to be one of the most contemporary places in all of Doldastam.

I opened the door expecting her usual immaculateness. Tilda always kept it looking like something out of a magazine showcasing trendy New York apartments. Instead, I was greeted by an unexpected mess—clothes were strewn all over her sofa, several cardboard boxes were stacked up in the living room, and dirty dishes were piled up in the sink.

Tilda came out from her back bedroom and gave me a sheepish smile. "I know, I know. It's a total disaster, but I haven't had time to clean."

"No, don't worry about it," I said as I made my way through the labyrinths of boxes and stepped over a glass punchbowl, which I assumed had been a wedding gift.

On the peninsula that separated the kitchen from the living room, Tilda had a fishbowl with two of the fattest goldfish I had even seen. Not only were they several inches long, they were completely rotund.

"These are Odin and Odessa." Tilda pointed to the one with the longer fantail flowing out behind it as it swam. "That one's Odessa. Odin is the fatter one. Kasper got them for me on my birthday in February." She opened the cupboard below them and pulled out a cylinder of fish food. "They were smaller when I got them, but they've just kinda ballooned. Usually when I'm on missions, Kasper takes care of them, but I think he over-feeds them, which is why they've gotten so fat."

Kasper had followed us, and he rested his arms on the granite countertop, leaning forward. "Thanks, dear."

"Well, it's true." Tilda shrugged and went onto explain the exact right amount of food to give the fish and how to properly care for them in case of some kind of fish emergency.

"I think I can handle that," I said when she'd finished.

"Knowing that you're taking good care of them and that you're watching the apartment will give me one less thing to worry about," Tilda said.

"Yeah, thank you, Bryn," Kasper added. "And not to change the subject, but what ended up happening last night with you at the palace?"

After Kennet and I had had our conversation, I'd gone home, since the night already felt exhausting. I'd texted Tilda to let her know I was okay, so she wouldn't worry, but I hadn't said anything more because I didn't want to ruin her wedding night with work talk.

"That's right!" Tilda put her hand on her face in distress. "I totally forgot to ask you about that! What happened?"

"It was just . . . strange." I shook my head. "Prince Kennet came from Storvatten to personally thank the King and Queen for helping, and I guess he wanted to thank me too."

Kasper's brow creased in bewilderment. "That is rather strange."

"Yeah, I thought so too," I agreed. "Apparently, he's the acting ruler now."

"What?" Kasper appeared as surprised as I'd felt when I found out. "I thought Lisbet was gonna get that."

"I don't know exactly what happened, but Kennet is the King now." I shook my head. "He got rid of Bayle, which is good, but the trial with Mikko is still on, which seems bizarre to me. I mean, if Kennet is in control can't he just make it go away?"

"Yes, unless he doesn't want to make it go away," he replied.

I chewed the inside of my cheek, taking in Kasper's response. "He gave Mina a necklace of sapphires."

"Buying her loyalty?" Kasper asked, and I nodded. "The exact same way someone bought Cyrano Moen's."

The way Kasper said that made something click in my brain. Pieces that hadn't fit together started falling into place.

"When Ridley and I went down to find Linnea before, Mikko barely spoke to us," I remembered. "Kennet worked as his liaison, and he kept saying that all the attempts at blocking the investigation were coming from Mikko, but how would we know that? Kennet could've just as easily been doing it himself. And Boyle refused to let anyone look at the records, so he could've easily fabricated evidence to frame Mikko."

"He planned the kidnapping of Linnea, and then he was involved in the investigation, so he could shift the blame however he wanted." Kasper straightened up. "And he wanted to shift it onto his brother."

"He wanted Mikko in jail so he could get the crown," I said, thinking aloud. "First he hired Konstantin to kidnap Linnea and make it look like Mikko either kidnapped or killed her. I don't know how he got in touch with Konstantin, but if Konstantin and Viktor Dålig are working some kind of operation with hired hands and weapons, they needed financing."

"And we saw how well Cyrano Moen was paid," Kasper added.

"Kennet told me that after he fired Bayle, Bayle had run off," I said. "But if Bayle has been working with Kennet this whole time to make it all happen, it would make sense for Kennet to send him away before they could question him and find exactly how he was tied to this whole mess."

I'd been suspicious of Kennet since I met him, but I'd also been suspicious of Mikko and nearly everyone else I met in Storvatten, so it had been hard for me to decide how culpable he might have been.

I looked over at Kasper. "Kennet did it all, didn't he?"

"I don't know if we can prove it, but yes. I think he did."

"He's here right now, celebrating with Evert and Mina," I said. "And they should know. They probably can't do anything, but they need to know they're aligning themselves with someone who has connections to Konstantin and is helping to finance the attacks on our kingdom."

"Holy shit." Tilda expressed my sentiments perfectly. "Evert is gonna be *pissed* when he finds out. I honestly wouldn't be surprised if he declared war on the Skojare."

She was right, and while that would have very negative ramifications for the Skojoare, it didn't change anything. The King needed to know the truth.

"I have to tell him, and it'll be better to do it before Kennet leaves," I said. "Maybe he'll just lock up Kennet, and we can avoid an all-out war."

I started to make my way to the door, since I didn't have time to waste.

"Wait. I'll go with you," Kasper said, then he looked over at Tilda. "I mean, if it's okay."

"You don't have to." I shook my head. "I can do this alone."

He turned back to me. "I know you can. But we worked in Storvatten together. This is kind of our job, which means I should be there too. I want to help you make this case." Then he looked to his new wife. "As long as it's okay with Tilda."

"The bed and breakfast will still be there in a few hours," Tilda told him with a smile. "You should go and do this. It's important. And besides, I wouldn't mind a little more time to make sure I've packed everything."

"Thank you." Kasper went over to her and kissed her quickly. "I love you."

"I love you too." She watched us go with an anxious smile, and as we walked out the door, she added, "Good luck."

recrimination

W e stood inside the meeting room, under the cold gaze of King Evert's coronation painting. Kasper stood rigidly beside me like a true member of the Högdragen, even though he was wearing a T-shirt and jeans instead of his uniform.

I had taken to pacing and chewing absently at my thumbnail. In my head, I tried to organize my thoughts and the best possible way to tell Evert about what was happening. It was important that he believe me, but it was also important that he didn't react rashly and attack Storvatten.

When we'd reached the palace, Elliot Väan had been standing guard at the door. Fortunately for us, Elliot had been Kasper's best man and was a good friend. Kasper managed to convince him to let us in and request that the King come and meet us.

The door opened behind us, startling me because I'd been deep in thought, and I turned to see Elliot holding the door open. A few moments later, almost as if she'd been deliberately trying to make an entrance, Queen Mina walked into the room. Elliot closed the door behind her, standing guard inside the room.

I wasn't sure what Mina had been doing before Elliot summoned her, but she looked more regal than ever. The train of her white gown flowed out over a foot behind her. Her hair was done up in twisted braids nestled at the top of her neck, and she'd donned a silvery fur stole that complimented the sapphire necklace.

Her crown—a platinum tiara encrusted with diamonds, including a massive one in the center—sat atop her head. Whenever she wore it, she seemed to carry her head a bit higher, lifting her chin slightly. I wasn't sure if it was to counteract the weight of the jewels, or if she was just putting on airs.

"Elliot claimed that you need to see the King urgently on important business." Mina walked around the table, eyeing Kasper and me with her cool gaze. She stopped directly across from us, beneath the painting of Evert. Instead of sitting down, she remained standing and rested her hand on the tall back of the King's chair.

"Yes, we did," I said.

"The King is very busy. As you can imagine, with the impending war, he has much to do and can't possibly take the time to meet everyone who wants to see him," Mina explained in a tone far frostier than the one I was used to hearing from her, and I wondered if she was suffering from a hangover that was making her so cross. "He has asked me to see you and find out if what you have to say is as important as you believe it is."

I glanced over at Kasper, but he kept his gaze straight ahead. This already wasn't going the way I'd hoped, and now I wasn't sure what to do.

The Queen could be maddeningly night and day. Even without a possible hangover in play, she vacillated from warmth and kindness to ice queen on a regular basis.

Mina didn't seem that open to hearing what we had to say, but I didn't know how else we'd get to talk to the King.

"Thank you for taking the time to see us, my Queen," Kasper said. "I know how busy your schedule must be."

"I'm often busier than the King, so let's get on with this, shall we?" Mina drummed her fingers along the back of the chair in impatience, causing the many rings on her fingers to sparkle in the light.

"We have reason to believe that Prince Kennet Biâelse is behind the events in Storvatten, not his brother King Mikko." I plunged right in, deciding that we had a better chance of getting through to her if we played it straight.

Mina arched an eyebrow but her expression remained otherwise unmoved. "Is that so?"

"We have a great deal of evidence to back up our claims, and we'd be happy to go over all of it with you and the King," Kasper said.

"You're getting ahead of yourself," Mina told him. "I haven't heard anything yet that would make me want to summon the King."

"In order to stage the kidnapping of Queen Linnea Biâelse three weeks ago, Prince Kennet enlisted the help of Viktor Dålig and Konstantin Black," I explained. "As a result, we believe that Prince Kennet may be funding Viktor Dålig and Konstantin Black's terrorist activities."

"Terrorist?" Mina nearly scoffed at the idea, totally overlooking the part where I connected Kennet to Konstantin. "Is that what you're calling them these days?"

With war preparations fully underway, I was floored by the Queen's response, but I pressed on. "They have used violence and fear by attacking our changelings, presumably to gain some sort of control over the Kanin, so yes, I would say that that's an accurate descriptor," I replied, matching her icy tone.

"Well, then, what's your great evidence that Kennet is connected to Konstantin? How did they meet each other?" Mina snapped. "These are high claims you're making, so what do you have to back them up?"

"We don't know how they met each other yet," I admitted. "But we know that Konstantin Black warned Queen Linnea of a plot against her, presumably because he and Viktor Dålig were hired to hurt her in some way. Possibly even kidnap or kill her."

"That proves that Konstantin was involved, but we already knew that. What more do you have to place blame on Kennet?" Mina persisted.

"He had the means to enlist Viktor and Konstantin's help," Kasper said. "He had access to all the same things as King

Mikko, but unlike the King, the Prince had a motive—he wanted the crown. So he framed his brother to get it."

Mina pursed her lips and inhaled deeply through her nose. "You're sure of this?"

I nodded. "I know he did it. And if you were to interrogate him, I think he'd eventually reveal his connection to Konstantin Black and Viktor Dålig."

"All right then. If you're sure." Mina looked past me to where Elliot stood by the door and motioned to him. "Let the Prince in."

"What?" I exchanged a looked with Kasper.

Kasper swallowed, trying to hide his nerves. "This is highly unorthodox."

I'd expected the King to interrogate Kennet himself, most likely with the help of the Högdragen. With that kind of pressure, I thought Kennet had a good chance of caving and confessing what he knew.

But with just Kasper and me accusing him, I couldn't imagine why he'd be honest in front of Mina.

"The Prince and I happened to be having lunch together when Elliot got me, and being the gentlemen that he is, the Prince offered to walk me down here," Mina explained. "And now it turns out be very fortuitous."

"Your Highness, with all due respect, I think we should talk this over with the King first," I said.

But it was already too late. Elliot had opened the doors, and Kennet entered the room with his usual swagger and walked over to join the Queen.

"What's all this?" Kennet asked, surveying Kasper's and my grave expressions.

"If you're going to accuse a man of something, you must be prepared to let him defend himself." Mina looked at me when she spoke, and her grey eyes were hard as stone.

"Accuse me of what?" Kennet appeared unnerved for a moment—his smile faltering and his eyes darting over to me—but he quickly hid it under his usual arrogance.

I met his gaze and kept my voice even. "I think you were behind everything that happened in Storvatten. You pulled all the strings to frame your brother and get his crown."

Kennet laughed, and I wasn't sure what exactly I'd expected his reaction to be, but he honestly didn't seem upset. His laugh wasn't one of nerves but his usual carefree booming one, like he genuinely found this whole scenario amusing.

"Bryn, you have made a terrible mistake." He scratched his temple and smiled sadly at me. "I didn't pull any strings."

"You're say you're not responsible for what happened in Storvatten?" Mina asked Kennet, but kept her eyes on me.

Kennet shook his head. "No, of course not."

"Now we find ourselves in a terrible predicament," Mina said. "You, Bryn Aven and Kasper Abbott, stand before me accusing an allied Prince of heinous crimes without any evidence to back it up."

"We do—" I began, but the Queen silenced me.

"He denies them all, and as a Prince, I will believe him over the unfounded word of two lowly guards," Mina went on, and I clenched my jaw to keep from yelling at her. "But had I believed you, your claims could have easily led to a war with a peaceful friend."

I lowered my eyes and swallowed hard.

"Ultimately, that would've led to the deaths of many innocent people—both Kanin and Skojare," Mina said. "Do you know what that means, Bryn? You attempted to cause the deaths of your own people and to hurt the King."

"That's not at all what I meant," I insisted desperately. "I was trying to defend the King and the kingdom."

"It's too late." Mina shook her head and attempted to affect a look of sadness, but it fell flat given her cold expression. "The damage is already done. And so you must be punished."

"Punished?" I shook my head, not understanding.

"Yes, both of you, actually." She looked between Kasper and me. "You both attempted to commit treason."

"*Treason?*" I shouted.

"My Queen, there has been a terrible misunderstanding," Kasper said, hurrying to defend himself.

"Elliot, arrest these two and take them to the dungeon until they can stand trial," Queen Mina commanded.

"This wasn't Kasper's idea. It's not his fault," I tried to argue for him.

"Elliot, *now!*" Mina raised her voice, and he hurried to comply.

Members of the Högdragen had a pair of iron shackles on the back of their belts in case they needed to restrain someone, and Elliot pulled them out now. He walked over to his friend, giving Kasper an apologetic look before locking the cuff around his wrist.

Then Elliot moved on to me, meaning to lock the other cuff around my wrist, but I pulled away.

"Your Highness, please, you have to listen to me," I persisted.

"I am the *Queen*." Mina sneered. "How dare you tell me what I have to do."

It was then that I realized my pleas were falling on deaf ears. There was no point in fighting, and I let Elliot arrest me.

castigate

The iron shackle around my wrist felt like it weighed a hundred pounds. Kasper and I walked with our heads down, saying nothing because there was nothing to say. Another guard had joined Elliot, in case we decided to put up a fight, and the four of us walked in silence through the cold corridors of the palace.

I heard hushed whispers as we walked by, but I never looked up to see who was speaking. As defeated as I felt, my mind raced to figure out how to get out of the situation. My father might be able to leverage his position as the Chancellor to get us free, and while I normally hated nepotism, I didn't want Kasper to spend years in prison for a crime he hadn't committed.

Both of us would most certainly lose our careers, but if we were lucky we might not have to forfeit our lives. There was a chance King Evert might not act as harshly as his wife, so hopefully we wouldn't end up in prison for life or exiled.

The highest punishment for treason was execution, but I had to believe it wouldn't come to that.

When we reached the cells located in the dungeon below the palace, we weren't the only ones in there. An old man with a long graying beard had gotten up from his cot to watch our arrival, holding on to the bars and pressing his emaciated, dirty face against them.

This was a long-term prison, which was why it only housed a solitary inmate. There was a jail behind the Högdragen dorms where everyday criminals were kept: thieves and tax evaders, drunks who needed to cool off, even the rare murderer.

The dungeon was for crimes against the kingdom.

The old man in the cell was unrecognizable from who he'd been when he was thrown in the dungeon over three decades ago, but I knew immediately that it was Samuel Peerson. In our textbooks, I'd seen pictures of him from when he'd been arrested in the 1980s. He'd been a young man then, protesting the King's high taxation.

It had been under Karl Strinne's reign, our current King Evert's uncle. Karl had been a much stricter King than his two predecessors, and so even though Samuel had been a Markis —a Kanin of good breeding and the heir to a fortune—King Karl had imprisoned Samuel for publicly disagreeing with him at a meeting, calling Samuel "a traitor" and "an enemy of the kingdom."

And here Samuel remained, wasting away in a prison cell. His skin was pale with years of no sunlight, his eyes bloodshot, and a few of his teeth appeared to be missing.

Even though the Kings who followed Karl were more lax in their rulings, they had never pardoned Samuel Peerson. They wouldn't undo the wrong that had been committed because they refused to undermine a King, even a long-dead one.

If Queen Mina decided that we should spend the rest of our lives in these cells, there was a good chance that King Evert wouldn't overrule her. It would seem like a weakness on his part, as if his wife had been allowed to act without his guidance and he didn't have a handle on the running of his kingdom.

We would die in here, if that's what the Queen wished, and after how she'd acted today, there was no reason to think she wished otherwise.

My eyes were locked on the sad, weepy eyes of Samuel Peerson. I stopped, frozen in my tracks, as I realized that Kasper and I couldn't risk waiting for a trial. Elliot had been leading Kasper along, and the guard that had been charged with me nudged the small of my back.

"Get moving," he barked, and I knew what I had to do.

He was standing directly behind me, so with one quick move I lifted my arm back and slammed the iron cuff into his head. He let out a groan, then fell to the floor unconscious. Kasper and I were still attached by the shackles, so when I moved to the side, he moved with me.

"Hey!" Elliot shouted in surprise and drew his sword on us.

"Elliot, don't do this," I said.

"Please." Kasper pleaded with his friend. "You know we didn't do what the Queen is accusing us of, and if you throw us in these cells, we'll end up just like him."

"They're right, boy," Samuel Peerson said in a hollow, craggy voice.

Elliot looked at the old man with a stricken look on his face, and I knew he had to be making one of the hardest decisions of his life. It was hammered into the Högdragen again and again that they must never disobey the orders of their King or Queen.

Finally, he let out a shaky breath and lowered his sword. He took the keys off his belt and tossed them to Kasper.

"You did the right thing," Kasper assured him as he hurried to unlock his shackle, then handed me the keys so I could take care of mine myself.

"I hope so," Elliot muttered and handed Kasper his sword. "Before you go, will you do me a favor and hit me on the head, so I have an excuse for letting you get away?"

"Okay." Kasper nodded. "And thank you."

Elliot closed his eyes, steeling himself for the blow, and Kasper raised the sword and slammed the bell handle into his head. Elliot cried out in pain and stumbled backward, but he didn't fall unconscious.

"Do you want me to hit you again?" Kasper asked.

"No, no," Elliot said hurriedly. His head had already begun bleeding, and he touched it and winced. "I'll just run and get the guards after you're gone, and tell them I was knocked out."

"Can you give us a ten-minute headstart?" Kasper asked.

Elliot grimaced. "I'll try."

"We have to get out of here," I said, because ten minutes wasn't very long at all.

He nodded, and we turned to make our escape. Before we did, I stopped and tossed the keys to Samuel, who reached his arm out of his cell to catch them.

"There's one key for the shackles, and one for the cell," I told him. "Get out of here as fast as you can."

He'd move slower than us, but since the guards would most likely be far more interested in catching us, Samuel actually had a good chance of making it out.

Kasper reached the top of the steps at the end of the dungeon before I did. They were curved, so I couldn't see the top, and I actually thought he might have left without me. But he was waiting with his back pressed against the wall, peering out around the corner.

"Is anyone coming?" I whispered.

"Two guards went around the corner, so just to be safe we should wait another thirty seconds."

"Once we get past here, we won't be going the same way, so you don't have to wait for me."

He turned back to look at me. "What are you talking about?"

"I'm going to find Kennet. Our only way out of this is getting him to confess his part in this. Otherwise we'll have to spend the rest of our lives on the run."

I wasn't sure how much knocking guards out and escaping a pair of shackles would do to help convince anyone I was innocent, but once I found Kennet and got him alone, I'd do whatever it took to get him to tell the truth.

And if I couldn't get him to admit everything, I would get

him to tell me something that would help me gather more evidence to convince Evert that he was working with Konstantin Black and Viktor Dålig. Evert would take his wife's side in many things, but he would never stomach any aid to his nemesis.

"I'll go with you," Kasper said.

I shook my head. "No, you need to take Tilda and get out of here as fast as you can."

"You think I want to drag Tilda and the baby along with me into a life in exile?" he asked. "I need my name cleared just as much as you do, so I'm going with you. We started this together, we finish this together."

I relented. "Okay."

Kasper leaned forward, craning his neck out into the hall, and it must've been clear, because he dashed out into the hall and I ran after him.

ambuscade

W e sat in wait behind the door of the en suite bathroom. I'd left it partially open so I could peer through the narrow crack. When the bedroom creaked open, I held my breath and leaned forward, trying to see the figure who had come in.

In the late 1800s, the Kanin had enjoyed an influx of cash thanks to a few well-placed changelings and the industrial revolution. That allowed Queen Viktoria to undertake a massive remodeling project on the west wing of the palace, including the installation of dumbwaiters in the guest rooms.

Guests of the palace were always dignitaries, and the Queen didn't want them to be forced to trek down the cold halls to the kitchen or wait for servants to bring up inevitably chilly food. (Even in the nineteenth century, we had a problem keeping the massive stone palace warm.)

All Kasper and I had to do was get down to the lower level beneath the west wing, which was separated from the dungeon under the east wing. That required a lot of moving quietly, hiding against walls, and dashing into broom closets and restrooms until guards passed by.

And it all had to be done very quickly. Right now, hardly anyone knew that we'd been arrested, let alone that we'd escaped, so our sneaking around was more of a precaution. But we were in no position to take chances.

Once we made it down to the west wing, I left Kasper to choose the appropriate dumbwaiter because he had more knowledge of the palace. As a Högdragen, he knew most of the ins and outs of the palace, since that had allowed him to better protect it.

Given the cozy relationship between Kennet and our King and Queen, we both surmised that he would most likely be staying in the finest room we had. That fortunately made finding the dumbwaiter a bit easier, because the nicest guest chamber was on the south corner of the palace, in a massive turret.

Once we made it up to the bedroom, I set about checking to see if it was Kennet's room. Thanks to the servants who made the beds and tidied up, it was nearly impossible to tell if the room had been used at all.

The heavy drapes were pulled back from the massive windows that ran along the rounded walls, leaving only sheer curtains to let light in, but I didn't know if that meant anything. Though it was a lush suite, I noticed absently that the French windows were in need of repair—the paint was chipping and the wood appeared warped.

Confirmation that we'd found the right room came from the

massive wardrobe across from the four-poster bed. When I opened it, I found a fur-lined parka and silver suits hanging up, including an all-too-familiar sharkskin one.

Kasper and I decided that our best course of action was to surprise Kennet, especially since we couldn't know if he had a guard or two in tow, so we hid in his bathroom. Kasper stood slightly behind me, leaning against the embossed wallpaper, with Elliot's sword still clutched in his hand.

We'd waited for what felt like eternity, but in reality, it couldn't have been more than ten minutes until the doors finally opened. I caught a glimpse of a shadow—someone moving in the room—but I couldn't tell who the person was, and if it was merely a maid instead of Kennet.

I leaned so close to the door that my nose brushed up against it, and finally he turned enough so I could see his face—it was Kennet. He took off his jacket and tossed it on the bed, and as far as I could tell he was alone. I decided to go for it.

The door didn't make a sound when I opened it, and Kennet stood in front of the window, pushing the voile curtains aside to get a better view of Doldastam.

While we'd been waiting, Kasper and I had decided it would be better if I took the lead with Kennet, since he and I had a bit of a history. But Kasper stayed only a step or two behind me with his sword drawn, so Kennet would know we meant business.

"Kennet," I said.

He whirled around, his eyes startled and wide, but within seconds, a smirk appeared on his face.

rivalry

Nothing can hold you back, can it?" Kennet asked.

"No thanks to you," I snapped.

"Bryn, that wasn't my idea," he reminded me. "You can't blame me for your Queen being overzealous."

"Yes, yes, I can. You did nothing to defend me."

"What should I have said? 'Yes, it's true what she says. It's all my fault. Lock me up and throw away the key'?"

"That would've been nice," I said dryly.

"Look, I didn't want you locked up, but I didn't exactly have a choice." Kennet held up his hands, trying to appear innocent. "You backed me into a corner."

I shook my head. "You're such a conniving weasel. I can't believe I ever found anything likable about you."

"Hey." He scowled. "I liked you too. And despite everything else that's going on now, I did have fun with you, and I'm sorry that things have gone the way they have."

"Everything you said was a lie," I hissed at him. "Your whole act was to keep me distracted so I wouldn't notice what was really going on with you."

"I'll admit, I was told to keep you occupied so you wouldn't get yourself into any trouble. But that doesn't mean I didn't enjoy my time with you." He tried to flirt with me, but it just felt forced and sleazy. "Some things can be both work *and* pleasure."

"You're so full of shit. You've only ever cared about yourself," I spat at him. "You've told me over and over that you love your brother, and look how you treated him."

His expression hardened. "I do love my brother."

"Spare me your lies, Kennet. We all know what you did."

"You know *nothing* about what I did!" he shouted. "Mikko hated being King. It made him miserable. He never should've been crowned in the first place. But he had to take the job, not because he was the most qualified, not because he was the best one in our family for the position, but simply because he was born first, and Father insisted that Mikko fulfill his obligations."

"So you have him imprisoned for life?" I asked mockingly. "That fixes everything?"

"Once this is all over and I'm officially King, I'll pardon him and set him free. He'll be fine, and he'll be happier in the end." Kennet tried to reason away his sins. "We both will."

"That doesn't change the fact that you tried to kill the woman he loves," I reminded him.

"Is that what Linnea told you?" Kennet rolled his eyes.

"That's some fairy tale fantasy she has. And that's all beside the point, since *I* never laid a hand on her."

"You hired the person who did," I countered.

He sighed. "You make it all sound so evil, but it wasn't. They told me that if I gave them sapphires, they'd help me dethrone my brother in a nonlethal way. Mikko has been so unhappy since he's been King, and I was honestly doing this for him as much as I was for me."

"If that's what you tell yourself, go ahead." I shrugged. "Maybe if you keep on going with that, your brother will pardon you after you confess."

He raised his eyebrows. "Confess? Why on earth would I do that?"

"Because this is over," I told him. "The Queen may be blinded by your lies, but as soon as King Evert hears about your involvement with Konstantin Black, he'll investigate and find out the truth. He's too paranoid to let it go, so you should make it easy on yourself and just admit what you know."

"Konstantin Black?" Kennet laughed. "I never even met the guy before you arrested him."

I shook my head in disbelief. "What are you talking about?"

"I never met him. I'd never even heard of him or this Viktor before you all started going on about them."

I narrowed my eyes. "Then who did you deal with?"

He tilted his head, a bemused smile on his lips. "You still don't get it, do you?"

"What are you talking about?"

"This is bigger than either of us." Kennet stepped closer to me, and from the corner of my eye, I saw Kasper raise his sword. "You think you can come in here and threaten me, and I'll just bow down and do as you say, but you've got *nothing* to threaten me with."

"I think you're grossly underestimating the situation," Kasper growled, and Kennet glanced over at him.

"You and your little sword are nothing compared to what would be done to me if I betrayed my allies," Kennet told him bitterly.

As soon as he said that, my mind flashed back to the dungeon on Storvatten, when Konstantin had still been in his prison cell and Bent Stum had been lying dead with his wrists slit. Konstantin insisted that Bent had been murdered to keep him from spilling the truth, and when I pushed him to tell me by whom, Konstantin told me nearly the exact same thing that Kennet just had.

Whomever they were both working for had them scared as hell.

"You killed Bent Stum," I realized. "So he wouldn't talk and ruin everything for you."

"I did what I had to do," Kennet admitted. "And I'll keep doing what I have to do."

His aquamarine eyes almost always seemed to sparkle, but now as he looked down at me, they seemed much more muted, almost glazed. The smile had gone from his face, replaced by a sad vacancy.

Then, without warning, he raised his arm and punched me in the face. It was so unexpected that I didn't have time to block it. And he was much stronger than I'd anticipated, especially for a Prince. I stumbled back, falling against the bed.

He'd hit me in my left eye, and the trauma to my head was enough to exacerbate my injury from Viktor. My eyesight blurred in both eyes. A white light replaced the vision in my right eye while my left eyelid began to puff up, closing off my sight.

For a few horrible seconds, I could only hear the sound of fighting going on around me—grunting, cursing, and then the clatter of the sword falling to the floor. I wanted to help Kasper, but I couldn't see, and I didn't want to blunder in blindly and make things worse. Kasper wouldn't use deadly force unless absolutely necessary (the sword was meant to be more of a threat) since we needed Kennet alive to clear our names.

Finally, the figures before me came into focus. They were rolling around on the floor, fighting over the sword. I started to move toward it, meaning to grab it, but Kennet got it first and rolled over onto his back, holding the sword pointed out in front of him as Kasper got to his feet.

"This game is done," Kennet said, standing slowly with his eyes and sword locked on Kasper. "You aren't going to let this go, which means that I can't let you go."

"It doesn't need to come to this," Kasper said, holding up his hands in a gesture of peace.

Kennet only smirked in reply, and in a moment of desperation, Kasper charged at him. I was sure he meant to get the sword away from Kennet again, but that wasn't what happened.

I was standing right behind Kasper, and I saw the sword come out his back—the sharp metal stained red as it poked out between his shoulder blades. The blood flowered out around it, darkening his white shirt.

Kennet's face paled, and he let go of the sword, allowing Kasper to stagger back. I rushed over, catching him just as he began to fall and lowering him to the floor, but I kept my arm around his shoulders, holding him up so the blade wouldn't move.

downfall

I t'll be okay," I said thickly, even though I didn't believe it.

Kasper stared at me, his dark eyes uncomprehending. He moved his mouth as if he meant to say something, but nothing came out. And then, as I held him in my arms, Kasper took his last breath and his body went lax.

"It had to be done," Kennet said in a low voice.

When I looked up at him, the only thing I felt was anger—a blinding rage I'd never experienced before. I knew I should try to control it, but just then, I didn't want to.

I jumped and charged at Kennet. He tried to block my attack, but I was faster than him and I hit him in the face, the stomach, the arms—anywhere I could reach. He stepped back, trying to avoid the blows, and he wasn't paying attention to his footing.

His fight with Kasper had left the rug rumpled, and he tripped on it and staggered back. I watched as he fell into the window. The glass didn't shatter, but the locks that held them shut were old, and under his weight the French windows swung open.

Kennet started falling backward, and while I was tempted to let him just fall, I needed him alive. I needed to know who he was working for and what was happening, so Kasper's death wouldn't be entirely in vain.

I ran forward, and I was nearly too late. I leaned out the window, almost throwing myself after him to grab his hand. I gripped it as tightly as I could, holding Kennet as he dangled over five stories above the ground.

"Pull me up!" Kennet yelled, his voice cracking in terror. "I'm sorry for what I did! Just pull me up and I'll do whatever you want!"

"Tell me who you're working for!" I demanded.

"Just pull me up and I'll tell you," he insisted, and his eyes were wild with fear.

The truth was that I was *trying* to pull him, but my grip on him wasn't good enough. I had to use one hand for balance, holding on to the windowsill so I wouldn't tumble out with him. Both of my hands had Kasper's blood on them, leaving them slick, and whenever I tried to lift Kennet, I felt him slipping away.

"Tell me first," I said, trying to pretend like this was my idea and I wasn't losing him.

"Bryn, *please!*" Kennet begged. "I'm sorry! Just help me!"

And I wanted to. As much as I hated Kennet, I wanted him to live so he could pay for what he'd done. But I couldn't hang on.

His hand slipped from my grasp, and he fell to the ground, screaming all the way until he hit the cobblestone courtyard below. I looked away so I didn't have to see the mess he'd become.

I turned back to the room, with the open windows letting in an icy wind behind me. Kasper lay on the floor. I didn't want to just leave him here like this, but I didn't know what I could do.

His eyes were still open, staring up at the ceiling, so I crouched down next to him and closed them gently.

"I'm sorry," I whispered around the lump in my throat.

Kennet had made a lot of noise as he fell, so it wouldn't be long before guards found their way up here to investigate what had happened.

I grabbed a chair and pushed it up against the door, propping it underneath the handle so they'd have a little more fight before they could get in. I went into the bathroom and washed the blood off my hands, trying not to think about where the blood had come from.

The Högdragen would be on the lookout for me, and one thing I'd learned from growing up in Doldastam was that my blond hair made me stand out like a sore thumb. I needed to cover up.

I ran over to the wardrobe and grabbed the parka, then I jumped back into the dumbwaiter and prepared to make my escape.

exile

Y es, sir. I understand. Of course, sir," Ridley was saying into his cell phone. "I will."

He stood in the living room, his back to me. He still wore the Överste uniform with the silver epaulets on the shoulder. When he hung up the phone, he ran a hand through his hair and let out a heavy sigh.

"Who was that?" I asked.

"Holy crap, Bryn!" Ridley turned around to face me, and his surprise was immediately replaced by relief as he rushed over to me. "What are you doing here?"

"Your back door was unlocked." I motioned to it behind me.

He pushed back the hood of the parka so he could see me more clearly, and he grimaced when he saw my eye, which had to be blackening by now. "Oh, Bryn."

"How bad is it?"

"I'm not sure if you're asking about your eye or the situation," he said. "But the situation is not good. I just got home from work, and the head of the Högdragen called to tell me that you'd been arrested for treason, escaped from prison, and then murdered Kasper Abbott and the Skojare Prince before going on the run again."

"It's not like that." I shook my head. "I never hurt Kasper, and I even told him he shouldn't come with me. Because Tilda—"

My voice caught in my throat as I realized what had just happened. Kasper had become my friend in his own right. He was good and capable, and he was dead. Not to mention what this loss would mean to Tilda. My best friend's husband of less than twenty-four hours and the father of her unborn baby had been killed.

But I couldn't let the full gravity of it hit me, because if I did I would just crumple up and sob.

"And the treason charge is bullshit. I would never do anything to damage this kingdom. I was trying to protect it. It was Kennet. He'd been supporting Konstantin, and I wanted to keep the King safe. And then everything happened so fast, and I got out of there as quick as I could. I took the dumbwaiter to the basement, and then I climbed up a garbage chute to the outside, and I had to sneak around town to get here as fast as I could. But I didn't do those things they say I did. I didn't."

"I know." Ridley put his hand on my face to calm me, since my voice had taken on a frantic pitch, and he looked me in the eyes. "I know you didn't do anything wrong. And you can explain it all to me later, but right now, we need to get you out of here before the Högdragen find you, because they won't believe you."

I nodded, because now everything was too far gone. I'd only been trying to make things right, but I didn't know how I could ever come back from this.

"Stay here," Ridley instructed me. "Lock the door behind me, and don't let anyone in." He started walking toward the door. "And hide, just to be safe."

"Where are you going?" I asked.

"I'm going to get you out of here," he said, like that explained anything, and then he left.

I did as I was told. I locked the doors and then went into his bedroom to hide. The shades were drawn, leaving it nearly dark even though it was still daylight. The afternoon sun was hidden behind an overcast sky, but the extra level of darkness was still comforting.

I leaned against the wall and slowly lowered myself to the floor. And I couldn't think. I tried to figure out my next course of action, but I couldn't. My mind felt numb and blank, and I couldn't process anything that had happened today. It felt like I'd slipped into a big white void that had swallowed me whole, and nothing was real anymore.

"Bryn?" Ridley's panicked voice was in the house, and I hadn't even heard him open the doors. Time no longer seemed to move in any coherent way, and I had no idea if he'd been gone for ten minutes or two hours.

"Bryn?" Ridley repeated, sounding more panicked this time, and he came into the bedroom. "What are you doing? Why didn't you answer me?"

"I don't know," I admitted.

He crouched next to me. "Are you okay?"

"I don't know," I said again. "But I will be."

His eyes searched me in the dark. I didn't know if he believed me or not, but we didn't have time to figure things out right now. "We have to get out of here," he said.

I got up and hurried after him, and that seemed to help. Moving reminded me that I was alive, and there were urgent things I needed to take care of if I wanted to stay that way.

Ridley had gotten an SUV from the King's fleet and parked it in the constricted alley behind his house. I pulled up my hood over my head, and he snuck me out the back door and loaded me into the back of the Land Rover. He covered me in a thick black blanket kept in the back for emergencies, and then he hopped in the driver's seat.

As he drove through town, he said nothing. Underneath the blanket, I couldn't see anything. I just listened to the sound of the car.

It didn't take long before I heard the SUV come to a stop and the window roll down.

"Where are you going?" a man barked, and by the tone of his question, I surmised it was one of the Högdragen guarding the gate.

"I have orders from the King," Ridley replied, sounding just as stern.

"That doesn't tell me where you're going," the Högdragen shot back.

"I am the Överste, Ridley Dresden."

By the sound of the rustling, I guessed that Ridley was pulling out his credentials to show the guard. It was a cross between a passport and an FBI badge, with all the specific information to prove exactly who he was.

"This still doesn't tell me what you're doing, sir," the Högdragen said, but with a bit more respect in his voice now. "Doldastam is on lockdown now."

"I know that," Ridley snapped. "But the King has sent me on a mission to follow up on a lead on Viktor Dålig. Do you want to stop the commander of the army from going after the man who tried to kill the King?"

"No, sir," the Högdragen replied. I heard the muffled sounds of him conversing with another guard but I couldn't understand what they were saying. Then, rather reluctantly, he said, "All right. Go on through."

The gates creaked open loudly, and the SUV started to move. At first, Ridley drove at a reasonable speed, but as soon as we were a safe enough distance away, he sped up, causing the vehicle to bounce around on the worn road.

I pushed the blanket off my head and sat up, looking around at the familiar trees that surrounded us. I wondered dimly if I'd ever see them again, but I had far more important things to worry about.

I climbed up over the seat into the front and sat down next to Ridley.

"How are you doing?" he asked.

"I've been better."

"I got passports and money from the safe." He motioned to a black duffel bag in the backseat.

"Thank you." I looked over at him, and I hoped he understood how much I truly appreciated what he'd done and risked to help me. Ridley reached over, taking my hand in his, and held it on the drive to the train station.

When we pulled into the parking lot, he turned off the car and got out. He grabbed the bag from the back, and I walked around the Land Rover. He took my hand again so we could walk together to the ticket booth, but I stopped.

"What?" Ridley looked back at me.

"You can't go with me. This is where we have to say goodbye."

He shook his head. "What are you talking about?"

"Kennet and Konstantin are just pawns. Somebody else is making the moves, and I need to find out who that it is and make sure they get some semblance of justice. I may never be able to prove my innocence, but I won't stand by and let everything I care about be destroyed."

"That's exactly why I should go with you," Ridley insisted.

"No. I shouldn't have let Kasper go with me, and I won't let you meet his fate," I said.

"Bryn—"

"And more than that," I cut him off, "my parents are still

in Doldastam. I don't know who is behind everything, and they could go after them in retaliation. I need you to go back and make sure they're safe.

"And Tilda," I went on. "She needs someone to help her now. And I need you to tell her that I didn't kill Kasper."

"Bryn, she knows that," he said.

"Tell her anyway, okay?" I persisted. "And tell her I'm sorry. I never meant for him to get hurt." I swallowed back the tears that threatened to form.

Ridley squeezed my hand. "Okay. I'll tell her, and I'll watch out for you parents and Tilda. I won't let anything happen to them while you're gone."

I kissed him then, knowing I might never see him again, that this might be the very last kiss we ever shared, and he set down the duffel bag so he could wrap his arms around me. For a moment, the world fell away around us, and it was only me and him and the way his lips tasted and his arms felt and how desperately I loved him.

He held my face in his hands and looked deep into my eyes. "When this is over, and your parents and Tilda are safe, I will come find you."

The train began to whistle as it pulled into the station, so we didn't have much time. I kissed him again, then grabbed the duffel bag and ran into the station.

five days later

The cell phone sat on the counter, the black screen staring up at me, almost taunting me to use it. It'd been five days, and every day had been a battle of will not to call Ridley to find out what was going on.

I didn't know if he'd gotten caught for helping me escape, and I wanted to know how Tilda was doing and if my parents were safe. But the Högdragen were probably monitoring his phone, and even though I'd gotten an untraceable prepaid phone, that could still mean trouble for him.

So I didn't call.

"What are you having?" the waitress on the other side of the cracked vinyl counter asked me, interrupting my staring contest with the phone.

"Um . . ." A badly worn laminated menu sat on the counter next to my phone, and I quickly scanned it to see if anything appealed to me. Most things sounded as if they were cooked in a vat of grease, and my stomach rolled in disgust. That was the price of stopping in dive diners like this, but I didn't know how long I'd be on the run, and these places had the cheapest food—even if all the food was repulsive.

"Just an unsweetened iced tea," I decided.

"Coming right up." She smiled at me as she took the menu. Even though she had the weary expression of someone who was at the end of a ten-hour shift, there was sympathy in her eyes as she looked at me, so I knew I had to look as bad as I felt.

The metal side of the napkin holder worked as an okay mirror, so I tilted it toward me to get a better look. My attempt at dyeing my hair hadn't worked, failing the way it always did since my hair refused to hold any color. The black dye had faded into a sickly grayish-blue, and in another day or two it would be gone entirely.

The black eye Kennet had given me had finally begun to heal. The first few days it had been an awful puffy purple, and now it was fading to a putrid yellow. I tried to cover it up with makeup, but it was still obvious that there was something going on with my eye.

It didn't help that I wasn't sleeping, so there were bags under my eyes, and my skin had an unpleasant pallor. I hadn't been eating well either, since it was hard to find anything that sat well with me on the road. I'd made the mistake of grabbing turkey jerky in desperation last night and ended up throwing it up.

So far, my only plan was to get south and lay low for a little while until I felt like most of the heat was off. I knew Evert wouldn't want to spare many soldiers to go after me, but he would probably send a few. The Skojare would definitely send some of their guards, not that I thought they'd be able to do anything.

But since I was accused of killing a Prince, other Skojare allies might send troops to help find me, like the Trylle or maybe even the Vittra. They lived farther south than we did, which meant I'd have to go even farther to get out of their range until everyone got tired of looking and went home.

I didn't know where I was exactly, but the last sign I'd seen had been for Missouri. I hadn't decided if this was far enough, or if I should keep going. I didn't know where the end of this journey was for me.

The waitress brought back my tea, and I pushed away the napkin holder so I wouldn't have to look at myself anymore. I leaned forward, letting my hair fall over my face as if I could hide myself, and went back to my staring contest with the phone.

I heard the stool next to me creak as someone sat down, which annoyed me since the entire bar was empty. There were plenty of seats for them to sit in without crowding me.

"Need any company?" the guy next to me asked.

"No, I'm good," I said firmly, and tilted my stool away from him a bit.

"A girl alone like you, I really think you could use a friend," he persisted, and it didn't look like he'd get the hint without more force.

"Listen—" I turned to him, preparing to tell him off—but when I saw I was face-to-face with Konstantin Black, the argument died on my lips.

He looked exactly the way he had in the lysa—his hair longer than it had been before, the raven curls framing his face. From the scruff on his cheeks it had to have been a couple days since his last shave, and he wore all black. His smoky gray eyes studied me, and he offered me a hopeful smile.

"So, what do you say, white rabbit?" Konstantin asked. "Friends?"

Crystal Kingdom

For Eric J. Goldman, Esq.—this book may be
the final chapter in one of our finest adventures together,
but I know there are still many more escapades
for us to enjoy.

friends & enemies

S o, what do you say, white rabbit?" Konstantin Black asked. "Friends?"

He sat on the stool next to me, his gaze unwavering. His thick eyebrows arched hopefully above the dark silver of his eyes, and the coal-black waves of his hair fell over his face as he tilted toward me.

All I could do was gape at him, too stunned to think or move. I didn't even know if he was really there or not. It would make more sense that I had unknowingly passed out in a random diner in Missouri and I was suffering from a stress-induced nightmare or possibly a lysa.

There was no way that Konstantin could be here with me. Not after I'd spent five days on the run from Doldastam after being arrested for treason and accused of murdering the Skojare Prince Kennet Biâelse and my friend Kasper Abbott.

I'd done everything in my power to stay under the radar—I

only used cash and a burner phone, and I hadn't even built up the nerve to actually use the phone and call anyone back home yet. I moved constantly and stayed off the grid in dive motels in small towns.

There was no possible way that anyone could've found me, not even Konstantin Black.

"Bryn?" Konstantin asked, since I'd done nothing but stare at him for the past minute.

Then, because I had to be sure he was real, I reached out and touched him, pressing on the black leather jacket covering his bicep, and he looked down at my hand in bewilderment. I half expected the coat to give way and him to disappear in a puff of smoke, but instead I felt the firmness of his muscle underneath.

"Are you feeling all right?" He looked back at me with what appeared to be genuine concern in his eyes, but I wasn't sure if I could trust him. "You really look like death warmed over."

"That's how you're going to sell the idea of friendship? By telling me I look awful?" I asked dryly.

Not that he was wrong. I wasn't sleeping or eating much, so I was even paler than normal. My attempts at dyeing my hair black to help mask my identity left my normally blond waves an odd gray color, since dye never really took hold in troll hair. The swelling around my left eye had finally gone away, but the bruise had shifted to a putrid yellow color that I wasn't able to cover completely with makeup.

"I'm selling it with brutal honesty," he said with a wry smile. "I want you to know that you'll get nothing but the truth from me."

I scoffed. "There's no way in hell I'm gonna believe that."

"Come on, Bryn. Try me." He rested his forearms on the counter, almost pleading with me.

"What are you even doing here? What do you want with me?" I demanded.

"I already told you—friendship."

I rolled my eyes. "Bullshit. Everything is always bullshit with you."

"How can you say that?" Konstantin shot back, incredulous. "I've been nothing but honest with you."

"Sure, sure. You've been nothing but honest when you attempted to murder my dad or when you tried to kidnap Linnea."

He pressed his lips into a thin line. "I already apologized about what happened with your dad." I glared at him. "Not that anything I say will ever make that okay, but you know that I regret it."

"How can I know that?" I shook my head. "I don't really know anything about you."

"Why are you being so combative?" Konstantin asked, his voice getting louder. "I'm only trying to help."

"You're a traitor who's been working with someone that nearly killed me!" I yelled back, not caring how loud I was being in the small diner.

"Yeah, well, right back at you!" Konstantin shouted.

The waitress came over, interrupting our heated conversation, and set down in front of me the iced tea I'd ordered. She stood with her hand on her hip, eyeing us both with suspicion. Before, she'd looked at me with concern despite her weariness, but with my bad dye job and Konstantin's agitation, it had to be obvious we were on the run.

"Is everything okay here?" she asked, her eyes flitting back and forth between the two of us.

"Yeah, it's fine," Konstantin replied curtly without looking at her.

"Well, you better keep your voices down, before you start upsetting the customers," she said with a slight Southern drawl, and she slowly turned and walked away.

Konstantin waited until after she had gone to the other end of the diner before speaking. "And I tried to save Linnea." He sat up straighter, indignant. "I did save her, actually. Without my intervention, she'd most likely be dead."

From what Linnea had told me, that sounded true enough. Since I couldn't argue with Konstantin, I turned the stool away from him and focused on my iced tea.

He sighed, then he leaned toward me, and in a voice just above a whisper he said, "I know what you're going through. Four years ago, I was almost exactly where you are. I know how frightening and lonely it feels when the kingdom turns against you."

I took a drink from my tea and didn't say anything, so he went on. "You and I have been on opposite sides for a while, and I've made a lot of wrong choices. But I'm trying to make up for them, and . . . now I'm alone, and you're alone. So I thought we could be alone together."

He leaned back away from me. "But I won't force this. If you wanna go through this all alone, then be my guest. Take on the world by yourself. I won't fight you." He reached into his pocket and tossed a few dollars on the counter. "The drink's on me."

I heard the stool creak as he got up, but I didn't look back. Not until I heard the door chime did I turn to watch him walking out the door, into the bright spring day. In a few more seconds he'd be gone, and I'd have no way to contact him or find out what he knew.

So even though I wasn't sure exactly how this friendship thing would play out, or even if this wasn't some kind of trick, I knew what I had to do. I cursed under my breath, and then I jumped off the stool and ran out after Konstantin.

tracking

W here are we going?" I asked. It might have been a better question to ask before I'd gotten in the black Mustang with Konstantin, but I hadn't wanted him to leave without me. And did it really matter where we were going? I had no place to be. No place to call home.

"I don't know." He glanced in the rearview mirror, watching the diner disappear behind us as he sped down the highway. "Do you have somewhere in mind?"

I shook my head. "No." Then I looked over at him. "But we should find someplace where we can really talk."

"How about a motel?" he suggested, and when I scowled at him, he laughed. "If I was going to murder you, I would've done it already, and if I was just looking to get laid, believe me when I say there are easier ways to do it than this."

"Why don't you come out with it right now? I think a talk is long overdue."

He smirked. "You sound so menacing."

I looked out the window, watching the lush greenery as we sped by it. Even with me moving all over as a tracker, it was always jarring to go from the harsh cold of Doldastam to the bright warmth of anywhere else. Home was so far away, and this felt like a whole other world.

"How did you find me?" I asked, still watching the full ash trees that lined the side of the road.

"It was actually quite simple," he said, and I looked back at him. He reached into the pocket of his leather jacket and pulled out a blond lock of hair held together with a thread.

Hesitantly, I took it from him. It was a pale golden color, with a subtle wave to it—exactly how my hair looked before I destroyed it with the bad dye job. This was my hair.

And all the pieces suddenly fell together. How Konstantin had been able to find me no matter where I was, like the hotel room in Calgary, or outside of Storvatten when I'd captured him. Even when he'd visited me in the lysa before.

Konstantin had been a Kanin tracker, from a long line of trackers, and thanks to his strong bloodline, he'd had a powerful affinity for it. Like many trackers, he had the ability to imprint onto a changeling if he had something from them—a lock of hair usually worked best.

It turned the changeling into a kind of homing beacon. Konstantin couldn't read minds, but he could sense extreme emotions in the trackee that meant they were in trouble. The recent events in Doldastam, along with my general fear and anxiety the last few days, would've turned me into a megawatt searchlight.

And Konstantin had been tracking me.

"Where did you get this?" I asked, twisting the hair between my fingers.

Like all trolls, changelings are born with a very thick head of hair, and a lock of hair is taken from them before they're placed with a host family. That way a tracker could find them later.

But I'd never been a changeling, and this hair felt much coarser than my hair had as a child. This had been taken recently.

"Why do you even have it?" I turned to look at him. "Why were you tracking me?"

He opened his mouth, then closed it and exhaled deeply through his nose. "That is a question that's best answered when we get to the motel."

"What? Why?" I sat up in the seat, putting my knee underneath me so I could face him better and defend myself if I needed to. "What's happening at this motel you keep bringing up?"

"Calm down." He held a hand out toward me, palm out. "You're already getting worked up, and I think when I start telling you things, you'll get even more worked up, and I've had enough fights in a car to know that it's better if we wait until we're someplace that isn't flying seventy miles per hour down the road to have a heated conversation."

His explanation sounded reasonable enough, so I relaxed a bit and settled back in the seat.

"For being on the run, this seems like a rather conspicuous and expensive choice of car," I commented, since that seemed like a safe topic.

"Conspicuous, maybe. Expensive, no," he said. "I kind of stole it."

"You really know how to keep a low profile," I muttered.

"Hey, I kept a low profile for four years. I know a thing or two," he insisted. "And I used persuasion, so it's not exactly like that owner is gonna report it to the police."

Persuasion was a psychokinetic ability trolls had where they could make people do what they wanted using a form of mind control. From what I knew about Konstantin, his ability wasn't strong enough to work on other trolls, but humans were much more susceptible to that kind of thing. So Konstantin probably hadn't had to try that hard to convince the human to part with his muscle car.

"So who exactly are you on the run from?" I asked. "Other than the Kanin, of course."

He hesitated, and his grip tightened on the steering wheel. "Viktor Dålig and his men."

"But I thought you were like Viktor's right-hand man or something. How'd you end up on the outs?"

"I told you back in Storvatten, when I was in the dungeon. I didn't want to get any more blood on my hands. That's why I warned Linnea. I wanted to make things right." He shifted in the seat. "And as you can imagine, that didn't exactly sit well with Viktor. I'd been on his shit list ever since I convinced him not to kill you."

"Thank you for that, by the way," I told him softly.

"You weren't supposed to get hurt." He glanced over at me, his eyes pained for a moment. "You weren't supposed to be down there."

While Linnea had still been missing in Storvatten, I had snuck down to the dungeon where Konstantin was being held to find out what he knew. I was desperate to find Linnea. But instead I'd interrupted Viktor helping Konstantin make his escape.

To prevent me from stopping them or telling anyone, Viktor had bashed my head against a wall repeatedly. Viktor had wanted me dead, but I'd suspected that Konstantin had intervened to save my life.

Still, I had a gash under my hairline to show for it. It had required six stiches, though it was nearly healed. The worst part of the injury was the vision in my right eye would get wonky sometimes, especially if I hit my head or somebody punched me.

"So why did Viktor finally kick you out?" I asked, changing the subject.

He shook his head. "Viktor didn't. Besides, he doesn't kick anyone out. Once you've served your purpose, you're dead." He shot me a sidelong glance. "You remember what happened to Bent Stum."

"You left, then?" I asked.

"Yeah. I'd finally had enough of it." He breathed deeply.

"Viktor doesn't care about anything but revenge. A lot of in-nocents are gonna die. And I couldn't be a part of it anymore, and I didn't know how to stop it."

I swallowed hard and sank lower in the seat. Konstantin hadn't really said anything that I didn't already know, but hearing it aloud didn't make it any easier to take.

Even if I were back in Doldastam, I wasn't sure how much I could do to help, but at least I would be able to fight along-side my friends—Ridley, Tilda, Ember—to protect the town filled with people I cared about.

Now I was trapped so far away from them. They were up against the worst thing ever to hit Doldastam, and I was powerless to help them.

THREE

ember

Bryn—   *May 13, 2014*
I'm not totally sure why I'm even writing this. I don't know how you'll get it, and if you do get it, I don't know if you'll even care. Hell, it might even be treason trying to talk to you. But I can't help it. It just feels strange not being able to talk to you about everything—especially with everything that's going on.

I just realized that I don't know if I'll ever see you again. I want to believe that I will, but the whole world feels like it's been turned upside down.

Kasper's funeral was yesterday. I kept expecting to turn around and see you there, coming in late, but you never did.

I don't know where to start with the funeral. Tilda has been trying so hard to hold it all together. I don't know how she's done as well as she has. It was almost creepy being around her. She was like a statue. She hardly ever cried. She'd just talk about the practical things that needed to be done.

Yesterday, she finally broke down. It was the first time she'd seen Kasper since he died. All fixed up in his Högdragen uniform, lying motionless in the coffin. The first thing she said when she saw him was, "He'd be so upset about his hair. It's not quite perfect."

And then she started sobbing uncontrollably. She basically collapsed, so her sister and I practically had to carry her back to her seat. To see Tilda like that . . .

The most heartbreaking part was probably Kasper's little sister Naima. She just cried and cried, and her mom kept trying to comfort her. But it's all so surreal and insane. There's no comfort in that.

The King and Queen came to give a eulogy, and it was all so bizarre. The King seemed so out of place. He kept sweating, and his face was all red, like he had a terrible windburn. The Queen kept doting on Tilda, almost pushing Tilda's own mother out of the way so the Queen could be the one to comfort her. When the King went up to give his speech, he mentioned a few things about Kasper—how great he was, how he died protecting his kingdom, and other generalities.

But it all seemed memorized, and he stumbled over the words a lot. Right after that, the King switched into this war propaganda speech. It was so gross and tactless. He started going on and on about how we can't let Viktor

Dålig do this to our people, and we can't trust anyone because Viktor can get to anyone.

Then he started saying that they would stop at nothing until you were captured, and that's when Tilda stood up and said that she didn't think that this was the time or place to discuss these things.

The King finally shut up after that, but I'm almost surprised he let her talk back. He's cracked down on everything since you've been gone. It reminds me of that book I had to read for an English class at a human school when I was tracking a changeling. 1984, I think. Everywhere you go, the King is watching, and he won't let you forget it.

There are even posters hanging up all around town saying just that. It's this weird black and white image of his face, but somehow his eyes are always following you, and it's super disturbing. Above it says, "THE KING IS WATCHING," and below it says, "TRAITORS OF THE KINGDOM WILL BE CAPTURED," with the Kanin symbol stamped over it.

Members of the Högdragen were going around tacking up all these posters—some of them are WANTED ones for you (you made the Kanin's Most Wanted list, that has to be kind of exciting, right?).

I wanted to tear them all down, but I didn't think now was the best time to deal with the wrath of the King. There was this freak rainstorm yesterday anyway, and most of them are all destroyed and hanging in tatters. But my mom said she saw Högdragen replacing them already today.

There are Högdragen everywhere, and they'll stop you for no reason and demand to know where you're going and what you plan to do there. The guards have even grabbed random people off the street to bring in them in for questioning.

They brought your parents in, too, but I suppose that's not random. Your father has been put on suspension from his job as the Chancellor, and your mother was fired from her job as a teacher. Your mother's job wasn't a direct order from the King, though. People in town started complaining that they couldn't trust her with their children, given what happened with you.

At least your parents are free, though, and that's more than I can say for Ridley. They brought him in for an "interrogation" the day after you left, and he hasn't come out since. I've tried to ask about him, but nobody knows what's happening.

They would tell us if they executed him . . . wouldn't they? Another tracker was talking about how they used to have public executions of traitors in the town square. I think that's what they'd do, if they decided to hang Ridley. So he must still be alive.

Östen Sundt has been promoted to working as the "acting" Överste, but they haven't given him the official title yet, so I'm hoping that's a good sign and it means that Ridley still has a chance to return to his position. To be truthful, though, I don't think anything is a good sign anymore.

I'm just keeping my head down, training and doing what they tell me. I visit Tilda most nights, because I'm afraid to leave her sitting alone in her apartment. I've tried to sneak around to see Delilah. We only just officially became an item, and both of us are getting nervous about what would happen if we got caught. At least I still get to see her training.

The King and Queen have such a stranglehold on Doldastam now. It's like they want to crush us before Viktor gets a chance to. I guess the King thinks that if he couldn't trust you, he can't trust anybody, and there is some truth to that. Except I know that he could trust you.

I know you didn't do the things they said you did, but I wish I knew what happened. What did you do? And why did you do it?

Will I ever see you again?

I know you can't answer these questions, at least not like this. But I do feel better talking to you, even if you can't hear me. And hopefully someday, you'll be able to read this.

Your friend (no matter what),
Ember

FOUR

impetus

It wasn't the worst place I'd ever stayed, but that was by a very, very, very small margin. The room smelled like dirty gym clothes and cigarettes, but the motel had met the requirements of small and secluded.

Konstantin had driven about an hour before finally spotting this sketchy-looking little motel off the edge of the highway. Based on the lack of cars in the lot, it appeared that we were the only ones here.

I tossed my duffel bag onto one of the two small beds in the room, and a plume of dust came out from the worn comforter. Konstantin had gone to the window and pulled the heavy drapes shut, casting the room in darkness.

"Sorry about that," he said and turned on a bedside lamp.

"The room sucks, but I don't care, because we're here." I had my arms crossed over my chest, and then I held out my hand to him, presenting him with the lock of hair. "Now you can tell me about this."

"That was the deal, wasn't it?" Konstantin grimaced before sitting back on the bed. "The long and short of it is that the Queen gave it to me."

My heart skipped a beat. "You mean Linnea?"

"No." He shook his head. "Mina. The Kanin Queen."

The room suddenly felt as if it had pitched to the right. The whole world seemed to go out of focus for a moment as I tried to comprehend the full of implications of what Konstantin had just told me.

"Why?" I asked breathlessly. "Why would the woman I was sworn to serve and protect want to cause me harm?"

"She didn't want to cause you harm . . . at first," he corrected me. "After the whole incident where you made off with Linus Berling before I could stop you, Mina just wanted to keep tabs on you and keep you out of the way."

"But why?" I pressed on. "Why was she involved with any of this?"

"The same reason as anyone else—she wants power." He shrugged helplessly.

"*Power?*" I scoffed. "She already has the fucking crown in the most powerful kingdom in the troll world. What more does she want?"

"Mina's power is contingent on Evert. He has the final say on everything, and if something happens to him, she's shit out of luck. She's under his thumb just as much as anyone else, and she hates it. She wanted to rule in her own right."

I'd taken to pacing the room, processing everything Konstantin was telling me. "And how does she plan to do that? If Evert's out of the way, they'll just find a replacement . . ." As soon as I said that, it dawned on me. "That's why you went after Linus Berling."

"Our plan was to remove as many of the next-in-line royals as we could until it would just make the most sense for the Chancellor to leave Mina in charge," Konstantin explained. "It wasn't a guarantee, but the idea was also that if the community was in turmoil, they might be reluctant to change horses midstream. And in the meantime, Mina is doing her best to make herself seem beloved by all."

"And she thought the best way to do that was to get hooked up with Viktor Dålig?" I asked.

Konstantin lowered his eyes. "It's not that simple. Viktor promised men to help the kingdom feel threatened. Mina wanted there to be the threat of war so she could step up and show everyone how well she could rule, and she would get Evert out of the way so she could 'crush' the enemy herself and no one would depose her."

I narrowed my eyes. "Get Evert out of the way how?"

"I don't know exactly. I wasn't privy to all the details of the operation."

"If Mina's got this great plan for war on her kingdom, why'd you end up sidetracked with the Skojare?" I asked.

"To get enough men for a war, we needed money, and Mina couldn't very well take money from the Kanin. I don't know exactly how it all started, but she was at some event or another hobnobbing with other royals, and she got to talking to Kennet Biâelse, and together they cooked up this great scheme where he would get her all the sapphires she needed in exchange for getting his brother dethroned."

I sighed and sat down on the bed across from Konstantin. "So that's how Kennet got involved. How did you?"

"I was the Queen's guard. I spent night and day by her side for a year." He stared down at a stain on the carpet, then swallowed hard. "She asked me to help her, and I couldn't say no. I went after your father for Viktor. It was his revenge for your father choosing Evert for the crown, and Mina said I needed to do it to strengthen our alliance with Viktor."

He sat at the side of the bed, with his hands holding the edge, and he gripped it more tightly every time he mentioned Mina. His brows bunched up, and his jaw tensed under his dark stubble.

"That's not good enough," I said at length, and he looked up sharply at me, his eyes flashing like freshly forged steel.

"What?"

"You took an oath," I reminded him, and then began reciting the key component to him: *"In times of war, I swear to defend the kingdom and fight our enemies. In times of peace, I vow to protect the King at all costs. It is my duty to kill if necessary, but never murder. A life must only be taken in preservation of the kingdom."*

As I was speaking, Konstantin looked away and groaned loudly. "Come on, Bryn. You've seen enough to know that life is never that black-and-white."

"My father was an innocent man," I growled at him. "You tried to kill him because the Queen didn't like being married but still wanted to be rich and powerful. Tell me what shades of gray I'm missing."

"I'm sorry about your father! I made a mistake!" Konstantin shouted and stood up. "But I was trying to protect Mina." He let out a rough breath. "I was in love with her."

I waited a beat before deciding to ignore his confession about his feelings for Mina—at least for the moment. "Protect her from what?"

"Evert." It was Konstantin's turn to begin pacing the small motel room. "He was cold and cruel to her. When we were alone together, Mina would cry to me and tell me how awful the King was to her. That's how the affair started between us. I only wanted to comfort her and make her happy . . . and it turned into something more."

"Evert can be cold." I agreed with his summation. "But I've never known him to be cruel to Mina. In fact, I've never seen him treat her with anything but respect."

It hadn't even been a week ago when I'd been in the King's parlor with Evert and Mina, both of them drunk on wine. He'd been so tender and loving with her, asking her what he'd done to deserve her, and she smiled at him.

Not to mention that Mina was constantly professing her love for Evert. I knew that abuse wasn't always obvious—people tended to do everything they could to hide it. But just the same, Evert didn't seem to fit the description Konstantin had laid out.

"I'm not saying I believe her *now*," Konstantin corrected me. "I'm saying I believed her *then*. I'll be the first to admit that I was far too blinded by love."

"Why didn't you just run away with her, then? Why did you resort to murder and treason?" I asked.

"I suggested it, but where would we run to? She grew up in Iskyla—a frozen, isolated wasteland that doesn't even have proper electricity. She wasn't going back to that, and she wasn't about to give up the life she'd created for herself.

"And killing Evert was out of the question, because he was the King. Somehow she convinced me that the only way for us to live happily ever after was for me to get rid of the Chancellor and start working for Viktor."

He shook his head at his own ignorance. "I don't even know how she did it. All I can say is that there is something very powerful about the conversations you have in bed with your forbidden lover."

I scowled, trying not to let myself think too much about Konstantin in bed with Mina, his arms entwined with hers as they lay in the satin sheets of her bed.

"If you loved her so much that you were willing to give up everything you worked for, everything you believed in, how can you go against her now?" I asked. "How can I trust you?"

He thought for a minute before finally saying, "I am still in love with the idea of her, the mirage that Mina showed me that was beautiful and warm and loving. But now I've come to know her well enough to see that that was nothing but a lie. The idea I had of her never existed."

"What made you realize that?" I asked.

"I'd started to realize that she was far more cold and calculating than I'd first suspected, but it was when she asked me to kill the changelings," he replied. "Initially we were only supposed to scare them off so they'd never go back with their tracker. But after Linus Berling, she told me to start murdering these innocent children . . . and that's when I knew her lust for power was the only thing that mattered to her.

"Well, that and her damn rabbit," he corrected himself.

Like many other Kanin royals, Mina had a pet Gotland rabbit. They were a symbol of hope and prestige for our people, and Mina used to carry hers around everywhere she went, until Evert made fun of her for it at a party once. Then she started leaving the white rabbit in her room, but she still brought it with her anytime she went on a trip out of Doldastam.

"If she's as awful as you say she is—and I do believe you that she is—then how did it take you so long to figure it out?" I asked.

"For starters, I couldn't see her that often, because I was a wanted traitor," Konstantin expounded. "It was very tricky for her to sneak out to nearby villages to see me, usually under the guise of visiting royalty or family members. Once I think she said she'd gone for a spa weekend in a human town, but she really spent it with me.

"So I only saw her for small glimpses, and she was always putting on a good show of being this helpless victim." He sighed. "And I—being the lovesick idiot I was—ate it up."

"Why has it been so long?" I asked, realizing that he'd been lying in wait for years. "Between your initial attack on my dad until Linus Berling, there was a four-year silence. Why didn't Mina command you to make a move sooner?"

"Viktor had been trying to gather more men, and Mina had been trying to gather more money," Konstantin explained. "But time was running out. Evert was getting more impatient about having children, and Mina refused to have kids."

I shook my head. "Why?"

"Because if something happens to Evert, then her kids will inherit all his power—not her."

"Holy crap. She really is power-hungry." Then something else occurred to me. "She's been plotting her attack for *four years?*"

Konstantin lifted his eyes to meet mine. "Honestly? I think she's been plotting her attack since the day she met Evert, and she is one determined bitch."

FIVE

exile

Lying on top of the covers, I was still fully clothed in my jeans and tank top. Konstantin promised me that he wouldn't murder me in my sleep, and even though we had struck an uneasy alliance, I still wasn't sure how much I could trust him.

In the darkness of the motel room, I lay awake for a long time, trying to process everything that Konstantin had told me. I reanalyzed every interaction I'd had with the Queen, and the more I thought about it, the more I saw that everything Konstantin had said added up.

It explained all kinds of little things about her—her insistence on wearing her crown so often, even when Evert didn't, her constant mood shifts from warm to icy, her unreasonable hatred of me.

And then everything that had happened with Kennet. She must have instructed Kennet to flirt with me in Storvatten in an attempt to keep me too distracted to figure things out. When Kasper and I had put the pieces together, we'd told her, and she'd had us arrested before we could find out her involvement.

For the first time, some of my guilt about Kasper's death had eased. There was no way that either of us could've known that Mina was involved, and she would've had us executed. Escape had been the smartest move we could have made.

I lay awake, letting my thoughts go over the scenarios again and again, because it was so much better than sleeping. When I closed my eyes, I knew that only nightmares awaited me. Horrific images of Kasper's death haunted me every night, replaying in nauseating clarity.

Other times, my dreams would start out nicer, with Ridley. We would be in the middle of nowhere, with the aurora borealis dancing above us, and he'd look down at me with that heat in his eyes that made my heart flutter.

He'd pull me close to him, and his lips would meet mine. Somehow, in the dream, I knew this would be the last time I'd ever be with him, and I kissed him desperately.

Then, without warning, he'd be ripped from my arms. An unknown force would pull him away, dragging him off into the darkness, and I would scream his name. I would run after him, but no matter how fast I ran, I never caught up to him.

Over and over, I had these nightmares of Kasper dying and Ridley being taken away. So I fought sleep as much as I could, but eventually it won out, and darkness enveloped me.

It didn't last for long tonight, though, before it was interrupted by bright blue water. It shimmered like sapphires, and it seemed to fill every corner of my vision. I could almost feel it, cool and delicious running over my skin.

I heard her shouting before I saw her—"Bryn! *Bryn!*"

"What?" I asked, and my voice sounded like a strange echo, bouncing off of everything.

Suddenly a hand gripped my ankle, yanking me under-water. I started to fight it, but I realized with some surprise that I could breathe easily in the clear water that surrounded me. Even though it should all be terrifying, I felt oddly re-laxed.

Linnea floated up in front of me, and the way her platinum-blond curls floated around her head made her look ethereal. Under the water, her eyes somehow managed to look even more blue than normal, but a worried expression aged her youthful face.

"Bryn," Linnea said again, and it sounded like she was speaking directly inside my head. "What's happened? Where are you?"

"I don't know where I am." I looked around, as if there would be some kind of sign telling me the exact location of my underwater dream.

"Not here. This is a lysa." Linnea took my hand, making me focus on her. "Everything is crazy in Storvatten. They say you killed Kennet."

"I didn't kill Kennet!" I shouted, then corrected myself. "I tried to save him, but I couldn't. But he was behind everything, Linnea. He's the reason Mikko was arrested."

Her eyes widened and she gasped. "*Kennet?* But he loved Mikko!"

"It's too much to explain now, but you have to believe me. Kennet was into some bad things, and you can't trust the Kanin Queen either. She was working with him."

"Who can I trust?" Linnea's lip began to quiver. "Everything is falling apart here. My grandma is trying to run things, but the board of advisers is pushing her out. They won't release Mikko, and they're trying to bring Bayle Lundeen back, but they can't find him anywhere."

"Don't let Bayle run anything!" I warned her. "If they find him, make them question him. He knows what Kennet was up to, so maybe he can help free Mikko."

The water seemed to grow colder. It had been the whole time, but I began to feel the chill running deeper in me. And it was getting harder to breathe. Each breath I took seemed to be equal parts air and water, and I was starting to choke.

"Don't trust the Kanin. Don't accept any aid from them," I told her as water filled my lungs. "Stray strong."

Her expression hardened with resolve. "I won't let anyone hurt me or Mikko anymore," Linnea promised me. "And I will clear your name, Bryn!"

That was the last thing I heard her say before the dream collapsed on me, and I woke up in bed, gasping for breath.

alliance

With one hand I tousled my damp hair with a towel, and with the other I pulled back the drapes, allowing the blinding sun to spill into the dark room. When my eyes adjusted, I half expected to see Högdragen or maybe Viktor Dålig's men outside, waiting to capture me.

But it was only an empty gravel parking lot on a relatively deserted highway. Being on the run made it awfully hard to not feel paranoid, especially when it turned out there was actually a conspiracy plotting against me.

"Anything exciting out there?" Konstantin's voice rumbled from behind me, making me jump.

I let the shades close, and I turned back to see him standing in the bathroom doorway. His dark curls were wet, and he was wearing only a pair of jeans. Seeing him shirtless, I realized that he was more muscular than I'd originally imagined.

While the smooth definition of his torso was a pleasant sight, his deep olive skin was marred by scars running all over his chest and arms. Some of them were undoubtedly from the days when he partook in the brutal sport of the King's Games, but some of them had probably been from more sinister actions with Viktor Dålig and his men.

On his chest, just above his heart, he had a black tattoo of a rabbit—the same tattoo many members of the Högdragen shared. They usually got it after they took their oath, and I was sure that Konstantin had been the same. He'd once been as young and determined as I had been, but somewhere along the line he'd taken a much darker turn.

"No, nothing." I lowered my eyes and tossed my towel on the dresser next to the small television.

"You used all the hot water," Konstantin grumbled absently as he picked his black T-shirt up off his bed. I peered over at him, watching as he pulled the shirt over his head, then quickly looked away once he'd gotten it on.

"Sorry. I guess I'm not used to sharing."

"I doubt this place had much hot water anyway." He looked over at me. "At least your hair's looking better now."

I tugged at a lock of my shoulder-length hair so I could get a better look at it. The faded gray had mostly washed out, and it was returning to its usual color again.

"So what's the plan now?" Konstantin asked.

"I don't know." I leaned back against the dresser. "What's your plan?"

"My plan was to find you, and I've found you." He

motioned in the air, making a checkmark with his hand. "Mission accomplished."

"You didn't have any idea what would happen after that?"

"Not really." He sat on the bed across from me, leaning back so he propped himself up on his arms. "I didn't know what would happen when I found you. But you've been on the run for some days now. Haven't you had time to come up with your next move?"

"No." I sighed. "I mean, I know what I want to do. I want to get back to Doldastam and avenge Kasper. I want to make sure my family and friends are safe, and I want to get the Queen out of there before she hurts anybody else, which probably means that I'd need to take on Viktor Dålig and his army along with the Kanin army.

"And then once all that is done, I want to go to Storvatten and make sure Mikko is freed and that he and Linnea are safe, and then I need to make sure they get a good, honest guard in place."

Konstantin let out a long whistle. "That's an impressive list you got there, white rabbit."

"I know. I just have no idea where to get started." I ran my hand through my hair. "And I don't know how I can possibly take on all of that by myself."

"Hey, you're not by yourself." Konstantin stood up and stepped closer to me. "I'm with you now. Remember?"

I stared up into his eyes, desperate to believe him. Not just because I was faced with an insurmountable task and I needed his help. But because there was something about him, something that still made me slightly breathless. It was almost as if nothing had changed since I was a kid.

I had trusted and believed in him then, and now I wanted nothing more than to feel that way again.

"I'm glad that you're with me, I truly am," I admitted. "But there's still only two of us, and we're enemies of the state. *No one* will believe us, and we can't defeat an army by ourselves."

Konstantin took a step back, considering this for a moment. "Maybe we don't have to."

"What do you mean?"

"I mean . . . Bent Stum."

"Bent Stum is dead," I reminded him.

He snapped his fingers. "Exactly! Bent was killed by Kennet Biâelse, who was working on orders from Mina."

I shrugged, since Konstantin hadn't told me anything I didn't already know. "So? How does that help us?"

"Bent Stum is Omte," he said, grinning.

"The Omte?" I shook my head. "They're unreasonable and grumpy and, quite frankly, they're kinda stupid."

"Trust me, I know. I spent months working with Bent." Konstantin frowned. "Bent was murdered, and that sucks, but he was awful to deal with. It was like working with the Hulk, if the Hulk was dumber and angrier."

"And you want to go to them for help?" I laughed darkly.

"Look, I get that it's not ideal. But the Omte already kinda hate the other tribes. They've always been jealous of them, because everyone else is richer, smarter, and more attractive. But the Omte are so much stronger. Their physical strength is unparalleled by any other tribe, even the Vittra."

"And you think they would help us over Bent? I thought the Omte Queen didn't care about him," I said, remembering what Ridley had said when he'd first been investigating Bent Stum after the Linus Berling incident.

"It doesn't matter." Konstantin shook his head. "The Omte are overly emotional and quick to anger. And now one of their people was killed in some kind of conspiracy between the Skojare and the Kanin? They'll be all over that."

"But I don't want the Omte to destroy the Kanin or the Skojare," I pointed out.

"I've heard the royals are smarter and more reasonable than the average Omte civilian. Maybe if we get a meeting with the Omte Queen, we can gauge how rational she seems, and we can go from there," Konstantin suggested.

I chewed the inside of my cheek, still not completely sold on Konstantin's idea. It wasn't an awful idea, but with a tribe as unpredictable as the Omte, I wasn't too keen on getting involved.

"Besides, their capital isn't even that far away," Konstantin added. "I think it's only a day's drive from here."

Unlike most of the troll tribes that preferred to make their homes in the colder temperatures of the north, the Omte had just kept moving south before eventually settling in the swamps of southern Louisiana. It was as if they'd done everything they could to distance themselves from the other tribes.

"All right." I relented finally. "What have we got to lose? Let's go see the Omte Queen."

commute

As the Mustang lurched along the gravel road, I leaned over into the backseat. Konstantin hit a bump, and I bounced up, hitting my head on the ceiling.

"Hey, what are you doing?" he asked.

I'd been reaching back to grab my duffel bag, but his bag was sitting beside mine, unzipped, and a flash of metal caught my eyes. Resting right on top of the clothes were two daggers, and I reached in and picked one up.

"What do you have these for?" I narrowed my eyes at him and held up the dagger for him to see. "These are the Kanin daggers you were given when you became the Queen's guard."

It had been a large ceremony in the palace. I'd been standing as near to the front as I could get, on my tiptoes to get a glimpse of it. They were beautiful daggers, with long sharp blades and ornately carved handles of silver and ivory.

"They're for protection," he replied gruffly. "And they're the only things I still have from being a Högdragen, so I'd like it if you stopped playing with them and put them back."

"Yeah, sure. Sorry." I leaned back over the seat and put his dagger safely back in his bag, then grabbed my own duffel before sitting back down. "I was just getting my own bag anyway."

"What for?"

"I don't trust that you know where you're going, and I'm hoping there might be something in here that could help," I replied as I unzipped the bag.

"I already told you. I've been to Fulaträsk before," Konstantin said, sounding indignant. "I went with Mina on a peace-keeping mission years ago, and I never forget how to get anywhere."

"As reassuring as that is, the sun is starting to set"—I gestured out the window at the amber skies showing through the branches of the willow trees that lined the road—"and I'd like to get where we're going by nightfall."

"That's a great idea, but if you packed a buncha maps to the troll capitals, you should've let me in on that sooner," he said with sarcasm dripping from his voice.

"I didn't." I dug through my bag, pushing through the clothes I'd picked up from thrift stores and garage sales over the last few days. "I didn't even pack this bag. Ridley got everything together."

As I moved a pair of jeans, the cell phone fell out of the pocket. I stared at it for moment, once again finding myself trapped under the tantalizing possibility of calling Ridley. It was a prepaid phone, so it was virtually untraceable, and I would do almost anything to be able to call Ridley and hear his voice and find out he was okay.

But I knew I couldn't risk it. It was still too soon, and if anyone in Doldastam found out I'd contacted him, he would be in serious trouble. Assuming that he wasn't already locked up for helping me escape in the first place.

"Who's Ridley?" Konstantin asked. "Wait. Wasn't he like the Rektor or something?"

"It doesn't matter." I brushed him off, since talking about Ridley still felt far too painful, and I buried the phone back in the bag. "But this looks like a standard bag for new trackers, which means that they pack it with a few emergency essentials, including a handbook . . ."

Finally, I unzipped a pocket hidden at the bottom of the bag and found the handbook. Since this bag was going out into the human world, we tried to keep the handbook as hidden as possible, in case the bag fell into the wrong hands. But it was a nice asset for trackers out on their first few jobs because it had tips and tricks, along with important information for them to remember.

It also had rundowns on all the other tribes in case you ran into them (which wasn't completely unheard-of, especially when tracking changelings in popular destinations like New York City or Chicago).

"Aha!" I held up the book to show Konstantin, but he seemed less than impressed.

"Does that have an address in it?" he asked with an arched eyebrow.

"Let me find out." I tossed my bag into the backseat, and then I got comfortable, sinking lower so I could prop my bare feet up on the dashboard with the handbook spread open on my legs.

The first few sections were all things to help trackers do their jobs better, and I flipped through them quickly until I got to the parts about the tribes. When I saw that there were only a couple pages on each tribe, my heart sank.

It didn't help that the top quarter of one of the pages on the Omte was a detailed sketch of their emblem—a brown-bearded vulture, staring at me with small black eyes. There were a few basic facts about the Omte, and finally, at the bottom, I found a sentence that seemed remotely helpful.

"The Omte capital of Fulaträsk is located in the wetlands in the human state of Louisiana," I read aloud. *"Fulaträsk has an estimated population of six thousand, making it the second most populated capital of the five tribes. They live under the rule of their King and Queen, Thor and Bodil Elak, who reside in the palace there."*

"That must be an older printing," Konstantin commented when I'd finished reading.

I turned back to the cover, and it looked new enough to me. "What makes you say that?"

"Because Thor died, like, three years ago," he said. "Bodil is still allowed to rule, though, because she and Thor have a little kid."

"How do you know this stuff?" I asked. "I don't even know this."

"I traveled with Bent for a while, remember? And he *loved* talking about all the stupid crap the Omte would get themselves into."

"What happened to the King?"

"There's a tavern in Fulaträsk called the Ugly Vulture." He shook his head, like he thought it was a dumb name. "According to Bent, it's a real roughneck place, although, also according to him, all the bars in Fulaträsk are really rowdy places. But the Ugly Vulture is apparently the worst."

The road had become narrow, so the swamp came right up to the edges of it, and Konstantin slowed down. As the sun continued to set, everything around us seemed to glow an eerie red.

"Thor really loved the Ugly Vulture," Konstantin went on. "That is one nice thing that Bent said about the Omte—their royals have no problem getting down and dirty with the commoners."

"How progressive of them," I said dryly.

"So anyway, I guess Thor got really drunk on eldvatten—"

"Eldvatten?" I interrupted him.

"It's this really, really strong alcohol that the Omte make. It's like a cross between wine and moonshine, but I have no idea what's in it," Konstantin explained.

"So the King is totally wasted at this point, and Bent didn't know the full details of it, but another patron starts getting mouthy with Thor," he continued. "So the King starts hitting this guy, and the guy gets pissed, so he rips out Thor's throat with his bare hands."

I gaped at him. "This is who we're going to for help? Their King died in a bar fight!"

"We don't have a lot of other options," he countered. "And besides, the King was drunk. He was probably less of a dick when he was sober."

I leaned my head back against the seat. "We are so screwed."

The car started to slow down, and I looked out the window, hoping to see a palace or some sign that we were getting closer. But it was only cypress trees and dark water.

"What's happening?" I asked.

"We've run out of road." Konstantin put the car in park and turned it off. "Now we get to finish the journey on foot."

everglades

The heat was oppressive. It's hard to explain exactly what it felt like to come from twenty-degree temperatures and snowstorms to more than eighty degrees and humid. The air seemed to condense on my skin, and bugs buzzed wildly around me.

As we waded through the bayou, with the murky water coming up to our knees, I hoped against hope that Konstantin knew where we were going.

"Watch for alligators," Konstantin warned.

I looked around the water, which was getting harder to see in the fading light, but even in bright afternoon it would be hard to tell a log from a large reptile. "There are alligators here?"

"I have no idea." He glanced back at me, smirking. "I don't know anything about what lives down here."

"I guess we'll find out, then, won't we?" I muttered.

A mosquito buzzed loudly around my ear, and I tried to swat it away to no avail. It finally landed on the back of my neck, and I slapped it hard to be sure I got it.

"You should be careful about making loud noises, though," Konstantin said as I followed a few steps behind him.

"Why? Will it attract alligators?" I asked sarcastically.

"No, but the Omte startle easily, and we definitely don't want them startled."

Beneath the water, the thick mud threatened to rip off my boots with every step I took, making it very slow going. I told Konstantin that there had to be an easier way to get to Fuläträsk, but he reminded me that the Omte didn't want to be found. They made it as difficult as possible for anyone to stumble upon them.

It had gotten dark enough that we needed to pull out our cell phones and use them as flashlights to help guide our path. But there was still so much around us we couldn't see, and the wetlands were alive with noise—frogs, insects, and birds were loudly chirping their nighttime songs.

Somewhere high above us, I heard the flapping of wings, but I couldn't move my light fast enough to spot them. I'd also heard the high-pitched squeaks of bats, so I figured that they were zooming around to feast on the plethora of bugs.

Occasionally I felt something swim up against my leg, but since nothing had bitten me yet, I tried not to worry about it.

Lightning bugs flashed around us, their tiny bodies twinkling through the trees and reflecting on the water. In the twilight, surrounded by the music of the animals and the still waters underneath the thick canopy of branches, there was something beautiful about the marsh, something almost enchanting.

"Bryn," Konstantin hissed, pulling me from my thoughts.

I'd fallen a few steps behind him because I'd paused to look around, but now I hurried ahead. He held out his arm, blocking me, when I reached him.

"Shh!" he commanded, and then he pointed toward where his light had picked up two glowing dots on a log, just barely above the surface of the water. It was an alligator, not even a meter away from us, and it looked massive.

"What do we do?" I whispered.

"I don't know. Back away slowly, I guess."

He kept the light on the alligator, and we started to move away when I heard the sound of flapping wings again. It sounded much too large to be a bat, and it was followed by more flapping. Whatever it was, it was very close by, and there were more than one.

I turned my flashlight toward the sky, and it caught on a huge brown bird flying above us. The bird circled us for a moment before settling down on a long branch, and I finally got a good look at it.

With its large wingspan, pointed beak, and thick feathers down its long neck, it was unmistakably a bearded vulture. Bearded vultures weren't native to this area—they were something that had been brought in with trolls from the old world, like Gotland rabbits and Tralla horses.

We were in Omte territory.

The cypress and willow trees around us towered several stories into the air, and from the corner of my eye I saw a flash near the top of one. I shone my light up toward it, and with the weak power of my TracFone, I could just make out the outline of a large tree house.

It wasn't exactly a luxury tree house, but it was much more than the average one you might find in a child's backyard. The wood seemed warped and worn, with moss growing over it, and a sagging porch was attached to the front. But it was easily large enough to house a family, and it even had a second story attached to the right side that climbed up along the trunk of the tree.

A large head poked out of the window, looking down at me. It was slightly lopsided, the way Bent Stum's head had been, with one eye appearing larger than the other.

"Konstantin," I said quietly. "I think we're here."

"What?" he asked.

No sooner had the words escaped his mouth than a massive ogre jumped out of a tree and came crashing down into the water in front of us, sending muddy water splashing over us. As soon as the water settled, the ogre let out a long, low growl, and I knew we were in trouble.

"I told you that we shouldn't startle them," Konstantin said.

NINE

monstrosity

I'd heard of ogres and seen pictures of them in textbooks, but I'd never actually met one in real life. I knew that the Omte occasionally gave birth to ogres and they had several of them living in their population. But it's one thing to read about massive, hulking trolls and it's another thing entirely to have one standing directly in front of you.

The ogre stood well over eight feet tall, and he had thick arms bulging with muscles like boulders. His whole body tilted to one side, with his right shoulder rising above his left shoulder, and his right hand was even bigger than his left. His head was massive, making room for a large mouth filled with uneven yellowed teeth. It all made his eyes seem disproportionately small, and he stared down at us with either rage or hunger—I couldn't tell which.

"Why disturb my home?" the ogre demanded, his voice booming through everything.

"We mean you no harm." Konstantin held up his hands toward him.

The ogre laughed at that, a terrible rumbling sound. "You no harm me! You *can't* harm me!"

"That's true," Konstantin allowed, and I wished that we'd brought some kind of weapon with us. We were defenseless if this giant decided he wanted to grind our bones to make his bread. "We only wish to speak to your Queen."

The alligator had begun to swim closer to us, but I'd hardly noticed it, since my attention had been focused on the ogre. It wasn't until the ogre lunged, swinging his massive fist out, that I realized how close the alligator had gotten. The ogre punched it, and sent it flying backward into the swamp.

Konstantin and I both took a step back, and I started to think that coming here might have been a very bad idea.

Then the ogre turned back to us with his beady eyes narrowed. "What you know of Queen?"

"We're Kanin," Konstantin explained. "We're allies."

"Friends," I supplied when the ogre appeared confused.

"Queen no tell me friends coming." The ogre bent down so he could get a better look at us, and the stench from his breath was almost enough to make me gag. "Queen tell me when friends visit."

"Well, it's a bit of a surprise, actually." Konstantin smiled, hoping to make light of things, but the ogre wasn't having any of it.

"Queen tell me to squash visitors," the ogre said. "Me think she want me to squash you."

"The Queen wouldn't want you to squash friends, though," I said, hurrying to come up with a reason for us not to end up like the alligator.

The ogre straightened up again and glowered down at us. He seemed to consider my proposition, but before he could make a decision, we were interrupted by the sound of a fan propeller coming from behind him. A headlight bobbed on the water toward us, and within a minute, an airboat had pulled up beside the ogre.

A woman stood on it, one of her thick rubber boots resting on the front edge. She appeared to be in her late twenties, and with smooth skin, large dark eyes, and a totally symmetrical body. Her long chestnut hair was pulled back, and she wore a black tank top that revealed the thick muscles of her arms. She wasn't much taller than me, but she could easily break me over her leg if she wanted to.

"What's all the commotion about, Torun?" she asked the ogre, but her eyes were on Konstantin and me.

"Squash visitors!" Torun told her, motioning to us with his massive paw.

"We're from the Kanin tribe," Konstantin rushed to explain before she became sympathetic with the ogre's position. "We're only here to talk to your Queen. We think we may have information that she may find useful."

She narrowed her eyes at me. "You look familiar." Then she tilted her head. "Didn't the Kanin just send us WANTED posters with your face on it? You killed someone important, didn't you?"

"That's part of what we would like to speak to the Queen about," I said, trying to remain unfazed.

She thought for a moment, then nodded. "All right." She leaned down and held out her hand to me. Her grip was almost bone-crushingly strong, and she pulled me up onto the boat with ease.

"But me squash!" Torun yelled plaintively as she helped Konstantin onto the airboat.

"Not this time, Torun," she said and turned the boat on. Torun splashed the water with his fists in a rage, and she steered us away from him, turning back.

There were no seats on the boat, so I held on to Konstantin to steady myself and hoped I didn't go flying off into the swamp as she picked up speed.

"Who are you anyway?" she asked, speaking loudly to be heard over the large propeller.

"I'm Bryn Aven, and this is Konstantin Black."

"I'm Bekk Vallin, one of the Queen's guards," she explained. "The Queen won't give you amnesty, if that's what you're looking for. But I'll take you to her anyway. She might be curious about what you have to say."

"Thank you," Konstantin said. "All we really want is an opportunity to speak with her."

Bekk didn't say any more as she drove us along, weaving through the trees. It was only a few minutes before we reached their palace anyway, and it wasn't exactly what I was expecting.

It was a square fortress, made of what appeared to be mud and stone, with thick layers of moss and vines growing over it. With the rest of the Omte living in tree houses, I'd assumed this to be higher off the ground, but it was nearly flush with the swamp, sitting on a small hill above it.

Konstantin and I followed Bekk up the muddy bank toward a massive iron door. Rust left it looking dark brown, and it creaked loudly when an ogre opened it, causing a nearby bearded vulture to squawk in protest.

Inside the palace, it was just as humid as it was outside, and moss grew on the interior walls. Slugs and snails seemed to have made themselves at home in here, and a giant spider had spun a web in the corner of a doorway.

Bekk said nothing as she led us through. Iron chandeliers dimly lit the way through the smallest palace I had been to. It reminded me more of the ruins of a castle in Ireland I'd seen in textbooks than of an active palace where trolls lived and worked.

A set of stairs ran along the side of the wall, jutting out from the stone with no railing or wall to keep one from falling over the other side. Bekk went up them, so Konstantin and I followed her.

At the top of the landing there were three heavy wooden doors, and Bekk pushed one of them open. It was a small room, with a dingy-looking bed, a metal toilet and sink in one corner. There were bars on the only window to prevent an escape, though bugs and birds could come and go as they pleased.

"You will wait here until I come get you," Bekk instructed us.

"Will that be soon?" I asked.

"It will be whenever the Queen decides," Bekk replied curtly.

Since we had no other choice, Konstantin and I went into the room. As soon as we did, Bekk shut the door loudly behind us, and we heard the sound of locks sliding into place. Just to be sure, Konstantin tested the door, and it didn't budge. We were trapped inside.

"Does this make us prisoners, then?" I asked.

Konstantin sighed. "It does seem that way."

confined

There was blackness, and then strong hands were on me, closing in, crushing me. I didn't remember anything before that, but all I knew was that I had to fight if I wanted to survive. I lashed out, hitting everything I could until I registered Konstantin's voice, crying out in pain.

"Bryn!" he shouted.

And slowly, the world came into focus. Early morning sunlight streamed in through the open window of our cell. Konstantin stood with his back pressed against the wall, wedged in the constricted spot between where I knelt on the bed and the mossy stone behind him.

I blinked at Konstantin, trying to understand what was happening, and without warning he lunged at me, grabbing my wrists and pinning me back on the bed.

"What are you doing?" I growled and tried to push him back with my legs.

"What are *you* doing?" he shot back, his face hovering just above mine as he stared down at me. "You started attacking me."

"I did not," I replied instantly, but then realized that I actually did remember hitting at *something*. So I corrected myself. "If I did, I was just protecting myself. What did you do?"

"You were moaning and freaking out, twitching your legs like a dog having a bad dream," he explained, his expression softening from accusatory to concerned. "I thought something might be wrong, so I put my hand on your arm—just to check on you—and you went ballistic."

I lowered my eyes. "I'm sorry."

"It's fine." He let go of my wrists and moved over so he was sitting next to me. "Are you okay now?"

"Yeah, I'm fine." I sat up more slowly and ran my hand through my tangles of hair.

Since there was only the one bed—a narrow, lumpy double mattress on a rusted iron bed frame—Konstantin and I had decided to share it last night. I'd honestly considered the floor, but there were centipedes and bugs of all kinds crawling all over it, and while the bed probably wasn't a much safer bet, I knew I wouldn't have gotten any sleep on the floor.

I'd slept as near to the edge as possible, rigidly on my side, and I was acutely aware of every breath he took and every time he shifted. Five years ago, if someone had told me that I'd share a bed with Konstantin Black, I would've been too excited to believe it, but now I had no idea what to think about any of this.

"What was the bad dream about?" Konstantin asked.

"I don't remember," I said honestly, but most of my nightmares were variations of Kasper dying, or of Kennet dying, or of me killing Cyrano, or of Ridley being ripped from my arms. None of them were pleasant to recall.

I got up and slid between Konstantin and the wall to the larger area of the room. My hair tie was around my wrist, and I pulled back my hair into a ponytail. My stomach rumbled, reminding me that it had been nearly twenty-four hours since the last time I'd eaten, and I had no idea when I'd eat again.

So, without anything better to do, I dropped to the floor and began doing push-ups. My jeans and tank top were both splattered with mud that had dried and become stiff, but I was hoping the more I moved, the more mud I'd lose.

"What are you doing?" Konstantin asked.

"I'm not just gonna sit and wait for the Queen to summon us. Assuming she ever does summon us." I looked up at him as I worked out. "Besides, we might have to fight our way out of here."

"And you think those extra twenty push-ups will help you fight off an ogre like that Torun guy?" he asked with a smirk.

"I'm doing a hundred," I grunted but didn't argue with him.

In truth, I had no idea how we could possibly escape from here. The Omte were much too strong for us to fight hand-to-hand. If they wanted us trapped in this tower forever, then that was what would probably happen.

Konstantin got up from the bed and walked over to the

window. His arms were folded over his chest, and the rising sun cast a long shadow behind him that overtook the room. When I finished my push-ups, he was still standing like that, staring through the bars.

I stood up and wiped the sweat from my brow. "I can't believe how hot it is for how early it is. How can people live like this?"

"It is actually kind of beautiful here," Konstantin said.

I went over to see what he saw. Our room was just above the tops of the trees, and from here we had a stunning view of the trees and the water below. A few birds flew by, their wings like arcs in the bright sun, and I had to admit that he was right.

"Do you think you could fit through these bars?" he asked.

"What?" I'd been looking past the window and now I turned my attention to the three thick bars that held us in the room.

"The bars." He started pushing at the stones that lined the window. "This place isn't in the best shape, so I think I could loosen a couple stones, and"—he glanced over at my waist, then looked back at the width between one bar and the window frame—"I think you could just squeeze through."

I leaned forward, poking my head through the bars and looking at the sheer drop many stories below to the muddy banks. The image of Kennet falling to his death flashed through my mind, and I looked away, hoping to stop the replay.

"Maybe, but then what?" I asked as I stepped back from the window. "I'll die on the way down."

"You can climb. There's grooves between the stones." Konstantin peered down. "If you climbed out carefully and went slowly, I think you could do it."

"Even if I can, what would you do?" I asked. "I'd probably just barely be able to squeeze through, and you're much broader than I am. You wouldn't be able to make it."

He turned back to me and shrugged. "So?"

"So?" I scoffed. "How will you get out of here?"

"I won't," he replied simply. "I'm the one that suggested we come here and got us into this. We don't both need to rot in this tower until the end of time."

I shook my head. "We'll come up with something so we can both get out of here together. I'm not leaving without you."

His mouth hung open for a moment, like he wanted to argue with me, but there was something in his eyes—a mixture of surprise and admiration—that stopped him. He seemed stunned that I meant what I said, and in all honesty, so was I.

I'd spent years plotting my revenge against him, and now I had a chance to leave him behind to suffer, and I wouldn't do it. I *couldn't* do it. After everything that had happened, and everything we had been through, I realized that Konstantin Black had somehow become my friend, and I wasn't going to let anything bad happen to him if I could help it.

The locks on the door started to creak, and we both turned

our attention back to the door. The heavy wood slowly pushed inward, and Bekk Vallin came in, carrying black fabric in her arms.

"The Queen has agreed to meet with you for breakfast," Bekk said, and she tossed the clothes at me. "She wishes for you to get changed and ready yourself for the meal, and I will come back and get you when she's ready to receive you."

"Thank you," I said. Bekk simply nodded and left, locking the door behind her again.

I set the clothes on the bed to see what she'd brought us, and the clothes smelled musty and looked worn, with holes and threads coming loose. My outfit was a black dress with a corset waist, off-the-shoulder sleeves, and a large ball gown skirt. It looked like something someone might've worn to a Gothic wedding. And then they'd been buried in it for a few months.

Konstantin's outfit was about the same—a worn black suit with a Victorian flare to it. He changed before I did—slipping off his muddy clothes and pulling on the new ones while I had my back to him. When he'd finished, he came over to help me lace up the corset in the back of the dress.

"I feel like Dracula or something," he said, looking down at himself. "But after he's been staked." He sighed. "There's still time for you to escape instead."

"No, we're doing this," I told him firmly. "It's our only chance of making things right. We have to get the Queen on our side."

carnivorous

A big black beetle scurried across the long wooden table, running directly toward the fried rabbit carcass in the center, and Helge Otäck walked over and smashed it with his fist. One might have expected him to wipe the mess off the dining table, but instead he left it and returned to his place standing behind Queen Bodil.

It felt like Konstantin and I had somehow slipped into a bizarro world, where everything was like a twisted version of troll culture, and nothing was quite right.

To start with, the dining hall was a rather small square room with no windows. It wasn't nearly as mossy or moldy as our room had been, but it was still dank. In compensation for the lack of windows, two large tapestries were hung on the wall, and they appeared to be depicting rather brutal Omte battles that I wasn't familiar with. The edges were frayed and coming loose, and I saw a huge brown spider crawling across one.

Two iron chandeliers hung from the ceiling, both of them lit with candles, and there were four torches on the wall. It seemed like overkill for such a small space, but the interior still ended up somewhat dim.

Like most meals I went to with royals, there was a massive spread of food covering the large table. Unlike every other meal I had been to, this one had lots of meat. Trolls weren't exactly vegetarian, and the Skojare especially had a fondness for fish. But we didn't eat it very often, preferring fruits, vegetables, whole grains, and some dairy, because everything else tended not to sit well with us.

But apparently the Omte felt differently. One platter was overflowing with whole crawfish, and I swear that I saw one of them still moving. Another had leathery soft-boiled alligator eggs on it, which the Queen insisted were delicious, but the thought of them made my stomach roll.

Four whole fried rabbits sat on a platter. Their heads were still on, which was especially unnerving, and I couldn't help but feel it was meant to be some kind of message for us as Kanin.

The only things that seemed edible were a bowl of figs and blackberries, but even they didn't look that good, thanks to the platters everything was served on. They were oxidized and dirty-looking, and despite my earlier appetite, I no longer wanted to eat anything here.

Queen Bodil Elak sat at the other end of the table from us, happily loading up her plate. On the back of her chair perched a large black-bearded vulture she'd introduced as Gam.

Bodil was only a little bit taller than me, making her small by Omte standards, and she was very pretty. Her long dark waves of hair were pulled up into a braided updo, and her gown looked similar to mine, although hers was in much better shape.

Her crown sat crookedly on her head, in large part because it looked like it had been bent many times, and given what I knew about the Omte, I imagined that it had been thrown against the wall on more than one occasion. It was a thick bronze, twisted around in an attempt to look ornate, but it reminded me more of an ambitious child's art project.

She wore a necklace adorned with large gemstones, along with several gaudy rings and a bracelet. All the gems appeared to be imperial topaz, an expensive amber-colored stone. And these were all very large rocks she had.

For her part, Bodil hadn't said much to us, other than insisting that the alligator eggs were delicious. It was her Viceroy, Helge Otäck, who had done most of the talking. He stood directly behind her, not eating anything, and he'd made all the introductions. He appeared much older than Bodil, probably in his fifties, but it was hard to gauge for sure because of how leathery and worn his skin looked.

Large and brutish, there was something very imposing about Helge. His scraggly light brown hair went down to his shoulders, and he wore just as much jewelry as the Queen. His eyes were the color of burnt caramel, and they were much too small for his face.

Along with the Viceroy and Queen, the young Prince Furston was here. He couldn't have been more than five, and despite the fact that a place was set for him, he hadn't sat down once. Instead he ran around the room, his dark brown curls bobbing as he laughed and squealed, and he'd grab whatever he wanted from the platters, preferring to eat on the go, apparently.

"Go ahead, eat," Bodil said in a way that sounded much more like an order than a suggestion. She stood up and reached over, roughly ripping off a leg from one of the rabbits, then sat back down. So far she'd eaten her entire meal with her hands.

"Yes, of course." Konstantin stood up first, serving himself an alligator egg and some fruit, before dishing up a similar plate for me.

"Thank you," I mumbled softly when he handed me my plate.

I took a sip of the eldvatten they'd poured for us in heavy chalices. It smelled like turpentine, but it didn't really have a flavor, unless "burning" and "fire" could be describe as tastes. I did my best to keep my expression even instead of gagging, and set the cup back on the table.

"So what brings you all here?" Helge asked, smiling in a way that reminded me of a viper.

"We've come to offer you information, and ask if you might be of some help," Konstantin said carefully.

As Bodil tore into the rabbit leg, ripping the meat off with her teeth, the vulture squawked and flapped his wings. She finished the leg quickly, then tossed the bone up to the bird, who caught it easily in his beak. Gam swallowed the bone whole, the brown feathers of his head and neck ruffling as he did.

"What information do you have?" Bodil asked, licking her fingers clean.

"Bent Stum," Konstantin said. "He was a member of your kingdom."

Furston suddenly darted over to me and grabbed a fig off my plate. Food already stained his face, and he laughed in delight before running away again.

"Bent was exiled over a year ago, and last we heard, he was dead," Helge said. "I'm not sure what information you have that could be useful to us."

"We know who killed him," I said.

"Furston, come sit with Mommy." Bodil held her hands out toward him, and the little boy ran toward her. She pulled him onto her lap, and he settled into the folds of her dress, quieting down for the first time since we'd gotten here.

"Do tell," Helge said, still smiling that reptilian smile of his.

"Viktor Dålig," I explained, lying to streamline the story. Viktor had ordered the hit on Bent, and while it hadn't been his hand on the sword, it might as well have been. "He's a sworn enemy of the Kanin, and he killed Bent to prevent anyone from finding out his plans of attack. He recruited Bent, used him up, and then killed him."

Helge inhaled through his nose. "That's unfortunate, but that's the path Bent chose when he left us."

"He didn't leave us," Bodil corrected him, giving him a hard look from the corner of her eye. "We exiled him."

Helge's smile had finally fallen away. "Bent broke the rules. He wouldn't fall in line."

"I told you when we exiled him that this could happen." Bodil ignored him and held her son closer to her. "It left him vulnerable to forces worse than he is, like this Viktor Dålig."

"My Queen, we've already discussed the matter. Bent wouldn't abide by the rules, and we must have order," Helge said. "And besides, we don't know if they're exaggerating about this Viktor Dålig. He may not have had anything to do with Bent's death. The Skojare said it was suicide."

"The Skojare were misled," Konstantin said. "I was there. I know Viktor did it." Helge glared at him, and one corner of his lip pulled up in an angry snarl.

"I believe him," Bodil decided. "Bent was my sister's son. He was strong-willed and arrogant, and he'd never have killed himself. I told you that when we heard the news. None of it made sense, and you wouldn't listen to me. Now we need to clean up the mess we've made."

As furtively as I could, I exchanged a look with Konstantin of pleasant surprise. With only limited communication between the Omte and the Kanin, I knew next to nothing of the royal family. In Ridley's conversations with the Queen after the initial incident in Chicago with Bent and Konstantin, she hadn't let on that she had a connection to him, but that was typical for the Omte. They were a very secretive people.

Now that I knew that Bent was so closely related to the Queen, it boded well for our plan to enlist the Omte to help us.

Helge bent over, lowering his voice when he spoke. "Perhaps now isn't the best time to talk about this."

"My sister will never forgive me for what happened to Bent, but maybe there's still time for me to make it right," the Queen said, turning to us. "Do you know where this Viktor Dålig is?"

"Not his exact location, but he's near Doldastam, planning an attack on the Kanin," Konstantin said.

Bodil narrowed her eyes behind her long lashes. "So that's what you wanted from us? To help you stop him from attacking?"

I nodded. "Yes. I thought we might share an enemy, and we could work together."

"As strong as you are, even sending a few of your people would do irrevocable damage to Viktor and his men," Konstantin elaborated.

"Why do you care what happens to the Kanin?" She shook her head, not understanding. "You've been banished."

"Everyone I love is still in Doldastam. I don't want them hurt or killed," I told her honestly.

For a few moments, the room was filled with a tense silence as Bodil considered what I'd said. The vulture ruffled his feathers, and a crawfish crawled free from the platter, moving slowly onto the table.

"All right," Bodil said finally. "We'll help you."

"My Queen, this Viktor Dålig has an army." Helge was nearly shouting his protests. "We don't need to get in the middle of the Kanin's fight."

"He killed Bent. No one gets away with killing one of our own," Queen Bodil said firmly. Her strong jaw was set, and her dark eyes were filled with resolve. "We must be the ones that punish him."

TWELVE

distrust

As Bekk led us up the long, winding staircase to our room,
I lifted the length of my skirt to keep from tripping
and tumbling to my death. I had to be careful because I'd
smuggled a few figs in it, since I had no idea when we would
eat again.

The Queen had directed us to wait in our room while she
consulted with the Viceroy and other advisers to come up
with a plan of attack. Helge had made it abundantly clear that
he thought we'd be waiting a long while.

"How did your meeting go?" Bekk asked, looking over her
shoulder at Konstantin and me.

"It went well, I believe," Konstantin said, but he didn't
sound very confident.

I gave him a curious look. "It was better than I expected,
actually."

"Me too." He met my gaze. "That's what makes me nervous."

"What exactly did you want from the Queen?" Bekk asked when we reached the landing. "If you don't mind me asking."

I looked over at Konstantin, who gave a noncommittal shrug. "I suppose if the Queen goes through with it, you'll find out anyway," I decided. "We asked for her help in fighting off Viktor Dålig."

The smooth skin of Bekk's brow furrowed. "I've heard that name before." She looked away, thinking. "I can't remember where, but it's definitely familiar."

"Maybe you've seen him on WANTED posters," I suggested, since she'd seen me on one. "He's been the Kanin's number one enemy for fifteen years."

"Maybe," Bekk agreed, but without much conviction. "Anyway, why do you think the Queen would help you with that?"

"Because he killed her nephew," Konstantin replied.

Bekk nodded. "And she agreed to it, then?"

"She said she would send people with us to help fight Viktor Dålig," I explained. "She's just deciding who and how many."

"For what it's worth, I'd be glad to go with you," Bekk said. "To see something outside of these walls, and to fight any enemy that's hurt our people. It would be a great privilege."

"Thank you." I smiled. "We'd be more than happy to have you."

She smiled thinly, then motioned for us to go back into our cell. When we were inside, Bekk paused before closing the door.

"We're a good people," she said. "But we're a temperamental people. We mean well, but we can't always be trusted. That's something you have to keep in mind."

I wanted to ask her what she meant by that, but I didn't think she'd really expound on it. She closed the door, leaving Konstantin and me standing in the middle of the room, and the locks clicked loudly.

Konstantin took his jacket off and tossed it on the bed. "Something doesn't feel right."

"What do you mean?" I went over to the sink and set my figs in it, since it seemed like the only clean place to store them.

"I don't know." He shook his head. "There's just something . . ." He trailed off and then lay back on the bed, letting out an exasperated sigh.

"Bodil seemed on board with everything." I went over and knelt on the bed beside him. "That Helge guy seems like a total snake, but I think she'll insist on sending at least a few men, and that will be enough for us to make a dent in Viktor's army. We might even be able to stop them before they get to Doldastam.

"Then, of course, all we have to do is get back and somehow get rid of Mina, but that's another problem for another day. We need to take all of this one step at a time," I said.

"You're right," he relented, but he still sounded defeated.

When he looked up at me, he seemed so forlorn. His gray eyes had never looked so soft and sad before.

The sleeves of my gown fell just off the shoulder, revealing the scar on my left shoulder, and he reached up and touched it. An odd shiver went through me as he traced his finger along the thin ridge.

"That's from me, isn't it?" he asked thickly.

I nodded. "Yes."

"I'm sorry, white rabbit." He ran his fingers down the scar to my collarbone, and it made my breath catch in my throat, then he dropped his hand. "I never wanted to hurt you."

"Why would you care if you hurt me?" I asked, forcing a smile. "You didn't even know me then."

The night Konstantin had attempted to kill my dad had been four long years ago. I'd only been a fifteen-year-old kid in tracker school, while he was older and a member of the elite Högdragen. We'd moved in entirely different circles, and I wasn't sure he even knew my name when he stabbed through the shoulder.

"You looked so hopeful that night. Your eyes were so wide and so blue when I talked to you." He smiled, looking both pained and wistful. "The whole world belonged to you for a moment."

It actually had been an amazing night. I'd felt drunk on happiness, and talking to Konstantin had added to that. Of course, that was before everything came crashing down.

His smile had fallen away. "And the look on your face when you saw me with your father . . . I broke your heart."

"I . . ." I started to argue, but it was then that I realized it was true. He had broken my heart. I swallowed hard and looked away.

"Why that night?" I asked. "Why did you have to do that when I was there?"

"Mina had been asking me to do it for weeks, and I had an opportunity." He hesitated before adding, "I almost didn't go through with it, and I think honestly my attempt was half-hearted. That's why your father was still alive when you walked in."

"You knew it was wrong," I said. "How could you do it at all?"

"I loved her, and I would do anything she asked." He breathed deeply. "But that can't be love, can it?"

"I'm not sure that I'm the one you should be asking. I've never been very good at love."

He sat up, moving closer to me. He used one arm to prop himself up, and his hand was resting right next to my thigh. "I know I can't get absolution. I don't deserve it. But do you think that I'll ever be able to make up for the things I've done?"

"I don't know," I admitted, meeting his gaze even though that made it hard for me breathe. "But I forgive you."

"You don't have to do that," he said softly.

"I know. But I want to."

He lowered his eyes, and abruptly, I got up. The air felt too thick, and I'd become acutely aware of the intensity of his proximity. I went over to the window, putting my back to him and breathing in the fresh air. And I wondered with mixed emotions how much longer Konstantin and I would be trapped in this room.

longing

I woke up with Konstantin's arm draped over me. I didn't know how or when he'd put it there, but there it was— strong and sure around my waist. Carefully and quietly, so I didn't wake him, I slid out from underneath it and got up.

A full moon shone brightly in the night sky, bathing our cell in white light. Konstantin slept in just his boxers with a thin sheet over him, since the heat had gotten even more oppressive. I'd only worn my tank top and panties to bed, but I'd tried to keep distance between us. It hadn't worked, apparently.

I stood next to the window, for a moment watching Konstantin sleep. His curls lying around his face, his dark lashes fluttering as he dreamt, his well-muscled bare torso— it was impossible to deny that Konstantin was a handsome man, especially when he was sleeping.

But something about this moment made me think of

Ridley, and how I'd snuck out of bed that cold night when all I'd wanted was to stay in bed with him forever. And despite whatever feelings Konstantin seemed to bring up in me, I still felt that way. I still wanted to be with Ridley more than anything.

The very thought of him made my heart ache. I missed him terribly, and I had no way of knowing if he was safe. If Mina was as insane as Konstantin made her sound, she could've locked Ridley up forever.

I knew that we needed to be here now, getting the Omte to help us put a stop to Viktor's army, but the second that was over, I needed to get back to Doldastam. I didn't care what it meant for me, but I would do whatever it took to make sure Ridley was safe.

My jeans lay on the floor in a rumpled pile, and I brushed a cockroach off them. I crouched down in the moonlight and pulled the TracFone out of my pocket. The battery was nearly dead, since it hadn't been charged while we'd been here and I'd used quite a bit of battery life on the flashlight.

It was after midnight, and according to the clock, that made it Friday, May 16. It had been over a week since I'd left Doldastam, since I'd last seen Ridley. Would it be safe enough to call? And it was in the middle of the night. Who would be monitoring his calls now?

I bit my lip, staring down at the flashing battery on the screen, and debating what I should do. All I wanted was to hear his voice, to know that he was okay.

And then without thinking, I started dialing a number I

had dialed hundreds of times before when I had been on missions. At that moment, the consequences didn't seem to matter. I just needed him.

I held the phone up to my ear, listening desperately. It seemed to take forever until I heard the sound of ringing—faint and tinny. I closed my eyes, and in my mind I was begging Ridley to pick up.

But instead of Ridley's voice I heard a despondent beep. I held the phone out, looking at it. The call had been dropped, and the message below the date warned me there was no service. I'd barely had a bar when I'd dialed in the first place, but I'd hoped that would be enough.

Now, staring at the useless phone in my hands, I wanted to scream or throw it against the wall. But I didn't want to wake up Konstantin and explain what exactly had me so upset.

So I lowered my head against my chest and wrapped my arms around my head and took deep breaths. My whole body was trembling, and my chest felt like it had been ripped out. I squeezed my arms tighter, trying to literally hold myself together.

The locks on the door started to click open, and I nearly did scream then. I jumped to my feet, and I saw that Konstantin had done the same—throwing off his covers and leaping out of bed. We were ready for whatever was coming our way.

Since Bekk had delivered us back to the room after we'd had our meeting, we'd had no visitors. I'd been right about taking the figs, or else we would've had nothing else to eat for the day.

And now someone was coming in, in the middle of the night.

I saw the orange flame of the torch before I saw the figure coming in behind it. He had to bow down to get in the door, but as soon as he straightened up, it became clear that it was Helge Otäck, the Viceroy.

"It's time for you to go," Helge said with that serpentine smile.

"What?" I glanced over at Konstantin. "Are the men the Queen is sending ready to go?"

"No, I'm afraid you won't be taking any men with you," Helge continued calmly. "The Queen spoke in haste today, and she's changed her mind about everything. So it's best for you to get out of here, since her hospitality has run dry."

"But the Queen—" I started to argue.

"The Queen wants you to go," Helge snapped. "And if you don't leave on your own, I'll get Torun and he can make you go." He smiled wider then, revealing his jagged teeth, and I had a feeling that he'd get a great deal of enjoyment from watching Torun tear Konstantin and me apart.

"Bryn," Konstantin whispered, probably sensing that I wanted to continue fighting with Helge anyway. "We need to go."

And since there wasn't anything more that we could say, Konstantin and I gathered our clothes and fled in the middle of the night, like prisoners making a break for it.

repossess

We'd sprung for the Holiday Inn, since we both needed a place where we could feel clean after our time in Fulaträsk. After we had made our way through the wetlands, Konstantin had driven for hours before we stopped, on the off chance that the Omte decided to give chase.

"It just doesn't make sense," I said for the hundredth time as I paced the room.

"It doesn't have to make sense. They're the Omte!" Konstantin was growing exasperated at having the same conversation with me. "Bekk even said they couldn't be trusted."

"But Bodil wanted to do this!" I insisted. "I know she did. The Queen was for it. It's her stupid Viceroy that interfered."

"That's probably true," Konstantin admitted. He rummaged through his duffel bag, tossing clean clothes on the bed beside him. "Since you seem too worked up to shower, I'll go first."

"Why would Helge talk her out of it, though?" I asked. "And did he even talk her out of it? Maybe the Queen was still for it, and that's why he made us leave in the middle of the night. We should've fought him."

"And what if he'd brought Torun up?" Konstantin turned to look at me. "What then? We'll somehow bring down Viktor's army after we've been torn limb from limb?"

"I don't know!" I stopped pacing and let my shoulders sag. "Why did Helge do that?"

"Because he was right." He walked over to me with his clothes in hand. "This isn't the Omte's fight—it's the Kanin's. They have no reason to risk their people for somebody else's fight."

"But—" I started to protest.

"It's just how it is, Bryn. We'll have to come up with something else." He put a hand on my shoulder to comfort me. "We'll figure it out, though."

"How?" I asked him plaintively.

"I don't know. We will, though," he assured me. "But first, I'm showering."

He left me alone in the main room and went into the bathroom. As soon as I heard the water running, I swore loudly, and then flopped back on one of the two beds. I closed my eyes and tried to think about where we could go from here.

If we went to the Vittra or the Trylle, they would just hold us captive until the Kanin could come retrieve us for a trial.

They were close allies, and since the Kanin had the largest army, they wanted to keep the alliances.

The Skojare were out of the question. With everything so crazy there, they wouldn't be able to help us at all, even if they wanted to.

There might be other expatriate trolls we could team up with, but it wasn't like I could post an ad on craigslist saying, "Troll seeking other trolls to combat evil troll army."

I opened my eyes when something occurred to me. How had Bent Stum gotten mixed up with Konstantin and Viktor? Bodil had made Bent sound like he was rebellious, but I doubted he wanted to attack the Kanin. At least not without an incentive from somebody else.

So how did Viktor enlist him?

That would be something I'd have to have a discussion about with Konstantin when he got out of the shower, but all my plans were interrupted when his duffel bag began ringing.

At first I thought it might be my phone, and my heart skipped a beat. But then I realized it was coming from his things, so I got up to check it out. His cell was sitting right on top of his bag, and the screen said BLOCKED CALLER, but I hadn't really expected any different for someone like Konstantin.

I glanced over at the bathroom, where the shower had just turned off. It would be easy to knock on the door and hand Konstantin the phone. But we were friends now, and allies. There shouldn't be secrets between us anyway.

Amanda Hocking

With that justification in mind, I answered the phone and grunted hello in as deep a voice as I could muster.

"It's done," came the gravelly reply.

Before I could say anything, the bathroom door opened, and Konstantin came out wearing only a towel around his waist. When he saw me holding his phone up to my ear, he rushed over and snatched it from me.

"Hello?" he said, casting an uneasy glare at me. "Sorry. I have bad reception here." He paused. "Okay. Thanks for letting me know."

And that was it. He hung up the phone and turned his attention to me. "What the hell were you thinking, Bryn? You could've gotten us both killed!"

"Why?" I demanded. "And who was that? What's done?" He turned away, so I grabbed his shoulder, forcing him to look at me.

"It was Viktor," Konstantin said, exhaling deeply. "Evert Strinne is dead."

FIFTEEN

notify

May 16, 2014

The King is dead.

Even writing the words, it still feels so unreal. King Evert Strinne is dead.

They announced it yesterday. He died in the early hours, just after dawn. The Queen says he was murdered, and everyone is in a panic.

This is the first moment I've had to sit and collect my thoughts about all of this, and I just have no idea what to think.

Murmurs around town are saying poison. Linus Berling told me his father had heard the King's lips were stained black from it. They'd been slipping it in his drink for over a week, and it finally took hold.

That explains how out of sorts the King seemed at Kasper's funeral. But that just leads to a much bigger, darker question—who exactly are "they"? The Queen says that we have a mole in our midst, but she'll root them out.

"We must be on guard always." That's what she said when she announced his death, perched on the balcony of the clock tower in the town square. Speaking to us all between tears while we all stared up at her anxiously, wondering what the fate of our kingdom will be.

And how can we be on guard any more than we already are? The Högdragen are everywhere, but they're not making us feel any safer. In fact, with them always watching, I feel even more vulnerable.

What if I accidentally do something and they think I'm the mole now?

In training today, I heard a few rumblings of your name, that you might somehow be behind all of this. I was quick to tell them to shut the hell up. You weren't even here. It's not even possible. And I know you would never do anything like this anyway.

The whole town is running scared, though. We're all eyeing up our neighbors. Are they the enemy? Do they know who poisoned the King?

Delilah came over last night. She didn't even care if anyone saw her. She was scared, and she needed to feel safe. So she came to me.

I held her in my arms for a long time, telling her that it would all be okay, when I wasn't so sure that it would be anymore. But she looks at me with those eyes of hers. (And those eyes, Bryn—they're unlike anything I've ever seen, dark chocolate and so big, I could get lost in them for days, and I wish I could, I wish I could just hold her and look at her, but there isn't time for that.) Everything is so royally fucked right now.

I've been thinking that you might be the lucky one because you're not here. The town is on lockdown. No one can leave or come back. There's a curfew. (But that worked to my advantage last night, because Delilah couldn't go home or she'd risk getting brought in for questioning, so she spent the night with me.)

You would be going crazy if you were here. That's something that you can take comfort in, at least. You're avoiding all the madness.

Today, the Queen appointed a new Chancellor to take your father's place. She said this isn't the proper time for an election, but with everything that's happening, they need someone doing the job.

There should've been an uproar. The Queen removed the people's only voice in our political process by cutting out the election. But nobody made a peep. We've all just accepted our fate.

In slightly better news, your parents are fine—they're making do with your father's pension, which the kingdom is apparently still paying. For now. Tilda is holding up okay. Or as well as one would expect given the circumstances.

Oh! I do have good news for you!

Tilda and I were walking through the town square this

morning to get breakfast. (I try to get her out of her apartment at least once a day.) I saw Ridley on the other side of the square, walking through a crowd.

He didn't look well, I'll be honest with you, but he was free. He was walking without guards. I called his name and waved to him, but he never looked my way. I wanted to run over to him, but Tilda stopped me.

"He heard you, Ember. I don't think he wants to be noticed right now," she said.

But she promised me that she would stop by his place tonight.

I just can't wait for this all to be over.

The snow has been melting, and it's been doing this weird cold drizzle thing all day. All the posters they'd had up were getting destroyed by the elements, so the Högdragen were out replacing them. The good news is that they took down the WANTED *posters of you.*

The bad news is that they replaced them with a reward being offered for anyone who knows anything in connection to the King's death. With the King being dead, he can't always be watching us anymore, so they replaced those with black and white posters of Queen Mina, looking twice as severe as Evert ever did.

The only thing it says is I AM ALWAYS WATCHING YOU, *but somehow I believe it more than I did the King.*

> *Your friend (no matter what),*
> *Ember*

duplicity

For a moment, there was only the shock of hearing that the King was dead.

To someone outside of the troll community, it would be hard to explain what it felt like to learn that the King was dead. The best I can come up with is to find out that the President and your favorite pop star had been killed at the same time, along with the Pope and the Queen of England.

It's this mixture of impossibility—even though Kings die all the time, they still have this bizarre sense of immortality to them. Then there's the reverence and loyalty. Despite our differences, Evert was *my* King, and I had sworn to protect him.

The wind felt like it had been knocked out of me, and I actually had to hold on to the dresser for support.

"Bryn?" Konstantin asked, moving closer to catch me if I needed it. "Are you okay?"

And that was enough to snap me out of it. I glared up at him, and there must've been something harsh in my eyes because Konstantin took a step back.

"Why is Viktor still calling you?" I asked, my voice a low hiss. "Why did he think you'd want to know that the King was dead?"

"I told you that I'd defected, and that's true." He hesitated. "But they don't know it yet."

"You lying asshole!" I shouted at him. "How could I have been stupid enough to trust you?"

"Bryn, it's not like that."

I turned away from him to start packing my bag. "Don't try to sell me your shit anymore, Konstantin. I'm not buying it."

"I did it to protect you!" he insisted.

I looked back at him in disbelief. "Fuck you." And then I couldn't control my rage anymore, so I lunged at him.

He grabbed my wrist before I could hit, and when I tried to kick him, he grabbed my other wrist and pushed me back, slamming me into the wall harder than he needed to. He held me there like that, pinning my wrists beside my head, and his body pressed against me, still wet from the shower.

"Let go of me," I growled, too angry to think properly about how to get out of the hold. I just wanted to hit *something,* preferably his handsome face.

"No! You have to calm down and listen to me!"

"I don't have to do anything you tell me!" I shot back.

"Bryn!" Konstantin yelled in exasperation. "Just listen to me for five minutes, and I'll let you go, and then you can do whatever the hell you want."

I grimaced and fought against his grip. His legs were pressed against mine in a way that made it impossible for me to kick. So I finally relented, since I didn't have a choice.

"Viktor sent me to find you and kill you," Konstantin explained. "He thinks you know too much about what's going on, and if you find someone that might believe you, he and Mina are screwed."

"So when are you planning on killing me?" I asked.

"I already told you—if I was going to kill you, I would've done it by now," he said, meeting my gaze evenly. "I went after you to keep you safe and because I didn't want to keep doing what they were doing. I'm done with Viktor and his men, but if I tell them that, he'll send people after us both and kill us. You can't just quit Viktor's army."

I pursed my lips, hating that his reasoning sounded plausible. "Why didn't you tell me this before?"

"I didn't think you'd believe me. Was I wrong?"

I looked away from him, considering everything he'd said. "I listened. Now will you let me go?"

"Fine." He sighed, then let go of me and stepped back. He stood with his hands on his hips, watching and waiting to see what I'd do.

"Who killed the King?" I asked, rubbing my wrists.

"Viktor didn't say, but I would assume that Mina did."

"How?"

"He didn't say that either, but when they'd spoken of it before, poison had been their top choice."

"Why did Viktor think you wanted to know?"

"I've kind of been his right-hand man. He's kept me apprised of everything."

I arched an eyebrow. "So when everything big is about to go down, he sent you out on an errand?"

"It was supposed to be quick. He thought I'd be back by now."

I walked closer to him, stopping so I was nearly touching him, and I looked up at him. "What does he think you're doing now?"

"Tracking you. I told him that you've been very elusive."

"And he believes you?" I asked.

"For now." He paused. "But he won't for much longer."

"What happens then?"

"He'll send men to kill us."

"So what do we do?" I asked.

"*We?*" A soft smile touched his lips. "Does that mean you trust me?"

I sighed. "I don't have much of a choice, do I?" I moved away from him and sat back down on the bed. "So what is our plan? Where do we go from here?"

"We keep moving. We can't sit still." He motioned to the bathroom. "You should shower, and then we should get out of here."

SEVENTEEN

summoned

From the window of our room, I could see the mountains behind us. Since Konstantin had gotten the phone call, we'd been driving nearly nonstop for over twenty-four hours until we finally stopped at a bed and-breakfast in Wyoming.

Konstantin had insisted on driving most of the way, so he crashed as soon as we'd checked in—sprawled out on top of the covers on the bed. It was a small room with a kitschy western feel, but it wasn't bad. Besides, we didn't need a credit card to check in, and the less of a paper trail we had, the better.

Between using a card at the Holiday Inn and our interlude with the Omte, Konstantin felt especially paranoid that Viktor would be able to find us if he wanted to.

On the long drive, I'd tried to talk about what to do next, but Konstantin seemed unable to think of anything beyond "get away right away."

And truthfully, I didn't know what to do or where to go from here. With Konstantin sound asleep, I decided to go outside to get some fresh air and think.

The bed-and-breakfast held eight rooms, and it was a quiet place. There was a wraparound porch with a few rocking chairs facing a magnificent view of the mountains. It was a bit chilly out—only in the fifties and breezy—so I had it all to myself, and I sat on one of the chairs, crossing my legs underneath me.

I still wasn't sure if I should trust Konstantin, but without him, I was completely alone and isolated with Viktor's men and Kanin scouts after me. With Konstantin, I wasn't much better off, but he knew a few more things than I did, and at least he was here.

One thing I did know for sure was that I couldn't stay on the run like this, not for much longer. Running wasn't accomplishing anything. Konstantin would argue that it was keeping us alive, and he was right, but to what end? What was the point of doing this if it meant constantly moving and looking over our shoulders everywhere we went?

Beyond that, I knew that with the King dead, things in Doldastam had to be descending into chaos. That was just what Mina wanted so she could be the one to save them. But only after she got rid of anyone who stood in her way. Things were only going to get worse before they got better—*if* they got better.

If Mina was willing to do all these awful things to those who loved her, like Konstantin and Evert, then what kind of monarch could she possibly be? She was vindictive, greedy, and remorseless. The kingdom could only suffer under her rule.

I rocked slowly in the chair, feeling the warmth of the sun, and wondering what my fate might be, when my pocket began to vibrate. It took me a few seconds to realize that my phone was ringing. I scrambled to get it out before it went to voice mail, and saw that it was an unknown caller.

I debated not answering it for a second, but then I realized that if Viktor Dålig or Mina had somehow gotten this number, I was already in deep crap whether I took the call or not. So I went for it.

"Hello?" I answered, feeling a little out of breath.

The caller waited a beat before saying, "Bryn?"

Relief washed over me so intensely I nearly cried, but I held it back. "Ridley."

"It is you, thank god it's you," he breathed in one hurried sentence. "When I saw the missed call on my phone, I thought it had to be you."

"How are you?" I asked. "How is everything?"

"Everything is . . . not good." He sounded pained. "Everything's falling apart, Bryn. I'm calling from a phone that Ember got me, and I don't think they can trace it. They shouldn't, since they don't know it exists. I had to talk to you. I had to know that you're okay. Are you okay? Are you somewhere safe?"

"Yeah, I'm safe. I'm okay. But what happened after I left? Are you all right?"

He hesitated for so long I was afraid that the call might've dropped. "I don't want to talk about that now."

My heart sank, and I felt like throwing up. "Ridley, I'm so sorry. I never meant to get you in trouble."

"No, don't be sorry. I did what I had to do to protect you, and I would do it again," he said. "And I'm fine now."

"Are you really? Promise me that you're okay."

"I'm okay. I am." He sighed. "I mean, I'm as okay as anyone else in Doldastam." He paused. "The King is dead."

I thought about lying to him, but I didn't want to lie to Ridley. Not now, not ever. "I know."

"You know?" The tension amped up his voice. "What do you mean, you know? How?"

"It doesn't matter." I brushed him off, because explaining Konstantin seemed like too much.

"Of course it matters!" Ridley was nearly yelling.

"Ridley, I just know, okay? Let that be enough for right now."

"Fine," he relented. "I can't talk long, and I don't want to spend this time arguing with you. I just called to tell you that you need to go to Förening and see the Trylle."

"What? Why? They're allies of the Kanin. They'll arrest me on sight."

"No, I don't think they will," Ridley said. "Ember talked to her brother, and he thinks that you might be able to sway the King and Queen into granting you amnesty."

"That's a huge risk to take. I can't end up back in the dungeons of Doldastam. They won't let me out of there alive."

"I know, but Ember seems convinced that the Trylle are your best hope. Her brother says that the Queen has granted amnesty before," he said. "And I know it's not safe for you out there, on the road alone like that. You need to get somewhere where you're protected."

"Okay," I said finally. "If it's what you think is best."

"I do." He breathed deeply. "I should get going, though."

"So soon?" I asked, hating that I could hear the desperation in my voice.

"Yeah. I can't raise any suspicions right now," he said huskily. "But it was worth it to hear your voice." He paused. "I miss you."

"I miss you too."

"Be safe, okay?" he asked, sounding pained again.

"You too, Ridley. Don't do anything dangerous."

"I won't if you won't," he said, laughing softly. "Good bye, Bryn."

"Good-bye, Ridley."

I kept the phone to my ear long after it had gone silent, as if I'd be able to hear him after he'd ended the call. Talking to Ridley had somehow left me feeling more heartbroken and yet rejuvenated all at once. I missed him so much, and I hated it that I couldn't be there with him and that I didn't know what he was going through.

But now at least I knew that he was alive and okay, and he'd given me a direction. I had to reach the Trylle.

parting

I can drive," I offered, not for the first time. The journey from our bed-and-breakfast in Wyoming to the Trylle capital of Förening on the bluffs of the Mississippi River was over twelve hours, and so far Konstantin had driven all of it.

"I took this car so I could drive it," Konstantin said, and pressed his foot down on the gas of the Mustang, pushing it over eighty to prove his point.

"I'm just saying. If you need me, I'm here." I sat slouched down in the seat with my bare feet on the dash and stared out the window at the world flying by.

He softened and let the speedometer fall back a bit. "I'm used to doing things on my own."

"Yeah, I've kinda figured that out."

"Are you sure that the Trylle will give you amnesty?" Konstantin asked, retreading a conversation we'd had a dozen times since I'd told him about Ridley's phone call.

"No, I'm not sure. But I trust that Ridley and Ember wouldn't send me somewhere to get hurt."

He didn't say anything right away. His lips were pressed into a thin line, and his eyes stayed fixed on the road before us. His knuckles momentarily whitened as he gripped the steering wheel tighter, then relaxed again.

"What?" I pressed, since Konstantin seemed anxious.

"Trust and love can be very dangerous things," he said finally. "I loved Mina, and I trusted her with everything, and you've seen how that worked out for me."

"Ridley and Ember are nothing like Mina." I paused as something occurred to me. "You trust me."

He glanced at me from the corner of his eye. "I do," he said, his voice low and gruff, like he hated to admit it, even to himself. "But everything's different with you."

"Yeah, I know what you mean," I agreed quietly.

I turned away to look out the window again. An odd tension settled in the car, and I felt like talking would only make it worse.

The roads became more winding, reminding me of a piece of string tangled up among the overreaching maples and evergreens. The car rolled up and down the hills along the bluffs, and between the branches I'd occasionally get a glimpse of the dark waters of the Mississippi racing along beside us.

When we reached the top of the bluffs, the road began to narrow, making it nearly impossible for more than one car to pass at a time. Fortunately, there weren't any other vehicles for us to contend with, so I didn't have to see how the Mustang would handle the sharp embankment that began right at the edge of the asphalt.

For a moment I could see the river clearly over the tops of the trees, and then the car was plunging down a steep hill, with Konstantin laying heavily on the brakes to keep us from going off the road and crashing into the trees.

The pavement leveled off a bit, and Konstantin pulled over as far to the side as it would allow and put the car in park.

"What's happening?" I looked around, searching for any sign of the Trylle palace, but it was only trees that surrounded us. "Why did you stop?"

"Förening's just up there." He motioned in front of us, but the road curved just ahead, so I couldn't see anything. "Maybe a quarter of a mile. You can walk it from here."

"I can," I agreed tentatively. "But why would I? Why aren't you driving?"

He turned to face me, a sad smile on his lips and his gray eyes hard. "I can't go with you, white rabbit."

I sighed. "I know that you don't know Ridley or Ember, and you have major trust issues, which I get, but—"

"Ridley doesn't know you're with me, does he?"

I hesitated. "No."

"And if he did, I doubt he would've suggested I go with you to Förening to ask for amnesty."

"The Queen is open to things here—" I tried again.

"Yes, but the difference between you and me is that *I* did the things I'm accused of. You didn't," he said, smiling wanly at me. "I would not fare as well there as you, and I would only hurt your case."

I pushed back my hair from my face and let out a heavy breath. For some reason, it hadn't occurred to me that Konstantin wouldn't come with me. We'd made it together this far. I thought we'd go together until the end.

"What are you gonna do?" I asked finally.

He shrugged. "I don't know. I'll figure something out. I always do."

"Will you go back to Viktor?" I asked.

"No." He shook his head with finality. "I'll do what I can to buy some time, to keep them from coming after me, but I'm not going back."

"Good."

Since there was nothing more to say, I smiled at him, and then opened the car door. Konstantin got out and walked around to the back of the car, so he could grab my duffel bag from the trunk. I went over to him, and we stood together awkwardly after he handed me my bag.

"Should we hug or something?" I asked.

Konstantin smirked. "I don't think either of us is the hugging type."

"That's true. So this is good-bye, then."

He shrugged one shoulder. "For now."

We walked back together until we reached the driver's-side door, which he'd left open. I gave him a small wave, then walked ahead down the road. The asphalt felt hot on my bare feet, but I didn't mind. Konstantin hadn't left yet, and I could feel him watching me, so I glanced back over my shoulder.

"I'll find you if you need me," he called to me, and he got into the Mustang. I made it around the curve, and then I heard his engine rev and the tires squeal as he sped off, leaving me to continue the journey on my own.

NINETEEN

compound

A massive gate blocked the road heading into the Trylle compound, not unlike the one in Doldastam. This one was shiny silver, whereas ours was made of worn iron. The guard shack appeared freshly painted sage-green, with vines growing up the side.

The guard manning the gate slid open the glass window and leaned down to get a better look at me. He wore a uniform of dark emerald, and he had eyes that nearly matched.

"This is private property," he said, not unkindly. "If you're lost, you need to head back up to the main road." Since he was Trylle, he probably wasn't used to seeing blond trolls and assumed that I was a human.

"I'm not lost," I told him. "I'm here to see Finn Holmes. He used to be a tracker, but I believe he's a guard now."

The guard pushed up the brim of his hat and narrowed his eyes at me. He scrutinized me for so long I was afraid he'd had a stroke or something, but finally, he nodded. He closed the sliding glass window, and I watched as he picked up a black phone that sat on his desk.

When he hung up, he glanced back at me, but he didn't open the window. I wasn't sure what was happening, but I knew I had no place else to be. I dropped my duffel bag on the road and I leaned against the gate, pressing my face against the cool metal so I could peer into Förening.

I spotted a few luxurious cottages, nearly hidden among the trees, all poised to take in the full view of the river below us. Knowing trolls, I was sure there were more that were camouflaged better. But still, it reminded me of an affluent gated community in northern California that I once visited while tracking a changeling. The Trylle were by far the most contemporary of the troll tribes.

My feet were sore from walking down the road, so I sat down on my duffel bag, using it like a chair, and leaned with my back resting against the bars. And I waited, and I waited some more.

Without warning, the gate groaned and started to move back. I scrambled to get to my feet before I fell over, then I turned around to see Ember's older brother Finn walking toward me. I wasn't sure what he'd been doing before I arrived, but he was dressed in black slacks, a dress shirt, and a vest. He wore variations of the same clothes every time I saw him, and I was beginning to wonder if he slept in them.

Finn walked with slow measured steps, and there was a rigidity to him that would make the Högdragen envious. His dark hair was smoothed back, and his mahogany eyes reminded me of Ember's, though hers were even darker.

"Bryn," he said, without any hint as to whether he was happy or upset to see me. He kept his expression and voice completely neutral.

"Thank you for meeting me like this," I said. "I'd heard that Ember had talked to you, and you'd agreed to help me."

"I did." He motioned for me come inside, so I grabbed my bag and walked through the gates into Förening. "How are you? Did you get here all right?"

"Yeah, I got here okay. I'm as fine as I can be."

"Good." Finn started walking ahead, so I followed alongside him. "Are you ready to see the Queen? I've told her about your arrival, and she's anxious to meet with you."

I wouldn't have minded a few minutes to gather my thoughts and get cleaned up. Especially since I was wearing jeans with holes in the knees, a tank top that showed my black bra strap, and my hair was just pulled back in a ponytail. But I also knew better than to keep royalty waiting.

"I can meet the Queen now."

"Good." Finn smiled for a moment. "She's a fair Queen, and there's no reason for you to worry."

"Thanks." I smiled back at him. "I'll try not to."

The roads inside Förening were even more winding than the ones that led to it, and it sort of felt like we were walking in circles until we finally reached the palace. Unlike many of the other troll palaces, which were designed more like castles, the Trylle palace was an opulent mansion.

Long vines grew over the three-story structure, nearly masking the bright white exterior, and the back was made entirely of windows. It sat perched on the edge of a bluff, with the back of the palace supported by beams overgrown with vines. It appeared as if it might fall off the edge and plummet into the river many feet below, but the Trylle had enough magic that I knew that would never happen.

Finn opened the grand front door, and I'd expected a footman to greet us, but the Trylle apparently had a much more help-yourself kind of operation. Inside the main hall, the floors were marble, and from the front door I could see straight through the house to the breathtaking view through the windowed back wall.

As Finn led me through the palace, I was once again reminded of the gated community in northern California and the mansions I'd seen there. The chandeliers on the ceiling, the velvet jade runner that lined the corridor, even the furnishings—it was all lavish but it was all so modern. Other than the paintings on the wall, which appeared to be of former Kings and Queens.

Finally we reached the throne room, where I'd be meeting with the Queen. Finn pushed open two massive doors with vines carved into them. I'd been here once before, when I'd visited Förening as part of a field trip in tracker school and had been given a tour of the palace. But the beauty of the throne room would never cease to impress me.

It was a circular room, with rounded walls, and the one behind the throne was made of floor-to-ceiling glass, to take in more of that stunning view. In all honesty, it felt more like an atrium with a domed skylight stretching high above. Vines grew over the ornate silver and gold designs etched on the walls, making this room feel much closer to nature than anything we had in Doldastam.

The throne sat in the center of the room, covered with lush emerald velvet, and I could've sworn that when I'd been here last, the throne had been red. It was made of platinum that swirled into latticing with bright emeralds laid into it.

Queen Wendy Staad sat in the throne, wearing a long flowing gown. The fabric was a deep evergreen, nearly black, but there was something iridescent about it, so when she moved, it would shimmer and change color.

Her dark brown curls were arranged perfectly, with one bright silver lock in the front. She appeared young, even though she was actually a few years older than me, but she had a severity about her when she smiled at me.

On either side of her there was a smaller chair fashioned in the same way as her throne. To her left was Bain Ottesen, the Trylle Chancellor I had met before in Storvatten. He was a rather slight young man with dark hair and features, so only his bright blue eyes gave away his partial Skojare heritage.

To her right was the King, Loki Staad. He sat rather casually for a King, tilting to one side and resting on his elbow, and he grinned when I entered the room. His hair was lighter than most Trylle's, and it was slightly disheveled.

"My Queen." Finn bowed slightly as he entered the room,

so I followed suit. "This is Bryn Aven of the Kanin. I told you about her."

I stepped forward and bowed again. "Thank you for taking time to meet with me."

"You've come here asking for our aid." The Queen folded her hands over her lap, and raised her chin slightly as she looked down at me. "Tell me exactly why we should do that, given that you've been charged with treason by one of our greatest allies."

TWENTY

correspond

Bryn—   May 18, 2014

I wanted to be the one to call you, but Ridley wouldn't let me. He said it's too dangerous, and even though I know it's true, I still wish I'd been able to actually talk to you.

Maybe I can soon though. If the Trylle give you amnesty. But they have to, right? Finn promised he'd help you. I know Queen Wendy has gotten stricter over the past few years. (Finn says that the battle with the Vittra changed something in her.) But you need help, and she has to see that. She has to be fair.

I say that as if anything in life is fair or right. After what happened to Ridley . . . I mean, I don't even know what happened with Ridley. Ever since he came back, he's been strange. He won't talk about anything. Tilda says I push too much and I need to just let him be but I just want to know that he's okay.

The funeral for the King was this morning. It was held inside the ballroom in the palace, and it was standing room only with people spilling out into the street. People turned out from other Kanin communities, but Queen Mina wouldn't let them in. She said that they could be spies for Viktor's army, so they had to wait outside the gates of Doldastam listening to the bells toll.

She wouldn't even invite any of the royalty from the other kingdoms, because she claims she can't trust them. She says that we can't trust anybody. During the funeral, the Queen spent most of the time swearing vengeance.

The worst part is that everyone ate it up. They were all cheering when she promised bloodshed to Evert's enemies. Not that I blame them entirely. Somebody in our midst murdered our King.

At the funeral, Ridley stood in the back by himself. When everyone started cheering, I looked back and saw him sneak out. I hope nobody else noticed because that won't look good for him.

I'm training harder with Delilah. We have to prepare for what's coming. I don't know what it is yet, but it's something dark and something big. And I can't let her get hurt.

I know this is terrible timing, but I can't help it. I'm falling head over heels for Delilah. I feel so guilty, since our whole world is falling apart, but my heart doesn't give a damn about time or place. All that matters is how we feel about each other.

But she has given me so much strength through all of this. I feel like I can do anything for her, and I will. I'll do whatever I must to keep her safe when this war finally begins.

Can I tell you an awful truth? I'm looking forward to this war. The tension and the waiting is maddening, especially when paranoia is running rampant.

I'm not sure if I should tell you this, but by the time you get this, hopefully everything will be all over, and you'll want to know about it. Even if it hurts to hear.

Astrid Eckwell tried to accuse your father of poisoning the King. It was right after the funeral, when everyone was milling about. She just stood up and pointed to him and said it was him. She was hysterical, and the guards eventually dragged her away.

Queen Mina silenced the crowd, reminding them that the Högdragen had already investigated your father. But that was all she said, so people kept giving your parents these awful glares until they finally slunk out. Well, they didn't slink exactly. You know your mother. She keeps her head held high no matter what anybody throws at her.

They should leave Doldastam, but I don't think the Queen will let them. No one can go in or out. Tilda has talked about making a break for it, but I don't know if she will. I don't blame her, though. I can't imagine having a baby here, even though she's not due for a few months.

You're so lucky that you're not here. I don't know if you're safe. I don't know if you'll ever be safe again. But I still think you're the lucky one.

> *Your friend (no matter what),*
> *Ember*

TWENTY-ONE

asylum

I t was the look in her eyes that caught me off guard. In the corridor, right before we reached the throne room, there had been a massive painting of Elora Dahl, the Trylle's most recent Queen before Wendy. Jet-black hair, flawless olive skin, dark piercing gaze—she was as beautiful as she was imposing.

But it was that look from the painting. Somehow, even in a rendering on canvas, Elora made me feel like I was two inches tall. And it was that exact look that Queen Wendy now shared with her mother.

I wanted to falter under her gaze, but I stood tall, with my shoulders back.

"I have been falsely accused," I told her coolly, and that caused King Loki to cock an eyebrow.

"That seems a bit like a convenient excuse, doesn't it?" Queen Wendy asked, unmoved.

"I was working in Storvatten, under direction of my kingdom," I explained. "The Queen there felt unsafe, and I, along with my comrade Kasper Abbott, was sent to find out the cause of her unease.

"Upon returning to Doldastam, I discovered information that tied the problems in Storvatten to the Prince, Kennet Biâelse," I went on. "When I tried to bring this to King Evert, Queen Mina blocked my attempts. Kasper and I explained the situation to her, and she accused us of treason and had us sent to the dungeon."

"What did you say that made her allege treason?" Queen Wendy tilted her head, appearing interested.

"She said that simply making any claim against an ally was treasonous," I answered.

Wendy sat up straighter and exchanged a look with her Chancellor, Bain. Then she looked back at me. "Go on."

"I was afraid that we'd be locked away in the dungeon, so Kasper and I escaped in order to clear our names," I said. "We went to Kennet's room, since he was staying in the Doldastam palace. He admitted to his involvement in the attempts on both Queen Linnea and King Mikko's lives in Storvatten."

Loki let out a surprised whistle, causing Finn to cast a harsh look at him. For their parts, Wendy and Bain appeared unfazed.

"An altercation ensued between Kennet, Kasper, and myself," I went on. "Kennet killed Kasper, and I began to fight with Kennet. During the struggle, Kennet fell out the window and died."

Bain leaned forward, resting his arms on his knees. "So you think Kennet was behind everything in Storvatten? What about when you arrested Konstantin Black and Bent Stum for the crimes against the Skojare kingdom?"

"Kennet admitted to hiring them to do his dirty work," I said, lying a little. "He wanted to be King himself, instead of his brother."

Kennet had confirmed that he'd hired someone—he just never talked to Konstantin himself. Mina had been the intermediary, but I thought if I accused Mina of anything without substantial evidence, Queen Wendy would question everything I was saying.

I didn't thinking aligning myself with Konstantin right now would help my case, and he was the only way I had been able to put all the pieces together. That meant that I had to leave out a few things and twist a few facts.

"But why wouldn't Queen Mina hear you out?" Wendy asked.

"Her reasons were never made clear to me, Your Highness," I said. "You'd have to ask her that yourself."

Wendy leaned back in her throne and exhaled. "I don't know what I should do with you." She considered for a moment. "I know the Kanin would want me to return you to them so they could devise a punishment for themselves."

"With all due respect, My Queen, if you send Bryn back

to the Kanin, they will execute her," Finn interjected. "Do you really think anything she's done deserves execution?"

"And you have granted amnesty before," Loki said with a sly smile, and Wendy cast him a look.

"Those were under vastly different circumstances," she said, almost whispering.

"I am inclined to agree with Finn," Bain said. He'd settled back in his seat and crossed his leg over his knee. "I worked with Bryn in Storvatten, and she seemed intent on serving her kingdom, not destroying it."

"Since both Finn and the Chancellor are vouching for you, and my husband seems to think it's a good idea, then we will grant you amnesty. *For now,*" Wendy said, emphasizing the fact that it could be revoked if she decided it should be. "Under one condition."

"And what's that?" I asked, feeling so relieved that I would've agreed to nearly anything at that point.

"Finn must keep an eye on you as long as you reside within the Kingdom of the Trylle." She turned her hard gaze to him. "Any trouble that Bryn gets herself into falls on you."

He nodded. "I understand."

The Queen looked back at me. "The King, the Chancellor, and I will continue discussing these matters. But for the time being, you are safe and you're free to stay here." She smiled. "Welcome to Förening, Bryn."

domestic

As soon as Finn opened the door to his squat cottage tucked away inside the bluffs, children dove at him—two squealing balls of delight with mops of curly hair. Both of them had mud smeared on their clothes, probably from a day spent out in the yard on the warm spring day.

Finn scooped up both of the kids with ease, holding one in each arm. I'd met them before, at Ember's house, since Finn tried to visit his family whenever he had a chance. Hanna, the little girl, was about five years old, and she was babbling excitedly about the adventures she'd had that day with her mom and her brother.

The younger boy, on the other hand, was much more observant than his older sister. Liam couldn't have been more than two, with chubby cheeks and dark brown eyes the size of saucers. He stared back at me over his dad's shoulder, studying me intently.

Finn's wife Mia came out from a back bedroom, shaking her head and making her ponytail bob. The long sundress she wore fell over the rapidly growing belly. It had only been a little over a month since I'd last seen her at Ember's birthday party, but by the way she looked now, it seemed like the baby must be due soon.

"Sorry about the kids," Mia said, offering me an embarrassed smile as she walked over to Finn and the kids.

"No, it's fine," Finn assured her, and gave her a quick peck on the lips.

"Since Bryn is here, I take it that the meeting went well?" Mia asked.

Finn nodded. "She'll be staying with us for a while, but that's what we'd planned anyway."

"I hope it's not too much trouble having me here," I said.

"It's no trouble at all." Mia smiled. "I'll take the kids to Liam's room to play, and let you get settled in." Liam allowed his mom to pick him up, but he turned his head, unwilling to take his eyes off me for a second.

And then suddenly it hit me, watching Mia and Finn with their children like that—this would've been Tilda's life. This should've been her and Kasper, and their unborn child, but now it never would be.

Because I had failed to act fast enough, Kasper had been killed, and this whole life was ripped away from Tilda and their baby. And now I couldn't even be with her. I couldn't even apologize for what had happened.

It all fell on me so hard, I was afraid my knees would give

way for a moment. I wanted nothing more than to collapse on the cool dirt floor and let the sadness overtake me, but I couldn't do that. I couldn't let it.

"Bryn?" Mia's eyes widened with concern. "Are you okay?" Then she turned to her husband, sounding panicked. "Finn, I think she's gonna pass out."

Finn dropped Hanna quickly but safely on the floor, then hurried over to me. "Bryn?"

"I'm fine," I said but my words sounded hollow. He put his hand on my arm to steady me, and I wanted to push it away, but I didn't have the strength.

"Have her sit down and get her a glass of water," Mia said, taking Hanna's hand.

Finn took my duffel bag from me, and I didn't even try to fight it. He led me over to the kitchen table and pulled out a chair for me. I sat with my head in my hands and let him fuss over me until the weakness finally began to subside.

When I looked up, Finn was standing over me with a worried crease in his brow, and Mia was sitting at the table beside me. I hadn't even heard her come back out.

"Sorry," I mumbled. "I don't know what that was about."

"No need to be sorry." Mia reached out, touching my forehead gently. "You're cool and clammy. Are you feeling sick at all?"

I shook my head. "No. I've just had a very long week."

Mia leaned on the table, studying me the same way her son had before. "When was the last time you've eaten?"

It wasn't until she mentioned it that I realized I hadn't in a very long time. While I'd been on the road, I'd hardly been able to find anything that sat with my sensitive troll stomach, and when I'd been with the Omte, they hadn't been much on feeding us.

"It's been a while," I admitted sheepishly.

"I'll make you something." Mia pushed back the chair to get up.

"No, you shouldn't be waiting on me," I said, glancing over at her belly.

She smiled and waved me off as she stood. "Nonsense. I've still got another month left with this one, and I can't just spend it sitting around." She rubbed her stomach. "I've got things to do."

"Do you need any help?" Finn asked.

"No, you sit down and talk to Bryn," Mia said as she began bustling about the kitchen.

Finn sat across from me. When I'd had my head down, either he or Mia had poured a cup of tea for me. He leaned across the table and nudged it closer to me.

"You should drink something."

"Thank you." I took a long sip, and the warmth of the drink felt amazing.

Finn's home, like many troll homes, was built sort of like a rabbit burrow—with most of it underground in the bluffs. This kept it warmer in the winter and cooler in the summer, which was nice on days like today when outside temperatures had risen into the seventies.

In a lot of ways, Finn's house was similar to Ridley's house back in Doldastam, except since it was a bit warmer here, they got to have more earthy features, like dirt floors and bushes growing around the doorway.

Remembering Ridley, and the times I'd spent in his house with him usually sitting beside a crackling fire talking about work, only made me feel worse. My stomach clenched and my heart throbbed painfully in my chest. I missed him terribly, and I wanted only to wrap my arms around him.

"You look like you have the weight of the world on your shoulders," Finn commented.

"I kind of feel that way," I said honestly. "I've made too many mistakes, and too many people are paying for them."

"I've had to learn a hard lesson, and I think you might need to, too." Finn leaned back in his chair. "Everything can't be your fault. You're not that powerful. The whole world isn't in your control."

I swallowed hard and stared down at my tea. "I know that."

"But it still feels like you should be able to prevent every disaster and protect everyone you care about from any pain?" Finn asked, and I nodded. "But you can't, so sometimes you need to trust that people can take care of themselves."

I thought of Kasper, and how he'd died trying to take care of himself. And Ridley, and how I didn't know what the Queen had done to him after I left. And Tilda, and how she was dealing with so much now. And Linnea, and how she was alone in Storvatten, trying to fight for her life and her husband's. And Konstantin, and how if Viktor or his men found him, things would end very badly for him.

I shook my head. "I can't turn my back on them, Finn. If I can help them, I have to."

"I'm not saying you should stand by and watch people suffer," Finn clarified. "But you can't save everyone. You can only do as much as you can, and then you need to move on."

"But . . ." It was hard to speak around the lump in my throat. "Kasper died."

"Did you kill him?" Finn asked me directly.

"No."

"Then it's not your fault."

"But I could've done more." I looked up at him. "I *should've* done more."

Finn leaned forward, resting his arms on the table. "Bryn, if you could have done more, you would have. That means you did everything you could."

I couldn't argue that, so I lowered my eyes again.

"From what I gather by what Ember's told me, and what you told the Queen, you've been trying to fight a massive enemy on your own," Finn said. "You've been taking on far too much for one person, and I think you should get some rest for a while."

"I can't," I insisted. "Not when people I care about might be in danger."

"You're no help to anyone if you're falling apart."

"That's the worst thing about Finn," Mia said, smiling at me as she set a heaping bowl of vegetable soup in front of me. "He's usually right."

"Thank you," I told her, and I used all my restraint to

keep from wolfing down the soup. I didn't think anything had ever smelled as wonderful or tasted as delicious in my life.

"You can stay here as long as you need to," Mia told me, as I devoured the soup. "Our door is always open to you."

I wanted to thank her for that, and tell her that I didn't think I'd be staying here that long. I couldn't just rest on my laurels, no matter if my body needed it or not. But I was far too famished to do anything besides eat.

reevaluate

Before this had become Finn and Mia's home, it had been the house that both Finn and Ember had grown up in. Ember's old room had become Hanna's, but she would stay in Liam's room tonight, so I could use her room. I'd tried to insist that they didn't need to go to any trouble for me, but Mia just did it anyway.

Despite my exhaustion, I lay awake in Hanna's slightly-too-small bed, my feet hanging over the end. A lighted mobile hung above the bed, casting shapes of the moon and stars over the ceiling.

The walls were a pale blue with clouds on them, and Finn had told me that Ember had been the one to paint the room this way when she'd been ten. I remembered her telling me about her childhood, when she would lay awake at night plotting her escape from this small boring house and her boring life. Ember had been determined to escape and have an adventure.

Now I couldn't help but feel a certain kinship to her, lying awake the way she had, wishing for an escape. Of course, I would happily trade all the troubles that were stretched out before me for a boring life with my friends and family again.

As soon as I thought it, I wondered if that was entirely true. Obviously, I would gladly get rid of Mina and Viktor and all the dangers that went along with them. But would I ever be content to just settle down and lead a normal life the way Finn and Mia had?

Before everything had completely gone to hell, Ridley and I had made plans to be together when this was all over. Of course, now it seemed impossible. I wasn't even sure if I'd ever be able to see him again.

But for a brief moment I allowed myself to fantasize about the life we might have led together. It wouldn't be exactly like Finn and Mia's life, since I wasn't sold on the idea of having kids myself. Staying at home and raising a family was great for people who wanted it, the way Mia so obviously did, but I wanted something different.

I could work as a tracker for a few more years, traveling and seeing the world. When I came home, Ridley would be there waiting for me, pulling me into his arms. Sipping wine by the fireplace in the winter, and riding the horses out to the bay in the summer. Arguing about the politics in Doldastam, or what movie to watch. And falling asleep at night in each other's arms.

We could have a life together.

Or at least we could've, before I'd been accused of treason.

But still, when I drifted off to sleep, I couldn't help but imagine the life that Ridley and I had almost had together. How we'd so nearly made it.

In the morning, I awoke to a little boy standing next to the bed, staring right at me. When I opened my eyes, there he was, and I almost screamed. Funny that after everything I'd seen lately, it was a two-year-old boy that nearly gave me a heart attack.

I wasn't sure how Liam would react to me picking him up, but I decided to give it a go anyway. When he didn't scream, I took that as a good sign, and proceeded to carry him out to the kitchen, where Mia was making breakfast.

She immediately apologized for him waking me, but I brushed it off. Besides, I honestly felt better than I had in a while. Getting a decent meal and a good night's sleep did wonders for the body.

I didn't even mind that since I'd picked Liam up, he refused to let go of me. Eventually, when he began tugging on my hair with his pudgy hands and poking me in the eyes, I realized where all his fascination came from—he hadn't seen many people who looked like me in his life.

After breakfast, I finally managed to detangle myself from Liam and headed outside to work out. I'd been trying to work out every chance I'd gotten, but since Konstantin and I had been on the move, and I'd been starving, exhausted, and anxious the whole time, I hadn't gotten as much done as I'd have liked.

Finn and Mia's house sat on a plateau, with a small field of grassy flat land extending out over the bluff. A split-rail wooden fence wrapped around it, preventing any animals or small children from tumbling over the edge.

Finn and Ember's mom used to use the land to raise angora goats, but since their parents moved, taking the goats with them, Finn hadn't picked up the tradition. The only animal he and Mia had was a solitary pony that Finn had apparently gotten as a birthday gift for Hanna.

The pony, rather inexplicably named Calvin, came over to investigate what I was up to. It was dark gray, with a long mane and fur around his hooves, so in many ways he appeared to be a miniature version of my Tralla horse Bloom, admittedly a much stouter version. He only came up to my shoulder, and he appeared bemused behind his thick bangs as he watched me stretch.

When I started running laps along the fence, Calvin trotted along with me, his short legs hurrying to keep up. But he quickly grew bored of that and went back to nibbling at the grass and flowers.

Eventually, I'd moved on to doing burpees—which was dropping down to a squat, getting in a push-up position, and then immediately jumping back to the squatting position and standing up again. I'd done about a million of them when I'd been in tracker school, but the last few weeks had taken their toll on me, and I was going way too slow.

Whenever I'd drop to the ground, Calvin would sniff my hair, as if it to make sure I was okay. I was on about my twentieth burpee when I heard the gate to Finn's property swing open. I stopped what I was doing long enough to look over and see the Chancellor, Bain Ottesen, standing just inside the gate.

"Finn's inside the house," I told him, wiping the sweat off my brow with the back of my arm.

"Actually," Bain said with a sheepish expression, "I'm here to see you."

hunted

With my heart pounding in my chest, I walked across the field to meet Bain. There weren't guards with him, so it felt safe to assume that the Queen hadn't decided to recant her amnesty and arrest me. But that didn't mean that she hadn't decided that it might be better for her kingdom if she sent me away.

Bain stepped carefully toward me, avoiding particularly muddy spots in the yard since he was barefoot. Because they had nicer weather in Förening than we did in Doldastam, the Trylle got to spend a lot more time free from footwear.

He was dressed nicely in black slacks and a dress shirt with a tie, and his brown hair was styled off his forehead. With his earnest expression and clean-cut appearance, Bain reminded me of those guys who went door-to-door dropping off religious pamphlets.

"What'd you want to see me about?" I asked when I reached him.

He pursed his lips for a moment. "I have some strange questions to ask you, and I don't know if you'll be able to answer them. But it would be helpful to us if you did."

"I'll do the best I can," I replied carefully.

Calvin had followed me over, and he began sniffing Bain. When Bain spoke, he began absently petting the pony.

"What do you know about what's happening in your kingdom?" Bain asked.

My stomach clenched, and I shook my head. "Not much. I haven't really been in contact with anyone there since I left. I briefly talked to the Överste, Ridley Dresden, but he wouldn't say much beyond the fact that everything is falling apart there."

"Did he tell you that King Evert was dead?" Bain asked, watching for my reaction.

"Yes, he did."

"And I am assuming that you had nothing to do with Evert's death?" he asked, and it did sound more like a formality than a serious inquisition.

"No, of course not!" I said, probably too forcefully. "I was in—" I stopped myself before I accidently let it slip that I'd been locked up in the Omte palace when Evert had died. "I was long gone by then."

"I thought as much." Bain looked away from me, staring out at the river below, and a warm breeze blew past us. "The Kanin Queen has begun acting very . . . strangely."

I tensed up. "How so?"

"About a week and a half ago, your kingdom sent out a blast of WANTED posters." He glanced back over at me. "Of you, obviously. But along with them was a letter stating that Doldastam would no longer be allowing visitors of any kind."

"That's insane. Did the letter say why?" I asked.

"Just that they were running an investigation. But that's not the really strange part," Bain went on. "It was signed by Queen Mina. And with the Kanin, every official letter or decree I've ever seen from them has been signed by the King. Sometimes the Queen cosigns, but she's never alone."

I shook my head. "The Queen is never allowed to make pronouncements like that, not on her own."

"When King Evert died, our Queen Wendy called to offer her condolences," Bain said. "Mina talked to her briefly, but she also informed her that, unlike every other royal funeral I've heard of, no other royalty was allowed to attend. Only those already living in Doldastam could go.

"Mina cited safety being her priority, but it all felt off to Wendy," he concluded.

"Holy shit." I exhaled shakily. "She has them completely isolated and totally dependent on her. Everyone in Doldastam is trapped."

"Which brings us to this morning and the strangest part about all of this." He reached into his back pocket, where he'd tucked a rolled-up tube of paper out of sight. "We received these, along with a lengthy letter."

He handed a tube to me, and I unrolled it to reveal two sheets of paper. The top one was a black-and-white poster of myself. The photo was the official tracker picture taken every three months. In it, I stared grimly ahead, my eyes gray and blank.

LARGE REWARD IF FOUND
WANTED: BRYN DEL AVEN
AGE: 19
HEIGHT: 5'5"
HAIR/EYES: BLOND, BLUE
COMMITTED CRIMES AGAINST THE KANIN AND SKOJARE
INCLUDING CONSPIRING TO KILL THE KANIN KING
AND SKOJARE PRINCE
SUSPECTED OF WORKING WITH KONSTANTIN BLACK

The beginning wasn't much of a surprise, but it was the last line that made my heart stop cold.

Mina knew that we'd been together. She knew that he'd helped me.

My hands were trembling slightly when I moved my WANTED poster to see the one behind it. And as soon as I saw Konstantin's face staring up at me in harsh black-and-white, my stomach lurched.

KANIN'S #1 MOST WANTED
HUGE REWARD FOR ANY INFORMATION
KONSTANTIN ELIS BLACK

And I didn't need to read anything beyond that.

They'd turned on him. They'd figured out that Konstantin had defected, and now they were sending everyone after him. It wouldn't just be Dålig and his men—it would be the entire troll community.

"But this doesn't make any sense," I said, trying to stop my hands from shaking. "Viktor Dålig is supposed to be the most wanted man. He already tried to kill the King."

"Not according to the letter Mina sent this morning," Bain said, and my eyes shot up. "She claims it's all a massive frame job perpetrated by Konstantin Black and you."

"What?" I shook my head. "No, that's not true at all. I mean, Konstantin—" I didn't know what to say about him, so I skipped over it. "I've only been trying to protect the kingdom! I would never do anything to hurt it!"

Bain held up his hand toward me. "Calm down. I didn't say that I believed Queen Mina. I just told you what she's saying."

I rolled the posters back up, since I hated looking at them. "I'm sorry. It's just . . . it's not true."

"Mina also said that she called off the war against Viktor Dålig," Bain said. I could only gape at him, so he went on. "She says that it's all smoke and mirrors put on by you and Konstantin, and that too many people have died. So she's just keeping Doldastam on lockdown until you and Konstantin are brought to justice."

"But . . ." I shook my head, not comprehending. "That doesn't make sense."

Konstantin and I had thought the plan was for Viktor Dålig and his army to attack Doldastam, and then Mina would come in and save the day, thus becoming an indispensable savior, so she wouldn't be dethroned.

But if she was eliminating the threat of Viktor, then how would she become a necessary hero? And what was even the point of building up the Viktor threat in the first place? And why was she so insistent on keeping the town locked down?

"The behavior of the Kanin royalty is increasingly erratic," Bain said. "So Wendy doesn't plan to tell them that you're here, and she's agreed to grant you amnesty as long as you need it."

That should have been a relief, but I barely even registered what Bain had said. My mind was racing to figure out what Mina was plotting, and what that would mean for everyone in Doldastam, along with myself and Konstantin.

"It's not the royalty—it's Mina," I said, and I looked up at Bain, imploring him to understand and believe me. "Mina is behind all these crazy things. She killed King Evert."

Bain took a step back. "We may not entirely trust the Kanin Queen right now, but that's a harsh accusation. You can't just go throwing that around."

"I'm not trying to stir up trouble," I persisted. "I'm saying that the people of Doldastam are trapped under the rule of an unfit and tyrannical ruler. They need help. *You* can help them. The Trylle have a great army."

"Slow down, Bryn." Bain shook his head. "Wendy granted

you amnesty. That doesn't mean she's going to go to war based on your word."

"It's not just my word! You've seen what Mina is doing!"

"We've seen Mina acting in a paranoid fashion, but she's also under a great deal of stress," Bain allowed. "And even if she is acting in ways that you or I or even Queen Wendy would think were wrong, Mina is still the acting monarch of the largest kingdom, with the largest army, and the largest wealth behind it. She is well within her rights. Not only are we outmatched, but action is unwarranted."

"What if I could prove it?" I asked, almost desperately. "If I could prove that Mina killed Evert, then she's not the rightful ruler. Which means that Wendy—as a Queen and an upholder of the troll kingdom at large—would not only be within her rights to deal with Mina, she would be obligated to."

Bain raised an eyebrow. "Can you prove it?"

"Not yet," I admitted. "But I'll figure out how."

strategy

How well do you know Queen Wendy?" I asked Finn directly.

He'd been doing the dishes when I came into the house, but he leaned back against the counter, arms folded over his chest, to talk with me for a minute. Mia had been putting down the kids for a nap in the master bedroom, and she walked out just as I asked the question.

He shifted his weight from one foot to the other and glanced over at his wife. "I know Wendy fairly well," he said finally.

"What will it take to get her to declare war on the Kanin?" I asked.

Finn leaned away from me, his eyes wide with surprise. "What? I thought you were trying to help your kingdom, not destroy it."

"I am trying," I insisted. "The Kanin Queen, Mina, is the

one who wants to destroy it, and I'm trying to figure out a way to get her out of power so she can't do any more damage."

Finn rubbed his temple. "You're trying to overthrow your Queen. I can see why she charged with you treason."

"I know how it sounds, but you have to believe me." I looked from him to Mia, but she just stood with one hand pressed against her lower back, looking nervous about the entire conversation.

"It's not that I don't believe you—I've been at the briefings with the Queen and the Chancellor. I know there's something sketchy going on in Doldastam," he explained. "It's just that I don't really know what the Trylle can do about it."

"You guys are so powerful! You can bring the hammer down on Mina!" I slammed my fist against my palm to demonstrate, and Mia held her finger up to her lips and motioned to the kids' rooms behind her. "Sorry."

"The Kanin have a huge army, and with Mina commanding them, they'd be fighting against us," Finn pointed out. "That means lots of innocent people—including my sister—would be hurt or killed."

"I don't want a civil war," I corrected him. "I want Mina deposed. Your kingdom has an army that's powerful and skilled enough that we'd only need a small number to pull off a covert mission. Maybe ten, twenty of your people could sneak into Doldastam and arrest her."

"And you think Mina would just acquiesce to the Trylle's authority?" Finn asked with a raised eyebrow. "That she wouldn't fight back and summon her guards to slaughter the twenty troops that had come in to capture her?"

"Then they could assassinate her," I replied simply, and Mia actually gasped at the mere mention of killing the Kanin Queen.

Finn exhaled heavily, looking rather grim. "Now you've stepped it up to murder?"

"It's not murder," I insisted. "Not when it's done in protection of the kingdom. If it's the only way to get Mina out of power, then so be it."

"I understand your anger and frustration, but that seems rather drastic and dangerous," Finn said.

"Your family is trapped in Doldastam, under Mina's cruel reign. Do you really want them to stay like that?" I asked.

"Of course I don't," he snapped. "But I'm also not going to suggest that the Trylle start a Kanin civil war when we have no grounds for it."

"What would be grounds enough?" I asked. "What do I need to find to sway Wendy into thinking that this is a good idea?"

"Short of the Kanin declaring war on the Trylle?" Finn shrugged. "I don't know."

"What do you have on the Kanin Queen?" Mia asked. "Do you have any evidence to tie her to any of the shady things that have been going on?"

"Not really," I said sadly. "There's stuff that Wendy already knows—like how Mina is acting strange and paranoid. But that's not enough in and of itself. I think she killed the King, but I can't go back to Doldastam to find out anything more."

"What about confidants or cohorts?" Mia asked. "The Queen can't be causing all this trouble entirely on her own. She has to have people working for her or at least a friend that she's telling all her secrets to."

Kennet Biâelse knew what was going on, but he was dead. Viktor Dålig would be far too dangerous for me to confront on my own, and I didn't have any idea about who might be working for him.

There was always Konstantin Black, but he wasn't a source that anybody would believe. He'd need evidence to corroborate what he was saying, and I knew he had none.

I shook my head. "Not anybody credible."

Then something occurred to me. Konstantin and I had been talking once, and I'd been surprised to realize that Mina had been planning all of this for four years. Konstantin had replied that he thought she'd been plotting to take the crown since the day she met Evert.

But that couldn't have just occurred to her. As power-hungry and greedy as Mina seemed, this wasn't a new thing. I bet she'd been trying to figure out a way to get the crown since she was a kid.

"I can't go back to Doldastam to dig up dirt on her, so I'll go back further," I said, looking up at Finn and Mia. "I need to go to Iskyla."

"Iskyla?" Finn asked.

"It's this tiny, isolated Kanin town way up in Nunavut. It's where Mina's from. And if she's been working on this for a long time—and I'm inclined to believe she has—she probably started out working with someone up there."

Now that I finally had a plan, I didn't want to waste another second, so I turned and hurried into Hanna's room. Finn followed a few steps behind me, telling me to wait a minute.

"Bryn, I don't know if this is a good idea," he said as I hurried to pack up my duffel bag. "You have all the tribes looking for you. If you go to a Kanin town, they'll arrest you on sight."

"Iskyla's off the grid," I told him. "I doubt they'll notice me."

"Have you looked in a mirror?" Finn asked dryly.

I'd finished my packing, so I turned back to face him. He stood in the doorway looking down at me, his dark eyes grave.

"Your parents and your sister are in Doldastam," I said. "Along with my parents and my friends and a whole lot of other innocent people. I can't just hide and wait for this to blow over. Unless *I* do something—unless people like you and me do something—this isn't going to blow over."

He breathed in deeply. "You're gonna need to travel fast. The kingdom has a few motorcycles in the garage that nobody ever uses. I'll get you one."

frozen

The plane dropped in the air, making my stomach flip, and I gripped the armrest tighter.

"We're just hitting a little turbulence as we come into town," the pilot said, attempting to comfort me. He'd turned back to offer the words of encouragement, but I'd have felt much better if he'd kept his eyes locked on the controls in front of him.

While I didn't ordinarily mind flying, this was easily the smallest plane I'd ever been on, and it seemed to tilt and lurch with every change of the breeze. The flight had been a very, very bumpy one, and it had turned into the longest three and a half hours of my life.

In Förening, Finn had gotten me a motorcycle, a few troll maps, and given me what money he could. I'd tried to decline the offer of money, but the truth was that I was running low on the cash Ridley had gotten me, and I needed the funds.

As a condition of my amnesty, Finn was supposed to keep an eye on me as long as I was in Förening. Once I went through the gate, I was on my own again.

Finn warned me that there was a chance Wendy wouldn't let me back in again. Since I'd already cast her pardon aside once, she might not grant it again.

But it was a risk I had to take. Stopping Mina trumped everything else, even my freedom.

After thanking Finn and Mia repeatedly for everything they'd done for me, I hopped on the motorcycle and spent the rest of the day riding up to Winnipeg. It was scary being back in Canada, closer to the Kanin and Viktor Dålig, but I hid in a motel for the night, with the curtains drawn.

It reminded me of the time I'd spent with Konstantin, and I wondered what he was doing and if he was okay. He'd left me without any means to contact him, saying only that he'd find me if I needed him. But I had no way of even knowing if **he** needed **me**.

Seeing him on the WANTED poster had been strangely jarring. I had seen his face on dozens of them before, but this one was different. Not only because Konstantin and I had become friends, but because this was a clear message from Mina—his behavior would not be tolerated.

But Konstantin had been on the run for a long time, and he was capable and smart. He could handle himself. I had to believe that, because if I didn't, I would have to face the harsh truth that he was a dead man walking, and there wasn't a thing I could do to help him.

That night, I slept fitfully—with my usual dreams of Kasper and Ridley mixed in with new ones of Viktor Dålig torturing Konstantin while Mina watched and laughed.

In the morning, I chartered the cheapest plane I could find, which I was now beginning to realize may have been a bad idea. When we landed safely, I was just as surprised as I was relieved.

In Nunavut, there were no roads connecting any of the towns. The Arctic weather made maintaining and traversing roads an impossibility. Planes were the best way to get from one place to another, but Iskyla was so isolated that it didn't even have a landing strip, and I'd flown to the nearest human settlement.

When I got off the plane, it was blustery and snowy, which reminded me of home, the way the cold always did. Spring was descending on the north, so it wasn't as bad as it could be. After the warmth I'd felt these past few weeks, I pulled my hat down more securely on my head to keep out the cold.

Fortunately, not too far from the airstrip, I found a place where I could rent a snowmobile. In my pocket I had a map to Iskyla, and I checked it three times before I headed out onto the icy tundra. The last thing I wanted to do was get lost up here in the middle of nowhere.

From what I could tell from my map, Iskyla was supposed to be roughly a hundred miles away from the town. I figured I'd be able to make it there in less than two hours. So when I still hadn't found the town, and I was rapidly approaching the two-and-a-half-hour mark, I started to get nervous.

I circled back around, trying to recalibrate. There were no major rivers or mountains nearby—nothing in the landscape to give any indication that I was close or way off. It was just a platitude of white.

Just when I was about to give up and go back, I caught sight of something in the distance. I pushed the snowmobile to full speed and raced toward it. Icy wind stung my face and threatened to blow back the fur hood that was keeping the snow at bay.

I was getting closer, and the town was starting to take shape. A few gray houses clustered together, and a couple more buildings. Beside one of the houses, a few huskies barked at me as I approached.

In towns of Nunavut, there were a few roads connecting houses to each other or to the local market and shops. This was no different, with the road coming to a dead end just at the edge of the town. A large, faded sign sat at the end of it, and I pulled my snowmobile up to it.

In big white letters it said: WELCOME TO ISKYLA. Below it: ᑐᖖᒐᓱᓯᑯ. Living in northern Canada, I'd had to learn some Inuktitut—the language of the native Canadian Inuit people. These symbols roughly meant, "Welcome to Ice," since *Iskyla* loosely translated to "iciness" from Swedish.

I looked at the small barren collection of houses before me, and I let out a resigned breath. I had made it to Iskyla. Now I just had to find somebody who would talk to me about Mina.

iskyla

I needed a place to warm up and a way to start asking around, so my best option appeared to be an inn just off the main stretch of road, aptly named the Frozen Inn, according to the warped sign that hung above the door.

Icicles hung precariously from the roof of the large square building, and the white paint chipped off the sides to reveal the gray wood beneath. The door creaked painfully loud as I opened it, and a gust of cold wind came up behind me and helped push me in.

Inside was a rather small waiting room, with worn mismatched furniture poised toward an old fireplace that was barely going. The carpet was a faded red, and the wallpaper looked like it hadn't been changed in a century.

A staircase with a dilapidated railing ran along the far wall, looking more like it belonged in an old farmhouse than a place of business. In fact, if it wasn't for the bar that wrapped along the east wall with a bell on it and a bulletin board behind it, I would've worried I'd walked into someone's home.

The door behind the bar swung open, and a girl of about fifteen came out. Her full lips and amber eyes were set in a surly scowl.

Five or six necklaces hung around her neck, all of them appearing handmade with leather straps and wood or ivory pendants. The thick straps of leather and hemp she wore around her wrists matched.

"Unnusakkut," she said, which sounded like *oo-new-saw-koot*. It was Inuktitut for "Good afternoon," but with more boredom and annoyance than I'd heard it pronounced before.

"Afternoon," I replied, since my Inuktitut was never that good.

In school, we had to learn English and French because most of our changelings were in Canada or the U.S., and we also learned Swedish because it was the language of our ancestors. We had some interaction with the Inuit people who lived around Doldastam, so we were taught basic Inuktitut, but I'd rarely used it, so my fluency had gone way down.

"Oh." She looked up at me in surprise as I unwound the scarf from my face. "Most of the people that stop in here are Inuit."

I pulled off my hat and brushed my hand through my hair. "I'm from Doldastam, actually."

She narrowed her eyes at me, and I realized that her left eye was slightly larger than the other, almost imperceptibly. Her nose was petite and turned up at the end, and her skin appeared fair and rather pale. Unruly dark blond hair landed just above her shoulders.

"You don't look like you're from Doldastam," she said, but I'd already come to the conclusion that she didn't exactly look Kanin either.

"Well, I am."

That's when I noticed the WANTED poster tacked up on the bulletin board behind her. The one that Bain had shown me. Right next to Konstantin Black, I saw a black-and-white photo of my face staring right back at me, and I realized that I might have made a mistake coming in here.

"Are you a half breed like me?" she asked. Her eyes brightened and she stopped slouching.

I nodded. "I'm Kanin and Skojare."

She smiled crookedly and pointed to herself. "Omte and Skojare."

I smiled back, hoping to earn some goodwill. "It's so rare to meet people that share a heritage like that."

"Maybe where you come from, but not so much around here. Iskyla is where they drop all the trolls they'd rather forget about — unwanted babies, outlaw changelings that can't hack it, half-breeds that don't fit in anywhere." She shook her head. "That's how I ended up stuck here."

"What do you mean?" I asked.

"My parents were unmarried royals that didn't want to lose their inheritance because of a bastard child, but apparently my mother loved me too much to just let me die out in the cold." She rolled her eyes. "So they dropped me here when I was a week old, and the innkeeper has been putting me to work for my keep ever since."

Truth be told, I didn't know much about Iskyla. It was very secluded, so we rarely had reason to talk about it. But since it was one of the most isolated towns in the entire troll community, it made sense that it had become a collective dumping ground.

"I'm sorry to hear that," I said, and I meant it. It had been hard enough for me growing up as a half-breed with parents who wanted me and loved me. I couldn't imagine what it must've been like for her growing up in a place like this without anyone.

She shrugged. "It could be worse." Then her forehead scrunched up and she tilted her head like something had occurred to her. "Hey, didn't the King die or something?"

I was taken aback by the casual way she broached the subject. Living in the Kanin capital and working for the kingdom, I'd gotten so used to the royalty being talked about with great reverence. But she seemed only vaguely aware that we even had a King.

Here in Iskyla, things were obviously very different. It was so disconnected from the rest of the kingdom—geographically and socially. It was like its own private little island.

"He did," I said somberly.

"I heard that nobody in Iskyla was allowed to go to the funeral," she said, then looked down and muttered, "Not that any of us would've gone anyway."

"Ulla!" a voice barked from the back room. "Stop wasting the guest's time and show her to her room."

The girl rolled her eyes again, this time even more dramatically than before. "Sorry. I'll get your room key."

She turned back around and went into the back room, where she and the innkeeper immediately began sniping at each other. As fast as I could, I leapt up onto the bar and leaned forward. I snatched the WANTED poster of myself off the bulletin board, crumpled it up, and shoved it into my pocket.

I'd just dropped back to my feet when the door swung open again. The teenage girl came out carrying a large metal key attached to a big carved chunk of wood.

"Come on." She motioned for me to follow her as she went up the stairs, each one of them creaking under her feet.

As I followed her up, I realized how tattered her layers of clothing appeared. The long tunic sweater was frayed at the edges, the fur on the hooded vest was coming out in patches, her heavy leggings were thin in the knees, and even her leg warmers had seen better days. Despite the cold, her feet were bare, and she had on pale blue toenail polish and a toe ring.

At the top of the stairs, she opened a door that had the number 3 painted on it, and she held it open for me. I slid past her into a narrow room with hardly enough space for the queen bed and a rocking chair. Several quilts were piled up on the bed, and a dusty arctic hare had been mounted on the wall.

I tossed my duffel bag on the bed and turned back toward her. "Sorry. I didn't catch your name."

"Ulla Tulin." She hung on to the door handle and half leaned on the door, so I didn't attempt to shake her hand.

"Bryn." I declined to give a last name, since that seemed less likely to trigger a connection to the WANTED poster. But either way, Ulla didn't give any sign of recognition.

"It was nice meeting you, and let me know if you need any-thing. We don't have any other guests, and I'm hardly ever doing anything, so I might as well be helping you."

"Actually, I did need your help."

She perked up and took a step in the room. "Yeah?"

"I was wondering if you know anything about a Mina Arvinge?" I asked, using Queen Mina's maiden name.

Ulla cocked her head. "That name sounds familiar, but I don't think any Arvinges live here now." She thought for a moment, staring off into space, then looked back at me. "Isn't the Queen named Mina? I'd heard someone say she was from here once, but I just thought they were lying. People come here to disappear." Then, sadly, she added, "Nobody ever ac-tually makes it out."

"I'm sure some people do," I said, attempting vainly to cheer her up. I neglected to address her connection about Mina and the Queen. The less she knew about what I was looking for, the better.

Ulla gave a one-shoulder shrug, like she didn't care one way or another. "There's only eight hundred and seventy-eight people that live here, so you'd think everybody'd know everything about everyone. But truth is, most people keep to themselves. We like our secrets here."

"Do you know of anybody named Mina?" I pressed on. "She probably moved away around five years ago."

"Five years ago?" Ulla repeated, thinking. "Kate Kissipsi had a couple sisters that left. I'm not sure when, but you could talk to her. She might know something."

"Do you know where she lives?" I asked.

"On the north side of town." Ulla gestured behind her. "I could take you there if you want."

"Could you? That'd be really great."

"Yeah." She smiled broadly, probably excited about the idea of getting out of the inn. "I have to make supper first, and you can have some. It's nothing exciting. Just boiled potatoes and ukaliq."

"Ukaliq?" I echoed, doing my best to make the *ew-ka-lick* sound she made.

"Sorry, arctic hare." Her expression changed to one of exaggerated weariness. "We eat so much hare." Then she shook her head, clearing it of the thought, and her smile returned. "I'll meet you downstairs in twenty minutes for supper, and then I'll take you out to see Kate."

visitors

W e have to walk," Ulla told me as she pulled on heavy kamik boots made of sealskin and lined with fur. "It's only about a mile north, so it's not that bad."

"Why do we have to walk?" I asked, bundling up the same way she was in the lobby of the inn.

"Because Kate doesn't like visitors, so it's better if she doesn't hear us coming." With that, she turned and headed toward the front door. "Let's go. We have to be back before dark."

Dark was still several hours away, but I didn't argue with her. I just followed her out into the cold. We went down the front steps, and then walked half a block. The streets were deserted, and if I didn't know any better, I would've thought this was a ghost town. But Ulla assured me that people actually lived here.

At the end of the block, we took a right turn onto a poorly

kept path. It had obviously been shoveled at some point in the winter, since it had less snow than the areas around it, but it was covered in snow.

"Why doesn't Kate like visitors?" I asked as we walked out of town.

"Nobody likes visitors here." Ulla spoke loudly so her voice would carry through the thick scarf she'd wrapped around her face.

"It seems like a lonely place," I said.

Ulla looked at me with a snowflake stuck to her eyelash. "You have no idea."

We'd walked for quite a while before Ulla pointed at what appeared to be a heap of snow on the ground, claiming that it was Kate's place. As we got closer, it finally began to take shape. It was so low to the ground that it had to be built like Ridley's house, with most of it below the surface. Snow covered it, probably both to camouflage it and to help insulate it during the harsh winters.

Dirty snow appeared to move near the front of the house, but when two gray and white drifts began charging toward us, I quickly realized it wasn't snow. Two massive wolves had been lying outside, but now they were running toward Ulla and me, snarling and barking.

"I forgot she had wolves," Ulla said.

I started backing away, since the wolves were rapidly approaching us. "We should get out of here."

"No, don't run!" Ulla snapped. "That'll only make them chase you."

"Well, I'm not exactly an expert in fighting wolves in hand-to-hand combat, so what do you suggest we do?"

The front door of the hut was thrown open, and a dark figure stepped out wielding a large shotgun.

"Magni! Modi," she shouted, and the wolves halted mere feet from pouncing on us. "Get back here!"

The wolf closest to me hesitated, growling at me once more, before turning back and running with the other one toward the hut. The home owner was still holding a gun, but she'd called the dogs off, so I took that as a good sign. I slowly stepped closer to the hut, and a second later, Ulla followed me.

"Who are you? What do you want?" the woman barked at us.

"I just wanted to talk to you for a minute. If that'd be okay."

She was cloaked in thick fur, and a hood hung low over her face, so I could only see her mouth, scowling at me. As she considered my proposal, it seemed to take forever, with the two wolves standing by her side.

Finally, she said, "You've walked all this way. I might as well let you in." Without waiting for us, she went back into the hut, and the wolves trailed behind her.

Since I wasn't actually sure how safe any of this would be, I turned to Ulla. "You can head back to town if you want. I can handle this from here."

"No way. This is better than anything that happens in town."

I didn't want to stand out here and argue with her, especially not when someone with a shotgun and wolves was waiting on me. So I nodded and went on.

Inside the hut, the walls were made of gray exposed wood, and there was a wood-burning stove, small kitchen table, and bed all in the same room.

It was surprisingly warm inside, and the woman had already taken off her fur and tossed it on the bed. Her long dark hair was pulled back in a frizzy braid that went to her knees. She wore a loose-fitting black dress with wool leggings, and, much like Ulla, she wore many pieces of wood and ivory jewelry.

When Ulla and I came in, she was busying herself filling up two metal dishes with chunks of meat from an ice chest. I took off my hat and scarf while I waited for her to finish. The wolves whimpered excitedly until she set the bowls down before them, and then she turned her attention to us.

Her eyes were dark gray, with thick lashes framing them, and without all the fur she appeared rather petite. She looked to be in her early twenties, but with her arms crossed over her chest, she gazed at me with the severity of someone much older and much more hardened by life.

"What do you want?" she demanded.

"Are you Kate Kissipsi?" I asked.

"That's what they call me," she replied noncommittally.

"I was just looking for someone, and Ulla Tulin"—I motioned to Ulla beside me, and she gave Kate a small wave—"thought you might know something."

"I live alone with nothing but Magni and Modi." Kate

looked over to where the wolves were chomping down on the semi-frozen red meat. "I don't think I can help you."

"Do you know anything about a Mina Arvinge?" I asked, almost desperately. "Anything at all?"

Her eyes widened for a moment, but her expression remained hard. Finally, she let out a heavy breath. "Ayuh. You mean my sister?"

My jaw dropped. "She's your sister?"

"I suppose I should make us some tea, then." She turned her back to us and went over to the stove. "Come in and sit down. You'll probably have a lot you want to talk about."

relation

S orry about the gun," Kate said, glancing over to where the shotgun rested by the door.

"It's no problem," I told her hurriedly, eager to get on with the conversation.

Ulla and I had taken off our jackets and sat down at the table while Kate prepared the tea. The metal teapot had begun to whistle, so she came over and poured hot water over the tea bags into chipped ceramic mugs.

"We've had problems with nanuqs this year, coming too close to the house and getting more aggressive than normal. The long winter's been hard on them," Kate explained as she sat down across from us.

Nanuq was one of the few Inuktitut words I remembered— it meant "polar bear." We had plenty of polar bears that lived around Doldastam, but they were almost never hostile. Still,

Amanda Hocking

I didn't want to start my interactions with Kate by doubting her claims.

"They call me Kate Kissipsi, but that's not really my name," she began, staring down at the mug. The larger of the two wolves lay close to the wood-burning stove, while the other lay on her feet. "We came here when I was seven, and nobody here wanted to take in orphaned children."

She looked up at Ulla then, who nodded solemnly.

"Too many babies and kids are dropped off here," Ulla said. "There aren't a lot of open hearts or open doors anymore."

"None of the Kanin would have us here, but we were eventually taken in by an Inuit family that lived nearby," Kate said. "That's when I adopted the name Kissipsi—it means 'alone' in Inuktitut, and that seems like the best word to describe my life.

"Arvinge isn't really Mina's last name either," she added.

As soon as she said it, it clicked with me. The Kanin had taken to using many Swedish words for official titles and names, even adopting them as surnames. It was so common, I hadn't thought anything of Mina's alleged maiden name until now.

"*Arvinge* means 'heir' in Swedish," I said, thinking aloud. And then everything began falling into place "And you came here when you were seven? It was in 1999, wasn't it?"

Kate nodded, but she hadn't even needed to confirm it. It all made sense.

I leaned back in my chair. "Holy shit. You're Viktor Dålig's daughters."

" 'Mina' was my dad's pet name for Karmin," Kate said. "She was the *only* one he gave a pet name to, but she was the oldest and his favorite." She let out an embittered sigh. "As soon as we got here, she started going by Mina Arvinge, trying to separate herself from the bad reputation our real name had garnered."

After Viktor had attempted to kill the King fifteen years ago, he'd been sentenced to death, but many felt that the harshest punishment had been saved for his three girls. Since the whole attack had been based on the fact that he felt that his oldest daughter, Karmin aka Mina, was the rightful heir to the throne, King Evert believed that his kids should be punished severely, even though they were only children.

All three of Viktor's daughters were stripped of the titles, their inheritance, and banished from the kingdom. Karmin was oldest, and she was only ten at the time. With their mother dead and their father on the run from the law, she had been left in charge of her younger sisters.

"After we were exiled, we had nowhere to go," Kate said. "We'd never been changelings. We'd lived our whole lives in Doldastam, and unlike trackers, who are trained in the human world, we knew nothing about it.

"Before we were sent away, the Chancellor brought us a bag of clothes and some money," she went on. "He told us to go to Iskyla. He said its people hardly ever followed the rules of the kingdom and no one here would even know who we were. And he was right."

The Chancellor at the time had fallen ill, which meant that my dad was working in his place. My dad had been the one to help the girls and send them somewhere safe. Years later, even knowing that he'd tried to help them, Mina would still send Konstantin to kill him in revenge for not crowning her Queen.

"Our father stayed away for a long time, and honestly, that's just as well," Kate said. "I wished he'd never come back."

Ulla leaned forward, resting her arms on the table. "Why? I would love it if my father visited, even once."

"Your father probably isn't completely obsessed with revenge," Kate countered. "To be fair, Mina was already preoccupied with it before he showed up. But once he came here around six or seven years ago, her preoccupation turned into her solitary drive. They talked only about how they would make everyone pay."

"How were they planning to make everyone pay?" I asked.

"I don't know." Kate shook her head. "I tried not to pay attention. My sister Krista and I never cared that much for it. Dad tried to get us to join, but Krista eventually fell in love and moved to Edmonton with her boyfriend. I stayed here, but I spent as much time outside and away from them as I could.

"The only plan I ever really knew about was when Mina

came to me and said she was going to a ball where she would make the King fall in love with her. It seemed ludicrous. I thought for sure Evert would recognize her, but she insisted that she'd only been ten the last time he saw her and now she was a woman of twenty.

"Not to mention that fact that Evert is our second cousin." She wrinkled her nose. "I know royals do that all the time to keep the bloodlines pure, but it's still always seemed so gross to me."

"But Evert didn't recognize her, and he did fall in love with her," I said.

Kate snorted. "Much to my surprise. She came back once after the engagement, and she tried to promise me riches and glory. I told her that I didn't want any of it, and I asked her to let it go. Vengeance never brings people happiness or peace. I said, 'What kind of life is it to be married to your nemesis?'

"Mina looked at me, with her eyes cold and hard, and she said, 'It will be my finest achievement, and I pity you that you'll never understand that.'" Kate grimaced. "And that was the last thing she's ever said to me."

"Did you know Evert was murdered last week?" I asked.

Kate lowered her eyes. "No. I'm surprised it took this long, but I guess Mina's plans are finally under way."

"Do you have any idea what she might do next?" I asked.

"Not anything specific," she said, looking at me with stormy gray eyes. "But honestly, I don't think she'll be happy until everything is suksraungiksuk."

I shook my head and didn't even attempt to repeat the word she'd used. "What's that mean?"

"There's not a literal translation in English," Ulla explained. "But it means 'destroyed' or 'finished.'"

"More like obliterated," Kate said.

THIRTY

nanuq

I awoke just after the sun started to rise, which meant that it was only four in the morning. After sleeping fitfully all night with my usual nightmares, I was happy for the reprieve that being awake provided.

We'd left Kate's hut not long after she'd confessed that Mina was her sister. Before we'd gone, I'd asked her why she'd been so open in telling us everything, and Kate had simply shrugged and said, "Why wouldn't I? Mina's never been much of a sister to me, and I have no reason to keep her secrets."

Ulla had been very excited about everything we'd found out, even though she didn't understand the implications of much of it. Growing up so isolated, she now fancied herself embroiled in plots of treason and espionage.

It had taken quite a bit of convincing for me to get her out of my room last night, telling her that I needed to get to bed early. But really, I just needed a chance to process it all for myself.

Once I did, everything Konstantin and Kate had said fit together perfectly, creating this portrait of a diabolical, unstoppable madwoman. Both Mina and Viktor had been incredibly patient, waiting *years* for their plan to come to fruition.

And now that it had, I was certain that Mina would do everything in her power to make sure that nothing got in her way. You don't plan something for a decade and let it all fall apart at the end.

I needed to get back to Förening. I thought I finally would have evidence to convince Queen Wendy that the Trylle needed to depose Mina. Assuming, of course, that Wendy believed me, since Kate wasn't about to leave Iskyla to testify.

I packed my bag and opened my room door to find Ulla on the landing just outside my room. She'd changed clothes from last night, and she was asleep, using her own bag as a pillow and her coat as a blanket.

When she heard the door open, she sat up with a start. "Finally. You're up."

"*Finally?*" I asked. "What are you doing?"

"I was waiting for you." She stood up and stretched. "I'm coming with."

"You can't come with. You heard what I told you last night. It's too dangerous."

"I know, but I can help," Ulla insisted. "And besides that, nobody wants me here. I have no reason to say."

"You may not have a reason, but I do. I can't afford to take you back with me. I have barely enough money to charter a plane and get back home myself," I explained.

"I've got money. I've saved up every dime and nickel I've ever made." Ulla reached into her jacket pocket and pulled out a surprisingly thick wad of cash. "I can pay my own way, and help you out."

I sighed. "How old are you?"

"Fourteen and a half." She stood up straighter, as if that would make her seem older. She was already taller than me, with slightly broader shoulders, probably thanks to her Omte genes. "I'm mature and strong for my age, though. I can help you."

I was about to tell her no, but the desperate, heartbroken look on her face finally made me cave. With everything that Ulla and Kate had told me about what it was like to grow up here, I didn't think it would be good for anybody.

"Fine, but if you slow me down, I'm leaving you behind," I said, which was more of an empty threat than I wanted to admit.

Ulla almost squealed with delight, but I silenced her and then walked past her and headed down the stairs. Taking her with didn't seem that bad, since I was just headed back to the Trylle. Ulla should be safe with the Trylle, and they could help her find a place in this world.

It wasn't until we'd taken the snowmobile to the nearest town that I realized that Ulla had never been outside of Iskyla before. She was amazed and entranced by every little thing, and I had to constantly remind her that we were traveling incognito and that she needed to stop making a scene.

Surprisingly, she handled the plane better than I did. Somehow the ride managed to be even more turbulent than it had been last time, and the pilot told me it was thanks to an incoming freak blizzard.

Our landing was twice as rough this time, but at least we made it alive. The pilot was right about the storm, though. A brutal wind was coming from the north, bringing with it heavy snow. Ulla suggested we get a hotel for the night and head out in the morning, but I suspected that she just wanted a chance to see more of the city.

I, on the other hand, didn't want to waste any time. I had information that I needed to get to the Trylle as soon as possible. Everyone in Doldastam was depending on it, whether they knew it or not.

So, despite travel advisories telling me not to, I rented an SUV and headed south. For her part, Ulla actually didn't seem to mind the storm or the slow going. I think she would've been thrilled by just about anything I did, though.

The first hour or so into the drive went okay. I barely went above thirty, but we were moving. And then we weren't. We hit a snowdrift so large, the SUV just couldn't get through it. We were stuck.

"Don't worry. I got it," Ulla said. She'd taken off her kamiks while I was driving, but now she slipped them back on, along with her heavy gloves.

"What do you mean, you got it?" I asked, but she was

already opening the car door and hopping out into the snow. "Ulla!"

I wasn't about to let her disappear into the snowstorm, so I jumped out after her. She'd gone around to the back of the SUV, and she'd put on what reminded me of old flight goggles. They were strapped on underneath the earflaps of her hat, and while they were comical-looking, they probably worked well at keeping the snow from stinging her eyes.

"What are you doing?" she asked me, like I was the one who had leapt out of the vehicle without explanation. "Is the SUV in neutral?"

"No. It's in park. Why? What are you doing?"

"I'm gonna get us unstuck." She flexed her arms.

It sounded ridiculous, but she did have Omte blood. She may not have been the size of the ogre Torun I'd seen in Fulaträsk, but she should have some of his strength.

"Be careful," I told her, but I left her to it.

I got back in the vehicle and put it in neutral. I adjusted the rearview mirror so I could watch. Her head bent down as she pushed on the back, and the SUV jerked forward a bit.

Then nothing happened at all for a few seconds, and suddenly it lurched forward, going straight through the snowdrift. Snow flew up around the vehicle, and it skidded to a stop on a clearer stretch of highway on the other side of the drift.

As soon as the SUV stopped, I put it in park and jumped out to make sure Ulla hadn't been hurt. After all, that had been an awfully big push.

"Ulla!" I shouted when I didn't see her right away, and I charged through the drift.

She was standing in the middle of the road, staring off to the right of her, but she didn't appear injured.

"Ulla," I repeated. "That was amazing."

"We should probably get out of here," she said flatly.

"What? Why?" I asked, and I looked to see where she was staring.

There, a few feet off the road and almost invisible in the snow, were two small polar bear cubs. The bigger, fluffier one hung back, but for some reason the smaller one thought it would be a good idea to trot toward us—its big eyes wide and excited.

Growing up near the polar bear capital of the world in Doldastam, there was one important lesson I had learned—wherever there was a cub, nearby was an angry mama bear.

"Let's go," I commanded.

Ulla started hurrying toward the SUV past me. I turned to join her, but it was already too late. The mama bear had come out of nowhere. The giant white beast growled and stomped between me and the vehicle. I had nowhere to run, but that didn't matter, because she wasn't about to let me run anywhere.

Before I could dodge out of the way, she swung at me with her giant paw, and that was the last thing I saw.

THIRTY-ONE

anguish

Searing pain. That's what kept waking me. I didn't remember sleeping or being awake. It was all one blur of pain.

My right side felt like fire, like I had been ripped open and filled with hot coals, and my head throbbed above my right eye. I remembered jostling. My body moving around without my control, bouncing and swaying.

At some point, I became alert enough to realize I was lying in the back of the SUV. From the driver's seat, Ulla kept looking back and telling me that everything would be all right.

I tried to tell her that I was okay and that she shouldn't worry, but all I could muster was a strange gurgling groan. In the back of my mind, I realized that I might actually be dying, but then the pain flared up, blotting out any rational thought.

Some time after that—I'm not sure how long, it could've

been five minutes or five hours—the SUV jolted to a stop, and I rolled forward, which caused enough agony that I screamed out.

Ulla apologized and asked if I was okay, but before I could respond (not that I would've been able to anyway), the driver's-side door opened and a male voice was yelling at her.

"Who the hell are you?" he demanded.

"Who the hell are you?" Ulla shot back.

"Where's Bryn?" he asked, and that's when I faded out again.

I wanted to stay conscious and find out what exactly was going on, but the pain was too much. It overwhelmed everything, and I blacked out.

Then I felt a hand on my face, strong and cold against my skin. I struggled to open my eyes, but my right eye wouldn't open. The vision in my left eye slowly focused, and I saw a face right above mine.

Dark gray eyes filled with worry, black curls falling forward—it took me a moment to realize it was Konstantin.

"Oh, white rabbit. What have you done?" he whispered.

"Am I dying?" I barely managed to get out, in a voice that sounded far too weak to be my own.

"No. I won't let you die," Konstantin promised me. Then to Ulla he shouted, "Drive faster! We need to get there *now*."

Gingerly, he lifted my head and rested it on his lap. It still hurt, but I tried to hide my wincing as best I could. He took my hand in his, and it felt sticky from blood.

"If it hurts too bad, just squeeze my hand," he said.

I wanted to tell him that it always hurt too bad. That the pain was so intense, I felt like I was suffocating, drowning in flames. But I didn't. I just squeezed his hand and waited for darkness to come over me again.

convalesce

Before I even opened my eyes, I felt the difference. My body still ached, especially on the right side, but it was no longer an excruciating fire burning me up from the inside out.

When I did open my eyes, they both opened with ease, which helped quell my fears that I had lost my right eye. They were both there, working properly, as I stared up at the mobile above me.

Sunlight spilled in through the open doorway, but the mobile still managed to cast a few dimly lit shapes of the moon and stars around me. My feet hung off the end of Hanna's small bed. I was back in Förening, at Finn's house.

I looked around, still getting my bearings, when I saw the dark silhouette of Konstantin leaning against the doorframe, backlit by the sun coming in from the front windows.

"What are you doing here?" I asked. I vaguely remembered him being in the SUV with me, but it all felt like a strange, terrible dream.

"I brought you here because you needed medical attention," he said, his voice low.

"But before you said that you couldn't come here because the Trylle would arrest you," I reminded him.

"That Ulla girl didn't know anything about where to go or what to do. I couldn't just leave you with her." He gave a half shrug. "Not if I wanted you to live, anyway. When we got to the gates, I talked to Finn, and he managed to convince the Queen to give me temporary amnesty since I was aiding an injured troll."

"Temporary?" I asked. "How long will that last?"

"I hope it lasts just long enough for me to get out of here without ending up in a dungeon," he replied glibly. His face was hidden in shadows, so I couldn't tell how concerned he really was about being locked up.

"How did you find me?" I asked.

"I'm tracking you, remember? I felt your panic, and I found you as fast as I could. I stopped your car just south of Winnipeg. Ulla didn't want to let me in at first, but I managed to convince her."

"You'll have to stop tracking me eventually," I told him.

"We'll see."

"I should probably thank you for helping me." I started pushing myself up into a sitting position, but as soon as I moved, my side screamed painfully.

"Easy, there." Konstantin rushed over. He put his hand

on my arm, helping me until I was sitting, and then he sat down on the bed beside me. "Finn got a healer to come in and help heal you, but she didn't do it completely. A couple medics fixed you up the best they could after the healer had finished."

Konstantin didn't say it, but I knew why she hadn't healed me all the way—she didn't want to waste her energy on a lowly half-breed tracker outlaw. To be honest, I was surprised she'd bothered helping at all.

"You would've died without it," he said, supplying a reason. A healer could be moved to help even the lowest of the low if they would die without intervention.

I lifted up my tank top to better inspect my wounds, but they were all bound tightly with bandages stretching from my waist to just below my breasts. Some blood seeped through, and I gently touched my ribs, which sent a searing pain through me.

"You've got quite a few stitches under there," Konstantin assured me as I lowered my shirt. "But at least she saved your eye."

I reached up and touched my eye, and unlike my side, it felt perfectly normal and pain-free. There wasn't any sign of injury that I could feel.

"The bear swiped you good across the face, but to save your eye, the healer had to fix it all completely," he explained. "Where the bear tore you open on your side, she mostly just closed up the internal organs. You lost a lot of blood."

"I'll have to thank her for that if I ever see her," I said, and I meant it. She hadn't needed to help me, especially since I wasn't even Trylle, and I was grateful that she'd gone out of her class to save my life.

Then I turned my attention to Konstantin. "How could you not tell me that Mina is Viktor's daughter?"

He inhaled sharply through his teeth. "I didn't know for sure."

"How could you not know?" I asked, incredulous. "You've been sleeping with her for years, and working with her dad? But somehow you never put that together?"

"They're not like a normal father daughter." He shook his head. "At first I thought they might be former lovers, but I quickly realized that wasn't the case because of how cold they were with each other. They were more like colleagues. Mina never called him 'Dad.' They never talked about family. The only thing they ever mentioned was revenge and how they were going to exact it."

"And you never asked?" I pressed.

"Of course I did! But Mina just told me not to concern myself with things like that."

"And that was good enough for you?"

"No!" Konstantin leaned forward and put his hands to his face in frustration. "Nothing was ever good enough for me with Mina, but she wouldn't ever give more. You don't understand what it was like with her. Everything was on her terms. *Everything.*"

"Fine. I can accept that you couldn't push Mina, but why wouldn't you have told me?" I asked. "You obviously had suspicions."

"Really?" He looked at me with an arched eyebrow. "What would've happened if I told you that Mina was Viktor's daughter, and it turned out *not* to be the case? Not only would that have destroyed any trust you had in me, it would've destroyed any credibility you had with whoever you'd gone to with that information."

I realized that he was right. If it had turned out that his hunch was wrong, it would've undone any progress we'd made.

By not revealing unsubstantiated ideas to me, he'd protected everything we were trying to accomplish.

"And does it even matter?" Konstantin asked. "Mina is an evil bitch regardless of who her father is."

"Well, now it matters, because the information might be enough to get the Trylle involved and help the Kanin," I said. "This is proof that Mina got the crown under false pretenses, murdered the King, and she should be dethroned."

"By dethroned, you mean executed." He looked down at the floor, his arms resting on his knees.

For the first time it occurred to me what this might mean to him. He'd once loved Mina, very deeply by his accounts, and even though he realized how awful she truly was, that didn't necessarily mean he'd want to see her dead.

"Yes. Mina will be executed. Are you okay with that?"

He breathed in deeply, then nodded. "I will be."

"You can tell me how you're feeling," I said, then added, "If you want this whole friendship thing to work and want me to trust you, you can't keep things from me."

"I think you know all my secrets now," he replied wearily.

"Thank you for coming back for me."

He smiled crookedly at me. "I'll always come back for you."

tisane

F inn led Konstantin and me down a narrow gravel trail. Hedges grew up around it, blocking out the world and reminding me of Alice playing croquet in Wonderland. The path curved around the palace, and I glanced back at Konstantin to make sure he was still following.

The Queen had invited us to join her for lunch, and Konstantin seemed convinced it was some kind of trick, so I kept expecting him to run off at any moment. But he'd agreed to come and even dressed up for it.

Finn had procured a black dress shirt and vest for him from someone in town. All Finn's clothes were slightly too small, since Konstantin was taller and broader-shouldered. Before we'd left the Holmeses' house, I'd told him that he cleaned up nicely.

He'd looked down at me, his eyes going over my body in a way that made my skin flush, and then he'd gruffly said, "You too, white rabbit," before quickly averting his gaze and walking away.

Mia had given me something—a lovely white dress with an empire waist and a subtle train in the back. It was slightly too small for me, squeezing a bit on my ribs, but fortunately, my wounds were healing up nicely. It had only been a little over a day since I'd arrived in Förening and begun recuperating, but the psychokinetic healing had lingering effects, causing accelerated healing long after the healer had stopped.

The trail opened up into a lush garden on the bluffs. The balcony from the palace hung over, leaving some of the garden in shadows, but the warm spring sun bathed the rest of it.

Brick walls surrounded the garden, covered in flowering vines, with large fragrant blooms of pink and purple. Fruit trees of all kinds populated the garden—with pear, plum, and fig being just a few that I spotted right away.

The gravel trail had given way to a soft, mossy covering that felt wonderful on my bare feet, and Finn led us deeper into the garden. Konstantin had to hold back a few branches to keep them from hitting him in the head.

In the center of a small clearing, surrounded by flowering trees of white and blue, was an elegant wooden table with high-backed chairs. Wendy sat at one end of the table, while her husband Loki sat directly across from her, leaving two chairs open on either side.

A spread of tea and fruits was laid on the table. As Konstantin took a seat next to me, I was again reminded of Alice in Wonderland.

"Thank you for joining us for lunch today," Wendy said, smiling at us.

I returned her smile warmly. "We're more than happy to."

"It seems like you're recuperating all right, then?" Loki asked as he leaned over and took a crumpet from a plate.

"I'm doing much better. Thank you," I said, alternating between looking at the King and the Queen. "I wanted to come see you yesterday, but Finn insisted I rest."

Finn was pouring himself a cup of tea and looked over at me. "You're better off taking your time and making sure everything is healing okay."

"Finn has always been the cautious one." Wendy laughed lightly, then turned her eyes onto me.

While she still held herself with the same authority I'd seen in the throne room, she seemed relaxed today. Her gown had been traded in for a peridot sundress, and the sunshine played well on her bronze skin. She'd done her hair more casually today, so the soft curls were ruffled by the breeze that went through the garden.

"We invited you to lunch to see how you are all doing and what your intentions are," Wendy said directly, looking from Konstantin to me.

Loki laughed. "You make it all sound so formal." With a softer gaze, he turned to us. "We're just curious to know how long you planned on staying."

"Since you granted me temporary amnesty, I hadn't intended to outstay my welcome," Konstantin said, speaking in the low, formal way a Högdragen would speak to authority. "I only wanted to make sure Bryn was stable, and now that she is, I am prepared to head out on my own again. If that's all right."

I shot him a look, unable to hide my surprise. He'd spent most of the past twenty-four hours with me, trying to get me to rest by reading to me, preventing Liam from climbing all over me, telling Ulla and me old Kanin stories, and just generally keeping me company. And he'd never once mentioned leaving.

I knew that he couldn't stay here forever, and I hadn't planned on it myself either. But I hadn't expected him to leave so soon, and the thought sent an unwelcome pang straight to my chest that had nothing to do with my injuries.

"If you want to go, we won't stop you. You're not a captive here." She'd leaned back in her chair, appraising him with the calculated gaze of a ruler twice her age. "But we're also not throwing you out."

Konstantin had taken a sip of his tea, and he dabbed at his mouth with an embroidered napkin before replying. "Thank you, but I think it's best if I take my leave sooner rather than later."

"What about you, Bryn?" Wendy asked. "Finn told me you absconded to find out what was happening with the Kanin. Did you find what you were looking for, or are you planning to leave again?"

"Thank you for extending your amnesty to me again, My Queen," I said as gratefully as I could, clearing my mind of thoughts about Konstantin's departure.

"You can thank my husband for that." Wendy turned her loving gaze to Loki. "He pointed out that if I want the Trylle to be a more welcoming, accepting kingdom, then it must begin with myself."

"What better way to do that than housing those that no longer have a home?" Loki asked.

"I cannot thank you enough for your hospitality," I said, and turned to face Wendy. "But there is something that I wanted to talk to you about. You know that there is a great deal of unrest in Doldastam right now."

The lightness fell away from Wendy, and she pursed her lips. "The loss of your King has had a tragic effect on the kingdom, and my sympathies go out to you."

"I appreciate that, but I was hoping that perhaps you'd be willing to go beyond sympathies," I said carefully, knowing that I may already be pushing my luck.

"I thought that Chancellor Bain already spoke to you and explained that while I am empathetic to the plight of your people, we are in no place to get involved with a possible civil war." Wendy spoke with the air of a Queen giving a procla-mation, but that was sort of what she was doing, so it made sense.

"I'm not advocating civil war," I clarified. "The Kanin people are innocent bystanders. It's only Mina Strinne that needs to be dealt with, and I have found new evidence that I thought you might find more compelling."

Wendy exchanged a look with her husband, her expression

unreadable. He shrugged one shoulder, then turned his attention to me.

"Go on," Loki urged me.

"Do you know who Viktor Dålig is?" I asked.

"The Kanin have apprised us on him previously," Wendy said. "We know of his attempts on the King Evert's life in the past."

"For years, he's been considered the greatest threat to the Kanin kingdom," I said, expanding on what she'd said. "I've just learned that Mina—Queen Mina of the Kanin—is actually Karmin Dålig, Viktor's daughter."

Wendy didn't say anything for a moment. She simply stared off at the garden while I waited with bated breath for her response. Still staring off in the distance, Wendy asked, "Can you prove that?"

"Her sister lives in Iskyla and confirmed it," I said. "If you were to send someone to do some digging, it would be easy to prove."

"I believe you, and that is very disturbing." Wendy finally faced me again. "But it does not change my stance."

"But Mina has no right to the crown," I insisted, barely able to keep my voice even. "She's not the rightful monarch of the Kanin. That's an offense to the entire troll kingdom."

"That may be so, but how would you propose we get the crown from her?" Wendy asked me. "We can't simply phone someone in Doldastam and ask her to surrender."

"We send in a reconnaissance mission," I said. "Konstantin and I are familiar with the palace and Doldastam at large. With as few as ten men, I think we could get in and kill Mina."

Konstantin made a soft, guttural sound next to me, but I kept my eyes on Wendy, so I didn't see his reaction.

"And if we are discovered?" Wendy pressed. "Either before or after the mission is completed, the results would be the same. The Kanin would declare war on us, rightfully so, since we'd just assassinated their Queen.

"And the war would not be with Mina, but with the actual Kanin people she's commanding," she went on. "The innocent people you want to protect." She shook her head. "I'm sorry, but we cannot do that."

Dark clouds began to roll in overhead, blocking out the earlier sunshine and warmth. A breeze came up, stronger and cooler than before, as the garden fell into shadows.

Loki offered me an apologetic smile. "We've had four years of peace after a war that cost us many innocent lives—both of the Trylle and the Vittra. So as you can imagine, we're reluctant to jump into another conflict so soon after that one, while our people and our kingdom are still recovering and rebuilding."

"What about the people of Kanin? She's trapping them and exploiting them. What will become of them?" I asked in desperation.

"If she's as cruel as you say she is, they will have to form an uprising themselves," Wendy said. "That's their only hope of regaining their independence."

return

T his is not what the Queen meant," Konstantin groaned.
He stood beside me, the top few buttons of his dress
shirt undone, glowering down at me with his arms crossed
over his chest.

Unlike him, I'd changed out of my borrowed clothes the
second we'd returned from lunch and put back on my ripped
jeans and tank top. After I'd given Mia her dress and thanked
her, I'd gone to Hanna's room to start packing.

"I don't understand." Ulla sat on the bed next to my bag,
with her knees folded underneath her, and looked from
Konstantin to me. "What exactly did the Queen say?"

"She said that the people of Doldastam need to rise up
against Mina, and I'm going to go back and get them started."
I stopped what I was doing to look around the room, which
had gotten rather messy over the last day or so. "Just as soon
as I find my passport."

"You don't need your passport because you're not going back," Konstantin said. "They will kill you on sight, Bryn!"

Liam toddled into the room, unfazed by the apparent tension, and crawled up onto the bed beside Ulla. He'd become just as fascinated by her unorthodox looks as he had been with mine, and when she pulled him onto her lap, he immediately began tugging on her dirty blond tangles of hair.

While Konstantin had been busy entertaining me, Ulla had been helping Mia around the house. She'd been sleeping in Liam's room and helping take care of him and Hanna, which seemed to make both Mia's and Finn's lives a bit easier.

"Who will kill Bryn?" Ulla asked, trying to follow along with the conversation as I went around the room, tossing aside toys and books in search of my passport.

"The guards. The Kanin. Maybe the Queen herself." Konstantin shrugged. "It doesn't matter *who*. But somebody will kill her. Mina can't let her live."

"I'll sneak in," I said absently.

"You are being ridiculous, Bryn, and you know it." Konstantin sounded exasperated.

"I'll go with you, and I can help," Ulla chimed in.

I shook my head. "No, you can't come. I told you I won't let you go anywhere dangerous."

"Why not?" Ulla whined. "I saved your life. If it hadn't been for me, that polar bear would've killed you."

"I know, and thank you." I paused long enough in my search to look at her sincerely. "But this is different. I'm not going to let you risk your life like that. You haven't had any training, and you're too young."

"I could say the same thing to you," Konstantin countered, giving me a hard look.

"What would you have me do?" I asked, nearly shouting at him. "Twiddle my thumbs and hope Mina isn't killing and torturing everyone I care about? No one will help me, Konstantin! The Omte said no. The Trylle said no. The Skojare don't have anybody left. If I don't do something, who will?"

"It's still early in the fight," Finn interjected, and I turned back to see him standing in the doorway. "There's still time for Wendy to change her mind."

"And what do we do until then?" I asked. "Wait for Mina to start killing innocent citizens off?"

"You're not the only one that has people there," Finn reminded me darkly. "You think I'm not worried about my parents and my sister? Of course I am. But I know that getting myself killed won't save them."

"He's right, Bryn," Konstantin said. "There has to be a better way."

Liam began to babble happily about something—I'm not sure what—and Ulla started to say that she could help me come up with a plan, while Konstantin and Finn were both staring me down, and suddenly it all felt like too much.

"Enough!" I held up my hands. "I just need everyone to go and let me think for a minute. Okay? I just need some space."

Ulla mumbled some kind of apology as she scooped up

Liam and headed out. Finn followed behind her, but Konstantin lingered a moment longer.

"Take all the time you need to sort this out," he said softly, then he left and closed the door behind him.

I sat back on the bed and ran my fingers through my hair. I wanted to scream in frustration, but that would only frighten Liam and Hanna, not to mention Ulla and everyone else. Finn and Konstantin were right, returning to Doldastam would be a suicide mission, but I didn't see any other option.

I couldn't just sit here and hope that something would change for the better. It had been over two weeks since I'd left Doldastam, but it felt like a lifetime. Two grueling weeks where I had no idea if my parents or my friends were okay, and from what I'd heard, things only seemed to be getting worse for them.

How could I just stand by and let it happen?

Someone knocked gently on the door, and based on the meekness of it, I assumed it was Hanna or maybe Liam. I still wasn't ready to talk to anyone, especially a child who probably wanted to play, but I didn't want to yell at them.

"Just go away for a little bit," I said as kindly as I could. "I'll be out soon."

The door creaked open anyway, and I was about to snap this time so they'd get the message, but then I saw who it was, poking her head around the door. Long chestnut hair, dark gray eyes, bronze skin, and her full lips in a timid smile.

It was my oldest friend, Tilda.

compatriot

At first I could only gape at her, in part because I wasn't even sure if she was real. But also because there was so much I had to say to her, so much that had happened since the last time I'd seen her that I hadn't been able to apologize for. Not that I'd ever be able to make up for it.

And top of all that, here she was, alive and safe. I'd spent so much time worrying about her, and now here she was at my bedroom door.

"Can I come in?" she asked quietly and opened the door a bit farther.

I meant to say, sure, or hello, or anything normal, but what tumbled out of my mouth was one big hurried, desperate apology, "Ohmygod, Tilda, I'm so sorry."

As soon as the words escaped my mouth, she began crying. In all our years of being friends, I'd only really seen her cry a handful of times, and never like this. These were big, heavy tears streaming down her cheeks, and she looked completely shattered in a way that I'd never imagined Tilda could be.

I wasn't sure if she hated me or not—I wouldn't blame her if she did. But at that moment, I didn't care. I rushed over and threw my arms around her. She leaned against me, letting me hug her, and sobbed into my shoulder. The fullness of her pregnant belly pressed rather painfully against the wounds from the bear attack, but I didn't care.

For a long time, we didn't say anything. We just stood that way—me holding her as she sobbed. Eventually, she began to collect herself and pulled away from me, wiping at her eyes.

"I'm so sorry," I said again.

She shook her head, sniffling a little. "You don't need to be sorry. I know that you never would've hurt Kasper or let anything happen to him. Not if you could help it."

"I never meant for things to happen the way they did," I said.

"What did happen?" Tilda asked, looking down at me with moist eyes. "I don't believe anything the Queen says, and nobody else was there. Nobody knows what really happened but you."

I motioned to the bed, and Tilda and I sat down. Then I began telling her the story of how her husband had been killed. How we'd gone to tell the Queen about how Kennet Biâelse and the Skojare head guard Bayle Lundeen had been working together to hurt the Skojare royalty. And how Kasper and I had escaped from the dungeon and went to confront

Kennet, and he'd gotten the best of us and killed Kasper, and how I'd fought with Kennet and he'd fallen to his death.

She didn't say anything as I spoke. She only stared at me, listening intently as I wove together the whole story. I even added in the pieces I'd learned from Konstantin, and how I'd found out that Mina was Viktor Dålig's daughter.

When I'd finally finished, she nodded once. "It's good that Kennet is dead. I'm in no shape to hunt him down and kill him, but that's what I would've had to have done. Thank you for getting rid of him for me."

"You're welcome," I said, instead of explaining that I hadn't meant to kill Kennet. I'd been hoping to get him to tell me who he was working for, but since Konstantin had filled me in later, it didn't seem to matter now.

And then I realized something. "What are you doing here? I heard Doldastam was on lockdown."

"It is." Tilda grimaced. "Everything has completely gone to hell since you left, and I couldn't stay any longer. There was no way I could have a baby there, so I had to get out when I could." She'd absently rubbed her stomach as she spoke.

"How far along are you now?" I asked.

"Almost five months." She smiled. "It's so weird because I'm already starting to feel more like a mom."

Hearing her say the word made me think of my own parents and how I hadn't heard anything from them since I'd been gone.

"Do you know how my parents are doing?" I asked.

Her smile fell away. "I've seen them around. I won't lie to

you—things are hard for them right now. They've both lost their jobs, and people don't trust them. But they're safe, and they're still together. They're as free as anyone else in Doldastam."

I let that sink in for a moment. My parents were safe, and they were together.

"How did you get out of Doldastam?" I asked.

"Pretty much the same way you did," Tilda said. "I snuck out with Ridley."

My heart skipped a beat at the mention of his name. "What do you mean, Ridley?"

"He can explain it to you better. He convinced Mina to send him out on an errand."

"He can explain it?" I asked, and my mouth suddenly felt dry. "What do you mean? Where is he?"

"He's here." Tilda motioned toward the door. "I think he's outside talking with Finn. But you can go see him." She slowly got to her feet. "Mia offered me tea when we got here, and I think I'm going to take her up on the offer."

I stood up, feeling dazed. "Tilda. I am glad you got out, and I'm really glad that you're safe."

She smiled. "Me too. And you have no idea how happy it makes me, knowing that you're safe."

We hugged again, this time quicker than before, and then she left me so I could find Ridley.

reserve

The clouds that had moved in earlier, darkening the lunch with Queen Wendy and King Loki, had brought rain along with them. It was a heavy garden shower, with thunder rumbling in the distance.

I stepped out into it, not minding the cold drops that fell on my bare shoulders, and looked around for Finn and Ridley. They weren't far from the house, standing underneath the awning that stretched past a barn that had once housed goats.

Ridley had his back to me as I approached, but the lines of his body were unmistakable to me. His strong shoulders, the narrowing of his waist beneath his loose olive jacket, the dark curls of his hair that could never be completely tamed.

When I reached them, Finn excused himself, and nodded at me as he walked toward the house. It seemed to take ages for Ridley to turn around to face me, but in reality, it was probably only a few seconds.

And then he was looking at me—the strong line of his jaw darkened by a few days' stubble, the richness of his olive skin, his lips barely parted as he breathed, and the dark mahogany of his eyes burning with an intensity that made everything inside me melt.

Ridley was really here. *My* Ridley.

It wasn't until then that I realized I'd been holding my breath, and I breathed in deeply. He lowered his eyes, hiding his gaze behind his heavy lashes.

"What are you doing here?" I asked finally.

"I came to find you," he said, his voice low and thick, and it sounded strangely far away. Like he was holding something back.

Calvin, Hanna's small pony, was out in the yard, running around and splashing in the puddles. Ridley turned, preferring to look out at the pony than at me.

The thatched roof of the awning had seen better days, and rain dripped in around us. It soaked the bales of straw stacked up beside us, and beneath my bare feet the ground was cold and muddy. Other than Calvin, we were alone. And Ridley wouldn't look at me.

A shiver ran through me, but it wasn't because I was cold.

"You're soaking wet," he commented, glancing at me out of the corner of his eye. "You want my jacket?"

I shook my head, but he'd already started slipping it off. He walked over to me and draped his jacket over my shoulders. His hand brushed against my bare skin, and he smelled cold and crisp, the way he always did. As he adjusted the jacket, he looked down at me. For a moment we were looking into each other's eyes, and all I could think about was the night we'd spent together.

Then he looked away and stepped back from me. I slipped my arms into the sleeves, which were still warm from his body heat. I wondered dourly if this was as close as he would get to touching me.

The distance between us felt immeasurable. The last time I'd seen him, he'd held me in his arms and kissed me deeply. He'd wanted to run away with me, but it had been dangerous, and I needed him to stay behind and make sure my parents and Tilda and Ember were okay.

Every night since, I'd had nightmares about him being ripped away from me. And as we stood here, with so much tension filling the gulf between us, I feared that all my nightmares had come true.

"Why did you come find me?" I asked. "You knew where I was. You sent me here."

"I had to get out of Doldastam," he said simply. "Queen Mina wants you captured and convicted, and I managed to convince her that I wanted that too. That you'd betrayed me so badly that I would go out and bring you back for her."

I swallowed hard. "Do you think I betrayed you?"

"No, of course not." He dismissed the idea immediately. "I just had to tell Mina that so I could get out of there."

"What's your plan now that you're here?" I asked.

He let his eyes rest on me. "Honestly, I don't have one."

"It's hard to know what to do when everything is falling apart."

Ridley rubbed the back of his neck, then turned away, again watching Calvin prance through puddles. Without looking at me, he asked, "You're working with Konstantin Black now? When did that start?"

"After I left," I said, realizing how much I had to explain to Ridley. How much had happened while we'd been apart. "He found me. He defected from Viktor, and he thought we might help each other."

"Have you been?"

"I think so," I said.

"He hasn't . . . hurt you or anything?" Ridley looked at me, and there was no jealousy in his eyes—only genuine concern.

I shook my head quickly. "No. No, nothing like that."

"Good. It's just . . ." He sighed. "For weeks, I didn't know what was happening with you. I was worrying about all the terrible things that might be going on."

"I had a run-in with a bear, but otherwise, I'm okay." I tried to force a smile, to ease some of the tension, but it didn't work.

"Finn told me about that," was all Ridley said.

"I worried about you too," I said, deciding that speaking from the heart might work better. "I thought of you every day, and I was so afraid of what might be happening to you." His jaw clenched, and he stared down at a small stone that he kicked at absently. "What happened after I left?"

"It's over now," he said, almost growling. "That's what matters."

"What does that mean?"

"It's getting cold out here. I think I'm gonna head back inside." Rather abruptly, he started to walk past me.

"Ridley," I said, but he just kept going.

I pulled his jacket more tightly around me and tried to make sense of what had just happened. This was not at all how I'd pictured my reunion with Ridley. There had been much more kissing.

I was so relieved to see him, to know that he was okay, but after that exchange, I had no idea how to feel.

From the corner of my eye, I saw movement. I quickly turned my head, but I couldn't see anything. Then it moved again, and in the shadows between the doorway to the barn and stacks of straw, I realized that I could see a black shirt, floating disembodied thanks to the chameleonlike skin of the Kanin.

Someone was there, spying on me.

THIRTY-SEVEN

derailed

I rushed over, preparing to get the jump on whoever it was, as my mind raced with thoughts of a Kanin spy stowing away with Ridley. Someone working for Mina coming to gather information and trap us.

But just before I punched at the black shirt, I heard Konstantin's voice. "Easy, white rabbit! It's just me!"

He appeared to materialize out of thin air—the brown brick of the wall and the dirty yellow of the straw quickly shifting to his normal skin tone. Konstantin had his hands up defensively, but since he had been eavesdropping on me, I punched him in the arm anyway. Not very hard, but enough to let him know that I was annoyed.

He scowled at me as he rubbed his shoulder. "That was uncalled-for."

"Why were you stalking me like that?" I demanded.

"I wasn't. I just came out to talk to you, and then you were in the middle of something, and I didn't want to interrupt the moment, so I just thought I'd hide out and wait for it to be over," Konstantin said. "And it's over now."

I narrowed my eyes at him. "That's creepy. Don't be creepy."

"What was going on with that guy anyway?" he asked. "Is he your boyfriend?"

I ran my hand through my wet hair and turned away from Konstantin. "Never mind."

"That's just as well. I didn't come out here to talk about him anyway."

"What did you come out for?"

"Mia got a call from the palace." He motioned vaguely behind me, in the direction of where the palace sat hidden among the trees a mile down the road. "Those friends of yours came in through the gate, so the Queen got word of it. She wants to meet with you and Ridley in the morning to discuss what's happening."

"Discuss what?" I asked.

"Probably why there's like half a dozen people hiding out in Finn's house, and how long everyone plans on staying here," he said.

I nodded. "That makes sense."

"I overheard Mia say that Ridley is the Överste now?" Konstantin asked.

"He was before I left. I'm not sure if he still is. I'm not sure about anything anymore . . ." I trailed off.

"Ridley's younger than me, and he wasn't on the

Högdragen, so I didn't really know him," Konstantin explained. "But you know how small the tracker school was, so I knew of him. He always seemed like a punk kid with a chip on his shoulder. I didn't know he had it in him to be the Överste."

"That was a long time ago," I reminded Konstantin. "He's grown up since then. We all have."

"Time does have a way of doing that to you."

He was right, and I realized how much the last few months had changed us—me, Ridley, Tilda, and even Konstantin. It was strange to look back and realize how much simpler things had been before I caught sight of Konstantin following Linus Berling.

"That one moment changed everything and put it all in motion," I said, thinking aloud.

Konstantin's thick brows rose in surprise, and then, as if reading my mind, he said, "When you got into my car in Chicago. It changed the course of my life entirely."

"Good. Your life needed a change of course."

He smirked. "That it did."

I turned away, staring out at the pouring rain around us. "Now where do we go from here?"

"I don't know. But I can't see anything good for you in Doldastam." He shook his head. "Only death and destruction."

gathering

An awkward night spent in Finn and Mia's increasingly cramped house did nothing to ease the tension between Ridley and me. I wanted to talk to him, to find out what was going on, but it was impossible to get a moment alone. There was always someone —usually Liam—in the way.

I'd taken the floor in Hanna's room, so Tilda could have the bed, and Ulla had gone back to Liam's room again. Ridley slept on the couch, while Konstantin strangely took the stables, insisting he'd gotten used to sleeping anywhere.

In the morning, I awoke with an awful crick in my neck. The bandages on my side were a bit bloodier than normal, probably from pressing too hard on the floor, but it was nothing that I couldn't survive.

First thing after breakfast, Ridley and I walked down to the palace for the meeting with Queen Wendy. We spoke very little on the way there, mostly commenting on the weather or the way the gravel stung my feet. Even though we were together for the first time in ages, the distance between us stretched further than ever before.

We'd been shown into the palace and left to wait outside the Queen's office. Presumably, she had some business to attend to before she'd let us in. There was no waiting area, so we stood in the hall just outside the office.

Ridley leaned back against the wall, staring down the corridor with a look of boredom and annoyance. The top few buttons of his shirt had been left undone, the way they usually were, but I noticed that his rabbit amulet was absent. It had been his gift from the kingdom upon becoming Rektor three years ago, and I'd never seen him without it before.

I wanted to ask him where it was or why he wasn't wearing it, but I doubted I'd get any kind of answer from him. Everything he'd said to me since he'd been here had been little more than a word or a grunt. It was like he couldn't even bring himself to speak to me.

I did my best to keep my head up and my expression neutral, like this wasn't breaking my heart all over again.

"One thing's for sure," Ridley said at length. "We can't all keep staying at Finn's house."

"I plan on leaving soon anyway," I told him honestly.

He jerked his head to look at me. "Why? Where are you going?"

"Doldastam."

His eyes darkened. "You can't go back there. Mina will have you killed."

"I didn't realize you even cared," I replied wearily.

"What are you talking about? Of course I care," Ridley said in an angry whisper.

I studied him, standing across from me. His hands were clenched on the chair rail that ran along the wall behind him, and his expression had softened. For one of the first times since he'd arrived in Förening, I could actually see the guy I'd fallen in love with.

"Do you?" I asked softly.

He stepped away from the wall and moved toward me. With only inches between us, he stopped, and looked down at me in the way that made my heart beat erratically. He had this wonderful, dizzying way of making the whole world disappear for a few moments, so it was only me and him, and all the rest of my fears and worries fell away.

Ridley opened his mouth like he meant to say something, but I'll never know exactly what it was, because the Queen's office door opened, interrupting us, and Ridley quickly stepped back from me.

Chancellor Bain leaned out into the hallway, hanging onto the door as he did, and offered us an apologetic smile. "Sorry to keep you waiting. But the Queen is ready to see you now."

"Thank you," Ridley said. He glanced at me from the corner of his eye and straightened his shirt, then followed Bain into the office.

I took a second longer to collect myself. Thanks in part to my much fairer skin flushing so noticeably, it was a bit harder for me to return to normal after moments like that with Ridley.

The Queen's office was smaller than I'd expected. The entire exterior wall consisted of floor-to-ceiling windows, which helped it feel a bit larger than it actually was. Two of the three interior walls were all shelves filled to the brim with books.

A large oak desk sat in the center of the room. Along the edges, vines had been carved into it, but that was a reoccurring theme throughout the room, with vines carved into crown molding and the frames around the window.

On the wall across from the desk were two large paintings—one of the previous Queen Elora, Wendy's mother, and the other was of Wendy, her husband, and an adorable boy of about three years old, presumably their son, Prince Oliver.

When I came into the room, Bain sat cross-legged in one of the leather chairs in front of the desk, while Ridley preferred to stand, leaving the other chair empty. Wendy was standing with her hands on the desk, leaning forward to look down at the papers spread over it.

"Can you close the door behind you?" she asked absently, still staring down at the papers before her.

I did as I was told, and when I came back to stand beside Ridley, I got a better look at what held her attention so raptly. It was a scroll, with a quartz paperweight placed at either end to keep it from rolling up. Still, a portion had flipped just enough for me to see the wax seal at the top—a rabbit pressed in white wax. The symbol of the Kanin.

Trolls weren't completely prehistoric—they would call or send e-mail, even text. It was so much faster than airmail, even though that scroll had probably been overnighted to a local town by FedEx and retrieved by a Trylle messenger. But we used scrolls for formal business, like invitations, gratitude, proclamations, and declarations of war.

I waited, holding my breath, to find out which one of those it was, although with Mina, I feared I already knew the answer.

proclamation

That Queen of yours has gone totally mad," Wendy said finally.

"She's no Queen of mine," I replied without thinking, and Bain smiled in approval, causing his blue eyes to light up.

Wendy straightened, but kept her eyes fixed on the scroll. "This just arrived, so it isn't what I'd invited you here to talk about. I only meant to ask you about your plans in Förening. But I know about your past relationship with the Skojare, so I'm sure you'd want to know."

"Know what?" I asked, instantly fearing that something had happened to Linnea Biâelse, or perhaps her husband Mikko or grandmother Lisbet.

The Queen finally looked at us, her dark tawny eyes sad. "The Kanin have declared war on the Skojare."

"What?" Ridley asked, sounding as shocked as I felt.

"Why would Mina do that?" I asked in disbelief. "She'd aligned herself with them to get their . . ."

And that's when it hit me. Mina had not been working with the Skojare as a whole—she'd been working with specific people, like the now-dead Kennet Biâelse and the now-exiled head guard Bayle Lundeen.

She had no one to get her the sapphires anymore, so she would have to take them by force.

"It's all here." Wendy motioned to the scroll. "Assuming you can make sense of her nonsense."

Ridley went over to read it for himself, but I sat back in the chair, feeling rather light-headed. Besides, it didn't really matter what reasoning Mina gave. I knew the truth.

"She's blaming Evert's death on Kennet, even though Kennet died before Evert did," Ridley said, surmising what he'd read. "She says Kennet had 'empoisoned' the wine he gifted them before he died, which is said to have killed Evert."

"Since she's accused me of killing Kennet, am I exonerated now?" I asked, not that I believed that that would actually happen. Mina would never let me go free.

"No, because you apparently killed Kennet in some sort of lover's spat, and you've been corrupted by the 'aberrations and unfettered debauchery' of Storvatten." Ridley stood up. "She keeps using all these abnormal words like that. I mean, they are words, but not ones that we actually use."

"Her language is odd, even for a proclamation like this," Wendy agreed.

"At the end, it says, when the Kanin are through, 'the ground will be *sanguinolent.*'" Ridley shook his head. "I don't even know what that means."

"It means 'tinged with blood,'" Bain supplied. "I looked it up."

"It's her British accent all over again." I rested my elbow on the armrest and propped my head up. "She's trying so hard to sound smart and important, because she's really just a spoiled, uneducated princess that got dropped in the middle of nowhere when she was too young to know any better, and nobody taught her how to act or grow up. Everything she pretends to be is just copied from Disney and Julie Andrews."

"Does that mean that she won't actually go through with all of this?" Wendy asked hopefully. "That this is all just part of her act?"

"Oh, no, she's definitely going to attack the Skojare. She's a monster," Ridley said, and that hardness had returned to his face, the same hardness that kept me at bay.

"She's going to slaughter them," I realized sadly, and looked over at Bain. "You worked in Storvatten. You know. They have no means of protecting themselves."

He nodded grimly. "Their guard is an absolute joke. The Kanin going after the Skojare will be like shooting fish in a barrel, pardon the pun."

Wendy's dark hair was up in a loose bun, but the silver lock fell over her forehead, and she brushed it back, causing her emerald bracelets to jangle. She walked around the desk, so she was closer to Bain, Ridley, and me, and leaned back against it.

"We want to help the Skojare, but we're in an awful position," Wendy began. "We're allies of both the Kanin and the Skojare, which means that technically we shouldn't get involved. But at the same time, I'm not about to stand by and let an entire tribe be destroyed.

"Mina sent that scroll asking us to rally behind the Kanin's unwarranted attack, which is so ludicrous." Wendy rolled her eyes. "I honestly don't know what she's thinking. But her overzealousness, I think, may be her downfall.

"However, that doesn't mean I can just jump into the fray," she went on. "I need to consult with advisers and talk to the board, and come up with the best possible solution I can."

I stood up. "I appreciate your position, and I know that you will do all that you can. Until then, *I'm* going to do all that I can."

"Meaning?" Wendy asked.

"I'm going to Storvatten, and I'm going to help prepare them for war."

tavvaujutit

W ait!" Ulla shouted, practically tripping over herself as she ran up the muddy embankment toward me. *"Wait!"*

I looked back up at the top of the hill, where Ridley, Konstantin, and Tilda were all standing at the SUV, making me feel like I was on the *Titanic* and they were escaping on the last life raft.

Instead of rushing up to join them the way I wanted to, I sighed and turned back to face Ulla. When she reached me, she was panting, and tears sparkled in her amber eyes.

"Ulla," I said as gently as I could. "We already discussed this. It's dangerous for you to come with us. Besides, you're a huge help to Mia and Finn. They need you here."

"I know, I know." She tried to shrug it off like it was no big deal, but the hurt was etched into her face. "I just . . ." Abruptly, she held her arm out, with a leather strap hanging from her fist. "I made you this, and I didn't want you to leave without it."

I held out my hand, and she unceremoniously dropped the necklace into my hand. Tied onto the strap was a piece of ivory. It had been crudely carved into a rabbit, but it was still unmistakable that that's what it was.

"Because Konstantin always calls you white rabbit," Ulla explained. "I thought it must be a nickname or something." She shook her head. "I don't know. It's probably stupid."

"No, it's great. Thank you." I dropped the necklace around my neck and smiled at her.

"Anyway, you should probably get going," Ulla said.

I nodded, and she hugged me gruffly. It was a case of her not knowing her own strength, and she nearly cracked my ribs when she squeezed me. When she let go, she started backing away.

"Tavvaujutit," she said, saying good-bye in Inuktitut— *tah-vow-voo-teet.*

"Tavvaujutit," I said, and she turned and jogged back to Mia and Finn's house.

I continued up the slope to the SUV. Tilda and Konstantin had gotten in the backseat, but Ridley waited outside, leaning against the driver's side. He didn't say anything when I reached him, choosing to just get into the vehicle instead.

Ridley started the SUV and headed down the narrow, winding roads of Förening toward the gate, and I leaned back in my seat.

"Just because I'm pregnant doesn't mean I won't hurt you

if you try anything," Tilda warned Konstantin, and I knew that she meant it.

Despite my assurances that Konstantin was on our side, Tilda was reluctant to trust him. I suppose having her husband killed by someone I'd trusted made her question my judgment, and I couldn't really blame her for that.

"I already told you, I'm not going to try anything," Konstantin said, exasperated. "I should've taken the Mustang."

"It's better if we ride together," Ridley explained to him again. "We'll draw less attention, and the last thing any of us want is to garner attention from either the Kanin or Viktor's men."

Konstantin let out a heavy sigh, and I looked up in the rearview mirror to watch him sulking in the backseat. "This is gonna be a long ride to Storvatten."

Yesterday, after we'd gotten back from the meeting with Wendy and Bain where they explained that the Kanin had declared war on the Skojare, we all sat down and talked about what we were going to do. I had already made up my mind that I was going to Storvatten, and Konstantin quickly volunteered to go with me.

Ridley had slowly warmed to the idea. Even though he wanted to do everything he could to avoid getting captured by the Kanin, he knew that the Skojare needed us, and despite his misgivings, he wasn't about to stand by and do nothing.

I'd wanted Tilda to stay behind in Förening, where she'd be safer, but she insisted on coming with us. She wanted to do something to help stop the people who were indirectly responsible for Kasper's death. And as of late, she'd been working as a captain in the Kanin army, helping train the soldiers. She would be an excellent asset for the Skojare in helping them get their troops in shape.

So we'd headed out to Storvatten that morning with a light drizzle following us everywhere we went. It soon became apparent that the eight-hour drive from Förening to Storvatten was going to be even longer than normal, thanks to the frequent pit stops needed by Tilda.

We weren't even halfway through the trip, and we were on our third break. We were on a relatively empty stretch of highway, so Ridley pulled over and Tilda ran out into the thick brush of the ditch.

I got out with Tilda every time, just in case she might need me. I doubted that she would, but I didn't like the idea of leaving a pregnant woman alone like that. While she ran through the ditch, I got out and waited next to the car.

"I told you this would be a long drive," Konstantin said, climbing out of the backseat.

"Why are you getting out?" I asked.

"I need to stretch my legs." He paced alongside the SUV, unmindful of the fact that the drizzle was getting heavier.

Beyond the ditch was a cold gray fog. We'd been taking back roads to avoid suspicion, and it had been a while since we'd crossed paths with another car. It felt still and eerie on the side of the road, and I was looking forward to getting to our destination.

I shivered and pulled my hooded sweatshirt more tightly around me.

Suddenly Konstantin tensed up, looking around like a hunting dog that's found its prey. I was about to ask him what was wrong when he said, "We're not alone."

And then Tilda screamed.

FORTY-ONE

strike

Tilda stood on the other side of the ditch, with brush between us, and her eyes were wide and frantic as she pointed toward us. "Behind you!"

Before I had a chance to look, Konstantin pushed me out of the way, knocking me to the ground, and he lunged at what appeared to be nothing—just empty space. But when Konstantin's fist collided loudly with his opponent's bare flesh, I saw the mirage-like shimmer of his skin. The chameleon coloring of the stark landscape around us changing to the tanned tones of Kanin skin.

"Get my daggers out of my bag!" Konstantin commanded.

As I scrambled from the ground, the guy Konstantin was fighting had finally shifted back to normal, and I realized that it was Drake Vagn. He'd once been a tracker in Doldastam, but he was more than ten years older than me, so I didn't really know him.

But I do remember the big fit he'd thrown when he'd been forced to retire six years ago. He'd eventually left Doldastam and the entire Kanin kingdom over it, and it had not been on good terms.

"You thought you could switch teams, eh?" Drake asked Konstantin, smirking as he punched him in the face.

Then came the loud sound of crunching metal, and the SUV lurched to the side, slamming into me and knocking me down. I lay perpendicular with the vehicle, squishing down in the mud as much as I could. For a brief second, the vehicle was actually over me—the metal entrails of it mere inches above my face. I'd turned my head to the side, watching as the tires skidded to a stop in the ditch beside me.

As quickly as I could, I crawled out from underneath toward the back of the SUV, and I got to my feet. Peering around, I discovered why it had suddenly lurched to the side.

A massive beast of a man was standing next to the driver's door, which had been severely dented in, causing the window to crack into a million pieces. That explained why Ridley hadn't gotten out yet—the angry hulk had punched in the door, momentarily trapping him inside.

Based on the hulk's size alone, I guessed he was Omte. He could easily push in the shattered window and grab Ridley, but he seemed to prefer glaring down at him, smiling like a shark. His dark hair went down his back in a thick ponytail, and he was shirtless, displaying a series of thick tribal tattoos that covered his torso.

Konstantin and Drake had moved their fight to the road,

matching each other blow-for-blow, and I registered the insults they were hurling at each other just enough to put together that they'd both been working together for Viktor before Konstantin had defected.

I opened the hatchback and saw that Ridley was crawling across the seats with the aim of getting out of the back passenger door. I grabbed Konstantin's worn leather satchel and hurriedly started digging through it.

Everywhere he went, Konstantin carried two long, sharp daggers. They had been his gift when he'd become the Queen's personal guard, and they were made with the highest-quality metal with ornate ivory carvings in the handle. They were beautiful, but most importantly, they were deadly.

I just caught sight of one of the blades in the bag when I felt a huge hand crushing me around my waist. I tried to hang on to the bag, but suddenly I was sailing backward, and I lost my grip. The bag tumbled to the ground, and I heard the daggers clattering against the pavement.

It all happened so quickly, and I was flying through the air before landing painfully against the damp asphalt of the highway. It took me a second to catch my breath, then I pushed myself up onto my elbows to see the giant stomping toward me with that awful toothy grin on his face.

Across his chest, he had the word MÅNE tattooed in huge black letters, and as he rapidly approached—he walked slow and deliberately, but he took giant steps—all I could think about was Ulla. She was a fourteen-year-old half-Omte and she'd pushed the two-ton SUV out of the snow. And this guy was at least a foot taller than Ulla, with hands the size of her head and arms thicker than her waist.

He was going to crush me with his bare hands.

As I jumped to my feet, my mind raced, trying to figure out how I could possibly fight someone as strong as this Måne guy. Behind him, I saw Ridley running toward him, wielding a huge chain. Based on the size of it and the hooks on either end, I guessed it was a towing chain that had been in the back of the SUV.

Ridley swung it hard, whipping Måne in the back. That would've been enough to knock a normal man down, but it barely fazed him. He stopped walking and turned to face Ridley, and he growled. Actually growled, like a wolf guarding a bone.

But Ridley didn't back down. He swung the chain again, harder, and this time the hook managed to take hold in the tough flesh of Måne's shoulder. I think Ridley's plan was to pull Måne down and tie him up with the chain.

But that's not what happened. Måne yanked the chain and pulled Ridley toward him, and I knew that I would have to act fast if I didn't want Måne to crush both of us.

I raced past Måne back toward the SUV and grabbed a dagger off the highway. Behind me, I heard Ridley let out a guttural moan that made my blood run cold.

When I turned back I saw that Måne had gotten the chain around Ridley's neck. He stood behind him, pulling the chain taut with his enormous hands, and as Ridley clawed futilely at the chain, his face had begun to turn purple.

I charged at Måne, and holding the dagger with both hands, I drove it into his back. I did it again and again, each time causing more blood to splatter back on me. It took five thrusts of the blade between his shoulders before he finally dropped to his knees. That brought him low enough so I could jab it into his spine, severing his brain stem, and he fell forward onto the road.

Ridley crawled out from underneath him, gasping for breath. His neck was red and raw and bleeding in a few places, but otherwise he looked like he would survive.

"Thank you," he said between breaths.

"Anytime," I said, then turned my attention to the fight between Konstantin and Drake.

It was still going strong, but Konstantin's face was looking more bloodied than Drake's. He was taking a beating.

I moved down the highway toward them. Drake had his back to me, and as soon as Konstantin looked at me, I tossed the dagger to him. He caught it easily just as Drake tried to come at him again. With one quick move, Konstantin sliced Drake's throat, and he collapsed to the ground.

Konstantin wiped the blood from his face, then stepped over Drake's body to walk to where Ridley and I were standing in the middle of the road.

"That's it, then," Ridley said, surveying the carnage around us.

Someone whistled loudly from the ditch, and I realized too late that we'd forgotten about Tilda. I couldn't see anything from where I stood, so I ran closer to the SUV, and then I saw them, standing in the brush just on the other side of the vehicle.

Bayle Lundeen—the former Skojare head guard—had one arm wrapped around Tilda, pressing her to him, while the other one held a knife to her throat. She had her hands on his arm, trying to pull it away, but he didn't seem to be budging.

"It's not quite over yet," Bayle warned me.

avenge

Konstantin rushed behind me, but I put my arm out to stop him, so he didn't go charging toward them. Bayle's knife was poised to slice right through Tilda's throat, and he raised his arm higher, making Tilda squirm.

Ridley came up beside me, and we stood frozen on the embankment, unsure of what the next move should be.

"You don't have to do this," I said, trying to remain calm, and I was acutely aware of the bloodied blade clenched in Konstantin's fist.

"I really didn't want it to come to this," Bayle admitted, but he didn't relax his stance.

When I'd been at Storvatten before, it had been hard for me to get a clear read on Bayle. He'd been standoffish but professional when Kasper and I interacted with him. We were never able to entirely discern what Bayle's role was in everything that had transpired in Storvatten, but as the head guard, he'd definitely had his hand in things.

It had been his guard, Cyrano, who attempted to murder King Mikko, and it had almost certainly been Bayle who falsified the safe records that got Mikko arrested. From the best I could gather, he'd been working with Kennet from the start of the fallen Prince's plan to dethrone Mikko.

If it hadn't been for Bayle, I wasn't sure how much Kennet would've been capable of on his own. But I doubt Mikko would've been arrested, which meant that Kennet wouldn't have come to Doldastam to pay Mina for her help, and then Kasper wouldn't have been killed.

"I worked my ass off for that *kingdom,* if you can even call it that," he said, his words dripping with venom. "For years. All I wanted was to be paid my dues! And Kennet came up with this plan, and it would all be so simple."

"It can still be simple," I said. "Killing an innocent will only complicate things."

Bayle snorted. "Since Kennet turned against me and deposed me, I've been sentenced to doing Viktor's dirty work. I'm up to my neck in blood! What's one more bitch?"

"Viktor will turn on you too," Konstantin warned him. "The same way he's turned on me."

"I'm not an idiot like you. I just wanna get *paid,*" Bayle sneered. "And right now, Viktor is offering a massive reward for delivering the three of you." He nodded toward Ridley, myself, and Konstantin. Then he looked down at Tilda, almost speaking in her ear. "What's one more body to add to the pile?"

"If you hurt her, you will not leave here alive," I growled at him. "I will kill you with my bare fucking hands, Bayle."

Bayle started to laugh. "Oh, you really think so?"

Something flashed in Tilda's eyes, and her body tensed up. Her expression hardened, and there was a resolve in her that I knew all too well from training with her. Tilda was a master of restraint, but she could destroy someone if she wanted to.

"Wait," Tilda said in a stilted voice. "This is Bayle Lundeen? Bayle, who conspired with Kennet? Bayle, who's one of the reasons my husband is dead?"

I nodded once. "Yeah. That's him."

For the first time, Bayle seemed to realize he might have bitten off more than he could chew, and he looked down at Tilda with new appreciation. Tilda may be pregnant, but she was still tall and strong, with muscular arms and powerful legs.

I was sure that when Bayle had first captured her, she'd been more docile so as not to risk him hurting the baby. But now she was pissed.

With one sudden jerk, she flung her head backward, smashing into Bayle's face. From where I stood several feet away from her, I heard the sound of his nose crunching. Before he could tilt the knife toward her, she grabbed his wrist, bent it backward, and, using her other arm as leverage, she broke his arm with a loud snap.

It all happened within a few seconds, and Bayle screamed in pain and stumbled back. His arm hung at a weird angle, and blood streamed down his face. But Tilda wasn't done yet.

With a swipe of her leg, she kicked his legs out from under him. He fell back into the mud, and Tilda kicked him hard in the groin, causing Konstantin to wince beside me. Then she jumped on top of him, punching him repeatedly in the face with both fists.

His body had gone limp, but I wasn't sure if that was because he was unconscious or dead. Either way, Tilda apparently decided that she wanted to be certain. She grabbed the knife that he'd dropped on the ground beside them, and she stabbed him straight through the heart.

And then she just sat there, kneeling on his dead body and breathing hard. None of us said anything or moved. It felt like she needed the moment to herself.

When she finally stood up, she shook her arms out, probably both because her fists hurt from hitting Bayle so hard and also to get rid of some of the blood.

"Do you feel better?" I asked her.

She nodded, still catching her breath as she walked over to me. "Yeah. We have to do something about these bodies, though. The humans will get suspicious."

"That girl is a fucking beast," Konstantin whispered as she walked by, and he looked at her with newfound admiration.

"You should see her when she's not pregnant," I said.

Tilda went into the SUV and used a bottle of water and a shirt from her bag to clean off the blood. Eventually, the rest of us would probably want to do the same, but right now we needed to focus on getting the bodies out of here before another car came by.

While Ridley and I went to grab Bayle's body, Tilda moved all our bags into the backseat so we wouldn't bloody all our things. Konstantin grabbed Drake's body, throwing it over his shoulder, and then dropping him unceremoniously in the back.

The challenge was not only moving Måne's massive body—which took all three of us—but also loading it into the back of the SUV. We had to fold him into a very strange position to get him to fit.

"There's still one big problem," Tilda said. While we stood at the back of the vehicle, beside the open tailgate, she was still sitting in the backseat and turned to look at us over the pile of bodies. "These guys were clearly Viktor's men, and they found us. How?"

Ridley shook his head. "When we left Doldastam, we threw out our phones, and we ditched the Range Rover and rented a car. I don't know how they could possibly track us." Then he looked over at Konstantin. "Unless someone told them where we'd be."

"They tried to kill me too, remember?" Konstantin snapped. "And how would I know that we'd be at this exact spot on this exact shitty road at this time while Tilda was taking a piss?"

"Then how did they find us?" Ridley asked defensively.

"Probably the same way I found Bryn." He turned back to the bodies and pushed Måne out of the way so he could dig in Drake's pocket. Then he pulled out a lock of dark curly hair and held it up to Ridley. "He was tracking you."

Ridley's face fell, and he ran a hand through his hair, as if he'd be able to feel a missing lock of hair. "Shit."

"Shit indeed." Konstantin gave him a hard look, then he slammed the hatchback shut. He walked around the car and got inside, leaving Ridley and me alone.

"I'm sorry," Ridley said, staring off at the empty field beside us. "I shouldn't have come. Mina knew I would lead her right to you. It's my fault."

"She tricked you," I said. "She's tricked all of us. It's what she's good at."

He set his jaw. "I should've known better."

"It's okay. We're all okay. You're the one that got hurt the worst."

His skin had been red and raw, but it was starting to darken as bruises began to form. He just shook his head. "You guys need to leave me here and go on without me. They could have more people tracking me. You won't be safe with me."

"Ridley, I'm not going to leave you on the side of the road. And even if they do track us, they'd follow us straight to Storvatten, where they plan on attacking anyway. We'll be fine."

He lowered his eyes, swallowing hard. "I'm sorry, Bryn. I shouldn't have come. I just . . ."

"You just what?" I stepped closer to him, and he lifted his eyes to meet mine.

"I just had to see you. I needed to know that you were all right."

I wanted to ask, *Then why are you pushing me away? If you just wanted to be with me, why are you being so distant?*

But I didn't think he would answer, so I just looked up at him, wishing I understood the pain in his eyes.

A car door opened and Konstantin leaned out. "We should probably leave before backup gets here."

FORTY-THREE

crusade

This was the first time Tilda had been to Storvatten, and her eyes widened as she took in the palace. With luminous walls tinged in aqua, curving to mimic waves, it rose from the still waters of the great lake like an enchanted sapphire.

Thick fog had left the palace hidden from the shore, since it sat several miles out in the water. Ridley, Konstantin, Tilda, and I walked almost halfway out on the dock that connected the palace to the land before it started to take shape, a shadow looming behind the gray.

And then there it was, in all its glory. Tilda—who wasn't easily impressed—actually gasped when she saw it. While I still found it magnificent, all the events of the past few weeks seemed to have left me somewhat numb to its magic.

As we approached the large wooden doors of the palace,

they opened before we'd even reached them. The entrance glowed pale white as we walked toward it, and an imposing man stepped forward, reminding me of an alien overlord descending from the mothership.

He was tall and broad-shouldered, especially for a Skojare. They tended to be more petite in frame—Mikko and Kennet Biâelse aside. His blond hair was cropped short, and he was clean-shaven.

The uniform he wore was that of the Skojare guard—a frosty blue, embellished with the insignia of a fish on his lapel. Even without the uniform, there was something very military about him. He stood at attention, with his head high and his blue eyes locked on us.

"I'm Baltsar Thorne." He greeted us formally but politely. He bowed his head slightly, and I noticed the thick black outline of a fish tattooed on the back of his neck. "I'm the new head guard for the Skojare."

Already he looked like a vast improvement from their last head guard, and I'd only just met him.

"It's really you!" Linnea squealed, and I heard her voice echoing through the main hall before I saw her. She dashed across the glass floor, her blue gown billowing around her, and she practically dove at me, hugging me.

When she let go, she stepped back to appraise me. Smiling broadly, she said, "It's really you. The guards at the shack at the end of the dock called up and said you were coming, but I didn't believe them."

"Your Highness," Baltsar said, carefully trying to wedge himself between us. "She has been accused of killing our Prince. It seems prudent to—"

"Oh, she didn't do it." Linnea waved him off, then she took my hand. "Let's go inside and get out of the cold, so we can talk. And you bring your friends—"

It was the first time she'd stopped to look at who was with me, but as soon as she saw Konstantin, her jaw dropped and her already large eyes widened.

"It's you," she gasped and let go of my hand. "You saved my life."

Konstantin lowered his eyes and shifted his weight from one foot to the other, already uncomfortable with her praise. Then she ran over to him and threw her arms around his waist, embracing him tightly.

For his part, Konstantin stood frozen in place with his eyes nervously flitting around. His arms were stiff at his sides, like he was afraid to even touch her.

"My Queen, it's not advised to . . . *hug* guests before we have a chance to vet them," Baltsar tried unsuccessfully to reason with her.

Incensed, she stepped away from Konstantin and glared at the guard. "This man saved my life! He's a hero! He doesn't need to be vetted! They're all guests of the kingdom, and they're all welcome inside."

Baltsar sighed, apparently realizing the futility of arguing with her. "If it's as you wish, Your Majesty."

"Come in, come in, everyone!" Linnea motioned for us to

follow her as she walked inside the palace, her platinum curls bobbing as she walked. Her dress was cut very low in the back, to just above her waist, and it compensated for that by having a long satin train that flowed out behind her.

Baltsar bowed slightly again and gestured for us to enter, so I smiled politely and followed Linnea inside.

"Just to let you know, there's a couple bodies in the back of the SUV you probably want to take care of," Ridley told Baltsar as he walked by.

"We already killed them for you, so it shouldn't be that much of a problem," Konstantin added.

"Pardon?" Baltsar asked, looking startled. "Who did you kill?"

"Don't worry," Konstantin said over his shoulder as we entered the grand main hall. "They were Viktor Dålig's men." When Baltsar still appeared puzzled, Konstantin elaborated. "The men that declared war on you."

Linnea had been walking ahead, intent on showing us all in and seeming to ignore the exchange between Konstantin, Ridley, and Baltsar, but as soon as the word *war* was uttered, she'd stopped cold.

In the rotunda, sandblasted glass shaped like waves surrounded us—opaque, with a hint of light turquoise showing through. Below us, the floors were glass, windows to the pool. Chandeliers sparkled with diamonds and sapphires, casting light all around us. It gave the effect of standing in a whirlpool, and right now Linnea was in the dead center of it.

"Well, the Kanin actually declared war," Ridley said,

correcting Konstantin in a conversational tone. "If you want to get technical."

"He seems like the kind of guy who'd want to get technical." Konstantin pointed toward Baltsar.

"That's true," Ridley agreed. "But either way, Viktor Dålig's men will attack the Skojare. They're probably helping the Kanin, so it's all the same difference."

"Yeah." Konstantin looked over at Baltsar. "The point is that we helped you by killing those men."

Linnea still had her back to us, and she turned around slowly to face everyone. All the lightness and playfulness that usually enveloped her had fallen away. Her skin had paled even more than normal, and the translucent gills on her neck weren't moving.

"Did you say war?" Linnea asked in a voice so soft I wasn't sure that Ridley or Konstantin had heard her from where they stood several feet back. Tilda and I were right behind Linnea, and even I barely heard it.

"Didn't you . . ." Ridley glanced over to me, looking for help, but I had none to give. "Didn't you get the proclamation? From the Kanin?"

Linnea shook her head once. "No. We've received no correspondence from the Kanin since they told us of Kennet's death."

"I saw it yesterday." Ridley motioned to me. "We both did. At the Trylle palace. Mina—um, excuse me, Queen Mina sent the scroll to the Trylle Queen declaring war on the Skojare."

"That's why we came here," I explained. "We wanted to see if you needed help preparing for it."

"Of course we need help," Linnea replied emptily, and then she looked past me at Baltsar. "Our worst fears have come true. They're going to kill us all."

defensive

M arksinna Lisbet Ahlstrom—the acting ruler of the
Skojare and Linnea's grandmother—stood with her
back toward the meeting room as she stared out at the dark
water that surrounded us. Her golden hair was up, and her
sapphire chandelier earrings hung past the high collar of
her jacket. Wavelike designs were embroidered in the cerulean fabric, and the hem of her jacket just hit the floor.

We were in the meeting room underwater, where half of
the room stuck out from the palace with a domed wall of glass,
creating a fishbowl effect. The last time I had been here, King
Mikko had been arrested. And now we were discussing war.

Baltsar, Ridley, Konstantin, and I sat at the end of the very
long table. Linnea had been too shell-shocked to be of much
assistance, and Tilda had feigned needing help to keep her
preoccupied. For the past hour we'd been in the meeting
room, explaining to Lisbet and Baltsar everything we knew.

While we spoke, Lisbet had paced the room, listening to us tell them about Mina's relation to Viktor, her involvement in Kennet's scheme, and her plot to steal the jewels now that Kennet and Bayle were out of the picture.

When we'd finished, she stopped and stared out at the lake. Night had fallen upon us, making the water too dark to see anything, but Lisbet kept staring out, as if an answer to all their problems would come swimming up to the glass.

"After he was killed, I realized that Kennet had to be involved in Mikko's imprisonment somehow," Lisbet said finally. "I wore black for three days until Kennet's funeral, as is customary, but I haven't worn it since. I mourned publicly because I had to, but I won't shed a tear for anyone that tries to hurt my granddaughter."

Then she turned to face us. In her sixties, she'd begun to show the signs of her advancing years, but she still carried the grace and beauty of her youth. She commanded the room like a Queen, even though she'd never really been one.

"What would you have us do?" Lisbet asked. "How do we stop this?"

Konstantin sat with his elbows on the table and his hands together in front of his face, almost like he was praying except that his hands were clenched too tightly. "You can't stop this. Once Mina has her mind set, there's nothing you can do to talk her out of it."

"What if we offered her our jewels?" Lisbet suggested, almost pleading. "We have so many, we must be able to spare a great deal."

"She wants them all." Konstantin lowered his hands. "And even that won't be enough. Since she's had to wait for them, she's annoyed. And she'll want you to suffer for that."

Lisbet rubbed her temple. "Then what do we do?"

"I've been working as the Överste for the Kanin," Ridley said. "And Tilda's been acting captain. We can work with your soldiers and get them ready. We know exactly how the Kanin fight and what they're skilled at."

Lisbet laughed darkly. "You say that as if we have soldiers."

"If Mina hasn't declared war yet, that means you might have some time," I said. "Time to gather people and get them ready."

"Unless, of course, she's planning a surprise attack," Konstantin corrected me, and I shot him a look. "Well, it's true."

"You have one huge advantage, and that's this palace." Ridley motioned around us. "It's an island fortress."

"And we have the spires," Baltsar said, referring to the five towers that rose from the palace. "I've been doing bow training with the guards, so they can man them and shoot at possible intruders."

"It's not a lost cause," Ridley said, trying to sound optimistic.

"There's something else I think you should do," I said. "You should release Mikko."

"Talk to that one." Lisbet pointed at Baltsar. "I want to let him go. I've known he was innocent for a while, but it's Baltsar and the Chancellor and some of the other royals that don't want him out."

Baltsar shook his head. "It's not that I don't want him released. There's not enough evidence to set him free. I was a Markis and I stepped down—I gave up my title and my inheritance because it was more important to me that Storvatten be kept safe. I took this job to make sure it was done right."

"You're going to war. You need him," I persisted.

"I'm the acting monarch. I have all the same power he has," Lisbet said.

"But you're not *King*," I told her emphatically. "Linnea may be Queen, but she's not strong enough yet to lead anyone into war. Mikko has power and presence. And he has a brother he needs to avenge. If it wasn't for Mina, I don't think Kennet would've ever done any of this. Mikko needs to be on the forefront, fighting for your kingdom."

Lisbet seemed to consider this, then she looked past me to Baltsar. "Do it. Let him go."

"Marksinna!" Baltsar protested. "I'm trying to bring order to this kingdom."

"And there won't be a kingdom to bring order to if we don't do everything we need to do!" Lisbet shot back. "Let Mikko go. He needs to be the one to end this."

FORTY-FIVE

valedictory

Dear Bryn—   *May 25, 2014*
*Everyone's gone and left, and it's lonely without you all.
Not that I blame Tilda and Ridley for getting out of here,
especially not after what happened to Ridley. But with all
of you gone again, the isolation feels so much more intense.*

*Thankfully, Delilah is still here. (She has become my
rock, my light, my only salvation in this claustrophobic
cage. Last night, I snuck into her room, carefully and quietly so none of the guards keeping watch would catch me.
We went under the covers in her bed, hiding away from
everything around us, and by the dim glow of the flashlight, we read poems by Gustaf Fröding, Karin Boye, and
Pär Lagerkvist, and her Swedish is so beautiful to hear.
Forgive me if I'm a little verbose today.)*

*I'm sorry for rambling on so much about Delilah. I
could go on for pages and pages about the beauty of her*

eyes and the scent of her hair and the strength of her spirit and the warmth of her arms and the taste of her lips . . . But I'm not writing you to go on about her forever (though I could). It's just the only time I feel even close to free anymore is when I'm with her.

It is so contradictory that life can be the worst it's ever been and the best it's ever been all at once. It's strange how love can blossom even in the darkest places.

And it certainly is dark here in Doldastam, and not just because you and Tilda are gone. I know I could've gone with Ridley the way Tilda did, and maybe I should've. My mom would've preferred it if I had.

Four years ago, we left Förening to escape all the turmoil there. We chose Doldastam because my mom's sister lived here with her husband, and it seemed like a quiet, safe place to live. My mom is starting to believe that there isn't a quiet, safe place in the entire troll kingdom, and at night, when she thinks I can't hear, she whispers to my dad about fleeing to live among the humans.

I wonder how you're finding Förening. It's been so long since I've been there. Are you sleeping in my old room? Finn says he hasn't repainted my room yet, so I hope you're enjoying the blotchy clouds I painted years ago.

Maybe I should have left with Delilah, gone back to my old room, gotten away from here. I'd certainly love to see Finn and Mia and the kids. But I couldn't go.

Not just because of Delilah, or even Linus Berling. I've been training with him as often as I can, and while he tries harder than anyone I've ever met, I still feel like he can't protect himself. And I know there's other people like him here.

For every Astrid Eckwell (who is a star pupil under the Queen's new paranoia campaign), there is a Linus Berling. And for every townsperson that screams about stringing up traitors like you, there is a Juni Sköld, disobeying the wishes of the town by still serving your parents in her bakery.(They have, unfortunately, been blacklisted from most of the shops here.)

There are still good people here, and they need someone like me to help them when it comes time to fight. I don't know when that will happen, but I feel it's gotta happen soon. I don't know how much more we can take of this.

Every day things get worse. Yesterday, Omte guards started appearing around town. You know how huge the Omte can get—all of them are over six foot, some over seven, with big heads and muscles bulging out everywhere. Apparently, where they're from is incredibly warm, and they're having a hard time handling the cold, so they're all bulked in winter jackets and hats and scarves even though it reached the forties.

Even with their ridiculous gear, it doesn't make them any less intimidating. They stomp around the cobblestones like they own the damn place. I've actually seen children cry at the sight of them.

Queen Mina held another meeting in the town square after they'd arrived. She stood on the balcony of the clock tower, still wearing all black, including this odd birdcage veil over her eyes. The Omte had arrived unannounced, and by the time she called the meeting, everyone was on edge and scared.

In her grandiose way, with lots of arm gestures and her fake British accent that annoys you so much, Mina explained that the Omte had come here to help protect us. We have so many enemies we needed a stronger guard.

(Though she didn't specify who any of these enemies were, and she hasn't mentioned the name Viktor Dålig in quite some time apparently he's no longer a threat? Just you and Konstantin Black. And now the Skojare, apparently, but I'm getting ahead of myself.)

She assured everyone that the Omte are here for our protection. Your mom and dad were at the back of the crowd, and I saw the nervous glances they exchanged with each other. I wanted to look as uncomfortable as they did, but since I'm part of the army, I had to put on my best smile and pretend like I thought this was totally brilliant and not complete insanity.

When the King died, Mina wouldn't even allow Kanins from other towns to come and mourn him. But now she'll open the gates to complete strangers from another tribe, a tribe we've had very little contact with over the past century?

Obviously something bad is going on, but I haven't been able to figure out what yet. It's hard when there's so few people I can talk to about this anymore. If I'm being honest, part of the reason I'm writing you this letter is just so I can sort it all out for myself. In your absence, you've become my sounding board.

After explaining the presence of the Omte, Queen Mina went on to announce that she discovered the culprit behind King Evert's murder—Kennet Biâelse. When the crowd cheered, I actually cheered along with them, because I thought finally you'd be cleared.

But, no. She actually raised the accusations, claiming that you were a coconspirator with Kennet. You actually helped him with the poison or some nonsense like that.

Then she concluded that the Skojare could no longer be trusted. You'd betrayed us because of your Skojare blood, and all Skojare are inherently evil.

It was at that point that your parents quickly and quietly made their exit. Unfortunately, they don't live that far from the town square, so I'm sure they could still hear all the vile things Mina was saying about the Skojare.

Later, after everything had died down, I brought a casserole over to them. My mom had made it for them with root vegetables, since she knows that the market has been refusing service to them. Your parents have mostly been subsisting on treats from Juni's bakery and the kindness of strangers.

Your mom was in the bath when I arrived, and your dad answered the door. He says that your mom spends most of the time soaking now. His temples looked grayer than they were the last time I saw him, but otherwise he *looked okay. He says he's just been reading and trying to keep his head down.*

They rarely leave the house, and they keep their thick drapes pulled at all hours since they caught some kids trying to peek in a few days ago.

When your mom came out of the bath, she hugged me and told me how happy she was to see me. I told them that you're safe, hiding in Förening, and she started to cry. Your dad teared up too, and he spent the next five minutes thanking me for helping you. I don't think I've ever seen two people look as relieved as they did then.

They'll need to escape soon, but with the Omte guard around now, it will be even harder than before. Fortunately, the Queen doesn't seem to have noticed that Tilda has escaped yet. Tilda's parents are covering for her, saying she's on bed rest with the baby, anytime anybody asks about her. I think her parents and I are the only ones that really know where she is.

As soon as I see a break in the defenses, I think I'll get my parents and your parents out of here. It's getting too dangerous. The Queen already turned on the Skojare. It won't be much longer before she singles my family out for being Trylle. We've always had the advantage of blending in better than you and your mom did, but nobody really blends in in Doldastam anymore.

Everyone is suspect.

I shouldn't even be writing these letters to you. If the wrong person reads this, I could end up in the dungeon, just for telling the truth about what's going on around here. To be safe, I'm even writing this in the wee hours of the morning, before the sun comes up. But you can never be too safe in Doldastam anymore.

I think this will be the last letter I write you. I have too much to do here. I can't risk getting caught over something silly like this. Besides, I'm not even sure if you'll ever be able to read these.

Until I see you again—
Ember

FORTY-SIX

torment

The meeting with Lisbet, Baltsar, Konstantin, Ridley, and I had gone on rather late into the night, and I'd been very relieved when I was finally able to go to my room. I had fantasies about falling asleep the second my head hit the pillow.

But, even as exhausted as I was, sleep could be a cruel mistress, and it eluded me. I tossed and turned, and spent most of the night staring up at the water spot on the ceiling above my bed.

The grandeur of the exterior of the Skojare palace was misleading. Even though the guest rooms had an air of luxury to them—fine linens, elegant furnishings, even the exterior glass wall that bowed out in the lake—the reality inside was quite different.

A bedroom underwater was cold and smelled musty. The

wallpaper in the halls was peeling, the tiles were warped, and I spotted a tuft of mold growing in the corner.

The dark water of the lake kept out most of the sunlight during the day, but somehow, even with the waning moon in the night sky, it managed to create an odd glowing sensation in the room. Like being in an aquarium, with the shadows of the moving water dancing across the ceiling.

Eventually I decided that I couldn't be the only one having trouble sleeping. I slid out of bed, and the tiles felt like ice on my bare feet.

Since I was still traveling with my thrift shop clothing, I didn't have much in the way of pajamas. I'd gone to bed in an oversized T-shirt with a kraken attacking a ship on it. The neck hole had been stretched out, so it kept slipping off my shoulder, exposing more of my skin to the cold.

I stuck my head out into the hall, and when I saw no guards in the vicinity, I crept out. Tilda's room was directly on the other side of mine, but I figured that between the pregnancy and brutally attacking a guy today, she probably needed her rest.

Instead, I made a beeline for Ridley's room farther down the hall. We'd hardly had a moment alone together since he'd arrived in Förening, and we needed to talk. There was something strange going on with him, and I had to find out what it was.

Slowly, I opened the door and peered around it. Ridley's room was a mirror image of mine, with the glass wall casting that bluish glow through it. Even though it was dim, I could easily see that the bed was messy, like it had been slept in, but it was empty.

I stepped farther into the room, scanning for Ridley, when suddenly someone grabbed me and threw me roughly against the wall, slamming my back into it. Within a second of me entering his room, Ridley had jumped out from behind the door, thrown me into the wall, and pinned me there with his body and his hand around my throat.

"Dammit, Bryn," he whispered when he realized it was me, and let go. "You scared the hell out of me."

"You're the one that attacked me," I said in a hushed voice.

"Sorry." He stepped back from me. "I heard someone sneaking around outside, and I thought it might be one of Viktor's men tracking me or something. I'm just jumpy."

"Viktor's men usually sneak into your room wearing over-sized T-shirts?" I asked, attempting to lighten the mood.

"I don't know how they'll come for me." Ridley's voice was low and somber, and his expression was a dark mask, hiding his normally handsome, playful face.

He stood shirtless across from me, wearing loose black pajama pants. They hung low on his waist, revealing the sharp ridges of muscles just above his hips and a thin trail of hair that started just above his pelvis and ran downward.

Part of me was aware of how sexy Ridley looked and how badly I wanted to pull him close to me. But the other part was all too aware of the gulf between us, and how it only seemed to grow wider and darker with each passing moment.

I rubbed my neck where he'd grabbed me and looked away from him.

"Did I hurt you?" he asked and moved closer to me. His hand was on my wrist, angling my arm back so he could get a better look at my throat. And his face tilted down, so close to mine, as he studied me.

I watched him—the way his hair fell over his forehead, his heavy lashes, his wonderful lips, the stubble on his cheek— as he touched me gingerly, and all I wanted was to be with him. To kiss him and feel him close to me again.

Instead, I whispered, "I'm fine."

He lifted his eyes to meet mine. "You sure?"

I nodded, and that was when I realized his neck had fully healed. The skin had been torn raw by the chain, and he'd been left with awful, thick bruises. But now it all looked normal.

"Your neck is better," I said in surprise.

"Lisbet had a healer fix it up. She wants me in top condition for the impending war."

He hadn't moved back from me, and his hand lingered on my wrist. His fingers were strong and warm on my skin, and I loved the way it felt when he touched me.

A heat burned in the pit of my stomach, a longing so intense it made my heart ache. Being so close to him, being able to touch him, but not really, not really hold him close to me, was killing me.

I looked down, really looking at him up close for the first time, and I noticed ridges on his chest and arms. They were perfectly straight raised bumps, half an inch thick and several inches long.

Without thinking, I reached out to touch one, and Ridley flinched and pulled back from me.

"I'm sorry. I didn't mean to hurt you."

He turned his back to me and shook his head. "It didn't hurt. When the healer fixed my neck, she healed those up too."

"What are they? What happened?"

"I just don't want to talk about it."

"Ridley." I moved closer to him. I lifted my hand, meaning to put it on his back, but I was afraid he'd flinch again, so I let it fall to my side. "Please stop shutting me out. What happened in Doldastam after I left?"

He looked at me over his shoulder. "Can you pretend like nothing happened in Doldastam? Can we just forget about it? At least for tonight?"

"If that's what you want."

"I do."

Ridley turned to face me, and held out his hand to me. I hesitated for a moment, but then I took it and let him pull me into his arms. For a moment, when I lay my head against his bare chest, with his arms strong and sure around me, I closed my eyes and tried to pretend that it was the way things were before.

But there was a stiffness in his muscles, a resistance that hadn't been there before.

"Even though you're right here, in my arms, you still feel so far away," I murmured, and saying it aloud hurt so much I could barely speak. "I can't do this."

"What?" Ridley asked, sounding startled as I pulled away from him and stepped back.

"I can't do this. I want to be with you, but only if you're actually here with me. I don't know what's going on with you or with *us*." I swallowed hard. "I can't keep doing this if you won't let me in."

He lowered his eyes and didn't say anything. I waited, hoping that he would finally say *something* real to me. But he didn't, so I turned and started walking away.

"Mina captured me as soon as I came back in the gates," Ridley said when I reached the door, his voice strong but flat. "The guards hauled me off in front of everyone with my arms in shackles."

I faced him, with my hand still on the door. His mouth twisted up as he spoke, and he kept his eyes locked on the floor.

"She tied me to a rack," he said thickly. "That's a medieval torture device. They tie you up by each one of your limbs, and then they pull. Slowly. *Agonizingly* slow." He motioned to his arms. "But that wasn't enough. Mina burned me—holding hot pokers to my flesh."

That explained the ridges on his arms, the ones I'd touched earlier.

"The worst part about it all," he said, shaking his head, "she never asked me anything. I wouldn't have told her, but she didn't even ask. She wasn't torturing me to find anything out—she was doing it because she *could*."

"Ridley," I breathed. I went over to him and reached out to touch his face. He leaned into my palm and closed his eyes. "I'm so sorry."

"No, Bryn, don't be sorry." He put his hand over mine. "Don't ever be sorry. Not about this."

"I don't know what else to say."

"You don't need to say anything." He lowered his hand, then stepped back, away from me, so I let my arm drop to my side. "It's late, and we have a long day tomorrow. You should probably head back to your room and get some sleep."

Startled by the abruptness, I didn't say anything at first. Then I nodded slowly and turned to leave Ridley standing alone in his room, wondering if I had failed him so much that we would never be able to reconcile again.

offense

That's not good enough!" Tilda barked, standing over a sweaty Skojare guard.

I'd been sparring with a different guard, but I stopped what I was doing to look over at her. For training today, she'd done her best to look every bit the part of a captain. Her hair was pulled back in a smooth ponytail, and she'd even gotten her hands on a frosty blue Skojare uniform. It fit her well, except that the jacket had to be left open to compensate for her growing belly.

Baltsar had set us up in the ballroom of the palace, since it had the most space. It was an opulent round room with white marble floors. Above us, the ceiling was domed glass, making this one of the few places I'd seen in the Storvatten palace that let in natural light.

The wallpaper had this magical quality, with a pale bluish sheen and a silver design etched into it, but when you looked at it, it seemed to move, like waves on the water. It was unlike anything I'd ever seen before. Every twenty feet or so, the wallpaper was broken up with a marble half pillar.

Baltsar and Ridley had organized the training today, separating the guards into groups based on their experience. Since taking his position a few weeks ago, Baltsar had already begun to rework the guard and hired thirty new recruits. On top of that, with the threat of war, many commoners and even a few of the royals had volunteered to join the makeshift army being built.

Tilda had been tasked with commanding the group of new recruits and volunteers, and she was running them through their paces like a drill sergeant. When they'd first been assigned to her, I'd heard the recruits snickering about how easy they'd gotten it because she was pregnant and a girl. None of them were snickering now.

At the back of the room, Baltsar was commanding his troop. While Tilda focused on more basic endurance and strength training, just trying to get them into proper physical condition, Baltsar was working on sword skills, while Ridley focused on hand-to-hand fighting.

For the most part, Konstantin and I just floated around, sparring with people and helping to show them proper form as needed. Right now Konstantin was standing with Ridley, discussing what to work on next, while Ridley's group ran laps around the ballroom.

Ridley had asked for Konstantin's opinion on several things today in regard to training, and that made sense since

Konstantin had a lot of experience as a tracker, a guard, and practical application in real life. Since Förening, the two had seemed to get along well, and Ridley appeared to trust Konstantin's judgment.

I'd had no input on what was happening today. Konstantin, Ridley, and Tilda actually all outranked me (discounting the fact that Konstantin and I had been exiled, of course). But that meant that while Ridley, Tilda, and Baltsar had to dress in uniforms like commanding officers, and the four of them had to worry and decide what everyone needed to focus on, I just got to get down and dirty.

I was in my tank top and yoga pants, sweating and fighting with whomever I could. And honestly, it felt amazing. In the chaos of everything around me, training in the gym was the one area I could always count on. This was the first time in a long time I'd had a chance to really work off all the aggression I had about feeling so powerless against Mina and Viktor Dålig.

So today, as I punched another one of Tilda's recruits in the jaw, I couldn't help but smile. It felt great to be back.

"Bryn!" Tilda shouted. "You're not supposed to be making contact, remember? This is just training. You don't want to break all the soldiers before they go to battle."

"Right. Sorry. I got a little overzealous." I waved at her, but by the look in her eyes, I knew that wasn't good enough.

She walked over to me, the trainees parting around her. "That's the fourth time I've called you out on it. We've been going at this all day. Why don't you take five?"

"No, I'm good. I don't need it."

"Bryn." She looked at me severely, and I realized it wasn't a suggestion. "Take a break."

"Fine," I said because there was no point in arguing with her.

I apologized to the guy I'd hit, then I turned and walked away. I tried not to storm off, despite my irritation. But both Konstantin and Ridley turned to look back at me, their eyes questioning. I just forced a smile and hurried on my way.

At the end of the ballroom were two large doors, and I pushed them both with my hands as hard as I could, blowing off a bit of steam. They flew open, and I heard a deep voice rumble in pain.

As the doors swung closed, I looked over to see that I had hit someone with the door. He straightened up, looking down at me with dazzling blue eyes, the thin gills under his jawline flaring when he exhaled. The chandelier directly above us was out, and his broad shoulders cast an ominous shadow over me from the light at the end of the hall.

It was the newly reappointed King, Mikko Biâelse. This was the first time I'd seen him since I'd been implicated in his younger brother's death, and he did not look happy to see me.

confrontation

B ryn Aven," Mikko said in a voice that rumbled like thunder. Linnea had once told me that Mikko was painfully shy, and I found that so strange. With his striking good looks, rather imposing size, and a voice like Odin, I'd never met anybody else who had a presence like his. He looked like he'd been created to be King.

I swallowed hard before replying with, "Your Highness," and bowing.

"There's no need for that." He looked uncomfortable for a moment, then folded his arms over his chest. "I heard that I have you to thank for my freedom."

"I . . . I, uh, that was more Marksinna Lisbet," I stammered in surprise. His words sounded kind, but he looked like he wouldn't mind snacking on my bones for breakfast.

"She said that you swayed Baltsar into action," he said. "While I was incarcerated, Linnea told me that you never stopped believing in me and fighting for my innocence. She insisted that you were our greatest ally."

"I . . ." I didn't know how to reply to that. It was an exaggeration, but there was some truth to it, so I said simply, "I just did what I thought was right, sire."

"It's unfortunate how rare it is to find someone who will do what's right."

He turned his attention toward the ballroom doors. A sliver of bright light spilled through the thin gap between the doors into the darkness of the hall, making a line across Mikko's face as he peered inside. Even out in the hall, Tilda could easily be heard, shouting her commands.

The King had apparently come to watch his new army training, and with his attention back on that and off me, now would be a perfect time for me to slip away. I could go down the hall, get a drink of water, and cool off.

But I hesitated, and it caused him to look back at me. "Is there something I can do for you, Bryn?"

"I wanted to say that I'm sorry about your brother," I said finally.

He sighed heavily. "So am I." His normally hard expression softened, disillusionment and sadness wearing down on his features. "And I'm sorry that you got pulled into that mess. Linnea filled me in on what happened, and I appreciate you acting as honorably as you did."

"Thank you," I said, stunned to hear Mikko actually thanking me for my involvement in his brother's death.

"I do wish that Kennet had been able to come to me with

his concerns instead of taking matters to into his own hands." He turned his eyes to the ceiling, and his exasperation gave way to anger. "But that's my father's doing. He always said that a real man would take what he wanted. Kennet was kinder than that, or at least he would've been without Father's influence."

From what I understood, Mikko and Kennet's father, the late King Rune, was not a good man. My mom had bordered on calling him a sadist. He had hoarded sapphires and let the palace and the kingdom fall into disrepair. He'd been more focused on maintaining his wealth than the welfare of anyone, including his own children.

Even after his father's death, Mikko had seemed afraid to undo his proclamations. The continuing policies of Rune had led to an inept guard and rifts in the kingdom. It was also one of the motivations for Kennet's attempt at overthrowing Mikko.

"Despite everything Kennet did, I do believe that he loved you," I said.

Mikko lowered his eyes. "I know he did. That's what makes it harder."

"I'm sorry. I didn't mean to upset you."

"No. In an awful way, this has all been good for me." He looked up at me, making eye contact for one of the first times since I'd met him. "I've realized that I need to step out of my father's shadow and lead in my own right."

"Queen Linnea has talked about the greatness she sees in

you," I said. "They need a strong leader, and I think you're the one to do it."

"The Skojare are good people, and they deserve a strong King." Mikko stood up straighter. "I must become that King for them."

I smiled. "I'm looking forward to seeing you in action."

"You can stay for as long as you want," he said. "I know things with your kingdom have become a terrible mess, but I want you to know that you are always welcome here. As far as I'm concerned, you have a home here in Storvatten."

A footman came running around the corner, going so fast he skidded on the floor. He caught himself, then raced toward us. As soon as he saw the King, he started yelling, "Sire! Sire!"

"What?" Mikko turned back to face him. "What's the matter?"

The footman reached us, gasping for breath. "The . . . they sent me to get you." He paused, gulping down air. "There's an army waiting at the door for you."

FORTY-NINE

unannounced

Mikko was about to go to the door by himself, but I ran back into the ballroom and grabbed Baltsar and Ridley. I wasn't about to let the King get himself killed when the Skojare had just gotten him back.

Konstantin and Tilda stayed back with the troops, preparing to command them if they needed to. The hope was that since the army had come to the door, they wanted to have some kind of sit-down with Mikko. Maybe he'd even be able to sway them away from battle and come to some sort of compromise.

That seemed unlikely, but at this point it appeared to be our only hope to avoid massive bloodshed.

Before I left, following Ridley and Baltsar behind the King, Konstantin grabbed my arm.

"Do not leave the King alone with her," he warned in a low

voice, referring to Mina. "She'll kill him the second she has the chance."

"I won't." I started to turn away, but Konstantin still hung on to my arm, so I looked back at him.

"Be careful," he said and finally released me.

I ran out after the King. He, Ridley, and Baltsar were walking quickly and purposefully toward the front door. Baltsar was talking to Mikko, telling him everything that he should do and say, and what response he advised based on what the leader of the army might say to him.

"What should we do?" I asked Ridley in a hushed voice as I fell in step beside him.

"Try not to let the King get killed, and try not to get killed ourselves." He glanced down at me. "That's the best I've got."

We reached the front hall, and I was doing my best to slow the racing of my heart. Seven guards—veteran ones who had been working around the palace and not training—stood at attention around the hall. Their hands were on their swords, ready to act if they needed to.

If Mina and Viktor had sent their full army, it didn't matter if the entire Skojare force were in the hall. They weren't ready, and they'd be slaughtered.

Ridley and I flanked the King on either side, while Baltsar went to open the large front door. Mikko stood tall with his head high, and it was definitely a good choice to release him from the dungeon. He was far more intimidating than Marksinna Lisbet.

Baltsar looked back at us, making sure we were ready, and the King nodded. So Baltsar opened the door.

Standing right outside on the dock was a small hobgoblin, maybe three feet tall. In some ways, hobgoblins were like miniature ogres, except that they were far more symmetrical in appearance. His features were humanoid, but his skin appeared slimy, with thick grayish brown hair sticking up wildly on his head. Like ogres, hobgoblins were insanely strong.

I'd met hobgoblins before, and I realized that I'd actually met this one in particular. He was Ludlow Svartalf, the right-hand man of Sara Elsing, the Queen of the Vittra. He'd accompanied her on trips to the palace in Doldastam before.

Just to the right and slightly behind him stood Finn Holmes, offering us an uneasy smile.

Standing behind both Finn and Ludlow were rows of troops, lined up down the dock. Most of them wore the dark emerald uniforms of the Trylle, but a fair amount had the deep burgundy uniforms of the Vittra, worn by both hobgoblin and troll alike.

"Queen Wendy Staad of the Trylle heard about the plight of Skojare, and after considering it, she decided to send half of her army to aid you in your fight against the Kanin," Finn explained.

"In addition, Queen Wendy and King Loki persuaded Queen Sara Elsing of the Vittra to join in the fight," Ludlow added in his low, craggy voice. "Queen Sara has sent a third of her army to join your fight."

Mikko appeared too stunned to speak for a moment, but

finally he managed to say, "I am forever grateful for your offers, but I am not sure that I can ever repay your kingdoms. We are not in a position to indebt ourselves so greatly to such powerful kingdoms."

"We are not asking for anything in return," Finn told him. "We are simply here to help you as you may need us."

"We are here to serve, King Mikko," Ludlow said, and he bowed before him. Finn followed suit, as did the troops on the dock—all of them bowing before the Skojare King.

masquerade

W e need to celebrate!" Linnea declared. "We're not all going to die, and if that doesn't call for a cele-bration, then I don't know what does!"

It was hard to argue with that logic, so I didn't even try, and neither did Mikko.

Since the Trylle and the Vittra had pledged their allegiance and a chunk of their soldiers to us yesterday, we had spent the entire time trying to combine our armies. It required more effort because each of the tribes had such different strengths.

Many of the Trylle had powers of psychokinesis, meaning they could move things with their minds or even start fires. Since the soldiers present were all lower-ranking trackers and civilians (and stronger abilities went along with the more powerful bloodlines of the royals), they weren't very power-ful, but they had did have some psychokinesis.

The Vittra were physically stronger than almost any other

tribe, possibly barring the Omte. Despite their smaller stature, hobgoblins were easily as strong as ogres, if not stronger. And while Vittra trolls were generally more attractive and smarter than the Omte, they could be just as quick-tempered and aggressive.

The Skojare could breathe underwater, which wasn't very useful for this fight. They were also the least skilled in combat, and the other two tribes were often frustrated by their inability to properly defend themselves.

More than once during training I saw a Vittra soldier throw a Skojare guard across the room in irritation. Ridley, Finn, and Ludlow were doing their best to keep order and get everyone working together, but it was no easy task.

It was during our training in the afternoon that Linnea came into the ballroom, excited about the cause for celebration. She insisted that everyone needed a morale-booster and a fun way to bond, and the way to do that was with a party in the ballroom.

With that, she tossed everyone out, telling us to go practice outside where the Trylle and the Vittra had set up camp in Storvatten. I spent the rest of the day out in the warm spring rain, teaching Skojare new maneuvers and fighting in the mud.

After a hard day of training, I walked down to my guestroom to wash off all the dirt in a warm shower. I'd almost made it to my room when Linnea came rushing down the hall toward me, carrying three garment bags in her arms.

"Bryn!" she called to me, nearly tripping on her long satin

dressing gown in her hurry. When I turned to face her, she realized how filthy I was, and she slowed down. "I was going to hand these off to you, but you'll get muck all over the bags. I'll just put them on your bed while you go shower."

"Why are you bringing me garment bags?" I asked.

"For the party." Linnea gave me a look like I was an idiot and brushed past me as she went into my room. "I know you weren't able to pack your finer clothes with you, so I grabbed a few gowns that I thought you might like and would fit you."

"That's very kind of you, but I hadn't planned on going to the party," I said as I walked more slowly into my room.

"Don't be ridiculous, of course you are." Linnea kept her back to me as she carefully laid out the bags on the bed. "You're integral to everything that's happening here, and you need to be here to mingle and get people to trust each other."

She unzipped each of the bags, pulling out the gowns a bit so I could see them. I'd owned some nice dresses in my life, but none as fabulous as these.

One was a rich navy-blue fabric that looked like liquid when it moved, and with a slit so high, I would be worried that my panties would show. Another was snow-white satin with diamond and lace embellishments creating an ornate illusion neckline. And the last was pale aquamarine, embroidered with flowing designs and sapphires, and a bit of tulle under the length filled out the skirt.

"And besides," Linnea went on as I stood, transfixed by the lavishness of the gowns, "you've earned it. You've been working so hard lately. You deserve a night to let your hair down."

I nodded slowly. "Okay. I'll go to the party."

She clapped her hands together. "I would hug you, but I don't want to get covered in mud. Now hurry and get ready."

In the end, it wasn't the logic of her arguments that won me over—although she had been right. It was simply the sight of the dresses. Something in the troll blood made it hard to deny luxury, which was why we all had such a penchant for gems and jewelry.

But also, a part of me just really wanted to wear a gown that was made for a Queen.

I showered quickly but thoroughly—there was no way I was ruining one of Linnea's dresses. Then I hurried back to try them all on and pick one.

While I'd been showering, Linnea had sent down a masquerade mask and a pair of pale sapphire earrings. The silver mask was gorgeous and delicate, its ornate flourishes encrusted with diamonds. Attached was a note that read, "Wear me."

The difficulty of the choice was made easier by the fact that the aquamarine one was snug in the chest, squishing my breasts in a very unflattering and uncomfortable fashion. While the darker navy dress felt like heaven on my skin, the slit felt too high, and it also had a plunging neckline, a combination that felt slightly improper for this party.

The white one fit perfectly, almost like it had been made for me. The illusion neckline allowed a hint of cleavage, and it was open in the back, showing off a bit of skin. While the length was longer than I normally liked, it was light and flowed away from me, so I didn't think it would be a problem to run or kick in if I needed to.

Once I'd finished with my hair and makeup, I went down the hall to admire myself in the full-length mirror of the bathroom.

Since I wasn't doing anything other than looking at my reflection, I'd left the door open, which allowed Konstantin to pause and whistle at me.

"Well done, white rabbit." He smiled crookedly at me, but his eyes were serious as they assessed me.

Something about the way he looked at me made my skin flush a little, and I turned to face him. "Thanks."

"It's kind of a shame I'm missing the party tonight," he said.

"Why aren't you going?" I asked in surprise.

Based on the way he was dressed, I assumed he planned to attend. He had on a simple black uniform, similar to the one that Ridley had worn as Kanin Överste, with epaulets on the shoulders, and a sword in a scabbard that hung from a belt around his waist.

While Ridley and Tilda had taken to wearing the shimmery blue uniforms of the Skojare, Konstantin had managed to dig up one that showed no allegiance. No color, no insignia, nothing to tie him to any kingdom.

"I'm walking the perimeter of Storvatten, along with some of the other guards," Konstantin explained. "Since we don't know when Mina and Viktor are going to strike, we're keeping a lookout."

"Damn." I looked down at my gown, suddenly feeling very silly. "I should change and go with you."

"No, no." He shook his head. "We've got enough guys going out. You should go. You should be happy."

I started to tell him that he should still come to the party if he got a chance, but he turned and walked away, leaving me standing there in my beautiful dress feeling flustered and alone.

dalliance

Given the short amount of time Linnea had had to put it all together, the ballroom looked especially impressive. Under the dark canopy of night displayed in the glass dome, twinkling lights had been strung around the room. Along the walls, tables had been adorned with shimmering linens, crystal centerpieces, and mood-enhancing candles. A buffet of savory and sweet ran along the wall at the end of the ballroom, with an ice sculpture of a fish.

In the far corner of the room, a small chamber orchestra had been set up. When I entered the room, they were just finishing an old Skojare song I remembered my mom singing, then they switched to an ethereal orchestral cover of "Bulletproof" by LaRoux.

I'd arrived late, so the dance floor was already crowded, all the guests wearing masks equally as beautiful as mine. It was a veritable rainbow in the ballroom, and not just because of all the beautiful dresses. All the highest royals were in attendance, along with the Skojare guards dressed in their frosty uniforms.

Most of the allies that had come to the party from the Trylle and the Vittra were men, dressed crisply in their dark uniforms of emerald and claret, but the Skojare women were more than happy to dance with them. After years of living in the rather isolated Storvatten, new faces were exotic and exciting, especially when they had come to save the kingdom.

I stood in the doorway for a moment, content enough to watch so many trolls coming together like this. Talking, laughing, twirling around on the dance floor together. Even at parties, like at King Evert and Queen Mina's anniversary party, everyone was still so segregated. Trylle danced with Trylle, and so on.

This was the first time I'd ever seen the kingdoms so commingled before. It was kind of amazing, and I wondered if Linnea's masquerade theme had helped this happen.

"I wasn't sure if you were coming," a voice said at my side, and I turned to see that Ridley had somehow snuck beside me.

He'd forgone the Skojare uniform, unlike many of the other attendees, and instead wore a simple, surprisingly well-tailored suit. It was pure white, with a satin and diamond finish, and he wore it with a black dress shirt. Based on the exquisiteness of it, I realized that Linnea had procured it for him the same way she had gotten my gown for me.

Since we'd been in Storvatten, Ridley hadn't shaved, leaving him with a light beard along his jawline and above his lip.

His hair was only slightly disheveled, like he'd styled it perfectly but couldn't help himself and ran his hand through it.

His mask was black and thicker than mine, more masculine, but just as gorgeous.

"I wasn't sure you were coming either," I admitted. Since we'd just been focusing on training and hadn't had a chance to talk since our late-night rendezvous, I had no idea where we stood.

"I'd never miss a chance to dance with you." He stepped back and extended his hand to me. He said nothing, but he didn't have to. The question was in his eyes.

Tentatively, I took his hand and let him lead me out onto the dance floor. I wasn't sure if the crowed actually parted for us, or if it just felt that way. Whenever I was with Ridley like this—when he was touching me, and his eyes were focused on me, and my heart was pounding so fast I felt dizzy and drunk—the whole world always seemed to fall away. Like we had become the center of the universe, and everything spun around us.

Ridley pulled me close to him and put his hand on my back—his hand warm and rough on my bare skin, thanks to the plunging back. We stayed that way for a split second—my hand in his, my body pressed against him, and him staring down at me.

I loved the darkness of his eyes. It seemed to overtake me.

And then we were moving. I let him lead me along, following his quick moves step for step. He extended his arm, twirling me out away from him and making my gown whirl out around me, before pulling me back to him again.

The crowd had definitely moved for us by then, creating a space in the center of the room where Ridley and I could show off the dancing we'd learned in school. All trackers learned it, but I had to admit that he was more proficient than most.

When he dipped me back, so low my hair brushed the floor, he smiled, and there was a glint in his eye. With one quick move, he pulled me back into his arms, holding me to him.

The song had changed, shifting to "Love Me Again" by John Newman, so we slowed. He kept his hands on my waist, and I let my hands relax on his shoulders. We were flirting, playing the way we had before, and it made my heart ache.

Because things weren't the way they were before anymore. Not even close.

My smile must've fallen away, because Ridley looked concerned—his eyes darkening beneath the mask, and his steps slowing as his arms tightened around me.

"Why did you come back for me?" I asked him finally, referring to what he'd said when he first arrived in Förening. "*Did* you even come back for me?"

"*Yes,*" he said emphatically. "Of course I came back for you."

"But why? Why, if you're not even really here with me?"

"I am here. I can't be with you more than I am right now."

His gazed shifted out to everyone else dancing around us. "This probably isn't the best place to get into it."

"There's never a good time to talk, not with everything going on here. I just want to know what's going on with us." I looked up into his dark eyes. "Is there even an *us?*"

He took a fortifying breath. "I came back for you because you're my first thought in the morning. Because you push yourself to be better, and in the process, you push everyone else around you to be better. You *make* everything better.

"You are far more courageous and stronger than anyone I've ever known," he continued. "And I never thought you'd ever want anything to do with me. I was certain I'd never be good enough for you.

"But when we kissed for the first time, under the lights of the aurora borealis, everything I'd ever felt about you was proven true," Ridley finished. "I came back for you because you're all I've ever wanted or needed, because I want to be with you always."

For a moment I was too stunned to say anything. I just stared up at him, my mouth hanging open and my heart pounding in my chest.

"You have me," I said simply. "You'll always have me."

His lips turned up slowly into a smile, looking both relieved and amazed. Then he leaned in, and I wrapped my arms more tightly around him. His lips had just brushed up against mine when I heard shouting over the music.

The orchestra finally stopped, and I heard Baltsar shouting, "Ridley! King Mikko!"

"What's going on?" Ridley pulled away from me, but kept his hand around mine. His eyes scanned the crowd, until it parted enough for us to see Mikko standing a few feet away with Linnea at his side.

Baltsar burst through the crowd, standing in the clearing between Ridley and Mikko. "There's been an attack on our men walking the perimeter. Two were seriously injured, and one was killed. We need a medic, and we need to make sure the area's secure."

"Mikko, you go with Ridley and get the men together to make sure we're safe," Linnea said. "I'll get the medic."

Ridley let go of my hand and started hurrying toward Baltsar.

"Who was hurt?" I asked, and it was hard to be heard over the distraught murmurings of the ballroom. I took off my mask and started pushing my way through the crowd, but they didn't part for me the way they had before. "Baltsar, what men were attacked?"

"A couple new recruits." He paused long enough to look back at me. "And Konstantin Black."

FIFTY-TWO

expiry

In the chaos that followed, I had to remind myself to breathe. Baltsar had said Konstantin's name, then had run off, and I stayed where I was as everyone rushed around me. I didn't know what to do, where I should be, and I looked around, hoping for direction.

Tilda had started commanding the Skojare guards, sending them to various posts around the palace so that any possible entrance would be protected. Marksinna Lisbet took control of the civilians who remained in the ballroom, assuring them that everything would be all right.

"Bryn." Tilda put her hand on my shoulder, momentarily pausing from giving orders. I turned to her, and she had a knowing look in her smoky eyes. She could always see through me, even when everything had gone mad.

"We've got this," she said simply. "Go."

I dropped my mask, letting it fall to the floor, and then I

was running, grabbing up the length of the gown and grateful that the fabric flowed enough to allow me to move as fast as I wanted to. I didn't know where I was going, not at first, but I couldn't slow down. I raced through the soldiers that crowded the halls.

Finally I spotted Linnea, dragging a medic by the hand as she ran in her own sparkly blue gown. She was way at the other end of the hall from me, rushing toward the south wing of the palace, but I could just see her platinum curls bouncing, so I followed them.

I managed to get to the room just after Linnea and the medic had arrived, and I stood in the doorway. It was a small room on the main floor, with a window that showed the stars reflecting on the lake outside. Two twin beds were in the room, but Linnea and the medic were blocking my view so I could only see the legs of the occupants.

And blood. Blood stained the white sheets and left a mess on the floor.

Ridley was already at work caring for the men before Linnea arrived. He'd taken off his white jacket and rolled up the sleeves of his shirt, and his forearms were stained red.

The medic started to take over, and Linnea tried to tell the wounded that everything would be alright.

"Dammit!" Konstantin growled, and I breathed in deeply for the first time.

"I know it hurts, but you need to let him do this if you want him to fix you," Linnea told him, her voice verging between comforting and scolding.

"I don't want him to fix me!" Konstantin shouted back.

"You saved my life," Linnea persisted. "I won't just let you die."

Ridley had been helping the medic tear back Konstantin's shirt so he could get to the worst of it—a horrible gaping wound in his abdomen. He'd assisted enough so that the medic could get his hands on Konstantin, pressing painfully against the gash in order to heal it with psychokinesis.

As soon as the medic got his hands on him, Konstantin started fighting it, trying to push them off. Linnea screamed when he threw his hand out, and she jumped back from him.

"Leave it be!" Konstantin commanded. "Just let me die."

"We need you," Ridley said, trying to hold Konstantin's arms down before he hurt himself or someone else. "Just let us help you."

I pushed past Linnea to get to his side, and when Konstantin saw me, out of surprise he stopped fighting. His eyes widened, and he grimaced. His hair was damp with sweat, and blood was splattered on his cheeks.

Since he'd relaxed some, I leaned on the bed beside him, taking his bloodstained hand in mine.

"Let them help," I said softly, imploring him.

He looked away from me, staring up at the ceiling. He gritted his teeth and breathed in angrily through his nose. That was as close to consent as we would get, so I looked to the medic and nodded.

The medic put his hands back on Konstantin, and he groaned loudly through his teeth. His hand squeezed mine to the point of being painful, but I just let him. It took a few moments, but eventually he began to relax.

I looked down, and the medic was panting as he took his hands off Konstantin. The wound was healed, and other than a fresh scar under the thick layer of drying blood, his abdomen looked completely normal.

The medic began to tell Konstantin to take it easy, and if there were other minor injuries in different areas, they would take more time to heal because he'd focused all his energy on the abdominal wound.

Linnea thanked the medic for his help and took him out to the hallway. Konstantin let go of my hand, so I straightened back up. In the bed across from Konstantin, a white sheet stained red had been pulled up over the man's head. The other guy who had come in with Konstantin hadn't made it.

"I hate to do it at a time like this," Ridley said. He stood on the opposite side of the bed, looking down at Konstantin. "But I have to find out about the attack. We need to so we can prepare ourselves."

"It was just a couple scouts," Konstantin said. "There were only two of them. We killed one pretty quickly, after he took out one of the guys I was walking with, but the second guy— he put up quite a fight." He grimaced at the memory.

"Did they say anything?" Ridley asked.

Konstantin nodded. "Yeah. I finally got my sword to his throat, and then he was quite chatty because he thought I'd spare his life. He said that Viktor sent them down to see how well armed the Skojare were. He said that Viktor is waiting to hear back from the scouts before sending troops."

Ridley folded his arms over his chest. "With them being dead, it ought to buy us a few days."

"That's the good news," Konstantin said. "The bad news is that both of the scouts were Omte, and not just any Omte. These were trained soldiers, which is why they did such a number on us."

"That doesn't make any sense." I shook my head. "I thought Viktor had just been picking up random trolls that had defected from other tribes, like Bent Stum."

"So did I," Konstantin replied wearily. "But we were wrong. The scout told me as much. Viktor and Mina have the Omte working for them now."

"Shit," Ridley whispered. "I need to go find the King and Baltsar to tell them this. It changes everything."

He walked around the bed, heading toward the door, but he paused and reached out, touching my arm gently. "You okay?"

"Yeah." I nodded. "I'm fine."

Ridley lingered like he wanted to say more, or maybe even finish that kiss we'd barely started in the ballroom. But now wasn't the time or place, and he knew it. He glanced back at Konstantin, then let go of my arm and left.

Konstantin closed his eyes and groaned. "You should've just let me die. They shouldn't have wasted their resources and the medic's energy on me, not when there's going to be many other soldiers that deserve it more."

"I'm not gonna let you die." I sat on the edge of the bed beside him.

He laughed darkly. "Death is something that's beyond even your control, white rabbit."

FIFTY-THREE

retaliate

O nce Konstantin was asleep, Linnea had a footman move the body of the recruit and begin preparing it for a proper burial. She stood out in the hall, watching them carefully and reverently carry the fallen guard away.

I left Konstantin's side to join her in the hall. Her mask rested in her hair, pushing back her ringlets so they stuck out haphazardly. She wrung her hands together absently, her eyes fixed on the retreating footmen.

"How are you doing?" I asked her.

"I haven't even been Queen for a year." She sounded as if she was speaking more to herself than me. "I turn seventeen on the sixteenth of June, and a week after that, it will be my one-year wedding anniversary. That will mark one year as Queen."

"It's been a very busy first year," I commented.

"At first, I think I was only playing at Queen, and if I'm

being honest, Mikko was only playing at King." She turned back to face me, her eyes moist. "We'd never really been challenged, so we were only going through the motions and having parties and putting on these silly costumes."

She lifted up the length of her gown and let it fall back down. "And now we must be the things that we were pretending to be. People are dying, and we must be the ones that protect them."

A solitary tear slid down her porcelain skin. "I feel like I've already failed."

"No, you haven't failed." I shook my head. "Despite how everything turned out tonight, the ball was a good idea. You need to create unity and order and a sense of happiness within Storvatten. While others are out fighting, you need to hold things down here, and when they come back, you take care of them. That's your job as the Queen."

"You really think I did the right thing tonight?" Linnea wiped away her tear.

"Yes, you did everything exactly right," I told her. "But you need to be strong. A Queen must never be seen crying."

She straightened up, pulling her shoulders back and raising her chin higher, and took a deep breath. "You're right. I need to be a leader."

I smiled at her. "You'll be a fine leader."

"I would hug you, but you're covered in blood." She motioned to the bright red splotches that covered the bodice of my dress, staining the lace and satin, from when I'd been attempting to comfort Konstantin.

"I'm sorry. I wasn't even thinking about it."

"Bryn." She gave me a hard look. "There are far greater things to worry about than my silly gown. I couldn't care a fig about what happened to that dress while in service to this kingdom."

I thanked her again, and she excused herself to sit with Konstantin. She didn't want him to be alone, at least not until she was absolutely certain he was better. I looked in on her before I left, sitting at the bedside of an injured outcast without a kingdom, and I wondered how many other Queens would do that.

With Konstantin in her hands, I felt safe heading down to the meeting room. The palace had settled down while I'd been in with Konstantin, now that the imminent threat of attack had been called off. Guards were still stationed around more than normal, but people weren't running around like madmen.

When I walked downstairs, I could even hear the orchestra from the ballroom playing. The ball was under way again, probably under the advisement of Lisbet. If we had been attacked, I imagined her still dancing to the music, like the orchestra that had played on as the *Titanic* sank.

I stopped only to wash the blood from my hands, and then I headed into the meeting room. Finn and Ludlow were seated at the long table, while Baltsar paced alongside it. Mikko stood at the head, his expression grave, and Ridley stared at the dark water outside, his back to the door. He glanced over at me when I came in the room but didn't turn around.

"It all depends on how many Omte they have with them," Finn was saying as I closed the door behind me.

"We're strong," Ludlow added. "But the Omte already outnumber the Vittra, and if they bring their whole army, I'm not sure how well we can hold against them."

"They'll break down the walls," Baltsar grumbled as he paced. "You get those ogres charging, and the walls will shatter underneath their fists. They'll destroy the palace."

"We have to stop them before they get to the palace," Finn said. "The battle needs to happen on land, far from the shore."

"And what if they beat us down and charge past us?" Baltsar argued. "You get the Kanin army and the Omte army and who knows how many others Viktor Dålig's collected, and they come charging at us? They'll trample our army."

"Once they get to the palace, it's all over," Finn said. "They'll break the walls, take the sapphires, and kill anyone who is left."

"I know!" Baltsar shouted. "That's my point. How do we stop them from taking the palace?"

"We go to them," Finn replied with a heavy sigh.

"We can't do that," I said, speaking for the first time since I'd entered the room, and everyone turned to look at me. "The people in Doldastam are innocent. They don't need to end up casualties of our war against their Queen. They shouldn't be punished for her sins."

"My family is there too," Finn reminded me, his eyes pained. "I know how great the risk is. But it's our only chance to stop the Queen and her armies before she destroys another kingdom. And once she's done with the Skojare, there's no telling who she'll go after next."

"We go to them," Baltsar agreed, sounding resigned to the idea. "We take the fight to Doldastam. We still might not win. They still outnumber us, and they're still much stronger. But if we lose, we give everyone in Storvatten a chance to escape. It's our best plan to avoid innocent casualties."

"You're suggesting we abandon the palace?" Mikko asked in his low rumble.

"I am suggesting that if we lose, yes, everyone behind in Storvatten fills their pockets with sapphires and disappears into the lake," Baltsar said. "It's the only advantage we have, that the other tribes can't follow us into the water."

"Konstantin and I know Doldastam and the palace inside out," Ridley said, referring to the fact that as a member of the Högdragen and Överste respectively they had been privy to all the plans and designs of the city. They knew it better than even Tilda and me.

He turned around to face the room. "Do we really have a chance of beating them? I don't know. But if we do, Finn is right. Our best shot is taking Doldastam before they come for Storvatten."

Mikko surveyed the room, waiting for dissenting opinions, but even I just lowered my eyes. It wasn't a perfect plan, and I wasn't sure that we wouldn't all end up dead anyway.

But it was still our best chance at defeating Mina, even if it meant risking the lives of the people I cared about most. The greater good of peace within the five kingdoms outweighed my own personal feelings.

"That settles it, then," Mikko said. "Since they'll be coming for us soon, we don't have time to waste. We leave at dawn for Doldastam."

älskade

With my bag slung over my shoulder, I closed the door to my guestroom in the Storvatten palace for the last time. It had a strange finality to it. I didn't know if I'd ever come here again or if the palace would even be standing in a couple weeks.

I started walking down the hall and paused when I reached Tilda's room. She sat on her bed, her legs crossed underneath her, and stared down at her belly as she rubbed it. Her wavy chestnut hair hung around her like a curtain.

I knocked on the open door, and she looked up at me with a sad smile.

"You're leaving already?"

I nodded. "It's time. Ridley's already upstairs."

Her smile became more pained, her full lips pressing into thin lines. I sat my bag on the floor and went over to sit on the bed beside her.

"I wish I was going with you," she said, almost desperately.

"I know. But the battlefield is no place for a pregnant woman, even one as badass as you."

"I know it's the right thing. I know that for the baby, this is where I need to be." She nodded, as if to convince herself. "But this is my war too. I should be with you, fighting alongside you."

"You've already helped so much. Everything you've done with the Skojare army, they're better because of you."

"It's just hard." She rubbed her stomach. "I think the baby wants to go too. He's been kicking a lot." Then she looked over at me. "Wanna feel?"

I wasn't sure that I wanted to, but I let Tilda take my hand and place it on her stomach. At first I didn't feel anything, then there was a sudden, soft pushing sensation on the palm of my hand.

"Did you feel that?" Tilda asked, sounding excited.

"Yeah, that's crazy." I let my hand linger for a moment, feeling another, stronger kick, and then I took my hand back.

"Did I tell you that I found out that it's a boy?" she asked, smiling wider now.

"No, you didn't. A boy?" I smiled. "That'll be great."

"I didn't find out the gender until after Kasper . . ." Her smile remained but her eyes were misty. "I mean, we could've. But we were waiting until after we were married. It's silly, but we wanted it to be like a wedding gift to ourselves."

She shook her head. "I don't know. It seemed like a fun idea at the time, but since we didn't know if it would be a boy or a girl, we didn't really talk about names yet. Not in earnest."

"Have you been thinking about anything now?" I asked.

"Älskade Kasper Abbott," Tilda said. "*Älskade* means 'loved,' and I want this baby to know that he's loved more than anything."

I smiled. "It sounds perfect."

"Thanks." She smiled and blinked back tears. "Anyway, I've probably held you up long enough. You should get going before they leave without you."

I leaned over and hugged her tightly. The two of us had never been much for hugging, but we both lingered in this one. Eventually I pulled away and stood up. I grabbed my bag off the floor and offered her a small wave before heading out.

"Bryn," she said, stopping me at the door. "In case I don't see you again, I just wanted you to know that you've been a really great friend, and I love you."

"I love you too," I said, rather awkwardly, since neither of us was usually very sentimental. "And take care of yourself."

Leaving Tilda alone in her room made me feel bad, but I knew that Linnea would be calling on her for help in the very near future. Linnea was going to be running the kingdom in her husband's absence, and Tilda knew quite a bit about keeping things in order.

I went up the winding staircase away from the bedrooms and up to the main floor. As I walked toward the main hall,

I was surprised to see Konstantin hobbling from the other direction, with his own bag over his shoulder.

He'd showered and cleaned up, looking better than he had in a while. Last night, when he'd been brought in, he'd been pale and clammy, on the verge of death, and now he appeared as he always did. Except with a slight limp in his left leg.

"What are you doing?" I asked. He'd stopped, waiting for me to join him.

"I'm going to Doldastam."

"But you need to rest," I reminded him. "The medic told you to, and you've got a limp."

He shrugged it off. "My leg is finishing healing. The limp will be gone in a day."

"Konstantin." I stopped walking, so he did too, and looked back at me.

"Do you really think I'm going to let anything prevent me from missing this fight?" he asked honestly.

"Fine." I sighed. "At least promise me you'll take it easy."

He shook his head and started walking again. "Nope."

FIFTY-FIVE

terrain

With so many of us in our motley of shapes and sizes, we had to avoid main modes of travel, including the train, which was how we usually crossed the vast Canadian territory to get to Doldastam.

Fortunately, winter had come to an end for most of Manitoba, and that made it easier for us to go off-road. To get where we were going, in many places there were literally no roads. We'd be relying on Skojare maps, GPS, and four-wheel drive to get us through.

The Trylle had been kind enough to bring their transports to us, which were modified all-terrain army vehicles. The majority of us managed to fit in the backs of those, underneath the tarp covers, while the rest crammed into the Skojare's small fleet of Jeep Wranglers.

In order for the humans not to spy us, we'd have to stay as far from their civilization and populated roads as we could.

We'd brought along a few of the Skojare tower guards to help cloak us. And if humans did actually see us, like when we needed a pit stop to gas up, several of the Trylle with us could use persuasion, and make them forget that they'd seen anything at all.

Once we got close enough to Doldastam, we'd leave the convoy and march the rest of the way on foot, since all our vehicles would be loud and obvious. That way we could have an element of surprise. The tower guards' cloaking ability worked well on humans, but it was much less effective on other trolls, especially when they were trying to hide such a large moving target.

I sat in the back of one of the transports, between Ridley and the back gate. The bench that ran on either side of the back was full of senior Skojare guards, and though they did their best to look confident, I could see their nerves showing through.

Konstantin had also chosen this transport, but instead of sitting on a bench, he lay on the floor, using his bag as a pillow. Some of the guards had complained, but Konstantin said he needed to stretch out his leg so it would heal faster, so they let it go.

Despite the bumps and jolts of the journey, Konstantin seemed to sleep through it, bouncing around undisturbed. It was a rough ride over rocky terrain, one that left me aching and sore whenever we stopped to stretch and take a bathroom break.

Through most of the ride, none of us really said anything.

It was hard to hear over the sound of the vehicle, and there wasn't much to say. *Are you scared that the Omte will literally crush you? Oh, me too!*

Ridley only spoke to me once, asking me if I wanted part of his lunch. Since his confession last night during the dance, we hadn't really talked, other than discussions of war and what we needed to do. But I didn't mind. There wasn't time for anything else.

When we got back into the transport together after one of our stops, he put his hand on my leg, gently squeezing when we hit a large bump, and there was something more comforting in that than anything he could've said.

By nightfall, we'd made it about two-thirds of the way through our journey, and we stopped to camp out. Driving off-road during the day was difficult enough as it was, and we all needed a chance to rest before we arrived at Doldastam. We'd known that we'd have to camp out, so we'd packed well for it.

It was in the low twenties, which made for a very chilly campout, so we hurried to set up our tents. A girl from the Trylle had asked to share a tent with me, and I'd obliged. Other soldiers had gotten fires going, but we set up our tent near the outskirt of the campsite, since I'd rather get sleep than stay up all night talking around a fire.

While she finished setting up the tent—a small white one, made of thick canvas that helped to keep the cold out and the heat in—I went back to the trucks to get thick animals hides to keep out the iciness of the ground.

When I went over to the truck, Ridley was already there, working beside Finn, helping to pass out hides and sleeping bags. Five others were already in line, waiting for their sleeping gear, and as I joined them, Ridley looked up at me, the dim lights from a nearby fire playing off the darkness in his eyes.

"We already have sleeping bags," I said as I reached the front.

"Hey, Finn, can you handle this?" Ridley asked, glancing back at the two people waiting behind me. "I wanted to talk to Bryn for a minute."

"Yeah, sure." Finn shrugged. "I think most everyone has got their stuff already."

"Great. Thanks." Ridley smiled briefly at him, then turned his attention to me.

"What did you want to talk about?" I asked.

He shook his head. "Not here." He turned, walking back between the covered trucks, so I followed him.

The majority of the vehicles were parked together at the edge of the campsite, creating an area that felt private and quiet, with large trucks blocking out the sound and most of the firelight.

"What's going on?" I asked Ridley when I felt like we'd gone far enough. I stopped first, and he turned back to face me. The moon above us illuminated his face, and he looked around me, as if expecting a spy to be following at my heels.

"Ridley, what is it?" I demanded, starting to feel nervous, since he wasn't saying anything.

He chewed his lip for a moment, staring down at me, and then, without warning, he rushed at me. His mouth pressed roughly against mine, cold and exhilarating against my warm flesh.

He pushed me back, and I began to stumble over my feet, but his arms were there, holding me up, carrying me until I felt my back pressing against the icy metal of the truck. His kisses were fierce and hungry, his teeth just barely scraping against my skin, sending delicious heat surging through my body.

But I matched his ferocity, wrapping my legs around him, burying my fingers in the tangles of his hair.

Almost instinctually, I began pulling off his jacket, desperate to get to the hot, hard contours of his body. Ridley moved his hands underneath my butt and thighs, gripping them firmly, as he carried me around the corner to the back of the truck.

Once he'd set me down, I started to scoot back, and he climbed up on top of me, his eager lips on mine. With quick desperation, his hands found their way under my layers of shirts, cold against my bare skin.

Ridley sat up, pulling away from me so he could hurriedly tear off his shirt. I don't think I'd ever undressed so quickly, and when my sweatshirt got stuck going up over my head, Ridley was more than happy to help.

He pushed it back over my head, but in his haste to kiss me again, he'd left my arms tangled in it, trapped behind my back. His mouth traveled lower, trailing down my neck.

His lips and the gentle scrape of his beard sent tingles all through me.

With one arm, he supported himself, and with the other, he unhooked the front clasp of my bra. My arms were still trapped behind me, but I'd stopped wiggling and trying to get free. I didn't want to stop Ridley from touching me.

He wrapped an arm around me, lifting me up so my back arched slightly, and then his mouth was cold on my breast. I moaned desperately, wanting more of him.

With that, he released me, so he could pull off his jeans. I finally got my arms free from the sweatshirt and tossed aside my bra. Ridley had turned his attention to my pants, pulling them off in one rough, fast move.

He crawled over me, his body above mine, and I stared up into his eyes. I put my hand on his cheek, and he tilted his head, gently kissing my wrist. He lips moved down my arm, until they found their way to my mouth again, kissing me deeply.

Despite the cold, his body felt like fire against me. He felt strong and sure, holding me, completing me.

And then I pulled him to me, unable to wait any longer. I raised my pelvis up, pushing against him, and with a shaky breath, he finally slid inside me. I moaned again, unable to help it, and he silenced me with his mouth on mine.

Soon I was breathing into his shoulder, digging my fingers into his back to keep from screaming, and he moved deeper inside me until he exhaled deeply and relaxed on top of me.

covet

W e stayed that way for a moment, neither of us wanting to untangle ourselves from each other. But eventually we had to deal with the cold.

The covered canvas kept some of the frigid air at bay, but not enough for us to lie comfortably naked for long. Ridley sat up and lay his jacket over me as a temporary blanket as he searched around for something to cover up with.

Underneath one of the benches, he found a silver Mylar blanket from an opened emergency kit, and he spread it over us. He lay down beside me and pulled me into his arms.

"Well, that was a nice talk," I murmured, resting my head against his chest and pressing myself closer to him.

"I actually did want to talk to you," he said, his words muffled in my hair.

"Yeah?" I pulled back a little and titled my head so I could look up at him. "What about?"

"I don't know when we'll be able to talk again," he said finally. "And I just wanted to be sure that you knew everything and understood how I really feel."

My heart skipped a beat. "Everything about what?"

"About why I've been so cold and distant." He stared at the canvas above us. "I never wanted to hurt you or push you away. It's just . . . when I was in Doldastam, while we were apart, and Mina had me locked up in the dungeon, she never asked me anything about you. Not once. The entire time I was there."

"You mentioned that," I said softly.

"I know." He nodded. "But I didn't say that she never talked about you. Because she talked about you a lot. Constantly, actually."

"What do you mean? What did she say?" I asked, tensing up.

"She talked about how strong and capable you were, and how you'd never had any trouble until you started getting involved with me." He looked down at me. "I don't know how she knew that we'd kissed or slept together, but she'd found out somehow."

I shivered, and not from the cold. I'd never told anybody about the night that Ridley and I had spent together. And all of the ways I could imagine she'd discovered that secret were creepy and disturbing.

He lowered his eyes, his voice growing thicker as he spoke. "Then she started telling me how I'd brought you down and destroyed your chances of being on the Högdragen, how all I did was ruin everything I touch."

"Ridley, that's not true." I shook my head. "You didn't do anything to me. I made choices on my own, and most of the ones that have gotten me in trouble have had nothing to do with you."

"I know. I mean, part of me knew that." He sighed. "But after you hear it, over and over . . . Eventually, her words just took hold somewhere inside me, and she had me convinced that I would be the death of you."

I put my hand on his face, forcing him to look at me. "It's not true. Nothing Mina said was true."

He swallowed hard. "When I was there, all I could think about was how I could get back to you, and how I was terrified of what would happen to you if I did. I couldn't live with myself if I hurt you."

"I know you'd never hurt me," I whispered.

He kissed me again, softer this time and less insistent. "I love you, Bryn," he breathed deeply. "And I want to spend all night with you like this, but we should get back and get some sleep."

"Tomorrow we'll arrive in Doldastam," I said with a heavy sigh. His arm tightened around me. "Are you scared?"

"Yes," he admitted. "But I'm mostly afraid that I'll lose you again." He rolled onto his side, so he could face me fully. He reached out and touched my face. "You have to promise that you won't do anything too risky, Bryn. I know that you'll fight, and that you won't shy away from trouble. But I can't lose you again."

"I promise," I said, but even then, I wasn't sure if it was a promise I could keep.

FIFTY-SEVEN

home

At the top of the hill, I lay down on my stomach. The ground beneath me was a cold mixture of snow and mud, and it soaked through my clothes, but I barely noticed. The sun had just begun to set, casting everything in a beautiful bluish glow as the sky darkened from pink to purple along the horizon.

From the hill, we could see beyond the thick pine trees that rolled down the valley going toward the Hudson Bay. And there, on the flat land, was Doldastam in a way that I rarely saw it.

I could see the four stone walls that surrounded it. Over twenty feet tall, the stones kept out most of the invaders of the past two centuries. The palace loomed along the south side of town, with its back to us. The sheer size made it appear like a castle, and the outside adornments and stained-glass windows definitely added to the effect.

The west side of town held the large brick mansions of the Markis and Marksinna, but most of the town consisted of smaller cottages, looking like a quaint village from another time.

Not too far from the palace was the stable, where my loft apartment had been. The huge Tralla horses were out in the yard beside it, and though I was too far away to see for sure, I imagined that I saw Bloom running out with them, with his silver fur and lush white mane flowing behind him.

In the town square, the clock tower soared above every-thing, and it began to toll for the last time of the night. Between ten p.m. and six a.m., the clock went silent.

My parents lived right off the town square, and I tried to pick out their place. But the houses were packed in tightly, like town homes, and they all had matching roofs. There was no way to know for sure, but I strained my eyes, as if I would somehow be able to see my parents through the walls.

On the far east side of town along the wall was the house Ember shared with her parents. It was easier to pick out, be-cause the houses were a bit more spread out in that area to make room for "farming." Ember's mother raised angora goats and Gotland rabbits, but I couldn't really see them.

I could see people walking around town, and though I wanted desperately to see a familiar face, they were all too far away to discern. Occasionally, I caught a flash of light from the epaulets of the Högdragen uniform, so I knew there were many guards out patrolling Doldastam.

Mixed in with them, I saw much larger figures bundled up

in brown coats. The Omte were inside, working with the guards.

Just outside the walls, a huge campsite had been set up in the valley. Personal tents were set up, along with larger rectangular marquee tents, where meetings could be held or meals could be served. Several fires were burning, casting plumes of smoke over the site.

Flying above the camp, bearded vultures circled. The Omte had brought along their birds. Legend had it that the Omte had chosen the vultures because of how much the Omte liked killing others. Since the vultures subsided mostly on bones, they would clean up the mess the Omte left behind.

"What do you see?" Finn asked. He stood back behind us, with Ludlow and Konstantin.

Baltsar, Ridley, and I lay at the top of the hill, scoping out Doldastam. Baltsar had a pair of binoculars, while Ridley and I were left gauging it with our eyes.

"It's definitely not good." Baltsar lowered his binoculars, so I held out my hand for them, and he passed them to me.

"What do you mean?" Finn asked. "Is it worse than we thought?"

I adjusted the binoculars, fixing them on the campsite outside the walls, and I immediately saw what the problem was. Not only were there a great deal of Omte soldiers, but members of the Högdragen and Kanin soldiers were mixed among them. It appeared that Viktor's army had fully acclimated with the Kanin and the Omte, and they were all blended together.

Konstantin had said that Viktor's army had been camping outside of Doldastam, and we were hoping that we could take care of them before moving on to deal with the Omte. Doldastam was too big to house the entire Omte army, so we'd assumed they'd also be camping outside the city walls.

Our plan had been to take out Viktor's men and the Omte without ever having to touch a Kanin. If we eliminated the first two threats, there was a good chance that Mina and her army would surrender, because at that point they would be outnumbered. Assuming we could take out Viktor and the Omte first.

But I wanted to avoid Kanin bloodshed as much as possible. These were people I had grown up with and trained with. They were good people, and they were going to end up dead.

fortified

S hit," I swore as I lowered the binoculars.

Baltsar stood up, wiping the mud from his clothes, and turned back toward Finn and Konstantin. "We're going to have to take on everyone all at once."

"We can't do that," I protested. As I got up, Ridley reached out and took the binoculars from me. "Innocent people will get hurt."

"You act like all the Kanin are saints and everybody else is a sinner," Konstantin said harshly. "Those Omte soldiers down there are just following orders, the same as the Kanin. And you don't have any qualms about killing them."

I shook my head. "It's different."

"It's different how? Because they're not like you? Because you didn't grow up with them?" Konstantin shot back. "Proximity doesn't make some people more worthwhile than others, Bryn."

"That's not what I'm saying. I don't want to kill anyone, but the Omte volunteered for this fight," I argued. "The Kanin were manipulated into it."

"You don't think the Omte were manipulated at all?" Konstantin arched an eyebrow. "You said yourself that weird things were going down in Fulaträsk."

And I had. I remembered how the Omte Queen Bodil had seemed eager to help Konstantin and me stop those who had gotten her nephew Bent Stum tangled up in the mess. She'd agreed to aid us in our quest to stop Viktor Dålig.

But later that night, her right-hand man Helge had done a total about-face. Not only had he refused to help us, he'd banished us from Fulaträsk in the middle of the night.

It all seemed very odd, and now it seemed even more suspicious that the Omte had aligned themselves with Viktor and the Kanin. Bodil had wanted revenge on Viktor one moment, and then she was apparently helping him the next.

The Omte were known for being finicky thanks to their short tempers, but this was ridiculous even by their standards.

"Fulaträsk?" Baltsar asked, looking from Konstantin to me with a quizzical expression. "When were you in Fulaträsk?"

Both Konstantin and I had failed to mention our excursion to the Omte capital city, since it hadn't been relevant before. But now, with the Omte so involved, it definitely wouldn't hurt for everyone to know.

"Finn." Ridley stood up, extending the binoculars toward Finn. "You should come see this."

"What?" Finn rushed up the hill, nearly knocking me over, and he snatched the binoculars from Ridley. "Oh, hell."

"What?" I demanded.

"My sister is with them." His shoulders slumped. "I just saw her go into a tent with Viktor Dålig."

"But she's not *with* with him," I said, almost insisting it when I looked at Baltsar and Ludlow, so they wouldn't think less of her. "Ember would only work with him to bide time. And this is what I'm talking about. We can't just storm Doldastam and hurt innocent people like her. We need to get them out."

"Most of the 'innocent' people down there would kill us on sight." Konstantin motioned toward the town. "They think *we're* the villains. So how do we decide who is safe and who dies?"

"Let's stop this before it gets too heated." Baltsar stepped in between us, raising his hands palms-out toward us. "It has been very a long day, and pressure is high. It's getting dark, so we should camp out tonight, and we'll come up with a plan of attack in the morning."

Below us, most of the troops were already setting up camp. We'd driven most of the day, and then spent the last four hours making the arduous walk toward Doldastam, through crowded forests and rough terrain. Everyone was exhausted, myself included, but that didn't stop the adrenaline from surging through me.

Baltsar managed to calm us down, and Finn agreed to a meeting at dawn with Mikko and all the captains. While everyone made their way back down the hill, I lingered behind to walk with Konstantin, who still moved more slowly because of his leg.

Ridley paused, looking back up at me with concern in his eyes. I nodded my head, motioning for him to go on ahead without me. He let out a heavy sigh, but he left me to argue with Konstantin on the side of the hill

"Why are you fighting with me so hard?" I asked him in a hushed voice.

"Because you've got to get the fantasy out of your head that you can ride in on a horse like some white knight and vanquish the dragon and save the kingdom," he replied wearily.

I stopped "I don't have that fantasy."

"You do," he insisted, and he stopped so he could look at me.

It had started to rain, and it was just above freezing, so the rain felt like ice. We stood on the side of the hill, among the trees that smelled of damp pine. The light was fading, thanks to the expanding cloud cover blotting out the setting sun, but I could still see the steel in his eyes.

"There is no such thing as a good war, Bryn," Konstantin said. "Good people will die. Innocent lives will be destroyed. And in the end, one unfit person will still hold the crown."

"But Mina is evil, and she needs to be stopped," I argued. "How do you propose we do that without war?"

"She does need to be stopped, and you're correct that this is probably the only way to do it," he agreed. "But that still doesn't make it good or easy or bloodless."

FIFTY-NINE

kingdom of ice

The flaps to the tent were frozen shut when we awoke, and when I kicked them open with my foot, ice shattered to the ground like broken glass.

My tentmate had found herself another place to sleep, and Ridley had taken residence in my tent. Despite our exhaustion, we had stayed up for a while, trying to concoct a plan to save our families from the worst of this war, but eventually we succumbed to sleep, our bodies pressed together for warmth, as the rain beat down on the canvas.

While we were sleeping the temperature had finally dropped enough to freeze, but the rain must've kept on for some time. When we emerged from the tent, the sky was beginning to lighten, casting us in an ethereal blue glow, and everything around was covered in a thick layer of ice.

Overnight, the world had turned into a frozen wonderland. Branches were encased in ice, their early buds trapped in crystal tombs. As difficult as it was getting around on the ice, there was something oddly magical about it. The way it changed the landscape completely.

Mikko held court in a large round tent, the sides of which now looked like panes of glass. He stood inside, hunched over a table with a map of Doldastam spread out on it, wearing a dark gray fur coat. Someone had made a pot of tea over a fire, and he sipped from a chalice as he studied the map.

The large hill kept our armies and the fires mostly hidden from Doldastam, but the Skojare tower guard cloaked any smoke or light that might be visible. Still, the guards' powers weren't very strong, so we kept the fires to a minimum.

Ludlow, Finn, and Baltsar were already in with him when Ridley and I arrived. None of them were speaking, so it didn't seem like we'd missed much.

"It's damn early for all this," Ludlow muttered, pouring himself a cup of tea.

Darkness only lasted for roughly six hours this time of year, and the plan before we'd gone to bed was that we wanted to hit Doldastam as close to daybreak as possible. Well, that was the old plan, at least. I was hoping to change it.

"If we go around—" Finn began to say, but I cut him off and stepped closer to the table.

"Sire, I would like to make a request," I said, and Mikko slowly lifted his head to look at me. "I would like it if you waited to launch the assault against Doldastam and allowed myself and a few others to sneak in past the walls so we can get people out before the bloodshed starts."

Mikko straightened up, resting his solemn gaze on me. "I know that you've grown up here, so you have friends and family to consider. But you can't evacuate half the town, at least not without everybody noticing."

"I'm not asking for half the town," I persisted. "I'm asking to get my parents out, and Ridley wants to get his mother." I motioned to Finn. "Finn's parents and sister are there."

Mikko's gaze hardened, and though I wanted to go on and on listing people I'd like to get out of there—like Tilda's parents, her sister and brother-in-law, and her three-year-old niece, or Kasper's family, which had already had enough loss. Even Linus Berling and his parents, who had been nothing but kind, a rarity among royals.

I knew Mikko's fear. I would evacuate the whole town if I could, but that wasn't an option. But I'd be damned if I left my parents trapped behind those walls. Tilda had told me that the town was already turning against them, and I wouldn't let them die there.

"Do you know a way that you can get in without being seen?" Baltsar asked, his curiosity clearly piqued.

"Yes, we think so." Ridley moved to the map and tapped on the east side of the wall. "There's a narrow pipe that drains out to the Hudson Bay. It wouldn't be large enough to sneak an army in, but a few of us should be able to go in undetected."

"I would like to get my family out of there," Finn said. "They have no part in this."

"I'd like to go too, my lord," Konstantin said, appearing behind us in the tent, and I turned to look at him. "I've already had to escape Doldastam once by going out through the sewers. I can get back through them."

Baltsar rubbed his chin, staring down at the spot on the map. "I would like to see the interior of Doldastam so I can plan my attacks better, but I don't think it's worth the risk."

"You've been looking for a weak spot in the wall," Konstantin pointed out, walking over to him. "And it's hard to detect from this distance. If we were inside, I could show you the weakest points, and you can decide where you want to attack."

Baltsar arched an eyebrow. "That would be invaluable information. Our only way into Doldastam will be by taking down that wall."

"It will only take us an hour, maybe two," I persisted. "Baltsar could gather information that would give us a great advantage in the war, and then we'll return. We can go to war without anything lost."

"Go, then," Mikko said, his thunderous voice rumbling with irritation. "Leave before anybody else decides to join you."

There wasn't time to waste. If we wanted to rescue our families, it would be best to use what little time we had before the sun rose.

Just before we left, Konstantin stopped me at the bottom of the hill. He held one of his prized daggers, the handle pointed toward me. "Take it, white rabbit. It'll come in handy if we run into trouble."

I'd planned to grab one of the swords from the arsenal, but

a dagger would be easier to carry. Not to mention that none of the weapons here would be as nice or as strong as Konstantin's.

"Thank you," I started to say as I tucked it in the back of my waistband, but he'd already turned and started walking up the hill.

Climbing back up the hill outside of Doldastam was much harder work than it had been last night, thanks to the ice. Once we reached the peak and looked down below, I had to pause to marvel at the beauty of it.

Even in the dim light, the ice made it all sparkle. Every inch of it was frozen. It looked like a kingdom made of crystal.

Ridley soundlessly came up beside me, and I didn't even know he was there until he started to speak.

"It's so strange to see the town this way." He exhaled deeply, his breath coming out in a plume of white fog. "I don't just mean the way the ice makes it look like diamonds. From up here, so far away, it looks like a quiet, peaceful little village. You'd have no idea about the lives it holds, or all the dark secrets it's hiding."

"I know," I agreed. "But it really is beautiful."

I looked over at Ridley. A strange expression was on his face, somewhere between wistful and pained. But I understood exactly, because Doldastam made me feel the same way. Homesick and angry and scared and happy and terrified.

Doldastam was the only home we'd ever really known, and it was home to everyone we'd ever really loved. And we were trying to save it, assuming that it didn't kill us or that we didn't destroy it in the process.

I reached out, taking Ridley's cold hand in mine. He squeezed it, the intensity of his grip promising me that somehow we would be strong enough to take this on.

"Ready to go back home?" he asked with a crooked smile.

"Are we going, or are you gonna stand up there all day having a chat?" Konstantin called up at us, and he was already a quarter of the way down the hill.

I tried to give Ridley a reassuring smile. "Let's go."

Then we were moving again, skidding down the hill, and sneaking around the camp. We stuck close to the bay, which put about four miles between us and Doldastam. There weren't any trees along the shoreline, but the distance from where the Omte and Viktor's men were camped made it nearly impossible for them to see us.

Eventually we reached the frozen stream that let water waste flow out from the town. It was in a trough dug eight feet down, so we were able to walk along it without fear of being seen. Assuming, of course, that no one came over and looked in.

Underneath the stone wall there was an iron grate to keep people or bears from getting in. Icicles hung from the bars, and Konstantin knocked them off. At the ends, where the grate met the wall, he used the handle of his dagger to hammer on the grate until it started to come free. Then, with Ridley's help, he pulled the grate back, creating a gap large enough for someone to slide through.

He stepped aside, looking at me, and then motioned to the gap. "Ladies first."

I smiled at him, then squeezed in through the gap, and entered Doldastam for the first time in almost a month.

burial

We came up in the cemetery. There were other access points, Konstantin explained, but most of them led into highly visible areas. This would be the least conspicuous place to climb up out of a sewer grate.

The cemetery was a narrow rectangle a few blocks from the center of town. Evergreen hedges created a living fence around the outside of it, providing us with some much-needed cover.

Thick, dark deciduous trees surrounded us, and their branches came together overhead, creating a canopy. In the summer, they bloomed brightly with flowers, but now icicles hung down from them, like diamond ornaments.

Almost hidden in the dim light, I saw a bearded vulture perched on one of the branches. It cocked its head, its sharp eyes locked on me. I held my breath, waiting for it to cackle and give away our position, but it only watched us before taking flight.

Four large mausoleums sat in the center of the cemetery, pointing to each of the four directions, and the royal family and high-ranking Markis and Marksinna were buried within them. Since plots were scarce, most people had burials at the bay. What few spaces were left were usually reserved for dödsfall—or a hero's death, someone who died in service to the kingdom.

We crept along, keeping our heads low in case guards were patrolling nearby, then Ridley stopped short, causing me to run into him. Konstantin was leading the way, weaving through headstones, with Baltsar and Finn following close behind.

I was about to ask Ridley why he'd stopped, but then I looked to see what he was staring it. It was a headstone, broken in half. The bloody carcass of a fish with its guts hanging out had been left on the stone, the blood and entrails frozen to the granite.

Even though it was broken, I could still make out most of the words, and I filled in the rest:

REINHARD MIKAEL DRESDEN
1963–1999
HERO TO THE KING
BELOVED FATHER AND HUSBAND

Ridley's father had been killed protecting the King during Viktor Dålig's revolt. He'd been revered as a hero . . . until Ridley had defected from Doldastam, and now, based on the dead fish, they were punishing Reinhard for Ridley's assumed loyalties to the Skojare. To me.

I put my hand on his arm and whispered, "I'm so sorry."

His jaw was set, and his eyes were hard. Then he shook his head once. "We just need to get out of here."

He turned and walked away. I wanted to right the stone and clean off the frozen blood, but we really didn't have time. And what would it matter if we did? The damage had already been done.

When we reached the edge of the cemetery, Konstantin, Baltsar, and Finn were long gone. I knew that Finn would go after his family, but I had no idea what Konstantin and Baltsar might be up to. Crouching beside the hedges, Ridley whispered that we should split up—he'd go get his mom, while I got my parents.

It seemed like the safest bet to get us out of here the fastest, so he kissed me briefly on the lips, then turned and darted in the opposite direction, while I dashed across the icy cobblestone streets toward the town square.

I was just thinking about how nice it was that I had yet to see a guard when I caught sight of two massive Omte soldiers marching right in my direction. I ducked into a narrow gap between two houses, just barely big enough to fit my body in sideways, and I started sliding through. In the middle, it started feeling very tight on my ribs, and I had to hold my breath so I could squeeze by.

When I poked my head out on the other side, I saw a member of the Högdragen patrolling at the end of the block, only three doors down from my parents' house. He kept going back and forth, walking the same beat. He'd disappear for about ten seconds, then he'd return.

I was not his commanding officer, but I knew for certain that he was supposed to be patrolling a larger area. But thanks to him being a lazy idiot, he was making it much harder for me to get to my parents' house.

By my count, I had twenty seconds to run down to my parents'. Since I had no choice, I made a break for it, running on the ice much faster than I should. When I tried to stop, I almost slid past their cottage, and I actually had to grab on to the side of it. Just in the nick of time, I jumped into the gap between my parents' house and their neighbor's.

Above the kitchen sink was a useless window. Well, my mom had always called it useless because it only gave her a view of the neighbor's wall. But today it was going to prove itself not useless as I jimmied it open and climbed inside.

I managed to squeeze in by grabbing on to the kitchen sink and pulling myself through. I'd been hoping for a more elegant landing, but I ended up tumbling headfirst onto the floor, knocking a few glasses down with me.

It was enough commotion to wake my parents, and the upstairs light clicked on. I'd just gotten to my feet by the time my dad came rushing down the stairs in his pajamas with his hair sticking up all over the place. He'd never been much for weapons, so he was wielding an antique Scandinavian sword that he'd gotten because of its historical value.

"I'm not afraid to kill you little punks," Dad growled and flicked on the kitchen light.

"Dad, it's me." I pushed back my hood so he could actually get a look at me, and he nearly dropped his sword in shock.

"Oh, my, Bryn." He just stood there staring at me for a moment, then he finally did drop the sword and ran over to me.

"Iver?" Mom called from upstairs. "Iver? Is everything okay?"

"Runa, get down here," Dad said, while giving me such a bear hug, I thought he might actually break me. But I hugged him back just as tight.

"Iver?" Mom asked cautiously, but then she must've seen me, because I heard her gasp.

By the time she'd reached me, she was already crying, and I let go of my dad with one arm so I could pull her into the hug.

"Oh, Bryn, we weren't sure if we'd ever see you again," she said between sobs.

"I know, I know." I finally pulled away from them. "I love you, and I missed you guys too. But we can talk about all that later. Right now we have to get out of here."

Mom nodded, wiping at her eyes. "I've got my bag ready. We've been waiting for our chance to escape. Just let me put on real clothes."

liberate

Getting out of my parents' house had been much easier than getting in. I didn't have a key, so I'd had to break in, but now we were safe to sneak out the back door.

Behind their house was a very small yard—a tiny strip of frozen grass separated by worn wooden fences. In the summer, my mom kept a garden there, and several of their neighbors kept chickens.

Most of the fences weren't very high, which was fortunate, since my dad had trouble jumping them as it was. Dad had always been more of an intellectual, and Mom fared much better at athletics than him, so she had no problem leaping over the fences.

We went down through the yards until we found two houses that appeared to be the farthest apart. Some of the spaces between houses were mere inches, but this gap was several feet. It was still tight to get through, especially with my parents' overstuffed rucksack, but it was much easier than the gap I'd used earlier.

From there, it was just a few mad dashes across the streets when guards weren't looking and hiding behind whatever was available. I led my mom and dad through the cemetery, around all the headstones, and as we got closer to our exit, I could see that Finn had beaten us there.

He was helping ease his mother down through the open hole. There wasn't a ladder down into the tunnel, so it was just a straight eight-foot drop to the bottom. He held Anna-li's hands, slowly lowering her down to his father, who put his hands on her waist and set her carefully on the ground.

I peered down into the hole, excited to see Ember after all this time, but she was conspicuously absent. Only Finn's parents waited in the tunnel.

"Where's Ember?" I whispered.

"She didn't come," he said in a low grunt.

"What do you mean, she didn't come?" I pressed.

Finn gave me a hard look. "I'm not going over this again. I barely managed to convince my parents to leave without her by telling them that their grandkids needed them. Ember refused to leave, and that's all there is to it."

That was apparently all he would say on the matter, because then he crouched, grabbing on to the edges of the hole, and dropped down into the sewer.

I motioned for my dad to go next, and Finn and his father

helped him. He landed with a bit of a clunk, but he wasn't any worse for the wear. Once he was standing, I helped lower my mom down.

I waited until she was safely on the tunnel floor. Above me, the sky was starting to lighten even more, and though I couldn't see it from where I sat crouched in the cemetery, I knew the sun had started its ascent above the horizon.

My parents had taken longer to get ready and get their things than I would've liked, but they were running away from the life they'd spent the past twenty years building. I couldn't blame them.

"Bryn, come on," my mom said, staring up at me. "Your dad and I will help you down."

"I have to go back and get Ember," I told her. "You go on with Finn and his parents. He'll take you back to camp."

"*Bryn!*" Mom nearly shouted, her voice cracking in desperation. "I'm not leaving without you."

"Mom, *go*," I told her. "I'll be fine. I have to do this. You and Dad need to get to safety."

"Bryn," Dad said, pleading with me to go with them. But I couldn't be persuaded.

"I gotta go. I love you guys. Stay safe." I placed the grate back over the hole, and my mom said my name again, but I didn't stay to hear more.

Since Ember had moved to Doldastam over four years ago, she'd instantly become one of my closest friends. She'd always had my back, even sometimes when no one else did. Because she was a couple years younger than me, I'd always kind of thought of her as a little sister. I was an only child, and her brother lived so far away, so we'd made each other family.

I wouldn't leave her here to die. I didn't know what Finn had done to try to convince her, but I would drag Ember out of here kicking and screaming if I had to.

The good thing was that Ember lived on the far east side of town where the poorer people lived, and that meant that guards weren't patrolling it so hard. The east also faced the bay, and the guards probably weren't counting on an attack from the water.

On the last half of my dash across town to Ember's farm, I didn't see a single guard. That made getting there much easier. I hopped the fence into the goat yard and ran over to her house.

The exterior had dark wood beams that ran along the outside, both for decoration and for support. Using the beams, I managed to climb up until I could reach the balcony that extended from her second story. That was far harder than it sounded, since everything had that nice layer of ice on it.

I grabbed the metal railing and hoisted myself up. For a moment I just lay on the balcony on my back, catching my breath and staring up at the fading stars. But then I was up, jamming open the French doors, and pushing my way inside Ember's house.

I'd just stepped through the doors and was about to say her name when I felt a hard punch slamming into my jaw, knocking me to the floor.

SIXTY-TWO

reunion

O h, Bryn, oh, my gosh, I'm so sorry!" Ember pounced on
me, hugging me while I was lying stunned on the floor.
"I thought you were a guard that caught my parents leaving."

"No, it's just me."

She sat back on her knees so I could sit up, and I rubbed
my jaw where she'd hit me. Then I just stared at her. It seemed
so unreal to be seeing her again.

Her wide eyes were so dark they were nearly black, and her
bangs landed just above them. Her long chestnut hair hung
over her shoulder in a thick braid. She wore shabby leggings
and a patterned long-sleeve thermal shirt, and I felt a tad envious knowing that she'd slept in a nice bed in a warm house
while I was out sleeping in the storm.

Her mouth spread into a toothy grin. "I can't believe it's
really *you*."

"I know. It's crazy."

We'd been apart for long periods of time before. I'd gone on missions tracking changelings, and so had she. But this time it felt different. So much had happened, and neither of us was sure that we'd ever see each other again.

And then, since she couldn't contain herself, Ember hugged me again, and this time I was able to hug her back.

"I'm not going with you," she said softly, still hugging me. I let go and pulled back. "What? Why the hell not?"

"I can't." She shook her head. "I don't have time to explain it all, but I can't. I have to stay here and help the people that are left behind."

"Ember, you're being ridiculous. Did Finn tell you about all the soldiers we have stationed out beyond the hill?" I asked. "It's going to be brutal here. You could die."

"I know, I do, but that's exactly why I have to stay," she said with a sad smile. "I can't leave everyone defenseless. Tilda and Kasper's families are still here, not to mention Juni Sköld, Simon Bohlin, and Linus Berling, and so many other of our friends." She paused. "I won't leave Delilah."

"Delilah?" I asked, and then I remembered.

The Marksinna whom Ember had been training with before. When I'd still been here, it had only seemed like a flirtation, but by the conviction I heard in Ember's voice, I guessed that their relationship had turned into something more.

"Ember, you can't risk your life for someone like this. You

need to do what you must to survive. That's what Delilah would want, if she really cares about you."

"Of course I can, and I will," Ember replied simply. "I love her."

"That's great, but—"

"I don't expect you to understand. I know that you'd never sacrifice anything for love," she said, sounding almost as if she pitied me. "For honor, for loyalty, for the kingdom, you'd give up anything. But love . . . you never had time for that."

Her words stung, probably harder than she'd meant them to, like a knife cutting straight through my heart. I wanted to argue with her, to tell her that I loved, that I loved very deeply. And not just her and Tilda and my parents, but Ridley and Konstantin.

It wasn't that I didn't have time for love, or that I wouldn't sacrifice for it. I had just been so afraid that I would lose myself and my place in the world, the way my mom had, the way Ember's mom had, and the way I had seen so many other women do before her. I refused to be sidelined by romance.

But when it came down to it, I would give anything for love. I would lay my life down for Ridley, if it meant I could spare him pain.

That's when I realized there was no point in arguing with Ember. Just as no one would be able to change my mind when it came to protecting those that I cared about, I wouldn't be able to change hers. Besides, Ember was nothing if not stubborn and loyal.

"You have to be careful," I told her finally. "All hell is going to break loose here."

"I know. You should go, before they start noticing that people are missing," Ember said. Then she suddenly exclaimed and jumped to her feet. "You're here!"

"Yeah?" I stared up uncertainly. "I've been here for a couple minutes."

"No, I mean—just wait." She turned and dashed back into her bedroom. A few seconds later, she came back carrying a handful of envelopes. "You can read these."

I took them from her, and as I flipped through them, I saw that *Bryn* had been handwritten on each one. "What are these?"

"I wrote to you while you were gone, but I didn't mail them because I had no idea where to send them." She stood with her arms folded over her chest. "Also, the Högdragen are checking all the mail going in and out, so that wouldn't have gone over well."

"Thanks, Ember." I stood up. "That was really nice of you."

She shrugged. "I missed you, and it was the only way I could talk to you."

"I missed you too." I smiled at her, and I tucked the letters in the back of my pants, next to the dagger, safely protected from the elements. "But I should go now."

"I don't know when I'll see you again," Ember said, and there was a hesitance on the word *when*, since it really should've been *if*. "Take care."

"You too."

I walked out of her house onto the balcony. I hung over the edge, and then dropped down carefully into the yard. I took a step backward and looked up to watch Ember closing the French doors.

Then I turned around and ran right smack into Ridley, who smartly put his hand over my mouth to prevent me from screaming.

"What are you doing here?" I hissed when he removed his hand.

"Looking for you. Finn told me you went back to get Ember, and I didn't want to leave you behind."

"What about your mom?" I asked.

"Finn is taking her out with the rest of the parents," he explained. "Where's Ember?"

I shook my head. "She's not coming." He didn't press any further, and it was for the best. "Do you have any idea where Konstantin and Baltsar went?"

"All I know is that Konstantin was trying to show Baltsar weak points in the town."

We hopped the fence out of the yard and started the trek back to the cemetery. We cut through alleys and backyards, taking much the same route I had on the way to Ember's house. But it was starting to get brighter out, and we no longer had darkness to help cloak us.

It had begun to snow, heavy wet flakes, and while it was only a flurry now, it felt like it could take a harder turn.

Two blocks from the cemetery, we paused, waiting in an

alley. An Omte soldier was patrolling the street, and Ridley stood with his back pressed against the nearest house, craning his neck around to watch the soldier. I crouched down beside him, trying to get a better look.

Both of us were so focused on the Omte soldier in front of us that we didn't notice anyone creeping up behind us, until I heard Helge Otäck's gravelly voice say, "Well, isn't this a nice surprise?"

SIXTY-THREE

overtaken

Helge Otäck was the Viceroy to the Omte Queen, and while that sounded like a cushy job, Helge looked more like an old biker than a politician. His leathery skin showed signs of a hundred bar fights, and his scraggly hair hung past his shoulders.

Even under the thick brown winter coat he wore, it was still obvious that Helge himself was a large man. He easily towered over us, making him appear strong by human standards, and he had the Omte strength to boot.

When he grinned down at us, I realized that two of his front teeth had been replaced with gold caps, but that was really all I had time to notice, because then Helge was moving.

Before either of us could act, Helge grabbed Ridley. Ridley tried to fight him off, hitting and kicking him any way he could, but it was futile. Helge wrapped one arm across Ridley's throat, and grabbed his hair with the other hand. Ridley clung on to his arm as Helge lifted him from the ground.

I pulled the dagger from the back of my pants and held it out toward him, not that I knew what to do to stop him.

Helge clicked his tongue at me. "Think carefully before you move with that knife, little girl. How long do you think it will take you to reach me? One second? Two? Because I can have your friend's neck snapped in half that."

"Just let him go," I said, watching Ridley struggle against Helge. "You don't want him. You want me. I'm the one that made the Queen's most-wanted list."

"Maybe so. But who says I can't have you both?" Helge grinned, and I heard a growl behind me.

I glanced over my shoulder to see a giant Omte soldier standing a few feet back at the opening of the alley. I turned again to Helge and kept my eyes on Ridley as my mind raced, trying to decide what to do. I could hear heavy footfalls as the Omte stepped closer behind me, and I waited, gauging his movements until I thought he was right behind me.

Then, in one fell swoop, I crouched and whirled around. I raised the dagger up quickly, jabbing underneath the jaw and straight up through the head of the Omte. His blood ran warm over my hand, and when I yanked the blade out, it made a sickening wet sound.

The body collapsed to the ground, and that should've been a relief, except there was another Omte guard standing right behind him. He saw what I'd just done to his friend, and he did not look happy about it.

He growled and lowered his head like he meant to charge at me, but just before he did, I saw movement to his left. An arm cloaked in a black jacket was wielding a long sword, and with the guard's eyes still locked on me, the sword sliced through his neck, decapitating him.

Baltsar stepped into the alleyway, holding his bloodied sword, and Konstantin pushed past him. He grabbed my arm, yanking me away. I looked back over my shoulder, at a grinning Helge holding Ridley hostage.

"Helge has Ridley," I said, trying to pull away from Konstantin.

"Helge also has guards coming. We can't fight them all, and we need to go before they get here," Konstantin said, still dragging me. I tried to dig my feet in, but the ice kept making them slip.

"They'll kill him," I insisted, barely able to keep myself from shouting, but I couldn't draw further attention to us.

Konstantin stopped long enough to turn on me. "No, they won't. Not yet. Mina will use him as bait. Let her."

I wanted to protest further, because it killed me to leave Ridley. And even though I knew Konstantin had a point, it felt like too great a risk.

Still hanging on to my arm, he broke the door in to a public outhouse. He went inside and kicked out the wooden base for the toilet. We couldn't risk being seen, which meant that we couldn't go back to the cemetery, so this would have to do.

Baltsar jumped in first, but I waited a moment longer.

Konstantin put his hands on my face, forcing me to look up at him.

"You can't save him if you're dead," he said roughly. "But I won't make you come with me. This is your choice."

He jumped down through the hole, and I looked back, as if I could somehow still see Ridley. I realized painfully that if Helge was going to kill Ridley, he would already be dead. Helge would've snapped his neck the second we walked away so he could go round up more of his guards.

It was either already too late, or I needed to get out of here if I wanted to come back with a rescue team. I closed the outhouse door, making it a bit more difficult for the guards to figure out where we'd gone, and I jumped down after Konstantin and ran after him through the sewers.

SIXTY-FOUR

tempest

By the time we made it back to our camp, the snow was coming fast and heavy, creating whiteout conditions. The wind had picked up, officially turning it into a late-spring blizzard. They were rare for Doldastam, but not unheard-of, and it started to feel like even the weather was against us.

My mom was waiting at the bottom of the hill for us to return. Finn and the families had arrived at camp before Konstantin, Baltsar, and I, even though we'd run most of the way back. I didn't know if Konstantin's leg was still bothering him, but he pushed himself on it just as fast as Baltsar and I.

Mom hugged me as soon as she saw me. But I just stood stiffly and didn't embrace her in return. Through the thick snowflakes, I saw Konstantin and Baltsar heading toward the King's tent, so I untangled myself from my mom and ran after them.

"If it keeps up like this, the men won't be able to see any of us commanding them," Ludlow was telling Mikko when I pushed my way into his tent. Snow came up behind me, forming a drift in his doorway.

Mikko stood on the opposite side of the table while his advisers, Finn and Ludlow, stood across from him. Baltsar moved up to take his place beside Ludlow, while Konstantin lingered by the entrance.

"As much as it pains me to say so, I agree," Finn said. "We should wait until the storm dies to make our move. We can't properly give orders or create a formation if we can't see anything."

"We can't wait. We need to go in and get Ridley." I stepped forward, but Konstantin put his arm out, blocking me and holding me back.

Mikko cast his severe gaze on me. "What's become of Ridley Dresden?"

"Give me a minute with Bryn," Konstantin said. "Baltsar, fill the King in."

Baltsar cleared his throat. "The Omte surprised Ridley and Bryn as they were retreating . . ."

I didn't hear anything he said beyond that because Konstantin had started pushing me out of the tent. When I tried to resist, he put his arm around my waist and carried me away.

"Put me down! What are you doing?" I demanded, but I didn't really fight him. After everything that had happened that morning, I didn't have the strength to defy him on things that weren't life-or-death.

He set me down once we'd gotten far enough from the

King's tent and the campsite that we could have some privacy. Bright white snow swirled around us, getting caught in his raven curls and eyelashes.

"I'm saving your ass," Konstantin said finally.

"How was that saving me?" I shot back.

"You were about to go in there and demand the King send a rescue mission after Ridley, even though you know that's suicide. Look around!" He gestured to the growing snowstorm. "We can't conduct our men in this, not if we want to win the war. And a rescue mission would only get us caught.

"Right now Mina only knows about me, you, Ridley, and Baltsar," he explained. "She already knew you, me, and Ridley were working together, and she'll likely assume that Baltsar is just someone else we picked up along the way. Even capturing Ridley, she hasn't found out anything new.

"But this army—" He pointed back to the campsite. "*That's* news to her. And if we go in with the kind of team we'd need to rescue Ridley, she'll figure out that we have a lot more muscle behind us."

He stepped closer to me, his gray eyes locked on mine. "Right now she has no clue what we're really up to, and we can't let her find out until it's too late."

I wanted to argue with him. I wanted to grab bigger weapons and gather all the men I could and storm the palace, tearing it apart until I found Ridley. But no matter how much the truth hurt, I knew Konstantin was right.

"I know it's hard setting your feelings aside to do the right thing." He smiled bitterly. "Believe me, I know better than anyone. But you can't let your feelings for Ridley—or for anyone—cloud your judgment right now." He paused, still looking down at me. "We need you, Bryn."

I breathed in deeply, relishing the way the cold air stung my throat and lungs, as snowflakes melted on my cheeks.

"I can't leave him there for very long," I said thickly.

"She won't kill him," Konstantin assured me, and with a gloved hand he gingerly wiped away the melting snowflakes from my face. "Not yet. She'll want to find out everything she can from him, and then she wants us to fall into a trap trying to rescue him. Ridley is strong and smart, and he's still alive. I promise you that."

I lowered my eyes. "He came back for me. It's all my fault."

"It is not your fault," Konstantin growled in anger, startling me into looking up at him. "Ridley chose to go back, and he wasn't paying attention in that alley either. You can't always take the blame for everything, Bryn. Sometimes bad things happen for no reason and sometimes they happen because other people fucked up. It's not always on you."

He sighed. "I'm sorry. I didn't mean to yell at you."

"No, it's okay. I think I needed to hear it." I brushed my hair back from my face. "So what do we do now?"

"You should go get your parents settled in. The snow will have us hunkered down for a while." He squinted into the on-coming storm. "Things are only going to get worse before they get better."

I wasn't sure if he was talking about the storm or the war, but it was true either way.

SIXTY-FIVE

disturbance

The tent was sagging low on me again, and I knew I would have to go out and scrape off the snow soon before it collapsed on me entirely. The batteries were going out in the little electric lamp, making it flicker dimly, but I tried to ignore that.

I lay on my back with one arm underneath my head, buried under my sleeping bag, with Ember's letters spread out around me. The snow hadn't let up yet, so the rest of the camp had gone to bed.

Everyone else around me was probably sleeping, but every time I tried to close my eyes, all I could think about was how last night Ridley and I slept curled up against each other, and tonight he was being held in Mina's torture chamber. The very last place on earth he wanted to be.

So I lay awake, reading through Ember's letters over and over again. It was my fifth time through reading her final letter, and it still made my stomach twist in knots. To read about how Doldastam had slowly collapsed, becoming a twisted dictatorship under the harsh rule of a paranoid mad-woman.

It also made me realize how much I'd missed out on in Ember's life, and Tilda's, my parents', and Ridley's. So much had befallen them, and I hadn't been able to help them with any of it.

I also missed Ember terribly. She had been shouldering such a huge burden these past few weeks, with Tilda reeling from Kasper's death, and Ridley dealing with the trauma of Mina's torture. Not to mention that Ember had taken time out to check on my parents when nobody else would. And all the other trackers and royals she was trying to train so they could protect themselves.

I wished I'd been able to talk to her more, and I couldn't wait for the day when this was all over so I could thank her for everything she'd done and tell her how proud of her I was.

Putting her letter down, I let myself indulge in a fantasy for a moment. One where there would be peace again, and Tilda, Ember, and I could go out together for a few glasses of wine the way we had before. And when I'd finished, I could go home and curl up with Ridley. Even though it hurt to think of Ridley, I couldn't help myself. I closed my eyes, remem-bering the feel of his skin against mine and the safety of his arms.

But it hurt too much, so I moved the thoughts along, try-ing to think of all the other things I would do when this was over. Like taking Bloom for a very long ride. And having dinner with my parents and asking my mom to make her gooseberry pie for me. And Konstantin would—

The thought of Konstantin jarred me out of the daydream. We had grown close, and he'd definitely become someone I could rely on. When this was all over, I did want him to be a part of my life still, but I realized painfully that I had no idea where he would fit in it.

A scuffle outside brought me from my thoughts, and I grabbed the dagger from where it sat beside me. I opened the flap, pushing back the foot of snow that had built up around the tent since the last time I'd cleared it away.

Next to the King's tent a campfire burned, and it cast enough light that I could see two guards dragging someone toward the large tent.

"Let me go," a woman insisted. "You've got it all wrong."

The guards didn't listen, so she broke free. With a few well-placed punches, she had knocked them both to the ground, and the ease of her fighting immediately made me think Omte.

I jumped out of the tent, wielding my dagger, ready to stop any Omte who dared come into our camp. She stood over the guards with her back to me, snow clinging to her dark hair and fur-lined jacket. When she turned around, I got a good look at her for the first time, and I recognized her.

In her late twenties and beautiful, especially for an Omte, she had the face of a warrior, with determined dark eyes and smooth olive skin.

"Bekk Vallin," I said, but I didn't lower my dagger.

When Konstantin and I had been to Fulaträsk, she had been kind to us, and even helped save us from the wrath of an ogre. But she had been a Queen's guard, and now she was sneaking into our base camp. So things didn't look good.

"Bryn Aven." Bekk sounded just as surprised to see me as I was to see her, but relief washed over her face. "I was trying to tell the guards but they wouldn't listen to me. I came here to help you."

I narrowed my eyes. "Why should I believe you?"

"Helge Otäck betrayed our Queen and our kingdom. He's dragged us into a war that we have no place in, all for a few gemstones." She wrinkled her nose in disgust. "He sold out our entire tribe. Queen Bodil doesn't see it yet, but I do, and I won't continue to do their bidding."

"So you're saying that you want to fight on our side?" I lowered my dagger a bit, and she nodded.

"I want to fight with whoever is going to kill Helge," she replied coolly. "And I'll help you however I can."

"I think I should take you to see King Mikko, and I'll let him decide what to do with you."

She nodded. "That only sounds fair."

dialogue

M ikko pushed in the canvas door to the round tent that had been used for planning our strategy, his long silver fur robe dragging on the ground behind him. Baltsar and Finn followed.

I'd gotten his footman to wake him, and he'd apparently decided to wake Baltsar and Finn too, but that was just as well. Bekk and I had been standing by his table, warming ourselves by the thick pillar candles that covered it.

As soon as he came and eyed up Bekk, his mouth turned down into a deep scowl. "I thought we'd decided we're taking no prisoners."

"I'm not a prisoner," Bekk said fiercely and stepped back from the table.

I put my hand on her arm in an attempt to calm her, and even through the thick leather of her jacket I could feel her thick muscles coiled. She could take us all out if she wanted to.

"She came here voluntarily to talk," I interjected hurriedly.

"What does she have to talk about?" Baltsar asked, eyeing her with the same suspicion as Mikko.

"Why don't you ask me yourself?" Bekk shot back, and I was beginning to wonder if bringing her had been a bad idea.

"All right." Mikko took a deep breath, and his broad shoulders relaxed a bit, as he attempted to start over from a less offensive position. "If you came into our camp tonight, risking a great deal, you must have something valuable to tell us."

Bekk responded by relaxing herself. "I do. I came to tell you about Helge Otäck. He duped Queen Bodil, and he's been working with Viktor Dålig. He's helped orchestrate the whole thing."

Mikko's brow furrowed. "Helge Otäck? I don't think I'm familiar with him."

"He's the Viceroy to the Omte," I said, and I bit my tongue to keep from adding that he was the bastard who was holding Ridley hostage.

"The Omte are working for the Kanin and Viktor Dålig. We all know that." Baltsar shrugged. "How is this exciting news to us?"

Bekk glared at him, her amber eyes seeming to blaze in the candlelight. "Helge helped orchestrate this whole thing. For over a year, Helge has been getting the strongest members of the Omte tribe exiled on the tiniest infractions, then passing them along to Viktor for his army."

"Why would Helge do that?" Finn asked.

"Viktor traded our men for a few sapphires. Helge has been selling off our tribe bit by bit for a few lousy blue rocks." Bekk shook her head in disbelief. "He even sent off the Queen's own nephew, and he got killed running errands for Viktor!"

The Queen's nephew was Bent Stum. From what I'd gathered from Konstantin, shortly after Bent had been exiled, he'd joined up with Viktor and was immediately paired with Konstantin to track down changelings. Viktor had brought Bent to help ensure that Konstantin would do his job.

"How do you know all this?" Mikko asked. "I'm not saying I doubt your story, but I can't imagine that Helge just confessed this all to you himself."

"I've never trusted Helge, but I started putting it together when we arrived in Doldastam and I met Viktor Dålig," Bekk explained. "I realized it wasn't the first time I'd seen him. He'd been sneaking around Fulaträsk before, whispering with Helge in the hallways of the palace.

"But last night I overheard Helge and Viktor talking and laughing about how their plans were coming together." Her lip curled in disgust. "They didn't even care if anybody overheard anymore. They think they've won already, that Viktor will be King of the Kanin and Helge will be King of the Omte, and then they will take out the rest of you, until the tribes and all your jewels are theirs.

"That's why I came here," she finished. "I can't let that happen. I'd rather see the entire Omte kingdom destroyed than those two bastards win."

Mikko stared at the floor, his hands on his hips as he

breathed in deeply through his nose. Baltsar and Finn exchanged a look, one that appeared as if they'd just realized they were in deeper shit than they'd originally thought.

"Thank you for coming here with this," Mikko said finally, and he lifted his head to look at Bekk. "What you have said is interesting, perhaps even valuable information, but it won't help us win this war or defeat Helge Otäck or Viktor Dålig."

"How about this, then?" Bekk challenged him. "The Högdragen and Kanin soldiers are inside the walls at night. If you want to avoid fighting the Kanin, attack at first light. It will only be Omte and Viktor's men on the outside."

Mikko nodded once. "Now, that might actually help."

Mikko, Baltsar, and Finn began talking among themselves, coming up with a revised battle plan. When it became apparent that Bekk and I were no longer needed, Baltsar told us that we should go rest as much as we could.

"Thank you bringing me to them," Bekk said as we walked back to my tent. I didn't know where else to put her, and it would be good if we could get some sleep tonight.

"Well, thank you for helping us," I said, then I stopped to look at her. "I do just have one favor that I'd like to ask you."

She cocked her head, appraising me. "You've got balls so big they'd make an ogre jealous. Whatever you want, I'm game."

SIXTY-SEVEN

battle cry

The snow came up past our knees, but we marched on down the hill toward Doldastam. Mikko led the way, with each of the captains leading their respective armies— Baltsar headed the Skojare, Finn the Trylle, and Ludlow the Vittra.

Konstantin, Bekk, and I had no real allegiance, so we simply walked near the front, following Mikko's long strides through the drifts. This time, since I wasn't sneaking around the town, I'd gone for a Skojare sword made of Damascus steel.

Before dawn even broke, we had started our descent down the hill. Most of the Omte were sleeping, and we'd nearly reached them before one of them caught sight of us and sounded the alarm.

Within moments the Omte were in formation. Mikko yelled his battle cry, and the war officially began.

I had a very singular plan—to get to the wall. I didn't want to be slowed down by fighting, but I would plow through anyone who stood in my way. Bekk had agreed to help me, and she quickly proved herself to be an amazing ally, knocking a giant ogre out of my way.

I'd drawn my sword, and I sliced through anyone who came at me. An Omte wielding an ax—I cut off his head. A scraggly ex-Kanin-looking guy with two swords—I cut off one hand, and then stabbed him through the chest.

I didn't think about what I was doing. I just moved on instinct, jumping over bodies and broken tents. The Omte had been living here for days, and bones littered the ground. It was a mess of garbage, rotting food, and expired campfires. It was like an obstacle course, but with murderous maniacs charging at me.

Bearded vultures circled above us, squawking their rage. All around me, I heard people crying out in pain. I saw a Skojare soldier fall to the ground, bleeding profusely from his neck.

But my mission was clear, and I couldn't save him. So I charged on.

Bekk stayed near me the entire way, stabbing or punching anyone who got too close. By the time we'd reached the wall, both of us were covered in blood. So far, none of it was our own, but that was bound to change.

I sheathed my sword and stared up the wall. It was still slippery from the ice and snow, and with all the fighting going on around us, it would be an impossible climb.

"Ready?" Bekk asked, right after stabbing a man through the head who had come running at us.

"Yeah, I'd better be," I said.

She grabbed me by the back of my jacket and the waistband of my pants, and with a grunt, she swung me back and then tossed me up. I flew into the top of the wall, with it hitting me right at the waist. I started to slip down, so I hurried to get a foothold. With my arms I brushed the snow out of my way and finally managed to get a grip on the wall and hoist myself up onto it.

I looked back down at Bekk and gave her a thumbs-up. She smiled and proceeded to punch someone so hard that his face actually caved in. I'd never seen anything like it, and I hoped I never would again. We were incredibly fortunate that she was on our side.

Then I stood up and turned my attention toward Doldastam. Since the Omte had sounded the alarm, the Högdragen and Kanin soldiers were filling the streets. I was near the palace, which was where most of them were running to—to protect the Queen.

"People of Kanin!" I shouted as loud as I could. The sounds of the battle were raging on behind me, but thankfully, the walls had a somewhat dampening effect. "Listen to me!"

Some of the people were still running around, but many looked up at me. I wasn't wearing a hood. I made no attempt to hide who I was, because I wanted them to know.

"Mina is not your true Queen!" I yelled. "You have been deceived! She killed your King! She's lying to you because she is Viktor Dålig's daughter!"

Some of the soldiers and even the panicked townspeople

gasped. Others were skeptical, but I knew they would be. I knew I couldn't reach all of them, but I hoped I could reach some.

Beneath me, the wall began to shake, and I glanced behind me to see that the Vittra hobgoblins had started going at it with an iron battering ram. They were knocking down the wall to make an entrance for our army.

The fight was still raging behind them, with the Skojare and their allies trying to take out as many of Viktor's men and the Omte as they could. Bodies littered the ground, blood staining the fresh snow, but it was hard to tell for certain if the fallen were allies or enemies.

Either way, the hobgoblins had decided it was time to move in past the wall, to get to the Kanin before they organized themselves.

"Do not let her deceive you any longer!" I shouted at the ever-gathering crowd. More and more were coming closer to hear what I had to say. "You have no allegiance to her, because she is a liar, a traitor, and a murderer! Rip off your uniforms and fight with us today! Fight against the oppression! Fight against the Queen! Fight for your freedom!"

In the crowd, I saw Ember standing with Linus Berling, both of them smiling at me.

Then a dozen Högdragen made their way to the front of the crowd, took a knee, and pointed their bows and arrows at me. The wall beneath my feet felt very unstable, and I knew I had overstayed my welcome.

Just as they began to fire, I threw my sword to the ground

on the village side and jumped down off the wall after it. The big drifts of snow helped cushion my fall, and I immediately rolled, attempting to limit the force on my legs and ankles. I grabbed my sword and scrambled out of the way to avoid getting hit by the stones that were tumbling down.

The hobgoblins had broken through, so the Högdragen turned their attention on them as the army began spilling in over the rubble. I ran back behind the buildings alongside the crumbling wall, toward the palace. Toward Ridley.

SIXTY-EIGHT

absolution

The sound of a little girl crying stopped me in my tracks. From where I stood, with snow coming up to my knees, I could see a back door to the palace half a mile away. It wouldn't be easy to break in, but that was all the more reason that I should get moving.

Just to my left was the wall, and to my right was the small dormitory where unmarried Högdragen lived. That meant this wasn't the safest place for me to stop.

All around me I could hear men and women screaming, the clash of swords, and stones crashing against each other as the wall continued to crumble. The sounds echoed off the remaining walls and outlying buildings, and became the continuous growl of battle. But over all that, I could hear the little girl crying, which meant she had to be close. Which meant that I might be able to help her.

I took a few steps forward, following the sound of the

crying, and I peered around the dorm. There in the corner, where the dorm met the Högdragen gym and the snow had drifted away, leaving a quiet spot, a little girl sat on the ground with her head buried in her arms.

I looked around, making sure there wasn't anyone lying in wait, and I crouched down and made my way toward her.

"Hey," I said softly when I got close, and she lifted her head.

When I finally saw her, I almost stumbled back in surprise. She looked so much like Kasper, it was like seeing a ghost. Since she was only ten, she had the chubbier cheeks of a child and her features were softer, more feminine, but she had his dark eyes beneath her black corkscrew curls, and his nose, and even his thick eyebrows.

It was Naima Abbott, Kasper's little sister, and I knew that I couldn't leave her.

"When the fighting started, I came here to get Kasper's sword," she explained with tears streaming down her cheeks, and I couldn't tell if she recognized me or not. "But I couldn't get in. I just wanted to protect my family the way Kasper would've."

"That's very noble, but Kasper would just want you to be safe." I held out my hand to her, the one that wasn't holding my sword. "We need to get you back to your family."

She looked at me uncertainly, then she sniffled and took my hand, and I tried to figure out what I would do with her.

I knew I couldn't take her into the palace with me, since that would be full of guards who wanted me dead, and there was a good chance she could end up as collateral damage.

The safest bet would be getting her back to her family, since her father was a former Högdragen and her other brother was going to tracker school. They could protect her, and if she stayed inside her home, odds were that nobody would attack her.

Neither side of the war wanted to hurt innocent children. But with her out on the street, and ogres throwing people around, and people killing each other, it would be far too easy for her to be hurt in the chaos of it all.

Fortunately, the Abbotts didn't live very far away from the palace. Unfortunately, that meant we wouldn't be able to avoid the fighting on our way to her home.

"I'm gonna take you home," I promised her. "But if I tell you to get down, you need to find the best hiding spot you can and hide, okay?"

She nodded, so I led her around the dorm, down the alleyway between the Högdragen facilities and the palace, and toward the main street. The worst of the fighting was concentrated half a mile down, where the hobgoblins had broken through the wall.

That didn't mean others weren't fighting down here, though. A Trylle soldier and a Högdragen were fighting each other rather brutally right on the street in front of us. The Högdragen was using a sword, but the Trylle had gotten a battle-ax, and they were mercilessly hacking at each other.

I pulled Naima behind me, trying to shield her with my body so she wouldn't see the worst of it, and I pushed up my hood, hiding my blond hair. If they saw someone running across the street with a child, I would attract less attention if it wasn't obvious that I was Skojare.

The Högdragen had knocked the Trylle to the ground, and it looked like he might be about ready to finish him off, so it seemed like a good time to make a break for it.

"Run," I told Naima, and then I bolted across the street, still holding her hand.

I was hoping that we could make it across unnoticed, but behind us I heard the angry growl of an ogre. We turned sharply off the main road, running down the narrow cobblestone street toward the Abbotts' house.

The heavy crunch of the ogre's feet destroying the cobblestones as he ran behind us began to speed up, and I realized that there was no way Naima would be able to outrun him. I wasn't sure if even I would be able to without her.

"Hide!" I shouted, and pulled her to the side, practically tossing her toward the thin gap between a couple houses. It was big enough for a normal adult troll to fit in, but an ogre would be unable to grab her.

With Naima safely out of the way, I drew my sword and turned back around to face the ogre charging toward me.

ogre

Grinning crookedly with his oversized mouth, the ogre slowed as he reached me, and I realized that it was Torun, who had so badly wanted to squash Konstantin and me when we came across him in the swamps outside Fulaträsk.

He was over eight feet tall, with arms like tree trunks. He was completely lopsided, with everything on his right side larger than that on his left. His right hand was much larger than his left, and he had it balled into a fist.

"Squash you now," Torun grunted with an angry laugh.

"Last time you caught me without my sword," I told him. "I won't go down as easy as you think."

Torun raised his right fist high above his head, and I waited until he started bringing it down toward me, to squash me. Then I lifted my sword and jabbed it straight through his wrist. He howled in pain and when he yanked his arm back, he took me with it.

I wrapped my legs around his arm, so when he tried to shake me off, I had a good grip, and I began twisting the sword, cutting through the tendons and bone. Ogres were bigger and stronger than regular trolls, but their bones broke just as easily as for the rest of us.

Realizing I wouldn't let go, Torun grabbed me with his left hand and threw me aside. I crashed into a house, and fell into a pile of snow. The landing had been hard enough that it left me dazed and out of breath for a moment, but I stumbled to my feet as quickly as I could.

Torun's massive hand was hanging on to his arm by a flap of skin and a few tendons. He cradled it with his good hand, crying out in pain, as blood poured out, soaking the street.

When he saw me getting up, he growled in rage, and I knew I had to finish him off quickly. He charged toward me, and I dove out of the way, so he crashed into the house and knocked himself off balance. The loss of blood seemed to be affecting him, and he stumbled backward.

My sword had fallen to the ground, and I grabbed it in a flash. I went up to his right side and stabbed between his ribs, straight into his enlarged ogre heart. Torun growled once more, and that was it. He slumped over and slid off my sword, onto the street.

I wiped the blood off my hand, then held it out to Naima. She hesitated before coming out, but she finally did, and we started running down the street.

We rounded the corner, Naima's house finally in sight, and a small Omte guard came out of nowhere. He had jumped out from between two houses, and now he was charging at me. I pushed Naima behind me, using my body as a shield.

The Omte raised his sword at me, so I blocked it with my own. Since that move would only leave us at a standstill, with him pushing his blade toward me while I pushed back, I kicked him in the stomach, knocking him back.

Moving quickly, I stabbed him through the chest before he had a chance to block me. I pulled my sword free, and he fell to the ground.

That was when I looked down the street again, and I saw Rutger Abbott standing in the middle of the street. His sword was drawn, and he had the rigid stance of a Högdragen. His face was much harder than Kasper's had ever been, but he had the same eyes as both Kasper and Naima.

I stepped out from in front of Naima and whispered, "Go to your dad."

Rutger had to have seen enough to know that I had just killed an ally of the Kanin kingdom. He walked toward me with cold deliberate steps. When Naima ran to him, he hugged her, but kept his eyes on me.

I was terrified about how this would play out. If Rutger believed the lies that Mina had told him, he would blame me for Kasper's death and believe me to be an evil traitor. With that in mind, he might very well want to kill me, and I did not want to fight Kasper's dad in a battle to the death.

"Go in the house," he told Naima.

She did as she was told, rushing toward the relative safety of her home, and leaving Rutger and me alone in the street.

At least for a moment. Other guards would surely be coming soon.

"Thank you for protecting my daughter," he said finally.

"I'm sorry I couldn't protect your son," I said.

He lowered his eyes. "Go, and finish this for him." That was all he said before he turned and walked back toward his house.

I looked back over the roofs of the cottages around us, toward the palace looming over everyone and everything, and I started running toward it, my legs moving as fast as they could.

conspire

On the way to the palace, I tried to avoid as many main roads and conflicts as I could. Not only because I wanted to get there as quickly as possible, but also because I wanted to avoid killing any Kanin if I could help it. And it was a bonus if I ended up not getting killed myself.

Still, I'd had to kill two more Omte soldiers before I found myself in close proximity to the palace. I crouched down next to Astrid Eckwell's mansion, with the body of Simon Bohlin in the snow beside me.

On my way here, I'd seen Simon, with his head lolled to the side, bleeding from a fatal wound in his stomach.

For a nearly year we'd dated, until I'd broken up with him because I was looking for something more casual. He had been a great tracker, though, which was one of the things that attracted me to him. We'd grown up together, and he'd always been kind to me in a school where a lot of kids hadn't been.

I couldn't leave him in the middle of the street to get crushed under ogres' feet, so I dragged him to the side of the house. I knew I couldn't move all the bodies, that I couldn't save everyone, but I couldn't bear the thought of leaving Simon out like that.

Leaning with my back against the cold bricks of the mansion, I tried to catch my breath and gather myself. I didn't have time to mourn Simon or anyone else who would die today. Not if I wanted to save Ridley and stop Mina.

I looked back out to the street, where the fighting raged on, just in time to see Ember, fighting her way through the crowd. Behind her was Linus Berling, and while he wasn't doing an amazing job, he was holding his own fairly well. He hadn't been killed yet, but he did appear to be bleeding from his arm.

Ember finally managed to break free from the fighting, and Linus chased after her, following the path she'd made. They ran right up to the mansion next door to Astrid's, diving over the fence and running around to the back door.

If I wanted to storm the palace, it wouldn't hurt to have someone like Ember at my side. She was a quick, strong fighter, and there were going to be many more guards left to face.

I decided to go to Ember and see if she would help me free Ridley. I ran around the back of Astrid's house, and then I jumped the neighbor's fence. I wasn't sure if I should knock or not, but since Ember had just gone in through the back door, I decided to try it for myself.

As soon as I pushed it open, Ember was there with her sword in my face.

"Oh, jeez, Bryn." She sighed and lowered her weapon. "You really need to start knocking." She opened the door wider for me, letting me in.

The door opened into the kitchen, where Linus sat shirtless at the kitchen table. A girl stood beside him, her dark hair falling around her, as she tried to clean up a nasty gash on his arm.

"Bryn." Linus tried to smile at me, but his injury caused him to wince instead. "When I saw you on the wall today, I was so happy that you were okay and fighting to get rid of that witch in the palace."

It had been nearly two months since Linus had first arrived in Doldastam, and in that short time he'd already grown and changed so much, even though he was barely eighteen. He'd spent time training with Ember, and his arms and chest had begun to fill out, with muscles bulking up his lanky frame.

Light freckles dotted his face, and he still had an openness to his expression, like he could never completely hide what he was feeling, but his eyes had darkened, taking some of the innocence he'd arrived with.

Around his wound, his skin had begun to change color, shifting to blend into our surroundings. When the girl tending his wounds tried to stitch up the gash on his arm, Linus winced, and the color intensified, making it almost appear as if his arm had disappeared, other than the parts stained red with blood.

"We just came here to fix Linus up, and I wanted to get

Delilah somewhere safe," Ember explained as she closed and locked the door behind me.

Delilah looked back at me, and I hadn't recognized her right away because I'd only met her once before. She was very beautiful, with dark almond-shaped eyes and a soft smile. In her jeans and tunic sweater, she appeared slender and tall.

"We got Linus's parents out of here already," Ember went on. "My brother is helping refugees escape. Since most of the fighting is going on around the back wall, Finn is leading evacuees right out the front gate and to your camp on the other side of the hill."

"I came back to help other people escape," Linus said, and he gritted his teeth when Delilah turned her attention back to fixing him up.

"My parents won't leave." Delilah scowled, and she began wrapping Linus's arm with gauze. "They're in the basement hiding in a panic room, and I'm actually surprised they haven't come back up here to drag me down with them."

"So that's what we've been doing—trying to help people evacuate." Ember looked me over, her eyes lingering on my bloodied sword. "What have you been doing?"

"I've been trying to get to the palace," I said.

I thought about explaining to her about Ridley, and how he'd been captured, and how I had to get him free before they killed him. But it all felt like too much to say aloud, and there was enough going on here. Everyone in this room had more than their share of problems to deal with.

"I saw you, and I wanted to make sure you were okay," I

said instead, my words sounding tight around the lump in my throat.

"I think we can handle it," Ember told me, trying for a reassuring smile. "I know you've got your work cut out for you."

A loud knocking at the front door interrupted our conversation. The kitchen was at the back of the house, so we couldn't see the door from where we stood, but we all turned toward it.

"I locked and bolted the front door," Delilah said softly.

But the knocking just grew louder and more intense, until it changed from knocking to someone trying to break down the front door.

adversary

Ember and I both drew our swords and moved closer to the entryway from the kitchen so we could see into the front hall, when the door came crashing in.

"Markis or Marksinna Nylen?" a man asked in the strong, clipped tones of a Högdragen. "Are you safe?"

"I saw her run in here!" a female voice shouted shrilly, and it was like nails on a chalkboard, so I placed it instantly— Astrid Eckwell. "Go inside and get her! She's the one behind it all!"

I grimaced, realizing that Astrid must've seen me coming over here. She had probably been holed up in her mansion with her family and their own personal Högdragen standing guard. But her contempt for me was so strong that she'd left the safety of her home to make sure that I got my punishment.

We'd grown up together, and Astrid had been unrelentingly vicious to me. She had been the first one to ever call me a half-breed, and she had made certain that it caught on as a cruel chant that the other kids would sing to me during recess.

It wasn't until my teenage years that I realized the sheer level of her hatred stemmed from jealousy and feelings of inferiority. Her house and most of her riches came from an inheritance that should've been my dad's, and would have been my own, had my grandparents not disinherited my dad for marrying a Skojare. The Eckwells—as second cousins to my dad—were the closest relatives and next in line.

Astrid only had her status because my dad had given it up. Her life should've been mine, and I think that secretly she was always afraid I would take it from her.

But I had never wanted her life, and now she was trying to get me killed.

"I'm here," Delilah said, stepping out from the kitchen before either Ember or I could stop her. "I'm Marksinna Delilah Nylen, and I'm here and I'm safe."

"Where is she?" Astrid demanded.

I leaned against the kitchen wall and carefully peered around the entryway to watch the scene unfolding. The Högdragen was Janus Mose, a tracker I'd gone to school with who was only a couple years older than me. He didn't appear as confident about their intrusion into the Nylens' home as Astrid did, and she pushed her way around him.

A war was raging on half a mile from her doorstep, and she wore a gown with a fur stole. It was typical of her arrogance and stupidity.

"I saw that Skojare traitor run in here, and if you're housing her, you'll go to prison too," Astrid said, sneering at Delilah. "Or you'll be executed. Janus could do it right on the spot."

"There's no need for that." Ember sheathed her sword and rushed out to the main hall.

Linus pulled on his shirt and stepped out from the kitchen. "You probably just saw us. Ember and I ran in here to get away from the fighting."

"I wanted to keep the Markis safe," Ember explained, standing beside her girlfriend.

"With all due respect, Markis Linus, you look nothing like a little blond half-breed traitor," Astrid told him, doing her best to keep her cool when talking to a royal who outranked her. "Bryn Aven is here, and I know it. And if you all keep covering it up, Janus will have no choice but to execute you all."

I gripped my sword tightly in my hand, but I didn't move. Not yet.

Theoretically, Astrid was right. In times of war, a member of the Högdragen had every right to execute those who were standing in the way of the kingdom or harboring traitors. But while Janus hadn't been the brightest guy I'd gone to school with, he'd gone through enough training to know that he shouldn't act rashly on the word of a spiteful Marksinna.

"Are you housing Bryn Aven?" Janus asked them directly, standing tall in his Högdragen uniform. The light coming in through the open windows caused his epaulets to shimmer, and he kept his expression hard but blank, the way Kasper always had.

"It's just us here," Delilah said, speaking as calmly as she could.

"Then where are your parents?" Astrid demanded, and she looked up at Janus. "They haven't left yet."

"My parents are in the panic room—" Delilah began, but she couldn't even finish her sentence before Astrid let out a delighted gasp.

"They have a panic room! They're hiding Bryn in there!" Astrid shouted, pointing wildly into the house. "Search the house until you find her."

"Is this really necessary?" Linus asked. "This all seems to be getting out of hand, especially with everything that's going on outside. You should take Astrid back to her house so she can be safe."

"As soon as we find the traitor, this will be all over," Janus told him firmly. "And then everyone can be safe."

That was when I knew that this wouldn't end peacefully, and I couldn't let Ember, Delilah, and Linus fight my battle for me. I stepped out from the kitchen. Astrid screamed when she saw me, but her eyes were wide with excitement.

"I told you she was here!" Astrid squealed.

Janus raised his sword, and his eyes were unforgiving and his jaw was clenched. I knew that look—he meant to kill me, with Astrid cheering him on.

"It doesn't need to come to this," Delilah said.

She stepped closer to him, perhaps meaning to reason with

him, but she didn't understand the severity of the situation. With the tension of the war, Mina's fabrications about me, and Astrid screaming in his ear, Janus was like a gun, cocked and loaded, just waiting for something to set him off.

When Delilah stepped toward him, that was it. He drew his arm back—he was going to kill her, the way he would kill anything that stood in his way. Everything unfolded so quickly, but it felt like slow motion—like the world had stopped and I could see it all but I couldn't move fast enough to change anything.

Linus shouted the word *stop*, but Ember was already moving, diving at Delilah and pushing her out of the way. Delilah fell to the floor just as Janus drove his sword straight through Ember, and she hit the floor with a sickening thud.

SEVENTY-TWO

allt är mitt

I ran at Janus, not caring if he was a Högdragen or if he truly believed he was justified in what he'd done. For a moment my anger blocked out any rational thought, and I was just moving.

Janus raised his sword, blocking me, but I was moving faster and faster. So each time he blocked me, I would move away and come at him quicker, until I finally found my opening. I drove my blade through his throat, pushing him back against the wall, until I'd pinned him there like a bug in a glass case. Blood poured from his throat, staining the dark fabric of his uniform.

I left him that way and turned back to survey the scene. Astrid stood with her back pressed against the wall, looking rightfully terrified. Linus stood off to the side of Ember with tears in his eyes, and Delilah was sitting with Ember, holding her in her arms as she slowly bled out.

I walked over to them and fell to my knees.

"Why did you do that?" Delilah asked through tears, and brushed Ember's hair back from her face. "You shouldn't have done that."

"Of course I should have," Ember said, her voice soft as she stared up into Delilah's eyes. "You're alive, and you're safe, and I love you. There is no greater thing I could do than die to save my true love."

"Ember, I love you," she sobbed. "What will I do without you?"

"Fight." Ember closed her eyes, but her chest was still rising and falling with shallow breaths. "And live. My love will go on with you, so live as long as you can."

"*Allt är mitt, och allt skall tagas från mig,*" Delilah said, reciting a Pär Lagerkvist poem in Swedish, sounding lyrical and beautiful. "*Inom kort skall allting tagas från mig.*"

While my Swedish wasn't as good as it should be, I thought what she said translated to, "All is mine, and all shall be taken away from me, / within moments all shall be taken away from me."

Then Ember took her last breath. Delilah leaned over and gently kissed her on the lips, and then she laid her head on Ember's chest and wailed like her heart had just been ripped out of her.

One of my best friends had just died, and I wanted to fall apart the way Delilah was doing, but I knew there wasn't time. Later, I would mourn for Ember the way she deserved.

But now I had to finish things so that she wouldn't die in vain. I needed to get Delilah safe.

I stood up and pulled gently on her arm. "Delilah. You need to let Linus get you to safety." I looked back at him. "You do know how to get the refugees out of here, right?"

He nodded, wiping at the tears in his eyes. "Yes. Ember showed me. I know what I need to do."

"Good. I need you to take Delilah out of here and keep her safe." I turned back to Delilah, since she still hadn't gotten up, and I pulled her to her feet. I put my hands on her face, forcing her to look at me. "Listen to me, Delilah. I know this is hard, but Ember died so that you could live. So you *need* to live. You have to pull yourself together, and follow Linus out of here. Do you understand me?"

She tried to stop her tears and nodded. "Yes."

"Good." I took Ember's sword and handed it to Delilah, since Linus already had his own. "Move quickly and stay safe." I looked from one of them to the other. "Both of you."

"I will," Linus assured me. "I'll finish what Ember and I started."

He stood up tall, looking more confident than I had ever seen him before, and I hoped I was doing the right thing, leaving him to protect the thing that meant the most in the world to Ember. But I had trust that she'd trained him right and he could do this.

Linus took Delilah's hand and led her out the front door, looking for the quickest escape route to the front gate, where

Finn could lead them to. And that meant I was alone with Astrid.

I turned back to face her, and she flinched. She hadn't moved from where she'd been before, with her back pressed against the wall.

"Bryn, I'm sorry. I didn't mean it. I didn't mean any of those things," she said in one hurried sentence, almost as if it were all one word.

I grabbed the sword from Janus's throat, which caused him to fall to the floor, and she cringed. I stalked over to her with slow, deliberate steps and Astrid began to whimper.

"Please, Bryn. I'm sorry. I didn't mean—"

Astrid kept right on talking until I pressed the blade to her throat, still warm from Janus's blood. Then her eyes flew open and her mouth flew shut. I didn't break the skin—I held the blade just hard enough so she could feel exactly how sharp the edge was.

"I could kill you right now," I growled. "And I should. But I'm not going to." I stepped back from her and took the sword from her throat.

"Thank you, Bryn. Thank you so much. I don't know—"

"But I'm not going to save you," I said, cutting her off.

Her hand was on her throat, rubbing where the sword had been. "What are you talking about?"

"There's a war going on, and I just killed your only protection." With my sword, I pointed to the window, where the fight was coming increasingly closer to the doorstep.

I grabbed her wrist and started dragging her outside. She

was pleading with me to stop, but it fell on deaf ears. As I pulled her out to the street, a Tralla horse came racing by, its heavy hooves pounding on the snowy cobblestones. With all the fighting, the fence outside the stables must've been broken down, freeing all the horses.

But that was the least of my concerns. I dragged her toward two hobgoblins who were just finishing taking down an Omte ogre at the edge of the fray. Astrid began to scream as soon as she saw them, since she was unaccustomed to them and frightened by their appearance.

"Bryn! Please! Let me go!" she begged.

"Hey, guys!" I yelled, and the hobgoblins looked over at me, and then I motioned toward Astrid. "She just had a soldier killed that was helping us, and she has close ties to the Kanin Queen."

"Queen Mina will have your head if any of you lay a hand on me!" Astrid shouted, her voice growing shriller.

Since she seemed like she would do just fine digging her own grave, I let go of her and started walking away. The two hobgoblins smiled before they pounced on her. I heard her screaming, but I didn't look back. I didn't need to.

bloodied

At first I'd been trying to avoid hurting any of the Hög-dragen. But after Janus, I would kill anyone who ran at me with a sword. I'd always known that war wouldn't be so black-and-white, but I'd come to realize that there was a darker shade of gray, where right and wrong came second to simply surviving.

I wanted to make a straight line to the palace and find Ridley, but the fighting made it hard to move quickly. I could make it a few feet, stepping over bodies, before I'd find myself in combat with someone else. My hands and clothing were soaked with blood, and there had to be a quicker way to get to the palace.

Then, almost like a guardian angel, I heard Bloom. I looked back and saw the massive Tralla horse running through the streets. His sterling mane flew behind him, and I whistled for him. He reared up on his back legs, braying loudly, and

I saw that the fur around his hooves had been stained dark crimson.

He saw me and raced toward me through the crowd, knocking over anyone who got in his way. When he reached me, I sheathed my sword, and I jumped up to grab on to his mane. I tried to hoist myself up, but Bloom was over seven feet tall at his shoulders, so I couldn't exactly just hop up on him.

Then I felt a hand under my feet, pushing me up, and I finally got high enough so I could swing my leg over. I looked down to see who'd helped me, and Baltsar smiled up at me before taking on a Högdragen guard.

"Go, Bloom," I commanded, but he didn't need more prompting. Even he knew that a war zone was no place to pause.

He charged ahead, his massive size chasing everyone out of the way. People either dove to the side, or he ran them over. I buried my fingers in his mane, leaning into him and urging him to go faster.

After losing Ember, I knew I had to get to Ridley as soon as possible. I couldn't waste any more time killing Omte or helping anyone. I couldn't let him die because I'd been busy somewhere else.

Delilah's last words to Ember, the poetry, pounded in my head like a death knell. I wouldn't let all be taken away from me. Not without a fight to the bloody end.

For so long, I had thought of love as a weakness—as something that would only make you distracted and vulnerable.

But what I'd come to realize was that love had only made Ember braver than she'd ever been before. Love made Tilda find the strength to carry on. Love made my parents willing to sacrifice everything for each other.

And love made me stronger. I would do anything to save Ridley. I would do *everything* I needed to do.

The massive door to the palace had already been knocked down, but after seeing the way the hobgoblins had handled the wall, I wasn't surprised. The door was over twenty feet tall, so Bloom ran through the opening with ease and straight into the grand front hall.

It was a massive stone room with high ceilings that rose several stories high and had iron chandeliers. The only natural light came through stained-glass windows that faced different directions. Right now the sun shone through the window depicting the Long Winter War, which left everything glowing red.

Other than a few dead bodies scattered around, the front hall appeared empty. The rest of the palace wouldn't be so easy for a horse of Bloom's size to maneuver around, and I really didn't want him getting hurt either. I swung my leg over and hopped to the floor.

"Son of a bitch," Konstantin said, and I looked over to see him coming in from a corridor off to the left of the hall. He looked up at Bloom, shaking his head.

"What?" I looked up to make sure Bloom was okay, but the horse seemed fine.

"I told you that you couldn't come in riding on a horse like a white knight, and so you had to go and prove me wrong." He smirked at me.

I stroked Bloom, telling him he'd done a good job, then I smacked him on the side and told him to get out of here. He did as he was told, racing back out through the doors again, and I turned to Konstantin.

"Have you found Ridley or Mina?" I asked.

He shook his head. "Not yet. I checked the dungeons for Ridley, but there was no sign of either of them there. I was heading to the throne room."

"You think Mina will be there?" I asked.

"She's obsessed with the crown, so it would make sense," he said. "And if we find her, I'm sure she can tell us where Ridley is."

I nodded. "Then I'm going with you."

The throne room was rarely used, except for coronations and the occasional ceremony. It was at the south end of the palace, straight at the end of a long, narrow corridor that led out from the main hall.

I let Konstantin lead the way, jogging a few steps ahead of me, but we both slowed when we saw someone standing in front of the doors to the throne room, blocking us.

Wearing only a leather vest to reveal the scars and tattoos that covered his thick biceps was Helge Otäck. His greasy hair hung around his face, and he grinned at us as we approached, showing off his gold teeth.

"Well, well, well. You thought you could just come waltzing up here—"

"I really don't have time for this shit," I muttered, so I took my sword and threw it at Helge like a spear, right at his stupid grinning mouth with his gold caps.

The blade went through, knocking out one of his teeth, and going out the back of his skull. His open mouth tore around the blade, making him look like a mutilated clown, and when I pulled the sword back, the top half of his head fell to the floor.

"Well done," Konstantin said. He kicked Helge's body out of the way, and then he pulled open the door to the throne room.

It was a small square room, with white velvet drapes hanging over the stone walls, from the ceiling down to where they pooled on the floor. Two thrones sat at the back of the room, and Viktor Dålig sat in the larger of the two, looking like he owned the place. But that wasn't what really caught my attention.

Hanging from the center of the room was a large metal cage. A black-bearded vulture sat perched on top of it, squawking at us, and Ridley was inside it, lying on the bottom with his clothes torn, looking badly beaten.

He lifted his head when the door opened, and I could see dried blood had crusted along his temple. He knelt at the bottom of the cage, looking down at me with fear in his dark eyes, and he clenched the metal bars.

"Bryn, get out," Ridley warned me frantically. "It's a trap!"

ensnared

T he white velvet drapes along the wall began to move, rippling like waves, and men dressed in black stepped out. There had been just enough space between the fabric and the cold stone to conceal them, and a dozen of Viktor's soldiers filled the small room.

Behind Konstantin and me, the doors slammed shut, and that's when Viktor threw back his head and began to laugh. His long, black hair swayed as he did. The dull red of his scar ran from just above his left eye down to his right cheek, a present from Ridley's father before Viktor had killed him.

"The prodigal son returns," Viktor said, grinning broadly at Konstantin.

"I was never your son," Konstantin spat at him.

I had my sword at the ready, waiting for the soldiers to attack, but Konstantin stood with his weapon at his side, his eyes fixed on Viktor.

Viktor's smile finally fell away. "I told you what would happen if you betrayed us. And I knew that eventually you would return to collect your punishment."

"No." Konstantin shook his head and pointed his sword at Viktor. "I told you that I would return to give you *yours*."

"Enough of this," Viktor growled. "Capture them. The Queen wants to torture them herself."

The soldiers started coming toward us, and Konstantin and I moved so we were back to back. Our only advantage was that it was a small space, so we could rely on each other. That, and Konstantin was the best swordsman I'd ever met.

I pushed down my fear, my worry for Ridley, my anger toward Viktor and Mina. I blocked out everything, leaving my mind blank, so when a solider struck out at me, I reacted only on instinct. I let my body move the way it had been trained to, blocking every attack, and lunging when I saw an opening.

From the corner of my eye, I kept trying to look for a way to free Ridley as Konstantin and I pivoted around the room, fighting off the soldiers as quickly as they came at us. The cage hung from the ceiling by a long chain, and I finally saw where it attached to the wall, in a small gap between the drapes.

Viktor sat on the throne in the center of the room, watching it all as if we were putting on a performance solely for his entertainment, and then I realized sourly that we were. He had staged this all with the expectation of trapping Konstantin or me here, and he'd lucked out by getting both of us.

Above, I heard the cage rattle, and I glanced up to see the

bird had taken flight, as Ridley started swinging the cage. He used his body weight to rock it, and I could see the anchor straining in the brick wall.

The cage had been meant to hold doves, which Mina released during special ceremonies. It hadn't been built to withstand the kind of tension Ridley was putting on it.

"Bryn!" Konstantin shouted, trying to direct my attention back to the fight.

I turned to see a soldier charging at me. I kicked him in the stomach, sending him flying back into the wall, and he dropped his sword to the floor. I ran at him and before he could get to his feet, and I stabbed him through.

Looking around the room, I realized that it was full of dead bodies, and Viktor's expression had turned to an angry scowl. We'd killed all but three of his men, and Konstantin was dealing with two of them.

The third ran at me, and I lunged at him, driving my sword through his stomach. Then Ridley shouted a warning, and before I could even think, his cage clattered to the floor mere inches from me.

I ducked out of the way just in time. I narrowly avoided getting crushed by the metal enclosure, but I dropped my sword in the commotion. The cage bounced over the bodies and crashed into the wall.

I ran over to help Ridley open the door, but as I did, his face blanched with horror.

"Bryn, watch out!" he shouted, and I whirled around just in time to see Viktor behind me, carrying a bloody sword.

SEVENTY-FIVE

reprisal

I felt the sharp point of the blade tear my clothes and pierce the tender flesh of the left side of my abdomen, just above my hip. I staggered back, my eyes scanning the floor for a nearby sword. Konstantin was busy on the other side of the room, finishing off the last of the men, so he couldn't toss me a weapon.

Viktor sneered at me, and I spotted my sword—the handle red with blood, lying a few feet to my left, directly beside the birdcage. But before I could make a play for it, Ridley kicked open the door to the cage. He climbed out and stepped toward Viktor, blocking Viktor's access to me.

"Enough games," Viktor growled at him. "It's time to finish this."

He lunged at Ridley, but Ridley dodged to the side and grabbed Viktor's arm. He twisted his wrist back, and even after Viktor dropped the sword, Ridley kept twisting until the bones in his hand and wrist finally made a loud cracking sound.

Viktor was bigger than Ridley, but he was also older and out of practice. And I knew that Ridley wouldn't let him get the best of him again.

Viktor let out a loud pained groan, and Ridley let go of him, allowing Viktor to stand up.

"I thought you were going to finish this, old man," Ridley growled at him as Viktor staggered back away from Ridley.

"There's still time," Viktor assured him with a sick smile.

Ridley moved toward him and kicked his feet out from under him, and Viktor fell back onto the bodies of his fallen men. He lay at an awkward angle, with his back curved up over the bodies and his head on the cold stone floor.

Ridley jumped on top of Viktor and grabbed him by his greasy hair, and he slammed his head into the floor three times. He wasn't dead—not yet anyway—but he wasn't really moving either.

"That was for Bryn," Ridley said as he got to his feet.

The scar that ran along my temple seemed to throb in sympathy, the one that Viktor had given me when he had bashed my head into a stone wall.

Konstantin had killed the last two men, and he stood on the other side of the room, catching his breath. With Viktor incapacitated, Ridley turned his attention to me.

"Are you okay?" he asked, his eyes darting down to where my blood was staining my shirt.

"Yeah, it's just a flesh wound." But it did hurt far worse

than I was willing to let on. Then I motioned to him. His shirt was unbuttoned in the front, revealing dark bruises all over his body. "Are you okay?"

"Hey, hey," Konstantin said, interrupting us.

When we looked over at him, he tossed his sword to Ridley, who caught it easily. I turned back to see that Viktor Dålig had gotten up and was stumbling toward us. Blood streamed down the side of his face, but he'd picked up a sword and managed to wield it with his shaky left hand, the one that Ridley hadn't broken.

Ridley stepped away from me and walked toward Viktor. Viktor tried to lunge at him, and Ridley countered by easily knocking the sword from him. Viktor stood before Ridley, with his head high, and began to laugh.

"What's so funny?" Ridley asked.

"I should've killed you the second Helge brought you in," Viktor said through his laughter. "I could've split you in two, just like I did your idiot father."

And that was the last thing Viktor ever said, because Ridley stabbed him in the stomach. Viktor stumbled back and collapsed onto the throne. He let out a few more raspy breaths before expiring.

"And that was for my dad," Ridley said.

"He would be proud of you," I said, trying to comfort Ridley.

He turned back to face me, and I stood up as straight as I could, with my hand pressed against the wound Viktor had given me. Ridley's eyes were dark, and he put his hand gently on my face.

"You sure you're all right?" he asked.

"Yeah." I smiled up at him. "As long as you're okay, I'm okay."

Konstantin took his sword back from Ridley and wiped the blood off on his shirt, then turned toward Ridley and me. "Shall we move on? There's still plenty more enemies to take down."

SEVENTY-SIX

chambered

The fighting had moved into the main hall of the palace. As Ridley, Konstantin, and I ran down the narrow corridor from the throne room, we could already hear the clash of swords. Baltsar and Bekk were fighting alongside other Skojare and Trylle allies against twenty or so Kanin guards and Omte.

Before we left the throne room, I'd torn off a strip from the white curtains and tied it around my waist, putting pressure on my wound to stop the blood loss. That helped some, but I could still feel myself moving more slowly than I should have. But I pushed myself on, refusing to quit or fail now, not when we were so close to defeating Mina.

Ridley had grabbed a sword, and when we reached the main hall, he joined the fight without missing a beat. Nothing that Viktor or Mina had done to him slowed him down, and I wished I had the time to admire that about him. Or admire anything about him. I wanted to relish the fact that he was safe and alive again, but an Omte soldier was trying to stab me.

I started fighting beside Ridley, but from the corner of my eye, I saw Konstantin running. He raced down the hallway toward the private quarters. I dodged the attack from the Omte soldier, and then I took off after Konstantin, running as fast as I could to catch up to him.

So far, the private wing looked untouched. The pearlescent tile wasn't stained with blood. The ivory drywall covering the stone had no holes or dents. None of the furniture was broken and none of the paintings were torn.

Konstantin had stopped where the hallway T'd, looking in both directions, and that's when I reached him.

"Where are you going?"

"To find Mina." He looked down at me. "I should finish this on my own. You don't need to come with me."

"Of course I'm coming with you," I insisted. "I want her dead just as badly as you do, and you don't know what she's up to."

"Yes, I do. She knows she's losing now, and she's going to make an escape." He turned to the hallway to the left, jogging ahead, and I went after him. "She's in her room, gathering everything she needs to start over."

The Queen's chambers were in the top of the tower on the south side of the palace. On the stairwell just outside the landing were two dead Högdragen soldiers, both with their throats slit. These were the first bodies we'd seen in the private wing so far.

"She killed them," Konstantin whispered. "They served their purpose, and she didn't want them taking her jewels."

He crept quietly across the landing, leading the way, and slowly pushed open the door. I peered in over his shoulder, and the room looked empty. Everything was in order—the satin bedding on the four-post bed was made, the lush white rugs were unruffled, and the sheer curtains were undisturbed over the windows.

I was about to ask if she was still here when I saw a small white rabbit hop across the floor. It was Vita, Mina's pet rabbit, and on every trip she'd ever gone on, she'd taken it with her. As far as I could tell, Vita seemed to be the only thing Mina really cared about. The rabbit scampered under the bed at the sight of Konstantin and me, hiding from us.

Then I heard a sound, reminding me almost of rain on a windshield, coming from the dressing room off the bedroom.

"She keeps her private safe in there," Konstantin whispered and pushed the door open farther. He crept into the room with his sword drawn, watching the half-open door to her dressing room warily.

I followed him inside, and he motioned for me to go toward a large armoire near one of the windows. It been painted white, but it was made out of wood, with an old legend carved into it with pictures—Odin gifting the Kanin people with the Gotland rabbits.

Konstantin came up beside me and quietly opened the armoire doors. From the dressing room, we could hear Mina softly singing an old Kanin war song to herself, and I heard the tinkling glass sound of jewelry and gemstones colliding with each other as she loaded up a bag.

"Get in," Konstantin whispered, his voice so soft it was almost inaudible.

I did as he commanded, stepping up into the armoire, thinking that he meant for us to hide in here until Mina came out of the dressing room. If she was packing up all her riches and planning to make a break from a kingdom at war, she had to have a weapon on her, and clearly she knew how to use a dagger, given that she'd left two guards dead on the steps.

The armoire was large enough that I could stand up in it, and with the lift at the bottom, it made me as tall as Konstantin. He looked at me for a moment, his eyes studying me.

Normally his eyes were cool like steel, even when he was vulnerable, but now there was a strange smokiness to them, masking his thoughts. His hair fell across his forehead, and I wanted to ask him what was going on, but he suddenly grabbed me. He put an arm around my waist, his hand strong and demanding on my back, and pulled me closer to him. Without waiting for my reaction, he kissed me roughly on the mouth.

His mouth was cold, but heat rushed through me anyway. Under his insistent desire, I felt something tender and passionate. I wasn't sure if I should embrace him or push him, and parts of me wanted to do both.

When he stopped kissing me, he kept his arm around my waist, and his eyes were filled with a yearning so strong, it took my breath away. Then he stepped back, and I still felt his touch lingering on my lips.

"I'm sorry, white rabbit," he whispered, and shut the doors. I heard a soft clicking sound, and I realized too late that he'd locked me inside the armoire. "I want you safe this time."

white rabbit

K onstantin," I hissed but didn't say more. I wanted to break down the doors and jump out, but I couldn't. Not if I didn't want to risk giving away his position.

Through in the gap between the doors of the armoire, I watched Konstantin back away. He'd trapped me, knowing that I wouldn't try to break out because it would mean risking his life.

Then, slowly, as he stepped back, I saw his skin begin to change. Going from its normal deep tan to blend in with the stark white of the Queen's chambers. He slipped off his shirt, kicking it underneath the bed, and stood against the wall beside the four-post bed.

His daggers remained tucked in the back of his pants, and he stood so that from his waist down, he was mostly hidden behind the abundance of linens on the bed. He'd almost disappeared completely.

Mina came out of the dressing room a few moments later, dragging a large suitcase across the floor with great difficulty. All her gemstones must've weighed it down quite a bit. Still in "mourning" over Evert's death, she wore a long black gown.

The satin of the bottom of the gown clung to the curves of her hips before flaring out around her feet. The top of her bodice went up to her throat, but it was made of a thin, open lace so that her breasts were almost entirely visible through the fabric. The sleeves went down over her hands, ending in a long point. Since the openness of the dress could provide no warmth, she wore a black fur stole around her shoulders, and its effect reminded me almost of glamorous, oversized epaulets.

"Vita, darling," Mina said, calling to her pet rabbit, and I noted that her British accent had grown even stronger since the last time I'd heard her speak. She'd completely devolved into the character she'd created for herself. "It's time for us to go."

Leaving her bag, she began looking around for the rabbit. She put one hand on the bed, and I noticed that even her nail polish was black, as she leaned down to look underneath the bed. With her back to him, Konstantin started moving slowly toward her.

"Vita," Mina cooed to the rabbit. "Come here, love."

Konstantin pulled the dagger from his pants, and his skin began to shift back to its normal flesh tone. I held my breath, watching through the crack, as he came up behind her.

"I know you're there," Mina said, her voice sharper than

it had been when she'd been speaking to Vita. "And I know that you're not going to kill me."

She stood up and turned around to face him, a smile playing on her lips. He glared down at her, his expression hardening as he seethed, and she began to laugh.

"You can't kill me, Konstantin. You love me too much."

He grabbed her and whirled her around, pulling her roughly against him so her back was pressed to his chest, and he held the dagger to her throat. The lace of her dress covered her throat, forming a choker-like feature, and his blade sliced through it. He didn't kill her, but he held the dagger hard enough to draw the faintest bit of blood.

"Please, Konstantin," Mina begged, sounding frightened. "You don't need to do this. Not after all we've been through. This is the moment we've been plotting for all these years. I have the riches! We can finally run off and be free together, just like you always wanted."

"*You've* been plotting," he corrected her, speaking into her ear like an angry lover. "I was only ever just doing your bidding."

"Konstantin, please. Don't be like this." She softened, trying to sound as gentle as she had when she'd spoken to her rabbit. "We've shared so much, and I don't know why you've taken such a turn. But I forgive you. I still want to be with you, even after all you've done. I still love you."

"After all *I've* done?" Konstantin growled, and then he threw her to the floor. She sat on the white rug looking up at him, and somehow managed to have tears in her eyes. "You are an evil, ruthless bitch, Mina. Don't act like I'm the one in the wrong here."

"Look, Konstantin, I know we've had our differences, and that you haven't always approved of the way I've taken care of things," Mina said. "But I just did what needed to be done. But that doesn't mean that I didn't love you. That I don't still."

She reached out, meaning to touch his pant leg, and he stepped back from her.

"I should've killed you years ago," he said harshly. "But I was too blinded by my own foolish love, and I hate myself for the parts of it that still linger on. The parts of my heart that I gave to you that I can never get back."

"Konstantin," she pleaded with him.

He inhaled sharply through his nose, and he turned away, trying to hide the emotions on his face. It was just the slightest bit of vulnerability, but that was all Mina needed. His back was half to her, and she could see the dagger holstered in the back of his pants.

With steathy fast reflexes, she moved, grabbing the dagger before I could even shout Konstantin's name. He started to turn toward her, but it was already too late. She stabbed him in the left side, digging the dagger right into his heart.

Konstantin didn't even try to fight back. He let his other dagger fall from his hand and stumbled back until he hit the wall, then slid down and sat slumped on the floor.

SEVENTY-EIGHT

gutted

"You think you couldn't kill me because you loved me?"
Mina sneered at him. "It was because you were *weak*.
That's why I *never* loved you. You were always a weak, stupid
boy."

I pounded on the armoire doors, and Mina turned back to
look at me. She cocked her head, realizing that she wasn't
alone, and picked up the dagger Konstantin had dropped on
the floor. I hit the doors again, harder this time, and they flew
open.

"Oh, I should've known." Mina snickered. "He brought
his dumb little bitch with him too."

"You've always underestimated me," I said. "But not
today."

I ran at her. She tried to stab me, and I grabbed her wrist,
bending it back until she dropped the dagger. Then I punched

her as hard as I could. Mina staggered back, her lip already bleeding.

"I know you always wanted to fit in, and you never could," Mina said, giving me a wide berth as we circled each other. "But I've the means for it. I've got the one thing you always needed, to be accepted—money. You let me go, and I'll give you everything you've ever wanted. Respect. Acceptance. A kingdom."

"You know, that's what Konstantin always thought you wanted," I said. "That if you had enough money, and the crown, and the throne, and the kingdom, eventually you'd be happy. But I don't think you really *wanted* any of it. You just wanted to destroy it all."

She smirked. "Greed is always such a great motivator, and I know it's worked for so many of those that have joined my team. But you're right. The truth is that I just wanted to take everything from those that had taken from me. I just wanted to see the Kanin obliterated from this earth."

"The only thing I want is to see you dead," I told her. "And that's something that I'm gonna have to do for myself."

She dove toward me, scratching at me with her nails, fighting the only way she knew how. I punched her again, and then I kicked her in the stomach. Mina doubled over, but she didn't go down.

As I walked over to her, I picked the dagger up from the floor, and I kicked her again. Mina started promising me all the money in the world, and I grabbed her by the hair, yanking her back up.

"Please, anything. I will give you anything and everything," she tried, pleading for her life.

"I would stab you through the heart, but I don't think you have one," I said, and then I slid the dagger across her throat. I let go of her hair, and her body fell lifeless to the floor.

"I wish I had the strength to clap," Konstantin said faintly.

He was slumped low on the wall, barely breathing, and I raced over to him. I knelt beside him, and he was starting to slide to the side, so I put my arms around him and held him up. His body felt cold and heavy, and I didn't know how much time he had left.

"Why did you do that, Konstantin? Why didn't you let me help you?"

"I didn't want you getting hurt anymore. You've already been hurt so much by the things I've done. This time I just wanted to protect you." He reached up, brushing my hair back from my face before letting his hand fall back down.

"You don't need to protect me. You never did."

"I know." He smiled weakly. "Do you remember when I told you that for love, I'd kill myself again?"

I nodded. "Yeah, when you were in the dungeon. You were talking about Mina."

"I would go through every awful moment, every terrible mistake, and even this knife to the heart. I would gladly go through it all again, but not for Mina. But because it brought me here with you."

A tear slid down my cheek. "Konstantin. There were better ways you could've ended up here."

"Maybe," he admitted, and his eyes started to close. "But I just wish I'd been deserving of your love."

"You always were," I told him, and a smile started to form on his lips before his last breath came out. I held him against me, crying onto his chest and wishing more than anything that I would hear his heart beat again. But it never did.

dödsfall

Bryn?" Ridley was calling my name from the stairs. I honestly didn't know how long I had been kneeling there with Konstantin.

I blinked my eyes, feeling as if I'd just woken from a dream, and looked around at the disarray of the Queen's chambers. A few feet away from me, Mina lay dead on the rug, which was now stained red. Her rabbit Vita hopped out from underneath the bed, inspecting the situation.

"Bryn?" Ridley yelled again and pushed open the bedroom door. "Holy shit." He stepped into the room, his eyes fixed on the Queen's body, and repeated, "Holy shit. She's dead."

Then he looked over at me. "Are you okay?"

"Yeah." The tears had dried on my cheeks, and I nodded. "I'm okay. Konstantin is dead."

"Yeah, I figured that." Ridley moved carefully toward me. "Are you ready to let him go?"

I looked down at the body in my arms. His skin had paled so much, and he felt like ice against me. All of the determination and life had drained from him. Everything about that body that made it so wonderfully Konstantin was gone.

I set him gently on the floor, and I held out my hand to Ridley, letting him pull me to my feet. I'd been kneeling for so long, my legs had gone numb and weak, and I had to lean on Ridley to keep from falling.

"Bryn." His arm was around my waist, and he put his other hand on my face, gently encouraging me to look at him. "Are you okay?"

"The kingdom is in chaos. Many of my friends and neighbors are dead. Ember is dead. Konstantin is dead. I killed the Queen." I shrugged my shoulders limply. "I honestly don't know if I'll ever be okay again."

"It will be okay," he promised me, with his fingers in my hair. "You're stronger than this, and you will be okay again."

"How can you be so sure?" I asked, looking up at him. In the darkness of his eyes, I saw the same despair that I felt, but also his perseverance pushing him on.

"Because I know you, and I know how much fight you have in you. You won't let anything keep you down for long." He ran his thumb along my cheek. "That's why I love you so much."

He leaned in, kissing me softly and sweetly on the mouth. We'd kissed more deeply before, more passionately, but this was a much different kind of kiss. This was relief and sadness and simply because we needed to. Because we were still alive, and we needed to remind ourselves that there was still so much left to live for.

"I need to go," he said softly. "I need to go tell King Mikko that the Queen is dead, so we can stop the fighting. With her and Viktor out of the way, there's no reason a truce can't be reached."

"Go," I told him as I stepped back from him. "Go and stop this before more people get hurt."

He nodded. "I'll be back for you."

I smiled weakly at him. "I know."

Ridley hurried out of the room, to put a stop to all the death and carnage. I picked up Vita before she hopped into any blood, and I carried her over to the window. I pushed back the sheer curtains to see what had become of my town, while absently petting the soft white fur of the rabbit.

So much of the snow had gone red with blood. Broken bodies littered the ground. Homes and buildings were smashed up in places, some destroyed entirely. Doldastam was in shambles, exactly as Mina had wanted.

But I couldn't let her win. The Kanin people wouldn't. They were stronger than this. I'd learned to be a fighter growing up here, watching people rise above their places in this world, and together, somehow, we would find the strength to put this back together.

We could not let anyone destroy us.

hope

June 7, 2014

In the days that followed, the ice began to thaw. The snow that had covered the town melted away, and while it wasn't exactly a heat wave, green began sprouting up in the patches of lawn between the cottages. In a few places, pink and purple wildflowers were beginning to blossom.

The sun shone brightly above, warming the chill in the air, as everyone gathered at the town square. Many of the surrounding businesses were still in various states of repair. The sign for the bakery where Juni Sköld worked still hung at a haphazard angle, but the broken panes of glass in the front window had been replaced.

The cleanup was still under way, as it would be for some time, but we were making progress. The people of Doldastam always managed to pull together when they needed to.

After Ridley had told King Mikko that Mina was dead, the King had attempted to end things immediately. The fighting still went on for longer than it needed to, but eventually Mikko was able to talk to the head of the Högdragen, and a cease-fire was declared.

The next few days were spent hammering out a proper truce, but once a new King was decided for the Kanin, everything went smoother. The Omte still seemed reluctant to put aside their resentments, but Queen Bodil called them back to Fulaträsk, so they had no choice.

While Linus Berling had been officially crowned three days ago in a private ceremony in the palace, today was meant to be his public coronation and an official celebration for the end of the war.

Since it was a celebration, the town square had been decorated accordingly. Ribbons of silver and white streamed from one building to the next, helping to disguise the damage, and large bouquets of fragrant white flowers were placed everywhere imaginable.

Folding chairs covered in white satin and accented with ribbons filled the square. Just beneath the clock tower, a large stage had been erected. Linus wanted to distance himself from Mina, who lorded over the town from the balcony, so he wanted to speak at our level.

From where I sat in the back row, I could see everyone, and the entire town had turned out. Juni Sköld sat a few rows in front of me, holding the hand of her new boyfriend, and looking as radiant as ever. Bekk Vallin had decided not to return to Fulaträsk, even after the Omte agreed to the truce, and she sat a few seats down from me, her arms folded over her chest.

Nearer to the front, Delilah Nylen sat with her parents, crying softly. We'd hardly spoken since Ember had died, but whenever I saw her, she looked so lost. I hoped that soon she could find the peace and strength to carry on.

King Mikko and Queen Linnea Biâelse sat in the front row, along with King Loki and Queen Wendy Staad of the Trylle and Queen Sara Elsing of the Vittra, all of them honored guests of the Kanin because of their help in the war. Queen Bodil Elak of the Omte had been invited, as a gesture of peace, but she had declined, saying that it was still too soon.

With the fighting over, Tilda had returned a few days ago, and she seemed to be doing better. Knowing that Kasper had been properly avenged seemed to ease some of her anxiety, but none of this could be easy for her. She sat beside her parents, and her mother kept gently rubbing her back.

Finn sat with Mia and their children, but his parents were noticeably absent. After what had happened here, and how they'd lost Ember, they had finally had enough. They'd left the entire troll world to start a life anew among the humans.

My parents felt much the same way, and they had taken up residence in Storvatten. Marksinna Lisbet Ahlstrom once told me that she'd do anything to thank me for saving her granddaughter, and I'd asked her to repay the debt by welcoming my mom back with open arms.

So she had, and after years of hating Storvatten, my mom seemed to be actually enjoying her return. She said it was all so much different than when she was a girl, more relaxed, and she was happy to reconnect with old friends and family.

Meanwhile, my dad was working with their Chancellor to help get the Skojare where they needed to be. Mikko and Linnea had been working very hard to improve things in Storvatten, and it looked like they might finally be on the right path.

With Linus taking the stage now, the tall platinum crown upon his head, I hoped I could say the same thing about Doldastam. Linus was less experienced than most of the townspeople would've liked, but his bloodline was the closest to Evert Strinne, so he was next in line.

As he walked across the stage, the crowd erupted in applause. No matter what differences had existed before, everyone here was ready for a change, for someone new to lead us to a better place, and their excitement came from the belief that Linus would be that leader.

I was optimistic because of his kindness and genuine empathy for the people. I wondered if growing up outside of the cold walls of Doldastam, unlike Evert and so many of our past Kings, had made him more compassionate, and I believed that with the right advisers and tutelage, he could stay that way.

Behind Linus in lavish chairs on the stage, his parents were seated along with the head of the Högdragen, and nearby was a large rectangle beneath a satin sheet. I had been asked to join him—and to wear onstage, I'd even been given a new crisp white suit with silver embellishments, including the platinum rabbit, our highest military honor. I'd elected to wear the suit, but declined the stage.

As one of his first acts as King, Linus had appointed me as his personal guard, and I'd accepted because I thought I could help steer the kingdom in the right direction and I could protect the King from corruption.

But I no longer craved the honor that went along with it. I didn't need or deserve the accolades. I just wanted to serve my kingdom.

He wanted to pull me onstage today to exalt me as a hero, but that wasn't something I could accept. I wasn't a hero, and in so many ways I still felt like I'd failed. Like I should've done more to protect the people. Nobody should've had to die.

"Thank you all for coming here today," King Linus said, speaking loudly so his voice would carry over the crowd. "We've all been through a great deal, and I know how hard it was for some of you to come out. So many of you have lost so much, and are in no mood to celebrate."

Delilah began to sniffle at that, and her father put his arm around her, pulling her close to him, and throughout the crowd I could hear others sobbing faintly.

"That's why today isn't about honoring me as your King." Linus stepped over to the side toward the sheet-covered rectangle. "It's about honoring those you've lost, everyone who laid down their life defending this kingdom so that we can all be here celebrating our freedom today."

He pulled back the sheet, revealing a white marble stone

ten feet high and five feet wide, in large black letters listing all the names of the people who had been killed. At the top was *Evert Strinne*, since he had been one of Mina's first victims, but there were many names below his.

Kasper Abbott, Ember Holmes, Simon Bohlin, and the names of so many others I had seen nearly every day in this town. So many lives that could never be replaced, voids that would never be filled.

Near the bottom, in letters just as bold and dark as everyone else's, was *Konstantin Black.*

A lump formed painfully in my throat. I'd been so afraid that nobody would know that Konstantin had died to protect the kingdom, or be aware of all the things he'd done to aid in this battle. I had been terrified that I would be the only one who mourned him.

But now everybody would know. For generations, people would see his name, and know that he'd died a true Kanin hero.

Linus continued his speech, telling Doldastam how he planned to honor the dead by giving the kingdom new life, but I'd heard all I needed to. I got up quietly and snuck away from the crowd, walking out of the town square.

I hadn't made it very far when I heard Ridley's footsteps behind me. The cobblestone streets were empty, since everyone was at the celebration, and I turned to face him.

His chestnut hair was slightly disheveled, and he brushed it back from his forehead. He'd left the top buttons of his shirt undone, the way I liked it, but his rabbit amulet was still missing. As soon as the fighting ended, he'd stepped down from his position as Överste and Rektor.

"What's going on?" His dark eyes were filled with concern as he looked down at me.

"I've spent enough time thinking about the dead lately," I said honestly. "I need a break from it. I think I just need some time to think about the future and try to feel optimistic again."

"I get that," Ridley agreed. "The last few weeks have been so dark, you need to start looking for something bright."

I nodded. "Exactly."

"Where you heading now, in search of your something bright?"

I shrugged. "Just back to my loft."

"Let me walk you home."

"You know you can always walk me home." I smiled up at him.

"I know. But I like it when you tell me I can anyway." He put his arm around me as we started walking across town toward my place.

"Have you decided what you're going to do yet?" I asked, looking up at him. "Now that you're not in charge of the trackers?"

"Not yet," he admitted. "But I've got time to figure it out."

"That's true," I agreed. "We've got the rest of our lives to figure it all out."

He kissed my temple. "And I think we've proven that together, we can take on anything."

GLOSSARY

Changeling—a child secretly exchanged for another.

Doldastam—the capital and largest city of the Kanin, located in northeastern Manitoba, Canada near the Hudson Bay.

Eldvatten—literally translates to "firewater." Very strong alcohol made by the Omte.

Förening—the capital and largest city of the Trylle. A compound in the bluffs along the Mississippi River in Minnesota, United States where the palace is located.

Fulaträsk—the capital and largest city of the Omte. It's located in the southern part of Louisiana in the wetlands, with many of the Omte residing in the trees.

Hobgoblin—an ugly, misshapen troll that stands no more than three feet tall known only to the Vittra tribes. They are slow-witted but possess a supernatural strength.

Högdragen—an elite guard that protects the Kanin kingdom.

They must go through a specialized training process after tracker school in order to qualify, and many students are unable to pass because of the difficult requirements in order to graduate. Members of the Högdragen are respected and revered throughout the kingdom, despite the fact that most are born lower-class, because of their skill and their unparalleled ability to protect the royal families and the kingdom at large.

Host family—the family that the changeling is left with. They are chosen based on their ranking in human society, with their wealth being the primary consideration. The higher ranked the member of troll society, the more powerful and affluent the host family their changeling is left with.

Iskyla—small Kanin arctic community in northern Canada.

Kanin—one of the more powerful tribes of trolls left. They are considered quiet and peaceful. They are known for their ability to blend in, and like chameleons, their skin can change color to help them blend into their surroundings. Like the Trylle, they still practice changelings, but not nearly as frequently. Only one in ten of their offspring are left as changelings.

Lysa—a telekinetic ability related to astral projection that allows one troll to psychically enter another troll's thoughts through a vision, usually a dream.

Mänsklig—often shortened to "mänks." The literal translation for the word "mänsklig" is human, but it has come to describe the human child that is taken when the Trylle offspring is left behind.

Markis—a title of male royalty in troll society. Similar to that of a Duke, it's given to trolls with superior abilities. They have a higher ranking than the average troll, but are beneath the King and Queen. The hierarchy of troll society is as follows:

King/Queen
Prince/Princess
Markis/Marksinna
Högdragen
Troll citizens
Trackers
Mänsklig
Host families
Humans (not raised in troll society)

Marksinna—a title of female royalty in troll society. The female equivalent of the Markis.

Ogre—similar to hobgoblins, except they are giant, most standing over seven-feet tall with superior strength. They are dimwitted and aggressive, and they are known only to the Omte tribes.

Omte—only slightly more populous than the Skojare, the Omte tribe of trolls are known to be rude and somewhat ill-tempered. They still practice changelings but pick lower class families than the Trylle and Kanin. Unlike the other tribes, Omte tend to be less attractive in appearance.

Ondarike— the capital city of the Vittra. The Queen, along with the majority of the powerful Vittra, live within the palace there. It is located in northern Colorado.

Glossary

Överste—in times of war, the Överste is the officer in charge of commanding the soldiers. The Överste does not decide any battle plans, but instead receives orders from the King or the Chancellor.

Persuasion—a mild form of mind control. The ability to cause another person to act a certain way based on thoughts.

Precognition—knowledge of something before its occurrence, especially by extrasensory perception.

Psychokinesis—blanket term for the production or control of motion, especially in inanimate and remote objects, purportedly by the exercise of psychic powers. This can include mind control, precognition, telekinesis, biological healing, teleportation, and transmutation.

Rektor—the Kanin in charge of trackers. The Rektor works with new recruits, helps with placement, and generally works to keep the trackers organized and functioning.

Skojare—an aquatic tribe of trolls that is nearly extinct. They require large amounts of fresh water to survive, and one-third of their population possess gills so they are able to breathe underwater. Once plentiful, only about five thousand Skojare are left on the entire planet.

Storvatten—the capital city and largest city of the Skojare, located in southern Ontario, Canada on Lake Superior.

Tonåren—in the Skojare society, a time when teenagers seek to explore the human world and escape the isolation of Storvatten. Most teens return home within a few weeks.

Tracker—members of troll society who are specifically trained to track down changelings and bring them home. Trackers have no paranormal abilities, other than the affinity to tune into their particular changeling. They are able to sense danger to their charge and can determine the distance between them. The lowest form of troll society, other than mänsklig.

Tralla horse—a powerful draft horse, larger than a Shire horse or a Clydesdale, originating in Scandinavia and only known to be bred amongst the Kanin. Once used as a workhorse because they could handle the cold and snow, now they are usually used for show, such as in parades or during celebrations.

Trylle—beautiful trolls with powers of psychokinesis for whom the practice of changelings is a cornerstone of their society. Like all trolls, they are ill-tempered and cunning, and often selfish. Once plentiful, their numbers and abilities are fading, but they are still one of the largest tribes of trolls. They are considered peaceful.

Vittra—a more violent faction of trolls whose powers lie in physical strength and longevity, although some mild psychokinesis is not unheard of. They also suffer from frequent infertility. While Vittra are generally beautiful in appearance, more than fifty percent of their offspring are born as hobgoblins. They are one of the only troll tribes to have hobgoblins in their population.

Biâelse Family Tree

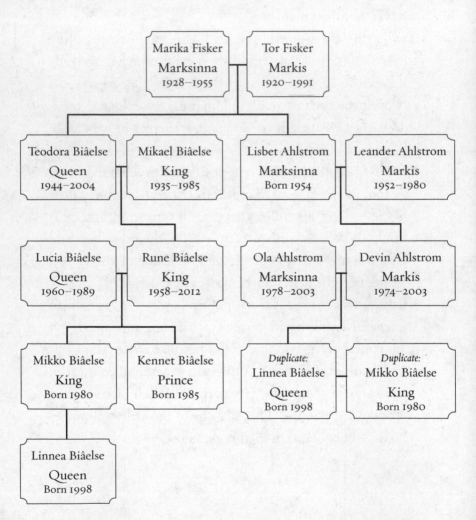

Marika Fisker
Marksinna
1928–1955

Tor Fisker
Markis
1920–1991

Teodora Biâelse
Queen
1944–2004

Mikael Biâelse
King
1935–1985

Lisbet Ahlstrom
Marksinna
Born 1954

Leander Ahlstrom
Markis
1952–1980

Lucia Biâelse
Queen
1960–1989

Rune Biâelse
King
1958–2012

Ola Ahlstrom
Marksinna
1978–2003

Devin Ahlstrom
Markis
1974–2003

Mikko Biâelse
King
Born 1980

Kennet Biâelse
Prince
Born 1985

Duplicate:
Linnea Biâelse
Queen
Born 1998

Duplicate:
Mikko Biâelse
King
Born 1980

Linnea Biâelse
Queen
Born 1998

Strinne Family Tree

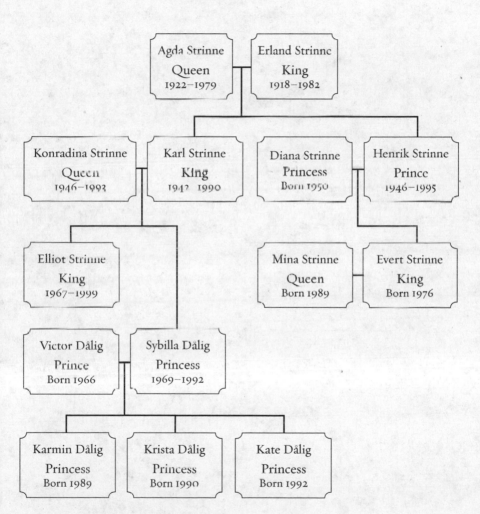

PRONUNCIATION GUIDE

Älskade Abbott—*Al-skah-duh Ab-bot*

Baltsar Thorne—*Bal-tsar Thorn*

Bayle Lundeen—*Bail Lun-deen*

Bodil Elak—*Buh-deel Eee-luck*

Bryn Aven—*Brin A-ven*

Cyrano Moen—*Sear-uh-no Moe-en*

Doldastam—*Dole-dah-stam*

Eldvatten—*Elld-vah-ten*

Evert Strinne—*Ever-t Strin*

Förening—*Fure-ning*

Fulaträsk—*Fool-uh-trassk*

Gotland rabbit—*Got-land*

Helge Otäck—*Hel-ga Oo-tech*

Högdragen—*Hug-dragon*

Iskyla—*Iss-key-la*

Iver Aven—*Iv-er A-ven*

Juni Sköld—*Joon-y Sh-weld*

Kanin—*cannon*

Lake Isolera—*Lake Ice-oh-lar-uh*

Linnea Biâelse—*Lin-nay-uh Bee-yellsa*

Lisbet Ahlstrom—*Liz-bet All-strum*

Ludlow Svartalf—*Lud-loe Svare-toff*

lysa—*lie-sa*

Måne—*Moe-nay*

Markis—*marquee*

Marksinna—*mark-iss-eena*

Mikko Biâelse—*Mick-o Bee-yellsa*

Mina Strinne—*Mee-na Strin*

Modi & Magni—*Mow-dee & Mahg-nee*

Naima Abbott—*Na-eema Ab-bot*

Omte—*oo-m-tuh*

Överste—*Ur-ve-sh-ter*

Ridley Dresden—*Rid-lee Drez-den*

Runa Aven—*Rue-na A-ven*

Skojare—*sko-yar-uh*

Storvatten—*Store-vot-en*

Tilda Moller—*Till-duh Maul-er*

tonåren—*toe-no-ren*

Tralla horse—*trahl-uh*

Trylle—*trill*

Ulla Tulin—*Oo-lah Two-lin*

Viktor Dålig—*Victor Dough-leg*

Vita—*Vee-tah*

Vittra—*vit-rah*

Royalty

Kanin
King Evert Henrik Strinne
Reign 1999–
Born 3/8/1976 in Doldastam
Crowned 1/17/1999
Married 4/12/2009
*Son of Prince Henrik Strinne and
Princess Diana Strinne, née Borling*

Queen Mina Viktoria Strinne, née Arvinge
Born 9/3/1989 in Iskyla
Married 4/12/2009
Orphaned daughter of Alva Arvinge and Viktoria Arvinge

Skojare
King Mikko Rune Biâelse
Reign 2012–
Born 5/7/1982 in Storvatten
Crowned 9/13/2012
Married 6/22/2013
*Son of King Rune Biâelse and
Queen Lucia Biâelse, née Ottesen*

Queen Linnea Lisbet Biâelse, née Ahlstrom
Born 6/16/1998 in Storvatten
Married 6/22/2013
*Daughter of Markis Devin Ahlstrom and
Marksinna Ola Ahlstrom, née Fisk*

Prince Kennet Tor Biâelse
Born 12/3/1985 in Storvatten
Son of King Rune Biâelse and
Queen Lucia Biâelse, née Ottesen

Trylle
Queen Wendy Luella Staad, née Dahl
Reign 2010–
Born 1/9/1992 in New York
Crowned 1/14/2014
Married 5/1/2010
Daughter of Trylle Queen Elora Dahl and
Vittra King Oren Elsing

King Loki Niklas Staad
Born 11/17/1987
Married 5/1/2010 in Ondarike
Son of former Trylle Chancellor Alrik Staad and
Vittra Marksinna Olivia Staad, née Härlig

Crown Prince Oliver Matthew Loren Staad
Born 10/6/2010 in Förening
Son of Queen Wendy Staad and Loki Staad

Omte
Queen Regent Bodil Freya Elak, née Fågel
Reign 2011–
Born 3/24/1978 in Fulaträsk
Married 9/1/2006
Widowed 8/13/2011
Crowned Acting Monarch 8/14/2011
Daughter of Markis Boris Fågel and
Marksinna Freya Fågel, née Dam

King Thor Osvald Elak
Reign 1992–2011
Born 4/2/1969 in Fulaträsk
Married 9/1/2006
Died 8/13/2011 in Fulaträsk
Son of King Draugr Elak and Queen Märta Elak, née Asp

Crown Prince Furston Thor Elak
Born 3/4/2010 in Fulaträsk
Son of Queen Bodil Elak and King Thor Elak

Vittra
Queen Sara Adrielle Elsing, née Vinter
Reign 2010–
Born 2/1/1977 in Ondarike
Married 11/2/1996
Crowned Acting Monarch 1/15/2010
Widowed 1/14/2010
Daughter of Markis Luden Vinter and
Marksinna Sarina Vinter, née Dron

King Oren Bodvar Elsing
Reign 1985–2010
Born 7/1/1914 in Ondarike
Crowned 11/23/1985
Married 5/19/1990
Annulled 7/30/1992
Married 11/2/1996
Died 1/14/2010 in Ondarike
Son of King Bodvar Elsing the II and Queen Grendel Elsing

Turn the page for a sneak peek at
Amanda Hocking's next novel

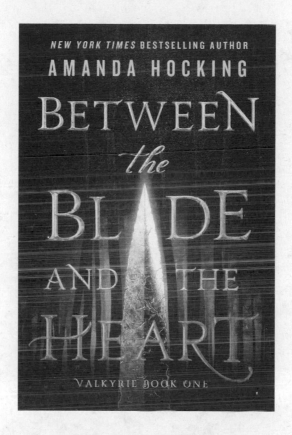

Available January 2018

ONE

The air reeked of fermented fish and rotten fruit, thanks to the overflowing dumpster from the restaurant behind us. The polluted alley felt narrow and claustrophobic, sandwiched between skyscrapers.

In the city, it was never quiet or peaceful, even at three in the morning. There were more than thirty million humans and supernatural beings coexisting, living on top of each other. It was the only life I'd ever really known, but the noise of the congestion grated on me tonight.

My eyes were locked on the flickering neon lights of the gambling parlor across the street. The *u* in *Shibuya* had gone out, so the sign flashed SHIB YA at me.

The sword sheathed at my side felt heavy, and my body felt restless and electric. I couldn't keep from fidgeting and cracked my knuckles.

"He'll be here soon," my mother, Marlow, assured me. She leaned back against the brick wall beside me, casually eating large jackfruit seeds from a brown paper sack. *Always bring a snack on a stakeout* was one of her first lessons, but I was far too nervous and excited to eat.

The thick cowl of her frayed black sweater had been pulled up like a hood, covering her cropped blond hair from the icy mist that fell on us. Her tall leather boots only went to her calf, thanks to her long legs. Her style tended to be monochromatic—black on black on black—aside from the shock of dark red lipstick.

My mother was only a few years shy of her fiftieth birthday, with almost thirty years of experience working as a Valkyrie, and she was still as strong and vital as ever. On her hip, her sword Mördare glowed a dull red through its sheath.

The sword of the Valkyries was one that appeared like it had been broken in half—its blade only a foot long before stopping at a sharp angle. Mördare's blade was several thousand years old, forged in fires to look like red glass that would glow when the time was nigh.

My sword was called Sigrún, a present on my eighteenth birthday from Marlow. It was a bit shorter than Mördare, with a thicker blade, so it appeared stubby and fat. The handle was black utilitarian, a replacement that my mom had had custom-made from an army supply store, to match her own.

The ancient blade appeared almost black, but as it grew closer to its target, it would glow a vibrant purple. For the past hour that we'd been waiting on our stakeout, Sigrún had been glowing dully on my hip.

The mist grew heavier, soaking my long black hair. I kept the left side of my head shaved, parting my hair over to the right, and my scalp should've been freezing from the cold, but I didn't feel it. I didn't feel anything.

It had begun—the instinct of the Valkyrie, pushing aside my humanity to become a weapon. When the Valkyrie in me took over, I was little more than a scythe for the Grim Reaper of the gods.

"He's coming," Marlow said behind me, but I already knew.

The world fell into hyperfocus, and I could see every droplet of rain as it splashed toward the ground. Every sound echoed through me, from the bird flapping its wings a block away, to the club door as it groaned open.

Eleazar Bélanger stumbled out, his heavy feet clomping in the puddles. He was chubby and short, barely over four feet tall, and he would've appeared to be an average middle-aged man if it wasn't for the two knobby horns that stuck out on either side of his forehead. Graying tufts of black hair stuck out from under a bright red cap, and as he walked ahead, he had a noticeable limp favoring his right leg.

He was a Trasgu, a troublemaking goblin, and his appearance belied the strength and cunning that lurked within him. He was over three hundred years old, and today would be the day he died.

I waited in the shadows of the alley for him to cross the street. A coughing fit caused him to double over, and he braced himself against the brick wall.

I approached him quietly—this all went easier when they didn't have time to prepare. He took off his hat to use it to wipe the snot from his nose, and when he looked up at me, his green eyes flashed with understanding.

"It's you," Eleazar said in a weak, craggy voice. We'd never met, and I doubt he'd ever seen me before, but he recognized me, the way they all did when their time was up.

"Eleazar Bélanger, you have been chosen to die," I said, reciting my script, the words automatic and cold on my lips. "It is my duty to return you to the darkness from whence you came."

"No, wait!" He held up his pudgy hands at me. "I have money. I can pay you. We can work this out."

"This is not my decision to make," I said as I pulled the sword from my sheath.

His eyes widened as he realized I couldn't be bargained with. For a moment I thought he might just accept his fate, but they rarely did. He bowed his head and ran at me like a goat. He was stronger than he looked and caused me to stumble back a step, but he didn't have anywhere to go.

My mother stood blocking the mouth of the alley, in case I needed her. Eleazar tried to run toward the other end, but his leg slowed him, and I easily overtook him. Using the handle of my sword, I cracked him on the back of the skull, and he fell to the ground on his knees.

Sigrún glowed brightly, with light shining out from it and causing the air to glow purple around us. Eleazar mumbled a prayer to the Vanir gods. I held the sword with both hands, and I struck it across his neck, decapitating him.

And then, finally, the electricity that had filled my body, making my muscles quiver and my bones ache, left me, and I breathed in deeply. The corpse of an immortal goblin lay in a puddle at my feet, and I felt nothing but relief.

"It was a good return," my mother said, and put her hand on my shoulder. "You did well, Malin."

TWO

————— ◆ —————

The crimson of the early morning sun glittered off the windows of the skyscrapers that towered above, making the glass look like fragmented rubies. In the heart of the city, dwarfed by all the buildings around it, sat the Evig Riksdag—the eternal parliament. Colloquially referred to as the Riks by Valkyries, it was where we all reported and got our orders from the Eralim.

The building's design made it similar to a concrete mushroom, with the lower twenty floors narrow and almost windowless, while the top ten floors extended far past the base, held up by metal beams. It was a feat of engineering that the top-heavy building didn't topple over. The austere appearance lent itself more to a government prison than to a place of celestial intervention.

A small computer screen was mounted next to the front door, and I placed my hand on it. A beam of light flashed hotly over my hand, analyzing it, then the screen flashed green. The thick steel doors slowly slid open, and Marlow and I walked inside.

The lobby was deserted, save for the half-dozen armed guards that were posted around the doors. Their black uniforms all had the same insignia on their shoulders—an eagle with the three horns of Odin. It was the symbol of the Vörðr, the powerful police force of the Evig Riksdag, mostly made up of sons of Valkyries.

The solid concrete walls enclosing the lobby gave the room a bunkerlike feel, but the black marble floors swirling with copper added a touch of elegance. Two bronze statues—men brandishing long swords, hunched under the shroud of their massive wings—were the only décor in the entire space.

But the Riksdag wasn't the kind of place that encouraged loitering or visitors of any kind. Security was of the highest priority. There had many attacks by immortals against the Riks, some that resulted in deaths of the Eralim and Valkyries that ran it, which was why the Vörðr needed to be the most elite police force in the world.

Many immortals took umbrage with the idea of being "returned," which was the vernacular the Riks used for killing. We weren't murderers—we were simply returning the immortals back to a world where they belonged.

Marlow and I took the elevator to the twenty-ninth floor, where we were greeted with a retinal scan before we could exit. A long corridor stretched out before us—more black marble floors and copper walls closing in on us. At the very end was a massive bronze door, and on either side stood Samael's personal bodyguards.

Godfrey Wright was the larger of the two, but both were hulking. Godfrey stood well over seven feet tall, with bulging arms and a shaved cranium. But what people usually noticed first was that he was a cyclops, with a solitary large eye above his nose.

The smaller and younger guard was Atlas Malosi. With light brown skin and cropped black hair, he had an open face and glittering dark eyes that made him appear much too friendly to be a guard.

He was the son of a Valkyrie, so he had the strength and height of one, but none of the supernatural ability that would make it possible for him to slay immortals. Only daughters could wield such power.

"How are you ladies doing this lovely morning?" Atlas asked, with a broad grin to match his broad shoulders.

"Just finished the job," I replied.

"I assume that it all went well for you," Atlas continued grinning.

"Is Samael in?" Marlow asked, cutting Atlas's chatter.

The smile finally fell from Atlas's face. "You know Samael. He's always in."

Godfrey was a man of few words, so he merely let out a grunt of agreement and gestured toward the door.

"Thank you." I smiled politely at the guards, but Marlow was already opening the door and heading into Samael's spacious office.

Samael had been assigned as my Eralim, because he'd been my mother's before me. His office was sparsely furnished—a large desk in front of the glass wall that overlooked the city, a few art deco chairs and a sofa, and objet d'art he'd collected over the centuries displayed on the shelves that lined the walls.

Samael himself was sprawled out on the black velvet sofa, absently reading something on his electronic tablet, but he broke out in a smile when he spotted us. While Samael was well over three hundred years old, he didn't look a day over twenty-five.

Lounging in black slacks and a dress shirt with the sleeves rolled up, he looked more like a college kid playing at grown-up than an experienced supervisor. Adding to that, he was incredibly handsome, with warm umber skin, bright aqua eyes beneath a strong brow, and a mass of shoulder-length chestnut curls with natural blond highlights coursing through.

His full lips always seemed on the edge of a smirk, one that even my stoic mother couldn't resist. As he walked over to greet us, Marlow pushed down her cowled hood and smiled brazenly at him.

"How is that you always manage to look so beautiful, even this early in the morning?" Samael mused, his eyes locked on my mother.

I rolled my eyes and sat in one of the several uncomfortable three-legged armchairs. I leaned back, propping my black moto boots up on the glass table to wait out Marlow and Samael's flirtation.

"You know work always brings out the best in me." Marlow smiled demurely at Samael, then turned and sauntered away from him, toward his desk.

He kept a crystal bowl on his desk, perpetually filled with treats like red bean paste covered in gold leaf or baby scorpions dipped in chocolate. As Samael turned his attention to me, Marlow grabbed a handful of whatever delicacy he had today, and as he spoke, she absently munched on it.

"So, Malin, how it did it go?" Samael asked me.

I looked past him to my mother, searching her expression for clues as to how she thought it went, but she just stared down impassively at the morsels in her hand.

"He's dead, so I think it went about as well as it could have," I said finally.

"*Returned*," Samael corrected me, then cast his eyes toward the ceiling, as if someone upstairs cared enough to eavesdrop on us. "He's returned, not dead."

The immortals weren't killed—they merely shed their mortal coil in a way that meant they could never walk the earth again.

That was one of the basic tenets of the world we lived in, and one of the first things we were taught in grade school. The gods had given us dominion over the earth, where humans, animals, and supernatural beings were all supposed to live in harmony as much as we could.

Valkyries were instated to return immortals to another realm—to an underworld called Kurnugia—and they could not come back.

Mortals couldn't return from the dead, either, but that was mostly because we had no afterworld.

That was how things were kept "fair." Immortals returned to Kurnugia, but mortals could not. When we died, we were left to rot in the dirt.

The dead must stay dead. That which is dead cannot rise.

"If you're going to be a Valkyrie, you'll have to get the lingo down," Samael went on.

"I *am* a Valkyrie," I replied pointedly.

"It may be in your blood, but it's not your job title yet," Samael said, sitting back down on the sofa across from me. "You know how the folks upstairs love paperwork and procedure."

"That they do," Marlow snorted in agreement, but I already had plenty of experience with the bureaucracy of the Evig Riksdag.

My training in their protocol had begun shortly after my eighteenth birthday, with classes at Ravenswood Academy, and it had still taken almost a year before I was able to start apprenticing alongside my mother. Then it had been another six months of testing and training and red tape before I had finally gotten a permit and been allowed to make kills, as long as it was under the close supervision of Marlow.

Since then I had killed—or, rather, *returned*—four immortals. Eleazar Bélanger had been my fifth.

"How are you taking to it, then?" Samael leaned forward, resting his arms on his knees, and something in the softness of his voice led me to believe what he was really asking was how I was coping.

There had been an entire course at Ravenswood Academy called Guilt and How to Handle It, and we discussed how some Valkyries couldn't deal with it. The responsibility of being an executioner was too much.

But I'd never felt guilt. I'd never felt anything but purpose. My

body was made to do this, and when there was too much time between jobs, I began to *crave* it. The way the electricity felt coursing
through me, the buzzing around my heart, the way the pressure
felt growing inside of me that wouldn't stop until I completed my
mission.

It was all relief and release.

"I can't imagine doing anything else," I admitted.

Samael looked back over his shoulder at my mother. "You think
she's doing well enough to go on her own soon?"

"She's ready to go now." Marlow absently brushed at the crumbs
on her black pants. "I know the Riksdag wants her to have seven
returns under her belt, so I'll be happy to shadow for the next two,
but she doesn't need me."

Samael looked back at me, grinning. "Well, it sounds like you'll
be a Valkyrie *very* soon."

My mother looked up, pride flashing momentarily in her dark
gray eyes. "She was born for it."